THE

BRIDES
TRILOGY

A 3-in-1 edition including

The Sherbrooke Bride
The Hellion Bride
and *The Heiress Bride*

THE
BRIDES
TRILOGY

A 3-in-1 edition including

The Sherbrooke Bride
The Hellion Bride
and *The Heiress Bride*

Catherine Coulter

G.P. Putnam's Sons
New York

G.P. Putnam's Sons
Publishers Since 1838
a member of
Penguin Putnam Inc.
375 Hudson Street
New York, NY 10014

ISBN 0-7394-1437-2

Printed in the United States of America

The *Sherbrooke Bride*

CHAPTER
═ 1 ═

Northcliffe Hall
Near New Romney, England
May 1803

"I SAW HER last night—the Virgin Bride!"

"Oh no, not really? Truly, Sinjun? You swear you saw the ghost?"

There were two shuddering gasps and fluttery cries of mingled fear and excitement.

"Yes, it had to be the Virgin Bride."

"Did she tell you she was a virgin? Did she tell you anything? Weren't you terrified? Was she all white? Did she moan? Did she look more dead than alive?"

Their voices grew fainter, but he still heard the gasps and giggles as they moved away from the estate room door.

Douglas Sherbrooke, Earl of Northcliffe, closed the door firmly and walked to his desk. That damned ghost! He wondered if the Sherbrookes were fated to endure unlikely tales of this miserable young lady throughout eternity. He glanced down at the neat piles of papers, sighed, then sat himself down and looked ahead at nothing at all.

The earl frowned. He was frowning a lot these days for they were keeping after him, not letting up for a day, not for a single hour. He was bombarded by gentle yet insistent reminders day in and day out with only slight variations on the same dull theme. He must needs marry and provide an heir for the earldom. He was getting older, every minute another minute ticked away his virility, and that virility was being squandered, according to them, for from his seed sprang future Sherbrookes, and this wondrous seed of his must be used legitimately and not spread haphazardly about, as warned of in the Bible.

He would be thirty on Michaelmas, they would say, all those uncles and aunts and cousins and elderly retainers who'd known him since he'd come squalling from his mother's womb, all those sniggering rotten friends of his, who, once they'd caught onto the theme, were enthusiastic in singing their own impertinent verses. He would frown at all of them, as he was frowning now, and he would say that he wasn't thirty on *this* Michaelmas, he was going to be twenty-nine on *this* Michaelmas, therefore on this day, at this minute, he was twenty-eight, and for God's sake, it was only May now, not September. He was barely settled into his twenty-eighth year. He was just now accustoming himself to saying he was twenty-eight and no longer twenty-seven. Surely his wasn't a great age, just ample.

The earl looked over at the gilded ormolu clock on the mantel. Where was Ryder? Damn his brother, he knew their meetings were always held on the first Tuesday of every quarter, here in the estate room of Northcliffe Hall at precisely three o'clock. Of course, the fact that the earl had only initiated these quarterly meetings upon his selling out of the army some nine months before, just after the signing of the Peace of Amiens, didn't excuse Ryder for being late for this, their third meeting. No, his brother should be censured despite the fact that Douglas's steward, Leslie Danvers, a young man of industrious habits and annoying memory, had reminded the earl just an hour before of the meeting with his brother.

It was the sudden sight of Ryder bursting into the estate room, windblown, smelling of leather and horse and the sea, alive as the wind, showing lots of white teeth, very nearly on time—it was only five minutes past the hour—that made the earl forget his ire. After all, Ryder was nearing an ample age himself. He was very nearly twenty-six.

The two of them should stick together.

"Lord, but it's a beautiful day, Douglas! I was riding with Dorothy on the cliffs, nothing like it, I tell you, nothing!" Ryder sat down, crossed his buckskin legs, and provided his brother more of his white-toothed smile.

Douglas swung a brooding leg. "Did you manage to stay on your horse?"

Ryder smiled more widely. His eyes, upon closer inspection, appeared somewhat vague. He had the look of a sated man, a look the earl was becoming quite familiar with, and so he sighed.

"Well," Ryder said after another moment of silence, "if you insist upon these quarterly meetings, Douglas, I must do something to keep them going."

"But Dorothy Blalock?"

"The widow Blalock is quite soft and sweet-smelling, brother, and she knows how to please a man. Ah, does she ever do it well. Also, she'll not get caught. She's much too smart for that, my Dorothy."

"She sits a horse well," Douglas said. "I'll admit that."

"Aye, and that's not all she sits well."

Only through intense resolve did Douglas keep his grin to himself. He was the earl; he was the head of the far-flung Sherbrooke family. Even now there might be another Sherbrooke growing despite Dorothy's intelligence.

"Let's get on with it," Douglas said, but Ryder wasn't fooled. He saw the twitch of his brother's lip and laughed.

"Yes, let's," he agreed, rose, and poured himself a brandy. He raised the decanter toward Douglas.

"No, thank you. Now," Douglas continued, reading the top sheet of paper in front of him, "as of this quarter you have four quite healthy sons, four quite healthy daughters. Poor little Daniel died during the winter. Amy's fall doesn't appear to have had lasting injury to her leg. Is this up-to-date?"

"I will have another baby making his appearance in August. The mother appears hardy and healthy."

Douglas sighed. "Very well. Her name?" As Ryder replied, he wrote. He raised his head. "Is this now correct?"

Ryder lost his smile and downed the rest of his brandy. "No. Benny died of the ague last week."

"You didn't tell me."

Ryder shrugged. "He wasn't even a year old, but so bright, Douglas. I knew you were busy, what with the trip to London to the war office, and the funeral was small. That's the way his mother wanted it."

"I'm sorry," Douglas said again. Then he frowned, a habit Ryder had noticed and didn't like one bit, and said, "If the babe is due in August, why didn't you tell me at our last quarterly meeting?"

Ryder said simply, "The mother didn't tell me because she feared I wouldn't wish to bed her anymore." He paused, looking at the east lawn through the wide bay windows. "Silly wench. I wouldn't have guessed she was with child although I suppose I might have suspected. She's already quite great with child. She may well give me twins."

Ryder turned from the window and swigged more brandy. "I forgot, Douglas. There's also Nancy."

Douglas dropped the paper. "Nancy who?"

"Nancy Arbuckle, the draper's daughter on High Street in Rye. She's with child, my child. She will have it in November, best guess. She was all tears and woes until I told her she needn't worry, that the Sherbrookes always took care of their own. It's possible she might even wed a sea captain for he isn't concerned that she's carrying another man's child."

"Well, that's something." Douglas did a new tally then looked up. "You're currently supporting seven children and their mothers. You have impregnated two more women and all their children are due this year."

"I think that's right. Don't forget the possibility of the twins or the possibility of Nancy marrying her sea captain."

"Can't you keep your damned rod in your pants?"

"No more than you can, Douglas."

"Fair enough, but why can't you remove yourself from the woman before you fill her with your seed?"

Ryder flushed, a rather remarkable occurrence, and said, his voice defensive, "I can't seem to keep my wits together. I know it isn't much of an excuse, but I just can't seem to withdraw once I'm there, so to speak." He stared hard at his brother then. "I'm not a damned cold fish like you, Douglas. You could withdraw from an angel herself. Doesn't your mind ever run off its track, doesn't it ever turn into vapor? Don't you ever want to just keep pounding and pounding and the consequences simply don't come into it?"

"No."

Ryder sighed. "Well, I'm not so well disciplined as you. Do you still have only the two children?"

"No, the babe died whilst I was in London. There is only Cynthia left now, a sweet child, four years old."

"I'm sorry."

"It was expected and just a matter of time so the doctors kept telling his mother. I went to London not just to see Lord Avery in the War Office but also to see Elizabeth. She'd written me about the babe's condition. His lungs never really properly developed." Douglas drew out a clean sheet of foolscap and adjusted last quarter's numbers.

"Your lust becomes more costly," he said after a moment. "Damned costly."

"Stop your frowns, Douglas. You're bloody wealthy, as am I. Greatuncle Brandon would be pleased that his inheritance to me is being put to such excellent use. He was a lusty old fellow until his eightieth year, at least that's what he told me. Bragged like a bat he did.

"You're always saying that our bastards are our responsibility and so I agree with you. I also agree with this plan of yours, for it ensures we don't miss any. What a general you would have made! A pity you had to sell out when you were only a major."

Ryder was chuckling when the estate room door opened. He looked up to see his youngest brother come somewhat diffidently into the room. "Ah, if it isn't Tysen. Come in, brother, our meeting is nearly done. Douglas has already told me my lust must soon poke holes in my pocketbook. Now he is completing his mathematics, truly a meager number, particularly when one considers what one could do with more available fields to plow and sow and tend."

"What meeting?" asked Tysen Sherbrooke, coming into the estate room. "What numbers? What fields?"

Ryder shot a look at Douglas, who just shrugged and sat back in his chair, his arms folded across his chest. He looked ironic, and if Ryder hadn't known him so well, he would have thought him annoyed rather than obliquely amused.

Ryder said to Douglas, "Look, brother, Tysen wants to be a vicar. It's important that he understand male frailties and that, without mincing matters, is basic lust. Attend me, Tysen, this is our quarterly meeting to determine the current number of Sherbrooke bastards."

Tysen stared, then turned an agonized eye toward Douglas. "Your *what?*"

"You heard me," Ryder said. "Now, you're nearly twenty-one, Tysen. It's time you come to our meetings. Isn't it time we included him, Douglas? After all, we don't want him sneaking in a bastard all unknown to us, do we? Think of our reputation. All right, my lad, have you gotten any of the local girls with child?"

Tysen looked apoplectic. "Of course not! I wouldn't ever do anything so despicable! I will be a man of God, a vicar, a shepherd who will lead a righteous and devout flock and—"

Ryder rolled his eyes. "Please, stop! It boggles the mind that a Sherbrooke could speak thusly and believe it. It makes one want to puke. Ah well, it's too bad that you are what you appear to be, Tysen, but one always hopes, particularly if one is of an optimistic nature."

"Does optimism go hand in rod with lust?" Douglas said to the room at large.

Ryder laughed and Tysen looked stunned. He knew his brothers were men of the world, that they understood many things that he'd scarce thought about, but this humor? A meeting to count up their bastards? Sweat broke out on his forehead. He began to inch toward the door.

"At least smile, Tysen," Douglas said. "A vicar can have a sense of humor, you know."

"Oh no," Tysen said. "It's just that—of course I can smile, it's just that—"

"You're not finishing any of your sentences, Tysen," Ryder said, his tone utterly irreverent. "You're repeating yourself."

"Well, a man of God can also share his boundless love with a specific sort of love. You know, I can also love a lady, and, well, I do!"

"Oh Jesus," Ryder said, turning away in amused disgust. "Do you want some brandy now, Douglas?"

"That's nauseating," Douglas said, "and I probably couldn't keep the brandy down, so no, Ryder." Then he took some pity on Tysen, whose lean cheeks were alarmingly red. "Who is the chit, Tysen? Surely as you're a future vicar, she's no actress or shop girl?"

"No," Tysen said, his voice strengthening, now bordering on very unvicarlike worship. "Her name is Melinda Beatrice and she's Sir Thomas Hardesty's daughter."

Ryder cursed. "I know the wench. She's silly, Douglas, and she simpers, for God's sake, and she acts as if she's better than everyone else, and she's got no breasts to speak of. Her eyes look watery, her elbows are bony, and she's got two names and her parents use both of them. It's beyond too much. Two names!"

"She will make a fine wife for a man of God!" Tysen would have further defended his goddess, but he stopped abruptly as Douglas slowly rose from his chair, staring at him. Ryder's insults were forgotten under Douglas's look, an expression that was alarmingly identical to their now-dead father's. Tysen began to step back, slowly, slowly, until he was hard against the closed door. Douglas said ever so softly, "You mean to tell me that at twenty years of age you've decided to fancy yourself in love with a girl who is your equal in birth and fortune? We are speaking of the Hardestys of Blaston Manor?"

"Yes," Tysen said. "I'm nearly twenty-one."

"Young fool," Ryder said dispassionately, flicking a dust mote off his sleeve. "He'll get over it within the month, Douglas. Remember how you thought you wanted that duke's daughter? When was that—yes, some three years ago, you fancied yourself tip over arse in love. You were home with that shoulder wound. Now, what was her name? Melissande—yes, that was it."

Douglas sliced his hand through the air, silencing Ryder. "You haven't spoken to Sir Thomas, have you?"

"Of course not," Tysen said. "You're the head of the family, Douglas."

"Don't forget it, no one else allows me to. Now, just promise me you'll not declare yourself when the chit smiles at you, or gives you a glimpse of her ankle. I've determined that girls must be born knowing all sorts of tricks to entice the unwary male, so you must be on your guard, all right?"

Tysen nodded, then said quickly, "But not Melinda Beatrice, Douglas. She's kind and honest. She has a sweetness about her, a goodness, that will make her a wonderful shepherdess to my flock, a helpmeet to cherish. She would never—" He saw that both brothers were on the verge of incredulous laughter. His jaw tightened, his brows lowered, his back stiffened, and he said, "That's not why I came in, Douglas. Aunt Mildred and Uncle Albert are here and want to speak with you."

"Ha! Preach to me is more like it. I suppose you told the servants to bag it and volunteered yourself to come find me so as to escape their eagle eyes?"

"Well, yes." Tysen paused when Douglas groaned, then went on in an apologetic voice, "Yes, you're right about their visit. I heard them speaking about the Marquess of Dacre's eldest daughter, Juliette, a diamond of the first order, Aunt Mildred was saying, and just perfect for you."

Douglas looked sardonic and remained silent as a stone.

"God grant you long life, Douglas," Ryder said with fervor. "I respect you and am grateful to my toes that you are the eldest son and thus the Fourth Earl of Northcliffe, the Sixth Viscount Hammersmith, the Ninth Baron Sanderleigh, and therefore the target of all their cannon."

"I respect you too, Douglas," Tysen said. "You make a fine earl, viscount, and baron, and I'm certain Uncle Albert and Aunt Mildred think so too. All the family agree if only you'd marry and—"

"Oh God, not you too, Tysen! Well, there's no hope for it," Douglas added as he rose from his chair. "Ah, Tysen, your gratitude will make me endure, no doubt. Pray for me, little brother. Our meeting for this quarter is adjourned, Ryder. I believe I'll speak to your valet, Tinker, and see if he can't sew your randy sex into your breeches."

"Poor Tinker would be appalled to be assigned such a service."

"Well, I can't ask one of the maids. That surely would defeat the purpose. I vow you would break our pact if one of the younger ones did the task."

"Poor Douglas," Ryder said as his brother left the room.

"What did Douglas mean about your pact?" Tysen asked.

"Oh, we have both vowed that any female in our employ is not to be touched. When you are safely out of love, and thus your wits are yours again, we will gain your assurances as well."

Tysen decided not to argue with his brother. He was above that. He would be a vicar; his thoughts and deeds would be spiritual. Also, to the best of his memory, he'd never won an argument with either brother, and thus said, "This girl they're going to batter at him about is supposedly quite wonderful."

"They're all wonderful with pillow sheets over their heads," Ryder said and walked out of the estate room.

Leaning against a dark mahogany Spanish table was Sinjun, her arms crossed, looking as negligent and indifferent as a potato, and whistling. She stopped when she saw that Ryder saw her, and said with a wonderfully bland voice, "So, how went the meeting?"

"Keep your tongue behind your teeth, brat."

"Now, Ryder, I'm young, true, but I'm not stupid."

"Forget it, Sinjun."

"How are all your Beloved Ones?"

"They all do very well, thank you."

"I'm silent as a soap dish," she said, grinned at him, blew him a kiss, and walked toward the kitchen, whistling again, like a boy.

CHAPTER
== 2 ==

THE EARL WASN'T frowning. He was anxious and he felt in his innards that something was going to happen, something he wasn't going to like. He hated such feelings because they made him feel helpless and vulnerable; on the other hand he knew it would be stupid to ignore them. Because the government was in disarray, and that damned fool Addington was dithering about like a headless cock, he thought that this anxiety in his innards must spring from his fear of Napoleon.

Like all Englishmen who lived on the southern coast of England, he worried about an invasion. It didn't seem likely, since the English ruled the Channel, but then again, only a fool would disregard a man of Napoleon's military genius and his commitment to the destruction of the English.

Douglas dismounted from his stallion, Garth, and strode to the cliff edge. Surf pounded at the rocks at the base of the cliff, spewing plumes of white-foamed water thirty feet into the air. He sucked the salt air into his lungs, felt it gritty and wet against his face. The wind was strong and sharp, blowing his hair about his head, making his eyes water. The day was cloudy and gray. He couldn't see France today, but when the sky was clear, he could see Boulogne from this vantage and the bleak coastline to the northeast toward Calais. He shaded his eyes and stared into the grayness. The clouds roiled and overlapped, but didn't part, rather they thickened and seemed to press fatly together. He didn't turn when he heard the horse approach and halt near him.

"I thought you would be here, Douglas. This is your favorite place to think."

He smiled even as he was turning to greet his young sister seated astride her mare, Fanny. "I see I shouldn't be so predictable. I didn't see you at breakfast, Sinjun, or at lunch. Was Mother punishing you for some infraction?"

"Oh no, I forgot the time. I was studying my—" She broke off, lightly slipped out of the saddle and strode toward him, a tall, thin girl, with long legs and wild pale hair that swirled thick and curly around her face, hair once held at the nape of her neck with a ribbon, no doubt, a ribbon now long lost. Her eyes were a vivid sky blue, clear as the day was gray and filled with humor and intelligence. All of his siblings had the Sherbrooke blue eyes and the thick light hair, though Sinjun's was lighter and filled with sunlight. All except him.

Douglas was the changeling, his eyes as dark as sin, his old nanny had happily told him many years before, aye, and he looked like a heathen Celt, all dark and swarthy, his black hair making him look like the master of the cloven hoof himself.

When he was very young, he'd overheard his father accusing his mother of cuckolding him, for his son looked like no Sherbrooke in either their painted or recorded history. His mother, Douglas recalled, had apologized profusely for what she accepted as her error in the production of this, the implausible Sherbrooke heir. Ryder was fond of telling Douglas that it was this un-Sherbrooke appearance that made everyone obey him instantly, for it made him appear so austere and forbidding.

But as Douglas looked at his sister, his expression wasn't at all severe. She was wearing buckskins, as was he, a loose white shirt, and a light brown leather vest. Their mother, he knew, would shriek like a banshee when and if she saw her young daughter thusly attired. Of course, their mother was always shrieking about something.

"What were you studying?"

"It isn't important. You're worrying again, aren't you?"

"Someone must since our government doesn't seem to want to concern itself with our protection. Napoleon has the best trained and the most seasoned soldiers in all of Europe, and they want to defeat us badly."

"Is it true that Fox will return and rout Addington?"

"He is ill, I hear, and the time isn't yet ripe enough for him to oust Addington. He is as misguided and as liberal as Addington, but at least he is a leader and not indecisive. I fancy you know as much as I do about the situation." He was well used to his sister's precociousness—not that precisely, but her erudition, the interest in issues and subjects that should have been years beyond her, things that would leave most gentlemen and ladies blank-faced with disinterest. And she seemed to understand him better than either of his brothers or his mother or the myriad of Sherbrooke relatives. He loved her very much.

"No, you're wrong," she said now. "You must have seen a lot when you went to London last week and spoke to all those men. You haven't yet told me the latest mood in the war ministry. Another thing, Douglas, you've armed all the men on our farms and some in the villages as well. You've drilled them over and over again." On the heels of her very adult appraisal, she giggled like the young girl she was, saying, "It was so funny watching Mr. Dalton pretending to beat away the Frogs with that gnarly stick!"

"He was best at retreating and hiding. I'd rather have trained his wife. Now she would be the kind of mean-boned soldier the French would fear."

Sinjun said abruptly, her light blue eyes taking on a gray hue, "I saw the Virgin Bride last night."

"I overheard you telling your friends. Your audience was most appreciative, albeit so gullible it was embarrassing. But, my dear girl, it is all nonsense, and you know it. You must have eaten turnips for dinner and it turned your dreams to phantoms."

"Actually I was reading in the library."

"Oh? I pray you won't tell your mother if you chance to peruse my Greek plays. Her reaction staggers the brain."

She smiled, distracted. "I read them all two years ago, Douglas."

He smacked his palm to his forehead. "I should have known."

"I think the most interesting one was called *Lysistrata*, but I didn't understand how the ladies could expect their husbands to just stop fighting just because they threatened to—"

"Yes, I know what the ladies did," he said quickly, both appalled and amused. He eyed her, wondering if he should attempt some sort of brotherly sermon, or at least a caveat on her reading habits. Before he could think of anything relevant to say, Sinjun continued thoughtfully, "When I went upstairs around midnight, I saw this light beneath the door to the countess's chamber, next to yours. I opened the door as quietly as I could and there she was, standing by the bed, all dressed in white, and she was crying very softly. She looked just like all the stories have described. She was very beautiful, her hair long and straight to her waist and so blond it was almost white. She turned and looked at me, and then she simply vanished. Before she vanished, I swear that she wanted to say something."

"It was turnips," Douglas said. "You forgot you ate them. I cannot credit the ghost. No intelligent person would credit a spiritual phenomenon."

"That is because you haven't seen her and you don't trust a female to report the unvarnished truth. You prefer vegetables for an explanation."

"Turnips, Sinjun, turnips."

"Very well, but I did see her, Douglas."

"Why is it that only women see her?"

Sinjun shrugged. "I don't know if it is only women she's appeared to. All past earls who have written about her have claimed it to be only women, but who really knows? In my experience, gentlemen aren't inclined to admit to anything out of the ordinary. They won't take the risk of looking foolish, I suppose."

Douglas continued, as sardonic as could be. "Your experience, hm? So you think our Virgin Bride was standing over the bed, bemoaning the intactness of her maidenhead, knowing that her bridegroom would never come? Thus she was doomed never to become a wife and a mother?"

"Perhaps."

"More likely the chit remarried within a year, bore sixteen children like every good sixteenth-century woman did, and died of old age, hair straggly and gray, and no teeth in her mouth."

"You're not at all romantic, Douglas." Sinjun turned to watch a hawk fly close overhead, its wings wide and smooth, a beautiful sight. She then gave Douglas a smile that was dazzling in its pleasure. It shocked him. She was a little girl, only fifteen, and this wondrous natural smile gave promise of the woman she would become. Actually, he realized, it scared the hell out of him.

"But I did see her, Douglas, and others have as well. You know there was a young lady whose husband of three hours was murdered and she killed herself when she heard the news. She was only eighteen. She loved him so very much she couldn't bear to live without him. It was tragic. It was written down in full detail by Audley Sherbrooke, the First Earl of Northcliffe. Even Father wrote of her once."

"I know, but you can be certain I shan't write a word about that nonexistent phantom. It is drivel and all reported by hysterical females. You can be certain that your Virgin Bride will end her ceaseless meanderings with me. Doubtless all our ancestors did their recounting during long winters, when they were bored and sought to amuse themselves and their families."

Sinjun merely shook her head at him, touching her fingers to his coat sleeve. "There is no reasoning with you. Did I tell you? My friends—Eleanor and Lucy Wiggins—they're both in love with you. They whisper and giggle and say in the most nauseating way imaginable that they would swoon if only you would smile at them." Then, after that girlish confidence, she added, "You are a natural leader, Douglas, and you made a difference in the army just as you're making a difference here. And I did see the Virgin Bride."

"I hope that may be true. As for you, too many turnips and lewd Greek plays. Oh, and give Eleanor and Lucy another couple of years and it will be Ryder who will draw their female swoons and sighs."

"Oh dear," Sinjun said, her brow furrowing. "You must make Ryder promise not to seduce them for he'll find it an easy task because they're so silly." Sinjun fell silent for Douglas was obviously distracted again.

He was thinking that he would protect what was his just as had his long-ago ancestor, Baron Sanderleigh, who had saved Northcliffe from the Roundhead armies and managed through his superior guile to convince Cromwell of his family's support, and after him, Charles II. Throughout the succeeding generations, the Sherbrookes had continued to refine the fine art of guile to keep themselves and their lands intact. They had provided mistresses of great mental aptitude and physical endowment to kings and ministers, they had excelled in diplomacy, and they had served in the army. It was rumored that Queen Anne had been in love with a Sherbrooke general, a younger son. All in all, they had enriched themselves and kept Northcliffe safe.

He shook his head, backing farther away from the cliff edge. There'd been a recent storm and the ground wasn't all that solid beneath his feet. He warned Sinjun, then fell into abstraction again as he sat on an outcropping of rocks.

"They won't leave you alone, Douglas."

"I know," he said, not bothering to pretend ignorance. "Damn, but they're right and I've been a stubborn bas—fool. I have to marry and I have to impregnate my wife. One thing I learned in the army is that life is more fragile than the wings of a butterfly."

"Yes, and it is your child who must be the future Earl of Northcliffe. I love Ryder dearly, as do you, but he doesn't want the title. He wants to laugh and love his way through life, not spend it with a bailiff poring over account books or hearing the farmers complain about the leaks in their roofs. He doesn't care about all the pomp and dignities and the knee-bending. His is not a serious nature." She grinned and shook her head, scuffing the toe of her riding boot against a rock. "That is, his is not a serious nature about earl sorts of things. Other things are different, of course."

"What the devil does that mean?"

Sinjun just smiled and shrugged.

Douglas realized in that instant that he'd made his mind up; more than that, he also knew whom he would marry. Ryder had himself brought her up during their meeting. The girl he'd fancied three years before, the beautiful and glorious Lady Melissande, daughter of the Duke of Beresford, who had wanted him and had cried when he'd left and hurled names at his head for what she'd seen as his betrayal. But three years before, he'd been committed to the army, committed to destroying Napoleon, committed to saving England.

Now, he was only committed to saving Northcliffe and the Sherbrooke line.

Aloud, he said, "Her name is Melissande and she is twenty-one, the daughter of Edouard Chambers, the Duke of Beresford. I met her when she was eighteen, but I left her because I had no wish to wed then. The devil, I was only home because of that bullet wound in my shoulder. It is likely she is long wed now and a mother. Ah, Sinjun, she was so beautiful, so dashing and carefree and spirited, and behind her was the Chambers name, old and honored, become dissolute only in her grandfather's day. There was little money for her dowry three years ago, but I didn't care if she came with naught but her shift on her back. Aye, her brother is another rotter, and even now he brings new odor to London with his profligacy. He is dissolute and a wastrel, gaming away any guinea he can get his hands on. It is likely that he will finish off the Chambers line."

"I think it noble of you not to be concerned with a dowry, Douglas. Mother says again and again that it is the only basis for marriage. Perhaps your Melissande has waited for you. I would. Perhaps no one wed her because there was no money, despite the fact she's a duke's daughter and beautiful. Or, what if she did wed another but is now a widow? It's possible her husband would have been obliging and died, and it would solve all your problems."

Douglas smiled at that, but nodded, again, comfortable with speaking aloud his thoughts and his plans to Sinjun. Yes, he had liked Melissande, found her careless ways fascinating, her clever manipulations intriguing. He'd also wanted to bed her very badly, had wanted to see her tousled and whispering endearments to him, adoration in her eyes for him.

Sinjun said quietly, "If Melissande is still available then you won't have to worry about spending time in London to find another appropriate girl."

"You're right," he said, rising and dusting off his breeches. "I will write immediately to the Duke of Beresford. If Melissande is still available—Lord, it makes her sound like a prize mare!—why then, I could leave immediately for Harrogate and marry her on the spot. I think you would like her, Sinjun."

"I'll like her if you do, Douglas. Mother won't, but that doesn't matter."

Douglas could only shake his head at her. "You're right. Do you know she's the only one who's never carped at me about marrying and providing the Sherbrooke heir?"

"That's because she doesn't want to give up her power as chatelaine of Northcliffe. The Sherbrooke dower house is charming but she disdains it."

"You sometimes terrify me, my girl, you truly do." He touched his fingers to her wind-tangled hair, then cupped her chin in his large hand. "You're a good sort."

She accepted this token of affection calmly, then said, "You know, Douglas, I wondered why the Virgin Bride would come at this particular time, but now it makes sense. I think she appeared because she knew you were planning to marry. Perhaps her coming is a portent; perhaps she is trying to warn you or your Melissande about something that will befall you if you aren't careful."

"Nonsense," said the Earl of Northcliffe. "However, you are still a good sort, even if you are overly fanciful upon occasion."

" 'There are more things in heaven and earth, Horatio, Than are dreamt of in your philosophy.' "

"Ah, Sinjun, and I shall say back to you, 'Rest, rest, perturbed spirit.' "

"You are sometimes a difficult man, Douglas."

"You sulk because I out-Shakespeared you?"

She poked him in the arm in high good humor. "You are too earthbound, Douglas, but perhaps that won't continue after you are wedded."

Douglas thought of the immense passion he fully planned to enjoy when he bedded Melissande. "Sometimes, my girl," he said, giving her a fatuous grin, "you are also delightfully perceptive."

The earl wasn't frowning when he returned to Northcliffe Hall. Everything would work out. He had the unaccountable Sherbrooke luck as did the first son of the Sherbrookes for the past untold generations. It would continue, for the Sherbrooke luck had never yet deserted him, and he would have no more worries.

He paused, standing next to his sister in the front hall, listening to the Northcliffe butler, Hollis, when their mother, Lady Lydia, swooped down on them, demanding that Joan come upstairs *immediately* and change her highly repugnant clothing and *try*, at least try, to *appear* the young lady, despite all the blocks and obstacles Douglas and his brothers—who positively encouraged the silly chit—put in her path.

"I gather we are expecting guests, Mother?" Douglas asked, after sending Sinjun a commiserating wink.

"Yes, and if the Algernons—Almeria is such a high stickler, you know!—if she saw this child in her breeches and her hair like—" She faltered and Sinjun said quickly, "Like Medusa, Mother?"

"A revolting witch from one of your dusty tomes, I dare say! Come along, Joan. Oh, Douglas, please refrain from calling your sister that absurd name in front of the Algernons!"

"Did you know that Algernon means 'the whiskered ones'? It was the nickname of William de Percy, who was bearded when every other gentleman was clean shaven, and he—"

"Enough!" said the Dowager Countess of Northcliffe, clearly harassed. "No more of your smartness, young lady. I have told you repeatedly that gentlemen do not like smartness in females. It irritates them and depresses their own mental faculties. It makes them seek out their brandy bottles. It sends them to gaming wells. Also, I won't hear more of that *Sinjun* nonsense. Your name is Joan Elaine Winthrop Sherbrooke."

"But I like Sinjun, Mother," she said, feeling her mother's fingers tighten painfully on her shirtsleeve. "Ryder named me that when I was ten years old."

"Hush," said the unknowing soon-to-be Dowager Countess of Northcliffe. "You aren't Saint John nor are you Saint Joan—Sinjun is a man's nickname. Dear me, you have that preposterous name all because Tysen decided you were Joan of Arc—"

"And then," Douglas continued, "he decided to martyr her and thus she became Saint Joan or Sinjun."

"In any case, I won't have it!"

Douglas said nothing. Since he could scarce even remember his sister's name was really Joan, he doubted not that their mother would have to hear Sinjun for many years to come.

Douglas took himself to the library to write and send off his letter to the Duke of Beresford. He wouldn't say anything about his plans until the duke had shown his approval of the scheme. And Melissande too, of course. He knew he could trust Sinjun to keep quiet about it. He realized he trusted his little sister more than his own brothers. After all, she never got drunk. He also liked the name Sinjun, but he hesitated to go against his mother's wishes. She was tied to many notions that appalled him, was occasionally mean and spiteful with both servants and her children and her neighbors. She was blessed with an intellect as bland as cook's turtle soup, was plump and pink-cheeked with sausage curls tight around her face, and carried at least three chins. She spoke constantly of her duty, of the rigors of bearing four children. He wasn't certain he loved her for she was vastly annoying at times. He knew that his father had endured her for he had told Douglas so before he'd died.

Was Sinjun right? Had his mother remained quiet in the eye of the marriage storm because she didn't want the wife to wrest the reins of control over the household from her? He tried to picture Melissande wanting to oversee Northcliffe, demanding that his mother hand over the chatelaine keys, but such an image wouldn't form in his mind. He shrugged; it didn't matter.

And what was wrong with a simple nickname like Sinjun?

CHAPTER
═══ 3 ═══

Claybourn Hall, Wetherby
Near Harrogate, England

"THIS IS DIFFICULT to believe, Papa," Alexandra said finally, her voice strained and paper-thin. She couldn't seem to take her eyes off that single sheet of paper her father calmly replaced on his desktop. "Are you certain it is the Earl of Northcliffe who wants to marry Melissande? Douglas Sherbrooke?"

"Yes, no doubt about it," said Lord Edouard, Duke of Beresford. "Poor fool." He smoothed his long fingers over the letter surface, then read it aloud again to his youngest daughter. When he finished and looked over at her, he thought for a moment that she was somehow distressed. She seemed pale, but it was probably only the bright sunlight coming through the wide library windows. He said, "Your sister will probably be ecstatic, particularly after Oglethorpe didn't come up to scratch four months ago. This should be a great balm to her wounded pride. As for me, why, I should like to throw my arms about Northcliffe and cry on his shoulder. Good Gad, the money he offers will save me, not to mention the handsome settlement he'll provide."

Alexandra looked down at the roughened nail on her thumb. "Melissande told me she refused Douglas Sherbrooke three years ago. He begged and begged to have her, she said, but she felt his future was too uncertain, that even though he was the earl's heir, it wasn't enough since his father was, after all, still alive, and that since he insisted on remaining in the army and fighting, he could be killed and then she wouldn't have anything, for his brother would become earl after his father's death. She said being a poor wife was very different from being a beautiful but poor daughter."

The duke grunted, a dark eyebrow raised. "That's what she told you, Alex?"

Alexandra nodded, then turned away from her father. She walked to the wide bow windows, their draperies held back in every season, regardless of the weather, because the duke refused ever to close them over the magnificent vista outside. His wife complained endlessly about it, claiming the harsh sun faded out the Aubusson carpet and the good Lord knew there was no money to replace it, for that was what he was always telling her, wasn't it, but the duke paid her no heed. Alex said slowly, "Now Douglas Sherbrooke is the Earl of Northcliffe and he wishes to come here to wed her."

"Yes, I give him permission and we will come to agreement over the settlement in short order. Thank God he's a wealthy man. The Sherbrookes have always used their money wisely, never depleting the estates through excesses, not forming alliances that wouldn't add to their coffers and their consequence. Of course his marrying Melissande won't bring him a single groat, indeed, he will have to pay me well for her, very well indeed. He must really care for her since the chances would have been excellent that she would have already been wed to another man. I must say too, in your sister's defense, that her consequence displays itself in equal measure to her pride."

"I suppose so. I remember that he was a very nice man. Kind and, well, nice."

"Hotheaded young fool, that's what he was," the duke said. "He was the Northcliffe heir and he refused to sell out. Not that it matters now. He survived and now he's the earl and that makes things quite different. All the Sherbrookes have been Tories, back to the Flood I dare say, and this earl is very probably no different. Staid and well set in his ways, I'll wager, just like his father, Justin Sherbrooke, was. Well, none of that has any bearing now. I suppose I should speak to your sister." He paused a moment, looking toward his daughter's profile. Pure and innocent, he thought, yet there was strength there, in the tilt of her head, in the clear light in her gray eyes. Her nose was straight and thin, her cheekbones high, and her chin gently rounded, giving the impression of submissiveness and malleability, which wasn't at all the case, at least in his experience with his daughter. But, strangely enough, she didn't appear to know she had steel in her, even when she argued with him. Her rich titian hair was pulled back from her face, showing her small ears, and he found both her ears and her lovely. She wasn't an exquisite creation like her older sister, Melissande, but she was quite to his taste, for there was little vanity or pettiness in her and there was a good deal of kindness and wit. Ah, she was the responsible one, the child who wouldn't gainsay her papa ever, the one who would do her duty to her family. Again, he had the inescapable feeling that she was distressed and he wondered at it. He said slowly, "I told you of this first, Alex, because I wanted your opinion. Even though your mother believes you to be much like the wallpaper—

quiet and in Melissande's shadow—I know differently, and thus I would like to know what you think of this proposed match."

He thought she trembled slightly at his words and frowned, wondering if her mother had perhaps tried to flatten her spirit again with her constant comparisons to her sister. He watched her closely. "Are you ailing with something, my dear?"

"Oh no, Papa. It's just that—"

"That what?"

She shrugged then. "I suppose I wonder if Melissande would have him now. She wants to enjoy another Season, you know, and we are to leave next week. Perhaps she would wish to wait to see what other gentlemen are available to her. She much savors the chase, she told me. Oglethorpe, she said, was a spineless toad and she was vastly relieved when his mama made him cry off before he cried on, so to speak."

The duke sighed. "Yes, your sister was right about him, but that isn't the point now. You know, Alex, that money must play a big part in any decision. Our family hasn't been in overly plump current for many years now, and the expense of London during the Season, the cost of staffing the Carlyon Street house, the price of her gowns and gowns for her mother, all of it together is exorbitant. I was willing to do it again as an investment, for I could see no alternative. Now with the Earl of Northcliffe proposing to her, I will get a settlement without having to endure London and all its costs." The duke realized, of course, that by canceling out another Season for Melissande, he was also preventing Alexandra from having her first Season. But the cost of it—he ran his hand through his dark red hair. What to do? He continued, saying more to himself, than to his daughter, "And there's Reginald, my twenty-five-year-old heir, gambling in every hell London can boast, raising huge debts to Weston his tailor, and to Hoby his bootmaker, even to Rundle and Bridge for 'trinkets' as he calls these supposed insubstantial baubles for his mistresses. My God, you wouldn't believe the ruby bracelet he bought for one of those opera dancers!" He shook his head again. "Ah, Alex, I've felt trapped for so long now, but no longer is my life falling down on my shoulders. You know well the economies I've tried to initiate, but explaining the necessity to your mother, well, an impossible task, that. She has no concept, telling me in a bewildered way that one must have at least three removes at dinner. Nor does Melissande. You, of course, understand something of our situation, but anything you do is insignificant. And Reginald—a wastrel, Alex, and in all truth I have little hope that his character will improve."

He fell silent again, a small smile on his mouth now. He was saved. He felt hope and he wasn't about to allow Melissande to toss her beautiful head and tell him she wasn't interested. Bread and water in a locked room would be fitting were she to go against him.

"What do you think, Alex? You do not mind about a Season? You are such a sensible girl and you understand there is no money and—"

Alex just smiled. "It's all right, Papa. Melissande is so beautiful, so sparkling and gay, so natural in her gaiety. If we went to London, no one would have paid me much attention in any case so I don't mind not going. I am not lying to you. It terrified me, the thought of meeting all those ferocious ladies—if their eyebrows twitch, you're forever beyond the pale—that's what Mama says. So, you needn't worry. I go along fine here. There are other things besides parties and routs and Venetian breakfasts and dancing holes in one's slippers." There were other things, but that list was woefully short.

"Once Melissande is wed to the earl, she will do her duty by you. As the Countess of Northcliffe, she will take you about so that you may meet appropriate young gentlemen. That is what is right and she will do it. And you will comply because that is the way one normally secures a husband worthy of one."

"Young gentlemen don't appear to be remarkably attracted to me, Papa."

"Nonsense. There are very few young gentlemen here about to see you, and those who are, look upon your sister and lose what few wits they possess. It is of no matter. You are a dear girl, and you are bright and your mind is filled with more than ribbons and beaux and—"

"When one isn't a diamond, Papa, one must cultivate other gardens."

"Is that your attempt to rephrase Monsieur Voltaire?"

Alexandra smiled. "I suppose so, but it's the truth. There is no reason to quibble about it."

"You are also very pretty, Alex. You surely don't wish to insult your glorious hair—why 'tis the same shade as mine!"

She smiled at that, and the duke thought, pleased, everything would work out all right now. The Earl of Northcliffe had just offered to save him from inevitable financial disaster and rid him of his eldest daughter at the same time, a set of circumstances to gladden any father's heart and purse.

"I trust Melissande will decide to take Douglas Sherbrooke this time," Alexandra said. "As I said, he is a very nice man and deserves to have what he wants." Her fingers pleated the folds of her pale yellow muslin gown, and her eyes remained downcast as she added quietly, "He deserves happiness. Perhaps Melissande will care for him and make him happy."

That was the sticking point, the duke thought, grimacing. He could

imagine Melissande making a gentleman's life a series of delightful en-
counters until the gentleman chanced to disagree with her or refuse her
something. Then . . . it made him shudder to think of it. He wouldn't
worry overly about it. It wouldn't be his problem. However, he would
pray for the Earl of Northcliffe once the knot was tied.

"I'll go fetch Melissande for you, Papa."

The duke watched his daughter walk from the library. Something
strange was going on here. He knew her well, for she was his favorite, the
child of his heart and of his mind. He remembered her sudden rigidity,
the trembling of her hands. And he thought blankly, as a crazed notion
bulleted through his brain—does she want the Earl of Northcliffe? He
shook his head even as he tried to remember three years before when
Alexandra was only fifteen, painfully shy, her beautiful auburn hair in
tight braids around her head, and still plump with childhood fat. No, no,
she'd been much too young. If she'd felt anything for Douglas Sherbrooke, why it had to have been only a girlish infatuation, nothing more.

He wondered if what he was doing was wise, then he knew that there
was no choice. The gods had offered him a gift horse and he wasn't about
to have it race away from him toward another stable, one doubtless less
worthy and less in need than his. If Alexandra did feel something for the
earl, he was sorry for it, but he couldn't, he wouldn't, change the plan. If
the earl wanted Melissande, he would have her. The duke sat down to
await the arrival of his eldest daughter.

The interview between the Duke of Beresford and his eldest daughter
proceeded exactly as the duke expected.

Melissande was in a towering passion within two minutes of her father's announcement. She looked incredibly beautiful in a towering passion, as she did in most moods. Her cheeks were flushed, her eyes—blue
as the lake at Patley Bridge in the late summer—sparkled and glinted.
Her thick black hair, darker than a starless midnight sky, shone vividly
even in the dim light of his library, and the artless array of curls that clus-
tered around her face bounced as her passion grew. She drew a deep
breath, tossed her curls another time, and nearly shouted, "Ridiculous!
He thinks he can simply *crook* his finger after three years—*three years*—
and I will not gainsay him at all, that I will come rushing to him and allow
him to do whatever he pleases with me!"

The duke understood her fury. Her pride was hurt, and the Chambers
pride was renowned for its depth and breadth and endurance. He also
knew how to deal with his daughter, and thus spoke slowly, empathy and
understanding for her feelings filling his voice. "I am sorry that he hurt
you three years ago, Melissande. No, don't try to rewrite the past, my

dear, for I know the truth, and it is a different recipe from the one you fed your credulous sister. But that isn't important now, save that you must keep in mind what really happened then. The earl spoke to me before he left, you know, explaining himself quite nicely I thought at the time. But as you can see, it is you who have the last word here, it is you and no other who caught his fancy and kept it, and now he admits that his fancy and his hand are eager to be reeled in by none other than you."

Melissande was doubtless the most beautiful creature the duke had ever seen. He found himself marveling even now that she had sprung from his loins. She was exquisite and she'd been spoiled and pampered since her birth. And why shouldn't she be petted and given whatever she wished, his wife would ask? She was so beautiful, so absolutely perfect, she deserved it. Judith would also say, doubtless, that Melissande deserved a duke, at least, not a paltry earl, even though he was one of the richest in all the land. But dukes weren't all that plentiful, any duke, one teetering on the edge of the grave or a young, almost presentable one. The father looked at his daughter now, watching her sort through his words, bringing a sense to them that would please her vanity and salve her wounded sensibilities.

"Still," she said after several moments of silence, "still he expects too much. I won't have him, Father! You must write back and inform His arrogant Lordship that I now find him repellent, yes, that's it, utterly repellent, just as Oglethorpe was repellent and a toad. I won't have him; I will wed another." She stopped, spun about, her white hands pressed to her cheeks.

"Oh dear, what if he feels that he broke my heart three years ago and that is why I haven't wed! What if he believes that I've pined for him? I can't bear that, Father, I just can't! What shall I do?"

The duke made soothing noises. Pride, he thought, damnable pride. Well, he'd infused her with all the pride that was in his lineage. Inspiration struck and he smiled to himself. "The poor fellow," he said in a mournful voice, shaking his head.

Melissande whirled about to face her father, blinking in confusion. "What poor fellow?"

"Why, the Earl of Northcliffe, of course. The man has wanted you for three years, has doubtless suffered more than you and I could possibly imagine. He wanted you, Melissande, but he felt great dedication for England, felt honor bound by what he believed to be his sacred duty. He did not dismiss his honor, despite his ardent desire for you. Surely you cannot fault him for that. And now he tries to make restitution. He pines for you. And now he bows himself before you, my dear, begging that you forgive his lamentable integrity, that you please consider that you will have him now." The duke wasn't about to tell his daughter that the earl had sold out some nine or ten months before. Even Melissande would wonder at the earl's depth of passion were she to know that he hadn't pushed to have her for nearly a year after he was free to do so.

"He was very distraught," Melissande said slowly. "Even as I took him to task for his devotion to his absurd duty, he did appear genuinely distraught."

"He is the Earl of Northcliffe, and his home is one of the premier estates in England."

"Yes, that is true."

"He has wealth and standing. He is still a man to be reckoned with in the government. I hear he still consults with the War Ministry, even with Addington." The duke paused, then added smoothly, "A man in such a position desperately needs a wife of grace and consequence to oversee his social obligations. He is also a handsome man as I recall. I hear he is much in demand in London drawing rooms."

"He is very dark, too dark. He is probably hairy. I do not like men so dark, but he is an earl."

"You liked him well enough three years ago."

"Perhaps, but I was very young. He was severe then; he is probably more so now. He did not laugh very much; he was far too serious. No, even his smiles were rare."

"He was suffering from a rather serious wound."

"Still, he rarely showed a glimmer of humor when I was amusing. It was a fault I saw but ignored then."

"But my dear, how could he be so very severe when he admired you? His admiration, as I recall, was quite remarkable in its scope." That was true, but he'd known that the earl, had he remained longer in his daughter's orbit, would have removed the blinders from his eyes. He fully intended to have them wed as quickly as possible.

"Not as remarkable as his devotion to his country!"

"Now his devotion would be to you, his wife, no longer to his country. You are an intelligent girl, Melissande. Surely with such a devoted husband, you would arrange matters quite to your liking. Ah, how you would shine when you took your rightful place as the Countess of Northcliffe in London society."

The duke stopped, knowing the seeds were all well planted, watered, and fertilized. Perhaps even a bit too much fertilizer. He must wait now and see if her mental powers were sufficient to bring the seeds to fruition. He hesitated to threaten her but he would do so should she refuse what he wanted her to do.

She was looking thoughtful, a circumstance that normally would have made him very wary, for her perfect brow was furrowed, a condition that she wouldn't have allowed had she been aware of it, for it diminished her beauty. It made her look remarkably human. Soon, thank God, another man would have to worry about her tantrums, her passions, her sulks, the inevitable scenes that gave him indigestion. Ah, but then again, the man who would be her husband would also have one of the most beautiful women in England in his possession.

The duke wondered if that would be enough. He liked the Earl of Northcliffe, believed him a fine young man. Since he was fit again, he probably did smile and laugh from time to time. The duke hadn't remembered him as being overly serious and severe. And now he would give him a prize that would gratify any man's soul.

He would give himself desperately needed funds to keep the ducal ship afloat.

CHAPTER
═4═

"BUT WHAT DO you think, Alex? Should I agree to marry Douglas Sherbrooke?"

Why, Alexandra wondered yet again as she looked at her sister, did people go through the pretense of asking for another's opinion? It was as if Alexandra, more than most, gave an impression that encouraged people to speak to her of their innermost thoughts, to ask her view, but of course, she wasn't to expect that they would ever heed anything she had to say.

Slowly she raised her chin and said clearly, "I think Douglas Sherbrooke deserves to marry the most beautiful woman in the world."

That drew up Melissande, for she'd been pacing her bedchamber like a healthy young colt, clearly involved in her own thoughts. "What did you say?"

"I think Douglas Sherbrooke—"

"Oh, all right, I heard you! Well, if I decide to wed him, you will have your wish, won't you?"

Alexandra eyed her sister thoughtfully, then said slowly, "I hope that Douglas Sherbrooke will believe so."

Melissande had very nearly convinced herself that becoming the Countess of Northcliffe would be quite the thing for her to do when their mother, Her Grace, Lady Judith, came into the bedchamber like a small whirlwind, spots of angry color on her thin cheeks, her hands fluttering, saying, "Your father says you will marry the earl soon—next week if it can be arranged! He says we won't go to London, there won't be the need to go! Ah, the man is impossible! What are we to do?"

Alexandra said mildly, "You know there isn't much money, Mama. London would cost Papa a fortune he can ill afford to spend."

"Stuff and nonsense! It is ever his plaint. I want to go to London. As for you, my girl, you must find a husband, and you'll not find one hanging over the garden wall watching you as you weed your infernal plants! After your sister chooses the gentleman she wishes, why then, the others will realize that you are to come next. They will put their feelings for your sister behind them and turn to you. As I said, your father has always complained that there is no money for anything, but there always is, except for your poor brother, who is quite unable to pry sufficient funds from your father to live like a young gentleman should live in London. It is disgraceful, and so I told His Grace."

Lady Judith stopped to catch her breath. "What did Papa say?" Alexandra asked quickly during this brief respite.

"He said I should mind to my own affairs, if it is any of your concern, my girl."

Alexandra wondered why her father had told his wife about the marriage plans, but decided he'd probably been forced into it somehow. She sat back and watched with a good deal of detachment as her mother and Melissande whipped themselves into a state of advanced outrage. It was ever so when one or the other didn't get her way. Eventually Alexandra rose and walked from her sister's peach and cream bedchamber, her departure unregarded.

Alexandra knew that Melissande would agree to marry the earl. She also knew that on that day, she would wish to be on another continent so she wouldn't have to see it, wouldn't have to live through it. She didn't want to face up to it, but she had to. She also knew there was no hope for it; she would be here, aloofness and silence her only defense, and she would be forced to smile and to greet the earl as a future sister-in-law should and she would have to watch him look at Melissande as he spoke the words that would make her his wife.

Alexandra had come to realize in her eighteen years that life could concoct many lavishly inedible dishes to serve on one's plate.

Northcliffe Hall

Douglas couldn't believe it, couldn't at first take it all in. He stared from the Duke of Beresford's letter to the other short, urgent scrawl dispatched by Lord Avery himself just that morning, brought to him by a messenger who awaited his reply in the kitchen, doubtless downing ale.

He picked up the duke's letter again. It was jovial to the eyebrows, filled with jubilation and relief and congratulations. Douglas was to marry Melissande next week at Claybourn Hall in the ancient Norman church in the village of Wetherby. The duke would become his proud papa-in-law in seven days. His new papa-in-law would also shove quite a few guineas into the needy ducal pocket once the marriage had taken place.

He picked up Lord Avery's letter. He was also to go to Etaples, France, as soon as possible, disguised as a bloody French soldier. He was to await

Georges Cadoudal's instructions, then follow them. He was to rescue a French girl who was being held against her will by one of Napoleon's generals. There was nothing more, absolutely no detail, no names, no specifics. If Douglas didn't do this, England would lose its best chance at eliminating Napoleon, for Georges Cadoudal was the brain behind the entire operation. Lord Avery was counting on Douglas. England was counting on Douglas. To hammer the final nail in the coffin, Lord Avery wrote in closing, "If you do not rescue this wretched girl, Cadoudal says he won't continue with the plan. He insists upon you, Douglas, but he refuses to say why. Perhaps you know the answer. I know you have met him in the past. You must do this and succeed, Northcliffe, you must. England's fate lies in your hands."

Douglas sat back in his chair and laughed. "I must wed and I must go to France." He laughed louder.

Would he sail to France to rescue Cadoudal's lover, as doubtless this female was, or travel to Claybourn Hall as a bridegroom?

Douglas stopped laughing. The frown returned to his forehead. Why couldn't life be simple, just once? He was responsible for England's fate? Well, hell.

He thought about Georges Cadoudal, the radical leader of the Royalist Chouans. His last attempt to eliminate Napoleon had been in December 1800, his followers using explosives in Paris that had killed twenty-two people and wounded well over fifty, but not harming any of Napoleon's entourage. Georges Cadoudal was a dangerous man, a passionate man who despised Napoleon to the depths of his soul, a man who sought the return of the Bourbons to the French throne; he counted no cost, be it lives or money. But evidently this girl's life he counted high, so high that he would renege on his plans with England if she weren't rescued.

Cadoudal knew Douglas, that was true, had seen him play the Frenchman several years before and succeed in a mission, but why he would insist upon Douglas and no other to rescue his lover would remain a mystery until and unless Douglas went to Etaples, France. And now the English government was backing Cadoudal in another plot. And the plot was in jeopardy because Georges's lover was being held prisoner.

When Hollis, the Sherbrooke butler for thirty years, who looked remarkably like a quite respectable peer of the realm himself, walked soundlessly into the library, Douglas at first paid him no heed. Once, many years before, when Douglas was young and prideful as a cock and equally jealous of his own worth, a friend had joked that Douglas resembled the Sherbrooke butler more than he did his own father. Douglas had flattened him.

Hollis cleared his throat gently.

Douglas looked up, and a black eyebrow went up as well in silent question.

"Your cousin, Lord Rathmore, has just arrived, my lord. He said I wasn't to disturb you but one simply doesn't disregard His Lordship's presence, you know."

"That is certainly true. To ask Tony to remain in a quiet corner to await someone's pleasure would never do. I'll come directly. I wonder what His Lordship wants? Surely not to press me about marriage."

"Probably not, my lord. If I may speak plainly, His Lordship looks a bit downpin, a bit tight about the mouth. Perhaps ill, although not of the body, you understand, but of the spirit. Were I to hazard a guess, knowing His Lordship's penchants, I dare say it would involve the fair sex." He looked off into the distance, adding, "It usually does, regardless of penchants."

"Damnation," said Douglas, rising from his desk. "I'll see him." He stared down again at the two letters. The messenger could wait a bit longer. He had to think, had to weigh all the alternatives open to him, he had to have more time. Besides, Anthony Colin St. John Parrish, Viscount Rathmore, was the son of his mother's first cousin, and a favorite of his. It had been six months since they'd been in each other's company.

His first view of his cousin did not gladden his heart. He looked depressed as the devil, just as Hollis had said. Douglas strode into the small estate room, closed the door firmly behind him, and locked it. "All right, Tony," he said without preamble, "out with it. What is wrong?"

Tony Parrish, Viscount Rathmore, turned about from his perusal of nothing in particular outside the window to look at his cousin. He straightened his shoulders automatically and tried for a smile. It wasn't much of a smile, but Douglas appreciated the effort, and repeated mildly, "Tell me, Tony. What's happened?"

"Hollis, I gather?"

"Yes. Tell me."

"That man should have been a bloody priest."

"Oh no, it's just that he isn't blind. Also he's rather fond of you. Now, talk to me, Tony."

"All right, curse you, if you must know, I am no longer engaged. I am now without a fiancée. I have been betrayed. I am alone and adrift. I am here."

Was Hollis never wrong? Still, Douglas was incredulous. "You mean to say that Teresa Carleton broke it off?"

"Of course she didn't. Don't be a simpleton. No, I did. I found out she was sleeping with one of my friends. Friend, ha! The bloody sod! Can you believe it, Douglas? The woman was to marry me—*me!*—she was to be my bloody wife. I had selected her with great care, I had nurtured her as I would the most precious of blossoms, treated her with consideration and respect, never doing much of anything except kissing her and not even with my mouth open, mind you, and all along she was actually one of my friend's mistresses. It is impossible to believe, Douglas, it is intolerable."

"It isn't as if she were a virgin to begin with, Tony," Douglas said mildly. "She's a widow, after all. I dare say you've continued sleeping with your lovers and I doubt not that some of them are friends of Teresa's."

"That's not the point, and you know it, damn you!"

"Perhaps not to you, but—" Douglas broke off. "It is over then? You're a free man now? Have you really broken the engagement or are you here to lick your wounds and consider your unanchored state?"

"Yes, I've broken it off, and I would like to kill the woman for her perfidy! Cuckolding me! *Me*, Douglas!"

"You weren't yet wed to the lady, Tony."

"The principle remains the same. I cannot take it in, Douglas, I can scarce convince my mind that it has really happened. How could a woman do such a thing to me?"

His cousin, Douglas thought, held a very good opinion of himself, and truth be told, so did most other people. No woman, so far as Douglas knew, had ever played Tony false. Indeed, it was always Tony who had stepped away, laughing, as carefree as Ryder when it came to the fair sex, until he met Teresa Carleton, a young widow who had, for some obscure and unfathomed reason, charmed Viscount Rathmore to his Hessian-covered toes and marriage had popped into his mind and out of his mouth within a week. Then she had proceeded to play the game by the same rules Tony employed. The blow to his esteem must be shattering. No wonder he was reeling from it.

"I can't go back to London now for I would see her and my temper is uncertain, Douglas, you know that. I must rusticate until I regain my balance, until I am once more in control—cold and hard in my brain once again—and in no danger of cursing that scheming slut and slapping her silly. Do you mind if I stay here for a while?"

The solution to his problem came to Douglas in a blinding flash, fully fleshed and brilliant, and he grinned. "Tony, you may stay here for the remainder of the century. You may drink all my fine French brandy; you may even sleep in my earl's bed. You may do anything you wish." Douglas strode to his cousin, grabbed his hand and pumped it, all the while grinning like a fool. "In addition, you, Tony, are about to save my life. Heaven will welcome you for what you will do for me."

Tony Parrish looked at his cousin, then smiled, a real smile, one filled with curiosity and humor. "I expect you will tell your expectations of my future bravery," he said slowly.

"Oh yes, indeed. Let's go riding and I will tell you all about it."

Tony's smile remained intact, his interest level high for about five minutes into Douglas's recital, then he looked astounded, aghast, then once again, he smiled, shrugged, and said, "Why not?"

Claybourn Hall

Why not indeed, Tony Parrish thought five days later, his eyes a bit glazed from the vision that stood not five feet from him. She was the most exquisite creature he had ever seen. Every feature complemented the other, and each was arguably well nigh perfect. None of his former or present mistresses, nor his former fiancée, Teresa Carleton, came near to her in the flawlessness of her features. He'd always believed fair-haired women were the most beautiful, the most delicate and alluring. By all the saints, not so. Her hair was black and thick with no hint of red, her eyes an incredible dark blue, slightly slanted upward and sinfully long-lashed. Her skin was white and soft and smooth, her nose thin, her mouth full and tempting. Her body was so precisely perfect in its wondrous curves that it made him break into an immediate sweat.

He felt his belly cramp. He felt himself pale. He just looked at her, unable not to, and watched a slow smile touch her mouth. She spoke, saying softly, "Viscount Rathmore? You are the earl's cousin, I believe?"

He nodded like a dimwitted fool and took her hand, turning it slowly, and kissing the soft palm. She knew her effect on him, he thought, her warm hand still held in his. She knew that he was stunned; and she would attempt to manipulate him, but he didn't mind. Odd, but it was so. Suddenly he felt her fingers tighten slightly in his grasp as he returned her smile. Was she also a bit stunned as well? He would soon see. He knew he had to regain his confidence, sorely diminished by Teresa Carleton. He had to regain his mastery. He could, if he wished, make this glorious creature bend to him. He could and he would . . .

His thinking stopped cold in its tracks. Her name was Melissande and he was here to marry her by proxy to his cousin, Douglas Sherbrooke.

Etaples, France

Douglas was in the middle of Napoleon's naval invasion stronghold, although anywhere from Boulogne to Dunkirk to Ostend and all points in between could be considered part of his "immense project." It was, actually, one of the safest places to be in France, particularly if one were an English spy, for there was no security at all and people came and went and looked and talked and listened and even drew sketches of all the ongoing work. Douglas marveled at the thousands upon thousands of men who labored around the clock in the basins and harbors and on the beaches, building hundreds of transports of all kinds. Alongside the score upon score of workers were soldiers, and they did little as far as Douglas could tell. There was constant activity everywhere.

Douglas wore a private's uniform, new and shining but three days before, and now appropriately soiled and wrinkled. He'd been scouting about as he'd waited for Cadoudal to contact him, gleaning information from the loose-mouthed officers and enlisted soldiers in the neighboring taprooms. All he could do was wait. His French was flawless, his manners just as they should be—commiserating with the enlisted men, joining in their complaints and grievances—and listening to the officers from a discreet distance, exhibiting due deference. All the talk was of an impending invasion simply because Napoleon had visited the many encampments along the coast two weeks before, assuring the men that soon, very soon now, they would cross that dismal little ditch and teach those English bankers and merchants that it was the French who ruled the land and the sea. Fine words, Douglas thought. Did Napoleon really believe that the English peasantry would rise up and welcome him as their liberator when and if he managed to cross the Channel, smash through the English navy, and land at Dover?

Two days passed. Douglas was bored and restless. As it turned out, he got Georges Cadoudal's instructions from a one-legged beggar who sidled up to him, stinking like rotted cabbage, and poked a thick packet into his coat pocket. The blighted specimen managed to get away before Douglas could question him. He read the letter twice, memorizing the precise instructions, then carefully studied each of the enclosed papers and documents. He sat back, thinking now of what Cadoudal expected him to do. He shook his head at the complexity of it all, the sheer heedless arrogance of it. Georges Cadoudal was imprudent at all times, outrageous upon occasion; he was at once brilliant and feckless; failure chaffed him and as of late, he'd known few successes, as far as Douglas knew.

It was obvious he'd spent hours formulating a plan to rescue this damned girl, this Janine Daudet. However, since Cadoudal was the brain behind the plot to kidnap Napoleon and create insurrection in Paris, setting the Comte d'Artois, the younger brother of Louis XVI, promptly on the throne, and since he held more than a million francs from the English government, Lord Avery was inclined to meet his demands. Obviously Georges couldn't take the risk of attempting a rescue himself. Obviously he knew that Douglas was an expert on General Honoré Belesain and that was why he'd asked for him specifically. Obviously, he believed Douglas would succeed. Douglas wondered if Georges knew of Belesain's scaly reputation with women. Damnation.

The following morning Douglas was fastening the buttons of his unfamiliar britches and straightening his stark black coat. Once he reached Boulogne, he would become an official functionary from Paris, sent by Bonaparte himself, to oversee the preparations for the English invasion. He devoutly prayed that Cadoudal's papers were in good order. With all the English money he'd gotten, Georges could afford the best forgers. Douglas didn't want to be discovered and shot as a spy.

At precisely twelve o'clock, looking every inch the officious functionary, whose authority in all likelihood exceeded his brains and his manners and his breeding, he made his way to Boulogne to the residence of General Honoré Belesain, not a difficult house to locate since it belonged to the mayor and was the largest mansion in the entire city. The general was the good mayor's guest. The good mayor, upon further inquiry, hadn't been seen in over three months.

Douglas did know just about everything about General Belesain. Nothing the general did could surprise Douglas. He was a brilliant tactician, a competent administrator, though most details were attended to by aides. He was vicious to both his prisoners and his own men, and he was more than passing fond of young girls. He fancied himself both the epitome of a military man and of a lover. Douglas knew that his wife, evidently long-suffering, was well ensconced in faraway Lyon with their four children. The general was on the portly side but believed himself a god amongst men. He lacked control and lost his temper quickly and with deadly results, as his men and the young girls he fancied discovered to their own detriment. In sexual matters, he wasn't known for his gallantry, even when in the best of moods. He many times drank himself into insensibility after he'd had sex.

The mayor's house was three stories, a soft yellow brick that had mellowed with age, large and rectangular, and covered with thick ivy. It was set back from the road, its long drive lined with full-branched oak trees, green and abundant in early summer. The mayor was obviously a man of substance. Or had been. There were at least a dozen soldiers patrolling the perimeter or simply standing guard outside the several doors to the house.

He looked up, wondering which of those third-floor rooms held Janine Daudet. He wondered if the general had raped her yet and then he knew that of course he had. Who would have stopped him? He prayed the general hadn't played his perverted games with her. He wondered if the gen-

eral had any idea who he was holding. There was no way of knowing because the general was more arrogant, more perverse, than any leader
Douglas knew about.

An aide, Grillon by name, Douglas knew, came to greet him in the
large entrance hall. He swaggered in his importance and in his fine scarlet uniform with all its braid, yet there was also an air of wariness about
him. He was uncertain face to face with this unknown man; he was also
a bully when he knew the rules and the players. Douglas gave nothing
away; he was enjoying the fellow's unease. He counted four more soldiers in the entrance hall.

"I am Monsieur Lapalisse. You, of course, know who I am. I will see
the general now." Douglas then looked about the house, quite aware that
the lieutenant was studying him closely. He tried for a supercilious expression, but it was difficult, for Douglas had never been good at sneers.
He saw a cobweb in the corner and that helped his lip curl.

"Monsieur Lapalisse," Grillon said at last, "if you will wait but a moment, I will inform the general of your presence and see if he wishes—"

"I am not in the habit of waiting," Douglas said, looking the young
man up and down and finding him lacking. "I suggest that you announce
me immediately. Indeed, let us go now, together."

Grillon fidgeted, then quickly turned on his heel. The general was suffering from a headache. He'd overindulged the previous night and was
paying the price today, the fool. He'd not known exactly when this
damned bureaucrat was to arrive, but he should have realized it would be
exactly when he didn't wish to see him. The general was also nervous
about this man's visit because no one higher in the government had noti-
fied him of it. Well, to hell with him.

General Belesain was standing behind his cluttered desk, eyes cold,
body stiff, his forehead furrowed. When Douglas entered beside Grillon,
he straightened to his full height, but Douglas wasn't fooled. His attitude
was both wary and defensive. Excellent, Douglas thought as he strolled
into the large salon as if he owned it. He gave the general a slight nod,
saying in his perfect French, "It is a pleasant day."

"Yes, it is," General Belesain said, taken off balance. "Er, I am informed you are from Napoleon's war committee, although I do not understand. He was here not long ago and expressed his pleasure at how his
invasion plans are progressing."

"A committee is such an amorphous sort of entity," Douglas said, striving yet again for a supercilious smile and a Gaelic shrug. "I am not a rep-
resentative of any committee. I am here as Napoleon's personal, er,
investigator."

The general stiffened even as his jaw slackened and his brain quickened. "Investigator?"

Had Napoleon somehow heard of the death of the two soldiers he'd ordered flogged the previous week? Perhaps he'd heard of the girl's beating, a girl whose relatives had a bit of clout? Damn the foolish girl. She'd protested, but he'd known she wanted him, the little tease, and thus he'd taken her, perhaps a bit roughly, but it wasn't as if she wouldn't recover to enjoy him again. She hadn't succumbed to his logic and his charms as had the woman he held upstairs in the small room next to his bedchamber.

Belesain believed Napoleon invincible on the battlefield, but he loathed him for his hypocritical bourgeois attitudes. He must tread warily. This man standing before him was nothing but a bureaucrat, a nonentity, obviously a lackey with few brains. But he did have power, curse him, which meant he, Belesain, would deal with him. If he couldn't deal with him, he would have him killed. After all, robbers and scoundrels of all sorts abounded on the roads.

"Yes," Douglas said. "As you doubtless know, Napoleon has always believed it imperative that plans and those carrying out the plans must be overseen. An endless task, no?"

"You have papers, of course."

"Naturally."

At three o'clock that afternoon, Douglas walked beside General Belesain through the encampment on the beach at Boulogne. The general hated this—this forced graciousness to a damned bureaucrat, this air of cooperation with a man he both feared and despised. He tried to intimidate Douglas, then ignored him, acting as though he knew everything and could control everything, and that made Douglas smile. Dinner that evening was with a dozen of Belesain's top officers in the mayor's dining room. By the time the lengthy meal was done, most of the officers were drunk. By midnight, three of them had been carried back to their billets by their fellow officers. By one o'clock in the morning, Douglas was more alert than he'd ever been in his life, waiting for his chance.

He prayed no one would discover he was really an English spy. He had no wish to die. After all, when he returned to England, it would be to his new wife, to Melissande—ah, how sweet her name sounded on his tongue—and she would be in his bed and he would keep her there until she conceived the Sherbrooke heir.

When the general challenged him to a game of piquet, Douglas gave him a bland smile, and his heartbeat quickened. "The wager?" he inquired, flicking a speck of dust off his black coat.

The general suggested francs.

Douglas showed mild irritation with such banality. Surely such a brilliant and sophisticated man as the general could come up with a more interesting . . . ah, a more enticing wager?

The general thought this over, then smiled, off center, for he was drunk. He rubbed his hands together and his eyes gleamed as he said, "Ah, yes, certainly. The winner of our little game, monsieur, will enjoy a succulent little morsel who currently lives with me here. Her name is Janine and she is very talented at pleasuring a man."

Douglas agreed with remarkable indifference.

CHAPTER
═══ 5 ═══

Claybourn Hall

ALEXANDRA COULDN'T BELIEVE it. She stood still as a stone by Melissande's Italian writing desk, whose surface for once held something other than a myriad of perfume bottles. She still wore her dressing gown, and her hair hung in a thick braid over her shoulder. She stared down at the single sheet of paper. She closed her eyes a moment, closed them against the knowledge . . .

You hoped this would happen.

Perhaps, perhaps not. Regardless, she'd kept silent. She'd watched. And it had happened. Melissande and Anthony Parrish, Viscount Rathmore, had eloped to Gretna Green the previous night. Slowly Alexandra picked up the paper upon which Melissande had scrawled her few sentences, words that had changed all their lives, words that were misspelled because Melissande disdained any attempt at scholarship. Alexandra was calm; she felt strangely suspended, as if something more were going to happen. She would have to take the note to her father. She would have to confess that she guessed what was happening between the two of them.

She hated herself at that moment, knew herself to be a jealous creature, petty and mean-spirited, who deserved no consideration from anyone.

After the duke had read the letter, he laid it carefully on his desktop, walked over to the wide windows and stared out onto the east lawn. There were four peacocks strolling the perimeter, three geese, and a goat tethered to a yew bush. After a near decade had passed, at least in Alexandra's mind, he turned to look thoughtfully at his younger daughter. He smiled at her then, actually smiled. To her astonishment, he said mildly, "Well, it's done, wouldn't you say, my dear? No big surprise, no startling revelations. No, I'm not taken aback by this, Alex, because Tony left me a rather fulsome letter, much more articulate than Melissande's, much more apologetic. His honor abuses him. We will see."

"Oh Papa, I knew, I knew, but I wanted . . ." Her father chuckled and shook his finger at her. "You too realized what Lord Rathmore would do, my dear?"

"Not that they would go to Gretna Green, but perhaps that they would refuse to go along with the wedding . . . I can't lie to you, Papa. But I hadn't realized that you also—"

Alexandra stood there, wringing her hands, her distress enough to make any fond parent soften. Her guilt was growing, not subsiding. The duke watched her for a moment, then said, "Yes, I knew Tony wanted Melissande and that she wanted him. I have never before seen two people more enraptured with each other so quickly. Tony is a fine young man—intelligent, witty, and blessed with good looks, an important ingredient to females. Further, he is nearly as rich as the Earl of Northcliffe. Doubtless he will offer a settlement to rival his cousin's; indeed in his letter he gives me his assurances. I imagine his guilt must prick him sorely, as I said—much greater than yours, Alex!—for did he not betray his cousin and take the woman the earl had chosen away from him? Ah yes, he despises himself for what he has done, now, of course, that he has done it, and there is no going back. Conscience, I've found, is all the more potent once the deed is done and irreversible. But despite this lapse, this quite unfortunate behavior, the viscount appears an honorable man. He will bring Melissande back here, and very soon. She, the minx, won't want to see us because she knows she's disaccommodated your mother and fears a great scold, but her husband will force her to come." The duke smiled into the distance. "Tony Parrish isn't a man to be wound around a woman's finger even though the woman is so beautiful it makes your teeth ache just to look at her. Aye, he will bring her back regardless of her pleas and her tears and her sulks."

"But I did guess, Papa, I truly did." There, it was out, all of it. She stood stiff and miserable, waiting for the parental tongue to flay her.

The duke took his daughter's hand and raised it to his lips. "All I regret is the immense bother occasioned by this irresponsible act. It is never a father's wish to have any of his offspring wed across the anvil in Scotland. A duke's daughter, in particular, isn't supposed to behave with such a lack of propriety." The duke paused then, and a myriad of expressions crossed his face. He said abruptly to Alexandra, "You want the earl so much, then?"

"You guessed that as well? Oh dear. It is revolting. I am as transparent as the fish pond."

"You are my daughter. I know you and I am rather fond of you."

"It's true. I have loved him, Papa, for three years, but now . . . now, I will not even have him as a brother-in-law."

She looked up at her father, desolation and pain in her fine eyes.

The duke said abruptly, "I just received a letter from your brother. I will tell you the truth, Alex. Even the settlement Tony will doubtless provide won't save this family. Your brother has left England in disgrace, on his way to America, he writes. He leaves immense debts behind him that will bankrupt me utterly. Even Tony's settlement, generous though I know it will be, won't settle the debts. I've been wondering what to do, thinking, worrying, struggling, but now . . . ah, now perhaps there is a ray of light." He turned on his heel and left the library, leaving Alexandra to stare speechlessly after him.

In approximately one hour Tony Parrish and his new viscountess would arrive at Claybourn Hall. She was sulking, enjoying a truly royal snit, he knew, and it made him smile. He'd informed her in no uncertain terms that they had to return to her father's home, that he had to make things right again. She'd pleaded and begged; she hated her guilt and didn't want her nose rubbed in it. She'd even cried on his shoulder, immensely beautiful crocodile tears, he'd observed aloud to his new wife, who had then promptly flown into a passion. He'd laughed. Outraged, Melissande had thrown one of her hairbrushes at him but he'd simply thrown it back at her. She was so stunned at his retaliation, she was dumbstruck. He left the room, telling her to be downstairs in ten minutes. Another hairbrush had struck the closing door. She'd come down in eleven minutes and he'd looked at his watch and frowned at her. He said nothing. She had obeyed him. She would accustom herself, in time, to obeying him without scenes and tantrums and without using any extra minutes.

They rode in a private carriage Tony had rented from a stable in Harrogate to take them to Gretna Green. This was the second day of his marriage and in an hour he would have to face his new papa-in-law, who would doubtless want to strangle him. But he had to return. It was the right thing to do. There was no choice. Besides he'd written to the duke that he would return to discuss the marriage settlement and to make amends as best he could.

He smiled at his bride's altogether lovely profile and didn't question that he wanted her very much, right this instant. He had but to touch her hand and he wanted her. He had but to hear her voice from another room and he wanted her. He had but to see her flushed with anger and yelling at him and he wanted her. Having her so close to him was more than he could bear.

He turned and said, "Take off your pelisse."

Melissande was in the throes of guilt, embarrassment, fury with her new husband for treating her with no consideration at all—he'd actually thrown the hairbrush back at her! "What did you say?"

"I said to take off your pelisse."

"I'm not at all too warm."

"Good."

She frowned at him, then unbuttoned the pelisse. He helped her remove it, tossing it to the other seat. He lightly touched his fingertips to her chin, caressing her, holding her head steady. He kissed her, lightly, not parting his own lips on hers.

"Tony!"

"Hush. Now, dear one, remove your bonnet. I can't kiss you properly with that nonsense on your head. Also it flattens your beautiful hair. Black as the most sinful night, your hair. I want to feel it cascading through my fingers."

Since his order also contained a very nice compliment, Melissande, mollified, removed her bonnet, tossing it atop her pelisse.

"Now," Tony said. His long fingers began on the long line of buttons that marched up the front of her gown. She gasped and slapped at his hand. "We're in a carriage, Tony! It is in the middle of the day! Goodness, you must stop, you can't do that, you—"

He kissed her again, pulling her onto his lap. His right hand was beneath the hem of her gown, moving up her leg, higher and higher until he touched the bare soft flesh of her inner thighs. She was squirming on his lap, and he knew it was from embarrassment, not coyness. It didn't matter. He wanted her and he fully intended to take her, right here, in the carriage, with her sitting on his lap, facing him, and he would come deep inside her. He nearly moaned aloud with the thought.

She continued to struggle and he said into her mouth, "You will be quiet now. You are my wife, Melissande, and you will learn, very soon now, that you will obey me. I want you and I intend to have you. I haven't taken you since last night because you were a virgin and thus sore from that plowing. But you have had time to recover. I will go easily with you. I want to see your breasts, to fondle them, to taste them with my tongue. You will leave your gown on and I will come into you after you've lifted your skirts."

She stared at him in disbelief, so adrift in uncharted seas that she could find nothing to say. The previous evening, she'd felt wicked, truth be told, because of what they'd done. She had shown the damned Earl of Northcliffe that she wouldn't be ordered about by either him or her father. Tony was lovely; he was gallant; he teased her mercilessly, making her want more. He fascinated her. He was like quicksilver. She'd quickly recognized the strength in him, the male stubbornness, the arrogance that was bred in him, but she'd never doubted that she could handle him. After all, she'd handled every other gentleman who'd chanced to swim into her ken.

He'd introduced her to sex in a very polished way. She recognized, vaguely, that he was immensely experienced but she was unable to appreciate his finesse. She found the entire procedure horribly embarrassing, and the darkness she'd begged for hadn't slowed him down a bit. He hadn't hurt her overly much. As for any pleasure from coupling, she sincerely doubted that such a thing existed. She knew that all she enjoyed was compliments and kissing and his wicked smiles, and perhaps the tip of his tongue lightly touching her ear.

And now he wanted to stick that man-thing of his up into her whilst she sat on his lap, fully gowned yet naked whilst he had his way with her, and all in a moving carriage!

"No," she said very firmly. "I shan't do that."

Tony merely smiled, and thrust his fingers upward until they were pressed against her woman's flesh. She paled then yowled. His right hand busily worked on the buttons over her breasts. She slapped at him, until finally he said in his sternest voice, "You are my wife. How many times must I remind you, Melissande? I know you received little or no pleasure last night. You were a virgin and that is why. You bled and that pleased me. However, I intend to rectify that now. You will accept pleasure from me. You will hold still and stop playing the outraged maiden."

But she didn't stop struggling, even when she felt one of his long fingers slide upward into her. She yelled, and he kissed her, hoping the carriage driver hadn't heard her.

"A delightful virgin, a beauty, and a spoiled handful," he said, his breath warm on her mouth. "That's what I married. I'm not complaining, don't misunderstand me. I had an excellent idea of your character before I ever nibbled that sweet spot just behind your left ear. But I will beat you, you know."

"You wouldn't! No, I shan't allow such a thing! Stop, damn you! Stop doing that!"

"Oh yes, I will beat you," he said as his thumb found her flesh and he began to fondle her. "And I have no intention of stopping. You will see that I shall do whatever I wish to with you." She was undoubtedly beautiful, absolutely exquisite, even with her eyes near to crossing in rage, and truth be told, glazed in utter incomprehension, for she'd never encountered his like before. She tried to jerk away from him. He merely removed his hand, pulled up her gown, her petticoats, and her shift, then bent her back so that she was lying across his lap against his arm. She was wearing her black leather slippers and stockings that were just above her knees, held there with black garters. From there on, she was naked to her waist, and he looked down at her and smiled.

"Very nice," he said only and splayed his fingers over her white belly. "Very nice indeed. I fancy I'll keep you. Were you a trout I wouldn't toss you back into the water. No, indeed."

"You cannot do this, Tony! My father will challenge you to a duel, he will cut your ears off, he will— I'm not a damned fish!"

"Dearest wife, your father wouldn't dream of telling me, your legal husband, master, owner, and lord, not to give you pleasure. And that is what I will do if you would simply close your quite lovely mouth and attend my fingers."

She opened her mouth to yell again at him, then realized the driver would probably hear her. She felt sunk with embarrassment, so mortified she held herself quiet until his fingers began to caress her in that very private place he'd touched the previous night. She hadn't protested much then for she'd still been feeling wicked, and it was dark in the bedchamber, and truth be told, she'd felt very powerful—ah, she'd eloped to Gretna Green!—so she hadn't fully realized . . . simply hadn't known that he would want . . . but now, now it was different. It wasn't black as pitch. It was daylight. They were in a carriage. He had actually looked at her, spoken easily as he'd looked, and she'd been naked and he'd touched her belly and other lower parts. It wasn't to be borne. Suddenly, she felt a deep piercing sensation that made her hips jerk upward against his fingers.

She stared up at him, not understanding, and saw that the damned sod was smiling at her, a knowing smile, a master's smile, so smug and satisfied that it was more than she could stand. She threw back her head and screamed at the top of her lungs.

The carriage jerked to a sudden halt.

Tony's smile didn't slip. He eased her up, helped her straighten her clothes, and waited for their coachman to appear at the window, which he did almost immediately. His eyes went at once to Melissande, and she realized that he must know what her husband had been attempting to do to her.

"Go away!" she yelled at the hapless man. "Ah, just go away!"

"Yes," Tony said easily, sitting back against the squabs, his arms folded over his chest. "Forgive my wife for disturbing you. Sometimes ladies, well, they forget themselves . . . you understand."

The coachman was very afraid he did understand, and, flushing, hurried to climb back to his perch. The carriage jerked forward.

Tony was quiet.

Melissande arranged herself with quick clumsy movements, so furious and embarrassed and disconcerted she wanted to shriek at him until she was hoarse. But it was difficult with him just sitting there, looking out the windows, saying nothing, looking bored. *Bored!*

She smashed her bonnet back onto her head, not caring that her lovely coiffure would suffer irreparable damage from her show of rage. She pulled on her pelisse and refastened the buttons, putting the wrong ones in the wrong holes and not caring.

He looked at her then and the smile was still on his lips. "You know, Mellie—"

"Mellie! What a horrid nickname! I hate it, it is perfectly dreadful and I—"

"Shut up, my dear."

"But, I—" She saw something in his eyes that she'd never encountered before in her twenty-one years. She closed her mouth and turned away, momentarily routed.

"As I was saying, Mellie, for you I betrayed my cousin. However, it isn't the sort of betrayal that destroys the soul. You don't really know Douglas nor does he know you. Lord, were he to have seen your games during the past few days, he would have been utterly disillusioned. He probably would have snuck out in the dark of night to escape you. He wouldn't have taken you to Gretna Green. Indeed, three years ago, I doubt you even saw him beyond a handsome man who praised your immense beauty. He left you because of his honor, because he felt he had to place his duty above matters of the heart. I will tell you truthfully, my dear, he doesn't love you. He remembered that he had desired you, had admired you, had laughed and been entranced by your carelessness, your seeming guilelessness. He remembered your beauty, nothing more.

"But he doesn't love you nor did he then. His family has been ruthless in their attempts to get him wedded so that there will be a Sherbrooke heir within the year. He saw you as a way to batten down his family, to wed himself to a beautiful creature, and save himself from having to travel to London to see the crop of available debutantes.

"Even as I knew I would have you, I was thinking of all the pros and cons of what I was doing. One thing I'm quite certain of though, Douglas will come to realize what a favor I did for him by removing you from the scene. One day he will thank me. You would have driven him mad, utterly mad." Tony now turned to his wife. He was looking very serious. "He is much more the gentleman than I am, you know. He would never have beaten you, no matter the provocation. He would have withdrawn from you, not at all what would bring you into line."

She said slowly, "I don't believe you. Douglas Sherbrooke does love me. He loved me then, he loved me for three years, and he still loves me.

He will mourn me the rest of his life. I will be his lost love. Aye, I have broken his heart by wedding you. He will hate you forever for what you have done. He will never forgive you."

Tony said quietly, "I hope it will not be so. I believe that only Douglas's pride will be a bit bruised. Then he will recover with alacrity when he sees what I must do to keep you under control. He will pump my hand in his gratitude. He will blubber all over me with thankfulness."

Melissande looked down at her gloved hands. "You speak as though you do not hold me in esteem. You speak as though I am not a person to be admired or loved. You speak as though you took me away only to save your cousin. I thought you adored me, wanted me desperately."

"Ah, that is true enough. Understand, just because I adore and want you doesn't mean that I am blind to your character. However, it isn't at all to the point. You see, what I have done demands retribution. I owe Douglas payment, of sorts, so that he won't have to start again at the beginning in his quest for a wife. Indeed, in my letter to your father I hinted as much."

"What do you mean?"

"I don't believe I will tell you, Mellie, not yet, because I have yet to be certain whether my notions are accurate." He gave her a crooked smile. "You see, I was thinking too much about you, about having you naked beneath me, to keep an excellent mental accounting of what I hoped would be true. Well, hopefully your father will have determined the accuracy by the time we return to Claybourn. Now, my dear, your bonnet looks quite dowdy. I suggest you endeavor to make yourself look a bit more charming, for we are nearing Claybourn."

He'd silenced her questions for the moment by appealing to her vanity. He watched her pull a small mirror from her reticule. She was efficient in her efforts, from long practice. She was so beautiful it made him shake. Her body was undoubtedly lovely—at least the parts he'd just managed to uncover and see and touch. He'd wanted to see her face when he took her virginity the previous night, but she'd been so frightened, so embarrassed, that he hadn't the heart to insist upon the lamp being lit. But what really shook him and surprised him as well was that no woman had ever affected him as she had. He had also known instantly that she was utterly impossible, spoiled, vain, as arrogant as he was, but it hadn't mattered. He'd wanted her. Despite Douglas, despite everything, he'd wanted her and he'd taken her.

Now the trick would be to live with her.

Another trick would be to bring her pleasure. The thought of a frigid wife was intolerable. It was nauseating.

The most important trick would be to pay Douglas back.

Odd, Tony thought, as the carriage bowled onto the long narrow drive of Claybourn Hall, but he hadn't given Teresa, his perfidious former betrothed, a thought since he'd met Melissande. He looked at his wife, saw that she was pale and that she was wringing her hands.

He rather hoped her father would yell at her. Then he, Tony, would step in. He was her protector, her master, her husband. Then, he prayed, he and the duke would come to another agreement.

Boulogne, France

Douglas won the piquet match. He hadn't even had to cheat. Belesain had been so drunk by the end of it, Douglas doubted he'd minded losing very much because as the winner he would have had to perform sexually, a feat he probably couldn't have managed. He'd given Douglas a key and told him to explain to the lovely wench he found in the small room that he was here to be pleasured. He said the wench loved threats and a bit of pain. Then, the bloody drunk fool had decided to accompany him. "Because," he said as they climbed the stairs to the third floor, "she isn't exactly trained fully as yet." Douglas watched him unlock the door and stride inside.

He followed, saying nothing. It was a spare room, with only a bed and dresser and a single circular rug in the middle. There was only one occupant, a single woman standing in the middle of the room. Was this Janine Daudet? The general grinned drunkenly at her and said with a flip of his hand, "Strip off those clothes."

The woman hesitated, then complied. He'd expected someone younger, though why he should have he didn't know. No, she wasn't really a girl, Douglas thought, looking at her more closely, but rather a woman in her mid-twenties. She was obviously scared and she was lovely, despite her pallor, the shadows beneath her very dark eyes, and her thinness.

Belesain waited silently until she'd stripped to her shift. Then he lurched to her, grabbed her chin painfully in his fingers and kissed her, fondling her breasts with his other hand through the thin lawn. Then, suddenly, he grabbed the front of her shift and ripped it off her. He laughed, saying over his shoulder to Douglas, "I wanted to see if you approved of her. Nice, eh? A bit thin for my taste, but her tits are nice." He pushed her back onto the bed, leaned over her, and said low, "You see this man, my girl? You do everything he wants you to do or . . . you know the punishment, don't you? I would like to remain and watch, but I am sorely tired." He straightened and turned to Douglas. "You are quiet. Don't you think she is lovely? Not a virgin, but not overused either. She belongs to me, and now, because she isn't stupid, she obeys my every command. Now you may enjoy her, but just for tonight."

He lurched out of the room. Douglas moved after him and listened as his footsteps receded down the corridor and then down the stairs. He listened to another door open and close on the second floor. Then he turned back to face the woman.

She was standing now by the bed, trying to cover herself with her hands. Douglas couldn't believe his good fortune but he wasn't about to doubt it, not for a moment.

His voice was urgent as he strode to her. "Is your name Janine Daudet?"

She was small, very fair, her hair falling straight down her back nearly to her waist. She had light blue eyes, very blond brows and lashes, and she was lovely.

"Are you?"

She nodded, taking a step back.

"Don't be afraid of me. I'm here on behalf of Georges Cadoudal."

Douglas wasn't able to keep his eyes on her face. He hadn't had a woman in a while. His body was responding with deplorable enthusiasm. "Do you know Georges Cadoudal?"

She nodded, still obviously afraid of him, not believing him for a moment, despite the flare of hope he'd seen.

"I wish you to dress, quickly. I am here to take you away, to Georges. We must hurry."

"I don't have any gowns."

Douglas looked around. "A cloak, anything. Come, we must hurry."

"I don't believe you." So there was some spirit left in her after all. She was nearly strangling on her fear but she still kept on. "I know that he gave me to you, he said so, and I know why he did it."

"It's because I won a wager."

"Oh no." She became even paler. Her rouged lips parted, then closed. She shook her head, then said in a rush, "He wants me to find out what you will tell Bonaparte when you return to Paris. He worries also that you are really a spy. I think he would prefer a spy to you being from Bonaparte because he fears Bonaparte will discover the wicked things he's done. He told me I must discover the truth or he will kill my grandmother."

"Ah." Douglas smiled down at her and gently began to run his hands up and down her thin arms. So, the general hadn't been drunk at all. The piquet, the wager, his loss, it had all been Belesain's plan to trap him. Not bad.

"Easy now," he said absently, trying to calm her, all the while thinking furiously.

"Where is your grandmother?"

Janine started. "She's at the farm, two miles from Etaples to the south. He says that he has a man there watching her and that the man will kill her if I don't do as he orders."

"If I know Georges, he's already taken care of any guards at your grandmother's farmhouse. I am really here to save you. Now, let's get you dressed in something. I am taking you and your grandmother to England."

"England," she said slowly, her dark eyes wide with surprise. "But we only speak French."

"It doesn't matter. Many people speak French in England and you will learn. Georges lives there much of the time and he can teach both of you English."

"But—"

"No, I can say no more. Georges wishes me to take you to London. You will be safe there until he returns to fetch you. There are chores he must attend to here first. Will you trust me?"

She looked up at him, worship and trust shining from her face and said simply, "Yes."

"Good. Now, listen to me. Here's what we will do." Douglas wondered, as he stared down into that pale tense face that held such radiant trust for him, why people in general and females in particular believed him to be some sort of Saint George. He hated it but at the same time he found it amusing. He thought of Georges Cadoudal, and fervently hoped she would remember him. After all, Douglas was probably a married man by now and he wanted no moonstruck female on his arm on his return to England.

CHAPTER
═══ 6 ═══

Northcliffe Hall
Five Days Later

DOUGLAS OPENED THE door of the library, saw a lone candle burning on the small table beside his cousin, and strode into the room, a tired smile lighting his face.

"Tony! Lord, it's good to see you and good to be home again." Douglas rubbed his hands together. "Ah, it's wonderful to be home and I fancy you know well my reasons."

"Douglas," Tony said, rising. He strode to his cousin and shook his hand. "I gather you were successful in whatever mission you undertook?"

Douglas gave him a fat smile and continued to rub his hands together. "Very successful, thank a benevolent God and a very stupid general who thought he could outsmart me. Ah, that dressing gown of yours is very elegant, but if you're not careful, your hairy legs stick out." He walked over to the sideboard. "You want some nice French brandy? I did promise you all you could drink until the next century."

"No, I think not."

Douglas poured the brandy, took a deep drink, felt it snake a warm trail all the way to his belly. "Hollis said you had to speak to me, that it was quite important, that it couldn't possibly wait until morning. I thought for a moment he was going to cry, but of course that's nonsense. Hollis never cries or yells or shows any unsuitable emotion. But it is nearly midnight, Tony, and I'm babbling because I'm about to collapse at your feet. Of course, once I see my beautiful bride, I imagine I'll forget all my fatigue. Still, I was surprised to see Hollis still up. What do you want?"

"I tried to tell Hollis to take himself off to bed, that I would await you in the entrance hall, but being Hollis, he refused."

Douglas took another long drink of his brandy, then sat himself in a deep wing chair next to his cousin's. "What's wrong?" There was dark silence, and Douglas suddenly knew that something he wasn't going to like at all was very near now, and Tony was the messenger. "You did marry Melissande, did you not?"

Tony looked at him full-face. "Yes," he said, "I did marry her." He drew a deep breath, knowing there was no hope for it, and blurted out, "I also married her younger sister."

Douglas had just taken another sip of brandy. He spit it out and choked on a cough. "You *what?*"

"I said I married two women." Anthony Parrish turned to stare into the fireplace, at the glowing embers. So much for his rehearsed explanation. He felt as tired as his cousin. In addition, he carried a burden of guilt that was well-nigh dragging him underground. "You may select to challenge me to a duel, Douglas. It will be your right. I will not fire against you, that I swear."

"What the hell are you talking about?" But Douglas didn't want to know what his cousin was talking about. He wanted to leave, right this minute, and go up to the huge master suite, to the huge master bed where Melissande awaited him. He didn't want to hear any more about Tony marrying two women.

"I didn't marry Melissande by proxy for you. I married her first over the anvil in Gretna Green, then once again later at her father's house. I then married Alexandra, her younger sister, by proxy, to you."

"I see," Douglas said. He rose, set his brandy snifter down carefully on the side table, nodded to his cousin, picked up a candle, and strode from the library.

"Douglas! Wait! You don't understand. For God's sake, come back here!"

But Douglas wasn't about to stop. He heard Tony coming after him and quickened his pace. A mistake, that's what all this was, no, it was a wicked joke, a joke worthy of Ryder . . . no . . . something else. He heard his cousin on the stairs behind him as he turned into the eastern corridor. He ran down the long hall to the master suite at the end. He pulled open the double doors, dashed inside, then slammed them closed behind him, and quickly turned the key.

He looked toward his bed, holding his candle high. The covers were as smooth as when he'd left Northcliffe Hall two weeks before. The bed was empty.

He walked to the dais and stood there staring down at that damned empty bed. He'd dreamed of this bed. Not empty like it was now. No, he'd dreamed of Melissande lying on her back in the middle, her arms open, inviting him to come to her.

He turned, furious, nearly beyond understanding anything. He looked toward the adjoining door and realized he was being a fool. Naturally she

wouldn't be in his bed, she would be in the countess's bedchamber next
to his. He was a stranger to her, somewhat, and it wouldn't be proper for
her to be in his bed, at least not yet. Not until he had, as her husband, formally fetched her into his bed.

He flung open the door to the adjoining bedchamber. This room was
smaller, its furnishings soft and very female; this was the room visited by
the resident ghost who didn't exist and never had existed except in bored
or fevered female minds. He saw that the bed covers were rumpled. But
this bed was also empty. It was then he saw her. It was a girl and she was
standing in the shadows, wearing a long white gown that covered her
from her chin to her toes. He couldn't see her all that clearly, but he knew
that she was very pale, and clearly startled. And was it fear he saw as
well? Fear of him?

Hell, she should be afraid, he thought, and took two steps forward. She
wasn't Melissande. She was a bloody stranger and she had the gall to be
here in his wife's bedchamber, standing there as if she belonged, staring
at him as if he were an intruder at the least, perhaps even a murderer. He
stopped dead in his tracks. "Who the devil are you?"

He sounded very calm, which surprised him no end. He was shaking
on the outside, his gut cramping on the inside, and he quickly set down
the candle on the stand beside the bed.

"I asked you who you are. What the hell are you doing in here? Where
is Melissande?"

"Melissande is down the hall, in the west wing. The bedchamber is
called the Green Cube, I believe."

Her voice was scared—high, thin, and reedy.

"I don't know you. Why are you here?"

The girl stepped forward, and he saw her square her shoulders. In the
dim candlelight he saw that she was small, slight of build, and her hair
was a rich dark red, long and waving down her back and over her shoulders.

"I was sleeping here."

"You aren't Melissande."

"No," she said. "I'm Alexandra. I'm actually your wife."

He laughed then, and it was an ugly raw sound, holding disbelief and
utter incredulity. "You can't be my wife, sweetheart, for I've never seen
you in my life. I believe you must be one of Tony's wives or perhaps one
of his many mistresses."

"You have seen me before, my lord, it's just that you don't remember
me. I was only fifteen at the time and you saw only my sister."

"Yes, and I married your sister."

There was loud pounding on the door in Douglas's bedchamber. He could hear Tony working the doorknob frantically. Douglas looked up, hearing Tony shout, "Douglas, open this damned door! Alexandra, are you all right?"

"I'm all right, Tony," she called out. She turned back to Douglas and said in a voice calm as a nun's, "Shall I let him in, my lord?"

"Why not? He appears to be married to everyone, thus it is his right to visit any number of female beds."

When the strange girl walked past him into his bedchamber, Douglas moved quickly to the hall door of this adjoining chamber, and was out the door just as Tony burst into his bedchamber. Tony saw him take off on a dead run toward the west wing.

"Douglas, damn you, stop! Where the hell are you going now? Oh, no! Stop!"

But Douglas didn't stop until he flung open the door of the Green Cube bedchamber. There, in the canopied bed, lay his wife, his bride, Melissande. She was sitting up now, looking dazed, then alarmed, framed in the candlelight. She met his gaze and blinked, pulling the sheet up to her chin.

"Douglas Sherbrooke?"

"Why are you in this room? What are you doing in his bed?"

"Because she's married to me, dammit! Douglas, please, come away, and let me explain what happened."

"No, I want to take my wife back to my bedchamber. I want her in my bed. You can't marry every woman, Tony. It's not legal except in Turkey. Truly, you must be a Muslim. So, I'll take this one."

"She's not your wife! I married her for myself, not for you. I've slept with her, Douglas! I took her virginity. She is my wife." Tony had begun on a roar but he managed to end on a lower, much calmer octave.

Douglas, very pale now, stared at Melissande. God, she was the loveliest creature he'd ever seen. Her black hair was tousled about her white face, her startling dark blue eyes large and deep and so seductive he could feel himself getting hard despite what was happening, despite the fact she was apparently married to Tony, despite . . . Douglas shook his head. He was tired, exhausted actually, but he'd ridden like the devil's own disciple to get home tonight, to his bride. He thought briefly of Janine and wondered how she would do here as a third wife. He shook his head and looked again toward his bride.

But there was no bride.

No, that wasn't right. There was a bride and her name was Alexandra and he'd never seen her before in his life even though she claimed he had.

He turned slowly to look at his cousin. "I want you to tell me this is one of your benighted jests."

"It's not. Please, Douglas, come with me back downstairs and I will explain everything."

"You can explain *this*?"

"Yes, if you'll just give me a ch—"

"You bloody bastard!" Douglas bared his teeth and lunged at his cousin. He slammed his fist into Tony's jaw, sending him sprawling. Tony rolled over and came up again, shaking his head. Douglas hit him again. This time, Tony grabbed Douglas's lapels and pulled him down with him. They fell with a loud thud, struggling, arms and legs flailing and thrashing.

Melissande screamed.

Alexandra stood in the open doorway, her candle held high. She saw Tony roll over on top of Douglas and smash his fist into his jaw. Douglas grunted in pain, brought up his knees and slammed them in Tony's back, lurching up. Tony hit Douglas again, harder now, making his head snap back.

Alexandra howled. She quickly dropped the candle to a tabletop and leapt upon Tony's back, pounding at his head with her fists, then jerking his hair. "Stop it, you brute! Let him alone!"

She pounded and pounded and jerked and jerked. Tony, so surprised by this unexpected onslaught that he froze, was quickly upended by Douglas. Both Alexandra and Tony went sprawling. Douglas grabbed Tony by his shirt and dragged him upright. He slammed his fist into his belly. Tony grunted, bending over, hugging his arms around himself. Suddenly, Melissande came flying through the air to leap upon Douglas's back, wrapping her legs around his waist. She pounded her fists at his head, screaming right into his ear, "Leave him alone!"

Douglas felt his entire brain begin to vibrate. His ears were ringing. She was pulling his hair out, still screaming at him, right into his ear. Then, the other wife, the small one, was tugging madly at Melissande, jerking her off Douglas's back. Both women went down together in a twist of white nightgowns and flying masses of hair.

Tony was still bent over, trying to regain his breath. Douglas felt as though he should be bald. His scalp throbbed from Melissande's attack. He stood there, surveying the disaster. He watched as the small girl untangled herself from Melissande, rose, and rushed to him. Her face was white, her eyes dilated. She was trembling and panting.

He stood silent as a stone as her hands went from his shoulders to his chest, then to the length of his arms. He still didn't move, didn't say a word. "Are you all right? Did he hurt you? Please, tell me if you have pain." Her fingertips skimmed lightly over his jaw and he jerked back just a bit. "Oh, forgive me, it's tender, isn't it? I'm sorry. It's not broken, no, but he hit you very hard."

Douglas shook his head, but otherwise he still didn't move. For the life of him he couldn't come up with one reason why he should move or say anything, for that matter. Her hands continued their journey over his body, feeling, lightly prodding. Finally, when she was about to drop to her knees and feel his legs, Douglas grabbed her wrists and pulled them together in front of her. He shook her to get her attention. He said very slowly, "I'm just fine. Leave me alone. Go feel him—your other husband." He looked beyond her to Melissande, who was standing beside Tony, her long black hair an incredibly soft curtain that hid her face from him. Her soft hands were on Tony's body.

Douglas stepped back from the second wife and looked toward the open doorway. He said quite calmly, "Hollis, please come in here."

Hollis, not one ounce of dignity lighter, stepped into the den of chaos. He said very gently, "My lord, should you care to accompany me, the others may then attire themselves in more suitable garb. I will serve brandy in the drawing room and they may join us when they wish. Come now, my lord. That's right. Come with me. All will be well."

Douglas allowed himself to be led away. He felt oddly numb now, even though his scalp still throbbed and his ears were still ringing. Melissande had strong fingers and even stronger lungs. He felt he should be someone else; he didn't want to be Douglas Sherbrooke because that poor fellow was an absurdity. He was a fool, a dunce, an ass, who'd nearly had all his hair pulled from his head and lost his bride. He heard himself say in a voice that didn't resemble his at all, "But Hollis, that girl jumped on Tony. Why would she do that? He said he'd married her. I've never seen her before. Why would that little twit seek to rescue me?"

"Don't concern yourself just now, my lord," came Hollis's soothing voice. "You must be pleased that she would try to protect you."

"Protect me! Damnation, she looked ready to fight to the death."

"Yes, my lord. It is fitting for her to do so. She is your wife, my lord, and your countess. Indeed, she has lived here for two days now and has gone along very well."

Douglas said very firmly, "No, she isn't my wife. That is quite impossible. I told you I'd never seen her before. Melissande is my wife. Her, I recognized. I will kill Tony for this." Douglas paused in his tracks, looking back over his shoulder. "Do you think if I leave that girl here she will kill Tony for me?"

"Probably not, my lord. Her violence was only brought on by his attack on you. Lord Rathmore is now subdued and thus she has achieved her aims. Come along now. Everything will look a bit differently in the morning."

"I can't sleep in the same bed with that strange girl, Hollis. I'm a gentleman. Since you allowed her to come into my house, I can assume, can I not, that she isn't a possible mistress? You say she's been here two days? No, I cannot like it or accept it. Even though she tried to kill Tony, I can't sleep with her."

"No, my lord. I understand your reasoning perfectly. Your sentiments are most commendable. Her Ladyship will appreciate your motives. Come along now. You need to rest and allow your mental parts to reassemble themselves."

With silence and coffee, not brandy, Douglas's mental parts quickly came together again, but that coming together built such rage in him that he choked on the coffee.

"I will have to kill him, Hollis."

"Perhaps not, my lord. You must listen to Lord Rathmore first. You were—are—quite fond of him, you know."

"Ah! There you are, you damned scoundrel!"

Douglas rose half out of his chair, only to feel Hollis's hand firmly on his shoulder. He subsided.

But he didn't want to. He wanted to go to bed and sleep for twelve hours, awaken and find that everything was as it should be. No, he wanted to kill his cousin.

Instead, Douglas, the man of normally fine-working mental parts and skilled strategies, said very calmly, "Tell me why you betrayed me."

Tony's hair still stood on end, the result of that other female's attack. He was still wearing his dressing gown, now ripped beneath the right arm and hanging longer on one side than on the other. He kept his distance. "Will you listen to me without trying to kill me again?"

"I'll listen. As for killing you, I dare say that will happen some morning soon at dawn."

"God, Douglas, don't talk like that! Damn, I didn't mean it to happen, but it did."

Hollis cleared his throat, saying gently, "Enough *mea culpas*, my lord. His Lordship is in need of facts. All this emotion is wearisome and not at all to the point."

"I fell in love with Melissande the moment I saw her and she fell in love with me. I know all her faults, Douglas, faults you can't begin to imagine, but I didn't care. I understood her and I knew that I could handle her. We eloped. Upon our return to Claybourn Hall, the duke and I decided that I would wed Alexandra by proxy to you. She was willing and the duke was more than willing. Indeed, he had just heard his wastrel son had not only left England in the dark of night, he had also bequeathed his father a mountain of debts. The duke was frantic and thus agreed, for your settlement in addition to the one I made him would rescue him and his family from disgrace. Still, I wasn't certain, Douglas, you must believe that, but there were so many good reasons for doing it, least of which Alexandra is lovely, she's a lady, she's not stupid, and you won't have to go to London and start all over again to find another wife. You have one and she's quite all right and here and you will get to know her and everything will be fine.

"Perhaps this angers you, perhaps you believe I did it just to try to placate you, perhaps everything I'm saying rings false to you, but I swear to you that I gave it great thought. I studied Alexandra thoroughly, and I swear she is worthy of you. She's a good sort. She isn't arrogant or vain. She's kind and steady and loyal—"

"You make her sound like a damned horse, Tony. Or a panting hound. She isn't Melissande!"

"No, lucky for you. Come, you saw how she defended you, her husband, nearly killing me! Truly, Douglas, you wouldn't be pleased for long with Melissande for your wife."

"Ha! You slippery sod, you make it sound as though you saved me from a fate worse than death. You want me to believe that you removed the plague from me and took it onto yourself, that you martyred yourself for me. You stole my wife, Tony! Damn you, it is too much, I have listened to your lame excuses and I—"

"My lord," Hollis said softly, his hand once more on Douglas's shoulder, "we must remain for the moment with the facts. Emotion is enervating and leads, evidently, to violence. I cannot allow more violence in Northcliffe."

"Where is my sister? Where are Ryder and Tysen and my mother?"

"Master Ryder insisted they all leave Northcliffe until everything was sorted out. He is an intelligent young man. Once he understood what had happened, he had the family gone from here within two hours. They, ah, are staying presently in London, at the Sherbrooke town house."

Lord, he'd very nearly taken Janine to the town house, but in the end, Lord Avery had seen to her lodgings. Douglas twisted about to look up at Hollis. "So, I'm alone in the house with this bloody wife thief?" Douglas rubbed his hands together and he smiled. "Excellent! That means I can kill him with no one the wiser, without Tysen preaching to me from his future pulpit, without Ryder laughing at me, without my sister and mother falling into a swoon. No, that's not true, is it, Hollis? It wasn't all Ryder's idea, was it? No, you were afraid there would be disagreements and so you convinced Ryder to remove them all. Ah, I don't mind, indeed I don't. Thank God, you sent them away. Now, I am going to kill this damned bastard cousin of mine!" Douglas roared to his feet.

"Please, no more, my lord."

Douglas stopped cold and stared at the same slight female who'd been upstairs in the midst of the fray. She was now standing in the open doorway, that same female who'd tried to protect him. The same one who was supposedly his cursed wife. He shuddered with the strangeness of it; it was absurd; it wasn't real; he couldn't, wouldn't, accept it.

"Tell me your name, at least," he said, his voice harsh, his fury boiling near the surface.

"My name is Alexandra Gabrielle Chambers. I am the Duke of Beresford's youngest child, but I am not a child, I am eighteen years old and a woman." She paused and he saw the strain on her face, really a quite pretty face, with rather luminous gray eyes that weren't stupid. She'd pulled her hair back and tied it with a ribbon at the nape of her neck. She had nice bones, a nice mouth, pleasantly arched brows and quite pretty small ears. It didn't move him one bit, none of it. She fretted with the sash on her pale blue dressing gown, then looked up to face him again. "Don't you remember me at all, my lord?"

"No."

"I suppose I have changed a bit. I was plump then and even shorter. I even wore spectacles sometimes to read, my hair was always in tight childish braids, so it was likely that you disregarded me entirely, but now—"

"I really don't care if you were bald and obese. Go away. Go back to bed. You can be certain that I won't come to ravish you tonight. I am not in the habit of bedding women who are strangers to me."

She paused a moment, drawing up, straightening just a bit more. She looked briefly at Tony, then nodded. "As you wish, my lord. I will sleep in the adjoining bedchamber if that is all right with you."

"Sleep in the corridor! Sleep with Tony for all I care. After all, he appears to have married you too."

"Really, Douglas—"

Alexandra turned without another word and left. She picked up a candle from a huge Spanish table in the entrance hall. She walked slowly up the wide staircase. What had she expected? That he would look at her and fall into raptures at the gift Tony had bestowed upon him? That he would compare her to Melissande and decide straightaway in her favor? That he would fall instantly and madly in love with her? That he would sing hallelujahs and donate his wealth to charities for what Tony had brought about? Or rather what her father had convinced her to do? Ah, her father . . . She remembered exactly what he'd said, how he'd begged her, pleaded with her, used her own feelings against her, how . . . Alexandra shook her head. No, it was on her head, no one else's, all of it. If she had wanted to toe the line, had really wanted to refuse, her father wouldn't have forced her to wed Douglas by proxy. But the money, he'd needed it so desperately, and he actually believed that the addition of both Douglas Sherbrooke and Anthony Parrish to the family would force his fatuous heir, Reginald, once he returned to England, to curb his wild, spendthrift ways.

Ha! She was doing it again, trying to find reasons to convince herself that what she'd done was right and just and really marvelous. When, in fact, there were no good reasons at all. Douglas had been betrayed by his cousin and by Melissande and by her father. And by her. She'd been hoping, desperately hoping that his reaction when he learned about her would be different, but now Douglas had come home and reality had presented a furious face. *It will be all right. You mustn't give up. It will be all right.* Her silly litany, Alexandra thought, climbing the stairs. Stupid and immature and . . .

Melissande was waiting at the top of the stairs, clutching her hands spasmodically to her bosom.

"Well?" she said without preamble. "Have they started fighting again? Have they drawn guns or their swords? Will they fight for me?"

"Are you palpitating?"

"No, don't be silly. What does that mean?"

Alexandra only shook her head. Nastiness toward the bone of contention between the two men was unworthy. "He told me to go to bed," she said, forcing all emotion from her voice.

"You knew this would happen, Alex. I warned you; I warned Father, but he talked you into going along with him. I warned Tony. All of you knew that Douglas wanted me desperately, not you. How could he ever want you or any other lady once he'd seen me? He doesn't even remember you, does he?"

Alexandra shook her head.

"It isn't that I mind you being a countess, Alex, though you certainly won't be happy being one. If your husband hates you, if he can't bear to look at you, if he leaves the room when you enter, how then can you be happy? No, I'm the one who should be a duchess or a countess, but here I am only a viscountess. But it is what I chose, isn't it? I chose Tony and he had no choice once I'd chosen him. Poor Alex! Poor Douglas! Are you certain Douglas isn't trying to kill Tony again?"

"Hollis will control both of them."

"A butler giving the orders," Melissande said. "I wouldn't stand for it were I mistress here. It is beyond strange."

"Yes," Alexandra said as she passed by her sister. She said over her shoulder, very quietly, "He wants you, of course, you're quite right about that. He probably will always want you."

Melissande smiled. "I told Tony the earl wouldn't forgive him. I told him, yet he chose to disbelieve me. I have found that men do not always accept the truth even when it is presented to them with sincerity and candor. They always believe they can rearrange things to suit themselves." Melissande paused a moment, then marred her lovely forehead with a deep frown. "I begin to think now that perhaps I made a mistake. Tony isn't the man I married. He wants to order me about, to treat me like a possession. He even told me he wasn't the gentleman Douglas was. He actually wanted to take liberties with my person in a carriage, Alex, in broad daylight, and not an hour from Claybourn Hall! Can you believe that? I couldn't allow such a monstrous sort of man-behavior. Perhaps Douglas isn't so indelicate, so uncaring, about a lady's sensibilities. Yes, I probably made a mistake. Why, do you know that he threatened to—" Melissande closed her mouth over further illuminations.

Alex stared in dismay at her sister. Melissande was now regretting marrying Tony? But how could that be? Tony certainly teased her, mocking her, but Melissande appeared to find this to her liking. Oh Lord. There were already too many untold ingredients in the pot. "Then why did you attack Douglas?"

"Because you had attacked Tony," Melissande said matter-of-factly. "It seemed the thing to do. Before Tony went downstairs to speak again with Douglas, he hugged me and told me next he would send me a dragon to slay. It pleased him that I acted the hoyden, that I yelled and nearly pulled out Douglas's hair. It is all very strange. He is quite unaccountable. Men are quite unaccountable."

Alexandra could only stare at her sister. "Tony will make things right with Douglas. The two of them are very close. Hollis said so."

Melissande shrugged. "I think Tony should suffer for what he did."

"But you did it right along with him!"

"Tony is a man; it is his responsibility."

"That's drivel," Alexandra said, and left her sister at the top of the stairs, peeking over the railing. She walked quickly down the long eastern corridor whose walls were lined with portraits of past Sherbrookes, many of whose faces and costumes sorely needed restoration. She went into the adjoining bedchamber and stood in the middle of the room, shivering. The bed was much smaller and shorter than the one in the master bedchamber. Alexandra supposed that since she was small and short, it didn't matter.

She remembered when Hollis had shown her through the master suite and she'd stood there and just stared at that huge bed, realizing for the first time that husbands and wives sometimes slept together if they wished to have children, that this was the bed where a child would be conceived. She didn't understand the process, but the thought of not wearing her clothing in front of a man made her brain clog and close down. Hollis, bless his astute soul, had said calmly, "I believe it wise to allow some time for His Lordship to accustom himself. You must be recognized as a wife, my lady, before you can be recognized as the Sherbrooke bride."

It was just that this room was so very cold and empty, much more empty than before Douglas had come home.

She snuffed out the candle and climbed into the bed, shivering violently between the cold sheets. She wondered if she would remain in this room for the rest of her years. For the moment, she had lost a goodly portion of her optimism about this marriage. Was Melissande right? Would Douglas ignore her or treat her badly?

She wasn't even a marriage of convenience, for Douglas Sherbrooke had paid dearly for her. Actually, he had paid dearly for Melissande and he had gotten her instead. And she hadn't brought him anything at all.

Tony had spent hours telling her about Douglas, reassuring her, reeling off anecdotes at a fine rate. She knew all his questions to her were to judge whether or not she was worthy of his esteemed cousin. At least she'd passed Tony's tests. He wanted her for a cousin-in-law, he said, and when she said she was already a sister-in-law, he'd gotten that gleam in his eyes that Melissande seemed to adore, and said, "Ah, then I shall have you so deep in my family that you'll never escape." Again and again he'd said Douglas didn't love Melissande, that she was merely a quite beautiful convenience for him, that he didn't know her at all, and would have been horrified to have found himself married to her, then hastened to add that he, Tony, most certainly did know her, but it didn't matter because he was him and not Douglas. All quite confusing, really.

So Douglas Sherbrooke didn't love Melissande. Ha! So now he was wedded to an unbeautiful convenience and he didn't love her either.

Alexandra burrowed deeper into the sheets, seeing her husband bursting into the bedchamber. She hadn't seen him for three long years. During the past two days she'd wondered if he'd changed, grown fat, perhaps, or lost his hair or his teeth, and then he'd appeared and she'd only been able to stand there gaping at him, utterly witless. He looked older, she'd thought, staring at him, a hard-faced man with dark hair and eyes even darker and a high-bridged nose that made him look utterly superior, utterly arrogant. As if to ruin the image of centuries of noblesse oblige, nature had added a cleft in the middle of his chin. Ah, but he was beautiful, this man who was now her husband, his body as lean and hard as his expression was severe, the most exquisite man she'd ever imagined.

Oddly enough though, Alexandra hadn't realized she loved him com-

pletely and utterly, with every ounce of feeling within her, until he'd
thrown his head back, yowled like a madman, and flung himself at his
cousin.

He was the man she wanted. Her natural optimism surfaced a bit. It
will be all right, she repeated to herself yet again. She was still awake
many hours later when she heard him moving about in the bedchamber
next to hers.

And what, she wondered, would happen on the morrow?

CHAPTER
═══ 7 ═══

"WHAT THE HELL are you doing here?"

It was seven o'clock in the morning, surely too early an hour for him to be here, in this precise spot, in the vast Sherbrooke stable. It was foggy, damp, and cloudy—all in all a dismal morning, a morning to match her mood and his too, evidently. The light was dim inside the stable and none of the half-dozen stable lads were about. The smells were comforting—hay, linseed, leather, and horse. Douglas was wearing buckskins, a dark brown coat, and Hessians that sorely needed polish. He looked tired, unshaved, tousled, and vastly irritated. To an objective person he would perhaps appear an ill-tempered dirty-looking brute. To her jaundiced eye, however, he looked immensely wonderful.

"I was going to ride, my lord."

"Oh? Perhaps my vision has become suddenly deficient for I don't believe I've seen any unknown horses in my stables. Where is this horse you were going to ride? I assume it is a horse. Even though I am apparently the ass in this drama, you cannot ride me."

Alex was silent a moment, then said calmly enough, "Mr. McCallum has given me Fanny to ride since I've been here."

"Fanny belongs to my sister."

"I know. She is a spirited mare with a sweet mouth and nice manners. I know how to ride, my lord, truly. You don't have to worry that I cannot handle her properly. Or would you prefer that I ride another horse?"

He was frowning ferociously at her. "So you brought no horse of your own?"

"No." Actually, her father had sold many of the ducal horses some two months earlier, clearing out the once glorious Chambers stables before he'd known about Douglas and his offered bounty, before he'd known he'd need more than Douglas's bounty to save Claybourn.

"You're wearing a riding costume, though it is not new nor is it even in last year's style. I may assume then that your esteemed blackguard thief of a father sent you away with at least enough clothes to cover you until you could wheedle some more out of me?"

As a verbal blow, it showed promise.

"I don't know. I had not thought about it."

He actually snorted and she heard an answering snort from one of the closed stalls. "That's Garth," Douglas said absently. "So you don't think about furbelows and ribbons and flounces—"

"Certainly, when it is necessary to do so."

"I cannot imagine Melissande not wanting lovely clothes and furbelows and all those other things you females clothe yourselves in to attract males and make fools of them. Why would you be any different?"

"Melissande is beautiful. She needs beautiful things and admires them and—"

"Ha! She doesn't need anything. She would look glorious in naught but her white skin."

As a verbal blow, it exceeded the last one.

"Yes, that is also true. What do you wish me to do, my lord?"

"I wish you to leave and turn all this damnable debacle into a nightmare from which I'll awaken."

It was difficult, but Alex remained standing straight, remained with a fixed pleasant expression on her face, forced herself not to scream at him or make fists or fall to her knees and wail. "I meant, do you wish me to ride Fanny or ride another mare or not ride at all?"

Douglas shoveled his fingers through his hair. He stared at the small female who everyone had informed him was indeed his wife. She looked pale in the shadowy light but that back of hers was as straight as if she had a broom handle bound tightly against her backbone. Her hair was tucked firmly up under a rather dowdy riding hat. One long tendril had come loose and was in a loose curl on her shoulder. The hair was a nice color, rather an odd dark red color, but it didn't matter one bit. It could be blue for all he cared.

She was a complete and utter stranger, this female.

He cursed, long and luridly.

Alex didn't move an inch.

"Oh, the devil! Come along, you may ride Fanny and I will judge if you ride well enough to continue mounting her."

Mr. McCallum, fifty, wiry, strong as a man of twenty, baked brown from decades in the sun, and married to a young widow of twenty-two, was standing outside the stable giving orders to a stable lad when the earl and Alex led their mounts outside.

"Good morning, my lord."

Douglas only nodded at him. As far as he was concerned, McCallum had betrayed him, giving this cursed female Sinjun's mare. As had that accursed bounder cousin of his, that damnable Tony who deserved to be shot, and his own butler, Hollis, as well.

"Her Ladyship has a nice seat and light hands," McCallum said, unknowingly stoking the embers of Douglas's fury as he stroked the horse's soft nose. "Ye needn't worry that Fanny will suffer from any bad handling."

Douglas grunted. Who cared if she were cow-handed? He didn't. Indeed, who had bothered to care about him? No one, not one single bloody person.

He gave Alex a leg up, then turned to mount Garth. The huge stallion, left in his stall to eat his head off for two weeks, snorted, flung back his head, and danced to the side, all in all, giving a fine performance.

Douglas laughed aloud with the pleasure of it. He spoke to his stallion, patted his neck, then without a backward glance, he urged him into a gallop.

Alex watched the stallion and the man for a moment, then said, "Well, Fanny, perhaps we should show him we're made of firm stuff and not to be left to choke on his dust."

She gave a jaunty wave to McCallum and followed her husband down the long drive bordered with thick lime and beech trees, now full-branched and thick and riotously green.

Douglas was waiting for her just beyond the old stone gatehouse. He watched her ride toward him. His expression didn't change. McCallum was right. She rode very well. It pleased him only to the extent that she wouldn't hurt Fanny's soft mouth. He merely nodded at her, and click-clicked Garth into a gallop. He took a fence into the northern fields of Northcliffe, watching from the corner of his eye as Alex gave Fanny her head and easily took the fence after him. He pulled up finally at the edge of the winding narrow stream that had been one of his favorite haunts as a boy.

When she pulled in Fanny beside Garth, Alex looked about her, and said with pleasure, "What a lovely spot. There is a stream much like this one on the Chambers land. When I was a little girl I spent many happy hours there fishing, swimming—though the water was usually too low for anything other than just thrashing about and getting thoroughly wet—all in all, having a wonderful time."

As a conversation effort it didn't succeed.

Douglas looked off into the distance toward the Smitherstone weald, and said without preamble, "Tell me why you did it."

Alex felt her heart begin to pound, low, dull thuds. The good Lord knew that there were many truths at work here. She would give him one of them and hope it would satisfy him, one that Tony had doubtless already pressed upon him the previous night. It was a good one, actually, the primary one, if one spoke from her sire's point of view. "My father desperately needed funds, for my brother has just fled England leaving mountains of debt on his shoulders, and any settlement Tony made wouldn't be nearly enough and— Don't you see, my lord? Time was of the essence else we would have lost our home and—"

Douglas slashed his hand through the air. Garth took exception to his master's peculiar behavior, twisted his head around and took a nip of Fanny's neck. Fanny shrieked, rearing back onto her hind legs. Alex, taken off guard, cried out in surprise, flailed her arms to find balance, failed, then slid off Fanny's rump, landing on the narrow path on her bottom.

She sat there, feeling as if her bones had been jarred into dust. She was afraid to move. She looked up at Douglas, who was calming his horse. He looked down at her, his eyes darkening to a near black, then quickly dismounted. Fanny, curse her hide, kicked up her back legs once more and wheeled about, galloping back toward the Sherbrooke stables.

"Are you all right?"

"I don't know."

"Luckily you appear well padded, what with all those petticoats and the like. Can you stand?"

Alex nodded. She came up onto her knees, felt a strange shock of dizziness, and shook her head to clear it.

Douglas clasped her beneath her arms and drew her upright. She didn't weigh much, he thought, as he continued to support her. She did, however, feel very female. Finally, he felt that damned broom handle stiffen all the way from the back of her neck to her waist.

He released her. She weaved about, then straightened. "I'm all right." She looked back toward the hall, obscured by two miles of trees and fields. "Fanny left me."

And it was his fault, Douglas thought, wanting to howl because it meant that now he would have to hold—actually *hold*—this girl in front of him. He didn't even want to look at her, much less be in her company, much less hold her.

He'd even have to talk to her, since it was all his bloody fault that she'd been thrown.

"You're obviously not as proficient a horsewoman as you claimed, else you would have been more alert."

As a verbal blow, it was the very best thus far, for it struck a killing blow to a pride inborn in her. She was not just a competent horsewoman; she was the best. She had ridden since before she could walk. She was beyond the best and above the best as well.

Her voice was as cold as the gaping shred in her pride. "Since your stallion is so ill-mannered as to take exception just because you fling yourself about on his back, yes, you are doubtless right." She turned away from him and began the long walk back to the hall.

Douglas watched her go.

He should apologize.

He should take her up on Garth.

Well, hell.

Her riding costume was dusty and he saw a rip beneath her right arm. A good length of the hem had come unstitched and dragged behind her in the dirt. Her riding hat lay in the middle of the road and her hair was falling down her back. She was limping just a bit.

He cursed, quickly mounted Garth, and went after her.

Alex heard him coming. She kept walking. At this moment, she hoped he would rot, every beautiful inch of him. Suddenly he swooped down, catching her around her waist, and lifted her up to sit sideways on the saddle in front of him.

"I'm sorry, damn you."

"That was most romantically done. Mrs. Radcliffe couldn't have penned a more dashing performance."

"Just because I didn't wish to argue with you or dismount again . . . What damnable drivel!"

"I could have walked," she said mildly. "It isn't all that far."

"You look like a ragamuffin. You look like a serving wench who's enjoyed half a dozen men but didn't please them sufficiently and got no coin for her labors."

She said nothing, merely sat with that straight back of hers, looking off toward the side of the road.

"I suppose I'll have to buy you a new riding habit now."

"It would appear that I didn't have to wheedle even a tiny bit."

"Since it was somewhat my fault—your fall, that is—I shall make reparations. Still, you should have been more alert, more prepared for the unexpected."

Alex was mild-tempered. She was patient and long-suffering; she knew how to endure; she knew how to hold her tongue to avoid distasteful scenes. She was never reckless. Even when her mother was at her pickiest, Melissande at her most demanding, she'd merely smiled and gone about her business. But with Douglas, her husband . . . how dare he continue to insult her riding ability? She simply couldn't help herself. She twisted against his arm, pushing at him with her entire weight. Caught unawares, Douglas went over the other side. He would have saved himself had Garth not decided that the extra weight on his back demanded that he make his master realize he wasn't to be treated like a common hack. Garth reared and twisted in the air. Alex managed to retain her balance, clutching wildly at Garth's mane. Douglas lost everything. He hit the road with a loud thunk, landing on his back, winding himself. The reins were dragging the ground and Garth immediately sidestepped away from his master.

Like Alex, Douglas just lay there, waiting to see if anything was broken, if anything had shaken itself loose.

He opened his eyes, still not moving, and said, "I will beat you for that."

"Tony said that you were a gentleman. Gentlemen do not beat ladies nor do they make such bullying threats."

"Being a gentleman pales when one is confronted with a wife one doesn't know, doesn't want, never did want, never even knew existed, a wife who is violent, heedless, without control." He drew breath to continue on this fine monologue when the ground shook and he watched, speechless, dust flying into his open mouth, as the female rode Garth—his stallion—away from him.

He nearly forgot to whistle.

Garth, thank heavens, heard him, stopped dead in his tracks, whipped about and trotted back to his prone master.

Alex was grinding her teeth. She stared down at Douglas, who was now sitting up in the middle of the road.

"I believe," she said clearly, "that you, my lord, are also in need of new riding clothes."

"These aren't really riding clothes. They're morning garb. Are you ignorant as well as a sham?"

"Sham? I am not!"

"Then why did you do it?"

Both Alex and Garth were motionless. She opened her mouth, then closed it. It was obvious that Tony had failed utterly to bring the earl around. She could repeat that her father had been in horrible financial difficulties, repeat that all the Chambers holdings would have been lost, that the heir had fled to America, that her father would have been disgraced, perhaps had to blow his brains out with the shame of it. She shuddered with the thought of how those offerings would be received. Then there was the other truth, but she couldn't, wouldn't, tell him that.

"No answer, hm? Well, I'm not surprised, particularly after all the drivel Tony was feeding me last night." Douglas got to his feet, queried his body, was satisfied with the response, and walked to his stallion. He picked up the reins, stroked the stallion's nose, and said slowly, "I am to believe that you were willing to sacrifice yourself on the marital altar because your beloved father was going to lose everything if you didn't? That you and your father convinced dear Tony—that traitorous sod—that it would save me having to find myself a proper female amongst the current batch of debutantes in London? That all of this was done for *my* benefit? But then you, honorable to your female toes, told your father you couldn't do it? Because of your nobility of spirit? Then he forced you?"

How could Tony have said that? It was ludicrous! Certainly she'd refused, at least at first she had. Before she could say anything, Douglas snorted, just like his horse. "Sorry, but I don't believe that. In this day and age, fathers cannot coerce their children to do anything against their will." Even as he spoke the words, they rang false and he knew it. Actually Tony had said nothing of the like but Douglas was probing, and the chit wasn't telling him anything that sounded reasonable.

Alex said quietly, "No, Papa didn't force me. He loves me, but I had to—"

"Yes, I know. You had to save him and sacrifice yourself. I hope you're pleased with my purchase, since I have paid dearly to have a stranger for a wife."

Alex straightened as tall as she could in the saddle. "I would that you would give me a chance, my lord, that you not despise me out of hand. I will make you a good wife."

He looked up at the disheveled female atop Garth. She was pale now and he wondered momentarily if she had been hurt in her fall, but then she added, "Tony said you would rather have a tooth extracted than spend a Season in London. He said the last thing you wanted to do was be forced to attend all the routs and balls and parties and sniff out available young ladies for your consideration. He said you felt like a plump partridge in the midst of well-armed hunters. He said you hated it."

"He did? And you believed him? I don't suppose it occurred to you during your spate of nobility that Tony would have said anything to try to find excuses for himself? To justify what he did to me?"

"I am sure that he still feels immense guilt. He is very fond of you."

"But more fond of your sister!"

"Yes, he loves her."

"He's a Judas and I should blow his brains out."

"He did not intend for it to happen. Surely you don't believe he married Melissande to thwart you? To somehow spite you? No, even in your foulest mood, you wouldn't believe that. Did he lie about your feelings toward going to London?"

Douglas looked down at his scuffed Hessians. Finkle would have a fit when he saw it. "No, but it wasn't up to him to make that decision for me. It is all a part of his justification, nothing more."

"I'm sorry."

Like hell she was! "You know, don't you, that I can have this farce of a marriage annulled and demand the settlement back from your black-hearted father?"

"Don't you dare speak of my father like that!" She waved a credible fist at him.

Douglas didn't move. He merely stared up at her, no expression on his face. "What am I to believe?"

Alex felt an awful wave of guilt for what she'd done to him. "I'm sorry, my lord, truly, but don't you think that perhaps you could allow me to be your wife for a while? By annulment, you mean you would send me home and the marriage wouldn't still be a marriage?"

"That's right. Our temporary union would be dissolved."

"Please, you must reconsider. I don't want to be annulled or dissolved. Perhaps in a very short time you won't mind my being here at Northcliffe, for I will keep out of your way. I will try to make things comfortable for you—"

"Women! Don't you think a man can be perfectly content without one of you hanging about his neck, handing him brandy and cigars?"

"What I meant was that I wouldn't be obtrusive and that I would make certain your house runs smoothly."

"It runs smoothly right now, or have you forgotten that I have a mother and more servants than I can count?"

She had momentarily forgotten the mother. He also had two brothers and a younger sister. Hollis had told her they were all visiting friends in London. But they would return soon to Northcliffe. Oh dear. Would they hate her, despise her as much as Douglas did? Would they follow his lead and scorn her? She drew a deep breath and said, "I had forgotten. I'm sorry." She leaned unconsciously toward him. "Please, my lord, perhaps you won't mind that I am in your home after some time has passed. Perhaps you won't even notice me after a while. I beg you not to annul me just yet."

"Annul you? You make it sound like a violent act." Douglas suddenly frowned; there was contempt in his eyes. "Ah, I begin to see the direction of your thinking or perhaps your sire's thinking. You hope to climb into my bed, don't you? You know that I cannot annul you—damnation!—obtain an annulment—if I take your virginity. That's what you want, isn't it? Once I take your precious virginity, then your precious father will be safe and all my money will remain with him. Did your father counsel you to try to seduce me?"

Alex could only stare down at him. She slowly shook her head. "No, I hadn't thought any of that and no, no one counseled me about anything."

He was silent, staring up at her.

"Truly, my lord, I know nothing of seduction. Surely seduction isn't something done between husband and wife. My mother told me that seduction was only done by wild young men who wanted to ruin innocent young ladies."

"Really? Did this motherly Delphi warn you of anything more specific?"

"That if a man ever flattered me or stepped too close to me or held my hand too long after kissing it, that I was to leave the vicinity immediately. He was up to no good, she said."

Douglas laughed, he couldn't help himself.

Alex brightened. She'd amused him, that or he was laughing at her. She waited, then said, "I will do my best to please you, to make you a comfortable wife. My temper is usually rather placid and—"

"Ha! You were beyond vicious, a shrew, a fishwife, and a less comfortable female I've yet to encounter. You knocked me off my damned horse!"

Alex frowned. "Yes," she said, surprise in her eyes and in her voice, "yes, it appears that I did, which is very strange. It is very unlike me."

Douglas saw that the top two buttons of her riding habit had come unfastened. He saw a patch of white flesh. Very soft-looking white flesh. He thought of her virginity and he thought of taking it, of pushing through her maidenhead. "Perhaps," he said, continuing to stare at her breasts, "perhaps I could be proved wrong. It is possible that you could be the one to demand an annulment. Perhaps you will want to leave Northcliffe as fast as your carriage wheels can roll away with you."

"Oh no, I want to be your wife—"

"Let's see, shall we? Unfasten the rest of the buttons. I can only see the curve of your breasts. I would like to see the rest of you. You're quiet? Is that a touch of pallor I see? You're shocked at my bluntness? I've assaulted your precious virgin sensibilities? Well, so there are ways to shut you up."

He was right about that, she thought, stunned.

"How old are you?"

"You know I am eighteen. I told you last night."

"Old enough to be a woman and a wife. You said that too. Oh, hell. Just be quiet, all right?"

"But I didn't say—"

"Damnation, be quiet or I shall demand that you take off that riding jacket and let me see your breasts and your nipples and your ribs. All your upper parts I've paid so dearly for."

Alex was silent as a stone.

Douglas eyed her, waiting, but she remained silent and still, that broomstick firmly in place down her back. He shrugged. "I will lead Garth. A good walk is balm to a weary soul."

She wondered why he'd gotten that bit of errant treacle, but was wise enough to keep her curiosity to herself. She watched him walk ahead of her; there was a jagged rip in his buckskins. She could see a patch of hairy thigh. Black hair. It looked rather nice to her. She looked down at herself then, jerked her chemise about, covering any hint of skin. She straightened again, and kept her eyes on the back of her husband all the way back to the stables.

This annulment business was still somewhat a mystery. She would have to ask Tony about it. She knew too little about marriage sorts of things. All she knew about virginity and virgins was that she was one. She would have to be in her husband's bed before she wasn't one anymore.

She should ask her husband, but she doubted he would take any question of that sort in a proper frame of mind.

He stopped suddenly in the middle of the road and turned back to face her. "I'm tired. Garth is tired. Get down and come here. We will rest a moment beneath that oak tree."

Alex slid from the saddle, saying not a word.

Douglas didn't bother to tether Garth, just left his reins loose. "Sit down," Douglas said, pointing to a grassy spot.

Alex sat.

Douglas sat also, a good three feet away from her. He leaned back against the thick oak trunk and crossed his legs at his ankles. He sighed, folded his arms over his belly, and closed his eyes.

"I am sorry you're so tired," Alex said. "Tony said you were on some sort of mission and that was why he'd come to us rather than you."

"Yes. I certainly made the wrong choice, didn't I? I certainly chose the wrong man to trust. Jesus, my entire life ruined because—"

"Was your mission successful?"

"Yes." He opened his eyes then and looked at her. Perverseness sang through his veins. "Actually, I would have preferred the lovely lady I rescued in France to be here rather than you. Her name is Janine and she's a woman, not a girl playing at being a woman, and she was more than interested in me as a man. She offered herself to me, without guile, without playing the coquette. However, since I believed I was a married man, believed that Melissande was awaiting me here, I didn't take her. Indeed, I pushed her away." He closed his eyes again.

"You are a married man."

"You, however, are not Melissande."

"This woman you rescued, she is French?"

"Yes, and a very important man's mistress."

"Surely you wouldn't want a mistress for your wife."

"Why not?"

"That's beyond foolish! You're only saying that to hurt me, to make me feel horrible. No man wants a woman who isn't all that is proper. It's all a matter of heirs. I heard my father saying that to a neighbor."

"There speaks eighteen-year-old wisdom and eavesdropping."

"Will you annul me?"

He was silent.

"Won't you at least give me a chance?"

"Be quiet. I wish to rest now."

Alex eyed Garth, who was placidly chewing thick grass at the side of the road. If she coshed Douglas, then he couldn't whistle for his horse and then the horse would take her back to the Sherbrooke stables. She sighed, closing her own eyes. The morning was warming and becoming clear. Soon the sun would shine fully.

Alex said then, "I had the oddest dream the first night I was here in your home, sleeping in the countess's bedchamber. I dreamed there was a young lady in the room and she was standing next to the bed, just looking down at me. I thought she wanted to say something, but she remained silent. She looked so sad and beautiful. When I awoke fully, she was gone, of course. A dream, yet it seemed so real."

Douglas opened his eyes. He stared at her. He said very slowly, "The devil, you say."

"Dreams are strange, aren't they? They seem so real, so tangible, but of course—"

"A dream, nothing more, nothing less. Forget it. Do you understand?"

Why would he behave so strangely about a silly dream? She nodded

"I understand."

CHAPTER
═══ 8 ═══

"YES, HOLLIS, IT'S indeed the one Sherbrooke you neither expected nor wanted to see. Yes, I know, you would probably like to see me at Jericho, but I'm back. The suspense was more than I could bear. I told Mother, Tysen, and Sinjun that I was going to the Newmarket races. They all believed me except Sinjun, no surprise there, she's a smart little chit, sometimes too smart, damn her eyes. But forget that. I had to see Douglas's new wife."

Hollis was dismayed. He stared at the windblown young man he'd known and loved all his life, a young man almost too vital and handsome for his own good, a young man who was far too young to be so very cynical. Now, facing him, Hollis was forced to smile. "No, not at all, Master Ryder, do come in, though I do understand that Jericho is quite nice this time of year. Yes, do come in. Give me your cloak. You will see that the new countess is a charming young lady. However, just so you will be properly advised, it may take His Lordship a bit more time to adjust himself to his good fortune. The new countess was, as you know, somewhat unexpected."

"Yes, and you decided Douglas should be left here alone to sort things out without family interference. I'll tell you, Hollis, Mother is fair chomping at the bit to chew the chit to bits. Poor little twit, I don't envy her when Mother returns. So Douglas didn't particularly approve the female Tony attached him to? Odd, I've never known Tony not to have exquisite taste in females, all except for that Carleton woman who somehow wrung a proposal out of him, which will remain a mystery in the annals of malehood into the misty future. Ah, well, Douglas is fickle and he is demanding as the devil."

"I don't believe fickleness is a particularly noble quality, Master Ryder, thus it doesn't fit well with His Lordship's character. No, it is all a matter of change, I believe. Abrupt change is difficult even for the best of men. The new countess, as I said, is all that a gentleman would wish for in a wife."

"Ah ha! I begin to understand. The chit isn't all that toothsome. She's nothing compared to the succulent Melissande, isn't that right, Hollis? Is that what you're trying to tell me in that wonderfully understated way of yours?"

Melissande, who'd immediately spotted this dashing young man with his fair good looks and his even fairer speech from the breakfast room door, thought a moment about being succulent, wasn't actually certain of its meaning, but decided the intent was obvious enough, and thus she cleared her throat and sang out, "Hello, I'm Lady Melissande. Who are you, sir?"

Ryder turned toward the unfamiliar voice and looked at the female standing there. To Melissande's utter amazement, this gentleman, unlike all the other male specimens of her acquaintance, did not turn to mesmerized stone at the sight of her; he did not metaphorically fall at her feet and lie there inert as a dead dog. She knew the sight she presented was enough to smite down the most jaded of gentlemen. Whatever was wrong? Was her hair not perfect? Was her figure not just as perfect, and the lavender of her silk morning gown beyond glorious against her white skin? Was his vision defective?

Of course nothing was wrong with her. Nothing was ever wrong. Still, he merely stood there, his head cocked to one side. For the life of her, Melissande couldn't see any incipient signs of besottedness about him, no sudden pallor or stiffening, no hint of soulful reverence in those lovely blue eyes of his. Ah, but maybe he was tongue-tied, and that was his afflicted reaction in the presence of her succulent self. Then he smiled and said, his voice lazy and smooth as warm honey, "I'm Ryder Sherbrooke, Douglas's brother. Where is the new countess? And what are you doing here?"

"She's with me, Ryder."

"Hello, Tony." Ryder grinned at his cousin, who'd come around his wife from the breakfast room. Ryder stepped forward and gripped his hand. "I am rather pleased you are still alive or is it still in question? Is Douglas still at your throat or have you convinced him that he is all the better off for this good deed you performed for him?"

"Look, Ryder, I—"

"No, cousin, Hollis didn't tell me any secrets, it's just that I had to come and see for myself. It's dashed good to see you in one healthy piece, Tony."

"I'm Melissande."

"Yes, I know. My pleasure."

Ryder immediately turned back to his cousin. "Is that a swollen lip I see, Tony? Perhaps that's a bruise on your cheek? So you did tangle with Douglas, did you? I trust you gave as good as you got."

"I'm Tony's wife."

"Yes, I know. My pleasure."

Ryder continued to his cousin, "Well, did you?"

"Did I what?"

"Punch Douglas in his pretty face."

"I got in a few good blows, but not enough. His wife attacked me."

"I'm Melissande. I attacked Douglas."

Ryder knew the glorious creature was miffed, and he was amused by it. Obviously Tony was meant to be an Atlas among men; he would need to be in order to control this delightful package of vanity that was his wife. If he didn't manage her well, he would probably wish rather to carry the world on his shoulders. It wasn't Ryder's problem, thankfully, so he said, "Come along, Tony, I want to hear all the details. Is Douglas here?"

"No, he and Alex are riding, I believe."

"Alex?"

"Alexandra."

"I'm Melissande. I'm Alexandra's sister."

"I know. My pleasure, ma'am. Come along, Tony."

Melissande was left standing in the entrance hall, staring after her husband and the unobservant clod of an oblivious cousin-in-law. Hollis gently cleared his throat. "Should you like anything, my lady?"

"No," Melissande said, her voice absent, for she was still suffering minor shock. "I must go upstairs and see what is wrong."

Hollis smiled after her, knowing that her mirror would soon enjoy her image and her puzzlement.

Five minutes later he wasn't smiling. His Lordship and his wife came into the hall, both looking as if they'd been dragged through a ditch. "My lord! Goodness! My lady, are you—"

"No, don't fret, Hollis." Douglas turned to Alexandra. "Go upstairs and do something about yourself."

As a dismissal, it was clear and to the point. Even though he looked very probably as bad as she did, Alex kept quiet. She went upstairs.

Douglas said to Hollis, "We both fell from our horses, but no harm done."

"Her Ladyship is limping a bit."

"It serves her . . . well, perhaps a bit, but she'll be just fine, don't fret, Hollis."

When told that his brother had come to grace the Northcliffe portals, Douglas cursed, cursed some more, stomped past Hollis, and stomped into the library. Three maids were peeking around the Golden Salon doors and two footmen were stationed unobtrusively beneath the stairs, staring out. Hollis, as was his wont, very gently sent them back to their duties.

"Ah," Ryder said upon Douglas's entrance. "Let me see your face. Tony claimed that you nearly beat him to a bloody pulp and you escaped without a mark. He said, of course, that he let you, that he only tried to defend himself."

"It was his wife who nearly killed me," Tony said. "She was first my sister-in-law, but now she shows me no loyalty. It isn't right of her. I feel flayed with treachery."

"Treachery! You damned cur! I'll—"

Douglas stopped. There was nothing more to say. What he had to decide now was whether or not to annul the marriage. And now Ryder was here. He looked with some dislike upon his brother. "All right, why are you here, Ryder? Is Mother all right? Tysen and Sinjun?"

"Mother is carping about you at full steam. Sinjun is reading voraciously, as usual, and Tysen was prosing on and on until Sinjun threw a novel at him. In short, everyone is just the same, Douglas. They all think me at Newmarket. I was curious, that's all. Where's the chit Tony married you to? Does she have a squint? Is she fat with several chins? Missing teeth? Flat-breasted?"

"Don't be an ass, Ryder," Tony nearly shouted. "Alex is lovely and sweet-natured and—"

"Sweet-natured! Ha! You would say so, certainly, since you married her to me! She's not Melissande."

"I saw Melissande, Douglas," Ryder said slowly, staring at his brother. "Tony was standing near her. I believe he's afraid that every man who lays eyes on her will lose his head."

"You saw her. He's justified."

"But you didn't appear to," Tony said thoughtfully to Ryder. "Why not?"

Ryder merely shrugged. "One woman's much the same as another. So long as they're warm and loving in bed, why then, who cares? Sorry, but I don't mean to insult your wife, Tony, it's just that . . . I will try to make her a fine cousin-in-law, all right?"

Tony chewed this over. He liked Ryder but he didn't understand him. This cynicism of his, this utter bland indifference toward women in general, hadn't led him to monkish tastes but rather to a satyr's appetites. No, he didn't like women particularly, yet he supported his bastards and their mothers. He never blamed a woman for becoming pregnant. It was perplexing. Women were sport to Ryder, nothing more, and he was quite willing to pay for it and accept the consequences. It was also a relief that Melissande was safe from his ogling. But Douglas . . . Tony turned to his cousin and said, "I understand you and Alex were riding. She's a superior horsewoman."

Douglas grunted.

"You are a bit disheveled, Douglas," Tony persevered. "What happened?"

"I fell off Garth; rather, that cursed woman you married pushed me off my horse. She fell off first and now I will have to buy her a new riding habit. Did you see the one she was wearing? Old and dowdy, doubtless all her other clothes are equally distasteful, and I'll wager it was all planned by her fond parent so I would be forced to buy her a new wardrobe. She looks a fright, Tony, damn you to hell."

Tony frowned. "That's odd. Melissande has beautiful gowns and the softest silk, er, feminine things."

Ryder said quickly, "There's a faint bruise by your left eye and over your right ear, Douglas. Any other battle marks?"

Douglas said nothing whilst he poured himself a brandy. He sipped it, then waved his snifter at Tony. "I am going to kill this miserable sot. Would you like to second me, Ryder?"

"You've a tear in your britches. And no, I truly cannot second you. I like Tony. I always have. Look, Douglas, it seems to me that you must allow a relative some latitude, particularly a relative of Tony's closeness. We spent much of our boyhood together. He has never before done you in, has he? No, you will be forced to say, and I must agree. Thus, it's just this one time that he has fallen off the cousinly straight and narrow. Only one time. Thus, forgiveness is—"

Douglas threw his brandy snifter at Ryder, who promptly ducked. The glass shattered against the brick hearth.

There was a knock on the library door.

"Come in," Tony shouted.

Hollis entered, carrying a massive silver tray with the Northcliffe crest emblazoned upon it—a lion with his front paws on a shield, looking both noble and vicious. "I brought some refreshments, my lord."

"Which lord?" Douglas said.

"You, my lord."

"Ha! You came because you feared I was trying to murder Tony again."

"It's wise to be vigilant, my lord. Here are also some rather tasty scones from Mrs. Tanner's kitchen, your favorite, my lord. And Master Ryder, here is your favorite strawberry jam. Come, my lord."

"What about me, Hollis?" Tony said.

"For you, my lord, there are thick slices of shortbread."

"Ah, you are a prince among butlers, Hollis."

"Yes, my lord."

Douglas cursed under his breath, Tony reached for a slice of short-bread, and Ryder had his hand around the jam pot.

Hollis stood back, feeling a modicum of relief. When he heard the footsteps from outside the library door, however, he felt himself pale. Oh dear, now wasn't the time for the two wives to make appearances. But there was naught he could do.

Both ladies came into the library. Lady Melissande glided forward on graceful feet; Lady Alexandra made solid thuds until she reached the thick Aubusson carpet. Lady Melissande's glorious black hair was in soft waves and ringlets about her face; Lady Alexandra's hair was a lovely color, true, but it straggled out of the crooked bun at the nape of her neck. She needed more time in front of her mirror. Lady Melissande's gown was a soft peach silk that draped over her womanly shape with subtle invitation—she'd changed from the lavender. Lady Alexandra wore a pale blue gown with nothing more memorable than a deplorably high neck.

With the two females standing side by side, Ryder understood his brother's sense of betrayal. He had a mouth full of scone and strawberry jam. He swallowed too quickly and choked and continued to choke. Alex calmly walked to him, and hit him as hard as she could with her fist between his shoulder blades.

She nearly knocked him over with the force of her blow. He stopped choking, however. Still red-faced, Ryder looked up at the young lady and quickly got to his feet. He studied her in silence for several moments, then nodded slowly.

He took her hand and kissed the wrist. "I'm Ryder, your brother-in-law. You're Alexandra."

"Yes. Are you all right?"

"You nearly sent my back through my chest, but yes, I am quite fine now. The bit of scone found its proper way down. Welcome to the Sherbrooke family. Did you really knock Douglas off his horse?"

Alex shook her head even as she said, "I didn't really mean to do it at the time."

"Ha! I recall making an observation about something quite bland and you coshed me onto the ground!"

"She is quite large and brawny, isn't she?" Ryder said. He lightly closed his fingers around her upper arm. "Ah, strong as an Amazon and as muscled as Squire Maynard's bull. She is terrifying, Douglas, she certainly is."

"You weren't at all bland," Alexandra said to Douglas.

"Neither am I," Melissande said.

Tony laughed. "No one in his right mind would ever call you bland, sweetheart."

"Would you call me succulent?"

Tony's face tightened ever so slightly. "I would but no one else would dare to."

"Ah," Melissande said and gave Tony a look so provocative it would sizzle any male's toes.

Douglas stared at her.

Ryder said to Alexandra, his voice easy, and oddly gentle, "Won't you sit down and join us?"

"I shall join you too," Melissande announced. She eyed her sister with grave perplexity. This was beyond strange, she thought, staring at Ryder, who was looking closely at Alex. Mirrors didn't lie. Perhaps poor Ryder was excessively myopic as she'd first thought. She turned back to her husband, saw that mocking gleam in his dark eyes, frowned, then turned to Douglas. Her soul found instant balm. His heart was in his eyes and both looked wonderfully bruised to her.

She gave him a sweet smile and nodded. "Please forgive me if I caused you discomfort last night."

Douglas shook his head.

"Come and serve me tea, Mellie," Tony said.

"I told you I don't like that horrible name!"

Douglas's right eye twitched.

"Come, Mellie," Tony said again.

"It's a lovely nickname," Ryder said, eyeing the heart-stopping creature, who looked ready to spit at her husband of two weeks. When she didn't react, he stoked the fire a bit. "I rather like the feel of 'Mellie.' It sounds rather mussed, comfortable, like a pair of old house slippers a man can slip his feet into and point them toward the fire."

Alexandra laughed. " 'Tis better than Alex. I would rather sound comfortable than like I was a man."

"No one would ever make that mistake," Ryder said.

Both Douglas and Melissande frowned together.

"Your gown is deplorable," Douglas said to his wife. "It is so out of fashion I doubt it was ever in fashion at all."

Her chin went up and the broom handle straightened alarmingly up her back. "It is blue, and blue is a very nice color."

"You look like a schoolgirl."

"Then perhaps you would like to buy me a new one? Or perhaps a dozen? Is my tone wheedling enough, my lord?"

Douglas realized this wasn't the time to show his ill-humor. He drew himself in and sought control, a commodity of which he'd been plentifully endowed until but twenty-four hours before. The chit had stripped it off him. He felt raw and exposed.

He picked up a scone and bit into it.

"Did you ride Fanny?" Ryder asked.

"Yes, she is a wonderful mare. However, I am uncertain if His Lordship is convinced that I ride well enough."

"You did fall," Melissande said. "That wasn't well done of you, Alex."

To Douglas's surprise, Alexandra said only, her voice quite apologetic, "It was unfortunate but I shall be far more careful in the future."

Douglas wondered if there would be a future. He had to get out of here and do some serious thinking. Annulment seemed the best answer. It seemed the only logical thing to do. He looked over at Alexandra. She was looking directly at him and he saw such wariness in her eyes that he winced. And there was fear also. Fear of him? Because of what she'd done to him, doubtless. The twit should be afraid of him, curse her.

Douglas rose quickly and nodded to the assembled company. "I have work to do with Danvers. The mail is doubtless here by now."

He left. As he closed the door behind him, he heard Ryder's laughter. The mail, however, didn't cheer him at all.

It rained in the early afternoon, a light soft drizzle that soon cleared away, leaving a very blue sky and very fresh air. Alexandra found Ryder Sherbrooke in the overrun garden at the west of the house, leaning against an oak tree, staring at nothing in particular, seemingly content to bask under the warm sun that filtered through the branches.

"Ryder?"

"Ah, my little sister. Am I an accident or did you search me out on purpose?"

She'd never met his like before, but oddly enough, she trusted him. "I asked Hollis where you were. He always knows everyone's whereabouts."

"True. Come sit here next to this fat nymph. What do you think of all these statues? Brought by my grandfather from Florence during his Bacchanal phase, so wrote one of his friends, Lord Whitehaven, an old roué who bounced me on his knee."

"I've never seen them before," Alex said, staring at the line of naked females, each in a startling pose. "This is my first visit to the gardens."

"In the depths of the gardens are all the naked male statues and the assorted couples. Grandfather evidently had some qualms about childish eyes and curiosity. The statues are nicely hidden. Do you like Northcliffe?"

"I don't know."

"Why do you bind your breasts?"

Alex nearly swallowed her tongue. She stared at him, mute as a snail.

"Sorry. I didn't mean to offend you. I am known for speaking my mind, what there is of it."

"How did you know?"

"I know women. There is nothing a woman can do that would fool me. The fairer sex is really rather obvious. Take your lovely sister, for example. Melissande will learn that life has a way of dishing out prunes along with the strawberries. She will play her games with Tony and he will allow them and doubtless enjoy them, within reason, of course. Already he controls her well despite his besottedness with her."

"You don't like ladies?"

Ryder gave her a surprised look. "Good Lord, I couldn't live without them. I doubt there is anything else in life to compare to the pleasure a man derives from a woman's body."

Alex gasped, she couldn't help it.

"Sorry, I did it again, didn't I? You're young, Alexandra, but you're not fluff. You've got steel in you and I dare say you will have to use it, very soon. Now, what do you want of me?"

"I came to ask you if you believed Douglas would annul our marriage and how I can make Douglas wait and just give me a chance before he does it."

"Ah, I thought that was the direction of his thoughts." Ryder looked at her closely. "I will tell you what I think, since you ask me. Douglas is very likely seriously considering an annulment. He has been clipped hard in the chin, so to speak. He is angry, feels betrayed, and wants to strike out. He is also stubborn and hard and untractable. After seeing your sister today, after seeing Douglas seeing your sister, I believe time is short. If you want to keep him for your husband, I suggest that you climb into his bed and seduce him. Continue until you're with child. Then there will be no question of annulment."

Alex stood very slowly, staring in mute fascination at her brother-in-law.

"I doubt Douglas has had a woman for a good while now. It's likely he will be amenable to your approach. Do it, Alex. Patience isn't a virtue in this case. Don't be Penelope."

Her hands were shaking. She thrust them into the folds of her gown. "I don't know anything about seduction."

Ryder laughed. "All females are born knowing about seduction, my dear. Just take off your clothes in front of him. An excellent start. You do understand about sex, don't you? About conception?"

There came a shout. It was Douglas. "Ryder! Come here, now!"

"Ah, the lord and master wishes my presence. He probably wants to send me back to London." He paused, looking down at his new sister-in-law. "I think you're a good sort, Alex. Now isn't the time to be patient with Douglas; you must act quickly. Also, if you're wise, you'll insist that Tony and Melissande remain here for a while. Comparisons are wonderfully enlightening sometimes, and my brother isn't stupid. Seduce him tonight; don't think about it, just do it. A man's brain can be diverted." Ryder wasn't so certain about Douglas's brain, but he didn't wish to discourage Alex.

Ryder left her then to stare after him in bemusement and to bemoan the poor condition of the garden and of her marriage. Her fingers itched to dig in the rich black soil. Why were the gardens so neglected? Rosebushes begged for pruning. She realized with a small smile that Douglas needed pruning too.

At dinner that evening, Douglas announced, "There was a letter from our plantation manager in Jamaica. There is trouble at Kimberly Hall. Ryder will leave on the morrow to deal with it."

"What sort of trouble?" Alexandra asked.

"Grayson wrote of strange doings, of black magic and visions from hell itself, murders and the like, of slave uprisings. You undoubtedly get the idea."

"Grayson excels in exaggeration," Ryder said. "If a fly flew past his head, he would call it a gigantic wasp and claim it was bedeviling him. This talk of perversions sounds interesting, but knowing Grayson, it involves nothing more than two noisy cats."

"Ah, but he is a good man and an excellent manager," Douglas said.

Ryder thought about his children and frowned. He'd dealt with all that needed to be done in his absence, but still, he would miss the little devils. He said aloud, realizing he'd been silent overlong, "I'll leave for Southampton early tomorrow. Thus tonight is my last chance to ingratiate myself with my sister-in-law. I like the pink gown, Alexandra. I have always said that deep red titian hair is complemented by certain shades of pink."

"Yes, it is," Tony said, frowning at Alex, as if he'd never really seen her before.

"The gown is old and is cut like a nun's habit," Douglas said. "It is as dowdy as the blue gown you were wearing earlier this afternoon."

The broom handle stiffened. Douglas raised his hand. "No, I didn't say I would replace any of your gowns, so I don't need more of your comments about wheedling. I was merely noting that your feminine display is sorely lacking."

"It's true a lady should attempt to display well," Melissande said.

Douglas looked over at Melissande. She looked so utterly feminine and unspeakably delicious that for a moment he was mute.

"Your display, Mellie," Tony said, caressing her bare upper arm, "would make our randy Prince George slip down in a puddle of his own drool."

Alex laughed. "I should like to see that. Will you take Melissande to London, Tony, so that the prince may see her and slip?"

"In good time," Tony said. "In good time."

"I should like to go now," Melissande said. "You have a town house I have never seen. I should like to give a ball and invite everyone important."

"In good time," Tony said. "First you must see Strawberry Hill, my family estate in the Cotswolds."

"A wonderful place to raise children," Ryder said. "Do you remember, Douglas, how we used to swing off that old maple branch into the spring, screaming at the top of our lungs?"

"Yes, and the time Tony broke the branch and nearly drowned because it struck him on the head when he hit the water."

"I should prefer London," Melissande said.

"You will prefer what I wish you to prefer, Mellie," Tony said very matter-of-factly.

Ryder said quickly, his voice limpid as that same spring in summer, "I agree that Melissande would enjoy London, but only if Tony was enjoying it with her. Since he prefers Strawberry Hill, why then, she will prefer it also. Melissande understands that it is a wife's duty and pleasure to obey her husband, to honor him by her every word and deed and soft caress. Don't you agree, Alexandra?"

Alex said with a smile, "I should like to see the branch that coshed Tony on the head and nearly drowned him."

"I should also," Melissande said, beautiful eyes wary, "but after I have enjoyed London, with my husband, naturally."

Douglas took a sip of the rich claret. He looked at Ryder over the edge of the crystal goblet.

"As I was saying," Ryder continued, "Strawberry Hill is a wonderful place to raise children. I have heard Tony say that he would like a good half-dozen children attaching themselves to his coattails."

Tony, who had never uttered such a longing in his entire life, smiled like an already besotted parent. He looked at Ryder from the corner of his eyes, then directly at his wife. She looked remarkably flushed, and frankly appalled. He cleared his throat and whispered in a voice that carried to every corner of the dining room, "Should we continue trying to begin our brood after dinner, Mellie?"

"Don't call me that!"

"But the other names I call you really aren't appropriate for the dining room. But if you would prefer, if you feel so very comfortable with all those here at the table, why then, who am I to quibble? How about honey-po—"

Melissande slapped her palm over her husband's mouth. He took her slender wrist between his long fingers and pulled it away. "Now, where was I?"

"Please, Tony."

He looked at her closely. "Did I truly hear a 'please'?"

She nodded.

He looked at her another long moment, then said calmly, "You have pleased me. Eat your stewed green beans, Mellie. They're quite delicious."

Alexandra, who'd been a fascinated observer, now looked toward her own husband. He was staring at Melissande and Tony and there was a deep frown on his forehead. As for Ryder, he was smiling at his turtle soup.

Two hours later, alone in her bedchamber, Alexandra stood irresolute, staring at the adjoining door. Ryder had said to seduce Douglas. Ryder said that all women were born knowing how. She wondered if Douglas would laugh at her if she tried. Ryder had said time was of the essence, that she must act quickly, that she mustn't wait patiently, like the faithful Penelope did for Ulysses. Very well then. She would do it and she would do it now. Before she lost her resolve.

Alex doused her candle and walked to the adjoining door. Slowly, she opened it.

CHAPTER
=== 9 ===

ALEX WALKED SLOWLY into the large master bedroom. Her eyes went immediately to the bed and she stilled. It was empty, the covers unruffled. She saw him then and walked quietly toward him. A branch of candles burned on a table beside the wing chair in front of the fireplace. There were only embers still burning, dull orange, throwing off little light and warmth.

Douglas sat in the chair, his long legs stretched out in front of him, crossed at the ankles. He was wearing a dark blue brocade dressing gown. It was parted over his legs. She stared at his legs, hairy, thick, strong. His feet were bare. They were long and narrow and quite beautiful to her. His chin was balanced on his fist.

She was scared silly; but she was determined, she had to be. It was very possible that her future with this man depended on what she did and how well she did it in the next few minutes. "My lord?"

"Yes," Douglas said, not moving, not looking at her. "I heard you come into my room. I never thought I should lock my door against a woman. What do you want?"

"I wanted . . . you're thinking about what to do with me, aren't you?"

"Yes, that and other things. I am also worried about Ryder voyaging to the West Indies. It is never a safe sailing. But he insisted that he be the one to go." Douglas turned then to look up at her. "Ryder said I should remain here and come to grips with myself and my marriage to you. He believes you a perfectly fine sort."

She said nothing.

Douglas looked over at her then. He brooded, stroking his fingers over his chin now. "Your nightgown is a little girl's, all white and long and high-necked."

"I don't have any others."

"The brass I will have to spend on clothing you begins to boggle the mind."

"There is nothing wrong with my nightgown. It keeps me warm and it is soft against the skin."

"It is a virgin's nightgown."

"Well," she said reasonably, "that is what I am."

"No self-respecting woman would wear such a garment."

Alex sighed.

"What do you want? Ah, I see. You wish to plead with me some more. You wish to further detail how indispensable you can be to me. You wish to bray on about your housewifely accomplishments. I beg you not to tell me you will also sing in the evenings to me and perhaps accompany yourself on the pianoforte. Why the devil do you have your hair braided? It looks absurd. I don't like it."

Alex never stopped looking at him. She hadn't thought about her braid; she should have, for a braid couldn't be considered remotely seductive. Melissande never braided her hair. Alex would learn. She set her single candle down on the table by his chair. She raised her arms and slowly began to unbraid her hair. As the plaits came loose, she tugged her fingers through the deep ripples, smoothing them out. He merely sat there, watching her, saying nothing.

When she finished, her hair was loose to the middle of her back.

"Bring some hair over your shoulder."

She did.

"There. Your hair is a nice color and it is of a nice thickness. At least the hair hides some of the hideous nightgown. Now, what do you want?"

There was really no hope for it. Either she opened her mouth and told him, or she left. He appeared impatient with her and saw her as naught but an unwelcome intrusion. It was daunting.

"Well? Get on with it. I can take anything except whining and wheedling."

She said without preamble, chin up, back straight, "I've come to seduce you."

"Ah, the female's final weapon," Douglas said. "I really shouldn't be surprised, should I? If naught else, I put it in your mind this morning. I should have known, should have guessed. When all else fails, bring out the female body and parade it about in front of the randy man's nose."

"My only problem is that I'm not certain how to go about doing it."

"That's twaddle."

"Perhaps if you could help me just a little bit, I could figure it out."

"Let me make something clear to you, something it's obvious you haven't considered in this plan of yours. I can still have this farce of a marriage annulled even if I take your virginity. Do you understand me? Who would know, after all? Would you or anyone in your family announce to the world that you were damaged goods?"

"You make me sound as if I would be a mangled parcel. Surely that is absurd."

"Oh no, a virgin who has lost her maidenhead is much worse off than a mangled parcel. Imagine your father's reaction. He would be appalled but would remain silent, for he would know that if he opened his mouth and announced what I had done, you would be utterly ruined and he would be a laughingstock. As for me, why, no one in our great land would regard me with one less whit of consideration."

"But why? That seems absurd. It seems hardly fair."

"Fair rarely has a meaningful place in anything. The fact is that men of our class aren't anxious to afflict themselves with wives who don't arrive in the marriage bed pure and untouched. Thus, if a female slips, it is kept quiet so the poor fool who does marry her is well and truly trapped. So, you see, no one would know what I did or didn't do to you. If I chose, I imagine I can take you with impunity for as long as I wished to."

"I cannot believe that gentlemen are so callous, so uncaring about the women they love."

"Ah, yes, there is the question of love, isn't there? But that doesn't come into this marriage, does it? You are a stranger, nothing more, just a stranger and—"

"In addition to seducing you, I must keep it up until I am with child. Then you couldn't annul me. But, you see, that is my problem."

Douglas's attention was fairly caught now. He'd used up most of his words, and he'd spoken truthfully to her but with no visible effect. Still, he couldn't believe the chit was standing beside him, dressed only in her virginal nightgown, her feet bare, her toes curled from cold, looking like some sort of pathetic sacrifice. But she was here and she appeared quite resolute. She wasn't a coward, he'd give her that. The question was, what was she? Would she do anything for her father, then? "Who told you to keep it up?"

"Ryder."

"Ah, my dear doting brother. Curse him to hell, but he must always meddle, it's his nature."

"But he didn't have time to tell me how to go about it, this seduction business, I mean. I am your wife, my lord. I am willing to become your wife and sleep in that bed. I am willing to sleep in that bed until I am with child. Do you not want an heir? Isn't that your primary reason for wishing to wed?"

"It was, but you are the wrong wife, as you well know, as I am tired of saying because repetition is beyond boring."

"I will give you your heir. I am young and healthy and I will give you a half-dozen heirs."

"I have never in my male adult life heard a woman offer to become a man's brood mare. Why, Alexandra? Another agreement with your villain of a father? Hell and damnation, just go to bed. You're a little girl, a virgin, and I haven't the inclination to show you anything or take your virginity or hear you whimper. I am tired. Go away."

Alex bent down, clutched the hem of her gown, and lifted it over her head. She tossed the gown to the floor. She stood there, arms at her sides, stark naked. She raised her head and looked directly at her husband.

Douglas froze. He opened his mouth. He closed it. He stared at his wife. He hadn't had any idea that she was built so very nicely. Her breasts . . . good Lord, he hadn't imagined, hadn't realized that . . .

"You bind your breasts. Why?"

"My nanny said they were too big. She said that the boys were staring at me and saying things that weren't nice. Because I had big breasts they assumed that I wasn't a proper young lady. My nanny taught me how to bind them."

"Your nanny was a stupid old prig. Your breasts are an asset, a fine one at that. Don't bind them any more. Now that I know what you've got, I want to see them."

"You are."

"This morning, when we were riding, I couldn't tell that you were so finely endowed."

"No."

Douglas fell silent. He was still staring at her breasts. They were high and very full, as white as her belly. They would fill his hands to overflowing. His fingers itched, his palms were hot.

She hadn't known how Douglas would react, but this conversation about her breasts, as bland as discussions about the weather, was unnerving. She saw him raise his hand, then lower it. He was still looking at her, oh yes, he was looking and his gaze was intent and, of all things, his eyes looked even darker. She forced herself to keep perfectly still.

"Pink goes nicely with red. I can see a pink nipple showing through your red hair."

Alex wanted to quite simply fold her body into a very small ball and roll away. But she didn't move. Her entire future was in this room, contained in this very minute. This man was her husband; she belonged to him more than she'd ever belonged to anyone else in her life.

Douglas tried to be blasé. He was an experienced man, a man who'd enjoyed many women, a man who was selective, a cold fish, Ryder had called him, because he could always control his passion. But, truth be told, he was stunned. Aside from the most beautiful breasts he'd ever seen in his life, breasts nearly too big for her slender torso, her waist was narrow, her belly flat, the curls covering her woman's mound, a soft dark red. Her legs were long and nicely curved. There was a mole on her belly, just below her navel. She looked very nice. She didn't look at all like a little girl. She stood straight and tall even though she was small. That damned broom handle against her backbone. He wanted to tell her to turn around so he could see her back and her buttocks.

Good lord. What was he to do?

"Come here," he said before his brain could countermand the order, and parted his legs.

She came to stand between his legs, still and silent, her arms still at her sides. Still he didn't touch her, merely looked and looked some more, now at her belly, and she knew it. It was almost beyond what she could bear, this intense study of her body by this man. Even she herself had never looked at her body as he was looking now.

Finally, after an eternity of minutes, Douglas raised his head and looked her in the face. "You do not displease me. Your female endowments are adequate. Should you like to part your legs so I may see the rest of you? No? That isn't part of your seduction plan? How far do you plan to go if I do nothing?" He looked away from her then, into the fire. "You say nothing. I have already brought you to stand between my legs. Cannot you think of anything to do yourself?"

Alex brought her hand up to cover her breasts, the other hand to cover her woman's mound. It was an absurd gesture, but she simply couldn't bear standing there any longer, exposed and open to him. His disinterest was obvious and it was so painful she couldn't bear it.

"You know, Alex," he said, looking back at her now, "not only can I take you again and again, I can prevent you conceiving a child. I can easily withdraw my sex from you before spilling my seed inside your body. I am not a boy; I am a man with a man's control. Don't look so damnably blank! You cannot conceive a child if my seed doesn't reach your womb. Thus I can freely take what is offered and still annul this farce of a marriage." He waved a hand at her. "However, tonight, this very minute with you standing here before me with only your white hide covering you, I find I have no interest. You are not Melissande. You are not the wife I wanted. Go away."

Alexandra felt beyond humiliation. She could scarce think for the pain roiling through her, the pain, the failure, the emptiness his words had carved out inside her. She stood there in front of him, not twelve inches away from him, because she was incapable of moving. She wasn't as embarrassed as she was devastated. He had rejected her, completely. He'd not been particularly cruel about it, just utterly matter-of-fact. He had made his feelings quite plain. Even though he had seemed to find her acceptable, he still didn't want her enough to take her and then discard her. He didn't want her for anything. Ryder hadn't judged his brother's feelings correctly this time. Ryder had been wrong. There was nothing more she could do.

She stepped away from him then, her blood pounding wildly through her, then ran from his bedchamber.

Douglas saw the flash of white skin. He heard the adjoining door close very quietly. He didn't move for a very long time. Then he rose and picked up her discarded nightgown. He looked toward her chamber. Then, very deliberately, he tossed the nightgown into his chair.

He knew what he'd done. He knew he'd kicked her and then kicked her again. But, damn her, he refused to be cornered, to be bribed and blackmailed with sex. He would never allow a woman to dictate to him, to try to make him lose his logic and his brain by flaunting her body. But the look on her face as he'd spoken. He cursed as he flung off his dressing gown. It landed beside her nightgown on the chair. He cursed as he climbed into his big empty bed and burrowed under the blanket. He felt disgusted with himself, but he wouldn't back down. He would do what he wished to do, and he wouldn't be coerced, certainly not by an eighteen-year-old chit with the most beautiful breasts he'd ever seen in his life.

In the dead of night Douglas awoke with sweat thick and clammy on his forehead. He held himself perfectly still. He'd heard a sound. He waited, completely awake and alert. He heard the strange noise again. It sounded like a woman. She was crying, low and soft, yet he heard her distinctly. No, it wasn't crying, rather deep moaning, hurt and raw. He knew that she was moaning because of a great pain. He didn't know how he knew this, but he did. He frowned into the darkness toward the adjoining room. This was absurd.

It was Alexandra, crying because he'd put her properly in her place. She was sulking; she had failed to get her way, and she was trying to draw pity from him. Crocodile tears, nothing more. That was it. He was a man, but he wouldn't be swayed by a girl's tears, sham tears because she hadn't managed to make him lose his head. But it wasn't crying . . . it was moaning, it was a deep, deep pain. He cursed and flung back the bed covers.

He walked naked to the adjoining door and quietly opened it. He knew it had to be Alexandra. It had to be, but still he was quiet, and the door made no noise as it opened.

He walked into the bedchamber. There was a narrow beam of moonlight coming through the window, slicing over the center of the bed. The bed was empty. No, wait, there she was, standing on the other side of the bed, staring down at it, and she was moaning softly, very softly, only he

would swear that her mouth didn't move, that she was making no sound
at all. But he heard the crying, the moaning, he heard it clearly in his
head. It was so quiet he couldn't imagine how he had heard her in his bedchamber. She was hugging her arms around her, and then she looked up
and saw him.

She was still now. He opened his mouth, but nothing came out. In the
next instant, she was gone, fading slowly like a soft white shadow into
that thin beam of moonlight.

"No," Douglas said, loudly and firmly. "No, dammit! I will not accept
this!"

He ran to the other side of the bed. Alexandra wasn't there. Damnation, he'd dreamed it, all of it. He felt guilty and he was having strange
visions because of his guilt.

Where was Alexandra? She was fast in hiding herself, he'd give her
that, the damned twit. There weren't many places to search. He looked in
her armoire. He even got on his knees and looked under the bed.

She wasn't here. She wasn't anywhere. It was the middle of the night.
Where the hell was she?

He saw her face then, clear in his mind. He saw her pallor, the humiliation in her eyes as his words had struck her, hard and remorseless,
words that wounded deeply. And he'd even thrown her sister at her while
she'd stood there standing still and solitary between his parted legs,
naked and vulnerable and terribly, terribly alone. And she'd run from
him, stripped of every shred of dignity, deeply wounded, but still he'd let
her go.

Well, hell.

It wasn't, thank God, as late as he'd first thought. It was just past midnight. Not many minutes after he'd fallen asleep then awakened so
abruptly. He dressed quickly and made his way quietly downstairs. He
didn't light a lamp, he didn't need one. He knew every foot of Northcliffe.
She didn't. There were a million places to hide but she didn't know of
them. No, she wouldn't want to remain here.

He didn't question how he knew this. He unlocked the massive front
doors and slipped into the cold dark night. The sliver of moonlight was
gone, covered now with dense gray clouds. It would rain soon, a thick
cold rain. The air was damp and heavy.

He hadn't thought of the cold and now he shivered from his thought-
lessness. He was wearing only a shirt, tight buckskin breeches, and boots.
The wind was rising, the storm was coming closer.

"Alexandra!"

The wind rustled through the leaves. A shutter banged against an upper-story window. He felt udden urgency. He ran toward the stables. They appeared deserted, naturally, all the stable lads in bed. He walked more quietly as he neared Fanny's stall. Then he stopped completely. Quietly, efficiently, he lit a lamp near the stable door. He lifted it and just looked.

Alex dropped the saddle, whirling around when the light struck her. She couldn't see anything because the light was in her eyes, blinding her.

"Who's there?"

She sounded scared. Good, she deserved it. He was furious now with her; she'd roused him from a deep sleep—well, it had obviously been some sort of nightmare—but still, it was her fault. She'd forced him to come looking for her. She'd made him worry; she'd made him suffer needlessly; she'd made him feel guilty.

"Please, who is there?"

He set the lamp down.

"You move an inch and I will beat you," he said and walked to where she was standing. Garth, recognizing his master, whinnied. Fanny twitched her head around and whinnied in response.

"Take off the bridle."

It was time to take a stand. "No," Alex said. She wanted to drop the saddle for it was very heavy, but she clung to it, holding it against her chest.

"You were planning to steal my sister's mare?"

"No. Well, just for a while. I'm not a thief. I would have returned her."

"Drop the damned saddle before your arms fall off."

Instead, Alex hefted the saddle onto Fanny's back. The mare twitched her tail and leaned around to take a nip of Alex's shoulder. It was close, but Alex managed to draw back in time.

"May I ask where you intended going?"

"Home. Now will you leave me alone? I'm leaving; annul the marriage, I don't care! Do you hear me, I don't care! Just leave!"

Douglas leaned against Garth's stable door and crossed his arms over his chest. "I had believed you many things, but not stupid. However, with the proof of your stupidity before me, I must bow to the obvious facts. You are incredibly stupid. You are a blockhead. Were you planning to ride Fanny all the way back to Harrogate?"

"Yes, but very slowly, and only at night. I also took some money from your strongbox in your desk."

"Dishonest and stupid."

"I have to eat. I would have returned it."

"Ah yes, your father who has all the guineas in the world would have paid me back. I think I shall beat you."

Alex knew a man's anger when she saw it. He hadn't been content to humiliate her. Now he wanted to beat her. Until she was bleeding and senseless? She wondered if he would use a riding crop. "Why did you wake up? I was very quiet."

He frowned. "I just did, that's all. I was in the army. I am a light sleeper." It was a lie but it would serve. He always slept like the dead and had very nearly died because of his habits two times in Italy. Thank the Lord for his valet cum batman, Finkle. "I'm a very light sleeper and I heard your every movement."

She didn't know how that was possible for she'd been so quiet she'd barely heard herself. But he obviously had heard her and followed, why, she couldn't begin to guess. "Why do you care if I leave? You don't want me here. I'm a stranger and I betrayed you as much as Tony did. So I am leaving and I will never return to bother you. Isn't it what you want?"

"I will tell you what I want when I want to tell you. You will take no action until I tell you to."

"That is absurd! You wish me to wait around like some sort of slave until you decide to boot me out? Damn you, my lord, it is you who deserve to be beaten!"

It all happened very quickly. Douglas was more amused than concerned when she grabbed a rake that was leaning against Fanny's stall and ran toward him carrying the rake in both hands over her head. Then, at the last minute, she lowered it, like a knight brandishing a lance in a tourney, and sent it into his belly with such force that he reeled to the side, then landed on his back. Then she struck the lamp and it promptly went out, plunging the stable into darkness.

He jumped to his feet, his belly feeling like it had a hole poked through it, only to have Fanny snort in his face and nearly run him down. He leapt out of the mare's way. He twisted about to see that damned girl riding bareback, her hair flying out behind her head, hugging herself low to Fanny's neck. The saddle lay on its side in the straw. She was riding like the devil was after her.

The devil would very soon be after her. Douglas was so furious, so disbelieving of what she'd done to him, that for an instant, he was overwhelmed with the force of his rage. He drew a deep breath, removed Garth from his stall, put a bridle on him and swung up onto his bare back.

He would, quite simply, kill her once he caught up to her.

Alex continued to ride like the devil. She was an excellent horsewoman and the feel of the horse against her thighs and bottom gave her a feeling of great control, much more so than the decorous sidesaddles society had forced upon females.

She pressed her face against Fanny's neck, holding her legs close against the mare's sides and whispering encouragement. The mare quickened her pace. Her neck felt warm against Alexandra's cheek, warm and alive and the mare was giving all she had. She was smooth-paced and fast as the wind and Alex simply gave her her head.

It was a good five minutes before it occurred to her to question what she was going to do. Fury, humiliation, and a profound acceptance of having lost, with no more recourse available, had doused her like a flood of cold water, and she'd acted without thought. It took only another minute to hear the thudding hooves of Garth coming after her.

The stallion was fast, no doubt about that, strong and fast, but not brutal, not like his master would be if he caught her. But why was he coming after her? Was it his male pride? His arrogance that no one should act without his precious Lordship's permission?

Alex shook her head against Fanny's neck. She wouldn't think about him, about his motives. It was true, she didn't want to do this; she didn't want to run away by herself, a female alone and thus vulnerable to every villain on the English roads. But she wasn't stupid. She fully intended to ride only at night and hide during the three and a half days it would take her to get back home. She had ten pounds of Douglas's money, surely enough to feed herself. No, she wasn't stupid. She would be very careful. Perhaps that was why Douglas was riding after her. Men gave women no measure of credit for accomplishing anything on their own. He probably saw her riding into the midst of thieves, heedless, reckless, unthinking. He probably thought his reputation would be damaged if something happened to his wife—she still was his wife. Ah yes, if something happened to his runaway wife. Such an eventuality would harm his pride, make his gentlemen friends raise their brows.

The rain came down quite suddenly, in thick cold sheets, washing away her body warmth and her thoughts in an instant. She gasped aloud. She hadn't counted on rain in her plans. She hadn't even thought about the possibility of rain. Perhaps Douglas was right; perhaps she was stupid.

Alexandra shook her head. What was a little rain? She wasn't a bolt of silk to fade and unravel. No, she would be fine. In all her eighteen years she'd never known a day's illness. Yes, she would be just fine if she managed to elude Douglas.

He was closer. She sensed him, she heard Garth's hooves. She turned to see him coming around a curve in the road, just as she went around a blind curve herself. It was her chance, perhaps her only chance. She quickly turned Fanny off the road into a copse of maple trees. She slid off Fanny's back and quickly pressed her nostrils together with her fingers to prevent her from whinnying to Garth. She held her breath.

Douglas passed by. He was riding hard. He looked magnificent on Garth's broad back, strong and determined even under the bowing rain, a man to trust and admire. And she would have admired him if she hadn't wanted to massacre him so badly.

Good, she'd fooled him. The rain was not quite so dense because the thickly splayed maple leaves slowed it. Alex patted Fanny's neck.

"We'll be all right, my girl. I'm not stupid and I won't abuse you. I am self-reliant and even though I haven't seen all that much of the world, I still know how to go on. We will be safe. You will like the stables at Claybourn, for they're very nearly empty and you'll have no stupid stallions to bother you."

Alex remounted, swinging herself up easily with the help of Fanny's thick mane. She headed the mare back onto the road. She had to be watchful. Douglas could turn back and she could run right into him. She kept the mare close to the edge of the road, ready to turn her off into the trees in an instant.

The rain continued, relentless and colder by the minute.

Fanny tired and Alex slowed her to a walk.

She would have missed him if she weren't being so vigilant.

CHAPTER
≡ 10 ≡

HE CAME OUT of the trees like a black shadow, yelling like a madman, Garth rearing up on his hind legs, Douglas big and frightening on the stallion's back. He got the stallion under control in a few moments, hauling him sideways, effectively blocking the road.

He smiled at her, an evil smile. "Got you," he said, satisfaction and rage mixed in his voice.

Alexandra pulled Fanny to a halt and simply sat on the mare's back, looking at him. "I tried," she said quietly. "I truly did, but you know, I couldn't bear to remain in the trees, hiding and growing colder by the moment. I was listening for you, that's why we were going so slowly, I was listening for I feared you would turn back and I would run into you. But you are very smart, aren't you, my lord? Very cagey. You simply lay in wait for me."

He remained silent, just looking at her. She thrust her chin into the air. "I am not going back, Douglas."

"You will do precisely what I tell you to do, madam."

"You make no sense. You don't want me. Is it your plan to humiliate me further? Do you wish to accompany me back to Claybourn Hall, a rope around my neck, perhaps, and hand me back to my father? To announce that I am worthless, that I am not deserving of your consideration? I had not guessed you to be so cruel."

Douglas frowned. His rage was justified, certainly it was. And she was putting him on the defensive, making him sound a veritable monster. He was a man, educated, fluent, well stocked in his brain, and yet, she was doing him in. No female had ever before managed it, but she was doing it quite nicely. He wouldn't stand for it. He would stop it now.

"Come along," he said. "We're going back to Northcliffe Hall."

"No."

"How do you intend to prevent me from dragging you back? Perhaps you're making ready to come after my guts with a rake again? Well, no matter what you're considering as a weapon, you will not try anything.

Not this time. I will tolerate no more of your violence. You will obey me and you will be quiet, no more of your disobedience. Come along now."

"No."

Alexandra whipped Fanny around and dug her heels into the mare's fat sides. In the next instant, a bolt of thunder rang out, making the earth tremble, making the trees beside the road shudder. Then there was a thick flash of lightning, ripping through the rain and darkness, white and jagged. It struck a maple tree.

Alex jumped, nearly losing her seat. She twisted about on Fanny's back and watched, so astonished and terrified, she couldn't believe what she was seeing. The lightning struck a thick branch at its base. The branch snapped, sending plumes of smoke into the air, and it slammed downward onto the road, not a foot from Garth's front hooves. The stallion, maddened with fear, screamed, twisted about, and entangled himself in the thick limbs and leaves on the maple branch.

Douglas didn't have a chance. He was thrown, landing at the side of the road. He didn't move.

Alex screamed, loud, shrill, terrified. She was at his side in an instant, kneeling over him, trying to protect him from the slashing dense rain.

He was still. She found finally the pulse in his neck. It was steady, slow. She sat back on her ankles a moment, staring down at him. "Wake up, damn you, Douglas!"

She shook him, then slapped him soundly.

"Wake up! I won't have this! You do not play fairly, not at all. You hold me here because you are helpless. It is not well done of you. No, I can't leave you like this. Wake up!"

He didn't move. His eyes remained closed. Then she saw the blood seeping from behind his left ear. He'd struck a rock when he'd fallen.

Alexandra didn't realize at first that she was rocking back and forth over him, keening deep in her throat, so frightened she thought she'd choke on it.

"Get hold of yourself, Douglas! Don't just lie there." There, it was her voice, and it was strong and she had to do something. Douglas needed her. She looked up. Both horses had bolted, probably back to the Sherbrooke stables. They were alone. It was raining like the very devil. Douglas was unconscious, perhaps dying.

What to do?

She leaned over him again, blocking the rain from his face. If only he'd regain consciousness. What if he didn't? What if he simply remained silent as death until he did indeed die?

She couldn't, wouldn't, accept it. She had to do something.

But there was nothing to do. She couldn't lift him or carry him. She could possibly drag him along the ground, but where to?

She cradled his head in her lap, bent over him, protecting him as best she could. She was cramped and so cold her flesh rippled then grew blessedly numb.

"My God, will you suffocate me, woman?"

She froze, disbelieving the voice she heard, the voice that was filled with irritation and annoyance, the muffled voice coming from her bosom. Slowly she raised her face and looked down at him. His eyes were open.

Her hair straggled about his face, a thick curtain of dripping strands. "Douglas, you're all right?"

"Of course I'm all right. Do you believe me a weakling? My head hurts like the very devil, but I'm just fine." He paused a moment, his nose not two inches from hers. "I preferred having my face buried between your breasts, though."

She could only stare down at him. He wouldn't die. He was too mean, too unreasonable, too outrageous, to die. She smiled as she said, "Both horses have left us. We're stranded. I don't know how far we are from home. It's raining very hard. There is blood behind your left ear. You struck your head on a rock, just a small one, but still a rock and thus hard, thus the blood. You were unconscious for a minute or two. If I help you up, you will simply become soaked." She stopped, not knowing what else to say, staring down at him.

Douglas silently queried his body. Only his head gave reply but it wasn't all that bad, just a steady deep throbbing. "Move," he said to himself.

He sat up, his head lowered for a moment, then he straightened and looked about. "See that narrow path there? We're near my gamekeeper's cottage. His name is Tom O'Malley, and of all my people, he's the one who won't faint with consternation when we arrive on his doorstep past midnight wet and in this piteous state. Come, Alexandra, help me rise, and we'll go there. 'Tis too far to walk back to the hall." It came into his head at that moment that she'd called the hall home. Stupid thought. She shouldn't have said it. It wasn't her home and it probably never would be.

Douglas remained silent until he was upright and realized he was a mite dizzy. Even more than a mite. Irritation was clearly in evidence as he said, "I must lean on you. Are you strong enough to bear some of my weight?"

"Yes, certainly," she said, and hunkered over, bracing herself as she wrapped her arm around his waist. She peered up at him through the thick rain. "I'm ready, Douglas. I won't drop you."

His head hurt. He was cold, he was dizzy. He looked down at the dripping female, scrunched against his side. She was half his size, yet she was trying to keep him upright. He couldn't help himself. He laughed. "A veritable Hercules. I don't damned believe it. This way, Alexandra."

He fell once, bringing her to her knees with him. "I hope it isn't stinging nettles," she said, her breath coming in short gasps as she pushed off the suspicious foliage. "Are you all right, Douglas? I'm sorry I dropped you but that root did me in."

He wanted to vomit, but he didn't, even though the nausea was great. He remained on his knees for a moment, knew he had to rise, knew he wasn't going to disgrace himself, and so he rose, his face white, his mouth closed, his bile swallowed. "No, it wasn't your fault. I was on my way down when you hit that root. I didn't hurt you, did I?"

"No, no," she said, scrambling to her feet. She was shivering with cold and slapped her hands on her arms.

"That isn't stinging nettles, thank the magnanimous Lord, or we'd be itching right now. Let's hurry. It's not far now."

Tom O'Malley's cottage sat at the end of the narrow path in the middle of a small clearing. It was clearly the home of someone who valued his privacy, a slope-roofed cottage of sturdy oak, but one story, and freshly painted, the grounds surrounding it clear of weeds. There were roses and honeysuckle, all well tended, climbing up the sides of the cottage. It looked like a mansion to Alexandra and as dark as a tomb.

"I don't want him to shoot us," Douglas said quietly, and began to lightly pound on the stout door, saying, "Tom. Tom O'Malley." He pounded harder then. "It's Lord Northcliffe! Come, man, let us in."

Alexandra didn't know what to expect, but the very tall, very gaunt-looking man of middle years, fully dressed, quite calm to see his master on his doorstep in the middle of the night, wasn't quite it. He had a very long, very thin nose and it quivered as he said in a low gruff voice, "My lord, aye, but surely 'tis ye. And this be yer new countess? Aye, and certainly she is for Willie at the stables told me about her and how she was comely and a bit slight, and light-handed with a horse. Welcome, milady. I'll build up the fire so that ye may warm yerselves. Nay, it matters not that ye are wet. The floor will dry, and 'tis but wood after all. Come in, come in. Don't tarry in this miserable rain."

"This is Tom O'Malley," Douglas said to Alexandra. "He and his mother arrived at Northcliffe from County Cork some twenty-five years ago, thank the heavens."

"Aye, 'tis me all right, milord, and 'twere twenty-six years before. Ah, 'tis blood on yer face, milord, and ye came to a grief, eh, and struck yer head." He efficiently took Alexandra's place, assisting Douglas to a plain high-backed chair in front of the fireplace. "Just rest yer bones, milord.

Milady," he added, turning to Alexandra, who was dripping very close to a beautiful multicolored handwoven cotton rug. She quickly stood aside, exclaiming, "Oh, it's lovely, Mr. O'Malley."

"Aye, milady, me blessed mother made it with her own caring hands, she did, aye, 'twere a wonderful woman she were. Come here now, and warm yerself. 'Tis dry clothing ye be needing now. Nothing fancy, ye understand, but dry."

"That will be wonderful, Mr. O'Malley. His Lordship and I thank you."

She moved swiftly to Douglas, who was sitting in the chair, staring blankly into the fireplace. "Your head still pains you, doesn't it?"

He looked up at her. "Build up the fire, please."

She did as he bid, then wiped her hands on her sodden skirt. He eyed her then said, "Actually I was just trying to credit that I was with you in the middle of the night in my gamekeeper's cottage. It isn't what one would expect. It isn't even on my list of worst nightmares."

Her chin went up and the broom handle down her back stiffened. "You wouldn't be here if you weren't so stubborn. You wouldn't even be here if you were better able to handle your horse."

As a verbal blow it wasn't bad. Douglas wanted to give as good as she'd just given, but he felt too rotten. He said only, "Make no more sport with me. Hush and move closer to the fire. No, don't look at me as if I'm drawing my last breath. My head hurts just a bit. Ah, Tom, with dry clothes."

Alexandra wouldn't move until Douglas went first into the small bedchamber to change out of his wet clothes. When he emerged, she smiled. He looked wonderful to her in his homespun trousers and handmade white linen shirt. The trousers were very tight on him and she found that she couldn't quite turn away as quickly as undoubtedly a lady should. The shirt laced up the front, but Douglas hadn't bothered lacing the rolled cotton strings all the way to his throat. For several moments, she forgot that she was wet and frowzy and bedraggled.

"Your turn, Alexandra. You look quite pitiful. Tom has no gowns, needless to say. You will be my twin, of sorts."

And thus it was that in ten minutes the lord and lady of Northcliffe Hall were seated on a rough-hewn bench in a gamekeeper's cottage sipping the most delicious tea either had ever drunk and wearing Tom O'Malley's clothes.

Their own clothing was draped over every available surface to dry. The earl said after a moment, "We thank you, Tom, for your hospitality. If you have extra blankets, Her Ladyship and I will sleep here, on the hearth."

Tom O'Malley stared and paled and gasped. "Nay and niver, milord!

Niver! Ask not such a repugnant thing from O'Malley. Me sweet mother would come back from her celestial mansion in heaven and thrash me till me nose bled off me face."

The earl remonstrated. Alexandra watched and listened to both of them. It was amusing and she knew Douglas would lose. Tom was pleading now, saying over and over, "Nay, milord, please don't make me, please. Me dear dead mother, aye, 'tis she looking upon us this minute and she's yelling in me ear, milord."

Douglas gave it up. His head was aching vilely and Alexandra looked ready to fall to the floor she was so exhausted. They adjourned to Tom O'Malley's bedchamber.

"That shirt comes to your knees," Douglas said to Alexandra across the narrow bed. "You might as well keep it on as a nightgown."

"Of course I shall! Did you fear I would pull it off and stand here naked before you again? Or perhaps parade about to provoke some interest in you?"

Douglas shook his head even as he said, "I don't think you're up to much parading." He shrugged, not looking at her. "Besides, you do things I don't expect."

"You needn't worry, my lord, that I will do anything unexpected now. You will be rid of me as soon as I can manage it. I will never disgust you again in that manner."

"I wasn't disgusted."

Alex snorted, a sound that was loud and quite odd in the small room. Douglas laughed.

"I had planned to wear Tom's shirt until it rotted off me, if necessary."

"I trust such a sacrifice won't be necessary."

"I hope so as well." She nodded as she looked about the small room. It was cleaner than her bedchamber had been at Claybourn Hall, its furnishings sparse but well made and well tended. The cover on the bed was soft and pale blue and beautifully knitted.

She unfastened the belt at her waist, then began unrolling the homespun trousers. There were at least eight rolls, and despite everything, she was giggling by the time she was ready to pull them down. She realized then what she had done and where she was, and froze. "Tom is very tall but so skinny that they nearly fit me everywhere else." She looked over at Douglas as she spoke. He had pulled the shirt over his head. His hands were on the waist buttons of the trousers. He looked at her when he heard the small gasp. He looked annoyed.

"For heaven's sake," he said, and pinched out the single candle. "I have no intention of shocking you the way you shocked me. Do women believe that men can't be embarrassed when they play the seductress? No matter, I don't want an answer from you. Unlike you, all my stripping will be done in the dark. Don't squawk."

When they were both lying on their backs, not two inches separating them, Alexandra said, "Tom didn't seem at all surprised to see us."

"Tom comes from a long line of phlegmatic O'Malleys. He's a good man, though I don't like taking his bed. He's as tall as I am and the damned bed is too short. I shall have to see about a new one for him. It's the least I can do."

Douglas moved, cursed when his elbow bumped her head. "Damnation, woman, your hair is still wet. Do you want to die of a damned chill? Spread it on the pillow to dry." He kept muttering about thoughtless, stupid women under his breath as Alex made a halo of her hair.

"You needn't use your foul language with me."

"Come, lie down and I'll spread the hair away from your head. You haven't done it right."

She could feel his warm breath on her cheek, his long fingers stroking through her hair, pulling out the wet ripples as he fanned it out. "There," he said, sounding bored. "Go to sleep now. I'm tired. You've quite exhausted me with your recklessness."

What to do, Alex asked herself again and again, indeed, the question plagued her until she fell asleep beside her husband in the gamekeeper's bed.

Douglas awoke feeling very hot and very aroused. His member was hard, uncomfortably so, and for an instant, he was disoriented. Never had he felt such intense desire, a desire so urgent, a desire that was pushing him, prodding at him, making him forget who he was, where he was. He realized that Alexandra's cheek was pressed against his bare shoulder, her bare right leg was resting on his bare belly. The linen shirt she wore was up around her waist and he felt every exquisite female inch of her. He wanted to touch her breasts, to feel their texture, their softness. He saw her standing there beside his chair, naked, her arms at her sides, her hands fisted for she was set on her course, and he, well, he had humiliated her thoroughly.

It hadn't been well done of him. But what was he to have done? To have taken what she offered would have admitted that he'd given in and accepted her, that she'd won, that her damned father had won, and all because she'd stripped down to her lovely white skin and let him look at her? She'd offered herself to him. He cursed now but it didn't help. His sex hurt, actually hurt with want. Well, why not? She was very nearly naked now, pressed up against him. Why shouldn't he feel lust? He was a normal man, wasn't he? He gave it up. None of it seemed to matter now. It was dark, they were alone, the rain was lashing heavily against the single windowpane and thudding loudly upon the roof. Everything that was real, everything that was solid, everything that mattered, everything that shrieked for decisions and consequences, was blessedly far away. It could all be ignored for a good long while.

He turned slightly toward her and his hand caressed her breast. She moaned. The low soft sound froze him, then made his heart pound frantically. He wanted to come inside her right this instant. Damn her, he hurt. He cursed again even as his hand cupped her, but only for a moment. He quickly unlaced the front of her shirt. He pulled it off her, shoving the shirt to her waist. Why didn't she wake up? He could barely see her, but he knew her breasts were magnificent. He wanted to touch her now, kiss her now, taste her. He didn't think, didn't consider a single consequence of his actions, merely lowered his head and took her nipple into his mouth. She tasted hot, so incredibly hot, and so sweet he couldn't bear it. He was in a sorry state, and he knew it.

He raised his head a moment, and again she moaned and then moaned again, her head falling to the side. He kissed her throat, as his fingers caressed her breast. He wanted her mouth. He wanted her to groan into his mouth, to fill him with the passion he was rousing in her. When his mouth closed over hers, he was aware again of the immense heat of her. So very hot she was, hot with passion, hot for him. Again she moaned.

He was nearly frantic now, his body surging, his sex swelled against her thigh. Why the hell didn't she wake up? "Let me get this ridiculous shirt off you." She moaned again and he paused, frowning down at her. Surely she should only moan if what he was doing to her made her feel passion.

"Alexandra," he said softly, and lightly tapped his palm against her cheek. Heat.

For a moment he simply didn't want to believe it. She moaned again, twisting away from him. Dear God, she wasn't moaning because she wanted him; she wasn't moaning to seduce him; she was moaning because she was burning with fever.

He felt like an animal; he felt guilty as hell, then he wanted to laugh at himself for his conceit. He shook his head, the seriousness of it washing over him. She was ill. She was very ill. He got hold of himself. His lust died a quick death. He saw then the many men bathed in fevers after battles. So many had died. Too many. But at least he knew what to do. It was still raining hard. There was no way to fetch a doctor. It was up to him. Douglas quickly rose and went into the front room.

"Tom," he said quietly.

"Milord, there be a problem?"

"Aye, Her Ladyship is ill. I need you to make her some herbal tea and

I'll bathe her with cold water to bring down the fever. Have you any special potions that would help her?"

Tom had no potions, but he had his dear mother's excellent herbal tea.

When Douglas returned to Alexandra, a lighted candle in his hand, he realized he hadn't even noticed that during his conversation with Tom he'd been quite naked. He shook his head at himself, set the candle down on the small table next to the bed, and quickly pulled on Tom's pants. He touched his palms to her cheeks, then to her shoulders. She was soaked with sweat. He pulled the damp linen shirt off her. Within moments Tom brought a bowl of cold water and a soft cloth.

Douglas straightened her arms and legs. He began methodically to wipe her down, long steady strokes from her face to her toes. When the cold wet cloth returned to her face, she tried to twist away, but he held her, saying quietly, "No, Alexandra. Hold still. You're the one who is now ill. Hold still."

She couldn't understand him, he knew. He wiped her face, holding the cold cloth still for several moments. She turned her face against his palm, trying to burrow into the cloth.

"Yes, you're hot, aren't you? No, I won't stop doing this, I promise. I know it must feel good. I know you're burning up. Trust me in this, at least." The cloth went down her throat to her shoulders. He lifted the cloth then and realized it was hot. The fever was heavy upon her.

He eased her onto her stomach. Again and again he stroked the cloth over her. He tried not to look at her, tried not to assess how he felt as he looked at her, tried not to acknowledge that his sex was swelled even though she was ill and not ready for him, that she probably wouldn't want him even if she wasn't ill.

"Alexandra," he said. "Listen to me now. You're ill but I fully intend that you get well and very quickly. Do you hear me? Stop this foolishness now. Open your eyes and look at me. Damn you, open your eyes!"

She did. She gazed up at him, her eyes clear. "Hello," she said. "Does your head pain you, Douglas?"

"Who gives a damn about my head? How do you feel?"

"I hurt."

"I know you do. Does this feel good?" He wiped the cloth over her breasts and down her belly.

"Oh yes," she said, and closed her eyes.

Douglas continued until Tom knocked on the door with his mother's special tea.

Douglas covered her and propped her up on the pillows. He sat beside her and held her up against his arm. "Wake up again, Alexandra. I want you to drink this tea. It's important that you drink liquids or you'll dry up and blow away. Come now, open your mouth."

She did. She choked on the tea and he slowed it to a trickle. He was patient. She drank the entire cup. Then she moaned again. He laid her back down and began again to stroke the cloth over her body.

At the end of an hour, the fever was down. She soon began to tremble and shudder with cold.

Douglas didn't hesitate. He crawled into bed with her and drew her against him. She sought him out then, trying to burrow inside him, her legs pushing against his, her face under his right arm. He smiled even as he tried to straighten her body. He was soon sweating but he didn't pull away from her; he pulled her closer, trying to cover every inch of her. Odd that she was so hot yet felt so very cold inside. This is very strange, Douglas thought as he leaned his cheek against the top of her head. Her hair, at least, was now dry. He was fully aware that she was his responsibility, fully aware that his hands were stroking up and down her back.

Damnation.

She moaned softly, her nose pressing against his rib, very close to his heart. He felt something altogether strange and unwelcome as her warm breath feathered against his skin.

He came awake when it was dawn, a gray dull dawn with the rain still pounding down, lessening but a little bit. He wouldn't be able to take her back to the hall. A carriage couldn't drive up to Tom's front door and he couldn't risk carrying her back to the road. She was too ill.

He forced more tea down her, cajoling her, threatening her, until the cup was empty. Tom left for the hall to get medicine from Mrs. Peacham and clothing for them both.

Douglas continued to hold her and wipe her with the wet cloth. Her fever rose and fell in cycles, endless cycles that scared him to death.

He was so scared he was praying.

He'd rather expected Mrs. Peacham to return with Tom, for she'd nursed all the Sherbrookes during his lifetime, but she didn't. Only Finkle, his one-time batman and valet, came back with Tom. Finkle, fit and strong, just turned forty, and nearly as short as Alexandra, said without preamble, "The idiot doctor is in bed with a broken leg. I will assist you, my lord. I've brought all sorts of medicines. Her Ladyship will be well in a trice."

Douglas tended her, alternately bullying her into drinking tea or eating Tom's thick gruel, and bathing her. Toward the end of one of the longest days of Douglas's life, he knew she was going to live. He'd forgotten his own headache and was surprised to feel the lump over his left ear where he'd struck the rock when he'd fallen.

He stood over the bed, staring down at her, knowing that the fever had broken, knowing that if only she would try, she would get well.

"Don't you dare give up now," he told her. "I'll thrash you but good if you dare to give up."

She moaned softly and tried to turn on her side. He helped her, then nestled the blankets snugly against her.

"She'll do," Finkle said matter-of-factly from the doorway. "She's got guts worthy of a Sherbrooke."

Douglas walked to the door and quietly closed it after him. He turned to his valet. "Don't give me any of your damned impertinence. She's only a temporary Sherbrooke, only a Sherbrooke through guile and betrayal, and just because she's ill, it doesn't make her my wife by default."

Finkle, in His Lordship's service for eleven years, said, "You aren't thinking clearly, my lord. She will live, thank the good beneficent being who dwells above us, and it is you who have saved her. Once you save a person's life, you cannot discard the saved person like an old boot."

"I can do whatever I wish to the damned deceitful chit. Do you so quickly forget what she and her father and my dear cousin Tony did?"

"Her sister, Lady Melissande, said her ladyship, the temporary one who lies here, was never ill. She said it was most likely a ruse to gain your sympathy, but that she said it was her duty to come and see for herself."

"Oh God," said Douglas, whipping around toward the door, as if expecting Melissande to appear at any instant.

"She's not here, my lord."

"How did you stop her?"

"I told her if Her Ladyship wasn't pretending illness, it was very possible that she could catch the fever herself and that a fever immediately ruined a lady's looks for the rest of her life. I told her a fever always left spots on a lady's face."

Douglas could only stare at his valet. "My God, that was well done of you."

"Lord Rathmore agreed that this was so, that he himself had witnessed such phenomena as nursing spots many times before. He said that it shouldn't deter her, though. He commended her on her selflessness. He nicely inquired if she would like him to drive her here to see her sister, to tend to her herself if she was indeed ill and not playacting. Lady Melissande shrieked. Quite loudly. Lord Rathmore laughed."

"You did well, Finkle, as did my cousin, the bounder. Now, since I must, since there is no one else, I will go back to the chit and see to her. Why didn't Mrs. Peacham come with you?"

"She and Hollis decided it wasn't the right thing to do."

"Ha! Hollis decided that and you know it, damn his interfering hide!

Why he wants this chit to remain as the Countess of Northcliffe is beyond me. You'd think he would remember where his loyalties should lie."

Finkle merely looked at his master. "You disappoint me, my lord," he said and left Douglas to himself.

"Well, hell," Douglas said. Within minutes he was under the covers next to Alexandra, knowing even before realizing it that she was cold again. Cold from the inside out.

He supposed it was later that night when she was snuggled against him, both of them naked and warm, that he considered accepting her. It would please her, no doubt about that. It would make her deliriously happy, no doubt about that either. After all, she'd tried to seduce him. She was a lady, a young lady of impeccable breeding and upbringing who had, nevertheless, stripped off her clothes in front of him. Well, he just might keep her. Perhaps she would come to suit him as well as any other young lady. The good Lord knew that her father would fall on his knees with prayers of thanksgiving to heaven. Everyone would be delighted, except perhaps him. Ah, but she would probably come to suit him as well as any other female.

It was a pity that she wasn't as beautiful as Melissande.

But no young lady on the face of the earth was as beautiful as Melissande.

There was no point in trying to locate another female to match her beauty. On the other hand, he wouldn't have to watch every man who came in sight of Alexandra for signs of complete besottedness. Nor would he have to worry that she would flirt with the men she'd rendered besotted. He frowned at that thought, for Melissande didn't just flirt; she flirted outrageously. She basked in the flow of compliments men rained upon her beautiful head. He wondered then, for the first time, if Tony hated the effect she had on every nondead male between the ages of ten and eighty who saw her. He wondered if some day he would ask his cousin.

He doubted it. He still wanted to kill Tony.

Alexandra cried out softly beside him. Without conscious thought Douglas kissed her forehead and drew her closer.

What to do?

He would think about it. He imagined the relief, the joy on her face were he to tell her that he had decided to keep her.

Why not make her deliriously happy?

CHAPTER
==11==

IT FELT REALLY rather good. She was alive, truly, honestly alive.

Alexandra took a deep breath and was relieved that it didn't hurt too much. She felt absurdly weak, so weak in fact that when she spotted the glass of water on the small table beside the bed, she didn't have the strength to get to it, and oh, did she ever want it.

She did manage to turn onto her side and raise her arm toward the glass. She was near to tears of frustration when the bedchamber door opened and Douglas looked in.

"You're awake. How do you feel?"

She stared at the water, saying in a low hoarse voice, "Thirsty. Please, I'm so thirsty."

He was there in but a moment. He sat beside her, brought her head against his shoulder, picked up the glass, and efficiently put it to her lips. "Why didn't you call me? I wasn't all that far away, no more than twelve feet."

She closed her eyes in bliss. The water tasted wonderful. Douglas allowed only a trickle but it was just fine with her. To swallow was a chore.

When she finished nearly half the glass, he set it down, but continued to hold her. He repeated, "Why didn't you call me? Tom's cottage isn't all that large, you know. I would have heard you."

"I didn't think about it."

"Why not? You haven't been taking care of yourself. I have been taking care of you and I've done a rather good job of it. You do remember that, don't you?"

"What day is it?"

He frowned down at her, but said, "It's Wednesday, early afternoon. You were very ill for only a day and a half. With my good doctoring, you'll be just fine now."

"How is your head?"

"My head is filled with its own importance again."

"Are we still in Tom O'Malley's cottage?"

"Yes, as I said, you should have called me if you needed anything. Finkle has returned to Northcliffe Hall to fetch a carriage. You'll be in your own bed soon."

"I don't have any clothes on."

"I know."

"I don't like it. You're dressed and I'm not."

"Should you like me to bathe you now and help you to dress? It's the old gown you were wearing but at least it's dry."

"I can do it myself."

"Nastiness won't help your recuperation." He held up his hand. "All right, stubbornness, then. I should realize that you're never nasty. No, don't berate me. You're not even stubborn, it's maidenly sensibility that directs your every word. I think I should simply bundle you up in blankets and take you back to the hall that way."

One hour later, the earl's crested carriage pulled up in front of Northcliffe Hall, the two matched grays blowing and snorting in the warm afternoon sunlight. The earl stepped out of the carriage carrying his countess in his arms.

Douglas stopped cold in his tracks when there came loud cheering from his staff. He stared toward Hollis, who was grinning like a wily old fox. He was responsible for this outpouring, of that Douglas had no doubt. He wondered if Hollis had paid the servants to give this wondrous cheerful homecoming. He would tell him a thing or two as soon as he deposited Alexandra in her bed.

She said nothing. He realized that her eyes were closed and that she was limp as a sweaty handkerchief in his arms.

He leaned his head down and whispered, "It's all right. It's natural for you to feel weak. Just a few more minutes and I'll have you tucked up."

"Why are all your people cheering?"

Because Hollis bribed and threatened them to. "They're pleased we're alive and back."

She retreated into silence again. He saw Melissande at the top of the stairs, looking so utterly delectable he swallowed convulsively. Her lovely face was pale, and she was wringing her hands. Her incredible eyes were brimming with tears of concern, yet she didn't move closer to her sister.

"Alex? Are you all right? Truly?"

Alexandra roused herself and lifted her head from Douglas's shoulder. "Yes, Melissande, I will be just fine now."

"Good," said Tony, coming up to stand beside his wife. "We hear from Finkle that Douglas has been taking very good care of you. He never left your side for a single moment."

Melissande said loudly, "I would have been the one to care for you, Alex, but Tony wouldn't allow it. He didn't want me to endanger myself, but oh, I wanted to. I did pray for you."

"That's right," Tony said. "On her knees every night."

"Thank you," Alexandra said, turning her face against Douglas's shoulder.

"You're not contagious any more, are you?"

"No, Mellie, she isn't contagious. You won't contract any spots."

"Don't call me that horrid name!"

Tony clutched a handful of Melissande's thick glorious black hair and bent his wife back against his arm, reminiscent of Mrs. Bardsleys's finest heroes. He then kissed her and kept kissing her until she was quiescent. He raised his head and grinned down at her, then over at Douglas, who looked fit to kill him.

He said calmly, belying the racing of his heart from kissing his wife, "I have saved you a great deal of vexation and aggravation, Douglas. One of these years you will realize it. Her temperament is not that of a devoted nurse. I have discovered that she needs constant attention to her various needs, and they are many and diverse. Believe me, Douglas."

Melissande gasped and struck her fists against Tony's chest.

He laughed and kissed her again, hard. " 'Twas a compliment, love."

"It didn't sound like one to me," Melissande said, her voice laden with suspicion. "Are you certain?"

"More certain than I am of the color of my stallion's fetlock."

"In that case, I'll forgive you."

"That is handsomely done of you, Mellie. Very handsomely done."

Douglas stomped away in angry silence toward the countess's bedchamber.

"Damned bounder," he said finally under his breath, but not under enough.

"He deals well with her," Alexandra said, wonder in her voice. "It is amazing."

Douglas cursed floridly.

"I can't imagine why my father would think you a good influence on Reginald. He has not heard the foul level of vocabulary you have."

"I see you're feeling much better. I'm relieved because I've gotten behind in my estate work taking care of you. I trust you'll keep to your bed for a while and leave me in peace."

He could feel that broom handle stiffening her back and he regretted his hasty words, but he'd said them and they would remain said. She'd deserved every one of them. She was stiff and starchy and she galled him, shoving him on the defensive, and it both surprised and angered him.

Alexandra said nothing. There was a young maid—Tess was her name, Douglas said—and she would see to her ladyship's needs. "Also," Douglas continued, "Mrs. Peacham will doubtless fill your craw to overflowing with advice and potions and all sorts of invalid dishes. Deal with her as you wish to but know that she means well."

He left her. Alex slept the remainder of the day. Mrs. Peacham herself brought a beautiful silver tray filled with at least a half-dozen selections to tempt a mending patient. "His Lordship said I was to stay with you until you ate enough," Mrs. Peacham announced as she sat herself down in a wing chair next to Alexandra's bed. It seemed to Alexandra that she counted every bite she took.

"Where is His Lordship?"

Mrs. Peacham looked uncomfortable, but for just an instant, then she nodded. "You know, my lady, gentlemen aren't really the thing in a sickroom. They're all thumbs and confusion and contradiction."

"He wasn't at all confused at Tom's cottage. He was a tyrant, but he knew well what he was doing."

"Well, now, that was quite different, wasn't it?"

"Yes, I suppose it was," Alexandra said, and began on another dish, this one of stewed potatoes and peas, that Mrs. Peacham uncovered for her. She spent the evening alone. Neither her husband nor her sister came to see her.

She felt very sorry for herself.

When she slept, it was fitfully. She dreamed, a similar dream to the one she'd had before. A beautiful young lady was standing beside her, motionless, just looking down at her. She looked all floaty and insubstantial, very beautiful but also frightened. It was strange. She wanted to speak but she didn't. Somehow Alexandra knew this. She wanted to warn her about something and Alex knew this as well even though she didn't know how she knew it. The lady came closer to her, bent down until she could touch her face, then she retreated suddenly nearly back to the door. Once she raised her arms in supplication. It was very odd. The dream ebbed and flowed until Alexandra brought herself awake at dawn. Because she'd been locked so tightly into the dream, because it had been so very real, she found herself looking into every corner of her bedchamber. Her room was empty, of course. She realized she needed to relieve herself. She reached for the bell but knew she couldn't wait.

The chamber pot was behind a screen not more than twelve feet from her bed. Just twelve feet. No great distance.

Alex swung her legs over the side of the bed. At least Tess had helped her into one of her nightgowns so she didn't have to worry about the dressing gown that was laid over a chair in the other direction from the chamber pot. She closed her eyes for a moment against the memory of Douglas dealing with her needs while she was quite without a stitch on. He'd looked his fill at her, that was certain, for there had been no one to gainsay him, no one else to see to her. She'd heard whispers that gentlemen were many times victims to their baser natures and that was why a young lady had to take such care with her person. If she did not exercise sufficient caution, why then, it would be her fault if the gentleman suddenly became a ravening beast. She'd been unable to exercise any caution whatsoever and evidently Douglas had been bored with what he'd seen; hadn't he already rejected her?

Well, she'd been ill and helpless then. She wasn't now.

She rose and quickly grabbed the intricately carved bedpost, clutching at a cherub's fat neck. How could she still be so weak?

She took a step, was successful, then took another. Three more shuffling steps and she had to release the cherub. The screen that hid the chamber pot looked to be two villages and a turnpike away still.

She sighed and released the cherub. She stood there, weaving back and forth, then gained her balance. "I will make it," she said over and over, her eyes on that screen. "I will not shame myself and fall into a heap on the floor."

When she weaved against a chair, then grabbed its back for balance, the wretched thing went skidding across the polished floor into the desk, jarring it so that the ink pot went flying, spewing black ink to the floor and onto the exquisite Aubusson carpet just beyond. Two books hit the floor with resounding thuds. Alexandra, so frustrated and furious that she wanted to yell, just stood there, dizzy and weak, wanting to kill.

The person who obligingly came through the adjoining door was a perfect victim. It was Douglas and he was hastily knotting a belt around his dressing gown as he came toward her.

"What is all the commotion? What the hell are you doing out of bed?"

She wished she had a cannon. Or a knife. Even a bow and arrow. "What does it look like I'm doing? I'm taking my morning constitutional. Doesn't everyone do that at dawn?"

"Damnation, you're destroying my home!"

She followed his line of vision to the awful stream of black ink that was quickly soaking into the carpet, raised her chin, and declared, "Yes, I am. I hate Northcliffe Hall and I fully intend to wreck everything before I leave. This is but my opening salvo."

Douglas, realizing that she was about to fall on her face, quickly strode to her and grasped her arms to hold her upright. "What are you doing out of bed?"

She couldn't believe how obtuse he was. "I was going down to the kitchen for some warm milk."

"Absurd! You couldn't even make it halfway across your room."

"Of course I can. I have a meeting with Mrs. Peacham to talk about replacing all the linens. The ones on my bed smell like moth bait."

"Alexandra, I would that you cease this nonsense and—"

"Damn you, don't be so stupid! I must relieve myself!"

"Oh, well that's different."

"Just go away. I hate you. Go away and leave me be."

Douglas frowned down at her. He was still firmly set upon his plan to make her deliriously happy by accepting her as his wife, but she didn't particularly seem in the mood to be the recipient of this proffered bliss. He'd left her alone the previous evening, wanting her to rest, wanting her to regain some strength before he made her the happiest woman on earth. And now here she was acting like a termagant, acting as if he were the devil himself, acting as if she weren't at all pleased to see him. And he was her husband and he'd taken fine care of her.

Unaccountable twit.

He scooped her up in his arms, saying even as she tried to push away from him, "Just shut up and hold still. I will take you to the chamber pot. No, keep your damned mouth shut."

"You will leave."

"Not until you're back in bed."

She subsided because she doubted she could get back to bed without his assistance. She should have rung for Tess. Douglas left her behind the screen. She managed, but it was difficult for her, knowing that he was standing just on the other side of the screen. He was so close and he could hear everything. It left her body nearly paralyzed.

When she emerged, finally, he made no remarks. He picked her up again, continued to remain thankfully silent until he'd tucked her under the covers in her bed.

"There, that wasn't quite such an appalling degradation, was it? You did take rather a long time with the chamber pot, but— Do you think you can sleep again or would you like some laudanum?"

"Go away." She gave him a brooding look, realized that she wasn't behaving well, and said in a voice that was as stiff as her back, "Thank you for helping me. I'm sorry I woke you. I'm sorry I hit that chair and that it bumped the desk and made the ink pot fall and the ink ruin that beautiful carpet. I will replace the carpet. I do have some money of my own."

"Do you now? I find that difficult to believe. Your precious father didn't have a bloody sou. Both you and Melissande left your homes without a dowry. You don't even have an idea of the settlement your father made with Tony, do you? For that matter, you don't even know if I'm going to give you any sort of allowance at all. Hell, if I do give you an allowance, and you graciously replace the carpet, why I'll still be paying for the damned rug after all."

"No you won't. I have thirty pounds with me. I have saved that amount over the past four years."

"Thirty pounds! Ha! That would replace a chamber pot or two, not a carpet of value."

"Perhaps it can be cleaned."

Douglas looked over at the ruined carpet, its exquisite pattern black as soot. "Yes, and perhaps one of Napoleon's ministers will throw a cake in his face."

"Anything is possible."

"You're too young to realize that idiots continue to survive in this world. Go back to sleep. You are absurdly confident and it is annoying."

So much for making her a happy woman, Douglas thought as he marched back into his bedchamber. How could she act so spitefully? What the devil was the matter with her? He'd been the perfect gentleman, the devil, he'd probably saved her life with the fine care he'd given her and what was his reward? She hated him. She told him to leave her alone. She destroyed one of his grandmother's favorite carpets.

Douglas fell asleep with the acrid taste of anger on his tongue.

It was Friday morning. Alexandra ordered Tess to dress her after she'd bathed. She still felt a bit weak, but nothing she couldn't deal with. It was time for her to leave. She was buoyed by righteous resolve and she prayed it would last until she was gone from Northcliffe Hall.

He'd rejected her. He'd treated her as if she were naught but a bothersome gnat, a sexless encumbrance.

She'd destroyed his grandmother's lovely rug.

He'd laughed at her thirty pounds. He had no idea how difficult it had been to accumulate that thirty pounds, penny by penny, hoarding it.

Not only had he rejected her when she'd been fool enough to attempt the disastrous seduction, he'd only cared for her because there'd been no choice.

It was a litany in her mind. It was something she would never forget. She stoked anger and resentment because it was better than the annihilating pain of his disinterest in her, his distaste of her.

She had failed, utterly, to win him over, to show him that she could suit him nicely, that she could and would love him until the day she passed from this earth. What had he meant about giving her an allowance? She quashed that inquiry; he'd not meant anything.

He still wanted Melissande. Everyone knew that he still wanted his cousin's wife. He still spoke of butchering Tony on the field of honor though nothing had come of it yet. Alexandra had heard the servants gossiping about it. Ah, and how they speculated and wondered.

Douglas hadn't come near her again after their one skirmish at dawn. She was glad of it. Her sister had visited twice, both times standing a good ten feet away from her and looking delicately pale in her concern. Alexandra had remembered Tony's kiss during her sister's second visit, and said, "You appear to like having Tony kiss you."

To her surprise, Melissande lowered her head and mumbled, "He is most outrageous sometimes. I cannot always control him. It is difficult to know what to do."

Control, ha! Melissande had met her match. "But you seem to like it."

"You don't know, Alex! You can't imagine what he does to me—to my person!"

"Tell me then."

"So, the earl hasn't bedded you. Tony rather hoped that he had. It would make it all so very legal then and we could leave and go to London."

"No, it wouldn't make it legal at all. Douglas said he could do just as he pleased to me, and our marriage could still be annulled."

"But if you got pregnant—"

"Douglas said that he can easily prevent that."

"Oh," said Melissande, who was now frowning ferociously. "But Tony insisted that—" She broke off, and her glorious eyes were narrowed slits, diminishing her beauty but making her all the more enticing for it.

"But what does Tony do to you?"

Melissande waved an impatient hand. "It isn't proper that I tell you what goes on. Tony is a madman and he insists upon ordering me about and then he does things that he really shouldn't do but the way he does them, well . . . However—" Again, she fell silent, and Alexandra was left wondering if what went on between a husband and wife wasn't to be devoutly wished for. She'd asked no more questions. Melissande had left, somewhat routed, and Alexandra found she was coming to believe that Tony was the perfect mate for her sister. She wondered how Douglas would have treated Melissande were he married to her. She doubted he would ever be nasty to her.

It didn't matter. There was nothing more for her here. She was well; she had no intention of having Douglas recognize that she was well, and allowing him to be one to take her back to her father. She would not allow him to serve her that final indignity.

She didn't deserve it. She deserved a lot of things, for she had been part of his betrayal, but she didn't deserve the kind of humiliation he would dish out. She would dish it up to herself, with no assistance from him. She pictured her father's face in her mind when she arrived at Claybourn Hall, alone, kicked out, soon-to-be-annulled. It was an appalling picture, but it was better than the one with Douglas gloating as he stood beside her, telling her father that she wasn't adequate, that he didn't want her, would never want her. She didn't want to think of what the lost settlement would mean to her father. In any case, there was nothing to do about it. She'd tried.

She waited until she knew that Douglas had ridden out with his estate manager, a man whose name was Tuffs, then made her way confidently downstairs. She paused, hearing Tony speaking to Hollis.

"I wish Ryder hadn't left before we discovered Douglas and Alex were missing. He was trying to help Douglas get his brains unscrambled."

"I agree," said the stately Hollis. "But Master Ryder is gone and there are none to assist His Lordship, save you, my lord. Has His Lordship, ah, ceased yet to demand your guts on a platter?"

"No," Tony said. "Hell, I grow tired of remaining here trying to make Douglas see that Melissande isn't at all the sort of wife who would suit him. Stubborn blighter! Why can't he see beyond her beautiful face to her altogether self-indulgent nature? I think it time I took my wife away, Hollis, to Strawberry Hill."

"I have come to understand that Lady Melissande would prefer London, my lord."

"So she would, but she will prefer differently when she comes to understand what it is I wish her to want."

If Alexandra thought it strange for a peer of the realm to speak with such intimacy to a butler, her brief stay at Northcliffe Hall had taught her differently.

"Perhaps it would be best for you to depart, my lord. Ah, but His Lordship's humors are so uncertain. I am concerned about Her Ladyship."

"I too, Hollis. But her illness at O'Malley's cottage—I can't help but feel it was a good thing. Douglas seemed affected, and he did care for her intimately. An excellent idea of yours that no one go back with O'Malley to the cottage."

Alexandra backed up a step. She didn't want to hear any more about intimacy or the machinations of Douglas's staff. She wasn't sure that Tony wouldn't try to stop her from leaving. Or Hollis, for that matter. Or Mrs. Peacham. She chewed on her lower lip, trying to figure out what to do.

Then it occurred to her that none of them dared touch her. They could rant and rave, but even Tony, easygoing, and an immense rogue with unlimited loyalty to his cousin, despite his ultimate poaching in Douglas's nuptials, wouldn't dare to lock her in a room, and that is what it would require, for she would not remain willingly.

She was still, and at this moment, the Countess of Northcliffe. She could do whatever she pleased. Only Douglas could stop her and he wouldn't. Still, because she wasn't completely daft, she waited until Tony drove out with Melissande. She'd heard Melissande say to Mrs. Peacham, excitement in her lovely voice, that he was taking her to Rye, a town of wondrous historic importance. "Yes, Mellie," Tony had said fondly, kissing her temple, "Rye was chartered in 1285. Edward the First, you know. It's lovely and I'll kiss you again on the cliff walk."

At one o'clock on Friday afternoon, Lady Alexandra, soon to be the discarded Countess of Northcliffe, armed with one valise and her own thirty pounds, walked firmly out the front door of the hall.

Hollis stood slack-mouthed in the entranceway, all his most convincing arguments exhausted in the dust, and with no discernible effect on Her Ladyship.

Mrs. Peacham was twisting her black bombazine skirts.

The earl was riding at the eastern end of the Sherbrooke property, inspecting two tenants' cottages that had suffered badly in the heavy rainstorm.

What to do?

Hollis tried again. "Please, my lady, you must wait. You aren't well enough yet to travel. Please, wait for the earl's return."

"I shall walk if you don't have a carriage fetched this instant, Hollis."

Hollis was very tempted to let her walk. She wouldn't get very far before the earl caught up with her. Damn the boy! Hollis couldn't be certain that he would go after her. He had the first time, but now? Why hadn't he come to grips with anything? He'd been foul-tempered with everyone since his return from O'Malley's cottage. Hollis didn't blame the countess. He put the blame squarely on the earl's shoulders. He deserved to be whipped. "All right, my lady," Hollis said at last, nearly choking on the bitter taste of defeat. He instructed a footman to have a carriage fetched from the stables and he also instructed the footman to have one of the stable lads search out the earl. "Have the lad find him quickly, else I'll have his ears in my mutton stew!"

Ten minutes later Alexandra was settled in one of the earl's carriages, John Coachman instructed to take her home. Her single valise sat on the seat opposite her. She was leaving only with what she'd brought with her.

Life wasn't going at all well.

When John Coachman suddenly pulled up the team at a shout from another carriage, Alexandra poked her head out the window to see what was happening.

She came face to face with an older woman who had the look of the Sherbrookes, a woman who simply stared at her, as gape-mouthed as Hollis had been.

A young face appeared, a quite lovely young girl who said happily, "Why, are you Douglas's new bride? How wonderful, of course you are! I'm Sinjun, his sister. This is marvelous! You are Melis—no, no, you are the other sister! Welcome to the Sherbrooke family."

Alexandra looked skyward. Her luck, which she'd thought was on the rise, she now saw plummeting to earth, and soon her face would be rubbed in the dirt.

The other woman, doubtless Alexandra's soon-to-be-annulled mother-in-law, sniffed with alarming loudness, and said, "I don't understand why you are still here. You shouldn't be out visiting tenants for it is not your responsibility. You are nothing compared to your sister, from all I have been told. You are nothing at all out of the ordinary. My son would never have selected you."

Alexandra felt the clout, but she said calmly, "You are certainly right about that. Your son doesn't want me. I am not visiting the tenants. I am leaving. No, don't say it. I am delighted to give you the pleasure of my departure."

She was on the point of telling John Coachman to continue, when the door to the other carriage opened and the young girl jumped to the ground. "Do let me ride with you!"

Alexandra closed her eyes, ground her teeth until her jaw hurt, and cursed, one of Douglas's colorfully lurid expressions.

The other woman yelled, "Joan, you will come back here this instant! The chit is going away, let her go!"

The girl ignored her, flinging open the carriage door and bounding exuberantly inside. Alexandra was facing her soon-to-be non-sister-in-law.

"Where are we going?" Sinjun asked, smiling brilliantly at Alexandra.

CHAPTER
═══12═══

ALEXANDRA STARED HARD at her sister-in-law. "I want you to get out, please. You heard what I said—I am not visiting tenants or anyone else. I'm leaving Northcliffe Hall and I have no intention of returning ever again."

Sinjun gave her the placid look of a nun. "I will go with you, of course. It's all the same to me. Please don't make me get out. I am your sister now by marriage and I'm not a bad person, really, and—"

"I don't assume you're a bad person, but I am leaving your brother, just as your mother obviously wishes, just as your brother wishes, just as, doubtless, the backstairs maids wish. I cannot be responsible for you. Goodness, I don't even know you or you me! You must go about your business. Would you please get out of the carriage?"

Sinjun found this complication profoundly interesting. So this was marriage in the making. It was far more engrossing than any of the Greek plays she'd read by candlelight at midnight in Douglas's library. It was closer to the Restoration plays she'd read by Dryden and Wycherley. Though she didn't understand all the speeches of the plays, she understood enough to laugh herself silly. She also knew enough not to tell Douglas that she'd read them. She had this feeling he wouldn't be at all amused.

"Why are you leaving Douglas?"

"Please, get out."

Instead, Sinjun waved to the other coachman and the carriage rolled away. Alexandra's mother-in-law was still looking out the window back at her. There was a look of confusion mixed with hopefulness on her face. She didn't attempt to halt the carriage.

"Now there is no choice unless you want me to walk. No, I didn't think you would. You must talk to me."

It was simply too much. Alexandra merely shook her head, opened the door, grabbed her valise, and stepped to the ground. She looked up at the homely appalled face of John Coachman. "Take her home, if you please."

"I can't," the coachman wailed. "His Lordship would feed my innards to the pigs. I can't! Please, my lady, don't ask me to do that. I can't leave you. 'Twould mean my throat being slit, my hide being whipped off my back!"

"I had not believed the earl so very vicious and unfair. It matters not. It is no longer my problem. In truth, I don't care what you do. Remain or return to Northcliffe. I will be the one to leave." She swung away and began walking. The valise was heavier than she'd believed. She would make do. She wouldn't stop and she wouldn't let her shoulders stoop.

Sinjun was soon at her side, humming under her breath as if she hadn't a care in the world, as if they were out for an afternoon stroll with nothing more on their minds than the varieties of butterflies they would see. The carriage was soon following some paces behind them.

"This is absurd," Alexandra said, so frustrated she was nearly shrieking. She whirled about to face Sinjun. "Why are you doing this to me? I haven't ever done anything to you that I know of. As I said, I don't even know you."

Sinjun cocked her head to one side and said simply, "You're my sister. I've never had a sister, only three brothers, and I can tell you it's not at all the same thing. Douglas has obviously upset you. He is sometimes a bit autocratic, perhaps even stern and forbidding. But he means well. He wouldn't strap John Coachman, believe me."

"He means well toward you but I am perfectly nothing to him. Go away now."

"Oh no, I shan't leave you. Douglas would feed my innards to the pigs too. He has very firm ideas about protecting ladies. A bit old-fashioned, but nonetheless, he is the head of the Sherbrooke family and takes his responsibilities very seriously. There are scores of us, you know."

"He doesn't take his marriage seriously. Go away."

"I did hear that he wasn't expecting you, but I paid no attention to that. Tony would never serve him up a pig in a poke, if you know what I mean. I've never seen Melissande but everyone says she is the most glorious creature in southern England, perhaps even in western England as well. But I can see Douglas quickly becoming very morose had Tony married her to him rather than to himself. I don't mean to insult your sister, but Douglas wouldn't deal with a female who knew she was beautiful and expected everyone to recognize her beauty all the time. Tony did the right thing, though I do hope he knows what he's doing. But what I don't understand is why—"

Alexandra stopped her. She said clearly and quite calmly, "Listen to me now. Your brother doesn't want me. He wants my sister. He loves her. Moroseness has nothing to do with anything. He doesn't care that she knows she's beautiful. He is perfectly willing to praise her eyebrows for the next fifty years. He wants to kill Tony. He is bitterly unhappy. I am leaving so that he doesn't take me himself back to my father and drop me on the doorstep of Claybourn Hall like some unwanted package. Would you not do the same thing, Sinjun? Would you not want to escape such humiliation?"

Her sister-in-law had called her Sinjun, and without hesitation. Sinjun smiled. "I am only fifteen so I don't perfectly understand what has happened. But I agree with you. Humiliation is not a good thing. Are you certain Douglas would humiliate you in that way? I cannot see him doing it. He isn't a cruel man."

"He wouldn't be to you."

Sinjun just shook her head. "Douglas took a birch rod to my bottom last year. He thought I deserved it but, of course, I heartily disagreed. I don't even remember what I did. Isn't that odd? Listen now, I cannot leave you alone. I fully intend to go with you. May I call you Alexandra? Perhaps even Alex? It is a man's nickname, just like mine. Do you have any money? We will need money, you know."

Alexandra stared at the young girl with frustrated awe. The Sherbrookes were a family beyond her comprehension and experience. She found herself nodding. She'd heard of tidal waves, but she'd never before imagined that she could experience the effects of one and not be close to the sea.

"Good, because Mother never gives me any money at all, except at Christmas, and even then I must account for every shilling, every penny, even to what I paid for her present. And she always criticizes my choices. Why, last Christmas, I hand-sewed a half-dozen handkerchiefs for Douglas and she said the linen had cost too dear and that my stitches were crooked and they should be tossed away. Of course Douglas didn't throw them away. He said he liked them. He uses them. It was humiliating now that I think on it. Perhaps I can understand just a little bit. I would like to be treated like a reasonable person, not patted on the head like a silly pug."

"Yes," said Alexandra.

Sinjun rubbed her hands together. "I am taller than you and much larger so I doubt I can wear any of the clothes in your valise, but perhaps we can buy me something else to wear on our way to your home. How far must we go? Several days away, I hope. I long for some adventure. Yes, it will be great fun, you'll see. Perhaps we'll even meet some highwaymen. How vastly romantic that will be! Don't you agree?"

It was then that Alexandra began to realize that she'd been firmly trapped and netted and by a guileless fifteen-year-old girl.

"I do so love to walk and enjoy nature," Sinjun continued, taking a skip. "I also know a number of quite interesting stories and that will pass the time. If I bore you, why then, you must tell me and I will be quiet."

Alexandra, overwhelmed, bewildered, and routed, could only nod.

"Douglas merely tells me to shut my trap, as does Ryder. Tysen—he plans to be a vicar—he wants to say the same things but he fears the fires of hell if he did say what he truly wanted to. His perceived path of rectitude is sometimes extremely annoying, but Douglas says we must be patient because Tysen is young and not yet thinking clearly. He says his belfry is still filled with nonsense. Tysen also fancies himself in love with a twit who makes me cringe she is so appallingly *good* and priggishly *proper*. Ryder just laughs at Tysen and says she has two names—Melinda Beatrice!—which is nauseating, and she simpers and has no bosom."

Alexandra gave it up. She eyed the sweet-faced very enthusiastic girl beside her. She turned and waved toward John Coachman.

"What are you doing, Alexandra?"

"Going home," she said. "We're going home."

"Oh dear, no adventure then. How disappointing. Perhaps someday in the future you and I can go seashell collecting. That's good sport. Come along then, let me assist you into the carriage."

It wasn't until five more minutes had passed that Alexandra noticed the quite smug grin on Sinjun's face. She stared and winced and shuddered as understanding hit her. The chit had knowingly done her in. Guileless, ha! Alexandra felt a perfect fool. Dear God, what malignant force had set her in the midst of this remarkably horrid family?

Done in by a fifteen-year-old girl who looked as innocent as a nun. It was very lowering, more lowering than falling off a horse and landing on her bottom.

Douglas stood on the bottom step of Northcliffe Hall, his hands on his hips. He watched the carriage pull into a wide arc and come to a halt not six feet from him. John Coachman looked triumphant. Relief flowed from his smile. Douglas was glad he'd sent his mother into the hall with orders that she remain there. Her initial impression of Alexandra hadn't been promising. He sighed even as he stoked his anger. Tysen stood at his elbow, telling him what Sinjun had done, how forward she'd been and how he should discipline the chit, but Douglas had only smiled, knowing rather that he would thank her.

He knew Sinjun. And he'd been right. She'd brought his errant wife back, and with little waste of time. She should have been born a male; she would have made a masterful general.

When the carriage door opened and Sinjun leapt out, Douglas didn't move. He stared beyond her. Finally, Alexandra emerged, her head down, her shoulders bowed. She looked defeated and that angered him even more.

"I see you came back," he said, cold as a fish on ice.

"Yes," Alexandra said, not looking at him. "I don't want to be, but it appears that I cannot even best the youngest Sherbrooke."

She was trying to hold her valise and that angered him even more. She was still recovering from her illness and yet she'd tried to leave him again—and carrying that damned valise herself!

"The Sherbrookes are competent, for the most part."

"May I leave now, my lord?" As she spoke, she raised her head and looked him squarely in the face. "I want to leave. May I have Your Lordship's august permission?"

"No." Douglas strode to her and pulled the valise from her fingers. "Come along now."

She didn't move. He was aware that every Sherbrooke servant was an avid watcher to the damnable melodrama they were witnessing, and that he was serving up meaty gossip for many winter nights to come.

He moved closer to her and said very quietly, "I am tired to death of your imprudence. You act without thought, you are reckless, and I will tolerate it no more. You will come with me this instant, and for God's sake, stop acting like I am going to beat you!"

She straightened her shoulders and walked beside him into the hall.

Her mother-in-law stood there, looking ready to breathe fire at her. Alexandra hung back. She didn't want this. She looked at the other young man, and knew him to be Tysen, the youngest brother who was in love with the twit of two names and no bosom. Sinjun was nowhere to be seen, but Alex knew she was watching. No Sherbrooke would pass up such a promising spectacle.

Douglas turned back when she stopped. "What is it now?"

"When are you going to take me back to my father?"

"What the devil does that mean?"

"You know very well that you don't want me to remain here. I simply left to save you valuable time and to spare myself further mortification at your hands. If you would but allow me to leave, you would never have to see me again." She paused and the bitterness crept into her voice. "I suppose you prefer to take me back, don't you? Will it give you pleasure to further humiliate me? To tell my father that I am sorely deficient and that you want all your money back?"

"Lower your voice, damn you!"

"Why? Your mother wants me here about as much as she would welcome the plague! My words must make her rejoice."

"Be quiet!"

"I will not be quiet! I no longer recognize you as my husband. I will no longer obey you."

"You are in my home! I am master here, no one else. You will do exactly what I tell you to do and that's an end to it! No more of your nonsense, madam."

And Alexandra, mild of manner and of quiet, thoughtful temperament, flew at her husband and struck his chest with her fists.

He let her strike him simply because he was frozen with shock and surprise. Her face was flushed, her eyes dilated. He very gently clasped her wrists and pulled her hands to her sides.

"No more, Alexandra, no more. Now, you and I have some talking to do."

"No," she said.

Douglas was a firm believer in reason and calm. He exercised beneficent control. He also was quite used to being the master in his home, he hadn't been bragging about that for it was the simple truth. He was not a despot nor was he a malignant savage. But his word was the law and his opinions the ones that counted. But this damned woman dared to go against him. It was infuriating and intolerable. He found himself uncertain what to do. In the army, any recalcitrant soldier he faced would simply have been removed and whipped or confined to quarters. But what did a man do when his wife disobeyed him in front of every servant and his mother and his brother and sister? If she struck him?

"No," she said again.

"Let her leave," said the Dowager Countess of Northcliffe. "She wants to go, Douglas, let her."

He bent on her a look she had never before received from him. "Mother, I would that you keep still."

His mother gasped.

Douglas ignored her and turned back to his wife. "If you don't come with me this moment, I will throw you over my shoulder and carry you."

As a threat, it was specific and precise. However, Alexandra didn't think he would want to provide more scenes for the servants' delectation. No, he was far too proud to do something so very indecorous. She turned on her heel and walked toward the front door, head high, the broom handle well in place.

In that instant, Sinjun shrieked, an unearthly sound that brought everyone's attention to her, including Alexandra's.

She was jumping up and down, shouting herself hoarse.

"Damnation, Sinjun," Douglas shouted. "Be quiet!"

"A rat, Douglas, a huge, awful, hairy rat! Look, over there! Right next to Alexandra! Oh my God, I can't believe it, it is going to climb her skirt!"

Alexandra grasped her skirts and ran into the nearest room, which was the Gold Salon. She slammed the door, stopped in the middle of the room, quickly realized there had been no rodent, that Sinjun had done it to her again. She'd prevented her from walking out on Douglas, perhaps prevented Douglas from humiliating her further . . . but it was quite possible that Douglas would have simply let her walk out. When the door opened, she didn't turn around. When the door closed and when she heard the sound of a key turning in the lock, she still didn't turn around.

"Your sister is a menace," she said.

"If you are careful, you just might save yourself a good thrashing. If you do, why then, you can thank Sinjun for rescuing you."

Alexandra walked slowly to a sofa and sat down. She folded her hands in her lap and remained completely quiet.

"Would you like a glass of wine? Brandy? Ratafia?"

She shook her head.

He was standing directly in front of her, his arms crossed over his chest.

"How do you feel?"

That surprised her and she looked up. "I am fine, thank you. Certainly well enough to travel back to Claybourn Hall. By myself, without your noble presence."

"I doubt that."

"Well, if I collapsed dead in a ditch, why then, it would result in the same thing, wouldn't it?"

"No, not at all. I wouldn't get my settlement back from your father."

Alexandra stood up. She held out her hand. "Give me the key to that door. I have been a fool to remain here for as long as I have, enduring your insults and your ridicule. I was wrong to believe that you would come to accept me, that you would realize that I would be a quite good wife for you. I was wrong in what I felt about . . . never mind. I have come quickly to despise you, nearly as much as you despise me. I won't stay here for another minute. Give me the bloody key."

Douglas ran his fingers through his hair, and cursed. "I didn't mean that precisely. What I meant to do was talk to you, not fight with you, not insult you or have you insult me. You don't despise me, surely you don't mean that. Nor do I despise you. Never did I have any intention of hauling you back to your father in disgrace."

"I don't believe you."

"Please sit down."

"Give me the key and I will leave."

Douglas closed his hands around her waist and lifted her. He carried her to a chair and sat her down in it. He stood directly in front of her, blocking any escape. "Now you will listen to me. I don't know how we have come to such a pass. I had thought you more reasonable, more—"

"Submissive? Malleable? Stupid?"

"Damnation, be quiet! None of those things. You're being absurd, you're trying to rile me." He began to pace back and forth in front of her chair. She watched him, not understanding and uncertain whether or not she wanted to.

He came to a halt, bent over, his hands clutching the arms of her chair, his face not three inches from hers. "All right, I will simply tell you what I have decided to do, decided in fact when we were still at Tom O'Malley's cottage."

She looked about as interested as an oak tree.

He straightened, looking down on her from his impressive height. "I have decided to keep you as my wife. I will not have this marriage annulled. Your father can keep the bloody settlement. You will suit me, I suppose, as well as any other female. You were right; you will make me a quite good wife. You carry a good bloodline; you have excellent breeding, at least you should. By keeping you, I won't have to travel to London to find a likely candidate and court her until I am demented with boredom. Tony was right in that, curse his bounder's hide. Of course, you are not all that I could wish for. You must learn to moderate your damnable tongue. I fancy I can assist you in improving your manners and your behavior toward me. So, Alexandra, there is no need for you to leave. There is no reason for you to act unreasonably. You are now my wife   I recognize you as such—you are now the Countess of Northcliffe."

He beamed at her.

Alexandra rose very slowly. He stepped back, still beaming at her, obviously eager for her to throw herself on his manly chest and weep her relief, to bless him for his wondrous nobility, to kiss his hands and vow eternal devotion and servitude.

She turned, very slowly, picked up the spindle-legged marquetry table beside the chair, raised it over her head and brought it down. He stared at her in disbelief, jerked out of the way, and the table crashed down on his shoulder, not his head. The key dropped from his hand and fell to the floor.

She picked it up and raced to the door. Douglas was shaking his head, furious, bewildered, a bit disoriented. He was fast, but not fast enough. She was out of the door in a trice, had slammed it in his face in the very next instant, and even as his hand closed over the doorknob, he heard the key grate in the lock. She'd locked him in.

He stared at the door.

The damned woman had locked him in the Gold Salon. The door was old and beautiful and stout and thick. It would take five men, at least, to knock it open.

Douglas had been a soldier. He was strong, he was wily, he'd lost few fights. Damnation, he even spoke French and Spanish fluently. And yet this female kept catching him off guard. It was beyond too much.

He gave it up and yelled, "Open this damned door! Alexandra, open the door!"

There was pounding on the outside of the door, and a babble of voices, but no sound of a key in the lock.

"Open the door!"

He finally heard Hollis's voice raised above the din, saying firmly, "Just a moment, my lord. Her, ah, Ladyship, has flung the key away, somewhere under the stairs we think, and we are currently searching it out."

"Stop her, Hollis! Don't let her get away!"

"There is no need for you to fret, my lord. Lady Sinjun has, ah, detained her as we speak."

It was simply too much. Douglas stood there like a fool, saying nothing more, simply standing there, helpless, unable to do anything at all. The door opened. He walked out into a press of servants and family. From somewhere Uncle Albert and Aunt Mildred had appeared. Everyone was yelling and jabbering in a cacophony that made his ears ring.

He stared over at his sister, who was sitting astride Alexandra, holding her down, stretching her arms flung over her head on the Italian black and white marble floor.

He shook his head. Northcliffe Hall had gone to seed faster than any army could lose a battle. He threw back his head and laughed.

"My goodness," came a familiar drawling voice from the open front door, "I say, Douglas, what the devil is going on here? Whatever is Sinjun doing sitting on Alex? Where did all these people come from? I believe it is nearly every Sherbrooke from London to Cornwall."

Tony and Melissande stepped into the entrance hall and quickly joined the bedlam.

CHAPTER

=== 13 ===

GIVEN THE EARLIER ruckus, it was an amazingly sedate group of people who were seated around the formal dining table that early afternoon for luncheon. Hollis was at his post, looking as unflappable as a bishop, unobtrusively directing two footmen to serve. Neither Harry nor Barnaby said a word. They appeared to be treading on eggs. Douglas sat at the head of the long mahogany table, and Alexandra, still as a statue, sat on his right, placed there by a gently insistent Hollis. The Dowager Countess of Northcliffe sat at the foot of the table.

Ah, Douglas thought, what a damnable mess.

He took a bit of thin-sliced ham and chewed thoughtfully. His mother had established herself quickly, before Alexandra had come lagging into the dining room. As for Douglas, he hadn't noticed until it was too late. He said nothing. No more upsets, no more scenes, at least for this afternoon. He couldn't begin to imagine what his mother would say when informed she was no longer the mistress of Northcliffe and that chair down the expanse of long table was no longer hers. She was, at the moment, looking rather pleased with herself, and that bothered him. Did she enjoy the immense embarrassment his wife had caused? Did she believe that he would remove Alexandra from Northcliffe? Did she believe she could still remain the mistress here even if Alexandra remained?

Of course, Alexandra seemed oblivious of her duty as mistress, the damned little twit, oblivious of the fact that the dowager was sitting in her, Alexandra's, rightful place. What to do?

He gave her lowered head a look of acute dislike. He'd offered her the earth and the moon and himself as a husband, and she'd flown at him like a damned bat, coshed him with a marquetry table, and locked him in the Gold Salon. She should have been grateful, happy as a grig, she should have thanked him for his generosity of spirit, for his forgiveness, for she'd been as duplicitous as Tony and her father. It really made no sense, particularly given her own behavior. Hadn't she stripped off her clothes and offered herself to him to make him forget about an annulment? On the other hand, perhaps he hadn't treated her all that well. He had rejected her, firmly and rather coldly. But no, that wasn't important any more. He'd saved her, taking excellent care of her when she'd been ill. He shook his head. All that was in the past, both the well done and the miserably done. What was important now was that he'd finally decided to accept her.

His humor at seeing his sister sitting on top of Alexandra, holding both her arms over her head in the entrance hall had faded quickly. Alexandra had looked furious, her face flushed, but Sinjun was the stronger and she hadn't been able to move. He'd looked at her when the laughter had burst out of him, really looked. Now he didn't think there could be a funny nerve left in his body.

There was only grimness. His wife was still recovering from her illness, yet she wasn't eating enough to keep her left leg alive. He wanted to tell her to eat more because she needed her strength, when in his mind's eye, he saw her wielding that damned table at his head. She'd certainly been strong enough to bring him low. He sighed as he looked over at Melissande, so beautiful she made the room and everyone in it pale into insignificance. He chewed thoughtfully, growing more depressed by the minute.

Finally, Sinjun broke the silence, saying cheerfully, "Well, isn't this pleasant! All of us together, and so many of us. It is very nice to meet you, Melissande. Since we are related, I hope you don't mind me being informal?"

Melissande raised her beautiful face, glanced with little interest at the eager young girl opposite her, and gave her a slight nod, saying, "No, not at all."

Tony said, "Call her Mellie, Sinjun. My dear, Sinjun is my favorite female cousin."

"I am your only female cousin, Tony!"

"Oh no, there are three maiden cousins, all with protruding teeth, who live with twenty cats, and knit me slippers every Christmas."

"Well, thank you, I guess," Sinjun said. "Mellie. I like that name."

To Alexandra's surprise, her sister actually smiled and said, "To the best of my knowledge Alex has never before been flung to the floor and sat upon. I could but stare. You are very enterprising."

To Alexandra's further surprise, Sinjun, for the first time since Alexandra had met her—what was it, two hours before?—kept her mouth shut and her head lowered after shooting Alexandra a guilty look.

When Aunt Mildred, an older lady of iron-gray hair, thin as a stick, with a pair of very sharp eyes, said in her fulsome voice, "All this is not what I am used to, Douglas," he knew that any calm at the dining table was at an end. He mentally girded his loins for Aunt Mildred's offensive, and he wasn't disappointed.

"Your uncle and I arrive with a message from the Marquess of Dacre, informing you of the imminent visit of his dear daughter, Juliette, who, as you know, is beautiful and sweet-tempered and immensely well dowered, to see this person on the floor and everyone yelling and babbling. Juliette is, incidentally, arriving tomorrow. She, I am certain, has never in her life spent even an instant lying on the floor, particularly with someone sitting on her. You have made a mess of things, Douglas. We discover you're already wed by proxy to *her*. We're told that Tony wed *her* for himself, the girl you had originally wanted to marry, not this one sitting next to you. It is passing strange, Douglas. And all of this without a word to us. It is perhaps an unwelcome omen that you are in danger of Becoming Like Your Grandfather."

Uncle Albert cleared his throat. "Er, Mildred refers to your father's father, Douglas, not your dear mother's father. The other father died on the hunting field, if you will recall, back in seventy-nine."

"All of us have heard of Dicked-in-the-Nob Charles," Tony said. "But didn't the fox turn on his hunter and frighten him so badly that the old earl fell off and broke his neck?"

"Tony, of course not," said Uncle Albert. "The horse wasn't all that frightened. It was a bit of bad luck, that's all. Doubtless Charles was thinking about his chemicals and not really paying attention. And don't be flippant, boy, it don't become you."

Aunt Mildred then turned on her spouse with ruthless speed. "Perhaps a hunting accident is what finally killed him, Albert, but he wasn't right in his brain well before then. His notions of behavior were really most unacceptable—I mean, having three talking parrots with him at all times!—and his experiments in the east wing caused the most noxious odors to float throughout the hall, making everyone's eyes water."

Douglas stared, fascinated. They'd all grown up with stories about their eccentric grandfather. Then he recalled the awful bit of news his aunt had dropped. He groaned silently, then said with ominous calm, "You say, Aunt Mildred, that the Marquess of Dacre's daughter is coming here?"

"Certainly. Your uncle and I invited her. It was time someone took a hand to correct this deplorable situation. You weren't behaving as you should, Douglas. Now, however, what you've done is beyond even what I can repair. You're married to *her* and not to this lovely girl over here who is married to Tony, and now dear Juliette is coming as well. It is quite a pointless tangle. I'm sure I don't know what to do. None of it is my fault. You will have to make arrangements to set everything aright."

And just how, Douglas wondered, was he to do that?

Aunt Mildred sat back and regarded her veal stew in awful gloom.

The Dowager Countess of Northcliffe said in a loud, clear voice, "I agree, Mildred. It is distressing, all of it. However, Douglas isn't to blame. It's Tony and this girl here. Tony took Melissande and left Douglas with this—this—"

"Mother," Douglas said, leaning forward, his voice low and deadly calm, "you will moderate your speech. I am master here and I will be the one to decide what is to be or not to be."

"Ah," said Sinjun, grinning at her brother, "that is the question, isn't it?"

Douglas gave it up. He had no control over anyone, even his fifteen-year-old sister.

The dowager continued after a moment, just a bit moderated. "Lady Melissande, should you like some more apple tart? It's quite tasty, one of cook's specialties."

Melissande shook her head and asked her husband in a lowered voice, "Who is this Juliette?"

"Ah, my love, Juliette is second only to you in her beauty. But second, I swear it."

"I would like to meet her," said Melissande. "She sounds charming."

Oh Lord, Douglas thought, that was all he needed, two exquisite diamonds glittering around his house making every man in their vicinity hard with lust, and numb in the brain, and incoherent in speech.

"Well," said Aunt Mildred, "there is no way to prevent her arrival unless a highwayman kidnaps her."

"Now that is a thought," Tony said, grinning toward Douglas who was looking at Alexandra. "What do you say, Tysen? You've been very quiet. Would you like to court this Juliette?"

"Oh no," Sinjun said. "Tysen is in love with Melinda Beatrice, but he will get over it soon enough." Then Sinjun made all the motions of praying.

Tysen looked ready to box his sister's ears. He restrained himself, saying with all the seriousness of a hanging judge, "I am shortly returning to Oxford. To complete my divinity studies. This Juliette indeed sounds charming, but I cannot remain. I am sorry, Tony."

That stopped all conversation.

Douglas looked over at Alexandra.

She had effectively removed herself, he realized. She'd closed down and moved inward. Oh, she was still seated in her chair, but the spark in her was effectively doused. She looked pale and cold and flattened.

Douglas couldn't bear it. He tossed his napkin on his plate and pushed back his chair. "Alexandra, you will accompany me to the library, if you please." Douglas had learned his lesson. Instead of merely walking out of the dining room, assuming she would instantly follow him, he remained standing beside her chair, waiting. She looked up at him and sighed. No more scenes, she thought, knowing that suddenly everyone at the table, Hollis and the two footmen, all of them were holding their breaths, waiting to see what outrageous act she would pull next.

"Certainly, my lord," she said, and allowed Harry to pull back her chair. She even placed her hand on Douglas's proffered forearm.

"Excuse us," Douglas said. "Please continue. Tony, do strive for a little conversation. And don't shred my character any more than has already been done."

"I shall tell an anecdote from our misspent youth," Tony said, his eyes on Alexandra.

"Oh yes, do," Sinjun said. "I remember both Douglas and Ryder were greatly misspent."

The dowager countess said in a penetrating voice just as Douglas and Alexandra were nearly out of the dining room, "Poor Douglas. Whatever will he do with that one? You were a wicked boy, Tony, to saddle him with the likes of her and keep this beautiful jewel for yourself."

Melissande, to Douglas's surprise, said, "Alexandra is my sister, ma'am. You will not speak of her in a displeasing manner, if you please."

"Hummmph," said the dowager countess.

"Well done, love," Tony said very close to his wife's beautifully perfect small ear.

"Yes," Melissande said, "I rather thought you would approve."

"You are learning," he said slowly. "Perhaps someday it will become a habit with you. You won't have to consider my reaction before you take action."

Alexandra didn't say a word. She walked beside Douglas across the entrance hall, looking inadvertently from the corner of her eye where she'd been ignominiously tripped up by Sinjun and straddled on the marble floor.

She felt stripped and exposed and completely alone. She felt defeated. It was a relief to be away from all those dreadful people, but now she was with Douglas, the only person in the world who could truly crush her.

Douglas led her to the library, shut and locked the door. This time, he offered her the key. "To save me from possible further physical attack," he said. "Although I see no furnishings in here you could use for another attack. Even you could not lift that wing chair. As for that hassock, don't be deceived by its lack of mass. It weighs more than you do."

She shook her head, moved quickly away from him, and stood behind a sofa, a dark brown leather affair that suited him immensely well.

He wished she would say something, but she didn't. He tossed the key to the desktop.

He drew a deep breath and fastened her with his major's eye. "All right, Alexandra, the time has finally come for us to get a few things straightened out."

She looked at him, no clue to her thoughts or feelings showing on her face.

He frowned. "You have made me a laughingstock. I am not particularly pleased about that. However, what's done is done. I am even willing to say that I did play something of a part in what happened, that I am somewhat to blame. Have you anything to say for yourself?"

"Your family made me a laughingstock. I am not particularly pleased about that. What's done shouldn't have happened, but it did. I'd further say that you played the largest part available. That's what I have to say."

"You're right, to a point. It wasn't well done of them. I won't let it happen like that in future. Now we will get back to you and your behavior."

She stared at him, mute.

"Were I you, I wouldn't say anything either. An apology would sound suspect since your behavior has been that of a bedlamite, of a thoughtless, feckless hoyden unworthy of the title of countess." Douglas came to a grinding halt. The diatribe was merited, indeed it was, but it wouldn't gain him anything, not after the rounds of fire in the dining room. Aye, given the likely penchant of her current temper, she just might try to hurl the sofa at his head. He moderated his voice. "But, as I said, what's done is done." He gave her a smarmy smile. "We must look to the future now."

"What future?"

"That is what I wish to discuss."

"I cannot see much hope for a future. Your mother is distressed that you are married to me. It is also obvious that she would dote on Melissande as a daughter-in-law. But since Melissande is out of the running, there is still this Juliette person, who, although second to Melissande in beauty, still rates quite highly in terms of comeliness. As for me, I appear to be off the other end of the scale. Your mother would never accept me. I don't fancy having to endure humiliation from you and then endure nastiness from her."

And Douglas said without thought, "I imagine my mother looks at Melissande and sees no challenge to her authority. You, however, are made of sterner stuff and couldn't be counted on to spend all your time on your clothing and planning for parties and balls. No, you would likely want to oversee the management of household affairs yourself." He stopped, both surprised and appalled at what had come out of his mouth.

She saw that he was chagrined and said, "Be careful, my lord, else I might take that as a compliment, regardless of your intentions."

"I didn't mean it," he said. "Melissande could most certainly be counted on to do her duty."

Alexandra could have told him that Melissande would be shown a torn sheet and look bewildered.

Instead, she said, "Melissande also enjoys watercolors. She's really quite talented. Whilst I am fully able to oversee darning sheets, she leaves such mundane tasks to those who haven't her talent."

Douglas didn't know what to say to that.

"However, I can sing. I am not Madame Belle Orzinski but I have been told that my voice is quite nice. Also, flowers and plants of all kind respond to me. The Northcliffe gardens are in horrible condition."

He said very quietly, his dark eyes glittering, "Are you trying to convince me that you would make me a good wife, Alexandra? You're trotting out your other sterling qualities?" He was pleased when she paled, obviously unaware of what she'd said until he'd pointed it out.

"No," she said. "I don't want to be your wife any more. I want to go home. You cannot force me to remain here, my lord."

"I can most certainly force you to do whatever I wish. It would behoove you not to forget that."

Instead of hurling curses at him, Alexandra drew a deep calming breath. She was moderate in her behavior and thinking, she was in control, she was mild-tempered and now she would prove it, both to herself and to him. She would not attack him. "You said you wished to speak to me. About what?"

That was well done, he thought, pleased. "There is a rip beneath your right arm. Either from hurling the marquetry table at me or having Sinjun sit on you and jerk your arms over your head."

"If I wheedle, will you buy me a new gown?"

"Probably."

"I don't want anything from you! You would throw it up to me endlessly whenever I chanced to displease you, which would be every other minute."

"A pity, because you've got me and all my bad habits. You've also got all my cursed relatives who have the sensitivities of goats, and a good two dozen meddlesome servants that come with me. No, don't hurl invectives at me. Your calm is refreshing, albeit unusual. Now, I told you that I wouldn't annul the marriage. I told you I accepted you as my wife. I have not changed my mind. Now, have you anything to say?"

"You are perverse."

"No more than you are."

He had a point there. She sat down, stretched and raised her arms to lie on the sofa back. She crossed her legs and dangled one foot. She looked amused. "So, I understand you now. You are doing this to avoid a scandal."

"No, but that's a good point. There would be a scandal, probably a vastly annoying one. But that isn't the reason. I think, once you have recovered your more temperate humors, that we can deal reasonably well together."

He was giving her what she'd wanted for the past three years, what she'd wanted so desperately that she'd even tried to seduce him. She'd taken off all her clothes and offered herself to him. And he'd turned her down and insulted her. Now she was dressed in a gown with a rip under the right arm and he was offering not to annul her. She couldn't quite grasp it. On the other hand, what real choice did she have? Wasn't this precisely what she wanted more than anything else?

She looked up at him then and said, "All right."

Douglas smiled. Something loosened inside him. He hadn't realized he was so very tense, hadn't realized he was so very apprehensive about what she would say.

"You look very different when you smile."

"I suppose you haven't seen much humor from me."

"No. I suppose you haven't observed much placid behavior from me either."

"No."

She blurted out, "What do you intend to do now?"

He cocked his head to one side. "What do you mean? Do you wish to go riding? Since Sinjun is here, you must ask her if you can ride Fanny. I will buy you another mount. Perhaps you can go with me. There is a stud over at Branderleigh Farm that sells mares with fine bloodlines."

"No, about this Juliette."

"Ah, a diamond of the second water."

"Yes! Currently being imported for your perusal. I can't bear it, Douglas!" Alexandra jumped to her feet and began pacing. "And I can't bear more comparisons, truly. This Juliette—goodness, named after a Shakespeare play!—will arrive and all your relatives will look from her to Melissande and then to me and they'll show their displeasure at what has happened. They'll be verbal in their displeasure. I can't bear it, Douglas."

"No, it wouldn't be pleasant for either of us. Let me think about it. Since I now know you won't be bagging it out of here, why then, I can set my brain to solving this particular problem. All right?"

She nodded numbly.

"You won't try to leave again, will you?"

"No. I doubt I could outsmart your sister."

"Will you prove it by giving me your thirty pounds?"

"No, never."

"So you don't trust me. All right, it seems that I'll just have to trust you first. Are you still hungry? You didn't eat much. Would you rather lie down and rest? I can ensure that you aren't disturbed."

"Yes," she said, desperation clear in her voice. "Yes, I should like that."

He gave her a long look, but said nothing.

CHAPTER
═14═

IT WAS ELEVEN o'clock at night. Alexandra was sitting up in her bed, bolstered up by three thick pillows, staring at the dying embers in the fireplace. The room was in shadow, the only light coming from a branch of five candles at her right elbow.

Would he come to her tonight?

Molière's play *The Misanthrope* lay facedown on her lap. She had just read the line "Women like me are not for such as you." And now she couldn't get it out of her mind. It read itself over and over. Poor Douglas, not only had he lost the first diamond, but the second diamond as well. She wondered what gem she could aspire to be. Perhaps a topaz, she thought, aye, a topaz, only semiprecious, not worth much, but still pleasant to look at. A solid sort of stone, surely, steady and to be counted upon. She picked up the play and turned a page, trying to force herself to read.

Would he come to her tonight?

A shadow fell across the white page of the book and Alexandra started. Douglas stood next to her bed and he was wearing a dressing gown of thick brocade, a rich blue with gold thread interwoven. His feet were bare. She looked up the length of him, met his dark night eyes, and said, "What are you doing here?"

He just smiled down at her and took the book from her hands. "Ah, *The Misanthrope*. And in English, unfortunately. You don't read French? It is much more amusing in French, you know."

"Perhaps," she said, "but I know the play well and like it more than well, even in English."

He flipped over several pages, then read, " 'Nothing but trickery prospers nowadays . . .' What think you of that, Alexandra?"

Ah, yes, her trickery, Tony's trickery. Douglas would never let it go, never. Her voice was dull as she said, "I think it is unkind of you to select that particular passage when there are so many other lines from which to choose."

"I was thinking of my sister, actually, and all her machinations. I was hearing her yowling at the top of her lungs about that huge hairy rat climbing up your skirt. I was seeing her laughing as she held you down on the floor. I missed you at the dinner table."

"I can't imagine why."

"It was rather boring, truth be told. Since you—the target—were no longer in their midst, all my relatives ate more than they should have and spoke of the weather. However, I did have to partner Aunt Mildred in whist. Do you play?"

"Yes."

"Then you will partner me next time. You cannot continue to hide in here, you know. Do you play as well as your sister?"

"Yes."

Douglas looked thoughtful. "I don't think now that it is that her play is so subtle. It is that she is so beautiful that one forgets the cards one holds and the strategics one has concocted."

"Your strategies will remain intact with me."

"Possibly. I really must insist, Alexandra. As mistress of Northcliffe Hall, it is your responsibility to see to my family and to my guests."

She looked up at him, her expression giving nothing away, and said, " 'I'm clever, handsome, gracefully polite; My waist is small, my teeth are strong and white.' "

Douglas laughed. "Now that's a line from the play I remember well. But you needn't trot out those particular qualities, my dear, for they are there for all to see. Shall we put Molière back on his shelf? Good." He then turned to look into the fireplace. "Didn't you expect to see me tonight?"

"I wasn't certain."

"Did you want me to come to you?"

At that moment she looked about as happy as she would welcoming the plague into her house. "I don't know. I'm very concerned about all this."

"About all what? What I'm going to teach you?"

"Yes."

"How very odd. I didn't expect one morsel of concern from the woman who came into my bedchamber not long ago and stripped off her nightgown and came to stand between my legs. Indeed, I hurried in here because I thought you just might repeat your performance. The husband is supposed to be the one to come to his bride on their wedding night, not the other way around. And this is our wedding night. Would you have trotted into my bedchamber, ready to do your worst to me? Truly, Alexandra, I didn't believe you had a modest bone in your very lovely body. Concern? Are you afraid that I shall beat you?"

"No, I was afraid that you would look at me again and not want me."

Douglas's mouth snapped shut. Dear God, he wished she had more guile. This honesty of hers was appalling, and he wished she would learn to keep it behind her teeth. "Well, I am your husband. This is the last time I will tell you that I have accepted this marriage. And now this marriage must be consummated if it is to be a real marriage."

She felt a frisson of both anticipation and fear. He did not sound particularly pleased to be in her bedchamber. He sounded as if this would be a chore for him.

"I am never certain what you will do. You are unpredictable. But I don't think you really wish to be in here, with me."

He waved his hand. "I am perfectly capable of enjoying myself with you. From this night on I won't be unpredictable when it comes to bedding you. You realize that I must be here, don't you? Do you understand about consummation, Alexandra? You do understand what we will do?"

He was still standing beside her, tall and broad, looking down at her from his commanding height. "Do you?"

"I know that you admire my bosom. You told me that. I assume that you weren't lying."

" 'Bosom' is a woman's word. What you have, Alexandra, is breasts. Full white breasts, large enough to overflow a man's hands. Yes, I like your breasts. They are most pleasing. They will be plentiful enough, certainly, to suckle my son. And until my son arrives, why then, they will suckle me."

"Suckle you? You are not a babe."

His mouth thinned a bit. "I will have to show you. Now, do you understand what is going to happen? I ask, Alexandra, because you are a virgin, and I have no particular wish to shock you or disgust you."

"Why would you do that? You make me angry, Douglas, but you've never disgusted me, save in your unregulated speech upon occasion."

"You might find my body disgusting. I am dark and hairy and large. I have heard that young ladies of quality occasionally are repulsed by the male body."

"Oh no."

"Surely this is a strange conversation," he said, frowning toward the fireplace. "Let us finish it. Consummation, Alexandra?"

"I know a little bit. I asked Melissande, but she—" She stopped when Douglas suddenly sucked in his breath. She felt a shaft of pain, deep and raw. He had thought of Melissande making love with Tony and it distressed him. But what could she expect?

"What did she tell you?"

He was trying to downplay his reaction, she would give him that. "She didn't tell me much of anything. She said it wasn't proper but then she got all flushed and stammered and I was left not knowing what to think."

Douglas pulled a loose gold thread from his sleeve. "It is common knowledge that Tony is an excellent lover."

"Common amongst whom?"

"At first amongst ladies, but then they talk to other lovers and husbands, and the gentlemen learn who amongst them enjoys success."

"So the more excellent the lover the more women the lover enjoys? It doesn't matter if he is married or not? Or if she is married or not?"

Douglas frowned. It was the accepted way of things, but he couldn't quite bring himself to tell her so. He said only, "I suppose so."

"What is an excellent lover? A man who is kind? A man who is very gentle? A man who kisses very well?"

"All those things and much more."

"It would seem to me that those things and much more would require practice and a good deal of experience."

"They do. Tony has years of both."

"And you?"

"I, too."

"And Ryder?"

Douglas laughed. "Ah, my younger brother was probably born an excellent lover. He has but to show himself and the ladies, as well as the females who aren't ladies, swoon and flirt and simper. However, he tends to forget himself in his own pleasure."

"What do you mean?"

"Never mind. Later. Perhaps when you know a bit more about things than you do now."

"Is it common knowledge you are an excellent lover?"

"I trust so. I have never been a selfish pig and I am careful to see to a woman's pleasure."

"You don't make it sound very enjoyable for yourself if you are being so careful about everything."

"Nature has dictated that sex is very enjoyable for a man, no matter the circumstance. It is to keep the race going, you understand. Pleasure is not necessary for a woman since she is only the recipient of a man's seed, and thus doesn't have to play an active role. She was deprived by Nature. It is a pity, but a man, if he's an excellent lover, will overcome Nature's oversight. I do enjoy overcoming."

"Even if you don't particularly care for the woman?"

"I don't generally have sex with women I don't care for. Except on rare occasion."

Well, she had asked and he'd told her the truth, a bit baldly perhaps, but it was the truth nonetheless.

"Yes," he continued, "for a woman, more care is required if she is to—" He broke off, then added, "I enjoy watching a woman find her release." He stopped at the look of pain in her eyes, intense pain and hurt. What the devil had he said? Perhaps it was just a maiden's fear. She didn't understand, but she would before this night was over.

Then she closed her eyes. "Then I shall forever be compared to all the beautiful women you've known and watched and enjoyed. And because I am ignorant and not a diamond, I probably will never find out what this release is all about, and you will be displeased with me. And then I will always lose and you will always feel sorry that you are wedded to me."

"But you just quoted to me that you are graceful with a narrow waist and white teeth. Ah, and handsome." He paused a moment, then said very quietly, "As to release, I will give you such pleasure that you will shriek with the joy of it. As for the rest of what you said, it's drivel."

"I don't know, Douglas. Perhaps when you begin this business, you will be sorry that I am the recipient of your excellent technique. You will feel as though you are wasting your excellence on such as me."

"I doubt that, for I have seen you and touched you and cared for you and your body pleases me, Alexandra. Very much. I am a man and not a boy. You may trust that I will take good care of you, that I will do what is just right at just the right moment to give you pleasure."

"It sounds very cold-blooded to me."

He only shrugged. It was, upon occasion, but he didn't intend to tell her that. "Do you know that this is all in all a very strange conversation to be having on one's wedding night? And that's what this is, Alexandra. Now, shall we?"

"No," she said. "I don't think so. Douglas, wait. Did you really want to come to me tonight?"

"Damn you, Alexandra, it's enough that I am here! It goes with me accepting you as my wife. No, don't look at me as if I will kill you." He grasped her arms and pulled her off the bed. "Sit down now," he said, then proceeded to push her down upon the counterpane. Her feet didn't touch the floor. They were bare, narrow, nice toes. Her nightgown was virginal; she looked about sixteen. But she hadn't braided her hair and it was really quite lovely, that deep red color, the waves thick and full, falling down her back. She'd brushed it and that must mean that she'd expected him to come to her. It was something, at least. Douglas took a step back from her and began to unfasten the belt around his waist.

"Oh dear, what are you doing?"

"I'm going to show you what a man looks like," he said and tossed the belt to the floor. Very slowly, he shrugged one shoulder and then the other out of the dressing gown. It fell to the floor and he kicked it away from him. Then, still looking at her directly in her eyes, he straightened, his arms at his sides, and stood there naked.

"Oh goodness," she said, her eyes immediately on his groin.

"I am not at all like you," Douglas said. He was watching her closely and he saw her eyes widen and glaze a bit. "With you looking at me with such interest, I tend to become quite enthusiastic. My brain has nothing to do with it."

"Oh goodness," she said again.

Still he stood there, letting her look her fill at him. Finally, to his relief, she nodded, as if coming to a decision. He hadn't the foggiest notion of what his next step would have been had she continued to look at him as if he were going to kill her.

"Your nightgown is in the way. Let's get rid of it."

He didn't wait, but pulled her to her feet to stand in front of him. He leaned down, grasped the hem of her nightgown and pulled it over her head. "Now," he said, "we are in the same boat, so to speak."

"You're very dark and hairy and big."

"Yes, and you're very white-skinned with no hair at all except between your thighs. Lovely, that."

"Oh goodness."

"Touch me, Alexandra. I would appreciate it very much."

"Where?"

"Anywhere that pleases you so long as it's between my chest and my thighs."

She pressed the open palms of both hands against his chest. Black hair crinkled against her flesh. She felt the thud of his heart, slow and steady. Slowly, very slowly, her hands came down.

He sucked in his breath. His sex grew thicker. His hands fisted at his sides, but he forced himself to stand still, to let her keep the control. He would be frightening her soon enough. When her hands were against his belly, his sex was throbbing and he prayed now that she wouldn't touch him.

"You're very big, Douglas."

He smiled painfully. "That's true, but you will learn that a man is made to give a woman pleasure. It is his role, that, and spilling his seed inside the woman."

"I can't believe this will work."

Then before he could think of anything to say, her fingertips lightly touched him. He jerked and moaned.

"Did I hurt you?"

"Yes and it was wonderful. Don't touch my sex again, Alexandra, else I might embarrass myself." Douglas couldn't believe it. He was the man Ryder accused of being a cold fish, the man who would control himself with an angel, and it was true. He'd never had to fight for control in his life. Yet she was touching him and it was making him crazy. He'd been without a woman for too long, that was it. But he hadn't, not really.

"But you are so—"

"So what?" he said between gritted teeth. Her hands were hovering over him, her face lowered, and she was looking closely at him, and he suddenly saw her on her knees in front of him, and she was going to take him into her mouth. He could practically feel the warmth of her breath on his sex. To have her take him into her mouth—the thought made him tremble and shake, and in that moment, he simply couldn't bear it any more. He couldn't call up a bit of cold-bloodedness. It was insanity and it had him. He jerked her close and pressed her hard against him.

"I want you," he said against her mouth. "Part your lips, now, now, yes, that's it," and his warm breath was inside her mouth and his large hands were stroking wildly down her back and cupping under her buttocks. Then he was groaning into her mouth, his tongue touching hers, and he was pressing her upward against him and he was hard and hot and his hands were on her bare legs now, feverishly stroking upward, and his fingertips pushed against her buttocks and touched her. She flinched, and in that instant, he realized she was scared. She was stiff as a board.

Douglas got hold of himself. Too quickly, he was going much too quickly. It wasn't at all like him. He was careful, slow, very deliberate, yet here he was, acting like a wild man. He, the excellent lover, was scaring the devil out of her. Ah, but he wanted to part her woman's flesh and he wanted to thrust into her this very second, this instant, deep into her, and hard, but he'd told her he wasn't a pig. Damn, he'd even bragged about how good he was to a woman. He had to gain control. She was a virgin and he wasn't. He was an experienced man, he knew how things were to be done. This grabbing and pawing and panting wasn't a sign of excellence. He drew a deep breath. He set her away from him and took a step back. He grabbed up his dressing gown and shrugged into it. He wouldn't spill his seed too quickly and leave her to wonder how he could ever believe himself a matchless bedmate.

"I'm sorry," he said, his voice raw and low. "I frightened you. I'm sorry." Then he laughed at himself. "You won't believe this, Alexandra," he said, grasping her arms and stroking them, up and down and up and down because he had to touch her, just have contact with her. "Never, please believe me, never have I felt so frantic before, so damned urgent. It's true and it shocks me that I could lose my control. I don't like it a bit.

It isn't at all like me. You're just a woman, truth be told, like any other woman, despite the fact that you're my wife. I'm not lying to you, Alexandra. No, don't look at me as if I'm a monster. I am not rejecting you, never that. That other time I was a fool and I want to make it up to you tonight. I don't want to hurt you, to frighten you. God, your breasts are lovely."

He was breathing hard, as if he'd just run to Northcliffe's north field and back. His sex was thrusting outward still. Alexandra pressed her palm against his heart. Fast pounding. He wanted her.

And she'd acted like a stupid ninny, freezing up on him. "Please, Douglas, I'm sorry I'm afraid. I won't act like a virgin again."

He laughed and it hurt. "You are a virgin." Yet he marveled at her unquestioned acceptance. She still looked wary, but also she was eager and he was more than eager to teach her.

"Come here."

She took the three steps until she was standing directly in front of him. "As you can see, I still want you very much. As I told you, I can't control my reaction. Do you want to stay here or come with me into my bedchamber?"

"I want to go with you."

Without another word, Douglas picked her up and held her tightly against him. Her breath was warm on his cheek and then she kissed him, a light kiss, one with her lips closed, a virgin's kiss, an innocent kiss a girl would give her uncle, and it pleased him and drove him mad with lust. He dropped her to her feet and took her hand, dragging her into his bedchamber. Once there, he turned to face her and pulled her up against him. She kissed him again, this time on his ear and then she lightly bit his earlobe.

He ran the last few feet to his bed. He was breathing hard, and it was going to be touch and go. "Now, listen to me," he said, forcing himself not to touch her, just to look down at her, sprawled in the middle of his bed. "I don't want you to touch me or kiss me again. I don't know what the matter with me is, but I can't take it, Alexandra. Do you understand?"

Even as he spoke the words, he remembered again Ryder telling him he was a cold fish. Cold, ha!

Her eyes were large with astonishment as she stared up at him.

"I know you don't understand, dammit, just tell me that you do, all right?"

"I understand, Douglas," she said, and reached up to clasp her arms around his neck, drawing him down. He fell atop her, his mouth was on hers, and he was kissing her again and again, whispering for her to part her lips, and when she did, he groaned into her mouth, and didn't stop.

"Alexandra." He said her name over and over, and he didn't want to stop kissing her, not until he had no more breath, not until he was dead, and then he'd stop, maybe. He managed to jerk off his dressing gown, but the touch of her flesh against his sent him over the edge. He was on top of her, hard against her belly and he wanted to fit himself between her legs. He reared back and pushed her legs wide apart. He fell on her again and his sex was pushing against her and he thought he would die if he couldn't come into her this instant, this very moment in time. He held on, but his tongue was wild in her mouth, deepening, his tongue touching hers, and the heat of her made his heart pound and speed up faster and faster. He raised his head and stared down at her. "I don't believe this," he said, and kissed her again. Her arms were around his back, her fingers digging into his shoulders, and she was moving beneath him and he jerked back to look down at her body, open for him, his for the taking, and he saw that she was pale, her face as white as her smooth belly, and he looked at her sprawled legs and felt himself tense and tremble, and he couldn't believe it. He sat back on his heels between her legs and stared down at her. "You are incredible," he said and his hands cupped her breasts, kneading them, and then he was leaning down, suckling her nipple and Alexandra, shocked, terrified until this moment, yelled.

Her back arched up, and at her response, Douglas went mad. His hands were all over her, everywhere he could reach, and he was pleased she was small and that his hands spanned her belly and at the same time his fingers were delving through the dark red hair that covered her woman's mound and she was wet and he was so relieved, so maddened with lust, that he simply couldn't wait to soothe her, to prepare her. He lifted her off the bed and brought her to his mouth.

Alexandra had no time for shock at this act. His tongue was hot and wet and all she could think of was, "Oh my God, something is going to happen to me!" And then it did, quickly, and she was screaming with the pounding and the scalding heat between her thighs and his mouth deepened and a finger gently came into her and she lurched up, her hands fisting in his hair and she shuddered and cried out and his words burned into her as she spun outside herself, yet deep into herself, and he was there, and he was saying, "Yes, come to me, Alexandra, come, come . . . yes. You're mine now and that is a woman's release . . . come."

The powerful burning and clenching eased and in the next instant, his fingers were stroking her there, parting her, and then he was easing inside her and she wanted to tell him to stop because it hurt and she knew it couldn't work for he was large and he would tear her, but his fingers were on her slick flesh again, probing and caressing, and she was sobbing with the power of it as he came more deeply inside her.

"Alexandra, look at me!"

She stared up at him. His face was taut, there was sweat on his brow, he looked to be in pain, and he groaned, his powerful back arching, and he lunged forward, and she screamed for the pain was deep inside her, tearing, rending, and there was raw pain and more pain. He came down over her, balancing himself on his elbows, but he couldn't stop himself. He was panting now, and he looked both incredulous and beyond reason, and he was pumping deep within her, hard and fast, and faster still, and the pleasure was forgotten and she was crying.

Then he froze over her. She was surprised that he was utterly still. She looked up at his face and saw the look of astonishment and intense satisfaction written there. Then he moaned long and deep, and his dark eyes were vague and wild and she felt the wetness of him at her womb. And it went on and on, and she was slick now and the pain had lessened.

Just as suddenly, he was lying on her, breathing painfully hard, crushing her into the mattress, and it was over and she was wondering what had happened and what more would happen. After some minutes, Douglas raised himself on his elbows. He looked down at her face. He stared at her for a very long time. He frowned.

He said finally, his voice harsh and angry, "My God, I don't believe this. It shouldn't have happened. It never has happened before. It wasn't what I wanted, expected. Damnation!"

He pulled away from her, aware of her flesh quivering as he pulled out of her. He rolled off the bed and stood there for a moment, staring at her. "Go to sleep," he said, and to her astonishment, he turned and left her, going into the countess's bedchamber, jerking the door closed behind him.

CHAPTER
═15═

THE SCREAM BROUGHT Alexandra bolting up in bed. It was loud, piercing, and it was coming from the countess's bedchamber, the bedchamber she wasn't in. She jumped out of Douglas's bed, realized she was quite naked, and grabbed the counterpane, wrapped it around her as she dashed to the adjoining door and flung it open.

There was a maid, Dora by name, fifteen and foolish and thin, and she was shrieking, her hands covering her face, and she was staring at the bed through her fingers.

Douglas was sitting up in bed, staring in some confusion down at his naked chest, now covered with hot chocolate. The white sheet came only to his belly.

Alexandra skidded to a halt, staring.

Douglas raised his head and yelled at the maid, "For God's sake, you silly wench, shut up!"

Dora clamped her jaws together. She began to wring her hands. Alexandra quickly came into the room, and Dora, seeing the mistress she'd expected instead of His Lordship who was amazingly naked, said, "Oh, my lady! Oh dear! 'Tis His Lordship and I thought it was you and I gently shook your—his—shoulder and he came up and he doesn't have any clothes on and it scared me so that I spilled the chocolate all over him and I burned him. Oh my lady!"

Alexandra looked at Douglas. There was chocolate matting the thick hair on his chest and staining the white covers. His hair was tousled, his jaws dark with whiskers, and he looked so beautiful to her that she couldn't understand why Dora had been shrieking. If she had discovered him thus, she would have leapt into the bed with him and kissed him until she was breathless.

She said to the maid, "It's all right, Dora. You may leave now. Fetch some warm water and washcloths and towels. Hurry now, His Lordship can't be all that comfortable with the chocolate on his chest."

Alexandra turned to her husband. "Are you all right? Did the chocolate burn you?"

He looked vastly irritated. "Dammit, no, but she startled the devil out of me, the hysterical little—"

"You probably scared her more, being in my bed."

She managed to hold herself quiet until Dora let herself out of the bedchamber. Then she laughed and laughed, so hard that tears pooled in her eyes. She hugged her stomach, bending over, still laughing.

"Damnation! Be quiet!"

"Yes, my lord," she said and laughed some more. Finally, Alexandra wiped her eyes on the edge of the counterpane, and looked at her husband.

Douglas, pulled from a deep sleep, doused with hot chocolate, and then shrieked at, shoved away the covers and rose from the bed. He was quite naked and Alexandra became quite still at the sight of him.

He didn't look at all like he had the night before.

"Good Lord, woman, stop staring at me!" It was then that Douglas looked down at himself. He drew in his breath. There was blood on his member.

He looked at the shrouded woman with long tousled dark red hair who was standing there like a half-wit staring at him, the woman he'd taken the previous night, that former virgin woman who was also his wife, and said, his voice deep and gruff, "Did I hurt you?"

She stared at him, unconsciously clutching the counterpane more closely. "Yes."

"Do you still hurt?"

She was terribly embarrassed, standing here with him perfectly naked, asking her questions that made the roots of her hair turn even redder. "A little bit. No, not really. Some, it's strange."

He walked past her into his own bedchamber, grabbed up his dressing gown and shrugged into it. He looked back at her, and said, "Come here."

Alexandra, her head cocked to the side in question, walked slowly to him. Without warning, he lifted her and laid her onto her back on the bed. He began unrolling the counterpane.

"Stop! Oh dear, what are you doing? Douglas!" She was swatting at him, but it did no good. Soon she was lying naked and he was looking down at her. "Part your legs."

She twisted away from him, but he grabbed her ankles and flipped her back. "Dammit, hold still, woman!"

"No, this is horrid! Stop it, Douglas! I might not be a virgin now, but this is still very embarrassing."

He came down on top of her. "Be quiet. I saw blood on my member, your blood, your virgin's blood, and I need to see if you're all right. Did you bleed much? I forgot to warn you. Were you frightened? Blessed hell, I'm sorry."

She stared up at him. "I don't know."

"What do you mean you don't know?"

"I feel sticky but I didn't look at myself. It was dark and you had left me."

"It's not dark now. Hold still, Alexandra." He rolled off her and shoved her thighs apart. "Damn," he said, "it's you who need the water Dora is bringing. You're a mess."

She was so humiliated, so utterly mortified, that she just lay there, her eyes tightly closed. She felt his big warm hands on her thighs, touching her, knew he was looking at her and it was a bright morning, sun flooding through the windows. She wanted, quite simply, to open her eyes and discover that she was ten years old again, waiting for her nanny to come fetch her for breakfast, and none of this was happening.

She felt the mattress shift and knew he was standing beside the bed now, staring down at her. "Don't move. I'll bring the water and bathe you."

She heard the master bedchamber door open, and she did move, faster than she'd thought possible. She buried herself in the sheets.

"My lord?"

It was Finkle, Douglas's valet.

"Go away!"

"My lady? Is that you, all muffled? Oh dear. Excuse me, oh dear."

"Finkle, is that you?"

"Oh my lord, forgive me, but I thought it was you but it wasn't, it was her—"

"No matter. I do understand, believe me. Go away and bring bathwater. Next time, knock. Her Ladyship still isn't certain which bed is hers. She has problems with direction, you know, and I have assured her that I quite understand."

When the door closed, Douglas looked down at the shrouded figure on his bed. It was his turn to laugh, which he did. She burrowed more deeply. Finally, he said, amusement filling his voice, "You can come out now. Finkle is quite gone. Can you imagine how I felt?"

"This is worse. Men don't seem to care who sees what. They have no modesty."

"This conclusion, I gather, is from your vast well of experience? Never mind. Get used to me seeing you, whenever and wherever I please. As for poor Finkle, with all those 'oh dears,' you and my valet could sing a duet. Come along, there's warm water in your room."

She came along, the counterpane trailing after her like a very long bridal veil.

She dug in her heels in the doorway. "I will bathe myself, Douglas."

"Nonsense, I need to see that you're all right. I am the one responsible for wounding you, though that is not the appropriate thing to say about the rending of your maidenhead, but no matter. I did it and I will tend you."

"You will go away. I cannot allow this. It is too embarrassing."

Douglas frowned. "Do you so soon forget what I did to you last night, madam? Do you so soon forget how you squealed with pleasure? Believe me, I was looking at you then. Now it's different, but just a bit. Be quiet."

"No." She fidgeted. "It was dark last night. You said the blood is natural?"

He heard the fear in her voice, and softened his own. "Yes. I should have warned you, but I didn't." He frowned, remembering how he'd felt so utterly stripped of everything comfortable, everything known and accepted at the power of his release, so completely unfamiliar to himself, an alien feeling he hated, that he'd reeled away from her and from the scene of his fall.

"Go away, Douglas."

Douglas picked up the bowl of warm water and set it on the tabletop next to the bed. He laid the washcloths next to the water. Then he turned to her. Alexandra tried to run but the counterpane tripped her up and she fell into his arms. He picked her up and dumped her onto the bed. He unrolled her, then said, "I am tired of playing Caesar to your Cleopatra, though you continue to unroll well. I am weary of telling you to be quiet and to hold still. I don't wish to tell you again."

She lay there, her head turned away, her eyes tightly closed, as he pushed her legs apart and bathed off the blood and his seed.

Douglas felt calm and in control even when his fingers touched her flesh and she quivered. He remembered he'd felt just as calm, just as in control when he'd tended her during her illness. No savage lust for him then and none for him now. It was finished, thank God. He was back to normal. When he decided to take her again, it would be accomplished with reason and logic and a modicum of involvement. No abandon, no frenzy. She would not disturb him again to the point that he lost himself entirely. He took one final swipe, then tossed the cloth aside. He turned back to tell her to get up when he looked down at her and discovered that he couldn't seem to look away from her. His calm fled from one short breath to the next. His task was done and so was his control. His vaunted control was a valueless memory. Now he couldn't stop looking at her, his fingers twitching at the closeness of her body. Her flesh was soft and pink and warm and he found that he'd begun to tremble. No, he wouldn't tremble at the sight of a naked woman. He never had before. His fingers dug slightly into her inner thighs. He wanted to stroke her, and he wanted to caress her with his fingertips and his mouth. And her breasts, he wanted to cup her breasts, to fill his hands with her breasts, he wanted to suckle her, to rub his cheek against the soft flesh and hear her heartbeat against his face.

He sucked in his breath. It was worse than it had been the previous night, this crippling lust, this alien urgency that turned him into a wild man, a man he didn't recognize, a man the logical side of him could not approve of. He felt blood pounding in his head, felt his muscles, his sex, tighten and throb. His sex was hard and he was filled with such desire for her that he was shaking with it. He tried to find a shred of reason in his brain, but there wasn't any, not even a thread. "Damnation," he said, and fell on top of her, parting her legs wider as he came between them.

"Lift your hips," he said, then lifted them with his big hands. He was panting now, close to shattering, so close to releasing his seed, and he couldn't understand it, couldn't begin to explain it, and then, suddenly, he thrust into her.

Alexandra cried out in surprise.

Douglas froze over her, but for just an instant. She was hot and very small, and he could feel her flesh accommodating to him; she was accepting him smoothly, so there must have been some desire in her for him as well. There was no force, only the soft acceptance of her, and he could feel every movement she made and it was exquisite and he felt everything he understood spinning away from him and he arched his back and thrust deeper and deeper still. She was crying and it was those small broken sobs that brought him a semblance of reason. He was pressed against her womb, so deep, yet it wasn't enough for he wanted his tongue in her mouth, wanted to have her breasts heaving and pressing against his chest.

"Alexandra."

She opened her eyes.

"Please, hold very still. Am I hurting you?"

"Not really hurt, it's just that I don't know what will happen and it is frightening."

"I promise the next time it will be very slow. I swear it to you, but not this time. Please, don't move. If you move I will go insane. Do you understand?"

She looked at him, at sea.

"Just say you understand."

"I understand."

"Good. Don't move. I don't know what's wrong with me. It is beyond my experience. This isn't acceptable to me or—" He felt her muscles clench around him and he groaned and tensed and heaved. He cursed and his eyes closed. He pushed deep then withdrew only to thrust forward, his hands digging into her hips as he lifted her higher.

He yelled when his climax hit him, yelled like a madman, yelled like he'd never yelled before in his life. Then he was flat on top of her and he was kissing her, wanting to consume her, tasting her tears, tasting the warmth of her mouth and still he was moving inside her, and he simply couldn't believe it, couldn't comprehend it and it just wouldn't stop.

When finally he calmed, he stilled above her. He'd done it again. He'd lost himself again and forgotten who he was and what he was. And it was this woman who had brought him to this ludicrous pass and he wouldn't accept it. He frowned. She was crying, her face pale, her hair tousled around her face.

"I'm sorry," he said, and pulled out of her. "Next time, I swear it will be slow and you won't be afraid. I'm sorry."

He stood there, stiff, his chest still heaving, looking at her sprawled legs. "I'm sorry," he said again, "but I can't—"

He turned quickly, his dressing gown flapping open, only to be brought up sharply by a very angry voice. "If you run away again, Douglas Sherbrooke, I swear I will leave Northcliffe Hall and travel to London and tell everyone that you are a pig and not an excellent lover. I will tell all the ladies that you have no control at all, that you're a raving lunatic, that you can't think of anything except yourself. Oh yes, and you're very hairy and you sweat a lot!"

"Damn you, it's your fault! If you weren't so—"

"So what? So extravagantly beautiful? So utterly perfect?"

"Well, no, you're not, not really, it's just that . . . it has to be your fault. No woman has ever before made me into such a fool, such an uncontrolled imbecile, and God knows you're not your sister so—"

"No, I'm not my bloody sister! I'm just me and you barely even can bring yourself to look at me!"

"That's been soundly disproved. All I have to do is look at you and go mad—Well, maybe not your face, but the rest of you and that's still you. You must be a witch. You've brought me low. It must be those breasts of yours. But there are your thighs and belly and . . . What have you done to me?"

"I have done nothing as yet, but I tell you that I am considering taking a sharp knife to your miserable throat!"

"Don't you dare threaten me! Well, blessed hell! The good Lord knows I was much better off before you thrust yourself into my life! At least I knew who I was and why I did what I did."

At least this time, she thought, staring at the newly slammed adjoining door, he had retreated to his own room and not to hers.

She pulled her legs together. She was very sore, deep inside, and her thigh muscles ached and pulled. She was also no longer a virgin. If she hadn't recalled the incredible pleasure of the previous night, she surely would have cursed him now for being an animal. As it was, Alexandra sighed and pulled herself out of the rumpled counterpane. She was a mess, he'd been right about that.

She gave the bell cord a jerk.

It was close to an hour later when Alexandra emerged from her bedchamber to see Douglas standing there, leaning against the opposite wall between two Sherbrooke paintings, his arms folded across his chest.

"You took long enough," he said and pushed off the wall. "I trust you're ready for your breakfast."

"Why not? Perhaps your mother will have put some rat poison in my scrambled eggs."

"I will eat off your plate, just as I slept in your bed. I will be your royal taster. Incidentally, that gown isn't at all what is acceptable for the Countess of Northcliffe."

"Give me a moment, and I will contrive a wheedle."

"No, you don't have to. Since I accepted you, why then, I must also clothe you appropriately. I particularly don't like the way all your gowns flatten down your breasts. Also, it can't be particularly healthful. Not that I want them on display when we select new gowns, but a bit more hint of cleavage would be nice. I won't have to be dependent entirely on my imagination to—"

"What are you doing here?"

He grinned down at her as he offered her his arm. "I thought you just might bolt. You were all but spitting fire at me, lying there on your back with your legs sprawled. I can't allow you to go to London and tell all the ladies how I have behaved." He gave her a bigger grin. "Not, of course, that they would believe you. They wouldn't. They would snigger at you. They would think you a jealous woman and a liar."

She wouldn't look at him. "I will leave for London as soon as I am certain your sister is nowhere around. I shall convince them."

"You won't leave."

"Stop grinding your teeth, it will do you no good. I will do whatever I want to do."

He said very quietly, "You could be with child."

That brought her face around and she gaped up at him. "Oh no, that can't be possible. You can't be that efficient. No, it isn't reasonable and you're making that up just to make me toe the line. Can it?"

"Certainly it's very possible." He placed the flat of his hand on her stomach, splaying his fingers. "I did spill my seed inside you twice. Don't tell me they were both such forgettable experiences that you'd already dismissed them?"

"How could I? The first time you hurt me and the second time you were a mauling savage."

Douglas frowned and removed his hand. "Yes, well, I didn't mean to. And you're lying about the first time. You squealed like a—"

"Be quiet! If that is supposed to pass for an apology, let me tell you, my lord, that it is sorely lacking. At least you didn't blame me again."

He gave her a brooding look. "I would be the same man if you weren't here, so what am I to do?"

"I believe I shall go sharpen a knife."

Douglas was grinning when he looked up to see his cousin approaching from the other end of the corridor. "Ah, if it isn't Tony, you traitorous sod. I would that you stay out of my sight. Where's your wife?"

Tony gave them a sleepy, quite sated smile. "Still asleep, doubtless dreaming of me."

Douglas's grin dissolved into a growl and Alexandra, so furious with him that she couldn't help herself, struck him hard in his belly with her fist.

He sucked in his breath, but smiled over the pain. "It's Tony you're supposed to attack, not me, not your husband, who made you scream with pleasure last night."

"Ah," Tony said, eyeing Alexandra's furiously embarrassed face. "About time, Douglas."

Alexandra couldn't cope with this outrageous man at her side. Had he no modesty, no discretion?

"I suppose it is also my fault that you speak so disgracefully, my lord? Just be quiet, and you too, Tony."

"A wife isn't a bad thing," Tony said, falling into step beside Alexandra. "Always there, beside you, ready to be kissed and stroked and fondled."

"A wife isn't a pet."

"Oh no, she's much more than a pet. What do you say, Douglas?"

It seemed to Alexandra that Douglas was concentrating on the stairs, not listening to Tony. He was probably thinking of Melissande, the clod. He was frowning and said abruptly, "Are Uncle Albert and Aunt Mildred still here?"

Tony yawned and scratched his elbow. "I suppose so. It's your house. You're the bloody host. You should know who is residing under your roof."

"You're here and God knows I don't want you to be."

As a complaint, it lacked heat, and Tony was pleased. He said easily, "Now, now, cousin, I would have thought all would be forgiven this morning. After all, at last you took Alexandra the way a man takes his bride and from the looks of her and the looks of you, I'd say—"

"Don't say it, Tony!"

"Sorry, Alex, you're right. Now, Douglas, I fancy that I will take Melissande to Strawberry Hill on Friday. Does that please you?"

"That's three more days of your damned company!"

"And my sister's," Alexandra said. "You should be pleased with half the bargain. You can sit about and brood and sigh and look melancholy."

"I would be pleased if you would contrive to hold your tongue, madam."

"I've never seen Douglas brood over any woman, Alex. Surely he would have more pride."

"Hello! Good morning, Alexandra! Goodness, you look pale. Didn't you sleep well? Is Douglas picking at you again? Good morning, gentlemen."

Alexandra looked at her enthusiastic young sister-in-law, who looked healthy and vigorous and repellently fit, and sighed.

"Hello, Sinjun."

"Good morning, brat," Tony said.

Douglas grunted at his sister.

"Is your mother in the breakfast room?" Alexandra asked.

"Oh no, it's far too early for Mother. She won't rise until nearly noon. Come along, Alexandra, there's no reason for you to dally. Only Aunt Mildred is there. She eats a lot, you know, so she won't say much. Odd, isn't it, and she's so thin."

Alexandra sighed again.

"Mother has the disposition of a lemon in the morning. Aunt Mildred is more like a prune." Sinjun frowned, then remarked to her brother, "It is difficult to imagine a prune eating a lot."

"You're abominable, you know that, Sinjun?"

"You aren't in a particularly excellent temper this morning, Douglas. Has Tony been twitting you again? Don't pay him any mind. I am so glad you're home and you're married to Alex. Shall we go riding after breakfast?"

"Why not?" said Alexandra. "I wish to mark the closest road to London."

Aunt Mildred was indeed occupied with two scones that dripped honey and butter. She gave Alexandra a look from beneath lowered brows but said nothing.

Alexandra felt Douglas's hand on her elbow, pulling her to a halt. She paused, looking up at him. "It's time you sat where you're supposed to."

She looked at the countess's chair and actually shuddered. "But it isn't necessary and—"

"And nothing. Be quiet and obey me. It will be a new experience for you. Here, sit down."

"You look very fine in that chair," Sinjun said. "Mother will gnash her teeth, but it is only right, you know, that Douglas's wife take precedence. You are the mistress here now. And, according to Douglas, a Sherbrooke must always do his or her duty and be responsible."

"A pity my cousin didn't heed any of the famous Sherbrooke maxims, the perfidious cur."

Aunt Mildred said to the table at large, "She is too small for that chair."

Douglas smiled down the expanse of table to his wife. "Should you like to sit on a pillow?"

Sinjun said, "Actually, Aunt, this chair is quite the right size for Alex. I must say that Mother overflowed it a bit. It is the chair in the formal dining room that must needs be cushioned for Alex."

"You're right, Sinjun," Tony said.

"No one requires your opinion, Anthony," Aunt Mildred said. "You have behaved abominably. Really! Marrying two girls and handing over the wrong one to Douglas."

"The scones are delicious," Sinjun said, and offered one to her aunt.

"Don't, I pray, say that to my wife, Aunt," Tony said. "Why, she lives to breathe the very air I breathe, she pines if I am gone from her for even a veritable instant, she—"

"I believe we should buy Alex a mare today, Douglas," Sinjun said, waving another scone in Tony's direction. "Now, you can't thrash Tony at the breakfast table. Oh, Douglas, I saw Tom O'Malley and he told me all about your and Alex's visit and how you took excellent care of Alex and how you sent him a new bed the very next day. He said it was heaven, it surely was, the first bed he'd ever owned that was longer than he was. Ah, here's Hollis. His Lordship is in need of coffee, Hollis."

"I see that he is indeed in need," Hollis agreed and poured coffee from a delicate silver pot. "Would Your Ladyship care for some coffee?"

Alex jumped. *Ladyship!* She looked into Hollis's kind face. "Some tea, if you please, Hollis. I haven't gotten the taste for coffee."

"I believe, young lady, that you are seated in my chair!"

"Oh dear," Sinjun said, "we're in the suds now and it isn't even close to noon."

The Dowager Countess of Northcliffe presented an impressive portrait of outrage. "Be quiet this instant, Joan, else you will spend the rest of the year in your bedchamber. I can see how you encourage her. Now, as for you, you will remove yourself."

CHAPTER
═16═

A SUDDEN THICK silence swallowed every sound in the breakfast room.
Alex looked toward Douglas. He was sitting perfectly still, his fork in
his right hand, suspended still as a stone in the silence. He gave her a
slight nod. So, he was leaving it to her. He was not going to intervene.
She swallowed, then turned to face her mother-in-law.

She said mildly, "You know, my name isn't 'young lady,' it's Alexandra. To be more precise, it's Lady Alexandra. I'm the daughter of a duke.
It is strange, is it not, that if we were at Carlton House, I would take
precedence over you. Even though I have taken a step down, nuptially
speaking, I still would take precedence. However, you are now my relative, you are much older than I and thus I owe you respect. I have never
understood why age demanded more respect, but it seems to be the way
of things. Now, should you like to call me Alexandra or Lady Northcliffe?"

The Dowager Countess of Northcliffe wasn't a twig to be snapped in
a stiff breeze, yet she saw the steel in the girl seated in her chair—*her
chair*—and was forced to reassess her position. Her son wasn't saying a
word. He wasn't defending her, his own dear mother. The dowager drew
in a deep breath, but she was forestalled by Hollis, who said very quietly,
"My lady, cook has prepared a special nutty bun for you this morning,
topped with frosted almonds and cinnamon. It is delightful, truly, and she
is waiting breathlessly for your opinion. Here, my lady, do sit here in this
lovely chair that gives such a fine view onto the eastern lawn. You can see
that the peacocks are strutting this morning. I have always thought it the
best-placed chair at the table."

The dowager wasn't certain what to do. It was her sham daughter-in-
law who decided her. Alexandra said quickly, clapping her hands in excitement, "Oh, I should very much like to see the peacocks, Hollis. Are
their tails fully fanned? How wonderful! Ma'am, would you mind if I sat
there this morning so that I can look at them? I had remarked before that
the placement of that chair was marvelous."

The dowager said, all three chins elevated, "No, I wish to watch them this morning. They are amusing. Well, Hollis, I am waiting to be seated. I am waiting for my nutty bun."

Douglas was impressed, very impressed. He looked toward Alexandra, but her head was down. That impressed him as well. No crowing from her, no gloating at this small but quite significant victory. She'd managed, with Hollis's help, not to turn the breakfast room into a battleground. He said then, "After breakfast, Alexandra and I are going to Branderleigh Farm to buy her a mare. Sinjun, would you care to accompany us?"

Sinjun had a mouthful of kippers and could only nod. It was Melissande who said gaily from the doorway, "Oh, how delightful! Tony, shouldn't you also like to buy me a mare? I should like a white mare, pure white, I think, with a long thick white mane."

She looked so exquisitely beautiful that Douglas's fork remained for several moments poised an inch from his mouth. Her morning gown was of a soft pale blue, plain, truth be told, but nothing more was required. Her hair had a blue ribbon threaded through the thick fat black curls. She looked fragile, delicate, immensely provocative.

"And a new riding habit, Melissande?" Sinjun said. "Pure white with perhaps a bright green feather in your hat? Oh, how lovely you would look. And seated on a lovely saddle atop a white mare, ah, you would look like a fairy princess."

"White makes her look sallow," Tony said matter-of-factly as he stirred the eggs on his plate. "It was with great relief I realized she wasn't required to wear any more white once she was married to me."

"Sallow! I am never sallow! Doesn't that mean that I would look a nasty sort of yellow? No, it is absurd. I am never, never sallow."

"Are you not, Mellie? In this instance, your mirror isn't telling you the truth. You must learn to trust your husband. I have exquisite taste, you know. Why, I was planning to toss away all your girlish nightwear. No more white. I was thinking of bright blues and greens—all silk and satin, of course—and slippers to match. What do you think, my love?"

Melissande was in something of a bind. "I am not ever yellow," she said, "but I should much enjoy new things."

"I thought you would. After we have visited Strawberry Hill for as long as I wish, why then, we will go to London and you will flail young male hearts with your incomparable beauty and your silks and satins."

"But I want to go to London now, Tony!"

"Should you like a scone, my dear?" asked the Dowager Countess of Northcliffe.

Douglas was looking at Melissande. He was also frowning, Sinjun saw. She smiled into her teacup.

"You must show everyone your lovely watercolors, Mellie," Tony said, watching his bride delicately tear apart a scone with beautiful slender fingers. "Douglas, she has done several of Northcliffe. I think you will be very impressed."

Melissande dropped her scone and smiled brilliantly at her husband, leaning toward him, her eyes sparkling. "Do you really like them, Tony? Truly? It is difficult, you know, what with the ever-changing light, particularly near the maple copse. Shall I try to paint the peacocks that everyone wishes to watch?"

"I don't know," he said, looking at her thoughtfully. "Perhaps you can begin by painting the mare I shall buy you. Not a white mare, please, Mellie, perhaps a bay with white stockings. I don't wish you to be trite."

"Trite! I am never—what precisely do you mean?"

"I mean that you would lack originality. You would be humdrum, run-of-the-mill."

Melissande frowned over this, then gave her husband a very beautiful smile. "Well then, my lord. You shall select a mare for me that is original."

"Yes, I shall. You will contrive to trust me in the future to always do what is best for you."

Melissande nodded slowly.

Sinjun shot Alexandra a wicked look.

The Dowager Countess of Northcliffe said in a very carrying voice to Aunt Mildred, "After breakfast, I wish to speak to you about Lady Juliette's arrival. We must have a small soirée for her, don't you think? Her importance calls for recognition and now that Douglas isn't here to wed her, why then—"

Oh dear, Alexandra thought, staring at Douglas, who looked now ready to spit on his fond mother. She forestalled him, saying quickly, "I should like to meet all the neighbors as well. A party for this Juliette would be just the thing, I think, for all of us to get acquainted."

"The party will be to introduce my wife," Douglas said, his voice as stern and cold as a judge's. "Lady Juliette, as our guest for as few a number of days as we can politely manage, will naturally be invited. Under no circumstance, Mother, will you intimate that it is a gathering in her honor. Do you understand me?"

"The peacocks have folded their tails," said the Dowager Countess of Northcliffe, and rose from the table. Her departure from the breakfast room was majestic.

Tony very nearly choked on his coffee.

Lady Juliette arrived not an hour later, just ten minutes before they would have escaped to Branderleigh Farm.

Sinjun moaned behind Alexandra. Alexandra would have moaned but she was older and a wife and so she straightened her back and drew a deep breath.

"The broom handle is back, I see," Douglas said, as he came to stand beside her at the top of the wide stairs that led to the gravel drive in front of Northcliffe Hall.

"What are you talking about?"

He waved a hand in dismissal and stared at the young woman who was being gently assisted from the ducal carriage by a footman in yellow and white livery. Another footman placed the steps beneath her dainty feet. A sour-faced maid followed her from the carriage, hugging a huge jewelry box to her meager bosom.

"Lady Juliette, daughter of the Marquess of Dacre," the footman called out.

"Do we curtsy?" Sinjun said behind her teeth. "Perhaps request a boon?"

"Be quiet," said Douglas.

The dowager countess was fulsome in her welcome. It was soon apparent that Lady Juliette was not only immensely beautiful, she was also immensely filled with her own importance. She also looked immensely pleased to be at Northcliffe Hall, until she saw Melissande. She was staring at the unexpected and unwelcome vision as the dowager was saying, "And, my dear Juliette, our Douglas here has gotten himself wedded. Such a surprise, but you will understand that—"

Lady Juliette stared blank-faced at the dowager. "He has married? Without seeing me?"

"Yes," said the dowager.

Lady Juliette wanted to leave immediately. She felt humiliated. The wretched earl had married, without even seeing her, Juliette, the most beautiful young lady in three counties. She was closer now to Melissande and her vision was at its sharpest. She went perfectly still. In a spate of inner honesty, Juliette had to admit that this Melissande, the earl's new wife, was possibly the most beautiful young lady in nearly all of England. Inner honesty led instantly to hostility and bone-deep hatred. He'd found and wed a lady more beautiful than she. It wasn't to be borne. He was a cad. He deserved to be skewered on the end of her father's sword.

"Where did Douglas meet you?" she asked, staring Melissande straight in the eye.

"Why he met me some three years ago when he was back in England because he'd been wounded in some battle. I don't recall now which one it was."

"Oh, then you married because of a family agreement? There was a prior entanglement?"

Melissande tilted her lovely head to the side in question. "No, we married because we were vastly suited to each other."

"But that is impossible!"

Douglas and Tony both stepped forward at the same time. Tony said easily, "I fear, my dear Lady Juliette, that you have come to a hasty conclusion. Melissande is my wife. Alexandra, her sister, is Douglas's countess."

There was another moment of heavy silence, then a babble of voices. Douglas finally said loudly, "Everyone hush! Now, Lady Juliette, allow me to introduce you to my wife, Alexandra."

Juliette looked at Alexandra upon the introduction and felt a good deal better. She said with a trilling laugh, "Oh dear, how very charming, my lord. You appear to have found yourself a wife in too short a time. This must have been the result of some old family agreement. Sometimes it is wise to take one's time. But it is still delightful to visit Northcliffe."

"Yes," Sinjun said in a voice loud enough for her to hear, "it is true, isn't it, what Tony said. Juliette is pretty but indeed a distant second to Melissande."

Douglas wanted to box his sister's ears.

Alexandra knew with chilling certainty that this houseguest would not add to any air of festivity.

She smiled when she heard Melissande say to Tony as they were turning to walk back into the hall, "Isn't it the oddest thing! Why, she doesn't like me and yet she doesn't even know me. Tony, I know well enough that I am beautiful, but you know, beautiful perhaps isn't the most important thing . . . well, even if it is, there are other things, such as a person's character, that should be considered, isn't that right?"

Tony kissed his wife in the full sight of anyone who happened to be looking. "You are wonderful and your character, in the not too distant future, should come to rival your beauty."

Sinjun said to Alexandra, "Good. Douglas didn't hear that. Tony is careful, you know, how he doles out the praise and the spurs. He's doing just excellently."

"Does nothing escape you?"

Sinjun looked startled. "Certainly, but this is important, Alex, very important. Douglas must be assisted to see everyone very clearly." She giggled, just like a little girl. "That Juliette is clearly a twit. I wonder if she is stupid as well as conceited? Douglas would like to box her ears even more than mine."

"Don't count on it," Alexandra said. "He is most appreciative of beautiful women."

Sinjun gave her a severe look. "Now it's you who act the twit. Don't talk such nonsense. Do you think we'll be able to leave Juliette to my mother and Aunt Mildred and go to Branderleigh Farm?"

"I sincerely hope so."

They weren't able to escape. For two interminable hours, Alexandra listened to a recounting of each of Juliette's conquests from her London Season. She turned finally to Melissande, who was examining one of Tony's fingers. "I understand that you are beyond having a Season now, Lady Rathmore. You were fortunate to find a husband after so many unsuccessful endeavors."

"Yes, 'tis true," Tony said in a mournful voice. "Just look at her. So hagged, so ancient, so long in the tooth. It was difficult for me to pull her off the shelf, she was set so far back and so very high up. It required all my resolution to bring myself to the sticking point. Even now I try to con vince her to wear a pillow sheet over her head, to spare sensibilities, don't you know. Aye, I wed her because I felt pity for her. I suppose that every other man on earth must also feel pity for her for they look at her from thirty feet away and become fools and addle-brained."

To Alexandra's surprise, she saw Melissande bite Tony's finger, then lightly rub her cheek against his palm. Then she looked at Douglas, who looked the perfect picture of a polite nobleman, standing with his shoulders against the mantel, his arms crossed over his chest. He was staring from Juliette to Melissande to Alexandra. There was no expression on his face, at least none that she could read. Comparisons in this instance brought on severe depression. It was time to do something, not just sit here like a stupid log.

She rose, smiled, and extended her hand to Juliette. "If you will forgive me I must see to our dinner. If there is anything you need, don't hesitate to ask. Welcome to Northcliffe."

She left the room, aware that her mother-in-law's face was brick red with annoyance. She'd lied; she didn't try to find Mrs. Peacham. She knew well enough that the dinner cook would present would make even a skinny ascetic eat until he groaned.

She went to the gardens where all the Greek statues were displayed. The grounds were in abysmal shape. She would have to speak to Douglas. She needed his permission to direct the Northcliffe gardeners, the lazy clods. There was a particularly beautiful rosebush that was being choked to death with weeds. Alexandra didn't hesitate, for her gown was old and quite unappetizing, as Douglas had told her. She dropped to her knees and began weeding. Soon, she was humming. Soon after that, she felt calm and even-keeled. She forgot Juliette; she even managed to forget her mother-in-law.

It began to drizzle lightly. The earth softened even more and she dug and plucked and smoothed down and lovingly tended. She was unaware of the trickle of water that fell off the end of her nose.

Finally, the rosebush was free. It seemed to glow in front of her eyes. The blooms were redder, larger, the leaves greener and more lush.

She sat back on her heels and smiled.

"My God."

She turned, still smiling, to see Douglas standing over her, eyes narrowed, his hands on his hips.

"Hello. Isn't it beautiful? And so much happier now, so much more healthy."

Douglas looked at the damned rosebush and saw that it was true. Then he looked at his filthy wife, her hair wilted with rain over her forehead, and forgot the rosebush. "Come along, it's time for you to dress for dinner."

"How did you find me?" she asked as she got to her feet and swiped her dirt-blackened hands on her already ruined gown.

"Melissande. She said that while she painted you made things grow. I have half a score of gardeners. There is no need for you to become quite so dirty."

She gave him a severe look that made him smile. "These gardeners are taking advantage of you, my lord. These beautiful gardens haven't been touched in far too long a time. It is appalling."

"I shall speak to Danvers about it."

"He's the head gardener?"

"No, he's my steward. He isn't here at the moment. His father is ill and he is visiting his ailing father in Couthmouth."

"It is the head gardener who is the one responsible, my lord."

"Fine, you may speak with Strathe whenever it pleases you. Tell him you have my permission. Come along now, you must do something about yourself."

"There is not much that can be done."

Douglas frowned. "I have wondered every time I see your sister why it is that she is always so superbly garbed and you are not."

"I would have had new gowns had I had a Season. Instead, Tony married me to you and thus there was no Season and no new gowns. Do not believe Melissande to be spoiled and pampered. Most of her gowns are from her last Season."

"I see," he said and Alexandra wondered just what it was that he saw.

Dinner that evening with two diamonds in the same room, eating at the same table, was a trial. Juliette spoke of Lord Melberry who was smitten with her and gave Melissande a superior smile. Melissande shrugged and said he'd bored her with his interminable talk of his succession houses. After all, commenting on the fatness of grapes paled after ten minutes.

Juliette told of turning down Lord Downley's proposal and how wounded he had been. Melissande laughed and said that Lord Downley had proposed to every woman who claimed to have more than a thousand pounds dowry. On and on it went.

At last Alexandra was able to rise and motion for the ladies to leave the dining room. She didn't notice that her mother-in-law gave her a very annoyed look. She immediately went to the pianoforte and sat down. She played some French ballads, trying to ignore the verbal flotsam around her.

"My parents are very fond of me," Juliette announced. "They gave me a beautiful name. Lord Blaystock told me they must have known I would be so beautiful." She turned very gray eyes toward Alexandra, who began to play a bit more vigorously. She raised her voice. "You parents must not have wished for what they got with you. Your name is manly, don't you agree, my lady?"

"Which lady?" Sinjun inquired. "There are so many here."

"You are very young to still be allowed amongst the adults, are you not? I refer, of course, to Alex. Why it is a man's nickname, to be sure."

"I have a good friend whose horse is named Juliette."

"Joan! Hush and apologize to Lady Juliette!"

"Yes, Mother. Excuse me, Lady Juliette. But it is a very nice horse, a mare actually, and she has the softest nose and the roundest belly and her tail, it is lush and thick, and twitches whenever there are flies or stallions around."

Douglas overheard the last and he laughed, he couldn't help it. His sister was the best weapon he'd ever had in his arsenal and he'd never before realized her wondrous capabilities. He was pleased that he had allowed her to remain downstairs this evening.

"Joan! Douglas, speak to your sister."

"Hello, Sinjun. Pour me a cup of tea, if you please. Alexandra, continue your playing. You are quite accomplished. It pleases me."

Tony went to sit beside his wife.

The dowager, seeing the evening spiraling downward, announced that whist was to be enjoyed. Douglas, grinning, asked Alexandra to be his partner.

Their opponents were Tony and Juliette.

Douglas wondered if his wife played as skillfully as she'd hinted. He wasn't left long in doubt. She didn't count all that well, but she played with verve and imagination, with a strategy remarkably similar to his own. That annoyed him as well as pleased him and he wondered, but just for an instant, how well Melissande would play if she wore a bag over her head. He and Alexandra won most hands. Tony groaned good-naturedly even when Juliette trumped a good lead or whined about a valueless hand.

Douglas had to hold his cards in front of his mouth so that no one would remark the unholy grin that overtook him when Alex did Juliette in, and the twit didn't have the brains to keep quiet. Oh no, she squawked. She threw down her remaining cards, rose and actually stomped her foot.

"However could you have known that I held the king of spades? Why, it is impossible. Why would you lead the ace, a bad lead surely? It is luck, all of it. Or it is that mirror I have been remarking."

That was quite beyond the line. Douglas rose himself and said in a very cold voice, "I believe you are fatigued, Lady Juliette. Surely such unmeasured words could not come from a well-rested mouth."

Juliette sucked in her breath and held her tongue, a difficult proposition in any circumstance, and allowed a very solicitous Uncle Albert to lead her out of the drawing room.

"She is beautiful," Sinjun said dispassionately, "but she is so very stupid. A pity."

"Why a pity, brat?" Tony asked, grinning over at her.

"Some poor gentleman will wed her, all enthralled with her beauty, and then wake up to find he's married to a stupid woman who hasn't any kindness."

Melissande came to stand beside her husband. Her hand rested lightly on his shoulder and his hand came up unconsciously to pat hers. "I pity you for playing against Alex. She is a killer. Papa taught her. Reginald tried to teach her to cheat, but she never did that particularly well. She always turned red whenever she tried."

"She needs to learn to count better," Douglas said.

"I venture to say that you will be responsible for teaching her many new things, cousin," Tony said, and rose, bowing to Alexandra, then saying his goodnights to the remaining company.

Alexandra actually sighed once she and Douglas were mounting the stairs.

"It was a long evening, I'll grant you that."

"Yes," she said, her voice suddenly clipped. Oh dear, would he insist upon coming to her again? Her step lagged.

Douglas stopped in the middle of the long corridor, took her shoulders in his hands and said very clearly, "Let me make this perfectly clear to you so you don't have to sigh again. You only have one choice. Do you wish to be in my bed or shall I be in yours?"

And even then, he took the choice from her. He lightly shoved her into his bedchamber, then closed and locked the door. He stood there watching her, his look brooding in the sluggish firelight.

"I will not frighten you tonight. I will be calm and subtle. I will control your pleasure just as I will control my own. I am an experienced man, a man of the world. I will be as tranquil and placid in my movements as that fire. Do you understand?"

She stared from him to the fire and back again.

"Say you understand, dammit."

"I understand." Then, she held out her arms to him, an unplanned gesture, and in the next instant, he'd lifted her and was carrying her to his bed. He came down over her and his hands were wild on her gown, pulling and jerking and ripping it to shreds. "It doesn't matter, dammit!" Then there were no words for he wouldn't stop kissing her. When he bared her breasts, his eyes blazed and he moaned even as he nuzzled her with his mouth, even as he suckled her. He was trembling, lurching over her, trying to cover her with his mouth and hands, all of her, even as he was jerking away her clothes and his.

And when she was naked beneath him, he had to rise to get off his trousers. He wasn't very graceful; he was frantic and ripped his britches. Then he was naked, splendidly naked. His body glowed in the firelight and she said, "You are so beautiful, Douglas."

"Oh no, no," he said, but he didn't fall on her this time. He pulled her legs apart and came down between them and lifted her to his mouth. "I won't allow you to hold back from me this time. No, I won't allow it. Do you like that, Alexandra? Dear Lord, you're hot. Yes, you're trembling. Please, tell me what you're feeling."

She moaned and dug her fingers in his hair, pressing him closer and closer still and she felt his warm breath on her flesh and it was too much. She screamed, her back bowing off the bed.

Douglas felt her nails digging into his shoulder, felt the frantic clenching of her muscles, and he was drawn into her pleasure, deep and deeper still. He didn't wait for her to calm. He thrust into her, lifting her as he rose. "Wrap your legs around my waist," he said once, then again, for she was oblivious, held in pleasure and surprise.

Her arms were around his neck and her mouth found his and as he came sharply up into her, his hands big and warm on her buttocks, she kissed him again and again, moaning softly, wringing all semblance of control from him.

He carried her to the large carpet in front of the hearth and just as he knew he would soon be lost, he also knew that he wouldn't be able to stand with the force of it, he lowered her to her back and came so deeply inside her he touched her womb.

When he came to his release, Alexandra was beyond anything in her experience. He heaved in her arms and she stroked him, feeling powerful and warm and she said without thinking, "I love you, Douglas. I've loved you forever."

He groaned, then fell to the side, drawing her against him. She felt the heat of the dying fire against her back and legs. She felt the strength of his arms around her waist. She felt the warmth of his breath against her temple.

But she felt cold in the next moment, for she realized what she'd said to him. She realized that he had remained quiet. She realized the power she'd given him. She felt his seed, wet on her thighs, and tried to move.

"No," he said, his voice low and slurred. "No." He scooped her up in his arms and carried her to his bed. "No," he said again as he pushed her between the covers. "I want my seed to stay inside you." He came in with her then, and covered them, holding her close. In the next moment, he was sleeping, his breath deep and rhythmic.

There was nothing like a young fool, she thought, and gave it up, nestling her face against his chest, feeling the hair tickle her nose. At least he hadn't tried to run from the room. She kissed his collarbone, letting her tongue glide downward to the small male nipples. She licked him and he sighed, deeply asleep, his arms tightening around her back, and she watched her breasts pressing against his chest, and she knew there was no going back now. She slept.

CHAPTER
═17═

"WHAT ARE YOU doing?"

Douglas turned to see Alexandra standing in the doorway. "I'm seeing exactly how bad this situation really is."

"But you're going through my clothes!"

"How will I know what you need if I don't? Curse that meddling twit of a sister of mine, but she was saying that if she was to attend that damned soirée, she must have a new gown. Then the chit shook her head and said no, she couldn't. Mind you, she spoke in the most mournful sainted voice you can imagine. Yes, she milked it wonderfully, saying it wouldn't be right, not since you didn't have anything new to wear. Then she had the gall to look at me as though I were abusing you. I, who assured you that you could wheedle me!"

"Just stop it, Douglas! I don't need or want any new gowns, it's ridiculous, and Sinjun should be smacked."

"The girl was right in this instance. Come on, Alexandra, be reasonable, if you please."

"All right, perhaps I do need a new ball gown, but I have my own money, Douglas, I don't want you to—"

"What? That infamous thirty pounds again? My dear girl, that wouldn't purchase the bodice for a flat-chested girl. Merciful heavens, the amount of groats alone to cover your upper works will empty my pockets. No, don't squawk. Be quiet. My mind is made up. I've arranged for a seamstress from Rye to arrive later this morning. She will take your measurements and then I will select a proper gown for you for the little soirée next Wednesday. From the looks of the remainder of these gowns, I will need to take you to Madame Jordan in London." Douglas snapped the door to the armoire closed. He pulled it open again, and began pawing through her slippers. "Ah, as I thought. You need coverings from your toes to the top of your head."

"Douglas," she said, desperation in her voice, "I don't need for you to buy me things, truly. All that talk about wheedling, it was silly jesting,

nothing more. Sinjun was just meddling, as you said. You're right about
the ball gown and I thank you, but no more, please. I don't think—"

"Be quiet."

"No, I won't be quiet! I am not one of your retainers you can order
about. Listen to me, I don't wish to be beholden on you, I don't—"

"Ah, so you would rather shame me wearing your damned rags.
Blessed hell, woman! I will not be called niggardly; I will not allow people to think I keep you on a skinny string. I imagine the gossip about us
is confused enough without adding the fact that my wife looks like a
dowd."

"But you don't particularly care what people think," she said slowly,
eyeing him. "I'm not a dowd. I only resemble a dowd if I have the mis-
fortune to stand beside Melissande. In truth, my gowns just aren't quite
up to snuff."

"Well, the chances are you will be standing next to her, so we must do
something. I have also decided that I will have your breasts kept well covered, no matter the cost. Not flattened down or bound or anything like
that, but camouflaged just a bit, giving only a hint of your endowments.
Perhaps even a hint is too much. I will have to give this more thought.
There are too many gentlemen who would ogle you and make you uncomfortable. Further, I won't accept any argument from you. Don't you
realize that if you allow your gowns to be at all low-cut, gentlemen will
be able to see you all the way down to your toes?"

"That's absurd!"

"No. You're not all that tall, and the result is that most gentlemen
would have the advantage of staring down at you. I will not have your
breasts on display for all those bounders to salivate over, so you can just
stop arguing with me."

"But I'm not arguing with you!"

"Ah, what would you call it? You're shouting your head off, yelling
like a bloody fishwife."

"All right! Take me to London, take me to see this Madame Jordan,
spend all your groats on my back!"

"Ha! Don't you mean your front?"

"Oh goodness. Douglas, please."

He grinned then.

"Blessed hell, you're as evil as Sinjun, damn you!"

"Not entirely. I see you've appropriated one of the favored Sherbrooke
curses. I've tried to curb my tongue around you but you've learned it
nonetheless. From whom, I won't demand to know. We will leave for
London after the soirée, all right? No, don't argue with me. You've al-

ready agreed and I hold you to it. Also, by then, that traitorous sod will have left with Melissande."

"And there's no reason for you to remain here if she isn't."

"Your syntax is nothing short of spectacular and you don't know what you're talking about. Now, if you continue to stand there, thrusting your breasts toward me, I will rip off that gown and then you will be late to meet with the seamstress."

He left her standing in the middle of her bedchamber, staring at nothing in particular, saying toward the armoire, "He is a strange man."

If Alexandra fancied Douglas would relent and allow her to be alone with Mrs. Plack, the seamstress from Rye, she was soon to see her grievous error. Sinjun lounged on a chaise longue and Douglas very calmly sat in the wing chair, crossed his legs at the ankles and folded his arms over his chest and said, "Pray begin, Mrs. Plack."

She wanted to order both of them out of her bedchamber but she knew from short but powerful experience that when Douglas had made up his mind, he couldn't be budged. She stood stiff as a stone while Mrs. Plack measured her. She raised her arms, stretched her full height; then she tried to slump just a bit so her breasts would not poke out so much, which made Douglas say sharply, "No, straighten your back!"

She did. Then she was allowed to remain while Douglas perused fashion plates until he found a gown that pleased him. "Except," he said, stroking his jaw, "remove that flounce at the hemline. It's too much. Ah, yes, the smooth lines and the raised waist will make her appear taller. Oh, and hoist up the neckline at least an inch."

"But, my lord, it will make Her Ladyship look provincial! This is the latest fashion from Paris!"

"An inch," His Lordship said again. "Raise it an inch."

"May I see?" Alexandra asked sweetly.

"Certainly," Douglas said and took her arm, drawing her to his side. "Do you agree that this will become you vastly?"

She stared down at the gown and swallowed. It was exquisite. "What color did you have in mind?"

"A soft pomona green with a dark green overskirt."

"I do not wish to look provincial."

Mrs. Plack heaved a sigh of relief. "Good. I shall leave the neckline where it is then."

"No," said Douglas. "I want her to be admired but I don't want her to be stared at."

Alexandra grinned up at him, saying nothing. She looked at his mouth and her eyes darkened. She loved his mouth, the feel of his mouth on her own; she saw his hands clench. She loved the strength of his hands, the frenzy of his mouth and his hands when he touched her, when he turned wild and savage and uncivilized, when she became the most important thing in the world to him.

"Stop it," he said beneath his breath.

"Hi ho," Sinjun said, yawning hugely. "I think you have chosen wisely, brother. Now, don't you think we can go buy Alexandra that mare?"

"You will remain and be measured for your own gown, Sinjun. I've selected it and Mother has given her approval. No, don't try to thank me—"

"I was going to take you to task for being so high-handed! I should like to choose my own gown."

"No, you're too young, too green. Don't argue with me. Alexandra and I will see you later. Thank you, Mrs. Plack. Don't forget, an inch."

"You were high-handed, you know," Alexandra said to her husband as they walked toward the stables.

He brushed a fly from his buckskin thigh. "You need it as does my impertinent sister." He kept walking, speaking quietly now, not looking at her as he said, "On your return to the Hall, I will take you back to that charming stream. I have decided that it is bedchambers with those big beds that make me lose my rationality and my perspective. Yes, it is the place rather than you that is responsible for turning me into a man with absolutely no finesse or *savoir-faire*.

"We will go to the stream and I will remain myself. I will take off your clothes, lay you down on your back and touch you and kiss your breasts and fondle you between your legs, and I will smile and talk to you while I caress you. Perhaps we will discuss the situation in Naples, from both Napoleon's and the Royalists' points of view. And I will wax brilliant because I am concentrating on my words and not on your body. My control will be uplifting, my experience will be at my brain's command. Then, when I decide that I wish to continue with you, why, I will do so, and I will go slowly and do all the things to you I haven't taken the time to do up to now. Well, more time, in any case, and you will scream and bellow until you are hoarse. And you will be very pleased that I am gentleman enough to have figured all this out."

He turned then to look down at her. She looked both amazed and incredulous and her face was hectic with color. He laughed. "You will be able to scream as loudly as you wish. There will be no one around save a few ducks and birds. Yes, I enjoy hearing you cry out in the middle of the day with the sun on your face and me pressing you into the warmth of the earth."

She poked him in his belly and he just laughed some more. She wanted to tell him that he could be as savage as he wished, but she hesitated, and then he said, "You will enjoy me even more when I return to being an excellent lover." She wondered how that could possibly be true.

At Branderleigh Farm they found a three-year-old mare of Barb descent whose sire was Pander of Foxhall Stud. She was spirited, soft-mouthed, long in the back, and black as midnight with a white star on her nose. She tried to bite Alexandra on her shoulder, Alexandra jerked away in time, and the mare then butted her chin with her nose. It was love at first sight.

"That's what I will call her," Alexandra said, skipping in delight next to Douglas after he had finalized the sale with a Mr. Crimpton. The new mare was tied to the back of the gig.

"Midnight? Blackie?"

"Oh no, that would be trite, and you know how much we must avoid that accusation!"

He handed her up into the gig then walked around to climb up into his seat. He click-clicked the horse forward. "Well?" he asked again some moments later.

"Her name is Colleen."

"There is no Irish blood in her."

"I know. She is an original."

He grinned. He realized he felt marvelous. He clicked the horse faster. He wanted to get to the stream and prove that he was the most controlled of lovers. He marshaled quite logical arguments for Napoleon's invasion of Naples while he drove. He was scarce aware that she was seated next to him. It was splendid. He was himself again.

He helped her down from the gig, and just that—the mere closing his hands around her waist to lift her down— sent his hands to her breasts and his mouth to hers and he kissed her and touched her, and was gone. He ripped her chemise to shreds. It was hard and fast and when he finally managed to raise himself off Alexandra, his heart still pounding so hard he could hear it, he said numbly, "I truly can't stand this, truly I can't. Blessed hell, it is too much for a man to suffer. There, you have even wrung the Sherbrooke curse out of me and I have tried hard not to use profanity in front of you. I've failed. Jesus, I'm nothing but a rutting stoat, a stupid man with no sense and fewer brains."

As for Alexandra, she doubted she would be able to move. He'd taken her quickly, as usual, and he'd been so deep inside her after he'd brought her to pleasure, making her scream as she lurched up, shafts of sunlight splashing through the oak branches onto her face. Her new mare had whinnied in response. Douglas had panted and heaved and said things to her that she guessed were very sexual, but she hadn't understood all of them. It was odd of her, but she rather wanted to ask him to translate so she could say them to him and understand what she was saying.

"Yes," he said, "far too much for me to bear." Then he leaned down and

kissed her. She parted her lips for him and it began again. "Damnation!"
he howled to the pure sweet air, then kissed her again and he was hard inside her and pushing more and more deeply only to withdraw, to find her
with his fingers and his mouth and it went on and on as she spun out of
control and yet turned inward, to him, to burrow inside his passion. She
didn't want him to be civilized; she didn't want him to do anything differently. She wanted him to be a pig.

She told him again that she loved him between kisses on his jaw, his
shoulder, his throat, her hands feverish on his chest and downward on his
belly. Her fingertips touched his sex and he shuddered.

"No, not again." He gently pushed her down onto her back. He stared
down at her, his eyes hard. "No you don't," he said. "Heed me well,
Alexandra. A woman says she loves a man because she has to justify her
own passion to herself. If she is abandoned, if she finds great pleasure,
why then, it must be love, not lust. You, particularly, are young and romantic; it is very important that you try to wrap your bodily pleasures in
more inspiring packaging. It is the way your female brain functions, bolstered by all those trashy novels you have doubtless swooned over, but
you will get over it if you will just be reasonable."

"You absurd clod!" Alexandra sent her fist hard into his jaw. He was
balanced on his elbow and the surprise of her blow sent him over onto his
back.

"You stupid boor! You mindless rutting stoat!"

"Well, the last of it is true, I already laid claim to that."

"Go to the devil!"

She was up and jerking on her clothing, panting and heaving, so furious with him that she was trembling.

"Alexandra, be reasonable. Stop it."

She didn't. If anything she jerked so hard a button went flying.

He came up on his elbows, lying stretched out, naked and sweating
and feeling very relaxed. He was even grinning at her. "Alexandra, why
become so distraught at the simple truth? Love is a poet's nonsensical
plaything and if he can bend one silly word to rhyme with another, why
all the better. It is as insubstantial as a dream, as meaningless as the rain
that flows through your fingers. Don't use it as a crutch or as an excuse
to enjoy me and yourself, you don't need it. You and I do well together in
bed. You respond fully to me, even though I seem to have this rutting-
stoat disease with you. Don't feel you have to cover it up with romantic
nonsense."

She was dressed now, though her stockings and boots were still on the
ground. Her hands on her hips, she said very slowly, very calmly, "I knew
I shouldn't have told you. I knew that you don't feel at all the same way

about me and I was afraid it would give you power over me. I was quite wrong. You care so little for me that power doesn't even come into it. I didn't realize you would mock my words and my feelings, that you would make sport at what I feel. Your cynicism is pathetic, Douglas. If it makes you feel any better, if it makes you feel as if your beliefs are justified, well, I don't love you at this moment. I should like to cosh you with a hammer at this moment. I would like to kick you on your backside. Instead, I think I will punish you in another way." She picked up his boots and his trousers and ran with them toward the stream. She stopped and threw them as hard and as far as she could.

Douglas bounded up to grab for his clothes, but he was too late. "Blessed hell!" He jumped into the stream to grab his boots and trousers and Alexandra untied the horse, bounded into the gig, and was off in the next moment. His shirt and jacket lay beside her on the plank seat.

She heard him yelling at her and just click-clicked the horse faster. He couldn't catch her, not in his bare feet, and he could whistle to the horses all he wanted, they wouldn't pay him any heed. Alexandra smiled. The cynical bounder. Retribution tasted very sweet.

Thirty minutes later, Douglas passed the yew bush that flew his shirt like a white flag of surrender. He'd wondered where his shirt had gone to. She'd taken it, damn her eyes. He was hot, sweating, and wished he had her neck between his hands, just for an instant, just long enough for him to squeeze and make her face turn blue.

Damned twit. Lust, good full-powered bone-deep lust, and like every other female in the history of the world, she had to make it into something more grand, more elevated than it really was. Doubtless if he encouraged her, she would begin to wax eloquent about a spiritual joining, a mating of their very souls. It wasn't to be borne.

His shirt stuck to his sweaty back. The afternoon sun was grueling. Another quarter of a mile and he spotted his coat flying from the lower branch of a maple tree.

When he finally stomped up the wide front steps of Northcliffe Hall, he was ready to kill.

Hollis greeted him, looking as bland as a bowl of broth. "Ah, Your Lordship is back from your nature walk. Her Ladyship told us how you lauded the lovely tulip trees that were bowed so gracefully over the stream; she said you strained your neck to see to the top of the poplar trees alongside the trails. She said you were humming with the lovely song thrushes and smelling the lilac flowers. She said you then wished to commune with the fishes and thus swam in the stream. She said how very kind you were to allow her to continue back here since she had the

headache. You look a bit hot, my lord. Should you like a lemonade, perhaps?"

Douglas knew that Hollis was lying and he knew that Hollis knew that
he knew. Why did everyone insist upon protecting her? What about him?
He'd been the one to have to leap into the stream and pull his boots from
bottom silt. He'd been the one to trudge three miles back to the Hall.
Lemonade?

"Where is Her Ladyship?"

"Why, she is communing with the nature that's confined here at Northcliffe, my lord. She is in the gardens."

"I thought you said she had a bloody headache."

"I fancy she cured that."

"Just so," Douglas said. The thought of her sitting at her ease on a
chaise longue, cool and sweat-free, would have sent him into a rage.
Douglas drew himself up. He shook his head at himself. All of this, it was
ridiculous.

A month ago he'd been a free man.

Two weeks ago and he'd thought himself married to the most beautiful woman in England.

And now he was shackled to a twit he'd never seen before and who tortured him. She also turned him into a wild man. She tortured him very well.

In the east gardens, Tony leaned negligently against the skinny trunk
of a larch, his eyes on his sister-in-law. She was filthy, sweat darkening
her hair, her hands were black with dirt. She was murdering a weed, her
movements jerky, and she was muttering to herself.

"I think things march along just fine," he said.

Alexandra paused and raised her face to Tony's. "Nothing is marching
anywhere, Tony. He doesn't like me, truly."

"You mistake the matter, my dear. He's accepted you as his wife. Too,
I've seen him look at you. I've seen him look violent with need and re-
plete with pleasure."

"He hates that. Until today, he blamed me for his loss of control whenever he touched me. Just two hours ago, he decided to blame the bedchambers and the beds. He planned to discuss philosophy or war or
something whilst he loved me." She sighed. "When that failed, he . . .
well, now he is probably intent on finding me and wringing my neck."

"What you did to him was splendid, Alex. I wish I could have seen him
dash naked into the stream to save his pants and boots. As I recall there
are many rocks to trip the naked foot."

"I know it isn't proper to speak like this, Tony, but I have no one else.
I was a fool. I told him that I loved him. I couldn't help it, it just came
out of my mouth. He told me that all I feel, that all he feels is just lust.

He said that love is nonsense and that the notion of a spiritual joining makes him physically ill."

"He really said that?"

"Not exactly. I am simply making the words fit his feelings more precisely. Actually what he said was worse—more insulting, more cynical."

"But now he is your husband and I swear to you, Alex, where a man finds pleasure, other pleasures usually follow, if the man and woman are at all reasonable. You love Douglas. Half the battle is won. More than half, for he goes crazy whenever he touches you. You will see. The soirée is tomorrow night. Melissande and I will leave the next day. You won't have to worry about my lovely witch any longer. Besides, I do believe that Douglas is already beginning to wonder how he would have dealt with her."

"I can't believe she allows you to call her Mellie."

"I dislike the name immensely. Mellie, bah! It sounds like an overweight girl with spots on her face. However, it is important that she bend to me completely. If I wish to call her pug, why then, she must accept it since it comes from me, her husband, her master."

Alexandra could but stare at him. "You are terrifying, Tony."

He grinned down at her. "No, not really. As much as I love your sister, I will not allow her to have the upper hand. Ah, I believe I see your errant husband striding this way. Normally a man will pause—just a moment, you understand—to look at the Greek statues, but not Douglas. He looks fit to kill. This should be interesting. Should you like me to draw him off?"

"No, he would challenge you to a duel or assault you right here." She shook her head, "Then I should have to attack you again, Tony."

"Very true. Ah, we are saved. Here is Melissande, carrying her watercolors. Now she is pausing to look at the statues and not with an eye to painting them either, I vow. She and Douglas are now met up and speaking. He must control his bile. He must be charming, no matter he wants to kill you. Yes, he appears to have stopped gnashing his teeth. You know, Alex, I have an idea, a thoroughly reprehensible idea."

She looked at him and understood and quickly said, "Oh no, Tony. It wouldn't work, it wouldn't—"

Douglas and Melissande came around a thick yew bush to see Tony on his knees in front of Alexandra, his arms around her, kissing her hair.

Douglas froze.

Melissande jerked back as if she'd been struck. She threw her watercolors to the ground, and yelling like a banshee, ran to the couple, grabbed Tony's hair and yanked with all her might. He fell onto his back, grinned up at her, only Melissande wasn't looking at him, but at her sister.

"You miserable husband stealer!" she yelled and threw herself on

Alexandra, knocking her over backward. "How dare you, Alex! You have a husband, and you have the nerve to try to take mine!" She yanked at Alexandra's hair.

"Stop it! For God's sake—"

Douglas grabbed Melissande and picked her up, shoving her toward Tony, who caught her and held her arms to her sides. "I'll make her bald, I'll make her two inches shorter!"

"Hush, Mellie, hush now."

Melissande turned on her husband and yelled not an inch from his nose, "Don't call me that horrid name! What were you doing, kissing her hair? I have beautiful hair, if you want to kiss hair, you will kiss mine! You faithless lout, I'll pull out all her hair and then you'll—Don't you dare try to kiss me now, you miserable clod!"

Douglas heard the yelling behind him, but he didn't move. He dropped to his haunches in front of his wife. She was shaking her head, as if to see if it were still on her shoulders. She was filthy, her face streaked with dirt, her eyes watering.

"Are you all right?"

"No, my scalp is on fire. I hadn't realized Melissande was so strong."

"It serves you right."

"Yes, quite probably, it does."

"I fancy it didn't occur to Tony that she would attack you. It's obvious his plan wasn't at all well thought through."

She looked up at him and saw that he knew exactly what had happened. "No, I imagine he was surprised. But pleased at the same time."

"Yes. Come along now, you're a mess, a greater one than I am. I won't bathe with you or we'll remain messes."

They rose and turned to see Tony kissing his wife very passionately.

Douglas said mildly, "Yes, Tony proved something, didn't he? Something he hadn't counted on. Now he is greatly pleased with himself."

Tony made love to his wife there next to a Greek statue and it was as violent and urgent a performance as his cousin would have given. Melissande actually didn't give a single thought to her lovely gown or to grass stains or to possible interlopers coming along. She lost her reason, all of it, and it was quite delicious. When she told him she loved him and she would kill any woman who tried to take him away from her, he grinned like a blissful fool and said with a good deal of satisfaction in his voice, "I believe that I love you as well. Your fierceness pleases me, as does your jealousy. Yes, you please me, very much."

As for Douglas: He sat brooding in his copper bathtub, his valet standing over him, wringing his hands, bemoaning the ruined boots and trousers.

CHAPTER
═══ 18 ═══

TYSEN SHERBROOKE STOOD tall and proud as a rooster, his eyes reverent as he said to Alexandra, "I would like to present Melinda Beatrice Hardesty. My sister-in-law, Lady Alexandra."

So this was the flat-chested simpering pious young woman Sinjun detested. Alex smiled at her. "I am charmed, Miss Hardesty. Tysen has told us all so much about you. I hope you will enjoy yourself this evening."

Melinda Beatrice, who knew her own worth, was nevertheless a bit shy with a countess, even though she appeared to be not a month older than Alex was. She gave her a graceful curtsy and said in her prim voice, "Thank you, ma'am."

"I trust you and Tysen will enjoy the dancing."

"Mr. Sherbrooke has asked my mama if I may dance with him. She has refused, naturally, for I'm not out yet."

"A pity," Alex said. "Perhaps you can play cards instead."

"Oh no, ma'am. Why, that wouldn't be at all proper and my mama would be most upset. Mama says that only wastrels play cards."

"Well," Alexandra said, shooting the love-slain Tysen a harassed look, "perhaps you and Mr. Sherbrooke can take a turn in the gardens. It's warm tonight so your dear mama surely can't object and there are so many adults just feet away to protect your reputation."

"Yes, I should like that," said Miss Hardesty. "If Mama won't object."

"What a twit," Douglas remarked as he watched his brother lead Miss Hardesty away. "I do hope Tysen will outgrow her. He goes back to Oxford soon, thank God." He looked back to his wife, whose bodice had been raised only a half-inch and frowned. He'd overheard Sinjun laughing about it. He'd said nothing, however, for when Alexandra had come earlier into the drawing room, looking toward him like a hopeful puppy, he was too busy thinking how lovely she looked to say anything. The green made her skin as creamy and white as her belly, and her hair, thick and redder than sin, was piled artfully atop her head, with several glossy tendrils trailing over her shoulder. He looked down at the expanse of rich white flesh and felt himself begin to shake. "Let's dance, otherwise I might be tempted to thrust my hand down your bosom."

"All right."

"All right what?"

She gave him a siren's smile. "Whichever you choose, Douglas."

He struggled with himself. As for Alexandra, she tried to keep down the bubble of laughter. As he continued to struggle, she stared with no little pride and relief over the ballroom that was gaily festooned with hanging blue, white, and gold crepe. Potted plants and thick bouquets were in every corner and on every tabletop, their scent fragrant in the warm evening air. There were at least fifteen couples dancing and another thirty standing or seated about the perimeter of the dance floor. Every invitation had been accepted except for Sir James Evertson, who'd had the bad manners to die just that morning. Everything was perfect and she had helped organize all of it. There was plentiful food and the champagne punch had been pronounced fit even for the pickiest matrons by Aunt Mildred. For the first time, Alexandra truly felt like the mistress of Northcliffe Hall. It was a heady feeling and she loved it. Her mother-in-law had harumphed a bit at some of her orders, but hadn't gainsaid her, at least to her face. Yes, she'd proved she could deal with her mother-in-law, at least in this.

She sought out Melissande, who looked like a princess, dancing with a young man who looked ready to collapse at her feet and pant.

Douglas, having finished his struggle, said finally, sounding just a bit shocked, "Are you trying to tease me, Alexandra?"

She smiled up at her husband. "What were we speaking about? You took so long to reply. Oh yes, it is your choice, Douglas. You insist that all I feel for you is lust. Well, then, since you're older than I, and far more experienced, I expect you're right. I accept that now. You're staring down at my bosom and it is only lust you feel. Now I am staring at your mouth and you must know that I want to kiss you, to feel you with my hands, all of you, especially over your belly and down to touch you, you're so hot and alive and smooth. All of it is lust. After all, you told me to be reasonable and that you are a man with vast experience in everything, so yes, lust it is." She gave him a wicked smile and held out her hand. "Dance, my lord?"

He wanted to smack her.

He was breathing hard. He was seeing her white hands stroking down his chest, her fingers splayed on his belly, her fingers curling around him, caressing him, and his muscles spasmed. "I'm going to the cardroom," he said and left her with a sharp nod.

Alexandra smiled. Let him taste his own turnips, she thought. Just let him believe that she felt nothing for him except his precious lust.

Lady Juliette seemed to enjoy herself, Alexandra saw. She's established herself and her own court far away from Melissande. She laughed rather a lot and loudly, but Alexandra didn't care. The chit would leave on the morrow.

When Hollis whispered in Alexandra's ear that the dinner buffet was ready to be served, she was startled at how quickly the time had passed. It was Tony who led her into dinner and Douglas who escorted Melissande. Juliette was on the besotted arm of a local squire who had been complaining at great length about his gout until he had seen Juliette.

"Douglas is still in a snit," Alexandra said to Tony as she forked down a bite of delicious salmon patty. "And all because I finally agreed with him about my feelings, rather my lack of them."

"Just lust, hm?"

"Yes. He puffed up like a haughty cardinal and took himself off to the cardroom. His mother isn't pleased with him. She blames me for his defection, of course. I am tempted to tell her exactly why he defected. I vow it would make her look at Douglas in a different light."

"And you as well, hussy."

Alex laughed. "True, but the look on her face would be worth it, almost."

"Are you pregnant yet?"

She dropped her fork. "Goodness. I have no idea. Oh dear, Tony, I hadn't thought about it. *Pregnant.* Why ever would you ask me that?"

"I heard the dowager speaking of it to Aunt Mildred. She just hopes you will do your duty before the year is out since that is the only reason Douglas was willing to marry in the first place. The precious heir, you know."

She gave him a stark look. "I suppose if I do not produce the precious heir within a year, Douglas will toss me out on my ear and try to breed with another female?"

"You make it sound like livestock on a farm. And no, Douglas will keep on trying manfully, I doubt not." Tony fiddled with a slice of bread, saying finally, "I know this is difficult for you to believe, but it's true. I've never in my adult life seen Douglas lose his control. In battle he was a cold-blooded bastard, never faltering, never losing sight of his goals, never forgetting a detail that would make a possible difference in an outcome. He was good, Alex, very good; he never lost his head. His men worshiped him because they knew they could trust him. He would never let them down.

"I have seen him so angry that another man would have exploded with the pressure, but not Douglas. Obviously I haven't observed him in bed with women in the past, but men being men, we do discuss things, and always, in the past, it's been something of a game to him. He enjoys having a woman lose her head over what he's doing to her; he enjoys controlling, setting the pace, deciding when and what will be done. You have shocked him to his Sherbrooke toes. He is reeling. I find it quite amusing. Also, Alex, I think your approach this evening was a master stroke. Ah, I wish I could stay and witness his downfall."

"Downfall. I don't like the sound of that."

"His upfall, then, his acceptance that he is very fond of his wife both in and out of bed and that it isn't at all a bad thing to be utterly mad about your wife."

"Do you know, if anyone overheard us, they would ship us off to that horrible Botany Bay. I have never even thought in terms of what we now speak about openly." She grinned. "As for Douglas, he knows no reticence, no shame—"

Tony grabbed her hand and kissed it, laughing. He looked over at Douglas to see his cousin frowning at him, murder in his dark eyes. As for Melissande, there was not only murder in her beautiful eyes, there was also dismemberment, if Tony didn't miss his guess. He was excessively pleased. He would never in his life forget their lovemaking in the garden. He rather hoped Melissande was pregnant. She certainly deserved to be.

"Ah, it is a pity to miss any of the drama."

Alexandra laughed. "You keep that up and you won't be alive for the rest of the drama."

The evening ended at two o'clock in the morning. Alexandra was still too excited to be tired, but the lavender feather on her mother-in-law's turban was listing sharply to port; Aunt Mildred was no longer tapping her toes to the beat of the music; Uncle Albert was snoring softly against a potted palm. Douglas emerged from the cardroom, five hundred pounds richer, to take his place beside his wife as their guests departed.

"You were a success," he said, "but I still don't like your breasts sticking out like that."

"I think you were a success yourself, Douglas, particularly with those black knee britches of yours molding your thighs and, well, the rest of you. I imagine all the ladies remarked on your male endowments."

She turned immediately to speak to Sir Thomas Hardesty and his wife, complimenting them on their lovely daughter, Melinda Beatrice, winking at a hovering Tysen whilst she did so. To her surprise Sir Thomas held her hand overlong and there was a definite loose look about his mouth. Douglas was stiff as a poker until they took their leave. "That damned old lecher. How dare he ogle you like that!"

"It wasn't really ogling," Tysen said. "He is shortsighted, that's all."

"You are becoming more of a fool by the day and it is excessively irritating. I should have sent you with Ryder. He would have beat the naïveté out of you."

"Well," Alexandra said after Tysen had given his brother an uncertain look and taken himself off, "Lady Hardesty was, I believe, ogling you a bit too."

"You will pay for your quite inappropriate observations, Alexandra." She gave him a sunny smile. "Why don't you call me Alex?"

Melissande and Tony came over and Douglas looked at the two sisters standing side by side. One was so achingly beautiful that it made a man's tongue stick to the roof of his mouth just to look at her; and the other . . . Good Lord, just hearing her laugh made him hard and sweaty, and made him think about her lying naked beneath him. She didn't look at all dowdy standing next to Melissande. He wanted to kiss the tip of her shiny nose.

Douglas couldn't wait to let his hands dive into her bodice and pull it away from her breasts. He followed her into her bedchamber, dismissed her maid, and did just that. When his hands were cupping her breasts, he sighed with pleasure, closing his eyes. Then, suddenly, he felt her hands on his legs, moving up and toward his groin. He froze. Then her hands were molding him and he wanted to yell with the pleasure of it.

"Ah," she said into his mouth as he kissed her, "I love lust, don't you, Douglas?"

"Blessed hell," he said and had her stripped within a minute. She gave no thought to the beautiful ball gown that had cost him at least one hundred pounds. She was too busy undressing him, stroking him, caressing him, staring at him as she touched him.

Again, there was no time, no overture, no prelude. He was on top of her, panting, his big body shaking, and she arched up against him and he came into her. She was ready for him, always ready, and the power of him made her cry out and lurch upward. She grabbed his head and brought his mouth down to hers and she kissed him, biting his lower lip, her hands wild on his shoulders and back even as she pushed upward against him, bringing him deeper.

For one single instant, Douglas managed to regain his sanity, and in that instant, she climaxed, and he watched her eyes go vague and soft and he kissed her mouth, taking the gasping cries into his. But it was just for an instant, one small instant, then he was raging over her again, beyond himself, surging into her, and it wouldn't stop. He felt her hands on his buttocks and that sent him over the edge. "Alexandra," he said, then collapsed on top of her.

They were lying half off the bed. He was very heavy but she didn't care. She wondered if it would always be like this—this fierce wild lovemaking, always so fast, so hard and deep. She knew she wouldn't mind a bit; she was always with him, just as frenzied, just as urgent. Douglas would accept nothing else. She said, when she was able to draw a complete breath, "Am I pregnant, do you think?"

"Yes," he said without hesitation. "I made you pregnant the first time I took you."

"Well, then, if you are right, I will be proved worthy. That's what everyone wanted, isn't it? A Sherbrooke heir?"

"Yes. As I recall, you volunteered to produce the heir."

"Yes," she said readily, "I'll give you half a dozen heirs if you wish. I should like to have a little boy who looks just like you, Douglas."

He didn't like the way her words made him feel. He grunted and said, "I am tired. You've worn me to a bone. Go to sleep."

"If you could control your lust, perhaps you would have more energy to talk to me."

"Go to sleep, damn you."

She did, a smile on her lips.

When Alexandra awoke the next morning, she was in her own bed but Douglas wasn't. She sat up, missing him, for it was his habit to awaken her with kisses, with his hands between her thighs, touching her, making her ready for him even before she was fully awake. She was alone. She didn't like it one bit.

I made you pregnant the first time I took you.

No, no, he couldn't know that, could he? She'd had no monthly flow since Douglas had taken her, that was true, but she was very unpredictable and thus she simply didn't know.

She rose and quickly bathed and dressed. Tony and Melissande were leaving today as were both Uncle Albert and Aunt Mildred. And Lady Juliette, thank the good Lord.

It was nearly two o'clock in the afternoon when the first of their guests, Lady Juliette, departed, berating her maid even as she said her good-byes to her host and hostess.

The dowager was frowning. "That girl was a severe disappointment, Mildred. I shouldn't have liked it if Douglas had wedded her."

"The girl is a shrew," Aunt Mildred said.

"She is divine, nonetheless," Uncle Albert said. "She is young and full of high spirits, that is all."

"She is a spoiled bitch and will only get worse as she ages," said his fond wife.

As for Tony, he had hugged Alexandra, whispering in her ear, "I am proud of you. Don't change. Keep going as you are now doing. All will be well."

As for Melissande, she gave her sister a long look and said, "I don't mind that you're a countess and I'm a viscountess. I do mind that you might want Tony. You will never have him, Alex, so you may forget it."

Alexandra looked at her exquisitely beautiful sister and wanted to giggle at the absurdity of it. "I promise I won't ever try to steal him from you again."

"See that you don't! You wanted Douglas Sherbrooke and you got him. If you have decided you don't want him now, it is too bad. You will just have to make do with him because Tony is mine."

"I shall try," Alexandra said in a humble voice.

Douglas, who'd overheard most of this, had a difficult time keeping his aplomb. He managed to say in a somewhat mellow voice to Tony, "We will see you in London?"

"Perhaps. If you would, Douglas, try to prepare everyone for my wife. It might prevent duels and I would appreciate it."

"She's already been there for a Season. They're all prepared."

"No, there is a difference this time. She is more . . . sympathetic now, more sensitive, and thus more vulnerable. Prepare them, Douglas. She's now a human goddess. You've seen her wrinkle her brow."

"All right, I'll tell everyone that you've trained her."

"Don't forget the discipline, my dear fellow."

Douglas laughed and punched his cousin in his arm. There was humor toward his cousin now, not the outraged bitterness of even the previous week. Alexandra felt a flood of hope. She was also relieved that Melissande hadn't heard this exchange. She would have broken Tony's arm.

They stood on the wide front steps of Northcliffe Hall until the last of the carriages bowled down the drive.

"Well," said the Dowager Countess of Northcliffe, "we are a small group again and will doubtless be downcast."

"Not I," said Douglas, looking down at his wife.

"Oh dear," said Sinjun, "stop looking at her like that, Douglas. I had hoped you would like to go for a ride."

"Not I," said Douglas again. "At least for a while."

"Well, I never!" said Douglas's fond mama, as she watched him grab his wife's hand and race into the hall.

Douglas heard Aunt Mildred say, "Now, Lydia, we all want an heir. Douglas is just doing his duty. He is a good boy."

He pulled her up the stairs to his bedchamber. He made love to her twice, quick and hard both times, and not once did he think about an heir. He stared down at her when he'd finished, breathing hard, his heart still pounding fast, but said nothing. He shook his head, dressed, and then immediately left her to go riding.

Alexandra stared up at the ceiling, not moving for fifteen minutes before she finally rose to pull herself together. As she bathed and dressed, she thought of the stunned look on his face when she said into his mouth just at the moment of his release, "Ah, Douglas, I lust for you so very much."

He'd snarled at her.

Douglas didn't come to her that night. Alexandra suspected he was brooding about lust and such in the library, at least she hoped so. She fell asleep in her own bedchamber. It was in the middle of the night when the darkness was heavy and thick when she awoke completely and very suddenly. She didn't move, not understanding. She simply knew she wasn't alone.

Then she saw her. The young woman she'd seen before, all white and floaty, her hair lustrous down her back, so blond it was nearly white, framing an exquisite face. She looked so sad and her hands were held out toward Alexandra.

"Who are you?"

Goodness, was that her voice, all thin and wispy with fear?

The figure didn't move, just stood there not three feet from the bed, her body shimmering as if she weren't really standing on the floor but rather hovering over it, her arms held out to Alexandra.

"What do you want? Why are you here?"

Again, the figure remained just as it was.

"I know you're called the Virgin Bride because your new husband was killed before you could become his wife. But I am not a virgin. My husband didn't die. Why are you here?"

Then the figure made a soft deep sound and Alexandra nearly leapt off the bed in fright.

Suddenly, everything was as clear as if the figure had spoken. Alexandra knew why she was here. "You want to warn me, don't you?"

The figure shifted subtly, deepening the lights and shadows.

"You're worried that something will happen to me?"

The figure shimmered softly and Alexandra suddenly wasn't certain whether or not it was her, no, not her . . . or was it? She was losing her mind, she was guessing a ghost's intentions. It was madness.

"What the hell is going on here? Alexandra, who are you talking to?"

The figure shuddered, gave off a soft glittering light, then simply faded into the wainscoting.

Douglas came through the connecting door. He was quite naked.

"It's all right. I was just entertaining my lover. But now you've chased him off."

She didn't realize her voice was shaking, that she sounded as if she were about to be shoved off a precipice, but Douglas did. He came across the room and looked down at her for just an instant before coming into bed with her. He drew her tightly against him, felt the shudders of her body, and simply held her. "It's all right, it was just a nightmare, nothing more, just a nightmare."

"Oh my," she said finally, her face buried into his shoulder. "It wasn't a dream or a nightmare, I swear it to you. Goodness, Douglas, I not only saw her but I also spoke to her. I started thinking I understood her."

"It was a dream," he said firmly. "That damned ghost is a collective figment. You dreamed her up because I wasn't here to love you until you were exhausted."

"You've seen her, haven't you?"

"Naturally not. I am not a silly twit of an empty-headed female."

"You have seen her, don't lie to me, Douglas! When? What was the circumstance?"

He kissed her temple and hugged her more tightly to him, pressing her face into his shoulder. When she spoke again, her warm breath fanned his flesh. "I told her that I wasn't a virgin and that you weren't dead; I asked her why she was here. She was warning me but I'm not sure it's me who's in danger . . . maybe it isn't, but then you came in and she left."

"Yes, I can just imagine it. She floated away, her shroud wafting romantically around her."

"I want to know when you saw her."

Douglas kissed her temple again, but his thoughts were on that night when Alexandra had run away from him yet he'd heard her crying in here and he'd come in and seen her . . . not Alexandra, but her, that damned ghost. He shook his head. "No," he said. "No."

He stiffened then. "My God, do you realize that I'm not attacking you? I haven't got you on your back? We've actually spoken together for at least three minutes, and we're here naked and—" She turned up her face then, and he felt her warm breath on his mouth and he kissed her.

"Well, damn," he said, and swept his hands down her back until they were cupping her buttocks and he was turning to face her, his sex hard and thick against her belly. Her arms were tight around his neck and she was kissing him wildly. It was difficult but he managed to get off her nightgown.

He was breathing hard and fast and when he knew that it was going to be closer than he'd thought, he lifted her leg and came into her. She gasped with the surprise and pleasure of it, and then she did more than gasp because his hands and his fingers were caressing her woman's flesh as his mouth was hot on her breast.

"Douglas," she said, and climaxed with a choking cry.

He pushed her onto her back to come more deeply into her and when she lifted her hips to draw him deeper, he cried out, tensing over her before pounding into her, his seed spewing inside her.

"Oh Douglas," she whispered against his neck. "She did sort of float."

"Blessed hell. She wasn't here, it was a silly dream. You were susceptible because you hadn't had me—like a tonic—before you fell asleep. You won't see that damned ghost any more tonight. Now be quiet." He pulled her on top of him, arranging the blankets over them as he did so. "All you'll think about is me. You understand?"

"Yes," she said, kissing his throat, his ear, his shoulder. "Just you and the wonderful lust you give me. Isn't it nice that we're leaving for London in the morning? Perhaps that's what she was trying to tell me. There were so many more men for me to lust upon."

"You are as amusing as a boil on a backside."

She laughed and kissed the spot behind his ear.

Douglas stared grim-faced into the darkness even as his hands stroked down her back and molded around her hips. He finally fell asleep with her breath against his neck, her breasts pressed against his chest, her heartbeat soft and steady against his.

The Sherbrooke town house was a three-story mansion on the corner of Putnam Place. It had been built sixty years before to grand expectations of an Earl of Northcliffe with more groats than good taste. Still, the Greek columns were inspiring to some—those in their cups, Douglas would say with a snort—and the interior with all its niches for statuary were filled now mostly with flowers and books, the abundant Greek statuary exiled to the attic. It was the same earl, Douglas told Alexandra, who had filled the Northcliffe gardens to overflowing with Greek statues. "So I have pleased myself," Douglas said, as he pointed to exquisite crimson brocade drapes that were drawn in the large central drawing room. "I expect that my heirs just might think I'm short in the upper works and do something else."

He frowned then, saying, "Perhaps you will wish to make alterations. I did nothing to the countess's rooms."

"All right," Alexandra said, still so dazed and overwhelmed by their actually being in London, a city of grace and wealth and poverty and excitement—and the smells—that she would have agreed to anything he said. He had pointed out everything to her and she'd gawked through the carriage window. Douglas grinned down at her. "A bit overwhelming, isn't it?"

She nodded, touching her fingertips lightly to a lovely Spanish table.

"You will grow accustomed soon enough. As for the house, Mrs. Goodgame will show you everything. Burgess, our plump London butler, is as efficient as Hollis. You can trust him. We will remain in London for two weeks, enough time for you to be fitted for new gowns and bonnets and the like and to meet society. Do you wish to rest now or can we visit Madame Jordan?"

Madame Jordan was genuinely French, born and raised in Rennes. She had six shop assistants, an impressive establishment in the heart of Piccadilly, and a doting eye for the Earl of Northcliffe. Alexandra stood there, an unimportant member of Douglas's entourage, listening to Madame and her husband discussing what was to be done with her. She was measured and clucked over. When she was to the point of screaming at Douglas that she wasn't invisible and she did have good taste, Madame suddenly splayed her fingers over Alexandra's bosom and went off with a salvo of rapid, intense French. Ah, Alexandra thought, grinning at Douglas, whose face was closed and hard, she wants my bosom to be fashionable. "I agree with Madame," she said loudly, and Douglas turned on her, a wonderful target for his ire. "Be quiet, Alexandra, or you will go sit in the carriage! This has nothing to do with you!"

"Ha! You want me to look like a nun and Madame disagrees, as do I. Give in, Douglas, and stop being strange about it. I am a woman like every other woman on the face of this earth, and all women are built just like me. No one will care, no one. If you insist that I be covered to my chin, why everyone will wonder if I have some sort of horrible deformity!"

"I agree with the countess," said Madame Jordan in perfect English "Come, my lord, you are too possessive of your bride. It isn't at all fashionable to wear your heart on your sleeve."

"I'm not," Douglas roared, slamming his fist on the glossy painting of a woman at least seven feet tall draped in willowy garments, as wispy and insubstantial as the ghost's had been. "It's just that she's too innocent and doesn't realize what men want and—" He ground to a stop. He was furious and felt impotent. He was outnumbered and outgunned and he knew it. Both women were regarding him with tolerant scorn. He had reason on his side, surely he did, only he sounded ridiculous. "Blessed hell! Do as you wish!" And he stomped out, saying over his shoulder, "I will await you in the carriage. Lower every bloody neckline to your bloody waist, I don't care!"

"Ah, I love a passionate man, don't you?" said Madame Jordan fondly, smiling after the earl.

"Oh yes," Alexandra agreed. "Your English is superb, Madame."

Madame nodded, not one whit affected by the contretemps. "I also speak German and Italian and a bit of Russian. I have a Russian count who is my lover, you know? He is probably as wild and possessive a lover as your husband, a wild man and he keeps my heart racing."

That sounded wonderful to Alexandra.

Before the afternoon was over, Alexandra was so weary she could scarce stand. She was also the proud owner of six new gowns, two riding habits, nightgowns, chemises. Goodness, the list went on and on. Douglas regained a proper mood after they left Madame Jordan's. Then he bought her bonnets and shoes and handkerchiefs and stockings and reticules, even an umbrella.

He was still a fount of energy when at last he handed her into the carriage. He shoved a stack of boxes away on the seat. Alexandra was so tired she didn't care if she was in London or in the Hebrides. Her head fell against his shoulder and he squeezed her against him, dropping a kiss on top of her head.

"It has been a long day. You did well. I was proud of you. For the most part anyway. I still am displeased by your necklines."

Alexandra wasn't about to touch that topic again. She chewed her bottom lip, then burst out, "You know everything about clothes. You and Madame Jordan were obviously well acquainted. Have you bought clothing for many women?"

CHAPTER
==19==

DOUGLAS LOOKED AT her thoughtfully, then shrugged. "It's really none of a wife's affair what a husband does, but I see no harm in educating you. Yes, it's something all females appreciate. I realized when I was no more than a very charming lad of nineteen years that I should gain expertise in the area of fashion and so I did. If a man wishes to maintain a constant supply of women, why then, he must adapt himself to their little vagaries."

"It sounds rather cold-blooded to me."

"Aren't you the least bit grateful for my generosity today? Six new gowns . . . two new riding habits. In addition, I even allowed you and Madame to have your own way. Won't you reward me suitably?"

It was very strange, she thought, and rather predictable that men always seemed to remember things differently. Alexandra sighed. "I am perfectly willing, but you never give me the chance to reward you, Douglas. You are all over me before I have a chance to do anything, and thus it is I who get all the rewards, and I never buy you anything."

"That is an interesting way of looking at it. Most women and men would consider you an oddity, that or a woman of immense guile." He frowned at her, as if uncertain of something, then said, "You still have the thirty pounds?"

"Yes. You mean, to have a constant supply of men I need to adapt myself to their little vagaries?"

"It doesn't work that way. Men are always in constant supply. Men are excessively easy to attach. Men won't ever simper or play the tease or make excuses."

"Come, Douglas, I may not have much experience, but what experience I have convinces me that the goose and gander apply here. The thirty pounds won't go very far. It wouldn't do for the mythical men to feel slighted, no matter how eager they are. Perhaps I could purchase several dozen of a single item and give them out as I go along. What do you think?"

"I think you're pushing me and it isn't wise. I think you need to be beaten. I think your humor needs silence and reflection. You are being impertinent and I won't allow it. Be quiet, Alexandra."

"Perhaps watch fobs," she said in an idle voice against his shoulder. "And I could have my initials engraved next to theirs on each one. Personalized, you know."

He said calmly, his voice controlled and cold, "If you provide me quickly with an heir, all the money I have spent on you will have been worth it."

Oh dear, she thought. She had pushed him and his retaliation was swift and rather brutal.

"If you tell me you don't mean that, I will be quiet and forget about the watch fobs and the humor."

"I won't tell you anything. Now, London is thin of company this time of year. However, there are still adequate amusements. The Ranleaghs' ball is tonight and it will suffice for your debut. You will wear the ball gown you wore at Northcliffe Hall. I have asked Mrs. Goodgame to assist you."

That evening, just after eleven o'clock, at the Ranleaghs' magnificent mansion on Carlisle Street, Alexandra came face to face with a woman who obviously knew Douglas well and wanted him still.

She was eavesdropping and she felt only a dollop of guilt. But in matter of fact, she was far more furious than guilty. They were speaking French and she couldn't understand a bloody word.

The woman was too pretty for her own good, slight, very feminine with her large eyes, in her mid-twenties, Alexandra thought, and her white hand was on Douglas's sleeve. She was standing very close to him, and leaning even closer, her breath doubtless warm on his cheek, the way Alexandra's was when she was kissing his face. Her voice was low and vibrant with feeling. Douglas was patting her hand, speaking very quietly, his French as smooth and fluent as could be.

Why had her father insisted she learn Italian? It was worthless. Ah, the woman looked so serious, so intent, so interested in Douglas. Who was she? Had Douglas bought her clothes? Was she offering him a reward?

Douglas turned at that moment and Alexandra pulled back behind a curtain that gave into a small alcove. A couple were there, passionately kissing, and Alexandra blurted out, "Oh, do excuse me!" She fled.

Since she had met nearly fifty people and remembered no one's name, she was quite alone. She saw Lady Ranleagh but that good lady was in close conversation with a bewigged gentleman who looked very important and somewhat drunk.

Since she had no choice, Alexandra stood on the edge of the dance floor, watching the couples dance a charming minuet. They performed flawlessly; they were all beautiful and rich and sophisticated and she felt like an interloper, a provincial with her gown a half-inch too high. At any moment, they would turn and point at her and yell, "She doesn't belong here! Get her out!"

"Dare I believe you are a lost lamb in search of an amiable shepherd?"

That was an interesting approach, Alexandra thought as she turned to look at the gentleman who'd spoken it. He was tall, and well built, his linen immaculate, and very fair-haired. He was probably not more than twenty-five years old, but his eyes, a very dark blue, were so filled with unhappy wisdom and weary cynicism that he gave the impression of being older. He was handsome, she'd give him that, and he did indeed look dazzling in his evening wear, but that glint of too much knowledge in his eyes was disconcerting. And now he was offering to be her amiable shepherd?

"I'm not at all lost, sir, but it is kind of you to inquire."

"You are Melissande's little sister, aren't you? One of the ladies pointed you out to me."

"Yes. You know my sister?"

"Oh yes. She is most charming, a glorious creature. Is it true that she married Tony Parrish, Lord Rathmore?"

Alexandra nodded. "It was love at first sight. They will be coming to London soon."

"I fancy Teresa Carleton won't be overpleased to hear who snapped him up. Ah, you don't know, do you? Tony was engaged to her, then suddenly, the engagement was no more. He didn't say a word, just left London. Teresa let it about that she didn't want him for a husband for he was proving to be unfashionably priggish in his notions. Ah, forgive me, my dear. I am Heatherington, you know."

"No, I didn't know. It is a pleasure to meet you, sir. What this lady said about Tony—if you are acquainted with him, you must know it is a clanker. Tony, priggish? It is too absurd. You know my husband, Douglas Sherbrooke?"

"So that is true as well. All know Sherbrooke, or North, as many of his army friends call him. He is a man not easily dismissed. I shouldn't like him for an enemy. And no one really believed Teresa. No, Tony is no prig."

"He is a great deal of fun and he and my sister deal well together. They are much in love."

He shrugged, staring at her intently. "What I find odd is you, my dear. You married to Douglas Sherbrooke. You appear warm and quite joyous, really, whilst your husband is a cold man, hard and severe, truth be told."

"My husband cold? Are we speaking of the same man, sir? *Cold?* It is too funny," and Alexandra laughed.

"Beecham, a surprise to see you." Douglas neatly inserted himself between the man and Alexandra. She said, frowning at her husband, "I thought he was Heatherington."

Douglas was infuriated with the young man who was nevertheless a seasoned roué. The dog had the gall to flirt with his wife. He said, "It is Lord Beecham."

"Heatherington is my family name," he said, giving her an intimate look. "I congratulate you, Northcliffe. She is charming. Very different from her sister. An original, I should say. I see that a quadrille is forming itself and I am promised to Miss Danvers, who fancies herself the soul of charm and discretion. I doubt she is worth your time, Northcliffe."

"No, she isn't," Douglas said.

Heatherington managed a shadow of a grin. "I doubt she's worth my time either."

"Keep away from that man," he added to Alexandra as he stared after Baron Beecham, who was making languid progress toward Miss Danvers. "He's known to have a woman's skirts over her head before he even has learned her last name."

"He is so young."

"He is but two years my junior. But you're right. His is a strange past. Keep away from him."

"He must have excellent fashion sense and a deep purse to have such success at such a tender age."

"It isn't funny, Alexandra. I don't like the way he was looking at you. Keep away from him."

"Very well, I shall, if you will keep away from that French hussy who had her hand on your sleeve and was practically speaking into your mouth."

"What French—" He frowned ferociously down at her. "Don't gesticulate so wildly. I can see every white inch of you to your waist. I will have that damned bodice raised before you wear that gown again."

"You will not distract me, Douglas! Who was that wretched hussy?"

He stared at her, surprise and satisfaction in his eyes, eyes that had grown darker if that were possible. "Good God, you're jealous."

She was, and it was humiliating that he had caught her at it. "If I knew anyone, I would walk away from you and go conduct a well-bred conversation with that person. But if I walk away, I will be alone and that isn't a good thing."

"Her name is no concern of yours. She is simply someone I know, nothing more."

"What was she telling you?"

He lied, but it wasn't clean and neat. "That her grandmother was ill."

"Bosh," Alexandra said.

"Very well. I went to France to rescue her and sent Tony to Claybourn Hall. The result wasn't quite what either of us had intended."

"Ah, so that is that Janine person you told me about. She's that bloody woman who offered herself to you."

"Your memory is beyond frightening. I won't say another word. I beg you to dismiss what I said that day. It makes no mind now. Stick to your own affairs, Alexandra."

"Come along then and dance with me since I don't wish to force you to more confidences, though the ones you gave me were meager indeed."

He danced with her, then took her into dinner, then introduced her to young matrons he hoped she would like. And he kept a wary eye open for Georges Cadoudal. Damnation, the last enemy he wanted on this earth was that maniac, Georges.

Why the hell wasn't the man in France where he was supposed to be? Maybe he was, maybe Janine was just hysterical. And that's who he'd been speaking to, Janine Daudet, the woman he'd rescued in France.

"I wish to meet Teresa Carleton."

"So, Beecham told you about her, did he? He enjoys making mischief. I wouldn't be at all surprised if he himself slept with the lady in question."

"Did she break off the engagement with Tony?"

"She didn't. He discovered she was bedding a friend of his. He nearly collapsed from shock and outrage. He came to Northcliffe to regain his mental balance and I looked upon him as my savior. He then went to Claybourn Hall and married my wife."

"Do you think, perhaps, Douglas, that you could rephrase that just a bit?"

"Why? It's the truth. Just because you pop out of the bottle doesn't change the facts."

She sighed. "You're right, of course. However, if you will change your words just a bit, I will reward you when we return home, if you don't reward me first, which you always do. You don't give me a chance, Douglas."

"Perhaps in fifty years I will."

That sounded like a fine commitment to Alexandra and she gave him a brilliant smile. Douglas, on the other hand, rethought his words, and wanted to kick himself. He cursed, drank too much brandy, then brightened. Too much liquor and it just might slow him down a bit. He was fuzzyheaded in the carriage. He was whistling vacantly on the way upstairs. Yes, maybe the brandy would work.

It didn't, but it had been worth a try. When finally he pulled out of her and rolled over onto his back, he crossed his arms over his head and concentrated on calming his breathing. "You will kill me," he said finally. "A man cannot continue like this. It isn't natural. It isn't healthy."

"What about me?"

He lowered an arm and placed his hand over her breast. Her heart was galloping. He grinned. "We'll be buried side by side in the Northcliffe family cemetery."

"I don't like the sound of that."

"You must give me an heir first."

"I thought ladies were supposed to feel ill when they were pregnant."

"Most do, so I've heard."

"I feel wonderful."

"When was your last monthly flow?"

It was dark and they had just made love and were now lying side by side on the large bed, naked and sated, but still it was embarrassing.

When her silence dragged out beyond his patience, Douglas said, "You haven't bled since we were married, have you?"

She shook her head and he felt the movement.

He lightly laid his palm on her belly. "You're very flat." He extended his fingers to her pelvic bones. "You're small, but not too small, I hope, to hold my child. But it is true that I am a big man, Alexandra. My mother complains bitterly even now that I nearly killed her with my size at birth. No, I don't think you're large enough. I will have a physician come and examine you."

"You will do no such thing!"

"Well, fancy that, she can talk," Douglas said.

"Douglas, listen to me." She came up onto her elbow and her hair fell onto his chest. "I am a woman and it is women who have babies. I won't allow any man other than you to touch me. Do you understand?"

"Who will deliver our child?"

"A midwife. My mother was delivered by a midwife. She doesn't care for men either."

He laughed at that, then skimmed his palm over her belly, down to cup her. He pressed her again onto her back. His hand was large and very warm. His fingers caressed and stroked her. She sucked in her breath. "You don't care for me, Alexandra? I am a man."

"I know you're a man, Douglas. What I don't understand is why anyone would believe you a cold man. Why, just look at what you are doing, and how warm your voice is. Cold! Ha!"

"Who told you that?"

"That young man you said was bad. Heatherington."

"Ah. He was perhaps seeing if you were unhappy with me, thus his comment."

"Why would he care whether or not I was happy? Ah, Douglas, that is very nice."

His fingers stopped but the warmth of his flesh was still there, settled against her flesh, and she shifted slightly. "You will make me forget what I was saying, Douglas, if you continue doing that."

"Accustom yourself for I will touch you whenever and however I please. Now, heed me well, Alexandra. I am a cold man, you could say, if you spoke starkly. By that I mean that I am a man who endeavors not to be overly fooled by artifice or guile. I am a man who lives by logic and reason and not by—" He broke off, his fingers moving over her again, and then he cursed even as he kissed her, rolling over onto her and sliding into her. It was as it always was: fast and hard and deep and she fell into the pleasure of it, crying out and holding him, burrowing into him, wanting him more than she could imagine and the feelings were deeper than he was inside her, so deep she couldn't remember how it had been before he had been with her. But she didn't whisper the words to him. She moaned when she found her release, biting into his shoulder with the power of it. And Douglas, he simply took her pleasure into himself and gave her his own, holding her tightly to him after his release and into sleep.

Alexandra came into the drawing room to see a slight, balding, middle-aged gentleman standing in front of the bow windows, rocking back and forth on his heels, staring at his watch, not across the street at the beautiful park. When he saw her he quickly put the watch back into his vest pocket and gave her a slight bow. She said, her head cocked to one side in question, "Our butler told me there was a gentleman to see me. It is odd since I don't know many gentlemen yet in London. For a moment I thought it must be Beecham, but no, I vow he would not be so indiscreet. It would not be his style. Who are you, sir?"

"I?" He stared at her, unblinking. "I? Surely, His Lordship said I was coming. Surely you must know who I am."

His astonishment at her ignorance was genuine and she smiled. "No, Burgess merely said there was a gentleman in here. Are you perhaps a playwright or an actor who seeks patronage? Perhaps a vicar who needs a living? If that is so, I regret to tell you that His Lordship's young brother will doubtless—"

"No! I am Dr. John Mortimer! I am a physician! I am one of the premier physicians in all of London! His Lordship asked me to visit you. As you know, he is concerned that you will bear his heir and that you are perhaps too small to complete the task successfully. He wished me to ascertain if this is true."

She stared at him, disbelieving. Douglas, curse his black eyes and hair, had been called out earlier in the morning and had not returned. So, he'd arranged for this man to come. Well, at least he hadn't yet returned, so that meant she wouldn't have to argue with him in front of Dr. Mortimer.

"Dr. Mortimer," she said, still smiling, but it was difficult, "I fear you have come for nothing. My husband worries overly. Besides, if I am already with child, then there is nothing to be done if I am too small, is that not true?"

Dr. Mortimer, a man who knew his own worth, which was great, and a man unused to a lady speaking so forwardly, a lady who treated him with such presumption, drew himself up and smiled kindly down at her. She was embarrassed, that was it. It was the only explanation for her odd behavior, though she didn't seem to be at all. Still, he chose his avuncular voice, one that always soothed nervous ladies, chuckled slightly at her foray into wit, and said, "My dear Lady Northcliffe, ladies, no matter their beliefs or what they think they believe—undoubtedly provided with good intent by their older female relations—don't have the ability to discern what is or is not appropriate for them. It is why they have husbands, you know. I am here to examine you, my lady, as requested by your husband. I will then tell your husband what is best for you when you conceive his heir. His concern for your size is laudable. As a physician, I take all factors into consideration and then guide you into the proper steps during the months until the child is born. Now, my lady—"

Alexandra couldn't quite believe that this pretentious, thoroughly irritating man, physician or no, had walked into her drawing room and was treating her like a half-wit stray. But it was Douglas she wanted to cosh, not this specimen.

She smiled sweetly. "Would you like a cup of tea, sir?"

He smiled back at her, showing teeth. "No, thank you, my lady." He fanned his hands in a gesture of spurious modesty. "My time isn't always my own, you know. Why, in an hour, I must be off to see Lady Abercrombie. She is a cousin to the queen, you know, and I am her private physician. It was difficult for me to come and see you this quickly, but your husband is well-known to me and I decided to oblige him in this. Now, my lady, it is time for us to go upstairs to your bedchamber. If you would like to have your maid present, that is certainly fine."

"Sir, we will not continue anywhere. I am sorry that you made this wasted trip. As I said, my husband worries overly." With that, Alexandra walked to the bell cord and gave it a healthy jerk. Her heart was pounding, she knew her face was flushed. Oddly, she still wasn't particularly angry at this condescending little man, for he was what he was. Ah, but Douglas, he was another matter entirely.

"My lady, really—"

She raised her hand to cut him off. "No, sir, please don't apologize. Do go along to Lady Abercrombie, the queen's cousin, who doubtless is on her toes in anticipation of your coming, and as a result her heart is beating much too quickly for her good health awaiting you."

"I wasn't going to apologize! Your husband pleaded with me to come here and—"

"I beg your pardon, sir, but my husband wouldn't plead with the king himself. It's obvious you don't know him well at all. Ah, Burgess, please see the good doctor out. He is in quite a hurry. He must see the queen, you know."

"No, no, it is Lady Abercrombie, the queen's cousin. Surely you can't wish me to leave!"

"I am certain the queen would swoon to see you as well, Dr. Mortimer. Now, good sir, if you would excuse me—"

Burgess was in an unenviable quandary. The earl had informed him of the physician's impending visit. He knew the countess hadn't been informed and that had bothered him. Knowing her just briefly, he still knew she wouldn't be pleased with what His Lordship had done. And now Her Ladyship was evidently booting out the good doctor. Burgess knew his duty. He also knew what was good for him. He drew himself up to his full five feet four inches and said calmly, "Dr. Mortimer, if you could come this way if you please."

"Good-bye, sir. How very amiable of you to call."

Mortimer wanted to be insulted; however, he was more confused by what had passed. He didn't understand how the young lady, countess or not, had managed to rout him, and thus allowed himself to be led out without a word by a butler who looked more like an ostler, bald, round of belly, needing only a large apron about his middle. He was also very short, not at all what Mortimer would have deemed proper in an earl's household. He stood for a moment on the front steps, staring back at the front door of the town house.

Douglas had hurried as quickly as he could to be here when the physician arrived. He imagined that Alexandra wouldn't be too pleased to see the man, but he was concerned and he'd wanted the physician to see her immediately. He wanted the man's word that she would be all right. The fact that he had no idea whether or not she was indeed pregnant didn't matter. If she wasn't now, she would be sooner or later. No, he was worried and he wanted his worries allayed by a man who should know what was what and Mortimer had been recommended by his own physician who'd tended him three years before when he'd been wounded.

Thus, when he saw the physician, standing outside his town house, staring foolishly back at the closed door, his greeting stilled in his mouth, and he frowned. Oh God, something was wrong. She was too small, he knew it; she was with child now and she would die and it would be all his fault. His voice was hoarse and urgent, but he didn't question it, saying, "Dr. Mortimer. Is my wife all right?"

"Oh, my lord! Your wife? She offered me tea, you know. Your wife is fine. She is not at all what I expected. She isn't as I am used to seeing in a lady. She is young, perhaps that is at the root of it. Most strange. I must go now, my lord. Ah, your wife, yes, my lord, your wife. I wish you all the best, my lord. Good luck. I dare say you will need it."

Mortimer continued in that vein as he walked quickly down the steps and into his waiting carriage.

Douglas stood, his hand on the front doorknob, staring after the doctor. He appeared vague; he appeared to ramble; he appeared not at all the way he'd appeared early that morning when Douglas had called upon him. Still, he would have said something if Alexandra wasn't all right. Wouldn't he?

He found her in the drawing room, standing by the bowed front windows, holding back the heavy draperies, staring out at the street and the park just beyond.

She looked over her shoulder at him when he came into the room but didn't say anything. She gave her attention back to the park across the street.

"I saw Dr. Mortimer on the front steps."

She didn't respond.

"He seemed a bit strange. He said you were fine, at least I think he did. He must have been very early."

She continued not to respond. That broom handle was stiff up her back.

"Look, Alexandra, I wanted to be certain you would be all right. Surely you aren't angry because I was worried about you. I know he is a man, but only men are physicians, and thus there was really no choice. I tried to hurry, to be back here when he came, but I was unable to. I would have been with you if I could have. Come, it wasn't all that horrible, was it?"

"Oh no, it wasn't horrible at all."

"Then why are you standing there ignoring me? Treating me as if I didn't exist? It isn't what I am used to from my wife. Don't you remember? You love me."

"Oh, surely not, Douglas. It is lust, nothing more. You convinced me of that. As for your precious doctor, why I hope the pompous fool falls into a ditch and succumbs to water in his mouth."

Douglas raked his fingers through his hair. "I'm sorry if he didn't treat you as I would have. No, no, I take that back. That is a truly appalling thought. Didn't you like him? Wasn't he gentle enough with you? Did he embarrass you more than he should have?"

She turned to face him now, her expression remote. "I told you last night I wouldn't be examined by any man—"

"Other than me."

As a jesting gambit, it didn't succeed. "That's correct. Your memory serves you well when it is your own ends you wish to serve. I was polite to him, Douglas, but we did not leave this drawing room—"

"You let him examine you here? Where, on the sofa? No? Then on that large wing chair over there? My God, that wasn't well done of you, Alexandra. It was indelicate of you and not at all wise. Why, Mrs. Goodgame could have come in. Burgess could have come in with the tea tray. A maid could have come in to dust, for God's sake. I would have expected you to demand that your modesty be preserved, that at least three female maids be present to keep careful watch. No, that wasn't—"

"He didn't touch me. I told you last night I wouldn't allow it. Did you disbelieve me?"

"You are my damned wife! You weren't at first, but then after I decided that you were, it became your obligation to oblige me—no, that sounds ridiculous. It became your damned duty! It is your damned duty! I want you examined. I don't want another man touching you, but he isn't really what you would call a man; he's a doctor, a sort of male eunuch, and he's paid to touch you and to know what it is he's touching. Dammit, Alexandra, what did you do to him?"

"Oh yes, your superior Dr. Mortimer is a man, Douglas! He spouted all your precious male nonsense. He treated me as if I were a child, a stupid child at that. Besides, how can he possibly know what he's doing? He isn't a woman; he isn't built like a woman. How can he know how a woman works and when something isn't working right?"

"I won't argue with you about this, Alexandra. I will ask him to come back. If you wish it, I will remain with you and keep an eye on him, if that is what concerns you. That is what I wished to do today. Now, enough. Would you like to go riding to Richmond? We could take a picnic. I wouldn't be able to attack you—to reward you, that is—there would be too many people about. What do you say?"

She could only stare at him. "Douglas, don't you realize what you did?"

"You are irritating me, Alexandra."

"You went against my wishes. You didn't even consult me. I will not tolerate that sort of thing, Douglas."

He turned red and actually yelled at her, "Damn you, you are my wife.

Can't you understand that if I get you with child, you could die? I don't want to kill you!"

"Why?" Her voice was now soft as butter, and Douglas heard the change and wanted to kick himself.

"Don't try your bloody guile on me, madam. Go change into your riding habit. You have fifteen minutes. If you are late, I shall lose you in the maze."

It was a start, Alexandra thought, as she climbed the stairs. It was a very promising start.

However, not half an hour later, she wanted to kick him. Her promising start had fallen into ashes.

CHAPTER
═ 20 ═

"DOUGLAS, WHO CALLED you away so early this morning?" Her question was one of random curiosity. However, Douglas stiffened alarmingly in the saddle. The stallion he kept in London, Prince by name, a huge roan gelding, didn't like the stiffening and danced sideways. Alexandra's mare, a foul-tempered chestnut, decided it was her rider's fault that the stallion was upset, whipped her head around, and bit her boot. She yelped in surprise.

Douglas said sharply, "I told you she wasn't like your mare at home. Pay attention, Alexandra."

She frowned at the back of his head. They were cantering sedately in Rotten Row. Douglas had decided they didn't have time to go to Richmond maze. It was too early by far for all the fashionable to be in attendance, which pleased Alexandra. It was a pleasant early afternoon, a light breeze ruffling the loose curls around her face. She said again, this time more than random interest in her voice, "Who wanted you so badly this morning? No one in your family is ill? Everyone is all right?"

"My family is now your family. Contrive to remember that, please. Also, it is none of your business where I go or what I do. A wife shouldn't meddle in her husband's affairs. Pay attention to your mount and—"

"Douglas," she said in what she believed a most reasonable tone of voice, "you are sulking because I didn't take that wretched doctor up to my bedchamber. I will continue not to take him anywhere, and unless you want to create a god-awful scene, you won't force me to. Now, what was all the urgency? I am your wife. Please tell me what is happening."

He remained mulish and silent and her imagination flowed into dramatic channels. "It isn't anything to do with an invasion, is it? Oh dear, the ministry doesn't want you back in the army, do they? You won't go, will you? Please consider well, Douglas. There is so much at Northcliffe Hall that requires your constant attention. So I don't think—"

"Be quiet! It has nothing to do with that, dammit! It has to do with a brilliant madman named Georges Cadoudal."

"Who is he?"

How had she managed to get him to spit out the name, he wondered, staring between his horse's ears. "It is none of your affair. Be quiet. Leave me alone. I won't tell you anything more."

"All right," she said. Georges Cadoudal. He was French and Douglas spoke French as if he'd been nursed on it at his mother's breast. She remembered the intensity of that French woman—that hussy he'd rescued, Janine—the previous night at the Ranleaghs' ball and said, "Is he involved somehow with that bawd who was trying to seduce you last night?"

Douglas simply stared at her. She couldn't know. It was just a guess and he was a fool. The last thing he wanted to do was worry her, to scare her. The absolute last thing he wanted was for her to pry into the absurd business. He dug his heels into Prince's sides and the stallion shot forward.

Alexandra wished she had a rock; she would surely throw it at the back of his head. But more than that, she was worried. How to find out who this Georges Cadoudal was and how it affected Douglas? She remembered the note brought to him by his valet, Finkle, who had come to London with them. Perhaps the note was still about somewhere. She resolved to find it. He'd said that his was now her family as well. Very well. She was his wife; it was time he realized that having a wife meant an end to his own counsels. She could be of help to him; he had to learn that.

She found the note. Finkle had deposited it carefully with His Lordship's other missives on his massive desk in the library. Alexandra frowned as she read it. It was from a Lord Avery. The scrawl, which was large and black, simply informed Douglas that this Georges Cadoudal was, it appeared, not in Paris where he was supposed to be, but rather back in England. Lord Avery was worried; he needed to speak with Douglas immediately.

Alexandra scrupulously refolded the letter, placing it back into the pile, giving no visual hint it had been moved. Douglas came unexpectedly into the room just as she finished. She flushed to the top of her forehead and quickly pushed away from the desk.

"Good day, my lord," she said and gave him an airy wave.

He was frowning; he blocked her escape. "What are you doing in here, Alexandra?"

She sent her chin upward. "Isn't this my house as well? Are there some rooms that I'm not allowed to visit? If that is so, it is only fair that you tell me where I am not to go and I will, naturally, obey you."

Douglas looked toward his desk, his frown still in place. "Your efforts to distract me have never worked. And, you have never obeyed me. Now, what is on my desk that was of such interest to you?"

As he took a step forward, she tried to duck around him. He caught her wrist in his hand. She felt his thumb gently caress the soft flesh and knew that if he continued, she would be on her back on the floor, or perhaps the sofa, and she would enjoy herself most thoroughly.

It was as if Douglas realized the same thing. He dropped her wrist. "Don't move," he said, "or I will see to it that you pay for your interest in my affairs." She wondered if he knew what he would do were she to duck out of the room. She decided the threat wasn't specific enough and was out of the room in an instant.

Douglas let her go. He'd find her quickly enough; he went to his desk and thumbed through the papers. When he found the note from Lord Avery, he cursed. Damn Finkle, why did he have to be so fastidious? Well, she knew very little more now than she had before. Still, he was worried. Georges Cadoudal wasn't predictable. From experience, Douglas knew that once Georges got a particular idea in his brain, he couldn't be budged from it. It was both an asset and a terrible drawback. Like now.

Douglas cursed. What to do?

His course of action was decided that very evening. He took Alexandra to a small soirée at the home of Lord and Lady Marchpane, a delightful older couple who were very fond of Douglas for he'd looked after their grandson in the army. They greeted him and Alexandra warmly.

As for Alexandra, she was wary, though Douglas had said naught to her of retribution or punishment. He'd appeared rather preoccupied, even when she'd presented herself in a new gown whose neckline wasn't all that high. He'd merely nodded at her and that had been that. She watched him from the corner of her eye. She would have preferred to have remained at the town house, with him. Perhaps she should apologize for her nosiness. She touched her fingertips to his sleeve. He looked down at her, saying nothing, his face expressionless.

"I'm sorry, Douglas."

"For what specifically?"

"For prying, but you made me so angry, not telling me what is happening. I am your wife, you know. I can be of assistance to you if you would but allow me."

His look was, if nothing, more remote. "I accept your apology though it is sparse as a gorse heath. As for the other, I cannot help but be aware that you are my wife. You are with me every blessed moment. I doubt I could relieve myself without you demanding where it is I went to and what it is I did. Ah, here is Teddy Summerton. He dances well. I will give you over to him. No, don't argue with me. You will do as I bid you. Do you understand me?"

"I understand," she said.

And she dutifully danced the next country dance with Teddy Summerton, a very nice young gentleman with a pallid complexion and large ears who appeared to worship her husband. When the dance was over, Douglas was nowhere to be seen.

Alexandra wondered if he were once again with that French hussy. She wandered slowly around the perimeter of the ballroom; some of the people recognized her and nodded. She nodded back, smiling. Where was Douglas?

It was a warm evening, the air heavy with impending rain. Alexandra went onto the balcony and leaned over the stone balustrade to peer down into the gardens below. There were lanterns hung at romantic intervals, but still there were many shadows, many dark places, and she felt a gnawing of fear.

She called out softly, "Douglas?"

There was no response. She thought she heard a rustle in the bushes to her left but couldn't be certain. She called his name again, then quickly skipped down the deep-set stone steps to the garden. Again she called his name. Then she fell silent. She quickly walked along one of the narrow stone paths, her ears on full alert. Nothing. Then, suddenly, she heard a man's deep voice that sounded like a low hissing, but she didn't understand what he was saying. Damnation, it was French he was speaking. She wanted to scream with vexation until she heard Douglas reply, in French, and he sounded both cold and remarkably angry.

Suddenly there came the unmistakable sounds of a scuffle. She didn't wait but ran full-tilt toward the fray. She ran into the bushes to see two men attacking Douglas. She watched with astonishment when he whirled about on the balls of his feet and struck one of the men hard in his belly with his fist, then as he turned, faster than the wind, his elbow struck the other man in his throat. It was all done so quickly she just stood there, frozen like a rabbit. The one man, rubbing his throat, yelled something in French at Douglas; in the next instant, both he and his henchman had melted into the shadows.

Douglas stood there motionless, rubbing the knuckles of his left hand, staring off into the darkness. She ran to him then, her hand on his arms, his shoulders, finally to cup his face. "Are you all right? You were so fine, Douglas. You moved so quickly. I couldn't believe it. You didn't need my help at all. Are you all right? Can you not speak? Please, Douglas, speak to me." As she spoke, her hands continued to caress him, to feel him, and still he stood motionless, his breathing deep and steady.

Finally, he raised his arms, grasped her hands in his, and lowered his face to within an inch of hers. "What the hell are you doing out here?"

Her hands stilled, but she didn't flinch away from him. "I was worried about you. I couldn't find you. I thought perhaps you would need me."

"Need you? Good Lord, madam, spare me your assistance! Now, we're leaving."

"But who were those men? Why did they attack you? I heard all of you arguing but I couldn't understand. It was in French, blast it. Why—"

He shook her, saying nothing, and dragged her back along the path to the town house. He was terrified for her, for the last thing Georges Cadoudal had shouted at him was a threat against her. Just as he'd destroyed Janine, he, Georges, would destroy Douglas's new wife.

He said nothing in the carriage, until she asked, "I've never seen anyone hit another like that. You didn't fight Tony like that."

"I wanted to thrash Tony, not kill him."

"Where did you learn to fight like that?"

He turned to look at her in the dim light of the carriage. He smiled just a bit, remembering. "I was in Portugal and I got to know some members in this gang of bandits in Oporto who were the foulest, meanest, dirtiest fighters I've ever seen in my life. They taught me and I managed to live through it."

"Oh. Who were those men who tried to hurt you?"

He took her left hand in his and held it firm. "Listen to me, Alexandra. You are to go nowhere without me, do you understand? Don't look at me like that, just trust me. Tell me you understand."

"Yes, I understand."

"Of course you don't, but it doesn't matter. The day after tomorrow, we are returning to Northcliffe."

"Why?"

"You will do as I tell you and ask no more questions."

She decided to let the matter rest. She knew him well enough to recognize that once he'd shut off the valve to his meager supply of information, it wouldn't again be opened. He was the most stubborn man she'd ever known. She leaned back her head against the soft leather squabs, closed her eyes, and began to snore.

She thought he chuckled, but she couldn't be certain. She now had a plan; not much of one, but at least it was a start; it was something.

The following day at just after eleven o'clock in the morning, Douglas returned to the town house. His meeting with Lord Avery had been short and to the point. Yes, Georges Cadoudal was here in London, not in Paris, where he should be with all the English government's groats and apparently he was out for blood, Douglas's blood.

Douglas sighed, handed Burgess his cane, and asked, "Where is Her Ladyship?"

Burgess looked pained but brave. "She is with a person, my lord."

"A person, you say? Is this person male?"

"Yes, my lord. It is a French male person."

He immediately thought of Georges Cadoudal and paled. But no, Georges wouldn't come here. Damn her eyes. Was she trying to spy on him by bribing some Frenchman she'd picked up off the street? "I see. And just where is she with this French male person?"

"In the morning room, my lord."

"Why did you not inquire the mission of this French male person, Burgess?"

"Her Ladyship said it was none of my affair. Her tone and words were very much in your fashion, my lord."

"It has never made you shut your mouth before!"

"Her Ladyship also asked me about my nephew who has a putrid throat, my lord. You have never shown such solicitude, thus, I favored her with my silence."

"Damn you. I didn't know you had a nephew!"

"No, my lord."

Douglas, still more intrigued than otherwise, walked quickly down the corridor toward the back of the house. The morning room gave onto the enclosed garden. It was light and airy, a delightful room. He hadn't been in here often. Sinjun had told him it was a room for the ladies and for him to stay away. He didn't knock on the door, just opened it quietly. He saw a long-faced young gentleman dressed in frayed black, sitting across from Alexandra. He was silent. She was saying slowly, "*Je vais à Paris demain. Je vais prendre mon mari avec moi.*"

The young man exploded with evident pleasure. "*Excellent, madame! Et maintenant—*"

Douglas said abruptly from the doorway, "I am not going with you to Paris tomorrow, Alexandra. Nor is there anything excellent about such a suggestion."

Under his fascinated eye, she flushed to the roots of her red hair, sputtered several times, then said to the French male person opposite her, "*Je crois que c'est ici mon mari.*"

"You only *think* I'm your husband?" Douglas nodded to the Frenchman, who was now on his feet, staring at him nervously, fiddling with his watch fob. A watch fob!

"What is he doing here, Alexandra?"

She was on her feet too and she was running lightly toward him, giving him a fat smile. "Ah, he is just a very nice young gentleman I met . . . well, yes, I met him at Gunthers' and I asked him to visit here and we could, well, we could talk about things."

"Things French?"

"I suppose you could say that."

"Are you paying him?"

"Well, yes."

"He is spying for you? Do you expect him to follow me and eavesdrop on my conversations and report back to you?"

She stared at him. "You really believe I would do that, Douglas?"

"No," he said shortly. "No, I don't, at least not in the usual run of things. But I do believe you would do anything you could think of to help me even when I don't require it or want it or need it and would, in fact, beat you if you tried it."

She cocked her head to one side. "You are saying several things there, Douglas, and I'm not at all certain—"

"Dammit, woman, who is this fellow and what is he doing here?"

Her chin went into the air. "Very well. His name is Monsieur Lessage and he is giving me French lessons."

"What?"

"You heard me. If you would now leave, Douglas, we are not yet through."

Douglas cursed in French with such sophisticated fluency that the young Frenchman was moved to give him a very toothy approving smile. He said something quickly to Douglas, and Douglas said something even more quickly back to him. Then the two men proceeded to speak in that accursed language, excluding her, making her feel like an outsider.

"Douglas," she said in a very loud voice, "Monsieur Lessage is my teacher. You are interrupting us. *S'il vous plaît*, please leave."

Douglas said something to Monsieur and the man grinned.

"I apologize, Alexandra, but Monsieur just remembered that he has another lesson to give, very shortly, and all the way on the other side of London." Douglas shook the man's hand, and money went from her husband's hand into the Frenchman's.

Alexandra wanted to hit him. She wished she could curse him in the fluent French he used so effortlessly. No, all she wanted was just one French curse word, just one. Her hands were fisted at her sides. She waited for the door to close, then bounded to her feet. "How dare you! He was my teacher, he was not at your beck and command! Ah, I would like to tell you in French just how angry I am!"

"Want to curse me out, hm?"

"Yes. *Oui!*"

"*Merde.*"

"What?"

"You may say *merde*. It means . . . never mind, it's a curse and it will relieve your spleen. Trust me."

"Merde!"

He winced, then grinned at her. "Feel better?" She said nothing, and he continued, "Why did you want to learn French?"

"To find out what that hussy said to you and why that man, Georges whatever, wanted to kill you last night!"

"Ah, so I was right. You are picturing yourself as Saint Georgina." He walked to the floor-to-ceiling glass doors that gave directly into the garden. He opened the door and breathed in the fresh morning air. "Alexandra, you were planning to rescue me again? This time with schoolgirl French?"

"If you won't tell me what is wrong, why, I must do something! It is my nature, I can't help it. I wish you wouldn't regard it as interference."

"A pity," he said, not turning to look at her. "Yes, a pity that you aren't more like your sister, a lady, I fancy, who is perfectly willing to wait to see what her husband wishes of her before hurling herself like a hoyden into one mess after another. Messes, I add, that have nothing to do with you."

"I wish you would be more clear in your condemnation, Douglas."

"In what way am I not perfectly clear?"

"That you love Melissande, still?"

He turned then to face her, this wife of his, and he saw the hurt in her eyes. It bothered him. He hadn't made love to her the previous night. He'd wanted to, Lord, that was nothing new, he always wanted her, but he had to teach her that she couldn't have him whenever she wished to, that he would decide when and where and how, and he'd had to show her his displeasure. Well, he'd done that and now he wanted her like the very devil. Her morning gown wasn't all that alluring, for God's sake, just a soft yellow muslin, yet he wanted to rip that very feminine row of lace from the neckline and bare her breasts. He wanted her breasts in his hands, he wanted to caress and kiss the soft flesh on the underside of her breasts. He wanted to press his face against her heart.

He sighed, and kept his back to her for he'd become hard, painfully so, just thinking about her damned breasts. He didn't like it at all.

And he said, to his own surprise, "No, I don't love Melissande. I never loved her but I wanted her. I suppose she was something of a dream to me, not a real woman, just this exquisite phantom that made my nights less lonely. No, I don't love her. I fear Tony was right about that, the damned sod."

"Tony loves her."

"Yes, he does."

And she wanted desperately to ask him if perhaps he couldn't bring himself to love her, just a little bit. But she remained silent. She did say, "I am as I am, Douglas. I cannot bear to think of you in danger. I cannot believe that you would prefer me to sit drinking tea when a villain comes up to plant a knife in your back."

"Perhaps if that were the case, you could yell at the top of your lungs for some assistance from a man."

"And if there were none of your precious specimens about?"

"Cease your games with me, Alexandra. I don't want you doing things I haven't approved. I want to know where you are, what you're doing. I do not want or require your interference in my affairs."

"You want a bloodless wife."

"Bloodless? Ha, do you so soon forget your screams and moans when I take you?" He shut his mouth for his sex was very painful now, his britches stretched.

He gave her a long brooding look. She was too close. "I wish you to remain here, in the house. Do not go out. Oversee our preparations to leave, early in the morning. Is that enough for you to do?"

She rose, her hands fisted at her sides. He simply wouldn't give over, she thought. She wondered in that bleak moment if he would ever give over. Perhaps not. She gave him a smile, ah, but it hurt to make her mouth move like that, but she did it, then just nodded to him, and left the room.

She walked up the wide stairway, not turning when she heard Mrs. Goodgame call to her. She walked to her bedchamber, walked inside, and locked the door. She stood for a very long time in the middle of the room, then slowly, she went down onto her knees. She wrapped her arms about herself and cried.

She was deep in her misery and didn't hear the adjoining door quietly open. Douglas, an order forming in his mouth, let the order die. He stared and felt a shifting hollow feeling in his belly. He hadn't really scolded her, for God's sake, nothing to bring on this misery. He couldn't bear it. He walked quickly to her, lifted her into his arms, and carried her to her bed. He came down on top of her, his mouth on hers, and he tasted her tears and sought to make her forget the tears, the pain, forget all but the pleasure he would give her. He jerked up her gown, shredded her stockings and flung away her slippers.

He unfastened his britches and came into her and she was soft and willing, quite ready for him, and it amazed him, this awareness of him that was deep in her, this yielding that was his even when he had hurt her. "Alexandra," he said into her mouth and thrust hard and harder still.

She opened her eyes even as she pushed upward against him to draw him deeper.

"I seems I must take you every day, for our health, you understand, otherwise we will grow quickly old and mean and testy. Do you understand? Tell me you understand."

"I understand," she said, and pulled his face down to hers. She was hungry for him, always this hunger, and she kissed him, her tongue in his mouth, taking the lead, and it both surprised him and made him instantly wild.

"Ah, don't," he said, but it was too late. Always too late with her and he surged into her and over her, panting and heaving, his eyes closed against the intensity of the feelings coursing through him, and that pressure, always building, and then, quite suddenly, he jerked out of her. Her eyes flew open but he only shook his head. He lifted her hips in his large hands and brought her to his mouth.

Alexandra screamed.

Then she groaned, softly, beyond herself, and it went on and on and he forced her to ease then he built the sensations again. He was controlling her this time but there was nothing she could do about it. She cried out, her head thrashing on the bed until finally, he left her and came inside her once more and he arched his back and yelled her name at his release.

When it was over, when he could find a breath, Douglas came up on his elbows over her, and said into her dazed face, "Don't you cry again. I don't like it. There is no reason for you to cry. I came to you, did I not? Did I not give you great pleasure?"

"Yes," she said. "Yes, you did."

He was still deep inside her. It was time for lunch. Absurd, the middle of the day and he was growing hard again. He forced himself to pull out of her.

"No more crying," he said and rose to stand over her. He straightened his britches.

"Why can't you trust me, Douglas?"

"You speak nonsense."

"Did I not try to save you from Tony?"

"That has naught to do with anything."

She managed to come up to a sitting position, pulling down her gown. She was wet with him and with herself, she supposed; she still felt the pull of the languorous feelings, the draining pleasure. She looked at her feet, bare, hanging over the side of the bed, not reaching the floor. "Very well, Douglas, I will do as you wish. I will not pry into anything. If you get into trouble, I shall be sorry for it, but I will do nothing. That is what you wish, is it not?"

He frowned. No, it wasn't, but it had been what he'd said.

"I wish you to arrange yourself. I am hungry. It is time for luncheon." He left her then, going into his own bedchamber, closing the adjoining door behind him. She sat there, staring after him.

"*Merde*," she said.

CHAPTER
═21═

DOUGLAS CAME AWAKE suddenly. He didn't know what had awakened him, but one instant he was deep in a dream, in a heavy skirmish near Pena, the French drawing closer and closer to his flank, and the next, he was staring into the darkness, breathing fast. He shook his head and automatically turned to reach for Alexandra.

His hand landed on smooth sheets. Foolishly, he ran his hands over her pillow and on the blankets bunched up at the foot of the bed. She wasn't there. She was gone. He felt panic surge, raw and painful in his belly. Dear God, Georges Cadoudal had taken her.

No, that was absurd. Georges couldn't have gotten into the house, up here into the bedchamber, and taken her, all without waking him. No, it was impossible.

Douglas was still wrapping the belt around his dark blue velvet dressing gown when he walked quickly downstairs, his feet bare and soundless on the heavy carpet. Where the devil could she have gone?

He quietly looked into the two salons, the breakfast room, the huge formal dining room. He paused in the wide entrance hall, frowning. Then, he walked quickly back toward the library. He stopped, seeing the flicker of light coming from beneath the door.

Very quietly, he turned the knob and looked in.

Alexandra was sitting at his desk, a candle at her left elbow, an open book in front of her. She was concentrating fiercely, her forehead furrowed.

He was on the point of charging in and demanding what the devil she was doing when he heard her say quite clearly, "So that is what *merde* means. Well, well, it is certainly bad enough and Douglas was right. It would relieve a person's spleen splendidly and very quickly." She said the word several times, then added aloud, "Of course it won't do much good in the long run. Come on, my girl, let's get to it."

He had a difficult time to keep the laughter in his throat, but he managed, for now she had begun repeating aloud in poor but understandable

French, "I won't go. *Je ne vais pas.* He won't go. *Il ne va pas.* They won't go. *Ils ne vont pas.*"

He stared. What the devil?

She was trying to teach herself French. All because she wanted to help him if she could.

Douglas simply stood there, staring at his wife, slowly shaking his head, grappling with what he saw and what was happening to him. Something deep and sweet began to fill him, something he hadn't felt before in his life, something new and wondrous and rich, something he'd never expected simply because he hadn't realized there was something to be felt and he hadn't known . . . hadn't known that he was lacking.

He continued to stare at her. She was sitting there in her white nightgown with its collar to her chin, her dark red hair in a braid that fell over her right shoulder. She was using her hands as she repeated the words in French. The candlelight flickered over her face, making her eyes luminous, breaking shadows on her cheeks and hair. She continued speaking, repeating endlessly the same phrases, over and over.

He could understand the French. If he really tried.

"I am helping him. *Je l'aide.* Ah, what is this?" She fell silent, then said very softly, "I love him. *Je l'aime.* I love Douglas. *J'aime Douglas.* I love my husband. *J'aime mon mari.*"

He stood there, letting the feelings expand and overflow in him, and then he smiled, a gentle smile that he could feel inside himself, and even that smile warmed him, made him feel incredibly lucky and that smile of his was his acceptance of her, of what she was to him and of what he knew he would always feel for her, his wife.

Very quietly he closed the door and walked thoughtfully back upstairs. He lay awake, reveling in the newness of his feelings, waiting.

When she eased into the bed beside him an hour later, he pretended sleep. For ten minutes. Then he turned to her and took her into his arms and began kissing her.

Alexandra gave a start of surprise, then returned his kisses with enthusiasm, as always. But there was no frenzy, no wild urgency this time. When he came into her, it was tender and gentle and slow, something he'd never been able to accomplish with her before, and he continued to kiss her, teasing her with his tongue, nipping at her lower lip, stroking her as he gave himself over to her. And it was good and she sighed in soft pleasure when it was done; she was bound to him now. She would be bound to him forever.

And when he knew she was asleep, he kissed her temple and said very quietly against her warm cheek, "*Je t'aime aussi.*"

Seven hours later, at the breakfast table, Douglas slammed his fist so hard his plate jumped and a slice of bacon slid off onto the white table-cloth.

"I said no, Alexandra. If Sinjun asked you to fetch her a book at Hookams, it is just too bad. I haven't the time to accompany you and you will go nowhere without me with you. Do you understand?"

She was silent.

"Tell me you understand."

"I understand."

"Good. Now, see to our packing. I'm sorry we can't leave this morning, but there is business I must attend to. I will return later." And just as he was at the door, he froze, hearing her say *"Merde!"*

He pretended not to hear her and was gone. Alexandra stared at her eggs and wondered why one could rhapsodize so stupidly in the middle of the night and imagine that it would last beyond a man's passion.

She remained busy the remainder of the morning although, truth be told, Mrs. Goodgame had little use for a mistress who was clearly distracted and really didn't care if her gowns were packed carefully in tissue paper or simply thrown into the trunk.

Douglas didn't return for luncheon. Alexandra was near to screaming with vexation and with fear for him. Why couldn't she make him promise that he would go nowhere without her in attendance? She tried to study her French but she was so angry with him that she spent most of the time searching for more curse words.

"You have the fidgets, my lady," Mrs. Goodgame finally told her, her voice weary with aggravation. "Why don't you take a nice ride in the carriage? There is nothing needing your attention here, I assure you."

So Douglas hadn't told his staff that his wife was to be a prisoner. Her mouth thinned. She would go fetch Sinjun her novel and Douglas be damned. However, just to be on the safe side, she removed a small pistol from Douglas's desk in the library that she'd come across the night before when she was resting from her French lesson, and slipped it into her reticule. She had no idea if it were primed. Just looking at it scared her; she prayed if she had to use it, the person she was using it on would be equally frightened just seeing it. She asked one of the footmen to accompany her, sitting next to John Coachman. What more could Douglas ask? She had two armed guards and a pistol.

Burgess did know that Her Ladyship was to remain indoors but he wasn't at his post when Alexandra slipped out, James the footman in tow.

The carriage bowled up Piccadilly, past Hyde Park corner to St. Edward's Street. John Coachman remained with the carriage and James accompanied Alexandra into Hookams. It was a drafty place, floor-to-ceiling shelves crammed full with books. It was dusty with little space between the aisles, but nonetheless, it had been pronounced a meeting place by the ton and thus the aisles were crammed with chatting gentlemen and ladies. Near the front of the shop, maids and footmen waited to relieve their mistresses and masters of their parcels. Alexandra left James to eye a pretty maid and allowed a harried clerk to lead her to where Sinjun's novel was. Ah, yes, there, on the third shelf. She reached for *The Mysterious Count* then froze when a man's voice hissed low into her right ear.

"Ah, the little pigeon leaves the nest, eh?"

It wasn't Heatherington, she thought. No, he'd been the sheep and the shepherd. She sighed and said, not looking back at the man, "Your approach is not to my liking, sir. It lacks originality. It lacks grace and charm. It lacks wit. You should hire someone to instruct you. I do like your affectation of a French accent though, but it really doesn't fit all that well with your excellent English. You don't reverse your words, you know?"

"Damn you, I do not mean to charm you! I speak three languages fluently!"

"Well, then, what is your purpose?" She turned as she spoke and stared up at a gaunt, very tall man, dark-haired, eyes blacker than Douglas's, garbed in gentleman's morning wear. She knew suddenly that this was Georges Cadoudal. Oh dear, this man's accent was quite legitimate.

"My purpose? Well, I will tell you. I have a very small and very deadly pistol here in my right hand and it is pointed at your breast. I suggest, madame, that you come with me, and keep that charming smile on your face. Consider me your lover and we shall deal together famously, eh? Let's go."

Alexandra saw the intent in his eyes, the cold hardness, the determination. "*Je ne vais pas!*" she shouted at the top of her lungs. She smashed *The Mysterious Count* in his face, hoping she'd at least broken his long nose. Then when he raised his arm to strike her, she screamed, "*Merde! Merde! Je vais à Paris demain avec mon mari! Aidez-moi!*"

He struck her against the side of her head, cursing all the while, whilst the patrons of Hookams stared in frozen shock.

"James, help! *Aidez-moi!*"

"Damn you," Georges Cadoudal hissed in her face, and then in the next instant, he was gone. James was at her side, shocked to his toes, knowing that he'd failed the mistress, but it had been so unexpected, the attack by the unknown villain.

"Are you all right, my lady? Oh dear, please tell me you're all right."

Alexandra shook her head to clear it. The blow had made her eyes blur and cross. "Yes, I'm all right." Then she looked at the novel she was holding and straightened out its ruffled pages. "I coshed him in the nose, James. Did you hear my French?"

"*Merde*, my lady?"

This time it was Heatherington, the man Douglas had told her would toss up a woman's skirts even before he knew her name, and he was smiling down at her, not the sardonic smile of a practiced roué, but a genuine smile. Oddly, there was a good deal of warmth in that smile. "Ah yes, I heard your magnificent French. Who is the poor soul who dared to agitate you?"

"He is gone," Alexandra said. She looked as proud as a little peahen. "My French scared him off."

Heatherington gave her a long look, then he laughed, a sound that was rusty because he hadn't laughed, really laughed in a very long time. It didn't go with the image he so carefully cultivated for himself. He laughed louder, shaking his head. "*Merde,*" he said. "*Merde,*" he said again, then turned away and left the bookstore.

Alexandra stared after him for a moment, then paid for her novel, ignoring all the whispering ladies and gentlemen staring at her. James walked very close to her until he handed her up into the carriage. They were at the Sherbrooke town house in twenty minutes. As James walked up the front steps just behind her, she stopped and said urgently, her fingers plucking at his coat sleeve, "Please, James, I don't wish His Lordship to know about the small, ah, contretemps, all right? It was nothing, nothing at all. The man was doubtless confused as to who I was, but nothing more."

James wasn't at all certain she was right. He was worried and rightfully so, for the first person he saw in the entrance hall was His Lordship and he looked fit to kill. In fact, he looked filled with anticipation to kill.

James had never before heard a man roar, but he did now. His Lordship straightened to his full height, and yelled at the top of his lungs at his wife who only came to his shoulder, "Where the hell did you go? How dare you disobey me! My God, Alexandra, you've pushed me too far this time! Bloody hell, it is too much, much too much!"

James retreated, bumping into Burgess, who glided into the fray without a tremor of agitation showing on his face.

"My lady, welcome back. Ah, I can see that James here stayed closely with you, as did John Coachman. His Lordship was worried, naturally, even though—"

"Damnation, Burgess! Be quiet! Believe me, she doesn't need your protection or interference." Douglas grabbed her arm and pulled her into the salon. He kicked the door shut with the heel of his boot.

"Trying to defend you, damn his traitor's eyes," Douglas said, shaking her now, his fingers digging into her upper arms. She said nothing, merely looked up at him. The shock of Georges Cadoudal's sudden appearance at Hookams had passed during the carriage ride home. Now, she was more calm than not in the face of Douglas's fury.

"I purchased Sinjun's novel," she said when he'd momentarily run out of bile.

"Damn Sinjun's bloody novel!"

"Douglas, your language is deteriorating. Please calm down. Nothing happened, really . . ."

He shook her again. "And now you compound your disobedience with a lie. How dare you, Alexandra? How dare you lie to me?"

No, she thought, it was impossible that he knew anything of what had happened at the bookshop.

"I ran into Heatherington," he said, seeing more deceit would come from her mouth.

"Oh," she said, then gave him a very tentative smile. Heatherington hadn't known a thing, not really. "It was just a man who didn't know what was proper—"

"It was Georges Cadoudal and he would have taken you."

"How did you know?"

"The good Lord save me from stupid females. Alexandra, you were screeching French loud enough for all of London to hear. I saw another gentleman you haven't even met and he told me about your *merde* at the top of your lungs. Everyone knows and I doubt not that I will receive a good dozen visits from people to tell me of my wife's exceedingly odd behavior."

"I said other things too, Douglas."

"Yes, I know. You're going to Paris with your husband tomorrow."

"And I screamed for help too in French."

"And another thing," he began, really warming up to his theme now, then stopped cold, for she'd pulled a small pistol from her reticule.

"I also took this. I'm not stupid, Douglas. That man couldn't have harmed me. I didn't leave the house without thought and preparation. I was bored, Douglas, please understand. I was bored and I wanted to do something. All went just fine. He tried but he failed. I also hit him on the head with Sinjun's novel. He didn't have a chance."

Douglas could but stare down at her. She looked so proud of herself, the little twit. She was completely convinced she was in the right of it. She was innocent and guileless. She had no more chance than a chicken against a man like Cadoudal. He took the pistol from her, his muscles spasming at the thought of having that damned thing turned back on her, and then walked very tall and straight and very quietly from the room. He didn't say another word.

Alexandra looked at the closed door. "He is trying very hard to control himself," she said to no one in particular.

He wasn't at home for dinner. He didn't come to her that night.

They left London at eight-thirty the following morning. Summer fog hung low and thick throughout the city, clinging like a dismal chilled blanket until they were well onto the road south.

Douglas sat silently beside his wife. She, curse her nonchalance, was reading Sinjun's novel. *The Mysterious Count*. What bloody drivel. Then he remembered Sinjun telling him about his Greek plays, and shuddered. This was probably filled with heroines swooning rather than taking off their clothes. "Why do you read that nonsense?" he asked, thoroughly irritated.

Alexandra looked up and smiled at him. "You don't wish to speak civilly to me, the scenery is nothing out of the ordinary, and I don't wish to nap. Have you a better suggestion than reading? Perhaps you have a volume of moral sermons that would elevate my thoughts?"

"I'll speak to you," he said, his voice on the edge of testy.

"Ah, that is very nice of you, Douglas."

He searched her words and tone for irony but couldn't detect any. He sighed. "Very well. I was worried about you. You must give me leave to worry, particularly when there is danger I know exists and it could touch you. All right, I apologize for leaving you alone, but you should have obeyed me."

"That is kind of you. I do appreciate your concern. I should appreciate it even more if you would explain the nature of the danger to me."

"I don't wish to. I wish you to trust me. Don't you understand the need to trust me? Tell me you understand."

She looked at his austere profile and said, "Yes, Douglas, I understand." She returned to her novel.

Douglas brooded in solitary silence for nearly an hour. Then he called out the window of the carriage for John Coachman to stop. They were deep in the country. There were no people about, no dwellings, no cows, nothing of any particular interest, just trees, blackberry bushes, and hedge rows.

Alexandra looked up, alarm in her eyes.

"No, it's just that I imagine you would like to stretch a bit, perhaps relieve yourself, in the woods yon."

She did wish to relieve herself, but she imagined that it was Douglas who had the need as well and thus the reason for their stopping.

He helped her down, clasping his hands around her waist, swinging her to him, hugging her close for a brief moment, then setting her on her feet. "Go to the maple copse. Be brief and call if you need me. French isn't necessary, but if you would like to, I shall be listening."

Alexandra smiled at him, saying nothing, and gave him a small wave as she walked into the midst of the maple trees. It was silent in the wood, the maple leaves thick and heavy, blocking out the sunlight. She was quickly done and was on the point of returning to Douglas, when, quick as a flash, a hand went over her mouth and she was jerked back violently against a man's body.

"This time I've got you," the man said, and she recognized Georges Cadoudal's voice. "This time I'm going to keep you." She had neither Douglas's pistol nor James the footman nor John Coachman. But she had Douglas if only she could free herself for just a moment, for just a brief instant.

She bit his hand and his grip relieved for just a moment. A scream was ready to burst from her mouth when she heard the whoosh then felt something very hard strike her right temple. She went down like a stone.

Douglas was pacing. It had been a good ten minutes since she'd walked into the maple wood. Was she ill? He fretted, then cursed, then walked swiftly toward the wood, calling, "Alexandra! Come along now! Alexandra!"

Silence.

He shouted, "*Aidez-moi! Je veux aller à Paris demain avec ma femme!*" Even as he shouted that he wanted to go to Paris on the morrow with his wife, he felt his muscles tensing, felt his mouth go dry with fear.

There was more silence, deep, deep silence.

He ran into the woods. She was gone. He looked closely, finally seeing where two people had stood. There'd been no struggle. There hadn't been a sound. Georges had taken her and he'd either killed her or knocked her unconscious. No, if he'd killed her, he would have left her here. Douglas continued his search. He quickly found where a horse had stood, tethered to a yew bush. He saw the horse's tracks going out of the woods, saw that the hooves were deeper because the animal was now carrying two people.

He had no horse. There was only the carriage. He couldn't follow. It was another hour before the carriage bowled into Terkton-on-Byne and he was able to obtain a horse that wasn't so old and feeble it swayed and groaned when it moved.

He was furious and he was scared. He was back at the maple wood in half an hour and he was tracking the other horse within another ten minutes.

He prayed it wouldn't rain but the building gray clouds overhead didn't look promising. Cadoudal was heading due south, toward East-bourne, directly on the coast. Was he intending to take her to France? Douglas's blood ran cold.

It began to rain two hours later. Douglas cursed, but it didn't help. The tracks quickly disappeared, but he had this feeling that Georges, the brilliant strategist, wasn't going to have an easy time of it with Alexandra. She wouldn't swoon; she'd try her best to get away from him and that frightened him more than soothed him. Cadoudal wasn't used to having anyone go against him; he was unpredictable; he could be vicious. Douglas plowed forward toward Eastbourne.

Just before he reached the town, soaked to his skin and trembling with cold, he knew that it would be next to impossible to find Cadoudal by himself. He would need much more than luck; he would need help. He needed many men to scour the inns and the docks and check into all the ships' passages.

He was tired, exhausted really, and knew that there was simply nothing more he could do. Yet he still rode into Eastbourne and stopped at three inns. None recognized his descriptions, that or they'd been paid by Georges to lie. Defeated, he mounted his horse, more exhausted than he was, and rode the fifteen miles to Northcliffe Hall.

Hollis took one look at His Lordship and called immediately for his valet. Douglas was bundled off to his bedchamber and put into a warm dressing gown. Hollis then deemed it appropriate for him to receive family, beginning with himself.

He said, "John Coachman told us what happened. I've sent out word and there are thirty men ready to do your bidding. You have but to give me instructions."

Douglas stared at his butler and wanted to fling his arms around the man. He said instead, his voice slow and slurred with fatigue, "Georges Cadoudal has her, Hollis, and I fear that he has already taken her to France. I did track him nearly to Eastbourne but it began to rain. I had no luck at the local inns."

Hollis patted his shoulder as if he were a lad of ten again. "No trouble, my lord. You will provide me with a description of this Cadoudal and I shall give it to all the men. They can be off within the hour. As for you, you will rest before you leave this chamber."

Douglas wanted to resist but he was so weary he merely nodded.

"I will bring you food and some nice brandy. Your brain will commence to work again very soon."

So it was that twenty-two men fanned out toward Eastbourne within thirty minutes, such an efficient general was Hollis.

He said to Douglas, "I also sent word to Lord Rathmore. I expect him shortly. His Lordship has never let you down before, you know."

Douglas grunted and sipped at the stomach-warming brandy. He'd eaten his fill, the fire in the fireplace was warm and soothing. He leaned back in his chair and closed his eyes. He slept deeply for an hour undisturbed, awoke and was greatly refreshed.

He opened his eyes to see Sinjun standing by his chair. For an instant he didn't remember and said, "Hello, brat. Where is Alexandra?"

The truth slammed through him and Sinjun watched as he paled.

"I'm sorry, Douglas. Despite what Mother says, I will accompany you to search for her. Shall I notify Tysen?"

"No, leave him be at Oxford." Douglas rose and stretched. "I don't believe this," he said to no one in particular.

"It's late, Douglas. Too late really for you to set out again. 'Tis nearly midnight."

"There are twenty-two men out searching, Sinjun. I must join them." He paused and gently cupped her face in his palm. "I thank you for wishing to come, yet I must ask you to remain here and run things. You know Mother . . . well, I want to be assured that all will be in readiness for Alexandra's return."

Douglas rode from Northcliffe Hall toward Eastbourne. It had stopped raining, thank the benevolent Lord, and there was a half-moon to light the way. He met McCallum, his head stable lad, at the Drowning Duck Inn on the docks in Eastbourne.

"Ah, Your Lordship needs a pint. Sit down and I will tell you what we've learned. I've made this inn a headquarters and each thirty minutes a group of fellows come to report their progress to me. That's right, drink your ale and sit down. Now just listen, my lord."

At two o'clock in the morning, five men trooped into the taproom to report that Cadoudal and Her Ladyship had taken a packet to Calais. Unfortunately they couldn't follow because of the contrary tides and the storm that was now blowing in. There was nothing they could do until the weather cleared and the tide changed.

Douglas told McCallum to send the men home. He arrived back at Northcliffe Hall at four o'clock in the morning.

He found himself going into Alexandra's bedchamber. He lay down on her bed in the darkness, staring up at the ceiling, exhausted but wide awake. He remembered every harsh word he'd ever said to her. He remembered the hurt in her eyes when he'd spoken of Melissande and how she would have acted the lady and done as her husband told her.

He felt pain wash through him, deep aching pain and an emptiness that was at once unusual yet not unexpected, not now, now that he'd finally come to realize that he couldn't live without his wife.

He heard her speaking French, saw her sitting at his desk, looking so very young, her voice clear and precise, her accent atrocious. He smiled even as the pain ebbed and flowed deep inside him.

He would find her; he had to. He couldn't now imagine facing a life without her.

The following day the storm had become a gale. No one was going anywhere. Rain splattered the windowpanes, and thunder shook the earth. Tree branches on the poplars were pressed nearly to the ground by the force of the wind. Douglas prayed that Georges had gotten Alexandra to France safely. He laughed harshly even as he prayed for that.

As for his mother, Lady Lydia sensed that the upstart wife who had been unknown to her son before she'd thrust herself into their lives had shifted in his regard. She wasn't stupid; she kept such thoughts as let the twit stay gone behind her teeth. As for Sinjun, she tried to keep her brother occupied.

It was no good. The storm raged outside and Douglas raged inside. Even Hollis was looking thin about the mouth. The entire household was tense, silent.

That night Douglas slept in Alexandra's room. He slept deeply simply because Hollis had slipped laudanum in his wine. He dreamed of Alexandra and she was standing there at the stables, laughing, patting her mare's nose all the while, telling Douglas that she loved him, loved him, loved him . . .

And then he was awake and Alexandra was standing there beside the bed, speaking to him.

CHAPTER
===22===

HE STARED THEN blinked rapidly. It wasn't so very dark in the bed-chamber and that was surely strange for it had been black as pitch when he'd gone to bed. But no, there she was, standing next to the bed, and he could see her clearly, too clearly really, and she was smiling gently down at him, saying, "She is all right." But she hadn't really said anything, had she? Yet he'd heard those words clearly in his mind.

It wasn't Alexandra. He reached out his hand and she stepped back very quickly, yet she hardly seemed to move, but he knew that he'd touched her sleeve, though he'd felt nothing, just the still air.

He felt a deep strangling fear, fear of the unknown, fear of ghosts and goblins and evil monsters that lived in cupboards and came out at night to bedevil little boys.

"No," Douglas said. "No, you're not bloody real. I'm worried sick and my mind has dished you up to torment me, nothing more, nothing, damn you!"

Her hair was long and straight and so light a blond that it was white, and the gown was billowing gently around her yet the air was still and heavy with the weight of the storm. He had, of course, seen her before, rather his mind had produced her before with a goodly amount of fanfare. She'd come to him that long-ago night when Alexandra had tried to escape him. She would have succeeded in escaping him had his mind not brought *her* to him.

Suddenly, without warning, Douglas saw Alexandra in his mind's eye. She was in a small room lying on a narrow cot. Her gown was wrinkled and torn. Her hair was straggling around her face. She was pale but he saw no fear. Her wrists and ankles were tied with rope. She was awake and he could practically see her thinking, plotting madly for a way to escape, and that made him smile. She had guts. Then he saw just as clearly the small cottage where she was and the village. It was Etaples.

Georges Cadoudal had a sense of irony.

He said aloud, his voice low and slightly blurred, "This isn't possible. You're not real. But how . . ."

"The storm will be gone early in the morning." The words swirled and eddied in his mind. She was leaving, gently and slowly she backed away and she was smiling at him and nodding slightly, moving backward, always moving, more like floating, and then she was simply gone.

Douglas refused to accept it. He leapt from the bed and he ran in the direction she'd gone. Nothing. He lit the candle beside the bed and held it up. The room was empty except for him. He was breathing fast, his heart pounding hard with the shock of it, the fear of it.

"You wretched piece of nothing, come back here! Coward! You ridiculous mind phantom!"

There was no sound save the rain beating steadily against the windows and the occasional branch slashing and raking against the glass.

He stood there for a very long time, naked and shivering and wondering. He had a headache.

At dawn the rain had slowed to a drizzle. At seven o'clock, the clouds parted and the sun came out.

Douglas came downstairs, fully dressed, and strode into the breakfast room. He drew up short. Tony Parrish was seated at the breakfast table drinking coffee and eating his way through eggs and bacon and kippers and scones.

He looked up and smiled at his cousin. "Sit down and eat. Then we'll leave. We'll find her, Douglas, don't worry."

"I know," Douglas said and joined him.

Tony waited until Douglas had eaten steadily for several minutes. "What do you mean you know?"

To tell the truth? Ah, no, not the truth, but it would be a treat to watch Tony's face change until he was regarding him like a Bedlamite. He just smiled, saying, "Georges Cadoudal took her to Etaples. We'll leave in just a few more minutes. We'll make the tide and be in France, with luck, in eight hours. Then we'll hire mounts and be in Etaples in the early morning."

"How do you know where she is, Douglas? Did Cadoudal leave a ransom note?"

"Yes," Douglas said and took a bite of toast. "Yes, it was a note. I would have left sooner but the storm prevented it. Is Melissande with you?"

"Yes, she's sleeping."

"Ah."

"While you're eating, tell me about this Cadoudal fellow and why he took Alexandra."

Douglas told him the truth, there was no reason now not to. He didn't tell him of Cadoudal's plan nor his million guineas from the English government to bring Napoleon down, sow insurrection in Paris, and put Louis XVI's brother, the Comte d'Artois, on the throne. But he told him of Janine Daudet and how the woman had told her lover Georges Cadoudal, that he, Douglas, was the father of her child. She'd been too afraid to tell him that it had been General Belesain or one of the men he'd given her to who had impregnated her. And then she couldn't take it back. She hadn't known that Georges would seek retribution until it was too late.

"The woman's mad!" Tony said. "Why should she serve you such a turn, Douglas? Good God, you saved her!"

Douglas toyed with a limp slice of bacon, memory ebbing and flowing in his mind. "It's quite simple, really, from her point of view. I rejected her."

"I don't understand any of this. What the devil are you talking about?"

But Douglas had pushed back his chair and stood. "I will tell you on the way to Eastbourne."

The air was crisp and cool and a slight breeze blew in their faces. Garth was full of energy and spirits and Douglas had his hands full controlling him. Both men carried pistols and knives. They both wore tall boots and buckskins and capes.

Douglas said finally to Tony, "She believed I didn't want to take her to bed because she'd been turned into a whore by General Belesain. It wasn't true, of course. As for the general, it's quite possible he used her as his own private whore, for visitors, for friends, whoever. He gave her to me for my enjoyment, no reason to believe that he hadn't given her to other men before I arrived. In any case, she was furious and hurt because I wouldn't bed her and she dished me up when she realized she was pregnant."

Tony shook his head. He cursed. Then he frowned, musing aloud, "I wonder why Cadoudal sent you a note. If he wanted retribution why wouldn't he simply take Alexandra and say nothing? He wants money?"

"No. He wants something else."

Tony started to ask what it was the man wanted, saw the closed look on Douglas's face, and held his counsel.

They arrived in Eastbourne in good time. Douglas had hired a weathered but worthy sloop. Their captain cursed the air blue. The crew didn't seem to mind, just went efficiently about their business. They were on their way within two hours. The tide was strong and swift.

They arrived in Calais seven and a half hours later.

She'd fought and struggled when he'd held her in front of him on his horse. He'd struck her with his pistol to keep her quiet. He'd struck her hard so that when she finally came to herself again, she had a deep pounding headache that made her want to retch. She was lying propped up against an oak tree. Since her hands were bound, she determined not to retch. She would be strong; she would control her body. She had scarce time to gather her wits when he was there, beside her, and he was forcing liquid down her throat. Before she lost consciousness she knew she smelled the sea.

She realized once she'd awakened that he'd drugged her. But how long ago? Where had he brought her now? She had no idea where she was, in a small house somewhere, since she was lying on a bed, securely bound, feeling dirty, hungry, and quite thirsty, but where?

She was alone. Any guards he'd left were outside the single door. Her thoughts were muzzy and she closed her eyes to try to regain clarity.

"So, you're awake. I'd hoped I hadn't killed you. I have never been any good guessing at amounts of laudanum. Of course," he added quickly, "I am good at everything else."

She opened her eyes. He was standing beside the bed, looking down at her. How had he come into the room so quietly? He looked tired, his flesh drawn more tightly over his cheekbones, his eyes more heavily lidded. His black hair was long and needed some soap and water. His clothing was that of an English gentleman, of good quality, but wrinkled and soiled. His expression was chilling. Still, oddly enough, she wasn't afraid, at least not at that moment, for Douglas was safe.

"I'm glad you didn't kill me too. I didn't hear you. You must have cat's feet."

He started, then shrugged. "Yes, I have many talents, and revenge is one that I take very seriously. I have perfected it to a fine art. I am a genius. It is unfortunate that you will never know of my fame, for I am also discreet. I leave nothing to chance, nothing to find, nothing to lead your damned husband to me. Your husband won't find you so you may quash your silly hopes that he will."

Still the fear simply wasn't upon her even though she was flat on her back, lying on a bed, bound. "I will tell you the truth, monsieur. I want only that my husband be safe. He is all that is important to me."

Georges laughed, a mean laugh that made his eyes look as black as satan's. "How very affecting! What a romantic child you are. Well, I imagine that this childish devotion of yours gratifies Lord Northcliffe at the moment. I also imagine that you are pleasing enough to his eye and young enough to give him passing pleasure. Men of his stamp aren't ever satisfied though, even with a little virgin with hero worship in her eyes. He would have played you false, probably by the end of summer."

Alexandra frowned at him. Because she loved her husband he believed her to feel hero worship for him? She wanted to inform him that she wasn't such a silly twit, but she said instead, "You are thinking of Janine."

Again, Georges Cadoudal started. "How do you know of Janine? Did he actually have the arrogance to tell you what he did to her? Did he boast about it? To you? His wife?"

"He told me that he rescued her in France and brought her to England."

"Ha! I trust Douglas Sherbrooke as much as I can trust any ruthless Englishman. He betrayed me. He raped her. That animal who was holding her prisoner gave her to Douglas because he'd won a card game, and he raped her repeatedly, hurting her, ripping her. Then he demanded her cooperation for she is strong, my Janine, and not easily subdued. It was his price for bringing her to safety in England, to me."

"Oh no, Douglas would never do that. He is a gentleman, a man of honor. You are wrong. This Janine lied to you. I wish I knew why she lied, but I don't speak French so I couldn't understand what she was saying to Douglas. I did ask him but he told me it was none of my business."

Georges Cadoudal had planned to ravish this little pullet, then send her back pregnant to Douglas. He didn't doubt his own virility for a moment. It would not take long. It would be an eye for an eye and then he would continue with his plan to kidnap Napoleon. But she wasn't at all what he expected. He shook his head, remembering how she'd reacted in that damned bookshop, screeching like a banshee in her absurd French. She'd even struck him in the nose with that book of hers. His nose hadn't been broken, but he hadn't liked the humiliation of it nor the pain. He looked at her now, brooding. Why wasn't she crying? Why wasn't she pleading with him to spare her, begging him not to hurt her?

"Just what do you mean you heard her speaking to Douglas?"

"It was at the Ranleaghs' ball. I saw her clutching at Douglas's sleeve. She looked as if she were trying to seduce him. I tried to listen, to eavesdrop if you will, but as I told you, I don't speak French. It was so provoking. I tried to get Douglas to tell me, but he wouldn't. He has too much honor to break a promise. I am very thirsty. May I have some water?"

He did as she wished, simply because she took him so utterly off guard. After he'd unbound her hands, watched her rub feeling back into them, he handed her the mug. He realized what he had done, but it was too late to jerk the mug of water from her hands. It was proof that he'd temporarily lost his control and his dignity and hadn't even realized it until it was too late. She finished it quickly, taking great gulps, so thirsty that water dribbled down her chin. She wiped it away with the back of her hand, then closed her eyes in bliss.

He stared at her and heard himself say, "Do you want more?"

"Yes, please. You are kind."

"Damn you, I'm not kind!" He stomped out of the door, slammed it behind him, and she heard the key grate in the lock. Alexandra would swear that she heard him cursing under his breath. She'd swear she heard at least one *merde*. At least Douglas had evidently taught her one of the most useful of French curses.

The moment she was alone again, the fear, stark and ugly, struck her full force. Lord, what had she done? She'd spoken to him as she would to a vicar, all trusting and confiding. She was a fool. He was probably now plotting how to torture her, to make her pay for what he believed Douglas had done to this Janine woman, the wretched lying hussy. Why had Janine lied like that about Douglas to her lover? After all, he had rescued her. To make him jealous? Surely that was going too far.

Alexandra lay back, closing her eyes, wishing that Douglas had spoken frankly to her so she could use the truth now with Georges Cadoudal. It was another minute before she realized that he had left her hands unbound. She couldn't believe it. She raised her hands and just looked at them.

New energy pounded through her. Alexandra untied the rope about her ankles. She stood and promptly fell back onto the bed. Several minutes of rubbing her ankles, of trying to stand and falling and trying yet again.

And when she could finally walk, she ran on light feet to the door. She knew it was locked but she tried it nonetheless. She turned back to the single window. It was narrow, maybe too narrow for her shoulders and her hips.

She could but try.

Douglas and Tony rode from Calais toward Etaples. The day was warm, the sun bright overhead. It was market day and the roads were filled with open wagons and drays and laden-down donkeys and farmers walking with their produce in bags slung over their shoulders. It would also be market day in Etaples. Perhaps it could be useful if they were forced to escape. Market days always were chaotic. Too, there were all the French soldiers, all the French carpenters and artisans and laborers and ship builders. Cadoudal was mad to have brought her here. It was beyond dangerous. It was foolhardy and it was precisely something that Georges would do. It was like laughing in the devil's face; it was like twitching his forked tail.

Tony said, riding close, "Did this Cadoudal fellow give you precise instructions, Douglas? You appear to know exactly where to go."

"Yes," Douglas said, looking between his horse's ears, "I know exactly where to go."

"I really don't understand this. What does he want from you?"

Douglas only shook his head. He couldn't get that damned insubstantial ghostly dream out of his mind. And it had been naught but a dream. He realized now that he'd been thinking so deeply, his thoughts so concentrated, about where Cadoudal had taken her, that he himself had come up with the likely solution. For some unknown reason, his mind had insisted upon giving further credence to his own deductions by providing him with a prescient ghost.

Yes, everything fit. Everything, once he knew Cadoudal had taken her to France. Everything, except the absurd ghost, the ridiculous Virgin Bride.

Even the house where he was holding her. It was the grandmother's farmhouse, and Douglas had seen the place. It was ideal for Cadoudal's purposes. Yes, everything fit.

Why the devil would a ghost give a damn about what happened to Alexandra?

He dismissed it; he needed to plan, to decide upon their best strategy. He realized that Tony had asked him another question, one he couldn't answer, one he didn't want to attempt to answer.

It was another hour to Etaples and then another ten minutes to the farmhouse.

Alexandra managed to twist enough to get her shoulders through the dirty open window. Her hips were more of a problem but she finally popped through, falling four feet to land on her face on the muddy ground. She lay there a moment, breathing hard, then lifted her head to get her bearings.

There was a small garden just beyond, filled with weeds and a few surviving vegetables. She was at the back of the farmhouse. There was a stable, dilapidated, with very old shingles hanging off the roof at odd angles. She heard chickens squawking. There was a goat eating what looked to be an old boot not ten feet from her. He chewed and looked at her with complete indifference.

She didn't hear any voices. There was no sign of life.

How long did she have before Georges Cadoudal returned?

That galvanized her. She kept low, skirting the vegetable patch, running toward the straggly stand of trees some thirty feet beyond. She was panting, a stitch in her side, when she slid behind one of the trees, falling to her knees, and peering back toward the farmhouse. She saw nothing except that goat, still chewing on the boot.

Now, where was she? She looked at the sun, hot now in the midday, and gathered her wits together. She wanted to go north to the English

Channel. But where the devil was she? Surely not too far away from the sea because she hadn't been unconscious for all that long. Had she?

She realized after five minutes of running that the trees were going to give out. There was nothing northward save an endless stretch of meadow, not even any low bushes, nothing to protect her, to hide her.

She couldn't remain here. It was now or never. She rose and began to run northward.

The sun beat down. She was bareheaded and soon she was light-headed from the heat and from hunger. Her breathing was rough and getting rougher. She was so tired she couldn't imagine being more so, but she forced herself to keep running, even walking quickly as the stitch in her side forced her to hobble like an old woman.

When she heard the horse's hooves pounding behind her, when she felt the earth shaking from the horse's hooves, she wanted to scream with fury, but instead, she just kept running.

She heard his voice and it was loud and mean. "You perfidious female!"

In the next moment, he scooped her up about her waist, bringing her against him and the horse's side.

Alexandra twisted around and struck at his face. She clipped his jaw solidly and knew a flare of success, but he jerked back and her next blow did nothing but glance off his cheek. He shook her like a bundle of rags and threw her facedown over the saddle. His hands were on her back to prevent her from lurching up. "Hold still, damn you!"

Alexandra felt bile rise in her throat. She tasted failure and she tasted fear and her own nausea. She was going to throw up. She tried desperately to control herself, but in the end, she couldn't. She vomited on the saddle, on his buckskins, on the horse.

The stallion went berserk at her uncontrollable jerking, the horrible retching noises. He reared violently, jerking the reins from Cadoudal's hands, flinging them both onto the ground. Alexandra came up immediately, her arms around herself, jerking and shuddering with dry heaves. Finally, the dreadful cramps stopped and she remained still, on her hands and knees, her head lowered, trying to control her breathing.

Finally she looked over and saw Cadoudal on his side looking at her.

She said, "I'm sorry. I tried to stop it but I couldn't. Is the horse all right?"

He could only stare at her and wonder if he hadn't struck his head when he landed on the ground. He shook his head now as if to verify that his brains were still inside his skull. His horse was grazing some yards away, looking quite unperturbed by all the ruckus.

"The horse looks to be fine, no thanks to you."

Her belly cramped again and she moaned softly, jerking once again with the dry heaves.

She was panting when she said, "I'm glad you didn't feed me. That would have been awful."

"Why are you ill? I didn't hurt you, dammit!"

"I don't know."

Georges Cadoudal rose and dusted himself off. He leaned down, clasped her beneath her arms, and drew her upright. He frowned at her. "You're a frowzy mess. You look like hell. I can't abide a woman who looks like you do."

Alexandra's eyes narrowed. "And you look like a man who's not been outside a brandy bottle in two nights. Ha! Telling me I looked awful!"

Georges Cadoudal laughed.

"Come along. I'm taking you back to the farmhouse."

She had no choice but to follow him. When they reached the horse, the animal slewed its head around and gave her a ruminating look. "I can't," she said, pulling back. "I'll throw up again."

She turned to look up at him. "You wouldn't be so cruel, would you? To make me get on that horse again?"

"I won't throw you across the horse on your stomach. That's what made you sick. If you promise to behave yourself, to just sit in front of me, we'll go slowly."

"All right."

It took only a few moments to return to the farmhouse. Alexandra had felt as if she'd run at least one hundred miles if not more. The stitch in her side was only now easing. With a horse, it took only a few minutes. It wasn't fair.

He dismounted first then lifted her down. "Go into the farmhouse. Drink some water. Sit down. If you so much as show your nose out the door or any of the windows, you will be very sorry."

Had it been one of Douglas's threats, Alexandra wouldn't have paid any attention. However, Georges Cadoudal was an unknown. He was cruel and ruthless and he'd shown himself to be quite determined. It was possible that he planned to kill her. Of course he had given her water to drink. It didn't quite fit together.

She went into the farmhouse, drank a little water, and sat down on one of the rickety chairs.

When he stepped through the door, kicking it closed behind him, she merely looked at him. He had washed his buckskins and the sick odor was no longer clinging to him.

She said, "Are you going to kill me?"

"No."

"What are you going to do to me?"

He eyed her.

"Will you ransom me? Oh, no!" Her face, already pale, was now paper white. And he knew what she was thinking. He would send the Earl of Northcliffe a note and he would come and Georges would kill him. He had never before in his life seen such naked pain. He wouldn't let it touch him. He had seen more death in his lifetime than this tender pullet would in a dozen lifetimes. He'd brought about more deaths than an English regiment.

She rushed into speech. "No, Douglas won't come to me, he won't, I swear it to you. He is in love with my sister, Melissande. He had to keep me, his cousin married me to him by proxy. It was all a horrible mistake. Douglas wants me gone, truly. Please, monsieur. Please, he won't care."

"I don't suppose you can cook? I'll just bet you are one of those utterly useless English ladies who never soiled her hands in her life."

"I am not useless! I am a fine gardener, though." She paused, then continued slowly, "I really can't cook anything that would look toothsome. I am sorry but in truth, I'm not at all hungry."

He grunted, then turned toward the small kitchen set back in the far corner of the room. He said over his shoulder, "Don't move."

She didn't. She sat there staring at the door, at him in the small alcove, at the thick layer of dust on every surface in the room.

"Where are we?" she called out.

"Be quiet."

"I know we're in France."

"How do you know that?"

She hadn't been completely certain, and she was pleased to have her conclusion so easily verified. She had remembered smelling the sea; then deep inside her, she remembered the rocking of a boat.

Some minutes later, he came into the room carrying two plates. One held slices of thick bread, the other a stew of sorts, reeking of garlic. Alexandra nearly gagged.

He said only, "Eat a piece of bread. It will probably settle your guts."

She chewed on the bread, trying to avoid looking at him downing the noxious stew.

The few bites stayed down. She looked toward the small crock of butter but was afraid to smear any on the bread. Georges continued to spoon down the stew.

When she couldn't bear it any longer, she said, "What are you going to do to me?"

He raised his head and simply looked at her. "I'm going to strip off your clothes first and I'm going to bathe you. Then I'm going to rape you as your husband did to my Janine. I will keep you with me until you are pregnant. Then I will send you back to Douglas."

She stared at him. Men were unaccountable. "But," she said, cocking her head to one side, "that doesn't make any sense, does it?"

He flung his spoon against the wall, rising from his chair, and leaning toward her, his palms flat on the rough wooden surface. "You will cease your unexpected prattle! I don't like it. It annoys me. Do you understand me?"

"No, I don't. It seems vastly stupid and just plain dishonorable and ungentlemanly to even consider doing such a thing. To force me? To keep me a prisoner and humiliate me like that? No, it isn't reasonable. Besides, Douglas says it can take a long time to create a babe. Will you keep me with you here for the next five years?"

He growled in fury, in frustration. "Damn you, beg me not to do it!"

She stared at him.

"Ah, be quiet!"

She was still quiet.

He said, "I am going to fetch you some bathwater now. I want you sweet-smelling when I take you."

She couldn't allow him to do that. She knew she wouldn't allow him to do that. The only problem was how to stop him. He was the stronger; he had hit upon this revenge and she realized that he was a man, who, once committed to a goal, couldn't be easily swerved from his set course. The thought of five years in her company didn't even seem to deter him.

What to do?

The main street of Etaples was crammed with stalls with people hawking everything from potatoes to blackberries. Tony and Douglas dismounted, leading their horses, pressing always forward.

Douglas cursed. They should have skirted Etaples but no, he'd thought he'd take a good look around in case they needed to hide here. How could he have forgotten the utter confusion and madness of market day?

It took twenty minutes and by the end of it, Tony was chewing on an apple and Douglas was eating a carrot.

"Well, we did need to eat," Tony said.

Douglas cursed again.

"Not long now. Er, Douglas, you're certain she' will be here at this farmhouse?"

"She will be there."

Douglas dismounted and purchased apples from a farmer. He threw one to Tony. "Eat your fill, cousin."

They continued on their way.

* * *

"You will take off those clothes or I will rip them off you."

She didn't disbelieve him, but neither could she imagine simply stripping down to her skin in front of him. He wasn't Douglas. No one was Douglas.

The tub of water was behind her, steam rising because he'd heated the water. It had taken a good half-hour but she hadn't managed to come up with a plan to escape him.

"Your face is filthy."

"I landed on my nose when I wriggled out of that window."

"Take off your damned clothes."

She was mute; she just shook her head.

He actually sighed. He looked unhappy. He looked uncertain. Then, he was on her and she fought him, indeed she fought him, kicking his shin and making him grunt in pain, but in but a few minutes she was naked and trembling, her clothing shredded and strewn on the floor around her.

"There." He lifted her under her arms and set her down into the tub of water. He handed her a cloth and a bar of soap. "Bathe. Do a good job of it."

He seemed completely disinterested in her. She was so relieved, so surprised, she said nothing, merely stared at him. After all, hadn't her mother assured her that once men saw a female form, they went berserk? Douglas had, but it had required several viewings before he had succumbed. Perhaps it took men time to get used to her before their animal urges consumed them. She prayed it would take Georges Cadoudal much, much longer. A decade perhaps.

"Wash your hair as well. It looks hellish. I don't like red hair on a woman."

Good, she thought and said, "All right."

He looked at her, that brooding look that raised more questions in her mind than answered them, then left her, cursing under his breath.

Alexandra bathed.

Unfortunately she was so exhausted, she fell asleep. She awoke with a start when Georges Cadoudal said from above her, "Damn you, the water's nearly cold. You fell asleep? That isn't normal, by God. You should be scheming something, you should be terrified of me, you should be screaming, piercing screams for help. Are you finished?"

She shook her head and pressed herself deeper into the water.

He frowned down at her as one would to a child. He grabbed the wet cloth, soaped it thoroughly, flattened it against her face, and rubbed vigorously.

She tried to yell but only got soap in her mouth for her efforts. Then she felt his hands on her breasts and froze.

CHAPTER
═══ 23 ═══

"LO AND BEHOLD," Georges said, staring down at her breasts. He shook his head even as she was trying to shrink away from his hands, but yet he was scowling. It was as if he were forcing himself to look at her. "You are well endowed. It is amazing. I should have remarked these breasts of yours before. I am disturbed that I didn't, but I am too tired, too concerned with all my future plans, and you have been naught but a vexing burden, but still—" He shook his head, frowning at himself.

Then he appeared to get himself well in hand. He rose and tossed her the cloth.

"Finish bathing and don't go to sleep again or it will be the worse for you."

She did, quickly. It was as if he had been watching her even though she knew he was in the other room, for the moment she stepped out of the tub, he was there, and he tossed her a thin ragged towel. She quickly wrapped it around her.

"Your hair," he said, and tossed her the other towel. "Did I tell you I didn't like red hair on a woman?"

"Yes, you were most specific. Could you leave please, monsieur?"

"No. I must look my fill at you. It will excite me, or it should, and allow me to get this over with quickly."

"I would prefer that you wouldn't."

He shrugged, an elaborate Gallic shrug that meant nothing and everything and she knew exactly what it meant.

She managed to get the towel firmly wrapped around herself, then took the other towel, more a rag really, to her hair.

He said, "Come into the other room. I've lit a fire. It is summer yet it is cold. I thought the fire would heat my blood as well as the room. I must try; it was my vow to myself."

She followed him into the outer room, her eyes on the front door.

"Even if you managed to escape me," he said dispassionately, "I can't imagine you running down the road wearing only a towel, your feet bare."

"You're right," she said and walked to stand in front of the fireplace. It was warm and it felt wonderful. She stood there, rubbing her hair, rubbing and rubbing until it hurt, wanting to put him off.

"Enough," he said finally, but he didn't sound or look like a man who wanted to ravish her. He sounded tired and angry and distracted.

She turned slowly and stared at him. He stared back, not yet moving. He opened his mouth, then closed it. He said something then in French and thrashed his fingers through his hair. "Well," he said finally in English, "damn you. Why you? Douglas should have to pay, curse his foul hide, but I cannot, I—"

She wanted to defend her husband, but what came out of her mouth was a sharp cry of pain. She pressed her hands to her belly. The cramp hardened and twisted and made her stagger against a chair. She was panting when it released her, only to cry out when it struck again.

"What the devil is wrong with you? You can't be ill. I don't like it."

Her face was white, her mouth twisted with pain.

"You shouldn't have any more cramps, it's ridiculous! You're not on the horse. You ate only the bread I gave you. Stop it, do you hear me? I told you I don't like this."

The cramp eased and she felt hot sticky liquid between her legs. She looked down to see rivulets of blood running down her legs. She raised her head to look at him.

"What is wrong with me? What is happening?" Then she cried out, falling to her knees to the floor. Tears were hot on her face; the blood was hot on her legs. The pain was building and building.

She fell back, drawing her legs up, hugging her belly, crying, trying to control the pain, but it was sharper and harder and she couldn't do anything save lie there.

Georges was on the floor beside her. He tugged the towel open and saw the blood on her thighs, the deep red streaks on the white towel. He swallowed. He didn't know what to do.

The door flew open to the farmhouse and Douglas came through, pistol in hand. "Get off her, you damned bastard! I'll kill you, you filthy sod!"

Tony was right behind Douglas. He saw Alexandra's white body, saw Cadoudal over her and felt himself raw with fury. Had the bastard already raped her? Oh God, she was bleeding, so much blood, too much blood. Had he brutalized her?

Georges Cadoudal whipped about, saw Douglas, and relief and hope flooded his face. But he had no time to say anything, for Douglas lunged across the room, jerked him away from Alexandra, and slammed his fist into his face. Georges yelled. Douglas struck him again, pummeling his ribs. Georges didn't fight back; he only tried to protect himself.

"Douglas, hold!"

Douglas hit him again before Tony's voice got through to him.

"Douglas, stop it now! Alexandra, she's hurt!"

Douglas reared up, his right fist hovering over Georges's nose, still straddling him, but looking at his wife. She was sprawled on her back and she was panting with pain and there was blood, so much blood.

His fist lowered and Georges quickly said, "No, no, don't strike me again. I can't remain defensive too much longer. I am a man, and cannot continue to allow this. Ah, but thank God it's you, Douglas. Quickly, quickly! She is having a miscarriage. Dammit, I don't know what to do. I don't want her to die. Ah, *mon Dieu!* Help me!"

"She's *what?*" Douglas's fist was not six inches from Georges's face.

Alexandra moaned and tried to draw her legs up.

"Look at her, Douglas. I didn't rape her. I swear I wouldn't have raped her in any case. Look, damn you! She is losing a child!"

Douglas took in the truth of the situation in that moment. He roared into action, rolled off Georges in an instant, and was on his knees beside his wife. "Georges, heat water and get clean clothes, immediately! Tony, go into the other room and fetch the mattress off the bed. We'll keep her here in front of the fire."

Both men were instantly in action although Georges did stagger a bit. Both were grateful to have something to do, anything.

Douglas was at his wife's side. She was moaning, her head thrashing back and forth as the cramps seized her. When they eased, she lay there panting, her eyes closed, gulping down deep breaths.

"Alexandra," he said, taking her face between his hands. "Alexandra."

She opened her eyes and stared up at him. To his astonishment, she smiled up at him. "I knew you would come. Please help me, Douglas. It hurts so very badly. Please make it stop."

"I'll help you, love." He picked her up in his arms and gently laid her onto the mattress Tony had laid close to the hearth.

"Now, listen to me. You're losing a babe. You are not so very far along so this will be over quickly, I promise you. Just hold on, love. Now, I'm going to press these cloths against you to get this bleeding stopped. No, don't fight the pain. That's right, hold my hand, squeeze as hard as you want to, that's right."

He felt a shot of pain go up his arm, her grip was so hard.

He prayed it would be over soon. He knew little to nothing about miscarriage, a subject never spoken about in a gentleman's presence.

Suddenly, her body stiffened, her back arching off the mattress, and she yelled. He felt the hot blood coming from her and it soaked through the cloth and onto his hand.

She looked up at him, her eyes dumb, then her head lolled back. She was unconscious.

Douglas kept the pressure against her.

"Here is the hot water," Georges Cadoudal said. "God, is she all right, Douglas?"

"She'll be all right. I'll strangle her if she isn't."

Georges looked oddly at him. "She told me you wouldn't come after her. She told me you loved her sister. She knew you wouldn't care what I did to her."

"She's sometimes quite wrong," Douglas said, not looking at Georges, not looking away from her face.

"I thought as much. She's unusual." He sighed, running his hands through his hair. "I couldn't have raped her, dammit. I'm telling you the truth. Damn, I could kill a hundred men without blinking an eye, but this one . . . I'm sorry I stole her, Douglas. It was wrong of me. You didn't rape Janine, did you?"

"No."

"The little one here was certain you hadn't. You're a man of honor, you see."

Douglas merely smiled.

Tony brought a blanket and covered her. He laid his palm on her brow. She was cool to the touch.

Georges Cadoudal turned away. To Douglas's astonishment, he looked as if he were in pain. He said, as if in confession to a priest, "I brought this on her."

Douglas looked at him, his mouth tight. "Tell me what happened."

"She escaped me. I'd given her water to drink and had forgotten to tie her hands again. She disconcerted me. I don't know how she did it but she managed to wriggle through that narrow window in the bedchamber. She landed on her face in the mud outside. She ran, she really did, ran and ran, but I chased her down. I threw her over my horse's back. She vomited."

Tony said, "I have been told that a miscarriage is a very natural thing. If a man's seed isn't meant to remain planted in a woman's womb, her body will expel it. It just happens sometimes."

"No, if I hadn't kidnapped her, it wouldn't have happened."

"That's right," Douglas said, not looking up from his wife's pale face. "I plan to beat the living hell out of you for that."

"For God's sake, Douglas," Tony said, "no one will ever know if he's to blame or not. You've already thrashed him. What's happened can't be changed. She will be all right and you will have your heir. Besides, if

Cadoudal really is to blame for it, he will go to hell and the devil will punish him throughout eternity."

"I doubt the devil will have time to punish Georges for this particular infraction. There are too many others." Douglas paused, then added, "Another thing, Tony, I don't give a damn about any precious heir." Douglas stared silently toward Georges. "If she dies, I will kill you. Then the devil can have his go at you."

"I accept that you would have to try," Georges said and shrugged. His left eye was already nearly closed from the blow Douglas had given him.

Tony said nothing. Georges moved over to the dirty front window of the farmhouse. Several moments passed in silence. Then Georges cursed and cursed again. Tony and Douglas looked up. Georges jerked open the front door.

Janine Daudet stood there, dusty and disheveled and alone, a pistol in her hand.

She grabbed Georges, shook him, yelling at him all the while in French. "Tell me you didn't ravish her, tell me—" Her voice dropped into stunned silence. "Douglas, you are here?"

"Yes."

"Who is that man?"

"He is my cousin, Lord Rathmore."

"Ah, the woman, your wife. What is wrong with her? All that blood . . . oh God, Georges, you didn't murder her?"

"No," Douglas said calmly. "She miscarried."

Tony watched the woman keen softly to herself, watched Georges Cadoudal gather her into his arms and attempt to soothe her. He gently removed the pistol from her hand and slipped it into his pocket. The woman was saying over and over, "It is all my fault, my fault, my fault."

"Enough of this caterwauling!" Douglas yelled. "Be quiet, Janine. It is certainly your fault that Alexandra is here, scared out of her mind I'll wager, because Georges threatened to rape her, as revenge for what I supposedly did to you."

"Ha," said Georges. "She wasn't scared, Douglas. She has steel, that one, all the way up her backbone. And she talks like no woman I have ever known in my life. She made me feel like a naughty schoolboy who should have a switch taken to his backside." But he knew he'd frightened her and he was sorry for it, but he simply couldn't bring himself to admit it aloud because that would make it real and that would make the guilt weigh so heavily upon him that he didn't think he could stand it. He didn't understand it. He'd killed with no remorse in the past and he would do whatever necessary in the future to bring the Bourbons back to the French throne. But this one particular woman was different.

"What are you doing here, Janine?"

She raised her head at Douglas's voice. "I had to come when I realized what Georges had done. I had to stop it. I knew I had to tell him the truth."

"And what is the truth, *chérie*?"

Janine pulled away from him, her eyes on her dusty riding boots. "He raped me—no, no, not Douglas—the general. Many times and he made me do humiliating things to him and to other men and he watched many times when he gave me to other men, and always, always, Georges, he threatened to kill my grandmother if I refused to obey him. The child I carry won't know his father for I don't know. Oh God!"

There was utter silence except for her low sobs.

"Why did you blame Lord Northcliffe?" Georges said. Tony started at the austere formality of his tone and his words.

"He was kind to me."

"A noble reason, surely!"

"It was close enough," Douglas said smoothly. "She feared you wouldn't want her if you knew what General Belesain had done to her. I was a better father for her child than any of those bastards."

Georges hissed through his front teeth, "All those bloody men should die."

"Quite possibly," Douglas agreed.

Tony said after a moment of tense silence, "All this is quite interesting, but isn't the scoundrel responsible for all this misery enjoying himself at this moment? All these bloody unknown men will remain unknown. Why don't we go teach this Belesain fellow a lesson he won't ever forget? Why shouldn't he be the one to pay for all this misery?"

Georges Cadoudal didn't often smile. He was merciless in achieving the ends for the causes he believed in. He couldn't afford softness and all lightness and humor had fled from his life many years before when he'd watched his mother and father and two sisters murdered by Robespierre. He was a man committed; a man committed didn't smile.

He smiled more widely.

"Jesus," he said. "How should I kill him? There are many methods, you know. Many, indeed. I have quite a range, a lot of choice. Shall it be slow? Shall we make him scream and plead and beg to know the final moment of his miserable life? Shall I use the garrote?" He rubbed his hands together, his eyes alight, his mind racing with plans and strategies.

Douglas said, "You forget that he is surrounded by more soldiers than I could count. He lives in a fortress. He has guards accompany him everywhere. He also knows me by sight and you and Janine."

They brooded in silence.

Tony said, "He's never seen me before."

"Oh no," Douglas said. "This isn't your fight, Tony."

"I don't know about that, it—"

Alexandra moaned softly; she opened her eyes to see Douglas over her, smiling gently. She felt his hand pressed against her. "Am I going to live, Douglas?"

He leaned down and lightly kissed her mouth. He said very quietly, "Oh yes. I have missed your impertinent tongue, madam. I have missed your pathetic flights of French. Most of all I have missed holding you against me."

She was crying; she didn't want to but the tears fell and trickled down the sides of her face. He wiped them away with his fingers. "Hush, love, I don't want you to make yourself ill. Hush. Now, just hold still. Are you warm enough?"

She nodded, gulping.

"I will continue the pressure for some more minutes. Then I'll bathe you and make you more comfortable."

"I lost our child. I lost your heir, Douglas, and that is all you wanted from a wife, from me. I did promise to be a brood mare but I've failed. I am so very sorry, but—"

"You will be quiet. It happened and that is that. I want you to be all right. You are what is important. Do you understand me? I'm not lying. It's the truth."

He hated the pain in her eyes, the pain of her loss, the pain of what she believed to be an irreparable loss to him. He would convince her otherwise. And eventually she would believe him. He started to say something but saw that she was no longer crying. Her eyes had narrowed. It was remarkable how she could be crying pathetically one moment and looking mean as hell the next. "What is that French hussy doing here? Did she follow you again, Douglas? I won't have it, I tell you! Tell me what to say to her, please."

"All right. Say, *'Je suis la femme de Douglas and je l'aime. Il est à moi.'* "

She looked at him suspiciously.

"You are telling her that you are my wife and that you love me. You are telling her that I belong to you."

"Say it again."

He did, slowly.

Alexandra opened her mouth and shouted the words to Janine Daudet.

There was stunned silence, then Georges said thoughtfully, "I prefer your rendition of *merde*, I think. It brought the entire Hookams bookshop your English aristocracy love so well to a standstill."

Douglas smiled, something he wouldn't have thought possible. As for

Alexandra, she was still thin-lipped as she looked at Janine Daudet. "Tell her, Douglas, tell her that if she ever again lies about you, I will make her very sorry."

Douglas didn't hesitate. He spoke rapid French to Janine. She stared from him to Alexandra, then nodded slowly.

Georges was rubbing his jaw as he said to Douglas, "Thankfully you didn't break it."

"You deserve that I thrash you within an inch of your life. However, I agree with Tony. I want to see Belesain pay for his crimes."

"Your eye is quite black," Janine said. "Did she do this to you?"

"No, but it doesn't sound odd to think that she would be quite capable of blacking both my eyes."

It was one o'clock in the morning. There was no moon. Dark clouds hid the few stars that would have shed light on the three men as they ran, bent low, from the shelter of one tree to the next.

There were no lights coming from the mayor's charming house in Etaples. There were four guards patrolling the perimeter. They were bored and tired and they spoke in low voices, trying to keep themselves awake.

The three men were on their haunches not fifteen yards from the guards. Douglas said low, "Tony, take down the one on the right. You take the one at the far corner over there, Georges."

"But that leaves two of them," Tony said.

"Don't worry, they're mine," Douglas said and he rubbed his hands together. He saw that Georges would disagree and quickly said, "No, I am a better fighter in the dark. Obey me in this. Once we're away from France, you can kill entire battalions, Georges."

Georges didn't like it. He was always the one in control, the commander of any and all raids. But he owed Douglas; he also respected his abilities, and thus held his tongue. Further, it hurt to talk because Douglas had hit him so hard in the jaw. Also it was difficult to see clearly. His right eye was now only a tiny slit.

They waited in absolute silence until the four guards were at their farthest points, then they scattered, hunkered down, appearing just shadows in the night.

Douglas planned to take the two remaining guards when they came together. He couldn't wait. He was grinning in the darkness. The dried mud on his face itched but he ignored it. The three of them were dark shadows on this particular night. He watched Tony make his way toward the guard. He remained relaxed. He grunted in satisfaction when Tony brought the man down, his forearm pressed hard into his throat, the only noise the man was making was a soft gurgling sound. As for Georges, he grabbed his guard, twisting his arms behind him and arching his back. He didn't kill him but Douglas knew he wanted to. He was relieved that Georges was sticking to their agreement.

Douglas readied himself. The guards were drawing closer. One was speaking and Douglas heard him say, "Ho, where's Jacques?"

"Probably relieving himself. He drank too much of that cheap wine."

They were nearly together. Douglas was silent and fast. He was on them before they saw him. He grinned and said in his flawless French, "Good evening, gentlemen!" He sent his right elbow into one man's belly and his left fist went into the other man's throat. He twirled on the balls of his feet, and slammed his foot into one guard's chin while his other hand struck the other guard dead center in his chest. Both fell like stones. Douglas quickly dragged the two men into the bushes and straightened. He gave a soft hooting sound and Georges and Tony were beside him in an instant.

"Well done," Tony whispered. "Remind me not to enrage you ever again, cousin."

Douglas grunted. They quickly tied the men and stuffed gags into their mouths. Douglas then led the way to the side of the house to the salon where he and General Belesain had played the card game so long before. The window was locked. Douglas gently broke it, tapping it lightly with the palm of his hand.

Tony made a cup with his hands and hefted Douglas up. He slithered through the window, dropping lightly onto the carpeted floor. In moments, Tony and Georges were with him.

Silently they made their way up the wide front stairs, shadows against the wall, low and swift.

There was one guard outside General Belesain's bedchamber. He was sprawled against the wall, sound asleep, his pistol on his lap.

Douglas tapped him with the butt of his own pistol over his right temple. He slumped over and lay on his side against the wall.

"Now," Douglas said. Very quietly he turned the knob to the bedchamber door. The door made no sound. Slowly, slowly, he pressed the door inward. It was perfectly silent. He stepped inside.

He looked toward the bed but couldn't make out the general's body. He took another step forward then froze.

"Ah, that's right," the general said low, not an inch from his ear. His pistol was pointed in the middle of Douglas's back.

"Who are you, eh? A thief breaking into this house? A fool, more like. I will see in a moment. You see, I heard you, for I have the insomnia, you know? I heard you; I hear everything."

Douglas didn't move. He didn't hear any noise from Tony or Georges in the hallway not two feet away.

A candlelight flickered and he was momentarily blinded when Belesain thrust it directly in front of his face.

"You," Belesain said and he was shocked. "I don't believe this, it makes no sense. Why are you here?"

Douglas said nothing.

"Ah, it matters not for you will die in any case. There is no reason not to kill you now, save for one small fact you must tell me. There are four guards. I cannot believe that you disabled all of them."

"He didn't," said Tony, and slammed the door into Belesain's arm. The pistol went flying. Douglas turned on his heel and smashed his fist into Belesain's stomach.

The man was wearing only a white nightshirt and presented a perfect target in the dark room.

Georges came through the door and grabbed Douglas's arm. "Now it is my turn," he said and struck the general hard on the jaw. He went down on his hands and knees and remained there, panting hard, moaning softly.

"He has gotten fatter since last I saw him," Douglas said.

"He could be skinny as a post and still be a pig," Georges said, and spit on the general. "Attend me, old man. I am Georges Cadoudal and I am here for retribution. You abused my Janine. You not only kept her prisoner, you raped her and let other men rape her as well."

"Cadoudal," General Belesain said dumbly, looking up. "God, it is you."

"Yes."

Tony looked dispassionately down at the general whose face had turned whiter than his nightshirt in his fear of Georges. "It is your decision, Georges. What do you wish to do with him?"

Douglas frowned. He prayed Georges wouldn't forget his promise not to kill the man. But he wasn't going to count on it. The rage on Georges's face bespoke pain and fury so deep it couldn't be easily assuaged.

The general said, "Your Janine, Cadoudal? I tell you she wasn't your woman. I had no need to ravish her. I offered her favors, jewels, money, and the like and she willingly came to me, willingly came to all the men who came to her room. They all paid her and she—"

Georges kicked him hard in the ribs, knocking him onto his side.

"That wasn't excessively wise of you, General," Douglas said. "I should say that it was rather stupid. Let's get it over with, Georges."

Tony saw that Georges was smiling in the candlelight. It was a terrifying smile.

"You know what they do to pigs, Douglas?"

The general didn't move.

"No," Douglas said, "but I imagine I am quickly to learn."

The general shrieked and tried to scramble away on his hands and knees.

"Hold, old man, or I'll put a bullet through your left calf."

The general stopped. He was panting hard; he was afraid. He'd been stupid to insult Janine. Now he said quickly, "I know you are an ardent Royalist. I know you want Napoleon exiled or assassinated. I can help you. I have information that will aid you. I can—"

Georges interrupted him easily. "Oh no you don't, General. You have nothing for me. I know you, you see. You are a fat bureaucrat who has no talent, but some power unfortunately. You are malignant; you are a parasite. It is true I hate Napoleon but I also hate fools like you who bleed those around them and torture them for their own enjoyment. Now enough. My friends and I don't wish to remain here."

Amongst the three of them, they dragged the general downstairs and out of the mayor's charming house.

They returned to the farmhouse by five o'clock that morning to find Alexandra sitting up, wrapped in a blanket, sipping on a cup of very strong coffee. Across from her, on the floor, sat Janine, her hands and feet securely bound, looking furious. She was cursing loudly, yelling to Georges when he walked through the door. All three men stopped short and stared.

"How could you do this?" Georges asked Alexandra, who looked quite fit, given that she'd looked white as death but hours before.

"I tricked her," Alexandra said. She took another delicate sip of her coffee. "I told her I didn't feel well and when she came to help me—unwillingly, Douglas—I hit her and then I tied her up. She deserves it for what she did to you, Douglas. Tell me you understand."

He couldn't help it. He was laughing. "I understand."

Janine was shrieking now in French.

"She's been doing that since I got her tied up, but you see, since I don't speak French, I cannot understand her. I have no idea what she's saying. Douglas, is she insulting me?"

Douglas grinned at his wife. "She probably started with you. Now she's insulting your grandchildren."

"Actually," Georges said, eyeing his mistress, "she is now quite fluently attacking your antecedents and all your former pets."

"I say," Tony said, "that we should untie her. She looks quite uncomfortable. What do you say, Alexandra? Do you feel you've punished her enough?"

Alexandra took another long drink of her coffee. "All right," she said at last. "I don't wish to stomp her into the ground, well, I do, but I'm not up to doing it right now, but I wish her to know that I am mean, that I will not tolerate such wretched behaviour toward my husband. She will never try to hurt Douglas again. Never."

Douglas turned and said something very rapid in French to Georges. He and Tony both laughed.

"What did you say?" Alexandra asked, her voice filled with suspicion.

"I said," Douglas said very slowly, smiling at his wife, "that once you are fluent in French, I will unleash you on Napoleon himself. Georges agrees that the Corsican upstart wouldn't stand a chance against you."

"I'm not sure," she said, frowning, her voice filled with worry, "you see, I don't think I'm feeling all that well right now at this particular moment. How long will it take me to learn that bloody language?" She paused, her eyes widening on Douglas's face. "Oh dear," she said.

She fainted. The coffee mug fell to the floor. Janine stopped cursing. Both Tony and Douglas were at her side in an instant.

"It shouldn't take her more than three months to spout French like a trooper," Tony said, as he gently laid two fingers against the steady pulse in her throat. "Stop shaking, Douglas, she'll be fine. It's the excitement, that's all."

CHAPTER
═══24═══

THE THREE MEN and Janine Daudet arrived at precisely six o'clock the following morning at the massive shipbuilding field that would shortly brim with workers, soldiers, sailors, cooks, prostitutes, hawkers of every item conceivable. They hid themselves and waited.

They remained hidden when the cry went up that General Belesain's headquarters had been breached. Guards were wounded and tied up and the general was gone.

There was some discussion as the men moved forward through the wide gates. Then there was utter silence.

At first there weren't more than fifty men and women; their ranks swelled to several hundred, all silent and staring. Then there was a giggle, a shout of laughter. More and more people arrived. The laughter grew. So did the general's curses and his threats, which ranged from cutting off arms and legs to pulling out tongues to flaying off the hide from every man and woman present. The onlookers paid no attention.

A man shouted, "Good Gawd, it's a pig, a big fat general sort of pig!"

A woman yelled, "Look at that little thing of his! Naught but a tiny sausage!"

"Aye, and that belly, bloated with all our local food he's sent his men to steal, the selfish pig!"

"A pig! A pig! Look at the pig!"

Georges looked at Douglas and then to Tony. They didn't have to take care and be silent. The noise was now deafening. They laughed and slapped each other on the back. Janine Daudet was so pleased she even hugged Tony.

General Belesain was standing on a four-foot-high wooden crate. He was tied securely to a pole, his arms pulled back so far that his back was arched, making his fat belly stick out obscenely. He was quite naked. Pig ears that Georges had stolen from a local butcher were tied on his head, a pig's snout tied around his face, poking out over his nose. The rest of him was fat and pink, no embellishments needed.

His men tried to get to him to free him but the crowd held them back. They weren't through with their fun.

Douglas finally motioned for them to leave. Janine said to Georges in some amazement, "You're laughing. I can't believe it. You never laugh."

He turned sober immediately. "I didn't mean to. It isn't well done of me."

Tony said, "A man should laugh; it gives him back his bearings; it makes him realize how absurd life can be."

Douglas said, nothing. He wanted only to see his wife. She'd wanted so much to come but he hadn't allowed it. She was too weak. She argued but he held firm. Now he wished he'd carried her here. She would have enjoyed herself immensely.

Now, he thought, he had to get them out of France and back home to England.

Three days later, Douglas, carrying Alexandra in his arms, followed by Tony, strode into Northcliffe Hall.

There was as much bedlam as there'd been the morning of General Belesain's unveiling, only this bedlam was joyous and welcoming. Douglas looked up to see Melissande coming down the wide staircase, looking more beautiful than a flesh and blood woman should look, breath-stoppingly beautiful actually, but he found that he just smiled toward her. She was looking for Tony, and when she found him, she picked up her skirts to her knees, and ran full-tilt until she could jump into his arms. She screamed at the top of her lungs, "You're safe, damn you! I was so worried, so—" She said no more for Tony was kissing her soundly.

Douglas still smiled.

He looked at his wife and saw that there were tears in her eyes. He was jolted into immediate fear. "You are ill? What is wrong? You have pain?"

She shook her head and wiped her eyes with the heel of her hand.

"Alexandra, we will be attacked by fifty servants, Sinjun, and my mother in under two minutes. Speak to me."

"She's just so beautiful."

"Who? Oh, Melissande. Yes, she is. Who cares?"

She stiffened in his arms.

He started a smile. "Why, you're still jealous."

"No, damn you!"

"Ah yes, you are, you silly chit. Answer me this, Alex. Can Melissande speak French?"

"No, she's horrible at languages, her accent even more atrocious than mine, but she paints so well."

"So, she couldn't have tried to save me like you did."

"That has less than nothing to do with naught."

Douglas merely continued his teasing grin. "I wonder how one would say that in French. Listen well, Alex—"

"You called me Alex!"

"Yes, certainly. If you prefer sweetheart, you will doubtless hear that as well. And stubborn and cherished and willful and wonderful. Now, listen to me. I think your sister is beautiful. Nothing new in that. But she isn't you. No, it doesn't matter now. What matters, to Tony, is that she is improving by veritable leaps and bounds under his tender tutelage. As Tony told me yesterday, one day soon her character just might begin to approach her beauty."

"Really, Douglas?"

"Really what?"

"Cherished?"

He kissed her. He heard laughter and slowly raised his head. There was Sinjun grinning at him like a fool. His mother stood behind her, her mouth pursed.

His mother called out, "Where have you been, Douglas? What is going on here? I demand to know now. Why are you carrying her?"

"Soon, Mother. As for the little one here, she has been ill."

"She looks quite well to me. Why is she wrapped in a blanket?"

"Because," Douglas said, walking toward his mother. "Because she's quite naked beneath."

"Douglas! You know that's not true." She was wearing one of Janine Daudet's gowns actually, a quite ugly gown really. Doubtless Janine's revenge for the coshing Alexandra had given her. Her feet, however, were quite bare and stuck out from the blanket. Douglas hadn't wanted to slow to buy her shoes. She hadn't argued. It was quite pleasant to be carried by her husband.

"Yes, but if she thinks you're naked, I'll get to escape with you all that much more quickly."

"What happened?" Sinjun asked.

"We will cover all that later." Douglas turned and raised his voice, saying, "We are all alive and well and home to stay. Thank all of you for being concerned."

The servants cheered. Hollis stood proudly, his arms crossed over his chest. Alexandra felt herself swelling with relief. Perhaps everything would be all right. Perhaps even her mother-in-law would come about. Perhaps Douglas really did cherish her. Perhaps.

Douglas carried her to his bedchamber. He kissed her, then eased her down to sit on the edge of the bed, pulling the blanket off her. "Mother doubtless believes you are a loose woman, that you must have burned your clothes to compromise me. I will tell her that I am already thoroughly compromised, that you have seduced me endlessly and I am used to it, that I can't do without your charms or your company. There was nothing more for you to do."

She was staring up at him, not moving, just sitting there, her legs dangling over the side of the bed, wearing Janine's gown that was too long and bagged around her.

She moistened her lips.

"Do you cherish me, Douglas? Perhaps just a little bit?"

"Perhaps," he said.

He walked, smiling to himself, into her adjoining bedchamber, soon to return with a nightgown. "Come, let's get you into this. You need to rest now."

He pulled the gown over her head, found himself staring at her breasts, then swallowed and quickly pulled the fine linen nightgown over her head, smoothing it down her body. "There." He put her between the covers, then sat down beside her and arranged her hair on the pillow even as he said thoughtfully, "Our marriage hasn't been so very smooth thus far. Do you think perhaps that you could moderate your actions? Perhaps think a bit before you hare off to do something outrageous? Like running away from me and becoming ill? Like getting yourself kidnapped and taken to a foreign country? Like trying to save me when you are really the one in jeopardy?"

She stared up at him, perfectly still as he continued to artfully arrange her hair on the pillow.

"I don't know," she said finally. "You are very important to me, Douglas."

He liked the sound of that. He leaned down and kissed the tip of her nose. "I have decided that if I keep you in bed for, say, three hours a day—not to mention the nights of course—you just might be too busy focusing on me or too busy recovering from lovemaking to bring gray hairs to my head."

"And would you also be too busy recovering from our lovemaking?"

"Never too busy to cease thinking about the next time I would haul you off to bed and have my way with you. You already occupy a great deal of my poor brain."

He frowned then as she remained silent. "Not just haul you off to bed to make love to you. I fancy also I'll haul you off to the stable, to the floor in the library on that soft rug in front of the fireplace. Perhaps also in the breakfast room with the morning sun streaming in on us and then on the formal dining table. You could clutch that ghastly epergne while I made you scream—"

She laughed and poked his arm.

"Tell me you love me, Alexandra."

"I love you, Douglas."

"Do you agree that a man needs to hear that every day of his life?"

"I am in full agreement."

"Good. Now, wife, I want you to rest. I will see to the family, censor our tale just a bit unless Sinjun has already pried all the facts from Tony, and store up all the recent gossip to tell you later on."

He kissed her mouth. He'd intended only a light, sweet kiss, but her arms went around his shoulders and she held him to her and parted her lips.

"You came after me," she said into his mouth. "You were worried about me."

"Naturally," he said, kissing her nose, her lips, her chin, his breath warm against her skin. "You are my wife, I love you, I will even go so far as to say that cherishing has a good deal to do with it. Are you satisfied now?"

"Do you know that a wife must needs hear that every day of her life?"

"I'm not surprised. No, not at all." He kissed her again, tucked the covers about her shoulders, and left her alone to rest.

Two weeks later in the late afternoon, Douglas came into their bedchamber. Alexandra looked up from her mending, smiling automatically. Good Lord, she loved him so very much.

"What do you have there?" she asked, trying not to look so besotted.

He was frowning. "I had to know," he said more to himself than to her. "I just had to know so I went looking in Sinjun's bedchamber." He spread out on her lap the items he'd found in the back of Sinjun's armoire.

Alexandra gasped. "It's a wig! Goodness, it looks like the Virgin Bride's hair! And that gauzy gown! Douglas, you can't mean it, no, surely not, I—"

"Can't believe that Sinjun was our ghost? Evidently so. Yes, she most certainly was. Here's the proof."

But Alexandra was thinking furiously, trying to remember when she'd first seen the ghost. She remembered quickly enough. Sinjun had been in London. She wasn't wrong. She started to tell Douglas when she saw that he was staring fixedly at the east windows. He was somewhat white about the mouth. He looked tense and stiff, his back and shoulders rigid. She said nothing.

Finally, he said firmly, turning back to her, "It was Sinjun all along. Just my little sister playing at being a ghost because she wanted to stir things up, wanted to have some fun at our expense."

Alexandra was shaking her head. She opened her mouth but Douglas raised his hand.

"Yes, it was just Sinjun, nothing more, nothing extraordinary, nothing ghostly. A real live human being, not a willowy phantom, not a creature who speaks but really doesn't but you hear it in your mind. No, nothing like that. It's true. It's very important that it's true. It will remain true. Tell me you understand this, Alexandra."

"I understand."

He kissed her, stood straight again, and said as he stared at the wig and the gown, "I have decided not to say anything about it to Sinjun. I don't wish to hear her denials, her protestations. I wish to let the entire subject alone. No, don't argue with me. My mind is made up. Do you understand?"

"I understand."

"Unlike my vaunted ancestors, I will never write about that accursed Virgin Bride, no matter the fact that she was of great assistance—in my mind, of course, nowhere else, naturally, and not really there as something substantial or nearly substantial. Since I will burn Sinjun's props, there will be no more appearances by that ghostly young lady. Never again. No one will have a word to say in nonsensical diaries in future years. That's the way it must be. I will accept nothing to the contrary. Do you understand, Alexandra?"

"I understand."

"Good," he said, kissed her again, and left her to look after him. She smiled as she shook her head, and returned to her mending.

The *Hellion Bride*

CHAPTER
=== 1 ===

Montego Bay, Jamaica
June 1803

IT WAS SAID she had three lovers.

Rumor numbered those three as: the pallid thin-chested Oliver Susson, an attorney and one of the richest men in Montego Bay, unmarried, nearing middle age; Charles Grammond, a planter who owned a large sugar plantation next to Camille Hall, the plantation where she lived, a man with a long-faced, strong-willed wife and four disappointing children; and a Lord David Lochridge, the youngest son of the Duke of Gilford, sent to Jamaica because he'd fought three duels within three years, killed two men, and tried unsuccessfully, because of his phenomenal luck at cards, to spend his grandmother's entire fortune that had been left to him at the tender age of eighteen. Lochridge was now Ryder's age—twenty-five—tall and slender, with a vicious tongue and an angel's face.

Ryder heard about these men in surprising detail—but nearly nothing about the notorious woman whose favors they all seemed to share equally—on his very first afternoon in Montego Bay in a popular local coffeehouse, the Gold Doubloon, a low sprawling building whose neighbor was, surprisingly enough to Ryder, St. James's Church. The crafty innkeeper had gained the patronage of the rich men of the island through the simple expedient of using his beautiful daughters, nieces, and cousins to serve the customers with remarkable amiability. Whether or not any of these lovely young girls carried any of the innkeeper's blood was not questioned.

Ryder had been made welcome and given a cup of local grog that was dark and thick and curled warmly in his belly. He relaxed, glad to be once again on solid ground, and looked about at the assembled men. He silently questioned again the necessity of his leaving his home in England and traveling to this godforsaken backwater all because the manager of their sugar plantation, Samuel Grayson, had written in near hysteria to Douglas, his elder brother and Earl of Northcliffe, describing in quite fabulous detail all the supernatural and surely quite evil happenings going on at Kimberly Hall. It was all nonsense, of course, but Ryder had quickly volunteered to come because the man was obviously scared out of his wits and Douglas was newly married and to a young lady not of his choice. Obviously he needed time to accustom himself to his new and unexpected lot. So it was Ryder who'd spent seven weeks on the high seas before arriving here in Montego Bay, in the middle of the summer in heat so brutal it was a chore to breathe. At the very least, what was happening was a mystery, and Ryder loved mysteries. He heard one of the men say something about this girl with three lovers. Had the men no other topic of conversation? Then one of her lovers had come in, the attorney, Oliver Susson, and there had been a hushed silence for several moments before one of the older gentlemen said in a carrying voice, "Ah, there's dear Oliver, who doesn't mind sharing his meal with his other brothers."

"Ah, no, Alfred, 'tis only his dessert he shares with his brothers."

"Aye, a toothsome tart," said a fat gentleman with a leering smile. "I wonder about the taste of her. What do you think, Morgan?"

Ryder found himself sitting forward in the canebacked chair. He had believed he would be bored on Jamaica with backwater colonial contentiousness.

He found himself, instead, grinning. Who the devil was this woman who juggled three men in and out of her bedchamber with such skill?

"I doubt it's cherries he tastes," said the man named Morgan, tilting back his chair, "but I tell you, young Lord David licks his lips."

"Ask Oliver. He can give us his legal opinion of the tart in question."

Oliver Susson was a very good attorney. He blessed the day he arrived in Montego Bay some twelve years before, for he now controlled three sugar plantations since all three owners were living in England. Not one of the owners seemed to mind that he was a competitor's attorney. He sighed now. He had heard every provocative comment and he never showed any emotion save a tolerant smile.

He said with an easygoing bonhomie. "My dear sirs, the lady in question is the queen of desserts. Your jealousy leads your tongues to serious impertinence." With that, he ordered a brandy from a quite striking young woman with wild red hair and a gown that offered up breasts as creamy as the thick goat milk served with the coffee. He then opened an English newspaper, shook the pages, and held it in front of his face.

What the hell was the woman's name? Who was she?

Ryder found that he really didn't want to leave the coffeehouse. Outside, the grueling sun was beating down, piles of filth and offal on all the walkways, thick dust that kicked up even when a man took a single step. But he was tired, he needed to get to Kimberly Hall, and he needed to soothe Grayson's doubtless frazzled nerves. Grayson was probably even now at the dock wondering where the hell he was. Well, he would discover all about this so-called tart soon enough.

He paid his shot, bid his new acquaintances goodbye, and strode out into the nearly overpowering heat of the late afternoon. It nearly staggered him and he found himself wondering how the devil one could even want to make love in this inferno. He was immediately surrounded by ragged black children, each wanting to do something for him, from wiping his boots with a dirty cloth to sweeping the path in front of him with naught more than twigs tied together. They were all shouting "Massa! Massa!" He tossed several shillings into the air and strolled back to the dock. There were free blacks in the West Indies, he knew, but if they were free, they couldn't be more ragged than their slave brothers.

On the small dock, the smell of rotting fish nearly made him gag. The wooden planks creaked beneath his boots, and there was a frenzy of activity as slaves unloaded a ship that had just docked. Both a black man and a white man stood nearby, each with a whip in his hand, issuing continuous orders. He saw Samuel Grayson, the Sherbrooke manager and attorney, pacing back and forth, mopping his forehead with a handkerchief. The man looked older than Ryder knew him to be. When he looked up and saw Ryder, Ryder thought he would faint with relief.

Ryder smiled pleasantly and stretched out his hand. "Samuel Grayson?"

"Yes, my lord. I had thought you hadn't come until I chanced to see the captain. He told me you were the most enjoyable passenger he's ever had."

Ryder smiled at that. The fact of the matter was, he hadn't slept with the captain's wife, a young lady making her first voyage with her much older husband. She'd tried to seduce him in the companionway during a storm. Captain Oxenburg had evidently found out about it. "Oh yes, I'm here, right enough. I'm not a lord, that's my older brother, the Earl of Northcliffe. I'm merely an honorable, which sounds quite ridiculous really, particularly in this blistering sun, particularly in the West Indies. I believe a simple mister in these parts is quite sufficient. Good God, this sun is brutal and the air is so heavy I feel as though I'm carrying an invisible horse on my shoulders."

"Thank God you are here. I've waited and wondered, I don't mind telling you, my lor—Master Ryder, that we've trouble here, big trouble, and I haven't known what to do, but now you're here and, oh dear, as for the heat, you'll accustom yourself hopefully and then—"

Mr. Grayson's voice broke off abruptly and he sucked in his breath. Ryder followed his line of vision and in turn saw a vision of his own. It was a woman . . . really, just a woman, but even from this distance, he knew who she was, oh yes, he was certain this was the woman who dangled three men so skillfully. When she bade them dance, they doubtless danced. He wondered what else she bade them do. Then he shook his head, too weary from the seven weeks on board the comfortingly huge barkentine, *The Silver Tide*, that he simply didn't care if she were a snake charmer from India or the whore of the island, which, he supposed, she was. The intense heat was sapping his strength. He'd never experienced anything like it before in his life. He hoped Grayson was right and he'd adjust; that, or he'd just lie about in the shade doing nothing.

He turned back to Grayson. The man was still staring at her, slavering like a dog over a bone that wouldn't ever be his because other bigger dogs had staked claim.

"Mr. Grayson," Ryder said, and finally the man turned back to him. "I would like to go to Kimberly Hall now. You can tell me of the troubles on our way."

"Yes, my lor—Master Ryder. Right away. It's just that she's, well, that's Sophia Stanton-Greville, you know." He mopped his forehead.

"Ah," said Ryder, his voice a nice blend of irony and contempt. "Onward, Grayson. Pull your tongue back into your mouth, if you please. I see flies hovering."

Samuel Grayson managed it, not without some difficulty, for the woman in question was being helped down from her mare by a white man, and she'd just shown a glimpse of silk-covered ankle. To render men slavering idiots with an ankle made Ryder shake his head. He'd seen so many female ankles in his day, so many female legs and female thighs, and everything else female, that he by far preferred an umbrella to protect him from the relentless sun than seeing anything the woman had to offer.

"And don't call me master. Ryder will do just fine."

Grayson nodded, his eyes still on the Vision. "I don't understand," he said more to himself than to Ryder as he walked to two horses, docilely standing, heads lowered, held by two small black boys. "You see her, you see how exquisitely beautiful she is, and yet you are not interested."

"She is a woman, Grayson, nothing more, nothing less. Let's go now."

When Grayson produced a hat for Ryder, he thought he'd weep for joy. He couldn't imagine riding far in this heat. "Is it always this unmercifully hot?"

"It's summer. It's always intolerable in the summer here," said Grayson. "We only ride, Ryder. As you'll see, the roads here are well nigh impassable for a carriage. Yes, all gentlemen ride. Many ladies as well."

Grayson sat his gray cob quite comfortably, Ryder saw, as he mounted his own black gelding, a huge brute with a mean eye.

"It's nearly an hour's ride to the plantation. But the road west curves very close to the water and there will be a breeze. Also the great house is set upon a rise, and thus catches any breezes and winds that might be up, and in the shade it is always bearable, even in the summer."

"Good," Ryder said and clamped the wide-brimmed leather hat down on his head. "You can tell me what's been happening that disturbs you so much."

And Grayson talked and talked. He spoke of strange blue and yellow smoke that threaded skyward like a snake and fires that glowed white and an odd green, and moans and groans and smells that came from hell itself, sulfurous odors that announced the arrival of the devil himself, waiting to attack, it was just a matter of time. And just the week before there'd been a fire set to a shed near to the great house. His son, Emile, and all the house slaves had managed to douse the flames before there'd been much damage. Then just three days before a tree had fallen and very nearly landed on the veranda roof. The tree had been very sturdy.

"I don't suppose there were saw marks on the tree?"

"No," said Mr. Grayson firmly. "My son looked closely. It was the work of the supernatural. Even he was forced to cease going against what I said." Grayson drew a very deep breath. "One of the slaves swore he saw the great green serpent."

"Excuse me?"

"The great green serpent. It symbolizes their primary deity."

"Whose primary deity?"

Grayson actually looked shocked. "One forgets that Englishmen don't know about these things. Why, I'm speaking of voodoo, of course."

"Ah, so you believe all this the work of the supernatural then?"

"I am a white man. However, I have lived in Jamaica for many years. I have seen things that would make no sense in a white world, perhaps things that could not exist in a white world. But the strangeness of the things happening, sir, it gives way to doubts."

Ryder had no more belief in the supernatural than he had in the honesty of a gaming hell owner. When Grayson paused, Ryder was frowning. "Forgive me, but I have no doubts. Simply mixing certain chemicals would produce the smoke and the strange-colored flames. It is a flesh and blood man, no great green serpent behind this. The question we must answer is why and who. Yes, who would do this?"

But Grayson clearly was not convinced. "There is another thing, Ryder. After the French Revolution, there was a revolt on Haiti led by a man named Dessalines. He butchered all the whites and forced many priests and priestesses of voodoo to leave Haiti. These people are powerful; they spread throughout the West Indies, even into America itself, and with them they took their demons."

Ryder wanted to laugh, but he didn't. It was obvious that Grayson felt strongly about this voodoo nonsense. And Grayson was right about one thing: a white man couldn't accept such things as being real, particularly not if he'd lived his entire life in England. He said, "We will see soon enough, I imagine. Ah, I didn't know you had a son."

Grayson puffed up like a proud rooster then he fidgeted with his light gray gloves. "He is a good boy, sir, and he does a lot for me—for the Sherbrookes—now that I am getting on in years. He is waiting for us at Kimberly Hall. He didn't wish to leave the plantation house unprotected."

They passed dozens more children, all of them ragged, all of them black, children of the slaves working in the fields, but these children were silent at the sight of the two white men riding in their midst.

Grayson said, pointing to the right and to the left of the narrow rutted road, "We are in the mangrove swamps now. Take care whenever you ride this way for crocodiles come out of the swamps and many times appear like fat logs lying across the road. They will normally eschew the presence of humans, but there have been stories where they didn't, very unpleasant stories."

Crocodiles! Ryder shook his head, but he kept one eye on the sides of the road. The smell of the fetid swamp water was nearly overpowering. He urged his horse forward. There came a flat stretch, the Caribbean on their left and field after field of sugarcane on their right, even climbing the hills that lay in the distance. And there were goats everywhere, sitting on low stone fences, chewing at flowers left on graves in the church cemeteries. There were egrets sitting on the backs of cattle, cleaning them of ticks, Ryder knew. And there were black men, tall, their bare upper bodies oily with sweat, working in the sugar fields, wearing only coarse trousers made of stout osnaburg. They didn't seem to notice the heat, their rhythm steady, as they plowed or pulled weeds or dug deeper trenches between the sugar plant rows. And there were women as well, their heads covered with bright bandannas, bending and straightening like the men in a steady rhythm. Not far away sat a white man on a horse, an overseer, sitting under a lone poinciana tree, its feathery, fernlike leaves shimmering in the sunlight, to see they didn't slack off. The whip in his left hand ensured their continued work.

It was utterly foreign to Ryder. It was exotic, too, with the thick, sweet smell of the frangipani trees that were thick alongside the dirt road, and the startling blue of the water coming into sight at unexpected moments. He was pleased he'd done reading on the voyage here. He wasn't completely ignorant of the local flora and fauna. But he hadn't read about any damned crocodiles.

"We are nearing Camille Hall," Grayson said suddenly, his voice falling nearly to a whisper.

Ryder raised an eyebrow.

"It's her home, sir. Sophia Stanton-Greville's home. She lives there with her uncle and her younger brother. There is one plantation between Camille Hall and Kimberly Hall, but as I understand it, her uncle is soon to buy it and thus add substantially to his holdings."

"Who is the owner?"

"Charles Grammond. Some say he wishes to move to Virginia—'tis one of the colonial states to the north—but it is a lame reason, one with little credence, for he knows nothing of the colonies or their customs and manners. He has four children who haven't become a father's pride, all of them sons, none of them ambitious or willing to work. His wife is difficult, I've heard it said. It's a pity, yes, a pity."

Ryder was certain he'd heard the man's name in the tavern. He said slowly, "I understand that this woman, this Sophia Stanton-Greville, has three men currently in her bed. I seem to recall that one of them is this Charles Grammond."

Grayson flushed to the roots of his gray hair. "You have but just arrived, sir!"

"It is the first topic of conversation I heard at the coffeehouse, the Gold Doubloon, I believe the name is. And I heard it spoken of in great detail."

"No, no, sir, she is a goddess. She is good and pure. It is all a lie. There are many men here who are not gentlemen."

"But it is the gossip, is it not?"

"Yes, it is, but you mustn't believe it, Ryder. No, it's a vicious lie. Don't mistake me. Customs, the local mores, if you will, are different here. All white men have black mistresses. They're called housekeepers here and it is considered a respectable position. I have seen men come from England, some to work on the plantations as bookkeepers, some to earn their fortune, and most change. They take wives and they take mistresses. Their thinking changes. But a lady remains a lady."

"Has your life changed, Grayson?"

"Yes, for a while it certainly did. I was my father's son, after all, but my wife was French and I loved her dearly. Only after her death did I succumb to local custom and take a mistress or a housekeeper. Life here is different, Ryder, very different."

Ryder subsided, letting his body relax and roll gently in the comfortable Spanish saddle. He closed his eyes a moment, breathing in the salty fresh smell of the sea, the coastline no longer obscured by thick clumps of mangrove. "Why is Grammond selling out then, in your opinion?"

"I'm not completely certain, but there are, of course, rumors. It was a sudden decision, that I do know. He and his family are leaving next week, I have heard it said. The plantation is quite profitable. It is said he lost a lot of money to Lord David Lochridge, a young wastrel with whom you must avoid gambling, sir, at all costs. It is said he has sold his soul to the devil, and thus his incredible luck."

Ryder turned to face Samuel Grayson, saying in a meditative voice, "There is every bit as much talk here as there is in England. I had believed to be bored. Perhaps we will have some mysterious manifestations this very night, to welcome me here. Yes, I should enjoy even a ghostly spectacle, if it is possible. Isn't this young Lord David reputed also to be one of her lovers?"

Ryder wondered if Grayson would have an apoplectic attack. He opened his mouth, realized that his employer was seated next to him and closed it. He managed to say in a fairly calm way, "I repeat, Ryder, all of it is nonsense. Her uncle, Theodore Burgess, is a solid man, as we say here in Jamaica. His reputation is good. He is amiable, his business dealings honorable. He loves his niece and nephew very much. I imagine that the vicious rumors of Miss Stanton-Greville's reputation hurt him very much. He never speaks of it, of course, for he is a gentleman. His overseer, however, is another matter. His name is Eli Thomas and he is a rotten fellow, overly cruel to the slaves."

"If Uncle Burgess is such a fine man, why does he have this crooked stick as his overseer?"

"I don't know. Some say he must have Thomas else the plantation wouldn't make any money. Burgess is too easy on the slaves, you see."

"And this Charles Grammond is selling out to the woman's uncle? This Theodore Burgess?"

"Yes. Perhaps Burgess feels pity for Grammond and is simply buying the plantation to assist him and his family. Burgess is the younger brother of Miss Sophia and Master Jeremy's mother."

"How do the girl and boy happen to be here on Jamaica?"

"Their parents were drowned some five years ago. The children were made wards of their uncle."

"I haven't heard the name Stanton-Greville. Are they English?"

"Yes. They lived in Fowey, in Cornwall. The house and grounds are in a caretaker's hands until the boy is old enough to manage for himself."

Ryder was silent, chewing over all the facts. So the girl had been raised in Cornwall. And now she was here and she was a tart. His thinking turned back to the problem that had brought him here. Ryder strongly doubted the supernatural had anything to do with the problems occurring at Kimberly Hall. Oh no, greed was the same all over the world. Gaining one's greedy ends evidently conformed to local custom. He said, "Did

Mr. Grammond have any problems before he agreed to sell to this Burgess?"

"Not that I know of. Oh, I see the direction of your thoughts, Ryder, but I cannot credit them. Burgess, as I said, has a fine reputation; he is honest; he gives to local charities. No, if Grammond were having financial problems or if he were being besieged as we are at Kimberly, Burgess certainly wouldn't be behind it."

Ryder wondered if Grayson spoke so positively about the Sherbrookes. He'd never met a man before in his life who deserved such accolades. Well, he would soon see. The island was small; society intermingled continuously and he would meet this Mr. Burgess and his niece soon enough.

Grayson directed them inland, away from the blessed breeze from the water. The air was heavy with dirt and the sickly sweet smell of the sugarcane. They came shortly to the top of a rise and he looked back at the Caribbean, stretched as far as the eye could see, brilliant blue, topaz in shallower water, silver-capped waves rolling onto the white beaches. He wanted nothing more than to strip off his clothes and swim in the Caribbean until he sank like a stone.

"All this is Sherbrooke land, sir. Ah, look upward at the top of the rise, in amongst the pink cassias." He heard Ryder suck in his breath and smiled. "They're also called pink shower trees. They're at their most beautiful right now. And there are golden shower trees, and mango trees and the ever-present palm trees. There, sir, just beyond is the great house. You cannot see it from here, but the coastline curves quite sharply just yon and is quite close to the back of the house."

Ryder drew in his breath yet again.

"Most of the great plantation houses here on Jamaica are built in the traditional manner of three stories and huge Doric columns, only here we have verandas and balconies off nearly every room, for fresh air, you understand. You will see that all the bedchambers are at the back of the house and all have balconies that face the water. The back lawn slopes down to the beach and is always well tended. You will be able to sleep, even in the deepest part of the summer, though I think you're doubting that right now."

"You're right about that," Ryder said, wiping the sweat off his face with the back of his hand.

It was nearly midnight. Ryder had thoroughly enjoyed himself in the warm water of the Caribbean for the past hour. There was a half-moon that lit his way. It glittered starkly off the waves. He felt for the first time as if he really were in paradise. He chose to forget the awful heat of the afternoon. It was so beautiful, the black vault of the sky overhead with the studding of stars, so calm, so silent, that he felt peace flow through him.

He wasn't a peaceful man. Thus, it was an odd feeling, but he didn't dislike it. He stretched out naked on his back, knowing full well the sand would likely find its way into parts of his body that he wouldn't like, but for now, it didn't matter. He stretched, feeling himself relax completely. He closed his eyes and listened to the sounds he hadn't heard before. He'd read about the coqui or the tree frog, and thought he heard some chirping into the soft darkness.

He also knew a turtledove when he heard it and sighed as the sounds became more distinct, each adding to his relaxation, his sense of well-being.

It was just so damned exotic here, he thought, stretching yet again, only to have the sand make him itch madly. He jumped to his feet, ran splashing through the surf then flattened into a dive into the next good-sized wave. He swam until he was exhausted, then walked slowly back to the beach. He realized he was ravenous. He'd been too hot to eat much at dinner and the strangeness of the food hadn't added to his appetite.

There were coconut trees lining the perimeter of the beach and he grinned. He'd seen a black man shinny up a coconut tree earlier. His mouth was already watering. But it wasn't as easy as it looked and Ryder ended up standing on the beach, rubbing a scraped thigh, staring with malignant hatred at the coconuts just beyond his reach.

There were other ways for the son of an English earl to get at a damned coconut. He found a rock and aimed it carefully at the coconut he'd selected. He was on the point of throwing it when he heard something.

It wasn't a coqui nor was it a turtledove. It wasn't like anything he'd ever heard in his life. He held himself perfectly still, lowering the rock slowly, silently. He listened hard. There it was again, that strange sort of low moaning sound that didn't sound remotely human.

His feet were tender, for he was an Englishman after all, but he managed to move silently enough through the trees that lined the beach. The sound became louder the closer he got to the great house. He ran lightly up the grassy slope toward the back of the house. He eased around the side so he could see onto the front lawn. He stopped behind a breadfruit tree and looked out onto the beautifully tended grounds. The sound came again and then he saw a strange light welling up from the ground itself. It was a narrow, thready light, blue, and it smelled of sulfur, as if it were coming up directly from hell and the moans were of the souls entrapped there. He felt gooseflesh rise on his body; he felt the hair rise on the back of his neck. Then he shook his head. This was beyond absurd. He'd said with absolute certainty to Grayson that it was naught but a mixture of chemicals. It was true, it had to be.

He saw candlelight flicker in one of the rooms on the second floor of the house. Probably Grayson and he was most likely scared silly. Then he heard a hiss from behind him and turned very slowly, the rock ready now, his body poised.

It was Emile Grayson.

Ryder smiled. He liked Emile. He was about Ryder's own age, intelligent and ambitious. He, like Ryder, wasn't the least bit superstitious, though he hadn't once disagreed with his father during dinner or their talk afterward.

"What is it?" Ryder said behind his hand in a deep whisper.

"I don't know but I do want to find out. Now you're here to help me. I've tried to make some of the male slaves keep watch with me but they roll their eyes back in their heads and moan." Emile paused just a moment, then added, "One slave did help me. Josh was his name. We kept watch several nights together. Then one morning he was found dead, his throat cut. I've had no more volunteers."

"Very well," said Ryder. "Go around to the other side of that damned light and I'll ease closer from this way."

Emile slithered like a thin shadow from tree to tree to work his way to the other side of the thready light. A neat trap, Ryder thought, pleased. Blood pumped wildly through him. He hadn't realized really how very bored he'd been during the voyage because he'd bedded two ladies, both of them charming, and from long experience, time passed more smoothly if one made love during the day and if one slept with a woman cuddled against one's chest during the night.

When Emile was in position, Ryder simply straightened, the rock still held in his right hand, and walked directly toward the light. He heard an unearthly shriek.

The light became a thin smoke trail, bluer now, the odor foul as the air of hell itself. A few chemicals, he thought, that's all, nothing more. But who was doing the moaning?

He heard a shout. It was Emile. He began to run. He saw the figure then; white flowing robes covered it, but there was a very human hand showing and that hand held a gun. Ah, was that a pillow slip over the man's head? The hand came up and the gun exploded toward Emile. Ryder yelled at him. "You bastard! Who the hell are you!"

Then the figure turned and fired at him. Ryder felt the bullet pass not three inches from his head. Good God, he thought, and ran straight for the figure. The man was tall and fit, but Ryder was the stronger and the more athletic. He was gaining on him. Any moment now he would have him. He sliced his foot on a rock and cursed, but it didn't slow him.

Then suddenly, without warning, he felt a shaft of pain sear through his upper arm. He stopped cold in his tracks, staring down at the feathered arrow tip that was sticking obscenely out of his flesh.

Damnation, the man was escaping. Emile, shouting hoarsely, was at his side in another moment.

He said blankly, "Where the hell did that bloody arrow come from? The man had an accomplice, damn him!"

"It's nothing! Get him, Emile!"

"No," Emile said very calmly. "He will come back."

With no more words, Emile ripped off the white sleeve of his shirt, then turned to Ryder, and without pause, without speech, he grasped the arrow firmly and pulled it out.

"There," he said, and began to wrap the shirtsleeve around the small hole that was oozing blood.

Ryder felt momentarily dizzy but he was pleased that Emile had acted swiftly.

"Yes," he said. "There." He looked up. "The bastard got away, curse him. Both of them." He looked back down at his arm. "When you've got me wrapped up, let's go examine the light and smoke, or whatever it is."

But there was no more smoke, no more thin thready blue light. There was, however, a faint sulfurous odor and the grass was scorched.

"Now," Ryder said grimly, "there are two of us. We'll catch the bastards who are doing this." He paused, feeling a burning sensation in his upper arm. "Why? Ah, that's the question, isn't it?"

"I don't know," Emile said. "I've thought and thought and I just don't know. No one has approached my father about selling the plantation, not a soul, nor is there any gossip, just that some voodoo priests or priestesses are displeased with us for some unknown reason. Please, Mr. Sherbrooke, come into the house because I want to clean the wound. We've got a good store of medicines and basilicum powder is just what we need."

"My name is Ryder."

Emile grinned. "Given the circumstances, all right, Ryder."

Ryder suddenly laughed. "Some guard I am," he said and laughed more. "I probably astonished our villain more than I frightened him. Jesus, I'm stark naked."

"Yes, you are, but I hesitated to point it out, particularly when the bastard was so close."

"I know. It's also difficult to call a man Mr. Sherbrooke when he's wearing naught but his hide."

CHAPTER
== 2 ==

Camille Hall

HE STRUCK HER ribs with his fist just below her right breast, hard enough to slam her against the wall. Her head snapped back and hit the top edge of the thick oak wainscoting.

Slowly, stunned, she slid down to the floor.

"Why the hell didn't you tell me, you stupid little fool?"

Sophie shook her head to clear it. She raised her hand and lightly touched her fingertips against the back of her head. A dizzying shaft of pain brought bile to her throat.

"Don't you dare tell me I hurt you. If it is so, it is your own fault."

It would naturally be her own fault. He was always careful never to strike her where it would show. Never. She moved her hand to her ribs. The pain made her suck in her breath, but that made it hurt even more. She took short, very shallow breaths and waited, praying that her ribs weren't broken, praying the nausea would subside. If he had broken some ribs she wondered how he would explain it. But he could come up with some plausible explanation. He always had in the past.

He was standing over her now, his hands on his hips. He was pale, his eyes narrowed with fury. "I asked you a question. Why didn't you tell me that Ryder Sherbrooke had arrived in Montego Bay?"

She opened her mouth to lie, but he forestalled her. "And don't tell me you didn't know. You were in town today, I saw you go myself. I gave you permission to go, damn you."

"I tell you I didn't—" She stopped, hating her cowardice, hating her voice that sounded thin as the batiste of her nightgown. She was silent a moment, feeding the rage that was bubbling up inside her. She looked at him squarely in his hated face. "I wanted him to be here, to catch you. I prayed he would come. He wouldn't believe any of that voodoo nonsense. I knew he could stop you."

He raised his fist. Then slowly, he lowered it.

He actually grinned at her and for a moment she saw what other peo-

ple saw—a man with humor and wit, a gentle man, a somewhat diffident
man of breeding and unquestioned gentility. In the next instant it was
gone and he was back as she knew him to be. "If Thomas hadn't shot him
with the arrow he might have. I was totally taken off guard. Certainly
Grayson's son, Emile, has been something of a thorn in my flesh, but this
young man, naked as a satyr, running at me yelling at the top of his lungs,
came as quite a shock. Then Thomas got him."

Sophie paled. "You killed him? You killed the owner?"

"Oh no, Thomas shot him through his upper arm. Thomas is always
careful. Strange thing, really, the fact that Sherbrooke was naked and carrying a rock, howling at me just like a damned Carib. Thomas says he was
probably plowing one of the slaves when he came out to investigate the
sulfur and the smoke and all those hideous moans we've perfected. I was
relieved that Emile Grayson stopped and saw to Sherbrooke."

She said nothing. By keeping the information to herself, she had en-
dangered a man's life. It hadn't occurred to her that he could be in any real
danger. She'd been a fool and he'd been the one to pay for it. She'd paid
too, but that was nothing new. At least he would be all right and she would
be as well, eventually. She slowly deepened her breathing as the pain in
her ribs eased a bit.

Uncle Theo moved away from her now. He pulled the chair away from
his small writing desk and sat down in it, crossing his legs at the ankles
and looking at her, his arms settled on his lean belly. "Stupidity doesn't
suit you, Sophia," he said finally, shaking his head. "How many times do
I have to tell you that obedience is the only choice you have? Loyalty to
me is your only choice. You just might ask yourself what would happen
to you and your precious Jeremy if I had been caught. You're underage;
you're the whore of the island; you would have no money, no place to
live; you would end up selling your body on the streets and Jeremy would
end up in some workhouse. Perhaps he could be someone's apprentice
bookkeeper and spend all his time in the trashhouse. No, miss, you will
not try to do me in again or I swear to you—" He paused, rose quickly,
and strode back over to her. She shrank back against the wall, she
couldn't help it, as he came down on his haunches beside her. He grabbed
her chin in his palm and jerked her head toward him. "I swear to you,
Sophia, I will kill you if you try such a thing again. Do you understand
me?"

She said nothing. He saw the hatred in her eyes and said more softly
now, "No, I won't kill you, I'll kill that pathetic brother of yours. Oh yes,
that's what I'll do. Now do you understand me?"

"Yes," she said finally. "Yes, I understand you well enough."

"Good." He rose then offered her a hand. She stared at his slender long fingers, the well-buffed nails, then looked him in the face. Very slowly, she pushed herself upright. He lowered his hand.

"You're stubborn but I don't dislike it in a woman. You hate me as well, and that is amusing. Now, if you were my mistress I would enjoy whipping that insolent look out of your eyes. Take yourself back to bed. I have plans to make. Ryder Sherbrooke is here finally. God, I waited a long time for Grayson to act, for the Earl of Northcliffe to react and send someone out here. And he sent his brother, just as I'd hoped. Now it is time to put my plan into motion.

"Ah, yes, my dear, since you have seen a frankly impressive number of naked men, let me tell you that this young man is built very well. He's an athlete and his body is lean and strong. Aye, you'll find that Sherbrooke is a fine specimen." He paused again, looking off into nothing in particular. "I think this will work quite nicely, but I must think about it in more detail. The man is not a fool. I was, I suppose, expecting another Lord David, but Sherbrooke isn't at all like that young wastrel. I will tell you in the morning what you will do."

At eight o'clock the following morning, Sophie was trying to fasten the front buttons of her gown. Every movement hurt. The flesh over her ribs had turned a fierce yellow and purple during the night. As she worked another button into its hole, she felt the pain so deeply she doubted it would ever ease. She stopped, bending over like an old woman. She'd sent her maid away; she couldn't allow Millie to see her, for it would start gossip and she couldn't allow that.

She couldn't allow that because of Jeremy.

When there came a light knock on her door, followed by her young brother's head coming around, she smiled despite the pulling pain. Jeremy came into the bedchamber. "Don't you want breakfast? It's growing cold and you know how Uncle Theo is. You won't get a bite to eat until luncheon."

"Yes, I know. Let me finish with these buttons."

Jeremy prowled around her room, forever curious, filled with a nine-year-old's energy. Always on the move, always restless, always ready to work as hard as any slave, only he couldn't.

She finally finished with the buttons. She happened to glance in the mirror and saw that she hadn't brushed out her hair. She looked pale and frowzy and about as seductive as a broken conch shell. Some whore she was. There were dark circles under her eyes. Ah, but it hurt to pull the brush through the tangles. Every stroke sent waves of pain through her chest.

"Jeremy, would you brush my hair for me?"

He looked startled and cocked his head to one side in silent question.

When she merely shook her head, he came to her, frowning. "Are you tired or something, Sophie?"

"Yes, I'm something." She handed him the brush and sat down. He did a poor job of it but it was sufficient. She managed to pull back the mass of chestnut hair and tie it at the nape of her neck with a black velvet ribbon.

"Now, Master Jeremy, onward to breakfast."

"You're ill, aren't you, Sophie."

It wasn't a question. She touched her fingers to his cheek for she saw the worry in his eyes, and the fear that something was seriously wrong. "I'm all right. Just a touch of a stomachache, I swear to you. Some of Tilda's wonderful muffins and I'll be right as rain."

Jeremy, reassured, skipped ahead of her. It was, at least, skipping to her. Perhaps to others it looked like clumsy ill-coordinated movements, but not to her. No, he was a happy little boy and he was doing marvelously well. She loved him more than anyone in the world. He was hers, her responsibility. He was the only person in the world who loved her, without question, without reservation.

Uncle Theo was in the breakfast room. The veranda doors, green-slatted, as were all the floor-to-ceiling doors in the house, were open and a slight breeze stirred the still air. In the distance the sea glittered beneath a blazing early morning sun. Just outside the open doors, the air was thick with the overripe summer scent of roses, jasmine, hibiscus, bougainvillea, cassia, frangipani, and rhododendron. During the hottest part of the day, the scent was nearly overpowering. But now, early in the morning, it was a paradise of smells and it stirred the senses. However, Sophie felt no stirring inside her this morning at the beauty of it. There was very little of anything that held beauty for her now. There had been very little of beauty for the past year. No, now it was closer to thirteen months.

Thirteen months since she'd become a whore. Thirteen months since other plantation owners' wives cut her directly whenever she chanced to see them shopping in Montego Bay. They didn't cut her here at Camille Hall; they admired her dear uncle much too much to hurt him like that. No, they were coldly polite to her here.

"There aren't any muffins, Sophie," Jeremy said. "Do you want me to ask Tilda?"

"No, no, love. I'll have some fresh bread. It's fine. Sit down now and eat your breakfast."

Jeremy did, with his usual enthusiasm.

Theodore Burgess looked up from his newspaper, the imported London *Gazette*, only seven weeks old, for English ships were regular in their arrivals.

He studied her face for a long moment, was content at the lingering pain he saw in her eyes, and said, "You and I will meet after you've eaten, my dear. There are things to discuss, and I know you always wish to accommodate yourself to my wishes. Ah, do eat a bit more. I know the heat is enervating, but you are growing too thin."

Jeremy continued oblivious, content to smear more butter on his roasted yam.

"Yes, Uncle," Sophie said. "In your study then. After breakfast."

"Yes, my dear, that is exactly what I wish. As for you, my fine lad, you will accompany me to the stillhouse today. There are some processes I wish you to learn. It will be hot as the fires of hell itself but we shan't stay long. Just long enough for you to learn something of the rum-making process and the steps Mr. Thomas takes to prevent the slaves from stealing and drinking all our profits."

The pleasure in Jeremy's eyes made her ribs hurt all the more.

Samuel Grayson had seen Ryder come back into the house, his thick pale brown hair dark with sweat, his white shirt stuck to his back, his face flushed red from the sun. He'd ridden over the plantation the entire morning with Emile, and now, at midday, he imagined Ryder was holed up someplace cool. He found him sitting on the veranda that gave off the billiard room. He was in the deepest shade, the one place where the breezes flowed continuously. He said quietly, seeing that Ryder's eyes were closed, "It's an invitation, Ryder, from Theodore Burgess of Camille Hall. There is to be a ball this Friday and you are to be the honored guest."

"A ball," Ryder said, opening his eyes. "Jesus, Samuel, I can't imagine trying to dance in this infernal heat. Surely this Burgess fellow isn't serious."

"There will be slaves waving woven palm fronds about to keep the air stirred up. Also the Camille Hall ballroom, like this one, is lined with slatted doors, all opening up from ceiling to floor. It will be quite pleasant, I promise you."

Ryder was silent for a moment. He was thinking about the woman who was sleeping with three men. He wanted to meet her.

"There's a boy waiting for your response, sir."

Ryder gave him a languorous smile. "We'll go, naturally."

Grayson left to write an acceptance and Ryder closed his eyes again. He didn't move much; it was too hot. He knew he couldn't go swimming just yet else he'd be baked within ten minutes by that inferno of a sun and his face and arms were already a bit burned. Thus, he sat there quietly and soon he slept.

When he awoke, afternoon shadows were lengthening and Emile was sitting beside him, his long legs stretched out in front of him.

"Your father says I will become accustomed," Ryder said. "I think he's lying to me."

Emile grunted. "A bit, but the summers are particularly brutal."

"Is it ever too hot to make love, I wonder?"

Emile laughed. "Yes, it is. I hear we are to go to a ball at Camille Hall this Friday night."

"Yes, I am to be honored. I think, however, that I would prefer swimming, perhaps even trying to shinny up a coconut tree again or even chase a villain who is wearing a sheet."

Emile grinned. "It should be amusing, Ryder. You will meet all the planters and merchants from Montego Bay and their wives. You will hear so much gossip your ears will ache. There is little else to do here, you see, except drink rum, which most do to excess, unfortunately. Also, Father is much taken with Sophia Stanton-Greville, and she is Burgess's niece and hostess. I don't doubt he would challenge any man to a duel if he dared say something insulting about Father's goddess."

"I also understand that she is a whore."

"Yes," Emile said, not looking at Ryder, "that's what is understood."

"This displeases you. You've known her a long time?"

"Her parents were drowned in a storm four years ago on a return voyage from England. Sophie and her brother, Jeremy, were given into the guardianship of Theodore Burgess, her mother's younger brother. She has lived here since she was fifteen. She is now nineteen, nearly twenty, and her exploits with men and thus her reputation began over a year ago. You are right, it displeases me and disappoints me even more. I had quite liked her. She was a spirited girl, fun and without guile or vanity. Indeed, I once thought that we might—but that's not important now."

"You know it as a fact then?"

"She meets her lovers at this small cottage that fronts the beach. I chanced to visit the cottage following a night she spent with Lord David Lochridge. David was still there, naked, and drinking a rum punch. The place reeked of sex. He seemed quite pleased with himself. He was rather drunk, which surprised me because it was only about nine o'clock in the morning. He spoke of her freely, her attributes, her skills at pleasing a man, her daring at flaunting convention."

"This woman wasn't there?"

"No. Evidently she leaves her men to wake up by themselves, that's what David said. However, there are slaves there to tend to them. None of the men seem to mind her habits."

"You believed this Lochridge?"

Emile's voice was emotionless, but still he didn't look at Ryder. "As I said, the place reeked of sex. Also, he was too drunk to make up something that hadn't happened. I don't like him particularly, but there was no reason for him to lie. The cottage is on Burgess land."

Ryder swatted a mosquito. He said, his voice meditative, "So she turns eighteen and decides to flout convention. It doesn't make a lot of sense, Emile. Surely no man would wed her now. Why do you think she started making herself available in the first place?"

"I don't know. She was always a strong-willed girl, spirited, as I told you, and very protective of her little brother. One of the planters called her a hellion because once she was angry at his overseer for calling her brother names and she smashed him on the head with a coconut. The man was in bed for a week. That was about two years ago. She could have wed any gentleman on the island for it is known that she is handsomely dowered. I have always been given to understand that females don't wish to have sex as much as men do. Thus, why would she want it so badly to give up everything that women are raised, even expected, to want?"

"There is always a reason for everything," Ryder said. He rose and stretched. "Thank God, I do believe it's cooling off, just a bit."

Emile grinned up at him. "I heard Father order Cook to make you something cool for dinner, a bowl of fresh fruit, perhaps, and some iced-down shrimp. No baked yams or hot clam chowder. He doesn't want you to shrink away for lack of sustenance."

Ryder swatted another mosquito. He looked off over the sugarcane fields shimmering beneath the sun, to the endless stretch of blue sea beyond. So beautiful it was, yet so alien. "As I said, there is always something that drives men and women to behave as they do. There are three different men involved, I understand, and there were probably others before these three. There is of course a motive, and you know something, Emile? I rather fancy that I will amuse myself and just find out what it is that makes this hellion part her legs for so many men."

"It is depressing," Emile said, and he sighed.

By Friday night, Ryder was actually beginning to believe that he could endure the heavy still heat, even though he was sometimes so hot it hurt to breathe. He had even swum that afternoon, but not long, for he didn't want to burn too badly. To his disappointment, after the incident his first night, there had been no other strange occurrences. No burning sulfur; no sheeted man; no moans or groans; no guns or bows and arrows.

Nothing at all out of the ordinary had occurred. He had met Samuel Grayson's "housekeeper," a young brown woman with merry eyes, a compact body, and a ready smile. She lived in Grayson's room and worked in the house during the day. Her name was Mary. As for Emile, he also had a "housekeeper," a thin slip of a girl who answered to Coco.

Her eyes were always downcast in Ryder's presence, and she never uttered a word that Ryder heard. She couldn't have been more than fifteen. Emile paid her no attention whatsoever, except, Ryder assumed, at night, when he took her to his bed. She cared for his clothing, kept his room straight and clean, and was utterly docile. Ryder was amused and put off by this custom, one considered quite respectable on Jamaica by all parties concerned.

Grayson, of course, had offered him a woman, and Ryder, for the first time in his adult sexual life, had refused. It simply seemed too cold-blooded to him, too contrived, too expected. That was it, he didn't want to do the expected thing. He laughed at his own conceit, at the affectation of his own behavior.

The three men rode to Camille Hall at nine o'clock on Friday night. It was just growing dark and the moon was full, the stars lush overhead. Ryder had never seen such a sight as this; it still made him stare.

They could see the lights of Camille Hall from a mile distant. There were carriages despite the condition of the main road, and at least three dozen horses, all tethered close to the great house and watched by a dozen small boys. The house glistened and shimmered. All the veranda doors were wide open.

Ryder saw her immediately. She was standing next to an older man at the very entrance. She was gowned in white, pure virginal white, her shoulders bare, her chestnut hair piled on top of her head with two thick tresses falling over her shoulder to lie on that bare white flesh. Ryder looked at her and smiled just as she looked up and saw him. He saw her go very still. He realized, of course, that there was something akin to contempt in that smile of his. He removed it. He relaxed. It didn't matter if she slept with every man on the island. It simply didn't matter.

But motives interested him. She interested him.

He walked beside a worshipful Samuel Grayson toward her. He saw upon closer inspection that she wasn't the heavenly beauty that Grayson saw her to be. She looked much older than nineteen. Her eyes were a fine clear gray, her skin as white as her bare shoulders, too white. But she was wearing more makeup than a girl her age should wear. She looked more like a London actress or an opera girl than a young lady at a ball in her own home. Her lips were thick dark red, kohl lined her eyes and darkened her brows. There was rouge on her cheeks and a heavy layer of white powder. Why did her uncle allow her to look a harlot in his own house? And that damned white virginal gown she was wearing, it was the outside of too much. It was as if she were mocking her uncle, mocking all the people present, perhaps even mocking herself.

Ryder heard the introduction and took her hand, turning it over and lightly kissing her wrist. She jerked and he released her hand slowly, very slowly.

Theodore Burgess was of a different ilk. A tall man, thin as a stick, with a gentle face yet stubborn chin, he seemed inordinately diffident. He also seemed oblivious of the nineteen-year-old girl who flaunted herself beside him. He shook Ryder's hand with little strength and said, "A pleasure, sir, a pleasure. Mr. Grayson has spoken often of the Sherbrookes and his esteem for the Sherbrooke family. You are most welcome here, sir, most welcome. You will dance, of course, with my sweet niece?"

Was the damned fellow an idiot? Was he blind?

The sweet niece looked like a painted hussy. Ryder turned politely and said, "Would you care to dance this minuet, Miss Stanton-Greville?"

She nodded, saying nothing, not smiling, and placed her hand lightly on his forearm.

He realized that she'd said nothing at all to Emile. She'd ignored him. More tangled and unexpected behavior. He became increasingly fascinated. His curiosity rose accordingly.

"I understand you and Emile have known each other since you were practically children," he said, then released her to perform the steps in the minuet.

When they came together again, she said, "Yes." Nothing more, just that flat, emotionless "yes."

"One wonders," he said when she was near him again, "why one would ignore one's childhood friend when one reached adulthood. Yes, one wonders."

It was several minutes before her hand was in his once more. She said, "I suppose one can wonder about many things." Nothing more. Curse the chit.

The minuet ended. To Ryder's relief, he wasn't sweating by the end of it. Grayson hadn't lied. The ballroom, brilliantly lit by myriad candelabras, was nonetheless fairly cool, what with the breeze coming from the sea from all the open doors, and the ever-swinging palm fronds waved by small boys all dressed in white trousers and white shirts, their feet bare.

Ryder returned her to her uncle. He said nothing more. He turned away, Grayson at his side, to be introduced to other planters. He looked back once to see her standing very straight, her shoulders squared. Her uncle was speaking to her. He frowned. Was the uncle berating her for wearing so many cosmetics on her face? He hoped so, but doubted it. Personally, if it were up to him, he'd hold her face in a bucket of water then scrub it with lye soap but good.

He danced with every daughter of every Montego Bay merchant and every planter within a fifty-mile radius. He was fawned over, complimented on everything from the shine on his boots to the lovely blue of his eyes—this by a seventeen-year-old girl who could manage naught else but giggles—simpered at until he wanted to yawn with the boredom of it. His feet hurt. He wanted to go sit down and not move for a good hour. Finally, near to midnight, he managed to elude Grayson, three purposeful-looking planters, two more purposeful-looking wives with daughters in tow, and slip out onto the balcony. There were stone steps leading down into a quite lovely garden, redolent with the scent of roses, hibiscus, rhododendron, so many more brilliantly colored blossoms that he couldn't identify. He breathed in deeply and walked into the garden. There were stone benches and he sat down on one and leaned back against a pink cassia tree. He closed his eyes.

"I watched you come out here."

He nearly jumped off the bench, she startled him so badly. It was Sophia Stanton-Greville and she was standing very close to him.

He looked up at her, not changing expression, making no movement whatsoever now. "I wanted to rest. I am not yet accustomed to the heat and every girl in that bloody ballroom wanted to dance."

"Yes. I understand that's what one does at balls."

She sounded cold, very aloof. She sounded as if she disliked him. Then why had she followed him out here? It made no sense.

He relaxed further, stretching his legs in front of him, crossing them at the ankles, crossing his arms over his chest. His posture was insolent. Never in his adult life had he been so rude in the presence of a woman. He said in a voice that matched her coldness, "What do you wish of me, Miss Stanton-Greville? Another dance perhaps, since it is a ball, as you so graciously pointed out?"

She stiffened, and again he wondered why the hell she was even here. She looked out into the darkness. "You don't behave as most men do, Mr. Sherbrooke," she said at last.

"Ah, by that do you mean that I don't drool on your slippers? I don't stare at your very red mouth or your doubtless delightful breasts?"

"No!"

"Then what is it that I don't do?"

She turned away. He saw her fingers pleating the soft muslin folds of her gown. She was very slender, and although her gown was cut high in the new fashion made popular by Josephine, he could tell that her waist was narrow. He wondered about her legs and hips.

She said, turning to face him, this time a ghost of a smile on her painted mouth, "You are brazen, sir. Gentlemen don't speak so baldly, surely not even in England."

"Not even to painted tarts?"

She sucked in her breath and he could have sworn that she actually reeled back in shock. She raised an unconscious hand to her cheek, and began to rub at the powder.

She stopped suddenly. She dropped her hand to her side. She smiled now, and the utter control of it made his eyes gleam. "No," she said calmly, "not even to painted tarts. I had been told you had some wit. I had thought to hear it, but evidently gossip was mistaken. You are rude and a boor."

He rose to stand over her, very close, but she didn't move away from him. "Now you draw blood," he said, "and you don't do it too badly. But not all that well either." He withdrew a handkerchief from his pocket and swiftly wiped it over her red mouth. She tried to jerk away, but he grabbed her about her throat and wiped her mouth yet again. He threw the handkerchief to the ground. "Now," he said, leaned down and kissed her hard on her mouth. He kissed her for a very long time. After but a moment, he gentled, and she knew his expertise was great, greater than any she'd known before. His mouth was caressing hers, his tongue seeking entrance, but not demanding. She allowed him to continue, not moving, not reacting.

Suddenly his hands were cupping her breasts and she jumped, she couldn't help it. "Shush," he said, his breath warm and tart with the rum punch he'd drunk. "Let me feel you. Is your skin as soft and warm as I believe it to be?" Just as suddenly, as he spoke, his hands were down the front of her bodice and cupping her bare breasts. He paused a moment, lifting his head, and staring down at her. "Your heart was pounding, but not fast enough, I don't think. Your breasts are nice, Miss Stanton-Greville. Is this why you came out here in search of me? You wanted me to fondle you? Perhaps you even wanted me to take you here in the garden? Perhaps right here beneath this beautiful cassia tree? The scent is strong; perhaps strong enough to cover the smell of sex."

She said nothing, merely stood very quietly, allowing him to caress her breasts. He kissed her again, deepening the kiss this time, his open palm against her heart. The heartbeat quickened just a bit and he smiled into her mouth.

"Is that it? Do you think to compare me to your other men? You won't, you know."

His breath was very warm, his tongue gentle and easy against hers. But she wasn't kissing him back. She was passive. He didn't understand her. He wanted a response from her and by God he was going to have it. He pulled his hands out of the bodice of her gown, grabbed the shoulders of the gown, and jerked it to her waist. In the pale moonlight her breasts showed soft and white. Not large breasts, but very nicely shaped, full and high, the nipples a pale pink. He leaned down and began kissing the warm flesh.

It was then that she laughed, a teasing, wicked laugh. He straightened from the sheer surprise of it and looked down at her. Graceful as a dancer, she spun away from him. However, she did nothing to cover herself.

"You are not bad, in the way of men," she said, her voice light and caressing, her breasts pale in the moonlight, her shoulders back, thrusting them outward. "No, not bad at all. You are bold, arrogant, a man who doesn't wait for a lady to issue an invitation. You should show more restraint, sir. Or perhaps it is an invitation you want, and you haven't the patience to wait for it?"

"Perhaps," he said, "perhaps. But I don't share, Miss Stanton-Greville. When I take a woman I am the only man whose rod comes inside her. There will be no comparisons, at least no immediate ones."

"I see," she said, that damned voice of hers now lilting and more seductive than any woman's voice he'd ever heard in his life. "For the moment then, you may admire me, sir," she said, and he stared at her breasts as she slowly and with infinite fascination pulled the gown back to her shoulders, gently easing it into place. When her gown was straight and she looked as if she'd done nothing whatsoever out of the ordinary, she said, "No, Mr. Sherbrooke, you have moved too quickly. You have displeased me with your excesses. You demand, not ask. On the other hand, I do not dislike your arrogance. It is refreshing. You do not mince matters. You speak what you think. I will think about you, Mr. Sherbrooke. I have decided that I will ride with you in the morning. You will meet me here at eight o'clock. Do not be late. I dislike waiting for men."

He wanted to tell her to take her riding habit and her horse and her damned orders and go to hell, but he didn't. He was looking at her mouth, clean now of the damned red paint. A beautiful mouth, truly. And she was still a mystery. Ryder couldn't resist a mystery.

He smiled at her as he reached out and lightly stroked his fingertips over her jaw. "An order for you. Do not paint your face. I don't like it. You will excuse me now, Miss Stanton-Greville."

He left her without a backward glance. He was whistling.

Sophie stared after him, unmoving, until he disappeared into the darkness. Her heart was pounding and she felt light-headed. She was terrified of him. She hadn't lied, he was like no man she'd ever known. She sank down on the bench and put her face in her hands. What was she going to do?

CHAPTER
══ 3 ══

RYDER SMILED AS he looked at the ormolu clock in the main salon of Kimberly Hall. It was now fully eight o'clock in the morning. She would be looking for him to arrive momentarily, yes, any minute now, and she would expect to see him riding up to the front of Camille Hall, just as Her Highness had bade him do.

Only he wouldn't be there.

When it was eight-thirty, he rose and stretched and went into the small breakfast room that opened onto a side garden. Both Emile and his father were there. Two house slaves were serving them, one of them Samuel's housekeeper, Mary, and she smiled at Ryder merrily, waving him to his seat as if he were her guest.

Ryder asked for fresh fruit and bread from the tall black man, James, who, like every black man, woman, and child on Jamaica, wore no shoes. It still disconcerted Ryder a bit. He downed the hot black coffee that tasted so rich here on Jamaica, saying nothing, for he was thinking about Sophia Stanton-Greville and trying to picture the look on her face now that she must realize he wasn't coming. He smiled as he chewed on the bread.

"I heard it said last night that you were riding this morning with Miss Stanton-Greville."

Ryder didn't look up at Samuel Grayson. He was afraid that if he did, he'd grin like a sinner, for Samuel sounded jealous. How many men were besotted with the damned girl? And, how the devil did anyone know about the plans he and Miss Stanton-Greville had made? Rather, the supremely confident order she'd given him.

"I would say that the persons reporting the phenomenon were wrong, wouldn't you? I'm here, eating my breakfast. James, please tell Cora the fresh bread is quite good."

"It was her uncle who told me," Samuel said. "He asked me if you could be trusted. He loves his niece very much and he is very anxious that no man take advantage of her."

Emile choked on his coffee.

Ryder leaned over and smacked him on his back. "Are you all right?"

"I won't stand for this, Emile," his father said harshly. "You will not speak badly of her, do you understand me? You will not act the leering young man."

"I said nothing, I merely choked."

"Damn you, boy, I won't tolerate your damnable impudence!"

"Samuel," Ryder said smoothly, interrupting him. "There is not a consensus of opinion on the virtue of Miss Stanton-Greville. Surely you know that."

"It matters not," Grayson said. "I know the truth."

"Let us speak of other matters then. There have been no further demonic spectacles. I'm disappointed, and yet at the same time, I do wonder why they ceased so abruptly with my arrival."

Emile said slowly, "It's true. Since you spent some hours in the bay before my father brought you to Kimberly, everyone or practically everyone would have known within twenty-four hours that you had arrived."

"Which means," Ryder continued thoughtfully, "that if they were meant to cease upon my arrival then the person responsible hadn't heard of my arrival before that first night."

"Exactly," said Emile.

"I am still not certain that there is a person behind this," Grayson said. "It isn't natural, all that you saw. You said yourself, Ryder, that there was no sign of the fire where you'd seen one. Perhaps it wasn't a person in a white costume, perhaps it was simply another manifestation of voodoo evil."

"It was a flesh and blood man," Ryder said firmly. "Also, the arrow that went into my arm was shot by a very real person. Thus, there were two villains at Kimberly that first night. A question, Samuel—do you know of any man nearby who is good at archery?"

"Good God," Emile said, startled. "I hadn't thought to ask. Yes, Father, let's think on that."

Both men were silent for several moments. Ryder ate the chilled fresh fruit and the crusty fresh bread. He thought of Sophia Stanton-Greville, waiting. Both the thought and the bread were delicious.

Samuel said, "Yes, I know a man who excels in the sport of archery."

"Who?" Emile and Ryder asked at the same time.

Samuel waved his hands in dismissal. "No, no, it makes no sense. I was thinking of Eli Thomas, Burgess's overseer. He is noted for his skill, but again, no, it makes no sense. Why would he come here and shoot Ryder? Also, David Lochridge is a devotee of the sport as is a Mr. Jenkins, a merchant in Montego Bay. There are doubtless others in the vicinity. Certainly too many to draw any sort of meaningful conclusion."

Ryder smiled. Another part of the puzzle brought out onto the table. Another link to that wretched little tart at Camille Hall who'd teased him and practically let him make love to her in the Camille Hall gardens with a hundred guests but yards away. He toyed with an orange slice. "Since the men who visited us that first night of my arrival didn't know I was here, why then, we can begin to narrow the list, because I met many gentlemen that first afternoon in the Gold Doubloon."

Emile got a piece of foolscap and a pen. They listed all the names Ryder could remember.

"Many aren't accounted for," Emile said. "More than many more. The count boggles the mind."

"Such as two of her lovers," Ryder said easily. "We can mark off Oliver Susson."

"Yes," Emile said, and his father threw his napkin down on the table and strode from the room.

Ryder frowned after him. "Why does he wish to be blind to this girl and what she is?"

Emile looked across the breakfast room to the oil painting of a sugarcane field. "He had selected her to marry me. He won't give up the idea. I think also that he is taken with her. Her wickedness teases him. You've noticed Mary, his housekeeper, is a little tease, and he is very fond of her. I tell you, Ryder, even if Sophia took him as one of her lovers, he would still defend her. You mustn't take his anger to heart. He is my father and he means well."

Ryder nodded and continued to eat.

Emile said after a moment, "You were to have ridden with her, weren't you?"

Ryder grinned at him. "Yes, but I will never allow a woman to dictate to me. I will tell her what I wish of her and when I wish it. I will do the asking, not she the telling."

"This should prove interesting."

"I trust so," Ryder said and drank the rest of his rich black coffee. "Do you have the time, Emile?"

"Yes, it's nearly nine-thirty."

"I believe I will go riding."

Emile gave him a crooked grin. "Good hunting."

"Indeed," Ryder said.

"Where is he?"

Sophie turned to face her uncle. "I don't know. I assumed he would be here at eight. He did not say he wouldn't come."

"You angered him, damn you!" He raised his fisted hand, but one of the house servants was coming onto the veranda. He lowered his arm.

He lowered his voice, but the anger was strong and vicious. "You put him off! You didn't succeed, Sophia. I am displeased with you. Must I do all the planning? No, don't say anything. I will decide what is to be done now. You've botched it and I wonder if you did it apurpose."

He began to pace the veranda. Sophie watched him with a disinterested eye and kept silent. She prayed that Ryder Sherbrooke would have the good sense to keep miles away from Camille Hall and away from her.

Burgess paused and approached her, sitting in a cane-backed chair close to hers. "You took Lord David to the cottage last night, did you not?"

She nodded.

"All went well?"

"Yes. But he was jealous of my attention to Ryder Sherbrooke. His is not a steady character. He is childish and self-absorbed. Once he has drunk sufficiently, he is not difficult for me to handle, but last night his jealousy . . . well, it doesn't matter now. It turned out all right."

"You dealt with him?"

"Yes."

"Grammond will be leaving next week."

"Yes."

"You may detach yourself from Lord David now. There is no more use for him."

"He will not go easily," Sophie said. "He's young and arrogant and considers himself to be my stud. He will not take it kindly that I no longer want him."

"You will think of something." Theo Burgess rose and walked into the house, leaving her alone with her endless round of useless thoughts.

When Ryder Sherbrooke rode up some ten minutes later she wished she could yell at him to leave, curse his male stubbornness. She knew men and she knew what he was doing. He was teaching her a lesson; he was teaching her that he would not take commands from a woman. He was punishing her, humiliating her. Well, let him try. If only he knew it was her wish never to see him again, that she would give just about anything for him to book passage on the next ship back to England. She didn't move, merely watched as he cantered up the long drive, dismounted, and tied his stallion to the post some ten feet away from her.

He strolled over to her, leaned negligently on the veranda railing, and said easily, "Good morning."

He frowned for she was wearing that awful paint on her face. It looked garish and tawdry in the morning sunlight.

"I told you to wash your face. You look absurd. You may be the tart, but there is no reason to advertise it."

Sophie stood up slowly. She looked at him for a very long time, saying nothing. Then, in that light, teasing voice, she said, "Are you here to take me riding or to dictate terms for a surrender?"

"Surrender," he repeated. "That sounds quite charming to me, particularly with regard to you, madam. First, go wash your face. Then I will take you riding."

"You are nearly two hours late, sir!"

"Am I? Dear me, how remiss of me. On the other hand, I didn't wish to ride two hours ago. Now I do. Go wash your face. I will give you ten minutes, no more."

"I wouldn't go to the trashhouse with you, damn you! Get out of here! Go back to England and be a boor there."

"Mr. Sherbrooke! How delightful to see you, sir. My niece mentioned that perhaps you would be coming to take her riding. Sophia, where are you going, my dear? Mr. Sherbrooke surely would appreciate your charming company."

Ryder was amused to see her so neatly trapped. "To freshen myself, Uncle."

"Excellent. Mr. Sherbrooke and I will have a cozy chat until you return. Such a sweet girl, my niece. Sit down, Mr. Sherbrooke, do sit down. Should you like a rum punch?"

"At this hour? No, thank you, Mr. Burgess."

"Ah, do call me Theo. I'm not quite that old."

"Then you must call me Ryder."

"I understand your brother is the Earl of Northcliffe?"

"Yes. He would have come here himself but he had recently wed."

"Ah. Do you plan to remain on Jamaica?"

"Only until we have dealt with the ghostly manifestations that seem to have plagued Kimberly Hall for the past four or so months."

"Mr. Grayson has spoken to me of these things. It's common knowledge that there are evil ceremonies and equally evil priests and priestesses on Jamaica who are capable of anything."

"They have stopped."

"Really? I'm vastly relieved, Ryder, but I wonder why."

"So do I." Ryder wanted to ask him about his overseer and his archery skills but it was too soon. He wanted to keep the upper hand. He sat back in his chair and gave Mr. Burgess a guileless smile.

A house slave brought lemonade at Mr. Burgess's request. It was delicious. Ryder noted that Miss Stanton-Greville had far exceeded her ten minutes. He finished his glass of lemonade and gently set the glass down on the polished mahogany-topped table next to him. He rose and extended his hand to Theo Burgess.

"I fear it grows late, Theo. Evidently your niece has become occupied with more important matters than riding with me. Good-bye."

He walked away, whistling, nonchalant as a clam.

Theo Burgess stared at him, then yelled, "Sophia!"

Ryder didn't pause. He strolled out onto the drive toward his horse. He heard a noise from above, and curious, looked up. She was standing on the balcony some twelve feet up and in her hand was a basin. He moved, but not quickly enough. A good amount of water whooshed down in a thick arc and landed squarely on the top of his head.

He knew he heard a laugh, but then she was crying out. "Oh dear, what have I done? Oh, Mr. Sherbrooke, how could I be so very careless! Dear me, I really should have looked. Do forgive me, sir. Do come in and I will give you a towel. Oh dear, oh dear."

He would give it to her. She'd gotten him quite nicely.

He called back, "Thank you, Miss Stanton-Greville. Actually the water feels very good in this heat."

"I will be right down with a towel, sir." She added with a voice of gentle sweetness so false he was forced to grin, "And do call me Sophia."

He turned back to the veranda and saw something very unexpected. It was Theo Burgess's face and it was ugly and mean and something very frightening moved in his pale brown eyes. Then, suddenly, whatever Ryder thought he'd seen was gone, and Burgess was distraught and concerned and waving his hands as he moved quickly toward him, even wringing his hands, exclaiming, "Come here, Mr. Sherbrooke, do come here and sit down. Ah, my niece was careless, but surely she will make it up to you."

"I have no doubt she will try," Ryder said.

The brazen jade.

Sophie had washed only the most vulgar of the makeup off her face. But Ryder Sherbrooke's face was shiny and dripping with nice clean water. She smiled at him, her eyes glittering her triumph even though the words that came out of her mouth would do justice to a contrite nun. She prattled nonsense like a brainless twit. She hung about him, offering to pour him more lemonade, offering him four more towels, perhaps even five for he was so *very* wet, even offering him a comb for his hair, even offering to comb his hair.

Finally, Ryder said, "No, thank you, Sophia. I feel quite dry. No more of your ministrations. I do hope that the bucket you accidently spilled on me contained fresh water and only fresh water?"

She blinked rapidly, her face paling creditably, then flushing, and settled finally into a patently false mask of chagrin. "Oh dear, I think so, but you know . . . oh certainly Dorsey must have changed it and cleaned out the bucket, but then again, sometimes she is lazy so perhaps not. Wait, sir, and I will ask." Then she struck a pose. "But you know, if Dorsey didn't clean it out, she would never admit it. So we will never know. Oh dear." She jumped to her feet and as she passed him, she sniffed rather loudly and wrinkled her nose.

She was quite good.

He rose to stand beside her. "Sniff again, Sophia. Yes, is there anything untoward? No? Excellent, I see that your face must weigh a bit less than it did. There are still cosmetics, but not enough to make me send you back to your room. Further, you have no more water to wash your face with, do you? Perhaps I now have some of your powder on my head? Come, let's go riding before it becomes too hot."

A boy appeared leading a beautiful bay mare with two white stockings. She nipped Sophie's shoulder. Sophie laughed, and patted her nose. "You naughty girl! Ah, you are ready for a gallop, aren't you?"

Ryder frowned. A completely different voice and a low, quite charming laugh.

He didn't help her to mount. She expected it, he saw that, but he merely mounted his own stallion and waited, not even looking at her.

The boy gave her a foot up. She looked over at Ryder, her expression as bland as his sister Sinjun's when she'd managed to beat him at a game of chess.

"Where would you like to go, Mr. Sherbrooke?"

"Since I am to call you Sophia, why don't you call me Ryder?"

"Very well. Where would you like to go, Ryder?"

"To the beach, to that very cozy little cottage I've heard so much about."

She didn't miss a beat, but he would swear that he saw her eyes widen, just a bit, in shock. But she said very coolly, "I think not." She gave him a seductive smile and a toss of her head. Her riding habit was of pale blue, her hat was a darker blue with a charming feather that curved around her face. It was very effective, that feminine head toss. "Besides, I do believe the cottage is perhaps still occupied. My uncle lends it out, you know. Yes, one never knows just who might be there."

"Oh? Your uncle, you say?"

Sophie kicked her mare, Opal, into a canter and off they went down the long, wide drive of Camille Hall.

She was brazen. There wasn't an ounce of shame in her.

He followed her, content to let her take the lead. They rode onto the road, following it only for a half mile or so, then she turned off it toward the sea. When they broke through the thin stand of mango trees, Ryder sucked in his breath. He'd never seen anything so beautiful in his life.

There was a stretch of beach that went on and on, disappearing around a bend a goodly distance to the east. The sand was stark white, pure and clean. The water was a light turquoise. The mango trees gave way to coconut trees that lined the perimeter of the white sand. The tide was going out and the different hues of the sand and water were startling in their beauty.

"It's incredible," he said before he thought to censor and give her only what he wanted her to hear. "I have never seen anything quite like it."

"I know. It is my favorite stretch. I swim here a lot."

He got control of himself and raised a brow at her. "Would you like to swim now?"

"I normally swim in a sarong. I don't have one with me."

"No matter. I really would like to see you. I already know that your breasts are quite adequate. Not all that large, but fine, really. No man I know of would complain about their size or their weight or their softness. But there is the rest of you—your hips, your belly, your legs, and your woman's endowments. I think a man should be able to see what he'll be getting himself into before he takes the plunge, so to speak."

She turned her head away, but for only a moment. "Oh? And do you believe a woman should have the same consideration, sir?"

"You may call me Ryder since it's likely we're going to become quite close. Why, certainly women should be given every consideration. Would you like to see me naked, Sophia? Now?"

He thought he'd gotten her, but not a moment later he knew he was wrong. She gave him the hottest smile he'd seen in his adult life. She ran her tongue over her lower lip and leaned her upper body toward him. "Why, I think that would be nice, Ryder. Perhaps you could pose for me. I could sit over there beneath a coconut tree and tell you which way to turn so I could gain every perspective I wished of you. A man's buttocks, flexed, you know, are sometimes quite delightful."

Good God, he thought, picturing exactly what her words had conjured up in his mind.

He flushed. He actually turned red to the roots of his hair.

Sophie saw that flush and her satisfaction wasn't at all subtle. She shook her finger at him. "Really, Mr. Sherbrooke, it's never wise to bait your hook when you don't know what you'll catch." It was difficult, but she'd managed it. She'd won for the moment. She'd been so outrageous she'd made him blush. She knew she must be the first woman to have accomplished such a feat, for he was polished, this Englishman with his clear blue eyes, polished and cynical and very sure of himself. But she'd known exactly what she was saying, for the first time she'd taken Lord David Lochridge to the cottage, he'd already been three-quarters drunk. He'd stripped off his clothes, eager to show her that his body was firm and muscled, much nicer than that old man, Oliver Susson's, and how once she saw him, she'd dismiss all the other men. He'd posed for her, even turning his back to her and flexing his buttocks, and thus it was he she was seeing when she'd said those words to Ryder Sherbrooke.

Ryder was furious with himself. He was so furious with himself that he wanted to howl. He wanted to dismount and kick himself. But he didn't. He wouldn't allow her the upper hand. Ha, she had it. He had to get it back. It was intolerable that a woman, a damned tart, could do him in.

"I enjoy taking chances, Sophia," he said finally, creditably in charge of himself and his voice again. "I haven't yet caught a shark or a piranha. Perhaps I've hooked an angelfish and the good Lord knows they're quite enjoyable to eat." He gave her an intimate smile, but Miss Stanton-Greville merely looked at him, one eyebrow arched, and Ryder would swear she had no clue as to what he was talking about. No, impossible, she was just toying with him again, pretending to innocence this time.

She said on a laugh, "Perhaps I should show you a rooster-tail conch. They're quite lovely but somewhat dangerous. They can cut you when you least expect it. Then there is the trumpet fish who is quite loud to other fishes and they avoid him. All in all a rather boorish fellow, one would say."

"I'm at a distinct disadvantage in this," Ryder said. "You could continue indefinitely whereas I have used up the sum of my marine life knowledge."

"Again, it isn't wise to bait your hook—"

"Yes, I know. I wouldn't want to hurt a tender mouth. However, some fish have tough little mouths and even tougher minds. As for their bodies, who can say? I wonder about their taste. Sour, do you think? Perhaps even deadly? Surely not sweet and juicy."

"Your similes are drifting rather far afield. Let's canter up the beach. There are some rather interesting caves in the low cliffs just beyond that bend ahead."

He followed her, appreciating the sea breeze that cooled him. He was angry with himself, not with her. She was what she was. The only problem was he wasn't certain exactly what that could be.

She dismounted, shaking her skirts, and led him up a narrow path that skirted jutting rocks and narrow crevices. There were gnarled bushes along the way. Finally, both of them panting from the heat, she stopped and pointed. There was a narrow opening into the side of the hill in front of them. Ryder stepped into the black stillness then out again. "So there really are caves. Have you explored it?"

"Yes. It's deep and has no other opening that I could ever find."

"Have you supplies in there?"

"What do you mean?"

"Oh, things like blankets, perhaps a sheet, a bottle of rum or two? Champagne to toast a successful completion?"

"I see. Do I come here occasionally with other people, that is what you're wondering." She looked momentarily thoughtful, nothing more. "No, not to date, but it isn't a bad idea. As I told you, it's quite possible there is a guest in the cottage even as we speak. It would be nice to have another place available to one, don't you think?"

"I think a man would have to be pretty desperate to be naked as a snake in a cold, damp cave, despite the skills of his companion."

"On the contrary. I have found gentlemen to be much alike. They tend to forget themselves entirely. They could be on the moon and dismiss it as unimportant when they are otherwise occupied."

Ryder suddenly remembered telling his brother that he would forget his very name once he was inside a woman, forget everything for the pleasure was so intense. Once again, he flushed. This time he managed to control it enough so he prayed she wouldn't notice. If she did, she didn't say anything. Damn her.

"To keep many men content when each knows about the other tends to support your theory."

"Crying uncle, Mr. Sherbrooke?"

"No, those are facts. A man has to be stupid not to face up to facts. My name is Ryder. I shouldn't like it if you screamed Mr. Sherbrooke when you have your first orgasm with me. It would make me feel very strange."

She didn't look a bit embarrassed. What she looked was appalled and utterly scornful. He merely smiled at her. "Would you like to go back to the horses? Incidentally, do horses get sunburned?"

She gave a lilting laugh.

It was late in the afternoon. Sophie sat in her bedchamber, wearing only a light shift for the air was heavy and still. She sat very quietly in a cane chair that faced the sea, in front of the open balcony. She was utterly silent. She felt utterly defeated.

She wouldn't be able to handle Ryder Sherbrooke. He wasn't like any other man she'd ever met, any other man she'd manipulated and seduced. It was true that she did him in, but that was because he'd simply never met a woman who spoke so baldly before. But he was already accustoming himself to her.

What to do?

She knew her uncle was in her bedchamber even though she hadn't heard the door open.

"Tell me what happened."

She still didn't turn to face him. She said in a flat voice, "We rode. I showed him Penelope's Beach and one of the caves. He is a man, Uncle, but a man unlike the others. He made no move to kiss me, no move of any kind, but he spoke frankly of sexual things."

"You will seduce him. Perhaps tomorrow night."

She turned then to face him. He was sitting on her bed, his back against the headboard. His face was framed by the mosquito netting, and for an instant, just the veriest instant, he looked good and kind and gentle, the man and mask he presented to the world now one and the same.

"You don't understand. He does what it is *he* wishes to do. He will tell me when he wants to bed me, not the other way around. I could probably walk around him naked and if he felt he didn't have complete control over me, over the situation, why, he would smile, say something outrageous, and stroll away. He would not even bother to look back to see my reaction."

Theo Burgess frowned. She was right. He'd spoken to Ryder Sherbrooke long enough that morning to see her point. It was valid and it irked him.

"Fine," he said, rising now. "We will simply get him to the cottage another way."

She said nothing. She felt very cold suddenly, very cold and very weary.

"Did he say anything about his wounded arm?"

She shook her head.

"He isn't a stupid man. I imagine he inquired as to who hereabouts could shoot a bow and arrow. He plays a game, but you and I, Sophia, we are the ones, the only ones who know the rules."

She hated the rules. They were his rules, not hers.

That evening she had to tell Lord David Lochridge that she wanted nothing more to do with him. She had no idea how to accomplish it, for he was young and filled with himself, and she knew that he wouldn't be able to imagine anyone not wishing for his wonderful self anymore.

Theo Burgess came up with the way to do it. For the first time in a very long time, Sophie laughed.

It was very late. Sophie arrived at the cottage. David's horse was tethered outside. When she entered he saluted her with a rum punch. He didn't appear too drunk yet. That should make it easier.

He rose immediately to embrace her. She danced away from him, laughing, her hands in front of her. "No, David, first we must talk."

"Talk," he said blankly. "How very strange you've become. Why talk?"

"I have something to tell you. It's only fair that you know the truth since I am very fond of you. I don't want you to be hurt, to perhaps go mad as many do, I am told."

Lord David drank the rest of his rum punch. "This is talk," he said, "talk that is very curious. What do you mean, Sophie?"

"I have the pox."

He turned utterly white. "No!"

"Yes," she said in a low, very sad voice. "The pox. There is no doubt."

"You didn't get it from me, damn you!"

"Oh no, certainly not. If I had, I wouldn't have to warn you, would I now?"

"Oh God," he said and actually moaned. "What if you've given it to me?"

"I don't think that would have been possible, not yet. You are still safe. But I fear it wouldn't be wise for us to continue as lovers."

He looked wildly about the small cottage where he'd spent a good dozen nights over the past two months. He looked at her, wondering, wondering at the strange fancies, the odd fragments of dreams, as he sometimes did when he was sober enough to assemble his thoughts coherently. But now, those fancies were nothing, less than nothing. Jesus, the pox!

"I'll go now, Sophie. I'm sorry. Good-bye."

"Good-bye, David. Don't worry. You'll be all right."

She watched him grab his hat, smash it on his head. He was actually running from the cottage, then galloping as if the great green serpent itself was after him. In this instance, Uncle Theo had been quite right.

She wondered if he was also right about David's reaction once he calmed down.

"He won't say a word to anyone. We needn't worry about that. No, he'll fear ridicule if he does. When he finds out that he hasn't caught anything, why then, he'll look at the other men and just smile and wish them the worst. That is his character, you know."

"He's that kind of man," Sophie said.

Before she fell asleep that night, Sophie wondered how Ryder Sherbrooke would have reacted had she told him she had the pox. She had an idea he would search her face for the truth then demand to examine her himself.

He was that kind of man.

CHAPTER
═══ 4 ═══

EMILE TOLD RYDER upon his return from Montego Bay late the following morning that Lord David Lochridge was no longer one of Sophia Stanton-Greville's lovers.

Ryder blinked. "Good heavens, she's worked very quickly. Astonishing, I would say, but difficult to accept. Didn't you tell me he was at her cottage just two nights ago?"

Emile grinned, pushed back a chair and sat down. "You don't suppose she's clearing out all the flotsam for you, do you?"

Ryder was thoughtful for a long moment. He said finally, very firmly, "One could be tempted to think so at first blush. However, I still can't see her doing something so blatant. She's a subtle female when she sees it is called for and, more importantly, she isn't stupid. She's many things, but not stupid."

"Really, Ryder, perhaps you're entirely wrong. Perhaps she wants to bed you. Perhaps she admires you and wants you, pure and simple. No ulterior motives. You aren't a troll, you know."

"There is nothing either pure or simple about Miss Stanton-Greville. As much as I would like to preen myself on my manliness, on my utter magnetism with women, I would be a fool to do so. No, Emile, if she does indeed want to add me to her string, there's an excellent reason for it."

"Fine. But why kick out Lord David, I wonder?"

"Perhaps," Ryder said, stroking his long fingers over his jaw, "just perhaps he's outlived his usefulness." But he was remembering his order to her that he wouldn't be one of many men in her bed. He would be the only one. He shook his head. No, he wouldn't be drawn into that conceit. This was really quite interesting.

"What does that mean?"

"I mean that everyone behaves a certain way for very solid reasons. If she dismissed Lord David, then there were very good grounds for her to do so. Remember, we spoke of motives. Lord David is young, handsome, a likely candidate if a woman wished to take a lover. But Oliver Susson?

Charles Grammond? They're middle-aged, overweight, or stoop-shoul-dered . . . no, Emile, the selection isn't random."

"Lord David is saying, of course, that he was tired of her but no one believes him."

"No, indeed."

"I stopped by the Grammond plantation to bid my good-byes to the family. They're leaving at the end of the week. I drank some rum with Charles and learned one thing of interest, but not until that boss-wife of his left the salon. What we had heard is true—he lost a bundle of money to Lord David. Didn't my father tell you of Lord David's phenomenal luck at cards?"

"Yes, he did and several others as well warned me to avoid him. This is interesting, Emile. So, as a result, he must leave Jamaica after selling his plantation, which, just as a matter of happenstance, is situated next to Camille Hall. Mr. Theodore Burgess—because he's such a fine, compas-sionate fellow—is buying the plantation. I do wonder what he's paying Grammond for it?"

"I can find out," Emile said. "I should have thought of asking but I didn't. Besides, his wife came back into the room. She quite terrifies me."

"No matter. There are more pieces of the puzzle falling in place with each passing day. Lord, it's hot."

Emile gave him an unholy grin. "It's not even noon, Ryder. I had thought to ask you to visit the stillhouse with me."

"Kill me first, for it's as close to hades as men have managed to get whilst still flesh of this world. I have wondered how the slaves tolerate it."

"They are quite used to it. Also, they all come from Africa, a country even more inhospitable than Jamaica."

"Still," Ryder said, then shrugged at the sight of Emile's housekeeper, Coco, shyly peeping around the door.

Emile turned and frowned at the girl. "What is it, Coco?"

The girl showed another inch of herself, but her eyes were on her bare feet now. "I—I must speak with you, massa. I'm sorry, it's important." Emile turned back to Ryder. "Usually she doesn't say boo to anyone, thus it must truly be important, so I'll speak to her. Excuse me for a moment."

Ryder wondered what Emile's housekeeper wanted. Then he felt the heavy, still air close in around him and he thought only of being naked in a snowbank on the very top of Ben Nevis, and wallowing and wallowing until he was freezing. He even thought fondly of a thick white fog swirling around him, making him cold to his very bones as he walked St. James's street to White's. Even a London drizzle, frigid and miserable, dripping down the back of his neck, sounded remarkably inviting at the moment.

He wondered why Sophia Stanton-Greville had dismissed Lord David Lochridge. He believed he knew why she'd taken him as a lover in the first place. He wondered how the devil he would verify what he believed to be true. But primarily, he wondered exactly why he'd been selected as her next lover. For the life of him he couldn't think of a thing to be gained by having himself in her bed.

Theo Burgess was pale with anger when he came into her bedchamber. "Damn your laziness. He hasn't shown himself in two days."

"I know," she said, turning slowly to face her uncle. "It's a game he's playing with me."

"Game or no, I want you to ride over to Kimberly Hall and do whatever you have to. I want him at the cottage and soon, Sophia."

He walked over to her, looked quickly around, saw there was no one in sight, and slapped her. She reeled back, bumping into a chair and careening to the side. She fell. She didn't move.

"Stand up. I'm not certain you understand just how very serious I am about this."

"I understand."

"Damn you, stand up or I'll have your brother fetched and just see how much he enjoys pain."

Sophie stood up. This time she was prepared for the blow, but still the fist in her ribs dropped her to her knees. More bruises, and the ones from his last beating had just begun to fade. She shook with rage and pain.

"Now I trust you understand. Get yourself dressed and put on your cosmetics. You're pale and sickly looking. That little tap I gave your face just might discolor a bit. Cover it up. Go now and hurry."

"Ryder Sherbrooke doesn't like my face painted."

"Then do as he would like. Don't just lie there like a lame dog."

An hour and a half later, just as the three men were preparing to sit down to luncheon, James announced the arrival of Miss Sophia Stanton-Greville.

Emile shot Ryder a quizzical look. Ryder was frowning slightly. He hadn't thought she would come here, to him. It wasn't her style, at least he hadn't thought it would be. Something must have happened to get her here, that, or someone must have put the spurs to her to come.

Samuel Grayson gave James a fat smile and actually rubbed his hands together. "Do show her in, James. Oh yes."

When she came into the dining room, a vision in a pale yellow riding outfit, with only a minimum of cosmetics on her face, Ryder's eyes glittered. He knew her face wasn't completely clean because to do a good scrubbing would require utter compliance to his wishes. She would give up a single battle, but not the war.

She was all laughter and charm. She was gay and witty and she played with incredible boldness to Samuel Grayson's besottedness. She cast Ryder sloe-eyed looks, remarkably seductive, really. As for Emile, she ignored him for the most part. She readily accepted Samuel's luncheon invitation.

Ryder was content to sit back and watch her perform. He had no intention of entering the fray until he had her alone. And he did indeed want to be alone with her. As for Emile, he was clearly distracted.

Near the end of the meal, Sophie raised laughing eyes to Ryder and said, "I'm here actually to ask Mr. Sherbrooke to visit a fascinating cave one of our field slaves just discovered. It is much larger than the one I showed him on Penelope Beach and it isn't quite so cold and damp because the entrance is larger and thus more sun can come in."

"You would make a charming guide, my dear," Samuel Grayson said in a voice so infatuated that it made Ryder nauseous. "Ryder normally stays out of the sun during this part of the day, the suffocating heat, you know, and he isn't yet used to it."

"Perhaps Mr. Sherbrooke would consider himself to have sufficient fortitude, to be a man of strong enough will, to bear up under the heat when the end result would be this charming cave."

Ryder recognized a bucket of bait when it hit him in the face. Ah yes, question a man's virility and he would leap onto the hook with no hesitation.

"I don't know," he said slowly. "Perhaps another time, Miss Stanton-Greville. I'm really quite fatigued."

"Sophia," she said, her voice testy.

"Yes, Sophia. You know I'm not all that strong and my fortitude appears to be at low ebb. Yes, I am a weak man, one who must take care of his precarious health."

"Surely you can survive a simple ride to the beach!"

"Do you have an umbrella I can hold over my head on the way there?"

"A hat should be sufficient."

"I'm also worried about my horse," he said. "He pretends to be a mean devil, but underneath he's just as weak and low-ebbed as I."

She sucked in her breath. He was slippery as a spotted moray eel. Then she smiled. "Very well, then. I'm off to visit the cave. Good-bye, Mr. Grayson. Thank you for the delicious luncheon."

"But you didn't eat anything," Grayson called after her.

Emile began to laugh. His father spun on his heel and hurried after Miss Stanton-Greville.

"You have her going every which way, Ryder. I fancy this has never happened to her before."

"Yes. But enough is enough. I think I will have to follow her now. She just learned an important lesson in control. Now it's time for a frontal attack."

"No flank? No coming around the back?"

"You're becoming impertinent, Emile," Ryder said, grinned from ear to car, and left.

Sophie didn't know what to do. She let a small slave lift her onto Opal's back. She sat there, staring blankly ahead of her. What to do?

She couldn't simply return to Camille Hall because Uncle Theo would know she'd failed. She shuddered at the consequences of that, unconsciously touching her fingertips to her cheek. It was a bit swelled from his blow. The powder covered it, but it didn't bury the memory of the pain, the humiliation. She would have liked to shout to that smug bastard, Ryder Sherbrooke, that she didn't wear makeup to look like a tart. She wore it to hide bruises, at least she had at first until Uncle Theo decided she looked more worldly, more seductive, painted like a whore. Of course he also realized that he could hit her more often without chance of discovery if her face was covered with cosmetics.

She had no choice. She would ride to the beach and loiter about before she returned home. Then she would lie to him. She would tell him that Ryder Sherbrooke had kissed her, had told her he wanted her. But then why wouldn't he want to take her to the cottage immediately? In her uncle's mind, a kiss made a man think instantly of bed. In her experience her uncle was quite right. Her brain closed down. She would deal with that when she had to.

Her decision made, Sophie urged Opal forward and made for the beach. It was called Monmouth Beach and it lay a mile farther east from Penelope's Beach. It was littered with jagged rock formations, the sand was a dirty brown from the swirling tides that crashed over and around the rocks. The cave was real. A slave had found it but yesterday. Opal picked her way carefully through the rocks, avoiding tide pools and battered tree limbs.

She didn't want to go to the damned cave. She pulled Opal to a halt, dismounted, and looked around. Within minutes, she was spreading the saddle blanket beneath a coconut tree and sitting in the shade, staring out over the brilliant blue sea. Her thoughts were, oddly, of her parents, of the last time she'd seen them four years before.

Her mother had been as strong-willed as a bull, beautiful of face and bountiful of figure, Corinna by name, a woman who loved her children very much, too much to take them on the journey to America, a journey she considered too fraught with danger. Her father had said "nonsense," but he didn't have her mother's strength of character and thus Sophie and Jeremy were fetched from Fowey, Cornwall, by their uncle Theo after the drowning of their parents, and brought to Jamaica. She remembered clearly her grief as well as her gratitude to her uncle. She had loved him, then.

She prayed her parents' deaths had been quick. Even now after four years she still repeated that prayer. Somehow she just knew that her mother had eased her father at the very end. It was the way her mother had been. She closed her eyes and felt the cool breeze from the sea on her face. She slipped out of her riding jacket and unfastened the top buttons of her linen blouse. She removed her riding hat, laying it gently atop her jacket, smoothing its curling feather as she did so.

Within minutes she was asleep.

When Ryder saw her mare, he smiled. So, she had come here after all. Perhaps that cave was really something. Then he saw her, leaning against that coconut tree, sound asleep.

Despite the heavy humid air, here on the beach, out of the sun, it was cool enough. He dismounted a good distance away from her, tethering his stallion close enough to some sea grass so he could graze.

He stood over her, staring down at her face, still now, and he realized that she looked very young despite the cosmetics that still coated her face. Very young indeed. Why, he wondered, why had she taken all those men to her bed?

Now she wanted him.

He dropped silently to his knees beside her. Very gently, very slowly, he began to unfasten the remaining buttons on her blouse. She wore a very plain batiste chemise beneath. No fancy frills or lace. He frowned and finished with the buttons.

But he couldn't peel the blouse off her because it was tucked into her riding skirt. He wanted her to remain asleep a bit longer.

He pulled the blouse back as far as he could then took a knife from his pocket and slit the chemise down the front to just below her breasts. Ah, he thought, as he eased the light material back, her breasts.

They were beautiful breasts. She stirred, but didn't awaken.

He waited a few minutes, then slowly eased her down until she was lying flat on her back. He waited longer, hoping she would remain asleep. She turned on her side, moaned just a bit, then fell back again. Smiling, Ryder then began to work up her riding habit, slowly, ever so slowly, until it was bunched at mid-thigh, and he could see the plain garters that held her stockings in place. Very nice legs, he thought, long and sleekly muscled.

He was still looking at her legs when he eased down beside her and waited for her to awaken.

He wasn't quite certain how he expected her to react when she did wake up. He supposed she'd look up at him, be a bit aroused already, and hold out her arms to him. He waited, picturing his hand easing up her inner thigh to touch her intimately, and she'd be eager, and she'd beg him to take her here, now. He looked at her mouth.

She awoke in the next instant, and out of that lovely mouth came an actual scream, loud and embarrassed and utterly horrified. The scream dwindled into a squeak then a gasp.

He sat up next to her. She was staring stupidly from him to her naked breasts down to her legs.

"Damn you, what did you do to me!"

"I kissed your breasts and you moaned and arched your back. You thrust your breasts into my face so I was forced to slit your chemise open to help you get what you wanted. But you're a greedy woman. You wanted more, so you came down upon your back and lifted your hips and I helped you by pulling up your skirt."

"No, no, damn you, that's a lie!"

Her face was red and she was actually sputtering. Ryder frowned. This was unexpected. Where were her teasing smiles, her outrageous, coy, very sexual remarks? He watched as she regained control, watched the blankness disappear from her eyes, watched the control and that damned cool smile set itself into place.

What Sophie was thinking was, *Did he see the bruises on my ribs? Dear God, please no.*

She got herself in control. Slowly, giving him a very tempting sideways smile, she pulled the sides of her chemise over her breasts and began to work the buttons closed again, all the while keeping her legs exposed to him.

When she'd finished, she slowly rose and stared down at him. She smoothed her skirt, then put her hands on her hips.

"You damned bastard," she said, surprised at the mildness of her voice. "Damn you, you came."

"Yes, I decided my manhood couldn't tolerate your obvious scorn."

"Most manhoods couldn't. You are no different."

"No, probably not."

"You had no right to do what you did to me."

"I wanted to take you off guard. I find you excessively unpredictable whenever I manage to do it. You shrieked, just like a maiden aunt. Most delightful. It sweetens the pot, one could say, all these varied and unexpected sides of you. I wonder how many other sides you will show me if I'm quick enough to catch you showing them."

"You have had your fun, Ryder."

"Oh, I haven't as yet begun, as you will see. But I do have a question for you, Sophia. Why did you dismiss Lord David Lochridge from your harem?"

"Harem? I think you're confusing your genders."

"It's the same concept. Why, Sophia?"

She shrugged and turned away from him for a moment, looking out over the sea. She was silent for a very long time.

Finally, she turned back to him and that damned flirtatious mask was well in place. "He bored me. He was a boy in a man's body. He cared only for his own pleasures, his own amusements. I grew tired of him, that's all."

"You're lying."

"Oh? Why would you say that?"

"You wish me to believe that you dismissed him because you wanted me and you remembered my demand that I be the only man in your bed and thus in your body?"

"Yes, I remember you saying that."

"What about Oliver Susson? Will you dismiss him as well?"

She shrugged, saying nothing.

"I won't become your lover until you do."

"Surely you are a bit overenthusiastic in your demands, Ryder. Surely it isn't up to the lady to make herself more appealing to the gentleman. I am already appealing; you should be slavering over me even as we speak. You should be begging me to allow you in my bed."

He laughed, a rich, deep laugh. "Sophia, let me tell you something. You are pretty, yes, even with the absurd paint on your face, but understand me. I have bedded many women whose beauty reduces yours to mere commonplace, to nothing out of the ordinary. From what I have seen of your body, it is pleasing enough. But understand me, I won't play your games. I won't wait in the wings while you spread your legs for seemingly every gentleman in the vicinity. I am not an uncontrolled boy, anxious to plow every female belly he can manage. I am a man, Sophia, and I have developed standards over the years."

"Years! What are you, twenty-five, twenty-six?"

"I had my first sexual encounter when I was thirteen. What about you?"

In that moment, he saw anger in her, at him, and it was barely leashed. He saw uncertainty then, as if she were arguing with herself whether or not to cosh him on the head if she could manage it. Then she smiled at him, that coy, teasing smile that made him hard as a rock.

"In short, Miss Stanton-Grenville, get rid of the others—all the others—or I will never bed you. I find I am already losing interest quickly."

"Very well," she said. "I will dismiss Oliver. Will you come to the cottage tonight? At nine o'clock?"

"Are there any others?"

"No."

"Ah, you already dismissed Charles Grammond, the poor fellow who lost all his money to Lord David?"

"That's right."

Ryder found that he was brooding, picking, but knowing at the same time that she would elude him. She would show him glimpses of herself, but she wouldn't drop her guard unless he pulled something totally unexpected, caught her completely off guard, like baring her breasts or pulling up her skirt.

He rose to stand beside her. He said nothing, merely stared down at her. He grasped her upper arms in his hands and pulled her up against him.

"Perhaps I don't wish to fall into the same bed that has held so many other of your men. Perhaps I would like to sample what you have to offer me right here, right now."

He kissed her, but she jerked her face away and his lips landed on her jaw.

He merely smiled down at her, clasped his arms beneath her hips and raised her, pressing her belly hard against his groin. He was hard and he knew she could feel him.

"Put me down, Ryder."

Her voice was calm and controlled. He didn't stop smiling. "On the other hand," he said close to her mouth, "perhaps I don't really wish to come into you right now. Perhaps what I really wish to do is pay you back. Give you a taste of retribution. Yes, that's exactly what I want to do."

He carried her to the water's edge. She knew his intent and began to struggle. He laughed as he waded out into the water, ruining his soft leather boots and not caring. He waded until the water lapped around his thighs.

She was screaming at him, pounding her fists against his chest, his arms, his shoulders.

He lifted her high in his arms and hefted her a good four feet into deeper water. She landed on her back, arms flailing wildly, and sank like a stone.

"There, you hellion," he shouted when her head cleared the water. Her chestnut hair was matted and tangled over her face and shoulders. She looked quite pathetic. "Don't attack me again unless you want to pay more reparations."

He laughed again and strode back to his horse. "I mean it, Sophia. I am a gentleman most of the time unless circumstances dictate another behavior. Understand me. I will never allow you to do your worst to me again without complete and utter retaliation."

As she stumbled through the water, her skirts dragged her first to one side and then to another. Her boot went into a hole and she went down on her face. She managed to regain her balance and rose, shaking her fist at him. He was on his horse's back, riding away down the beach. He was still laughing.

He stopped and she heard him shout over his shoulder, "Tonight. Nine o'clock. Don't be late! Ah, and make certain the place is aired out."

Sophie paced the cottage, aware that her uncle was watching her from the corner of his eye. She said finally, "I'm afraid of him."

"Don't be a fool," Theo Burgess said. "He's just a man, a young man, not all that experienced, surely."

"You're wrong. I get the impression he's slept with more women than there are on Jamaica. Him and his damnable standards."

Theo shrugged. "Get him drunk. You know how to do it. It's nearly time for him to arrive. I'll be close by. You know what to do."

"Yes," she said and wished, quite simply, that she could drop to the ground and die.

But that would leave Jeremy alone.

She stiffened her back, but the fear wouldn't go away. She had to get control, she had to manipulate him. She was good at it, for she was bright, and the good Lord knew she'd had a lot of practice.

At exactly nine o'clock, there came a light tap on the front door of the cottage.

Sophie opened the door. He stood there, giving her a lazy smile.

As he stepped past her into the cottage, he said, "Your attempt at a seductive gown is more of a success than not, I should say. However, harlot-red really isn't your color. I think a soft green would be more the thing. To avoid laughter, you should avoid any shade of white. Also, the whalebone pushing up your breasts is an artifice I deplore. A woman has breasts or she doesn't. A man who knows women isn't fooled. But you will learn. Come into the light so I can see your face."

Sophie followed him dumbly. She was right to be afraid of him.

He clasped her chin in his long fingers and raised her face into the full candlelight. "Ah, no makeup, or hardly any. I am pleased that you wish to satisfy my demands. Now, should you like to strip for me now or should we talk for a while? Who are your favorite philosophers, for example? Ah, I can see by your expression that you have read the great minds throughout all the centuries. Yes, there are so many you are very likely completely conversant about. Let's select only the second half of the last century. French."

She drew back, moving away from him to stand behind a wicker chair. "I like Rousseau."

"Do you now? Do you read him in French or do you read him in English?"

"Both." She turned away from him and quickly poured him a glass of rum punch. She handed it to him. "It's warm tonight. While we speak of Rousseau, why don't you drink a bit."

"I don't like Rousseau. I find him nauseatingly imprecise in his thoughts and rather foolish, truth be told, in his aspirations of the earth's possible perfection in his hands, using, naturally, his absurd methods."

Ryder raised his glass and toasted her. He drank it. It was tart and cold and quite delicious. He hadn't realized he was so thirsty. He didn't particularly care for rum, but this didn't taste all that much like rum. He took another drink. It was really very good.

"I think Rousseau is a gentle man, one who wishes what is best for both men and women. He believes that we should quit the infamy and decadence of the world and return to a simpler life, return to nature."

"As I recall, this matter of nature was never defined."

Ryder drank more punch. It slid down his throat, tasting better than anything he'd ever drunk in his life. He finished the glass and handed it back to her. She poured him another.

"As I said, the fellow is a fool. What he should have preached is that men must control women or they will lose all sense of what and who they are, for women can control men through sex. The more skilled the woman, the more dangerous she is to a man. You, for instance, Sophia. I wonder what you want from me. I wonder what I have that you could possibly lust after, other than my body, of course. It is true that I am a Sherbrooke and thus the plantation belongs to my family, however—" Ryder broke off. He felt suddenly quite warm; he felt, really, quite wonderful, relaxed, but yet the need for her was growing hot in his blood. She looked soft and sweet to him, so willing, so anxious to please him. Now she was holding out her arms to him and she was speaking to him, but he didn't understand her words, which was odd, but he really didn't care. He downed the rest of the rum punch, rose from his chair, and walked to her. He took her into his arms and began kissing her. Her breath was warm and sweet and she opened her mouth to him and he reveled in her. His hands swept down her back to cup her buttocks. As he had that afternoon, he lifted her against him and moaned at the delightful sensation.

He released her for a moment, then stepped back and began to pull her gown from her shoulders.

She laughed softly, so very sweetly, and slapped his hands away. "No, Ryder, you'll rip the material and it was expensive. I had it made just for you. I am sorry that you dislike the color. I will have another made in the shade of green you deem proper for me. Now, let me remove it. Let me become naked just for you. Yes, sit down here and watch me. Tell me what you want me to do. Here's another rum punch to cool you whilst you watch me."

Ryder took one sip of the rum punch. He leaned his head back against the chair cushion. His eyes were slitted as he watched her, standing in front of him, her hands on the buttons at the front of the harlot-red gown.

It was the last thing he remembered.

"He's unconscious."

"Excellent," Uncle Theo said, stepping into the cottage. He walked to Ryder and examined him closely. "Yes, this is excellent. No, Sophia, don't leave. I would like you to see him. It is quite possible that being the sort of man he is, he will question you, and you must be prepared. If there is a mole or a birthmark on his thigh, why then, you must be able to remark upon it."

She stood back as her uncle dragged Ryder Sherbrooke to the wide satin-sheeted bed. He undressed Ryder swiftly, for he'd had a lot of practice. When Ryder was sprawled on his back, quite naked, Theo laughed. "My God, he's still aroused. Look at him, Sophia. Didn't I tell you he was an excellent specimen?"

She didn't want to, but she did look. She supposed he was beautiful, for he was lean and nicely muscled, light brown hair covering his chest and thinning out to his belly, but she found him terrifying, particularly his sex, which was thick and hard. Uncle Theo turned him over on his stomach. His flesh was smooth, his back long, the muscles deep and firm. There were no moles or birthmarks.

Uncle Theo turned him again onto his back. "Ah, he is ready because in his mind it's you he will bed." Theo turned and called out, "Dahlia! Come in now, girl."

A very beautiful young girl, no more than sixteen, with light brown skin and brown eyes, stepped into the cottage. She sauntered over to the bed and stared down at the naked young man. She stared a good long time.

"He be a treat," she said and gave Theo Burgess a big smile even as she lightly touched Ryder's belly.

"Excellent. I won't have to pay you then."

"He not that much a treat," she said. She slipped out of her dress. She was naked beneath, her breasts pendulous and very large, her hips round and supple. Sophie turned away only to have Uncle Theo grab her arm. "I think you should watch, Sophia. Again, he might ask questions, make comments and—"

"I won't!" she yelled in his face, jerked free of him, and ran from the cottage.

She heard Dahlia laughing softly, heard her say in an utterly happy voice, "Ah, look at how much bigger he get and all I do is touch him with my fingers! Ah, yes, massa, this nice boy be a treat."

Sophie fell to her knees. She felt nausea roil in her belly but she wasn't sick. She was beyond being ill. At first she would have been, but not now. No, too much time had passed. She'd seen too much. She hugged her arms around herself and rocked back and forth.

She heard Dahlia crying out in the cottage, heard her laughing and groaning and encouraging Ryder to come deeper into her, to caress her breasts. She wondered if Uncle Theo were standing there, watching. She knew he'd done it before. She wondered if he'd taken Dahlia to bed himself. She heard Ryder then. Heard him moan, heard him yell. Oh God, it was too much.

She crept away.

CHAPTER
══ 5 ══

RYDER WOKE SLOWLY. His first reaction was one of incredulity, for he felt both slightly drunk and sated. He also felt utterly relaxed, but strangely vague. But it was morning, he knew that, and he was drunk? He'd never been drunk in his life upon waking. It made no sense. Nothing made any sense at the moment.

He sat up in the strange bed, and held his head in his hands, trying to understand. He realized then that he was naked, and remembered where he was and what he had done here in this bed for most of the previous night. Actually, he should be completely exhausted but he wasn't.

He'd been in this bed with Sophia Stanton-Greville.

God, she'd been incredible, her skills beyond the ability of any woman he'd ever bedded before. He rose slowly, shaking his head to clear it. The front door opened and an old female slave came in, giving him a wide toothless grin, saying in just short of a cackle, "Good morning, massa. Aye, 'tis fine you be this mornin'." He started to cover himself, but the old woman merely shook her head. She couldn't have cared less if he was wearing a gentleman's morning wear or was as naked as the Sherbrooke Greek statues he and his brothers had gawked at when they'd been boys.

She offered him a bath and breakfast.

True to form, Sophia had left him alone.

He was just one of many. She hadn't cared enough to stay with him. Oddly it hurt and made him angry, in equal parts. He was just another man and she'd not cared.

He eased himself down into the bath. He tried to remember the previous night in detail, but most of the specifics eluded him, which was surely very strange. He remembered kissing her at first, then he could almost feel again her mouth caressing him expertly and he shuddered with the memory. He remembered her riding him hard and fast, his hands kneading her large breasts, caressing them, lifting them, and he'd screamed like a wild man when his climax had hit him.

She'd screamed as well. And she'd spoken to him, urged him on, telling him what she liked, telling him what a man he was. He remembered it quite clearly, her voice soft and deep. He remembered her breasts in his hands and how they'd thrust forward when she'd arched her back over him.

Ryder didn't remember pleasuring her though, and that was odd for he hadn't lied to her. He was an excellent lover. He never left a woman unsatisfied. But he hadn't taken her in his mouth as she had him. He couldn't remember kissing her either, except at the very beginning of the evening, and surely that was even more odd, for Ryder loved kissing, sliding his tongue into a woman's mouth, stroking her, bringing her closer and closer as he used his hands on her body to heighten her pleasure.

Why hadn't he kissed her? Was she so abandoned that she could climax with him simply inside her? He hadn't even fondled her with his fingers, at least he couldn't remember doing so. He shook his head again, shaking away a slight dizziness. He still felt mildly drunk and he hated it, and the damnable vagueness.

He rose from the bath and the old slave handed him a towel. She didn't show any interest in his body at all. No, he thought, the anger building stronger than the drunkenness, she was so used to seeing naked men here—Sophia Stanton-Greville's men—that she didn't even pay attention anymore.

He dressed in freshly pressed clothes—good God, did the cursed woman think of everything?—and ate fresh fruit and warm bread. He shook his head at the offered rum punch. Jesus, he thought, watching the old slave drink it when she thought he wasn't looking. The drinking here was beyond good sense and control. He should know, he'd done enough of it the previous night.

When he left a few minutes later, he turned in the doorway of the cottage and looked back toward the bed, now freshly made up by the old slave. The interior still smelled of sex.

He hated himself for what he'd allowed her to do to him. She'd obviously kept control the entire time. He again remembered her shriek of pleasure and wondered if it had been feigned. Odd, for he wasn't certain and surely that couldn't be right. Ryder knew women. No woman could feign pleasure with him. But she could have and he simply didn't know. He remembered then the glasses of rum punch he'd drunk when he'd arrived the previous evening at the cottage. How delicious it had been, how cool and refreshing, and then all he remembered was the warmth he felt, the hard arousal, the urgency, the incredible sex that had gone on and on until he'd finally fallen like a good soldier in battle.

He walked to his horse. Sitting beneath a mango tree was Emile, chewing on a piece of turtle grass, his hat pushed to the back of his head.

"So," Emile said only, rising, and dusting off his breeches. "Are you ready to go home?"

"Yes," Ryder said. "I'm more than ready."

Emile asked him no questions. As for Ryder, he was cold sober now, his head so clear it ached. The more he tried to remember each detail of the previous night, he found he simply couldn't call it forth. Except that he'd spewed his seed in her mouth, his back arcing off the bed the release had been so powerful, that and her sitting astride him, riding him hard, her hands busy on his body, pushing him until he couldn't bear it, and again, he'd screamed his release.

Something wasn't right. In fact, something was very wrong. He was still frowning when he and Emile rode down the long Kimberly Hall drive. Ryder listened with half an ear to the rhythmic humming and singing of the slaves as they worked in the fields.

"Emile," he said finally, "have you ever seen a crocodile in the middle of the road in the mangrove swamps?"

"Yes, I have. It's terrifying, really."

"Something is very wrong," Ryder said.

"What do you mean?"

Emile was dancing around the issue. He didn't want to call Sophia Stanton-Greville a whore if Ryder was now enthusiastic about her. He was uncertain; he was trying to be diplomatic.

From one instant to the next, Ryder realized the truth, clear and shattering. It was her breasts! He'd fondled Sophia's breasts two times. He knew the texture of her flesh, the size of her, her weight, his hands could even now mold themselves in the shape to hold her breasts.

The woman who'd taken him twice the night before wasn't Sophia Stanton-Greville. The breasts were all wrong. It was that simple. If it hadn't been Sophia, then it had been another woman, and that meant something that made him want to howl in fury. He turned to Emile and said, "There was something in the rum punch she gave me last night." There, he'd said it aloud. And it was true, of that he was certain. But he couldn't tell Emile he was basing everything on the size and feel of breasts.

Emile was clearly incredulous. "You mean to say she drugged you? Good God, why?"

"I woke up alone, just as you told me would happen. What was strange was that I was still feeling drunk. Something else even stranger is that I can remember certain things, but all the details of the night are gone from my memory." He shook his head for there was something of a flaw in his theory. "If there was something wrong, if she has indeed been drugging men's rum punch, why wouldn't her other lovers have come to realize it and said something or confronted her with it?"

"I would say that you are the man with the most experience of all the men she's taken to that cottage. Perhaps the others simply remembered the pleasure and didn't question a thing."

"Perhaps," Ryder said. "Perhaps." He was thinking that more than likely, none of the other men had ever seen and caressed Sophia Stanton-Greville's breasts as he had. Just that other woman's, and thus the fools didn't realize the truth. Perhaps he wouldn't have either, at least at first.

He laughed aloud then. She'd be brought down all because of her breasts.

At five o'clock that evening, Ryder realized there'd also been a man there. He could actually hear his voice, but he couldn't remember the words he'd said. Did that make any sense? It had to. Who the hell had stripped him naked? He certainly couldn't remember taking off his own clothes, much less Sophia Stanton-Greville's.

She'd drugged him, seduced him, then brought in another woman to make love to him. It was clear enough. Ah, yes, and there was Uncle Theo who'd come in to see to his clothing. It must have been Burgess, there was no one else.

Ryder rose from the chair, a very grim smile on his mouth. He bathed and dressed carefully. He was coldly and calmly furious. He was going to drop in at Camille Hall. He had no doubt that he wouldn't be invited to stay for dinner.

Sophie wanted to eat in her room but Jeremy came bursting in upon her. "What's the matter, Sophie?"

Always he was afraid that she would become ill and die as their parents had died. She hastened to reassure him. "I'm just fine, love. I've quite changed my mind about eating here in my room. Give me a moment and I'll comb my hair."

Jeremy sat in a chair watching her brush her hair, chatting all the while.

". . . Uncle Theo had Thomas take me with him to the north field today, just for two hours, not more, because of the heat. It was fascinating, Sophie, but several times Thomas used his whip on a slave. I didn't think it was necessary but Thomas said he had to because they were lazy and had to taste the whip to remind them what would happen if they didn't work. He kept calling them lazy buggers."

Thomas was a cruel monster. Sophie hated him. She fastened her hair at the back of her head with a black velvet ribbon. She rose and looked in the mirror. In the old pale yellow muslin gown she looked about sixteen. The only discordant note was the faintly greenish bruise on her left cheek. She had no intention of putting on the powder. It didn't matter. Besides, in the dim evening light, no one would notice. And if Uncle Theo did, why it would probably give him pleasure.

She said over her shoulder, "If you were master here, Jeremy, would you keep Thomas as your overseer? Or another man like him who would whip the slaves?"

Jeremy chewed on his lower lip, swinging his legs, his energy overflowing despite his mental contemplation.

"I don't know," he said at last. "Uncle Theo seems to think Thomas is very good. He trusts him and allows him to do just as he likes. It's just that—"

"What?"

Jeremy shrugged and rose. "Well, I've known most of the slaves since we came here over four years ago. Most of them are my friends. I like them and they like me. I don't understand why you would want to hit someone you liked. And it's so hot in the fields, Sophie. I know I wanted to rest after a while. They never get to rest."

She ruffled his hair and kissed his brow, risking a little boy's horror at such a motherly act. Jeremy squirmed away from her and out of her bedchamber. "Come on, Sophie!"

She drew to a stop at the bottom step of the stairs. She stared, her heart pounding. There, standing in the large open foyer, was Ryder Sherbrooke, looking like an English gentleman from his brushed pale brown hair to his glossy Hessian boots.

Uncle Theo had just welcomed him in.

Ryder looked up and saw her. He blinked, he couldn't help it. The tart in the red gown from the night before bore no resemblance to this young girl standing there, mouth agape, staring at him as if he were the devil himself come to claim her for the fourth circle of hell.

Theo Burgess turned at that moment and a spasm crossed his face. Damn the girl, she looked like a virgin of fifteen, certainly not like she should look. He wanted to hit her for her defiance; he disregarded the fact that Ryder Sherbrooke was entirely unexpected.

"Hello, Sophia," Ryder said very calmly. "Your uncle has seen fit to take me in. I am to dine with you. Ah, and who is this?"

"I'm Jeremy, sir. I'm Sophie's brother." Jeremy walked with his clumsy gait, his hand outstretched.

Ryder smiled down at the boy and shook his hand. "How do you do, Jeremy? I hadn't realized Sophia had such a large younger brother."

"Sophie says I grow faster than the swamp grass. I'm nine years old, sir."

"He's a good lad," Theo said, his voice testy.

Sophie was standing there, frozen, waiting. Would Ryder look at Jeremy with contempt or pity? She didn't know which was worse. People had looked at him with both and it was all horrible. Ryder had been a perfect gentleman thus far but she didn't trust him, not an inch. Perhaps he hadn't yet realized that Jeremy wouldn't grow up to be perfect like him.

Jeremy beamed up at the man he recognized immediately as a real gentleman. He was young and handsome and well dressed, and there was a very nice smile on his face, a smile that reached his eyes. Jeremy also realized that he must be here because of Sophie. He turned to his sister and called out, "He's having dinner with us, Sophie. Isn't that grand?"

"Yes," she said, forcing a smile that was ghastly. "That's just grand."

Ryder saw the marked resemblance between brother and sister. He also saw that Jeremy had a lame left leg, probably a clubfoot. It was a pity, but it didn't seem to slow the boy down a bit. He was a handsome lad and seemingly well adjusted. He chattered all the way into the dining room to Ryder, who found him both amusing and intelligent. He reminded him very much of Oliver. Ah, how he missed Oliver and the other children.

Theo Burgess tried to sidetrack Jeremy, but it didn't work. It seemed that the man was truly fond of the boy. He didn't order him to be quiet. He merely shook his head at him and smiled at Ryder as if to say, What can I do?

Sophie said nothing at all.

"My sister is the best rider in the entire area," Jeremy said. "Maybe on all of Jamaica, but I've never been to Kingston so I can't be certain."

"Thank you, Jeremy," Sophie said, smiling at her knight, a quite beautiful unconscious smile that made Ryder draw in his breath. She looked about fifteen and that smile lit up her face. It made her look very different, very appealing, really, and he didn't like it. At that instant he realized it was the very first time he had ever seen her smile.

What the hell was going on here?

He looked down at the delicious curried shrimp with pineapple. He speared a shrimp and chewed it thoughtfully. The boy was speaking again, telling his uncle and Ryder about his hours spent with Thomas in the fields.

Sophie noticed that he didn't mention Thomas whipping the slaves.

The dinner was pleasant, finished off by mango pie topped with warm cream. The rich Jamaican coffee was thick and black and wonderful, as usual.

Ryder bided his time. He enjoyed the boy. He shook his hand when he was dismissed to his bed. When Theo Burgess asked him if he would like to adjourn to the veranda where it was much cooler, he readily agreed. Every man he'd met on Jamaica imbibed rum in the evenings. It was time for the ritual to begin. It was time to put his plan into action.

He wasn't surprised when Sophie excused herself to follow Jeremy upstairs. Nor was he surprised when Theo called after her, "You will join us, my dear, when you have seen to your brother. Don't forget, Sophie."

"I won't forget, Uncle," she said, and Ryder heard something odd in her voice, something he didn't understand at all. "I'll be down shortly."

Ryder set out to make himself a congenial companion. He was amusing, his anecdotes of the first order. He encouraged Theo Burgess to talk and once he started, Ryder sat back, thinking about what he hoped would happen.

When Sophia came out on the veranda, she was carrying a tray and on that tray were glasses of rum punch. Ryder wasn't at all surprised.

"How delightful," Theo said. "I'm glad you remembered, Sophie. I trust the punch is up to the Burgess standards? I assume you enjoy a rum punch in the evenings, Ryder?"

"Why, most assuredly, sir," Ryder said.

So this was it.

He accepted the glass Sophia handed to him. He thought her hand shook a bit. But no, he must have imagined it.

Theo proposed a toast. Ryder clicked his glass to theirs and then pretended to drink.

He then rose, glass in hand, and walked to the wooden railing, leaning his elbows on it, and looking out toward the glistening sea in the distance. There was a half-moon and the scene in front of him was spectacular. But he really didn't see it. He turned to face Sophia and Theo, made a toast to this beauty he really didn't see, and again pretended to drink. As he turned away again, he dumped the contents of the glass into the vivid pink blooms of the hibiscus bush just below the veranda. He hoped he hadn't killed the plant.

Now it was time to act. He turned, smiling widely, showing his empty glass, and said, "Why don't we take a bit of a stroll, Sophia?"

She didn't want to. She wanted him to just leave. She didn't want him to be sprawled naked in the cottage with Dahlia leaning over him, fondling him. She didn't want to hear him yell again in his man's release.

"Yes, Sophia, go along, my dear."

"Do bring us each another glass of that delicious punch."

"Yes, an excellent idea," Theo said and he felt the blood speed up, felt the triumph. Sophia had been quite wrong about Sherbrooke. He was only a young man, not all that intelligent or sly, quite easy really, quite predictable. In a sense it was disappointing. There was no challenge in him, not really. Sophia had been wrong.

Sophie brought each of them a fresh glass. Again, Ryder accepted the glass she thrust toward him. He offered her his arm. "Let's walk a bit. It's a beautiful night, isn't it? You can tell me some more of the island's history."

"Oh yes."

He drew her into the garden on the eastern side of the house. It was darker here, but the scent of all the flowers was stronger, nearly overpowering. There was no one about, just the two of them, each with a glass of rum punch in his hand.

He said easily as he walked slowly beside her, "You don't look the whore tonight."

"No."

"However, last night was something of a sensation, wasn't it? Quite memorable, but not really, but surely I am quite wrong. It must have been memorable."

"Yes, of course it was. You seemed to enjoy yourself."

"And you, Sophia? Did you enjoy yourself as well?"

Still, she kept walking, and showed him only her profile. "Naturally. I wouldn't have wanted to make love with you had I not expected pleasure from it. You are quite competent as a lover."

"You screamed quite loudly when you climaxed."

She was silent as the night.

"I found your skills quite adequate, more than just quite, actually. Did you enjoy taking me in your mouth? You took me so deeply I feared I would gag you. But you didn't gag, at least I don't think you did."

"I think such things should be left to the cottage, don't you, Ryder?"

"Let's stop a moment. What is that bush over there? Yes, that one with the wispy yellow leaves?"

He took her glass from her, saw her stiffen slightly, then ease, as relaxed as could be, when he set both glasses on a stone bench. And he knew, simply knew, that she was memorizing that her glass was the one on the left. Well, it wouldn't matter. When she turned away from him, he slipped the packet of powder from his pocket and quickly poured the contents into her glass, stirring it with his finger.

"It's a yellow poui tree, actually, it's just very small as yet."

She turned and waved him forward. "You see, the flowers are in clusters. They're quite delicate and won't last long, perhaps only another week."

He admired the yellow poui tree.

When he turned back, she was already at the stone bench and she'd picked up her glass. She was obviously taking no chances. As he'd assured Emile, she wasn't stupid.

He picked up his own and raised it in a toast. "To our evening. You gave me great pleasure. I trust we will spend another together very soon."

"Yes," she said and clicked her glass to his. She sipped it, found it remarkably delicious, and drank deep.

"Finish it off, Sophia, and if you like, we'll stroll about a bit more."

His rum punch went onto the ground and hers went straight down her throat.

Ryder said, "You have beautiful breasts, but I've already told you that. However, I remember last night that your breasts seemed even larger. Isn't that curious? I suppose it must have been my lust, my fevered urgency for you that made me imagine such a strange thing."

"Perhaps."

"Why do you say perhaps?"

"You'd drunk a bit more than you should have, but you seemed to enjoy it very much. I didn't wish to take away from your enjoyment."

"It was very kind of you."

She kept walking. Why wouldn't he simply collapse? He'd drunk two glasses, surely it was enough. Uncle Theo had made it stronger tonight. But he sounded chirpy as a blue jay and his step was light and bouncy. She hated him and herself. If it weren't for Jeremy, why she'd . . . she didn't know really what she would do.

Ryder stopped and turned to face her. "I'd like to kiss you, Sophia. Odd, but I can't remember kissing you at all last night, except of course just a few forays before you pushed me away so you could strip off that scarlet whore's gown for me. It's odd, for kissing is something I much enjoy. Why didn't we kiss, Sophia?"

"You wanted me quickly. As you said, there was fevered urgency. There was no time."

"Now there is." He kissed her and she let him. She tried to force herself to kiss him back but she couldn't. She was a fraud and a cheat and she was very, very afraid of this man. Ryder was well aware that she was letting him touch her, not reacting, suffering him. It was enraging, but he wasn't overly surprised and oddly enough his anger soon stilled.

He gently pushed her away, holding her in the circle of his arms. "How do you feel, Miss Stanton-Greville?"

She looked up at him. "Why so formal, Ryder? After all, you are now my lover. None other, just you, and you will remain my lover, won't you?"

"Oh yes. You're marvelous. If I close my eyes, why I can see you taking me into your mouth, I can feel your tongue on me, the warmth of you.

Yes, you gave me great pleasure. Tell me though, Sophia, isn't there something I can give you? Something you would like to have? I had thought to bring you a piece of jewelry but I didn't have time to go to Montego Bay. What would you like, sweetheart?"

Yes, she thought, bitterness filling her, he had to pay the whore. She wished she could tell him Dahlia's name and send him to her; let her get the gift. But no.

"Well," she said slowly, giving him a dazzling smile, "perhaps there is something I would enjoy."

"Yes? Just tell me and it's yours. A bauble, perhaps? A diamond or a ruby? Of course I want you again, tonight."

She didn't tell him. She sighed softly and fell against him, quite unconscious.

Well, hell, Ryder thought, as he lifted her. She'd succumbed more quickly than he'd expected. He gently laid her out of sight in the midst of colorful jasmine bushes, smoothed down her skirt, and rose. He gave her a small salute.

And he thought, as he walked quickly back to the veranda, now it's your turn, Uncle Theo. I suspect you'll be fairly easy, you old bastard.

And Theo Burgess was remarkably easy. There was only one old slave to see him when he carried Theo over his shoulder, quite unconscious, to his bed.

Sophie woke slowly. She felt strangely suspended, somehow separate from herself. Her head felt light, her thoughts scattered and vague. She felt slightly dizzy. It was morning, the sun was shining through the window.

But that couldn't be possible. The morning sun didn't shine in her window.

She forced herself to sit up in bed. She shook her head, wondering at the strangeness of how she felt. She felt somehow drunk but surely that was odd.

She swung her legs over the side of the bed. It wasn't her bed. She realized then that she was perfectly naked.

She cried out. She stared blankly around her. She was in the cottage, quite alone. She simply sat there, tugging the sheet over herself, staring at the far wall. What had happened?

Ryder Sherbrooke had happened. Somehow he'd discovered what she and Uncle Theo had done to him. And he'd gotten revenge.

She wondered if he'd taken her as Dahlia had taken him two nights before. How did one tell? She rose slowly, dropping the sheet. The room was warm and she felt perspiration on her brow from the heat of the room, and from the heat of her fear.

What had he done to her?

She looked down at herself. She looked just the same. She remembered long ago that Uncle Theo had assured her that she'd remain a virgin. But how could one tell if a female was a virgin or not? She hadn't asked him. God, she didn't know.

What to do?

Sophie saw her clothing lying neatly over the back of a wicker chair. They were the same clothes she'd worn the night before. He'd brought her here to the cottage and stripped her to her skin. It was beyond embarrassing. She had to know what he'd done to her. She had to find out what he knew.

She thought of Uncle Theo and blanched. Then, of course, she realized what must have happened. Ryder had drugged her, then Uncle Theo. He'd done a fine job of it. He'd paid them back in kind.

She dressed quickly and combed her hair, tying it at her nape with the same ribbon she'd used the night before. She looked at herself in the mirror. Did she look different? Was that how one knew that one wasn't a virgin anymore?

She looked pale, nothing more that she could see. She had to know. She left the cottage and walked quickly back to Camille Hall.

Uncle Theo wasn't there. A slave told her that the massa hadn't come down yet.

She realized then that it was only seven o'clock in the morning. But she couldn't wait. She called for Opal to be saddled.

CHAPTER
═6═

RYDER WAS ALONE on the front veranda drinking a cup of coffee. It was still very early, but he knew, deep down, that she would come and very soon. She wouldn't be able not to. She would have to know what he'd done to her and he couldn't wait to tell her.

When he saw Opal cantering up the drive, he smiled in anticipation, both his body and his mind becoming instantly more alert. He didn't rise, merely sat back and watched her ride closer and closer.

Sophie dismounted and tethered Opal to one of the black-painted iron posts. She was shaking. That would never do. She wiped her hands on her skirt and forced her shoulders back.

She walked up onto the veranda and simply looked down at him. She hadn't expected him to rise as a gentleman should in the presence of a lady and, indeed, he didn't. After all, she was about the furthest thing from a lady that breathed.

Ryder smiled up at her, a predator's smile, a quite evil smile really. "Good morning, Sophia. You haven't changed your clothes, I see. You couldn't wait to see me again, then? Would you like some breakfast? Coffee, perhaps? You must keep your strength up, particularly after your exertions last night."

He was going to toy with her. Very well then, she wasn't an inexperienced twit when it came to men. She'd well learned most of their vagaries during the past year, their little conceits, their need to dominate and rule. She smiled back at him and tossed her head. "I should like some coffee, thank you."

"Do sit down."

She waited for him to return, her mind working feverishly, but blank of ideas. When he handed her the cup, she took it and sipped it slowly, all the while watching him take the wicker chair opposite her. He leaned back, as indolent as a lizard warming himself in the sun, and crossed his arms over his chest. He leaned the chair back on its hind legs. She wished it would tip over and he would cosh himself on his damned head.

"It's very early for a visit," he remarked to the wisteria that was spilling wildly over the railing of the veranda.

"Yes," she said, "very early indeed, yet you are up and dressed, almost as if you were waiting for someone to arrive. It will be hot today."

"It's hot every day. Did you wish to speak to me about something in particular? Or perhaps you wanted to see Samuel, who's so besotted with you he nauseates me with his endless effusions? Or perhaps Emile, your childhood friend whom you now ignore?"

"You."

He gave her a lazy nod, then fell silent. The silence stretched long between them.

"Well?" he asked at last. "It's not that I have something urgent to do, it's just that I do bore rather easily. You are pushing the limits, Sophia."

"What did you do to me?"

"I beg your pardon?" An eyebrow shot up a good inch. He was pleased with the utterly sincere puzzlement in his voice.

"Damn you, don't play with me further. Please, did you take me to the cottage?"

"Yes."

"Did you take off my clothes?"

"Yes. I also folded them neatly for you. I am a man of orderly habits."

"Did you . . . that is to say, did you become intimate with me?"

"Do you mean did I become intimate with you before I folded your clothes neatly? Or after?"

She said nothing, merely stared at him. He shrugged, looked at her breasts, and smiled. "Become intimate, Miss Stanton-Greville? Why in heaven's name wouldn't I have taken you, or, as you so quaintly put it— become intimate with you? Isn't that the whole purpose of having a lover? Your body is mine, you told me that quite clearly. I don't particularly like females in my bed who are more unconscious than not, but parting your legs and coming into you did indeed serve my purpose . . . my purpose as your lover, naturally. You did arch your back just a little bit. No, unfortunately, I don't think you enjoyed it, even though you did moan once or twice." He struck a thoughtful pose. "But wait, I recall you moaned when I kissed your breasts, or perhaps it was when I was caressing your buttocks and I turned you on your stomach. You certainly didn't scream as you did the other night, though. Of course, you were in no shape to ride me, so it was I who did the mounting and the riding. You're quite soft, Sophia, and very giving. You gave me some measure of enjoyment. Last night, of course, I was full-witted and felt every shred of feeling to be felt from plowing your belly." He was just getting into the full swing of his splendid monologue when she jumped to her feet and yelled at him, "Damn you, stop it! Just stop it! You forced me, you raped me! You're an animal!"

"Forced you," Ryder said blankly. "An animal? Surely not, Sophia. I'm your lover."

"You drugged me! You took me when I was unconscious. You're no lover, you're a perfidious bastard! I hate you!"

He laughed then, a full, deep, rich laugh that made her skin crawl. God, she wanted to hit him, to hurl something heavy at his head, to kick him. She couldn't stop herself. She rushed from her chair and at him, her hands fisted. It took a lot of strength, but she managed to push his chair backward, sending him sprawling. Unfortunately she didn't move back quickly enough. Ryder caught her ankle and jerked her down over him. He held her wrists so she couldn't strike him.

He looked up at her face, flushed with fury, at her breasts, heaving up and down, and said, happy as a vicar at a wedding, "How passionate you are, Sophia. Perhaps next time you can be as full-witted as I was this time and we can speak together while we make love. It will enhance your enjoyment, and mine as well, I hope, not that I'm complaining all that much."

She struggled and he was well aware of her body pressing onto his. She was truly enraged, quite unaware that her belly was grinding against him. He was hard; surely she felt him. But he had her firmly held. He merely waited until she realized she couldn't hurt him. But she struggled a good three minutes more. Finally, her voice low and mean, she said, "Let me go, damn you to hell."

"You know, Sophia, no woman has ever attacked me before with evil intent. Attacked me with laughter and sexual intent, certainly, for I much enjoy playful women and many of them seem to know it. But this violence? I'm uncertain of the rules here. Should I hold you another five minutes to be certain you're well tamed?"

She felt rage and fear. Tears were burning her eyes. She had no more words. She simply shook her head.

Ryder saw the tears but he knew she wouldn't let them fall. "If I release you, will you try to do me in again?"

She shook her head again, and he guessed she was now really beyond words. He had won. Quite simply he'd demolished her. She deserved it. He released her wrists. She rolled to her side and was on her feet in an instant, staring down at him.

Ryder rose slowly. He set his chair back in its place, then motioned for her to be seated again.

It was as if it had never happened, she thought numbly, for the first words out of his mouth after he'd sat down again were, "Drugged you?

That is what you said, isn't it? What a novel idea. What a grotesque thought. Who ever would think of something so perfidious as drugging? Why, that lacks all honor, all honesty. The deceit of such an act boggles the mind. Goodness, it's very early in the morning for such jests, but since I have nothing urgent to do, as I told you, and you certainly aren't boring me now, why, do continue spinning your fairy tales."

"I was a vir—" Her voice fell like a stone off a cliff. Good God, telling him she was a virgin would make him howl with laughter. She shook her head, trying to get hold of herself. He knew about the drugging; she'd been almost certain. "You drugged me. You must have put something in my rum punch. And then you took advantage of me." The words weren't what she would have liked to have said but there was nothing else in her mind. They were the ineffectual words of an outraged maiden. She also realized that if more words were to come out of her mouth, they wouldn't be the right words either and he would only laugh all the more at her.

"Did I tell you that my very first afternoon in Montego Bay I heard you had three lovers? I heard descriptions of the three men in question. Why, Oliver Susson even came in and was needled mercilessly about you, all envy of course. Now, unless you took all these gentlemen in strange and exotic ways, then it's impossible that you've been a virgin for a very long time. Ah, yes, don't look so surprised, Sophia, and please don't protest. There are few words I know well that begin with 'vir.' I am relieved that you stopped yourself before you finished out that truly ludicrous lie. Virgin . . . another deceit that boggles the mind."

"No," she said, defeated. "I won't lie." But she was thinking, *I didn't feel any different this morning. I even looked in the mirror. I looked just the same, yet he says he took me and knew I wasn't a virgin.* She didn't understand this, but she remained silent. Evidently a man couldn't tell whether or not a woman had been touched. Evidently a man had to take a woman's word for her innocence. Given her reputation, her word was worthless and she knew it, so that was that. She was about as innocent as any harlot in Montego Bay. She saw he was grinning at her, and that grin was filled with triumph and satisfaction and more than a dollop of malice.

"Please, Ryder, please tell me the truth. What do you know? How did you find out? What do you want? I admit it's over now, I know that even if Uncle Theo doesn't yet, but, please, oh God, please—" She stopped. What was she prepared to ask him anyway? There was nothing she could do now to prevent him from doing precisely what he wanted to do. She could hear his laughter if she attempted to tell him about Jeremy. Slowly, feeling as numb as a slept-upon arm, she rose from the chair. She stared at him blindly, turned, grabbing up her skirts, and ran down the front steps of the veranda.

He called after her, his voice loud and carrying, "It was your breasts that did you in, Miss Stanton-Greville. From that I deduced you must have drugged me. You see, it wasn't all that remarkable of me to have figured it out. Yes, indeed, a woman's breasts are hers alone, not to be pawned off on another. The other breasts were nice really, but much too large. No, I prefer yours."

She didn't turn but he would have sworn that her entire body jerked at his words.

Ryder watched her run away. He let her go. He didn't say another word. So she'd wanted to protest that she was a virgin. He shook his head at that nonsense. Even though another woman had bedded him, he still doubted very strongly that Sophia was as innocent as she looked now, as she'd looked the previous night, in that mussed girlish muslin gown, her face washed clean of cosmetics. No, it was highly unlikely. She'd led him on, teased him expertly, enticed him, let him fondle her breasts as would an experienced courtesan, setting the pace unless he managed to knock her off guard.

He watched her gallop her mare full tilt down Kimberly Hall's drive. He watched her until she disappeared from his sight.

He rose and stretched. He really had to decide what he was going to do now. It was a pity he hadn't discovered the purpose of the game with him, but he would, he didn't doubt it for a single moment.

Uncle Theo was waiting for her in his study. His face was pale and his hands were shaking slightly. He wore no kindly gentle mask for her. She knew fear, and kept as much distance as she could between them. She shut the door behind her and watched him slowly rise.

"Where the devil have you been?"

She expected this, and recited in a low voice, "I awoke in the cottage, naked in the bed, quite alone. I had to know what happened so I rode to Kimberly Hall. Ryder said he'd taken me since he was my lover, and what was all the fuss about.

"I accused him of drugging me. I started to tell him I was a virgin but I didn't because I knew he wouldn't believe me."

"He drugged both of us, the damnable bastard!"

At that, Sophie felt a fierce joy, despite what Ryder had done to her. It was over now, finally over.

"Damnation! How did he know? None of the others ever wondered about a thing."

"I don't know." But he saw she was lying, and knowing there was no hope for it, she said quietly, "Very well. He said he knew that the breasts of the woman of that night weren't mine. He had fondled me before, twice, seen me, felt me. That was how he knew. He said all women were different from each other."

"That's absurd! He knew Dahlia's breasts weren't yours!" he cried, his words slightly slurred because his tongue was thick with rage. "Ridiculous. You're lying, damn you, Sophia!"

Theo Burgess stopped cold, whirled about and stared at his niece. "By God," he said very quietly, "you told him, didn't you? You went to him and you told him. You fell for his charm and his man's body and you told him!"

"No! I despise all men! He is no different."

"You hate me so you used him to get back at me. Well, it won't work. I'll figure something out and you'll do as you're told. Oh no, it's not over, Sophia. It won't be over until I say it will."

"It is over. He knows. Not all of it, but he knows enough. He will do something and you can't stop him."

"He knows because you told him. Don't lie to me further, you damned little bitch!"

She saw the darkening of his eyes and knew what was coming. He was on her in an instant. He struck her hard and she slammed against the doorframe. She grabbed the knob to keep herself upright, then wished she hadn't, for he struck her again. Rage flowed through her, rage and strength she didn't know she possessed. The pain disappeared, leaving only the rage. She whirled away from him, regaining her balance. She picked up a lamp from a table and hurled it at him. It struck his arm.

He was screaming at her, cursing her, and she knew that if he got to her again, he wouldn't stop until she was dead.

A slave's face appeared at the veranda window, then quickly disappeared. She ran behind his large desk, grabbing books and throwing them at him, but he kept coming, closer and closer, and his fists were large, his knuckles white with the strain, his face brutal.

She saw the letter opener. She didn't think, she was beyond thought. She grabbed it and ran straight at him.

"I won't let you hit me again! Never again! I hate you!" She struck as hard as she could. She felt the end of the blade slide into his shoulder with sickening ease.

She was crying, her vision blurred. She looked at the letter opener, the mother-of-pearl handle sticking obscenely out of his flesh. She watched him look from her to the letter opener. His expression was bewildered.

"You stabbed me," he said slowly. He looked up at her again and he screamed, "I'll take care of you now, you damned little bitch! I've given you everything, you and that miserable little cripple. Stab me, will you."

He caught her arm, bent it until she knew it would snap, then released her, shoving her hard against the wall. She was trapped now in the corner of the room, and he was on her, hitting her again and again . . . her ribs, her face, again and again.

Until she slumped unconscious onto her side.

When she came to, she was still lying on the floor where she'd fallen, sprawled on her side. The pain drove all efforts at coherent thought from her head. Her body clenched and twisted in on itself; she moaned softly, unable to keep the sounds to herself. At least he hadn't killed her. Nor was her arm broken. That was something.

She lay there for several more minutes, not moving, scarcely breathing. She had learned to deal with pain but it was more difficult this time. He'd showed no restraint at all. He'd beaten her here in his study, a room that the slaves could enter at any time. Usually he was so careful, waiting until she was in her bed and coming into her room and beating her there with little to no chance of discovery.

Had he beaten her so badly because he had no intention of continuing his gentle, kindly fiction to anyone, the slaves included? Did he finally accept that it was over and he simply no longer cared? Even had she not stabbed him, she knew he still would have beaten her badly.

Perhaps he was dead. If so, she was a murderess.

Sophie tried to sit up. The pain was bad but she managed it. She couldn't remain here. If a slave came in and saw her, the truth would be out all that much sooner, and then Jeremy would find out as well and her mind balked at that. He wouldn't keep still. He would try to protect her. He would attack Uncle Theo. She saw both of them in a heap with their few possessions in a pile of refuse in the middle of Montego Bay. Oh, Jeremy, oh no, not her little brother. She'd been responsible for him for four years. She would be until she died.

No, she had to be wrong. Uncle Theo wouldn't do anything immediately. No, at the very least, she'd wounded him. He would be too weak to do anything yet. But he'd sworn to her that it wasn't over yet. He'd beaten her because he'd been so furious at Ryder Sherbrooke. No, he'd try to continue the fiction, he simply had to. Yes, she was wrong.

She drew a deep breath, gripped the edge of the desk, and pulled herself to her feet. She felt dizzy and nauseous but finally she managed to control it. She had to get out of here until she could keep from crying out in pain. She would need all her cosmetics this time to hide what he'd done to her.

She passed a mirror but didn't look at herself. She crept out the side door of the study, holding her sides. She walked the near mile to the cottage, bent over like a frail old woman, breathing in short, jerking gasps.

It was too much. This time she had to do something. It had to end. Either she did it or Ryder Sherbrooke would. But she didn't think she'd have time to take action. She hurt too badly. Time seemed to stop. She wondered if she would die. She thought of Ryder. He was furious and primed for revenge. What he'd done to her was just the beginning, and that gave her hope.

When she finally reached the cottage, she began to cry. She couldn't stop crying nor did she try. The tears burned down her bruised cheeks.

She staggered into the cottage and, very slowly, walked to the bed. She eased herself down on it and let the pain flood over her in relentless waves.

Ryder wanted more answers. He was through with games. He rode to Camille Hall. Sophia wasn't there. The house slave didn't know where she was. The slaves he saw were acting strangely but they wouldn't tell him anything. Uncle Theo wasn't there either, not that Ryder was ready to face him down just yet.

Ryder paused a moment at the end of the long drive, wondering where she could have gone after she'd ridden away from Kimberly Hall. Then he knew. Without hesitation, he directed his horse to the cottage. If she wasn't there, she'd probably ridden to Penelope Beach, her private place, she'd told him.

At first he thought he'd been wrong. There didn't seem to be anyone about. He walked through the door and became very still.

She was lying on her side on the bed, fully dressed, her legs drawn up. She appeared to be deeply asleep.

Ryder walked very quietly to the bed and stared down at her. He took her arm and pulled her onto her back. He sucked in his breath in disbelief. All burgeoning ideas of further punishment fled his mind; incredulity took its place, then a rush of sheer rage. He stared down at her face; he couldn't believe it. Jesus, what had happened to her? But of course he knew. Uncle Theo had beaten her.

Even her heaviest cosmetics wouldn't cover these bruises. He realized his hands were fisted. She moaned and he saw her hands flutter about her chest.

As gently as he could Ryder undressed her. He guessed that she was as much unconscious as she was asleep. When he got her gown and slippers and stockings off her, he was still left with her chemise.

Again he drew his knife and cut if off her. The sight that met his eyes made him go very still. From just beneath her breasts to her belly she was covered with ugly bruises. Uncle Theo had hit her hard many times. He'd shown no mercy. It came to Ryder then that the night before when he'd stripped her, it was possible that there had been remnants of bruises over her ribs. But he couldn't be certain. The light had been dim. But now the evidence was there for all to see.

Jesus, the man was an animal. Lightly, he touched his fingertips to the worst of the bruises, just below her left breast. She moaned softly, flinging her arm out, then letting it fall. She'd come here to the cottage to hide away as would a wounded animal.

He straightened. The first thing he needed was laudanum, explanations could wait. When she awoke he could only imagine how bad her pain would be. He would have to leave her to fetch medicine. That, or he could simply wrap her up and take her back with him to Kimberly Hall.

She began to cry, low deep sobs that tore at him. Tears seeped from beneath her lashes. She was unconscious and still she was aware of the pain to such an extent that she was crying. Was she crying about all the rest of it as well? The months upon months of deception?

Ryder didn't hesitate. He wrapped her as gently as he could in a blanket and carried her out of the cottage. It was not easy to get her and himself onto his horse's back but he finally managed it. He prayed she would remain unconscious until he could get her back to Kimberly Hall.

When he arrived at Kimberly Hall, Emile was standing on the front steps, pulling on gloves. He started forward, eyes widening in surprise. "What the hell is this, Ryder?"

"Come with me and I'll explain what I can. First, Emile, get some laudanum, water, strips of cotton, cream, whatever. If I'm not mistaken, her dear uncle Theo beat the hell out of her."

"Jesus," Emile said and hurried away.

Ryder carried her to his bedchamber. It simply didn't occur to him to take her anywhere else.

He pulled back the mosquito netting and laid her as gently as he could upon her back. He covered her with the blanket. He didn't want Emile to see her naked.

When Emile came back into the room, he said, "My father wants to know what's going on. I put him off. You should tell him what you think appropriate."

"Thank you, Emile. Just leave the things. I'll take care of her."

Emile hesitated. "Would you like Mary or Coco to help you?"

Ryder just shook his head. "No, I'll see to her. I don't suppose there's such a magical item as real ice here?"

"Of course. Ah, you want it for her face, to reduce the swelling. I'll fetch some immediately." Emile quietly shut the door on his way out.

Ryder peeled the blanket off her and set to work. When he knotted the last of the strips of cotton over her ribs, having made certain they weren't

broken, he rose slowly, studying his handiwork. She was still unconscious.

He had a glass of water with laudanum ready the moment she woke
up. He studied her face as he waited. Slowly he reached out and gently
glided his fingertips over her brow, her nose, her jaw. He slipped his finger into her mouth and pressed against her teeth. Her teeth were still
strong and nothing was broken, thank God. Ah, but the pain she would
suffer.

Sophie didn't want to wake up. She knew if she did, she wouldn't be
pleased about it. And she wasn't. The pain hit her in vicious waves and
she gasped with the force of it.

His voice came from above her. He was saying over and over that she
would be all right, that he would make certain Uncle Theo never hurt her
again. She was to trust him. "Trust me," he said yet again.

She opened her eyes then and stared up at Ryder Sherbrooke.

"Trust you?" she said, shuddering with the pain those two simple
words brought her.

"Yes, please, Sophia. Trust me. I'll see that everything will be all right.
Here, drink this."

Ryder saw equal amounts of pain and wariness in her eyes. He understood, he couldn't blame her, but he was determined. He gently lifted her
head and forced all the drugged water down her throat.

He eased her back down. "Now, don't say anything. There will be time
later to find out exactly what happened. No, don't try to talk. Just listen.
Nothing seems to be broken. I've bound up your ribs. Your face is another
matter. I'm going to wrap ice in a cloth and cover your eyes with it. Hopefully the cold will keep the swelling down, all right? If you feel something very cold, don't be alarmed. Now, just hold still."

Her eyes were closed when a light knock came on the door. It was
Emile and he was carrying cloths and a bucket of ice chips.

"Thank you," Ryder said. "If Theo Burgess shows up here, come and
get me."

Once alone with her again, Ryder wrapped the ice in the cloths and
laid them over her eyes and across her face. She flinched and he said quietly, "Just hold still, Sophia. It will numb your face and the pain will
lessen. Also, I gave you laudanum. Don't worry, please."

She tried to force the words from her mouth. "Jeremy," she said, but
knew it was but a whisper of sound in her mind. She felt the laudanum
pulling at her and tried one more time. "Jeremy."

Ryder's face was very close to hers. He made out her brother's name.
He felt a frisson of alarm. If Uncle Theo had beaten her so badly, what
would he do to the boy?

"Uncle Theo, I stabbed him. He won't come here, at least not today."

"You what?"

"I . . ." Her head lolled to the side.

Ryder didn't hesitate. He found Emile, who was pacing in the front entrance hall downstairs. "Have Coco stay close to her. The laudanum I gave her put her to sleep. Tell James not to allow anyone from Camille Hall in here. No one. As for your father, Jesus, tell him whatever you think best."

Emile nodded and was gone in an instant. Ryder took his place pacing. When Emile returned, he said, "Now what?"

"You, my friend, you and I are going to beard the lion in his den. Hopefully the damned lion isn't dead. I'll tell you all about it on the way."

Sophie gritted her teeth. The pain kept coming, kept pounding through her, surging and swelling until she thought she couldn't bear it. Then it would lessen, retreating and flattening as a wave receding from the shore, but she knew it would return again and again and there was nothing she could do about it. It wouldn't ever stop, not ever. She was trapped in it, helpless, and completely alone. She'd failed and now she was paying with this ghastly pain. There was nothing she could do to help anyone.

"Please don't cry, Sophie, please. Here, drink some water. Ryder said you'd probably be really thirsty."

She sipped the water, nearly choking. Then she realized that it was Jeremy who was here with her. Jeremy, her little brother. She raised a hand and pulled away the cloth from over her eyes. She could open her eyes without too much effort. The swelling had gone down. She saw Jeremy was standing there beside her, worry and fear etched deeply into that beloved face.

"I'm all right, Jeremy," she whispered. "Don't worry. I probably look much worse than I really am."

"Shush," Jeremy said. "Ryder said you'd try to talk to me, and he said I was to tell you to be quiet. He said I could tell you what was happening. All right?"

"Yes."

"You are to lie very still. Ryder said that you'll be just fine. He said nothing was broken, but your ribs and your face are badly bruised. He said to be very still, Sophie."

"Yes."

"Uncle Theo changed," Jeremy said slowly, and he was frowning as he said it. He didn't understand, that was clear to her, but she didn't say anything, merely waited for him to continue. "He saw me come into the house with Thomas and he started yelling. He was holding his shoulder and I saw blood seeping through his fingers. He screamed at me that he was through with the two of us."

"He didn't hit you, did he?"

"Oh no. He just told Thomas to lock me in my bedchamber. He said he'd take care of me later. He didn't hurt me like he did you. But he was very angry and he was calling you a liar and a slut and a whore and other words I didn't understand. He said I was nothing but a crippled little bastard and he'd see to it that I never, ever inherited Camille Hall or got control of our home in Fowey. He said he'd see you in hell where you belonged."

Oh God, Sophie thought, wishing she could reach out and fold Jeremy in her arms. Yet he sounded very calm, detached, as he spoke, and that frightened her even more.

"I was going to climb down the trellis off my balcony when the door burst open and Ryder came in. He said we were leaving. He said you were here and he was bringing me to you. He said everything would be all right."

"Uncle Theo?"

"He wasn't there. I guess he went off with Thomas to see to his shoulder. Did you hit him, Sophie?"

"Yes, I stabbed him with a letter opener."

He seemed to take her bald words quite in stride. "I was afraid, Sophie," Jeremy said after a moment. "I was afraid that he would send in Thomas with his whip and he would whip me like he does the slaves. And I didn't know where you were or what he'd done to you."

She felt such relief that for an instant, the pain faded into near insignificance. She didn't hear the door open, but suddenly Jeremy turned and his face lit up.

"Is she all right?" It was Ryder's voice, low and deep.

"Yes, sir. I told her to be quiet, just as you told me to, and just let me talk. She's been pretty good. She tried, sir. She did stab him."

"Yes, I know. Now, my boy, would you like some pineapple betty? Cook said every young man she knows loves her pineapple betty."

Jeremy shot a look back at his sister.

"No, it's all right. I'll be here. Go ahead, Jeremy."

Ryder didn't say anything until Jeremy had left the room.

"Are you ready for some more laudanum?"

"No, please, it makes my mind fuzzy."

"It's better than the pain. Jeremy is safe and I swear to you he will remain under my protection. There is no reason for you to be a martyr. No, keep quiet, Sophia. Here, drink this."

She did and within minutes her eyes were closed and her breathing had deepened.

Then she said in a soft, slurred voice, "My name is Sophie. I've always hated Sophia."

"I prefer Sophie as well," Ryder said, but she was asleep.

He placed fresh ice packs over her face then settled back in a chair. He stretched out his legs, crossing them at the ankles. He steepled his fingers and lightly tapped his fingertips to his chin. His eyes never left her. What the hell was he to do now?

He thought fondly of home, of his brothers and Sinjun, his sister. He thought of his brother's new wife, Alex, and wondered how she was faring with the earl, a very stubborn man.

If Samuel Grayson hadn't written all in a dither about strange happenings here, why then he would still be in England, enjoying his children, enjoying his mistresses, riding the southern cliffs, the wind whipping his hair in his eyes, without a worry in the world.

Now he had two big human worries. He realized that his life to this point had been exactly as he'd ordered it up. He'd done precisely what he'd pleased because providence had made him the second son, and thus his brother was the Earl of Northcliffe. An equal share of good fortune was the immense wealth left to him by his uncle Brandon. He realized with a start of self-contempt that he'd played with his life, taking what he wanted, never really thinking about consequences because he'd even managed to control those quite well. Most who knew him liked him, he knew that. He was charming, he brought laughter into a room with him, he was honorable in his dealings. He shook his head, seeing himself clearly. He was honorable for the simple reason that there was never any reason for him not to be honorable, no challenges to his honor, to his integrity; he'd never really had to prove himself. One could praise him about the children, perhaps, but that was different, that was something deep within him that he had to do. It was a pleasure to do; it was easy to do; they made him feel blessed, not put upon.

But now things had spun quite beyond his control. He didn't want to be involved in this mess, but he was. He stared over at the beaten girl on his bed. She'd managed to stab the bastard. She had guts. He couldn't walk away from this. He couldn't walk away from her. He cursed quietly, with great fluency.

There was nothing for it.

CHAPTER
═ 7 ═

SUNLIGHT POURED IN the bedchamber, warming Sophie's face. She opened her eyes and queried her body. The pain was less than it had been yesterday. Two days now, two days of lying here and wondering what had happened and what would happen now. She hated the helplessness. She had to get up; she had to do something, what she didn't know, but she knew the first step was to get her feet on the floor. She managed to pull herself upright, groaned with the rush of pain in her ribs and fell back again, panting. She closed her eyes and waited, counting slowly to ten. At least she could close her eyes, even blink, without pain. The ice Ryder had kept on her eyes for the past two days had markedly reduced the swelling. Ah, but her ribs. She tasted blood and knew she'd bitten her lower lip. But it didn't matter. Who cared? She got control of the pain, finally. Still, she didn't move. She was afraid to move, it was that simple. When she finally opened her eyes again, Ryder was standing beside the bed, looking down at her.

"Good, you're awake. I've brought you breakfast. I'll bring Jeremy along to see you once I make certain you're in good enough condition not to scare the devil out of him. I had to let him see you the first time because he wouldn't believe that you were alive. But it did scare him; he was brave about it and continues to hold up well. I am proud of him and so should you be as well." He smiled at her as he spoke, and he was very matter-of-fact. The last thing she needed was an outpouring of sympathy and pity, and he knew it.

"I did what I thought best for him and for you. No, hold still. I'm going to lift you. Don't try to do anything yourself."

When she was propped up against the pillows, he set the tray on her legs. "Before you eat, perhaps you need to relieve yourself?"

"No," Sophie said, staring at the fork beside her plate.

"Don't be unnerved. It really doesn't suit you. Surely you can handle any impertinence out of a male mouth. Come now, after the long night you must have to—"

"All right, yes! Would you please take this tray and leave me alone."

He grinned down at her, pleased with her outburst that brought color to her face, and called out, "Coco, come here and assist Miss Stanton-Greville."

He turned back to her. "I suppose you would like me to remove myself?"

"At the very least."

"Ah, it pleases me to allow you to resharpen your knifely wit on my poor male head."

She paled. It infuriated him. He leaned down, his hands on either side of her face. "Dammit, Sophie, don't think about your uncle! Lord, had I been with him, I wouldn't have stabbed him, I would have wrung his mangy throat. Now, stop it."

"You don't understand."

"I understand a lot more than you think I do."

She looked up at him, wondering, but afraid to ask him what he meant. "Thank you for keeping Jeremy away." He merely nodded and left the bedchamber.

When he returned, Sophie was eating her breakfast. No, he was wrong, she was actually pushing the soft baked yams around her plate. She didn't look quite as frightful as she had the day before or the day before that. He needed to examine her ribs, but he would wait a bit for that.

"Eat. I won't leave you alone until you finish everything. Does it hurt to swallow and chew? I imagined that it still did and that's why you have the soft yams again. I had Cook put some brown sugar on them."

"Thank you. They're quite good, really. I'm just not very hungry."

"You're worried and I told you not to. Eat."

"Why are you being like this?"

He turned toward the open wooden doors that gave onto the balcony. "Like what?" She waved her fork at him, winced because the slight movement brought her pain, and continued silent.

"Well, I really can't see myself making love to you in your current condition. No, don't throw the yams at me, you might hurt your ribs. I will tell you something. Even the bruises in all their splendid color are preferable to those cosmetics you smeared on your face."

"My uncle demanded the cosmetics. He said they made me look more like a woman should, more sophisticated."

"Yes, and I imagine you also had to use them to cover bruises. Am I right?"

"I will be well enough to travel very soon now."

"Oh? Where do you intend to travel to? A young girl with a little boy and no money?"

He regretted his sarcasm, though she'd deserved it, and said quickly,

"I will decide what will be done after you're completely well again. You're not to concern yourself about anything. As I told you, Jeremy is just fine and I'm keeping a close watch on him. When I'm not with him, Emile or Samuel is. All right?"

"Why are you being so nice?"

"Does that come as a shock to you? I suppose you're really not used to nice men."

"No."

"Finish your breakfast and then we'll talk. It's time, don't you think? I cannot continue to battle shadows. I must know the truth."

"You're so smart I would have thought you would have already figured out everything. Didn't you just tell me that you understood more than I gave you credit for?"

No, he thought, he wouldn't strip her just yet to see her ribs.

"I don't like the way you're giving orders, Ryder. I'm sorry, you are being nice to Jeremy and me, but after I'm well again, I will see to us. We are not your responsibility and—"

"Shut up, Sophie. You're really quite wearying."

"Go to the devil!"

He grinned at that. "Who was it who told me you were a regular hellion?"

"Some miserable man, I doubt not. Hellion—what nonsense! None of you can bear the thought of a woman making decisions for herself, being responsible for herself. You must always rule and order things to your own satisfaction, and you dare to call it protecting her. Well, let me tell you, I won't have it, do—"

"Shut up, Sophie. If you want to expend ire, why, then, let's redirect it. Let's talk about Uncle Theo."

"Is Uncle Theo alive? Are you certain?"

"Yes, I am certain. Your aim wasn't all that good."

"It is not a good thing to stab one's uncle."

"Nor is it a good thing to beat one's niece."

She sighed, leaned her head back, and closed her eyes. He studied her in silence for several minutes. Her hair was loosely braided and hung lank and dull over her right shoulder.

"Would you like to bathe? To have your hair washed?"

Her eyes flew open and there was such hope and excitement that he laughed. "Very well, if you finish your breakfast, I will see to it."

She ate everything on her plate and promptly fell asleep. Ryder removed the tray and sat down on the chair beside her bed. What a damnable mess. He realized fully that he was in it up to his neck, perhaps beyond. What he was going to do about it was still unknown. He looked at Sophie—yes, she did look like a Sophie, young and vulnerable and soft. She didn't look like an elegant, cold Sophia. He looked beyond the ugly bruises and saw the fine high cheekbones. Her nose was thin and straight, her eyebrows nicely arched and slanted, her lashes thick. Perhaps in another time, in another place, in different circumstances, he would have taken her as his mistress and shown her that men could really be quite useful when it came to making a woman happy. But the time was now, and the circumstances were godawful. He continued to study her. She was really quite nice-looking and that realization surprised him. Her chin wasn't rounded and soft, it was stubborn and solid, that chin, as was her jaw. He imagined she was a hellion even when she was a little girl. Ah, but she was loyal. She would do anything for Jeremy. Anything at all.

And now what was there for her to do?

He had bath water brought to the bedchamber and poured into the large copper tub. Now was as good a time as any to have a look at her ribs. Very slowly he drew the sheet down. He was unfastening the buttons on one of Samuel's borrowed nightshirts when her eyes flew open. She stared up at him, not moving, not saying a word.

"What are you doing?"

"I'm going to look at your ribs. The bandages must come off in any case if you're to have a bath."

"No."

"Sophie, I know your body very well, as well, I imagine, as you know mine. I admit the circumstances are a bit peculiar here but I am the only one who has taken care of you. You will hold still and let me look at your ribs. If you continue being stubborn about it, I will tie you down."

"No, damn you!"

"You won't get your bath."

"No."

"How many men have seen your body besides me? Surely more than the three you entertained when I arrived. Surely you can't have an ounce of modesty left."

She turned her face away. He eased her out of the nightshirt then methodically began to untie the bandages from her ribs. He paid no attention to her breasts, to her white belly. He was staring at her bruised ribs and feeling bile rise in his throat. He wanted, quite simply, to kill Uncle Theo with his bare hands.

He gently ran his fingertips over each rib. "Tell me how bad the pain is," he said. Her breathing was shallow. His hand brushed against her left breast.

She shuddered.

"All right. You're better. Now, I'm going to help you into the bathtub."

Why not, she thought. It didn't matter. He was quite right. He had seen her and taken her and probably looked his fill of her the night he'd drugged her. It made no difference. She allowed him to ease her to the side of the bed. She was naked and he was holding her, lifting her now to her feet. Her knees gave, and when she fell against him, he held her upright, pressing her against him. His breath was warm on her temple. She would have been terrified of him but she felt too weak, and the pain was rippling through her. He knew, of course, damn him.

"Is the pain bad?"

"No, I'm just weak, that's all. Ryder, I can manage, truly. Would you leave me alone now?"

"Be quiet, Sophie."

He eased her into the copper tub. She sighed with pleasure and he grinned down at her. He unbraided her hair and smoothed out the ripples.

She managed to wash most of herself and he washed her hair. It took a long time, and she was white with fatigue and trembling with weariness when they were finished. And pain, he guessed. He toweled her dry as matter-of-factly as he'd rub down a lathered horse. That thought made her smile and he saw that small smile and wondered at it as he wrapped her hair in another towel.

He carried her to a rocking chair by the open louvered doors and sat down, holding her in his lap. "Time for a rest for both of us. You've worn me out. You've a lot of hair. Lean your head against my shoulder. That's right."

"I'm nothing to you."

"What does that mean?"

"I mean that I'm naked and you have seen me and taken me and yet you don't care. I'm nothing to you."

His arms tightened about her and he felt her wince and immediately loosened his hold.

"Would you prefer me to slaver all over you and make you uncomfortable by staring at your breasts?"

"No, you already did that. It was just a game to you, it meant nothing. It's just that—"

"That what?"

"I don't understand you."

"Sometimes I don't understand myself," he said. He began to rock her back and forth. She was asleep within two minutes.

No, he thought, he didn't understand and it was driving him mad.

He carried her back to bed and laid her on her back. He decided to leave her ribs unbandaged. Very gently he removed the towel from her hair and smoothed out the tangles with his fingers, fanning her hair about her head on the pillow to dry.

He looked at her flat belly and at the soft nest of hair below. She really was quite lovely, he thought, as he pulled a sheet over her, and she'd known men in only one context. They wanted her body, nothing more. Well, she had a very nice body, but he wasn't moved at all.

He had no intention of ever being moved by this woman, at least any more than he already was.

He was eating luncheon with Samuel, Emile, and Jeremy, when James came into the room and said, "Mr. Thomas is here, Mr. Sherbrooke. He wants to see you."

Jeremy's fork fell to his plate, his face suddenly white. Ryder nodded to James, saying, "Show him into the salon, James. I shall be there presently. Now, Jeremy, pick up your fork and eat those delectable shrimps. I asked your sister to trust me. I'm asking the same of you. If you don't get color back into your cheeks, I'll stake you out in the sun. If you think I will allow Thomas or anyone else to get near you, you are sorely mistaken. Do you understand me, young man?"

"Yes, sir," Jeremy said, his eyes searching Ryder's face. Ryder saw the fear, the uncertainty, and he felt something move deep inside him. He buffeted the boy's shoulder as he passed his chair. "Emile plans to teach you all about rum this afternoon."

"I already know a lot about rum."

"Emile will show you things you've never seen before, won't you, Emile?"

"Indeed."

"Eat your lunch. You'll need your strength."

Ryder heard Jeremy say to Emile as he left the dining room, "Do you whip the slaves, sir?"

"No," Emile said matter-of-factly. "They're our workers. Without them we wouldn't produce much sugar. We depend on them. If I hurt them, why then, they couldn't work and then where would we be?"

"Thomas beats the Camille slaves."

"Thomas is a stupid man. Ryder will doubtless see to his education."

Ryder smiled in anticipation. He wished he'd spoken to Sophie but he hadn't wanted to awaken her. Well, doubtless Thomas was here because Uncle Theo still wasn't well yet. Good. It seemed that she'd plunged that letter opener nice and deep.

Sophie woke up just as the sun was lowering, splashing the sky with all shades of pinks and reds. She was alone. She rose and relieved herself, then found the man's nightshirt she'd been wearing and slipped it over her head. Her ribs ached and pulled but the awful tearing pain was now bearable.

She walked slowly to the balcony and raised her face to the still evening air. Soon she would be well enough to leave Kimberly. Soon she would have to leave Kimberly, she and Jeremy. But where would she go?

Ryder was right about that. She had nothing, no money, nothing except a harlot's reputation.

She stared blankly into the pink and golden twilight, listening to turtledoves, frogs, crickets, and the myriad other night creatures that she normally didn't hear because she was so used to them.

Ryder paused in the doorway. He saw her standing there in the ridiculous loose nightshirt, her hair thick and flowing down her back. She looked sixteen. But he knew when he saw her eyes there would be weary cynicism there.

"Come back to bed," he said quietly, not wanting to startle her.

She turned slowly. She was no longer weak and hurting. She was standing now, a grown woman, and she had to deal with him. She said calmly, "I'm tired of that damned bed. I wish to remain standing for a while. You said you wanted to speak to me. Let's do it."

She was back to normal. It pleased him enormously. "As you will," he said easily. "Thomas was here."

Had he expected her to gasp? To shudder with fright? To totter toward him and beg for his protection? She didn't do any of these things. Her expression was remote and remained remote. She looked calm and serene. She was really very good. He walked to her and stopped directly in front of her. He raised his fingertips and lightly touched her chin, the tip of her nose, ran his fingertips over her eyebrows. "The bruises are fading. By tomorrow you won't be such a fright."

She didn't move. "Then I won't request a mirror until the day after tomorrow."

"As I said, Thomas came here."

"I assume you handled him?"

He grinned. "No, I pleaded with him to allow you to remain here for a little while longer. He beat me into the floor but decided to let you stay. However, he said he'd come back and—"

She jerked. It was just a small sort of shiver really, but he'd discovered that during the past few days he'd become attuned to her, noticing small movements, small reactions, that gave her away.

"Don't be a fool," he said. "Now, let me tell you about a very unmemorable meeting. Lord, the man's a villain and utterly without a conscience. I met him in the salon. Did you know that James, our footman, isn't fond of Thomas? Why, I do believe James's eyes got meaner than a snake's when he said the man's name."

"Thomas is an animal. James has a brother who is owned by my uncle. Mr. Grayson tried to buy him but my uncle refused. Yes, Thomas is a swine."

"Well, yes he is. Hush now and let me tell you of our rather boring conversation."

Ryder had walked into the salon in high good humor, nearly rubbing his hands together in anticipation. He stopped, smiled, and said, "I believe your name is Thomas? Fancy seeing you here at Kimberly Hall without your bow and arrows and that very charming white sheet both you and your master enjoy wearing. I particularly applauded the white hoods. Ah, but my manners. Would you care for some coffee?"

"I have come for Mr. Burgess's niece and nephew."

"Oh?" Ryder smiled benignly at the overseer. He was tall, exceedingly thin, save for a belly that protruded between his vest and his breeches. His hair was grizzled and very short and there was beard stubble on his jaw. He looked as if he hadn't slept much or bathed or changed his clothes in several days. His eyes were cold, very cold, and Ryder doubted if he'd ever been filled with the milk of human kindness.

"I do owe you for that arrow you put in my shoulder."

"I'm sure I don't know what you're talking about," Thomas said. "If you please, Mr. Sherbrooke, Mr. Burgess is anxious to see his niece and nephew. He is naturally concerned for their welfare."

"Ah, doubtless that is so. How could anyone ever question his feelings? However, whatever makes him think they could be here?"

"There is talk. Everyone knows. The gossip is that Miss Stanton-Greville is living here openly as your mistress, and in return for her favors, you also took in the boy. It distresses Mr. Burgess. Bring them down now and they won't bother you again."

"Why don't you sit down, Thomas."

"Damn you, Sherbrooke, you have no right—"

"No right to what? To rescue a girl who's been beaten senseless? To take a small boy out of a locked room?"

"Hellfire, one of her lovers beat her! I locked the boy in his room to protect him!"

"One of her lovers beat her," Ryder repeated slowly. "Which one, I wonder? Perhaps Oliver Susson? Now, he's certainly a vicious brute, isn't he? No, I think you must be mistaken. He'd already been dismissed, and according to my sources, he didn't seem at all upset by his dismissal. Who else? Charles Grammond, perhaps? I hear his wife's a regular tartar, perhaps she did it?"

"Damn you, Sherbrooke! Get them!"

Ryder smiled. "You will now listen to me, Thomas. I think you're a conscienceless bastard. I will have no more dealings with you. Your master, however, is another matter. Tell him he will hear from me shortly. Now, if you attempt to bring back some of your cronies to Kimberly Hall and cause a ruckus, I will come after you. I will kill you and I will do it very slowly. Do you understand me?"

Thomas didn't know what to do. He'd told Mr. Burgess that this man wasn't like the other men here on Montego Bay. This man was hard and smart. "As I told you, Sherbrooke, one of Sophia's lovers beat her. Her uncle tried to stop it. If she's told you differently, it's because she's ashamed of her notoriety. Now, be sensible. Why would you want to be saddled with a little cripple and a whore?"

Thomas didn't get out another word. Ryder smashed his fist into his jaw, a hard, clean blow. Then he drew back his right arm and sent his fist into the man's belly. Thomas yelled as he fell like a stone to the floor.

"James! Ah, I'm glad you're here. Didn't go very far, did you? Well, I very much do need your assistance now. Please ask another strong man to take this vermin back to Camille Hall and dump him there. In the dirt. On his face."

"Yes, massa," James said and he was smiling. "Dat man a bastid, a real bastid. He look good flat on de floor. No, not a bastid, he be a serpent."

"His fangs should be dangling loose, at the very least," Ryder said as he rubbed his knuckles. He frowned down at Thomas. "He's got a big belly. That's not good for a man. No, not at all healthy."

He rubbed his knuckles again as he finished speaking, thinking again how good it had made him feel to vent his rage on that mangy bastard. He looked at Sophie and grinned just as he had before to James. "That's all that happened. Nothing more. James and another fellow took him away."

She said, "I'm glad you hit him. I hope you struck him very hard. I've wanted to many times. He's a horrible man. Good heavens, you enjoyed that!"

"Perhaps," Ryder said with obvious relish. "The man's a rotter." He fell silent then and he gave her a brooding look. "However did you manage to get yourself into this ridiculous mess?"

"What do you mean, sir? Ah, you wonder why I chose of my own free will to become a whore? Perhaps why Jeremy decided to become a cripple? I would that you be more specific."

"You were much easier to handle on your back. You're all vinegar again."

"A pity, for you will never see me like that again."

"Not even when I make love to you again?"

Another very small jerk of her shoulders. Yes, he was getting to know her quite well.

"Sit down, Sophie. I'll keep my distance. I don't wish to frighten you."

That got to her. Ryder was pleased; he was even grinning shamelessly when she said, "You don't frighten me. No man frightens me."

"As a matter of course I would believe you. You appear quite skilled with men. However, I am not other men and I do frighten you. You will admit it eventually and then, I daresay, you'll be more careful around me. Sit down before I pick you up and set you down."

She sat down, smoothing the nightshirt over her legs. It occurred to her then that it must surely be odd to be here in a bedchamber with a man wearing only a man's nightshirt, and that made her smile.

She said then without preamble, "Kimberly Hall belongs to you, not to your brother, the Earl of Northcliffe."

Ryder stared at her, his mouth open. "What did you say? No, that's absured, that's utter nonsense. Wherever did you get such an idea?"

"Be quiet and attend me. Kimberly Hall belonged to your uncle Brandon. When he died, you inherited his fortune. However, Oliver Susson neglected to attach the specifics of this property to the will he sent back to your family. At the time it was truly an oversight. Also, at the time, I believe your father had just died and thus there was some confusion because the new earl hadn't sold out yet of the army. Thus, everyone believes that Kimberly belongs to the family—your older brother—not you, to be exact."

"By God," Ryder said, staring at her.

"Are you not rather rich for a second son?"

"Yes."

"Well, now you are even richer for this plantation is yours."

"I begin to see why Oliver Susson was one of your lovers."

"Naturally."

"I did tell Emile that there were always motives. Particularly where you are concerned, Sophie. You would never have become a slut without very strong motives."

"Understand me, Ryder. I don't care if you own all of Jamaica. My uncle wanted this plantation and he thought my talents would give him an excellent chance at it. Don't get me wrong, I was to be used just to soften you up. In his final estimation, he didn't think you would care about living here, or care about the uncertainty of sugar profits, and thus, you would sell out to him, stuff the guineas in your aristocratic pockets, and sail happily back to England."

"And at the appropriate time I would have been told by Mr. Susson that Kimberly Hall belonged to me."

"Yes."

"And with you as my delightful mistress—you and that other woman with the big breasts of course—I would be delighted to sell to your uncle. Did he intend to send you back with me to England? As my mistress?"

"I don't know what he planned."

"Why did you agree to this?"

Her look was hard and cold. "Don't be absurd. You're so excellent at assigning motives, why have you let down here? Jeremy was to be his heir if I cooperated. If I didn't cooperate, he said he would throw both of us out. Jeremy is lame; he would never be able to make his way here."

"And naturally, you could."

She didn't react in any way, merely said in that same cold voice, "Quite probably."

"Lord David became your lover so that he would fleece Charles Grammond."

"Yes and he performed admirably."

"And Charles Grammond was your lover so he would be quite amenable to selling his plantation to your uncle."

"Yes."

"How did you ever manage to rid yourself of Lord David?"

She smiled. It was an impish smile, a young smile, and he found himself reacting to it. He realized it was the first genuine smile he'd ever seen from her. "I told him I had the pox."

"Good God, that's wonderful."

"I would have probably told you the same thing once you had sold Kimberly to my uncle."

"Ah, but the difference is that I wouldn't have simply believed you."

"That's what I told my uncle. I told him you weren't like the other men. I told him you weren't stupid. I told him that he should be very cautious with you, perhaps even fear you. He refused to heed me."

"You aren't making much sense about this fear business, but no matter. He didn't listen to you. He wasn't afraid enough of me, more's the pity."

"No. He measures all men with himself as the standard. He'd heard you were a womanizer, a young rakehell with no more morals than a tomcat. He thought it would be marvelously easy."

"I'm not a—" He stopped and frowned down at his bruised knuckles. Jesus, what an appalling thought. His mind shied away from it. He swallowed, then shrugged negligently. "Well, he was wrong, wasn't he?"

"About you being a womanizer? A tomcat? No, surely not. If you'd been like the other men, you wouldn't have realized that it wasn't me."

"Are you telling me that you didn't sleep with any of them? That it was always this other woman?"

She looked at him steadily. "Would you believe me if I told you that I had not?"

"Probably not." He raised his hand to cut her off. "No, attend me, Sophie. I have never before met a woman with such a repertoire of feminine tricks as you have, and believe me, I've been treated to the best. I wish I knew the female equivalent of a rakehell or a tomcat. You surely fit the mold. You're remarkable in your scope of seductive devices for one so young. Now, enough of that. It's not important. Back to your dear uncle. It still takes me aback that I own Kimberly Hall."

"It's true."

"But what if I hadn't come here? What if my brother had come instead?"

"Uncle Theo considered that unlikely. You see, he knows all about your family. He even hired a man back in England to find out everything he could about the Sherbrookes, about you. The man wrote back with a goodly number of details."

"He did all this before he and Thomas began their little scare campaign?"

"Oh yes. It was all well planned. Uncle Theo knew that Samuel Grayson was superstitious and could be manipulated. He knew if he played on his fears, why, he was bound to write to your brother, begging for help. And he did. He even told my uncle that he was going to write. Of course, my uncle encouraged him to write, encouraged him in his superstitions, stoked the fires, so to speak."

"I begin to believe that Uncle Theo deserves to have me wring his miserable neck."

"The man my uncle hired wrote that your brother had many responsibilities and that it was highly unlikely that he would come; your younger brother is at Oxford studying to become a man of the cloth. That left you and your fifteen-year-old sister. Naturally it was you who came. Everything went just as he'd planned. He simply misjudged you, that's all. He assumed you'd be like Lord David—frivolous, narcissistic, rather stupid, and wanting only to sleep with me. He was wrong; he simply wouldn't recognize that he'd failed. You never for a moment believed there was anything supernatural about the incidents, did you?"

"Of course not," Ryder said, his voice clearly abstracted.

"Nor did you ever want to become my lover."

"No. Yes. I don't know. I don't share."

"What are you going to do?"

"Oliver Susson agreed not to say anything to my brother or to me until your uncle decided it was the right time?"

She nodded.

"Did Jeremy know any of this?"

"No, I tried to protect him as best I could. Also, Uncle Theo was always very careful to treat him well, both in private and in public. Even
now, everyone believes both Jeremy and I are very lucky. Indeed I imagine the gossip is that Uncle Theo is too loving, too sentimental, to even
realize that his niece is a whore."

"Yes, that's what I've heard. You're tired. It's time for you to rest and
for me to do some thinking. I want this mess resolved and soon."

She didn't sleep for the simple reason that she was too frightened
about the future. But she did lie on that damned bed for three hours, her
mind squirreling about frantically.

CHAPTER
═══ 8 ═══

SOPHIE WALKED QUIETLY down the upstairs corridor of Kimberly Hall to the bedchamber where Jeremy was sleeping. She wanted to speak to her brother, to reassure him, to make him promises that she prayed she'd be able to keep.

She quietly opened the door and peered in. The room was small, but as in all the other chambers, there were floor-to-ceiling louvered doors that gave onto a balcony and those doors were wide open. She smiled. Jeremy many times slept on his balcony at Camille Hall. He was probably doing the same here. The mosquitoes never bothered him.

He wasn't in his bed. She still smiled even as she walked slowly to the balcony. He wasn't there either. Her smile froze.

Oh God.

She'd seen him today, briefly, and he'd been very quiet, too quiet. He'd looked at her for a very long time and she'd known he was troubled, but she hadn't said anything to him because Ryder had come in. And that was why she'd wanted to see him now.

But he was gone.

Of course she knew where he was. He'd gone back to Camille Hall to face down Uncle Theo for beating her.

Uncle Theo would hurt him badly, perhaps even kill him, for now there was no reason for him to pretend to kindness, to affection, for either of them. She realized she was breathing in huge gulps that made her ribs throb and ache. She leaned forward, hugging her arms around her.

When the pain drew back, she still didn't move, just stood there, very still, staring out onto the beautiful scene before her, but not really seeing the glistening waves beneath the near full moon. The stars were points of cold white in the sky, a sky empty of shifting clouds. Slowly, she turned and went back to her own bedchamber. She found her gown in the bottom of the armoire. It was ripped and soiled but she didn't care. She dressed quickly, ignoring the pulling and aching in her ribs, her mind set on what she had to do. She merely shook her head when she realized she had no petticoats, no chemise, no stockings, nothing but the gown.

Nor could she find her shoes. No matter, she'd go barefoot. She crept down the front stairs as quietly and stealthily as a thief, and into the small estate room that was also the Kimberly Hall library. There was a gun case there, thank God, a tall oak affair with glass doors. It wasn't locked. She knew guns and thus picked out a small derringer. If she had to protect Jeremy, she would shoot whoever it was at very close range. She had no intention of missing.

She slipped out of Kimberly Hall five minutes latter, walking quickly down the graveled drive, ignoring the small rocks digging into the soles of her feet, welcoming the evening breeze that stirred tendrils of hair on her forehead.

It was a beautiful night, a still night. Her heart pounded in slow, steady strokes. If only she knew how long Jeremy had been gone. She was afraid, but she was calm. It was about time she took over responsibility for herself and for Jeremy. Dear God, please give her enough time to prove herself.

It took her twenty minutes to walk to Camille Hall, cutting through canefields, keeping in the shadows as much as possible. She cut her feet but ignored the jabs of pain, even ignored the blood when she felt it sticky and cold on the soles of her feet.

There was light coming from several windows, but she couldn't see anything, no shadows, no sign of her uncle or of Thomas or any of the servants. Where the devil was Jeremy?

She ran bent over from bush to bush, getting closer and closer to the great house. She slithered up onto the side veranda to where her uncle's study was located. It was then she heard the voices.

It was Uncle Theo, and he sounded amused. He also sounded quite drunk. "So, you little bastard, you decided to come back here and whip me, eh?"

"Yes. I'm not a bastard. My mother was your sister and she was my father's wife. I'm here because of what you did to Sophie. I can't allow you to hurt my sister and get away with it. You *beat* her!"

"She deserved it, and as soon as I get my hands on her again, I'll whip her until she's begging for mercy."

"I won't let you. Ryder won't let you."

Ryder Sherbrooke, the young man Theo wanted very much to kill. Ah, but he had the boy here, the useless little cripple. He grinned down at Jeremy. "And just how do you think you'd ever stop me, whelp? You couldn't even keep your whip. I have it now, don't I?"

"I will think of something."

There came the hissing sound of a whip cutting through the air. Then she heard a sharp cry. It was Jeremy. Uncle Theo had struck him with the whip.

She thought she'd felt all the rage of which she was capable. She'd been wrong. The wooden door was partially open. She slipped through it very quietly to see Uncle Theo, his shoulder heavily bandaged, wearing a dressing gown, standing over Jeremy, the whip raised again in his right hand.

"I'll give you another taste, Master Jeremy, just to show you how important you are!"

"If you do, you filthy wretch, I'll put a bullet through your belly. I don't want you to die quickly. I want you lie on the ground, holding your belly, feeling your guts rotting from the inside out while you scream and scream."

Theo Burgess froze, but just for an instant. Slowly, very slowly, he lowered the whip and turned to face his niece.

"So, you discovered the little cripple was gone and came galloping to his rescue."

She ignored him. "Come here, Jeremy. Keep your distance from him. That's right, come to me now."

Jeremy's face was white with pain, his eyes hollow with failure. She understood both feelings very well, and said, "It's all right. This time, we've won. You're very brave to come here. That's good, come to me now and we will leave soon."

"You think so, do you, slut? Don't count on it. All I have to do is call out and at least ten slaves will be here to do my bidding in an instant."

"It won't matter because you'll be belly-shot. Go ahead, Uncle, yell as loud as you want because it's the last sound you'll make without agony. I want to kill you very badly. You're a coward, whipping Jeremy, who's half your size. I suppose your utter lack of any feeling surprised even me, but just for a moment."

Theo Burgess didn't know what to do. He shook his head, trying to clear his thoughts from all the rum he'd had to drink for the damnable pain in his shoulder. He believed the girl. She'd stabbed him, hadn't she? Lord, he should have continued hitting her until she was dead, but he'd had to stop because the blow she'd dealt him was making him dizzy and light-headed. He looked at her now, feeling renewed pain in his shoulder, despite the huge amounts of rum he'd drunk, remembering the bitter torture of that damned letter opener, remembering how Thomas had pulled it out and how he'd tried to keep silent but had failed and screamed. Even then it hadn't been fair. He hadn't fallen into blessed unconsciousness. Oh no, he'd stayed with the torment and it hadn't let up for a very long time. He'd sworn to make her pay. He had to make her pay and he would.

He said at last, very pleased with the indifference of his voice, "You know, my dear, if you kill me, you won't have a thing."

"The rum has curdled your wits. Jeremy is your heir. He will have everything."

"Oh no. He isn't my heir for the simple reason that I don't have a will."

"Will or no will, we are your closest relatives, and thus when all is said and done, Jeremy will inherit Camille Hall. Of course my father's house in Fowey is also his."

"Did dear Oliver Susson tell you that when he was plowing your belly?"

"That you believe your own fiction rather points to a failing mind, doesn't it, Uncle? I have two bullets in this derringer. Jeremy, let me see how badly he hurt you."

Her brother turned his back. The single stroke of the whip had cut through his shirt. Thank God the skin wasn't broken, but the long diagonal welt was ugly and red, the flesh rising around it. She sucked in her breath. "You're a monster, truly. Now, as I said, I have two bullets. If that whip had drawn even a fingertip of blood, I would have shot you in your belly. However, you are lucky, Uncle. I won't shoot you at all, this time. I'm simply taking Jeremy back with me to Kimberly Hall. You will leave us alone, do you understand? You won't come there nor will you send Thomas again. Now, we will leave. Don't move an inch."

"And just what will you do when Ryder Sherbrooke tosses you and the boy out of Kimberly?"

"That isn't your concern."

"Thomas told me you were installed in Ryder Sherbrooke's bedchamber. Everyone knows now that you're his mistress. Your reputation is—"

She actually laughed. "Look at my face. Can even you imagine a healthy man being interested in bedding me now? My ribs are even more violent shades of purple and green than my face. Believe me, even if I wanted to be in his bed, even if he'd wanted me there, I would have been unable. You saw to that. Now, Uncle, I want to leave here with Jeremy."

"To go back to that damned Englishman?"

"You're a damned Englishman, remember?"

"As I said, he'll remove you quickly enough. I hear he bores easily and no one woman could ever hold him. My agent in England wrote that he had women climbing over themselves to become his mistress. No, you ugly little slut, you couldn't hold him for more than a night."

"I don't want to hold him. I don't even want to be in the same room with him. He can have a dozen more mistresses for all I care. However, he does seem honorable, something new in my experience in a man. He has protected Jeremy. I grow tired of this. Jeremy, go outside. I'll follow."

"But, Sophie—"

"Go!"

The boy backed away from her, his face white and set.

She lowered the derringer to the level of Theo Burgess's left knee. "Perhaps," she said in a very low, very mean voice, "just perhaps I've changed my mind. I would like to know that you're hobbling about for the rest of your damned life, a cripple, a no-account cripple."

Theo Burgess shrieked, "No, damn you, no!" He rushed toward her, flailing his arms madly.

Suddenly the candelabra crashed to the floor and the room was plunged into darkness.

Sophie's finger inadvertently jerked the trigger. The derringer fired, a monstrous loud noise in the small room. She heard an anguished yell. Someone struck her arm but she managed to hold onto the derringer, and this time she pulled the trigger on purpose. Then something struck her on her temple and she slumped to the floor. She heard Jeremy yelling and she smelled something acrid, something she vaguely recognized. She managed to open her eyes, trying desperately to hang on. She saw only darkness and a strange glowing orange light. And the sounds—snapping and hissing and a windy sort of whoosh.

The light muslin draperies were aflame, billowing upward as if caught in a great wind, flaming outward, the heat intense. The room was on fire.

"Jeremy," she whispered, "run, please, you must run. Go to Ryder. He'll take care of you. You can trust him." She choked on the smoke even as she closed her eyes and her head lolled back on the wooden floor.

She awoke coughing, her throat raw and burning. She felt someone's arms around her, felt a man's hands rubbing her back as she coughed and wheezed. She heard his voice: "It's over, Sophie. Jeremy is safe. It's over. Shush, don't worry now and don't try to talk."

Ryder. His voice, his hands on her back. She leaned against him, shuddering from the rawness in her throat, trying not to swallow because it hurt so much.

"Where is Jeremy? Is he all right, truly?"

"Be quiet and I'll tell you everything. We're here at Camille Hall. Jeremy had very nearly managed to pull you out of the room all by himself by the time Emile and I got here. The fire is out and the damage isn't too bad. Only the study was pretty well destroyed and the veranda outside charred a bit. Naturally there's smoke damage and the smell in the house is godawful. Uncle Theo is quite dead."

It hurt so much to talk, to say the words, but she did, wheezing them out. "I must have killed him. My derringer went off and I heard him yell."

"Did you now? Well, that was well done of you. However, when you're well enough again, I will have to thrash you at the very least for what you did. If Coco hadn't seen you running barefoot down the Kimberly Hall drive, why then you very probably would have died in that fire, Jeremy along with you, for the boy wouldn't have left you in there to die."

"The magistrate, Mr. Sherman Cole, will see that I'm hanged."

"I see no reason why he would want to hang you."

She tried to pull away from him but he held her firmly.

"Yes he will. He wanted me to take him as my lover but there was no reason to and so Uncle Theo had me refuse him. He was nasty about it, and threatened me. Uncle Theo thought it was amusing. He said he could handle Cole if the need ever arose. And he also said I was to keep up a light flirtation with him so that if Uncle Theo ever needed something from him, he'd come running when I smiled at him."

"But you didn't keep flirting with him?"

"No, I slapped him and stomped on his instep when he tried to kiss me. He's repellent. It was about three months ago."

"I see. Well, then, my dear girl, I guess it must be I who shot Theo Burgess, trying to save you and Jeremy. But why? After all, Burgess is known only as the loving, ineffectual uncle, isn't he? I must think on this. Perhaps there is another resolution to all this. Yes, let me think on it."

"Where is Thomas?"

"I don't know. I haven't seen him. I'll ask."

"I wanted to shoot Uncle Theo in his knee so he'd be a cripple like Jeremy, to make him live with a limp just as Jeremy has had to do—dear God, he'd actually taken a whip to Jeremy—but I swear to you, I didn't pull the trigger intentionally. The candelabra suddenly crashed to the floor and everything was dark and I jerked accidently on the trigger. Then someone hit my arm and I pulled the trigger on purpose to protect myself."

"Tell me all of it and don't leave out a thing. Quickly, I don't know how much time we have."

By the time she was finished speaking, her throat was so raw she could barely speak in anything but a hoarse whisper.

"I'm giving you over to Samuel now, both you and Jeremy. He'll take you back to Kimberly Hall. Now, no more words from you, no arguments, no nothing. I'm in charge now and you will do exactly what I tell you to do. The first order is that there is to be no talking from you for at least twenty-four hours."

"My head hurts."

Ryder frowned down at her and lightly touched his fingertips to the bump over her temple. "Good God, you didn't tell me that someone struck you on the head."

"I forgot."

"All right, talk, but make it quick." When she'd finished, he was frowning. She opened her mouth, only to feel his palm over her lips. "No, now be quiet. Here's Jeremy. Emile was seeing to him while I talked to you."

The boy was on his knees beside her, stroking her filthy face, her hands. "Oh, Sophie, your feet! What happened? What did you do?"

She'd forgotten her damned feet.

Ryder yelled for a lantern. When a slave brought it, he lowered it and looked for a long time at her feet, saying nothing. Then, "From the top of your head to your very toes, you've managed to do yourself in. Jesus, Sophie, your feet are a mess. See that Coco bathes them when you get back to Kimberly."

Ryder watched Samuel drive away with Sophie and Jeremy. He himself had carried her to the carriage. He was hot and sweaty and covered with smoke and grime from the fire. He was also in a devil of a mess and in an equally foul mood.

Where the hell was that bastard, Thomas? Actually, truth be told, Thomas worried him more than Theo Burgess. At least Theo tried to keep up appearances; Thomas couldn't give a good damn about anything. Ryder had no doubt that it was Thomas who had struck Sophie and hurled the candelabra to the floor.

Ryder left Emile in charge of Camille Hall and took himself back to Kimberly for a few hours' sleep. When he awoke he was told that Miss Stanton-Greville was still sleeping. He frowned but said nothing. He was thinking about her damned bloody feet, curse her. Just after he'd finished eating breakfast, Mr. Sherman Cole arrived from Montego Bay.

Sherman Cole looked like the father of one of Ryder's mistresses, a draper in Rye who was greedy and sly. He was very fat, double chins wobbling over his collar, had a monk's tonsure of gray hair, very sharp eyes, and thick lips. The thought of him trying to kiss Sophie made Ryder want to gag.

Still, he shook the man's hand and offered him coffee. Mr. Cole wanted not only coffee, but sweet buns, which, when a tray was set before him, he eyed with more intensity than Ryder would have had gazing upon a beautiful naked woman.

Ryder merely sat opposite him and looked over his right shoulder, unable, for the most part, to look at the man's face. It was not an elevating sight. He listened to the man speak even though his mouth was many times full and thus his words a bit slurred.

"Yes, Mr. Sherbrooke, as you know, I am the magistrate, the man in

charge of all civil and criminal disturbances. I am the law here on the island, the power of the law resides with me. I was shocked to learn that
you were involved, that you had brought Miss Sophia Stanton-Greville
back to Kimberly with you. I don't know how you came to be involved
with her, but I am certain you will tell me soon enough. Please have the
girl fetched here. I will question her now."

My God, Ryder thought, steepling his long fingers. He looked over
them at the man who had just consumed four sweet buns. The man was
not only a pig, he was also pompous, condescending, and thoroughly irritating. As to his manners, he had none. There were crumbs on his coat
and on his chin. The man needed to be stripped and tossed to the crocodiles in the mangrove swamps. It would doubtless keep them busy for at
least several days.

"I think not, Mr. Cole," Ryder said mildly. "You see, she is suffering
from breathing in too much smoke and thus cannot speak without a lot of
pain. Perhaps in several days you can return and she might be better."

Mr. Cole frowned. He wasn't used to having anyone go against his expressed wishes. He was the man in charge; he was a leader of men, truly
the law here, and it was his word, his orders, that counted. "I want to see
her," he said again, obstinate as a pig.

"No."

"See here, Sherbrooke—"

"*Mr.* Sherbrooke, Cole."

Sherman Cole was quite obviously taken aback and becoming angrier
by the minute. But he wasn't stupid. Was Sophia Stanton-Greville already
this man's mistress? Was he set on protecting her? He pursed his lips. He
held himself silent, having learned that a man or woman felt compelled
to fill in silences and thus provide him with information, but this young
man didn't say a word. He sat back in his chair, his fingers still steepled,
and, damn his eyes, he looked bored.

It was infuriating. Mr. Cole drew a deep breath, looked quickly down
at the tray but saw there were no more sweet buns there, and frowned
again. Food helped him sort through his thoughts, it always had, even
when he'd been a child. "I want her," he said.

"A pity. You must accustom yourself, sir. You will never have her."

"That isn't what I meant! My dear young man, I am married, my wife
is a charming lady, really quite charming. I mean that I must speak to her,
and I must tell you, Mr. Sherbrooke, that I suspect foul play here. I suspect that she murdered her uncle in cold blood and then set fire to the
great house."

"This is a rather remarkable theory. May I inquire as to what brought
you to this incredible conclusion?"

"The girl isn't what she seems to be, rather she is exactly what she seems, only her uncle wouldn't recognize it or accept it. You must have heard—perhaps you even have firsthand information—she's a slut, a high-priced harlot with no morals at all. I think her uncle finally realized the truth and she killed him when he threatened to toss her out. Aye, that's what happened." He stopped, gave Ryder a patented hanging judge's look, and announced, "I am here to see justice done."

Ryder laughed, a deep, rich laugh. "Your theory is beyond amusing, Mr. Cole. However, you must realize that it is also rather libelous."

"I have a witness, Mr. Sherbrooke."

"Do you now?"

"Yes, Thomas, the overseer."

Ryder laughed again, more deeply, more richly, more genuine amusement than before.

"Sir!"

"Mr. Cole, Thomas is a villain, as I must assume you already know. I don't believe it wise to take testimony from a villain. I propose another theory, one that differs from yours quite substantially. However, there is just as much motive, just as much rationale for mine, as for yours. Thomas is a bounder. I suspect that Mr. Burgess discovered Thomas was cheating him, that or he was abusing the slaves too much, and he fired him. Put very simply, Thomas killed him. As luck would have it, Miss Stanton-Greville and her brother were there at Camille Hall and thus she proved to be a perfect scapegoat for Thomas."

"Thomas is a man and she is a—"

"No, he's a bastard, no-account, cruel, mean as a snake."

"That doesn't excuse Miss Stanton-Greville. Why, she's nothing more than a—"

"I wouldn't say anything were I you, Cole. She and her brother are under my personal protection. Indeed, I will be applying shortly to become the guardian to both of them. Oliver Susson will be handling the matter."

"Ah, I see the truth of the matter now."

"Do you, now? Pray, just exactly what do you see?"

"She is, as I intimated before, your mistress."

Ryder said in a voice reminiscent of his father's whenever he was tired of an individual's impertinence and wanted him gone, "Perhaps she will be someday. I'm not as yet certain I wish to bed her and keep her. However, I do feel an obligation to Jeremy and she comes along with him. He is, after all, Theo Burgess's heir. His interests must be protected and I can see no other man to do the job. Now, Cole, do you wish to say anything else? No? Why then, why don't you have Thomas fetched in your august presence? Perhaps with your obvious interrogation skills you can induce him to tell the truth." Ryder rose and merely waited for Cole to heave himself to his feet, which he did, reluctantly.

"I just might find more evidence to convict her!"

"More, Cole? As of this moment, you haven't even a pinch, nary a dollop. Get Thomas and you've got your killer. Now, I have many matters to attend to. I trust you will excuse me. Oh, should you care for more sweet buns to take with you?"

Sophie quickly ran back up the stairs. She'd seen Mr. Sherman Cole ride up the drive. She'd had to know what he would say. Nothing he said was unexpected. Ryder had handled him brilliantly. But then Ryder had spoken. . . . She felt deep, very deep pain and it wasn't in her ribs or in her burned throat.

"I am not as yet certain I wish to bed her and keep her."

He was no different from any of the other men. She guessed that he would demand her in his bed as payment for seeing to Jeremy's protection. Then he would tire of her and that would be that. At least she'd be free, at last. She and Jeremy would live in peace at Camille Hall. Everything would be all right. In a year and a half she would be twenty-one and deemed old enough to become his guardian.

She managed to climb into her bed and pull the sheet to her chin before he was standing there in the doorway, looking at her, saying nothing for a long time.

"Mr. Cole was very amusing."

"Was he? Am I to be arrested?"

"You still sound like a foghorn. No, you won't be arrested. I venture to say that Thomas just might be the one to hang. Wouldn't that solve all our problems?"

She turned her face away from him and said in a very low voice, "Why was Coco awake so very late last night? You said she was the one who saw me leaving."

"Coco is pregnant. She was feeling ill and thus had her face in the cool night air on the balcony."

"Oh."

"Would you like to hear everything that is going to happen now?"

She wanted to scream at him that she'd already heard everything and for him to shut up and just go away, but she couldn't. She merely nodded.

He censored judiciously, so well in fact that if she hadn't overheard the entire exchange between the two men, she wouldn't have suspected a thing.

Ah, but he left out the damning things.

"I don't think so," she said when he finished.

"You don't think so what?"

"I don't need you to volunteer your services as guardian. I am nearly twenty. Mr. Susson can be Jeremy's guardian until I reach twenty-one, then I will be his guardian. Camille Hall now belongs to him. Yes, I will be his guardian."

"No."

"You are very nearly as young as I am. How could you possibly set yourself up to be my guardian? It's absurd."

"I am nearly twenty-six, not so very young an age."

"Not so great an age either."

He grinned suddenly. "My brother would like to hear you say that. The poor fellow is only twenty-eight and all the Sherbrookes were pounding and pounding at him to get himself wedded and produce an heir."

"What happened?"

"He did marry, just before we received the letter from Samuel Grayson."

"Well, I feel sorry for his poor wife if that is why he married her. To breed heirs."

"I wouldn't feel sorry for Alexandra," Ryder said slowly. "I must admit, however, to being interested in learning what has happened between the two of them. But that's all beside the point. I will go to Montego Bay and speak to Oliver Susson. I will tell him the race is lost, so to speak. I will engage him to handle this situation and if he does it well, why then, I won't beat him to a bloody pulp."

She was quiet. Too quiet. He frowned down at her. "Attend me, Sophie. This is what is going to happen so accustom yourself. If you try to leave Kimberly Hall again, Emile has instructions to sit on you."

"Why are you doing this? Do you even realize what you're doing? You are volunteering to take a nine-year-old boy into your guardianship along with his nineteen-year-old slut of a sister. Why would you want this kind of responsibility?"

"I don't know," Ryder said. He tried to shrug it off, but couldn't quite manage it. He said slowly, "I am twenty-five. I am the second son, an honorable, not a lord. All my life I've done precisely what I wanted. All my life I've laughed and played and loved and enjoyed myself. When my father died, well then, there was Douglas to take care of things because, after all, he was the new earl. He was the responsible one. And I continued as I had. There was no reason for me to change. No one expected anything else from me. As for the other, well, none know of it and it is none of their business and besides it is no great or grave responsibility."

"What other?"

He simply shook his head and looked irritated with himself.

Sophie held herself silent.

He shrugged. "So," he said, "now I am responsible for both you and Jeremy. You will depend upon me and upon no one else. Just me. No, just shut your mouth, Sophie, and shake hands with your new guardian."

He hadn't really expected her to do anything but continue to squawk. She thrust out her hand and he took it in his. She stared up at him, saying in her tortured raw voice, "I do trust you with Jeremy. I do."

"You must learn to trust me with yourself as well."

"Oh no."

"How are your feet?"

"My feet? Oh, I forgot about them. They're fine, nearly well, in fact."

"Yes, I'll just bet they are." Ryder pulled the sheet off her. Her feet were lightly bandaged. Blood had soaked through the white cloth. "Why is there blood on the bandages?"

From walking on them downstairs and then running back upstairs.

"I don't know." Actually, she hadn't felt a thing. Odd, that.

"Sophie, it's obvious you got out of that bed. What did you do?"

"I had to relieve myself."

"Yes, certainly, that sounds like the exact truth. And reaching the chamber pot—all of six feet away—did this. Where did you go, Sophie?"

She looked at her hands. There was still grime under her fingernails. She said absolutely nothing.

"You need a guardian more than Jeremy does."

She looked then at her feet and wondered how she could have possibly forgotten them. Even dashing up and down the stairs to eavesdrop on Ryder and Mr. Cole hadn't hurt her. But now, looking at them, seeing the bloody bandages, she began to feel throbbing pain.

"I will see to them. There's no reason for you to remain, Ryder."

He cursed, fluently and loudly.

Within ten minutes he'd removed the bandages and was washing her feet with soap and hot water. She was trying to keep from crying out. He saw her white face and gentled. He called her a fool and kept cleaning the cuts. He called her a stupid twit when he lightly rubbed at a gash that was ugly and still bleeding.

When he poured alcohol over both feet, she nearly leapt off the bed it hurt so bad. But he grabbed her shoulders and forced her onto her back. "I know it must sting like the very devil but you deserve it. Damn you, don't move. I don't know where you went walking but I'll find out and don't think I won't. Now, I'm going to do it again, just to make sure. If you dare to move, I will tie you down. Scream instead."

She yelled at the top of her lungs when he forced both feet into an alcohol bath. He held them there and she choked on the pain and on her tears.

Jeremy came flying through the door. His fists were up, his face was red with anger and determination.

Ryder stopped him with a look and a simple, "I'm helping her. Come here and hold her hand."

Jeremy clutched Sophie's hand until finally Ryder was satisfied that he'd done all he could. He lifted her feet out of the alcohol and swung them back onto the bed. "Now, we're not going to do anything for the moment, just keep them on top of this clean towel. No walking or I'll thrash you and I daresay Jeremy will help me."

"Yes, Sophie, don't you move. How could you? Coco took care of your feet last night. What did you do?"

"I'm your sister," she said, her voice so raw and hoarse that she was barely understandable. Jeremy didn't understand but Ryder did, and he did sympathize. He was no relation whatsoever to Jeremy, yet Jeremy was perfectly willing and ready to obey him, not her. He leaned down and patted her white cheek. "Jeremy will visit with you for a while. Keep an eye on her, my boy, and don't let her move except to relieve herself. You're in charge, Jeremy. Don't let me down."

"Oh no, sir."

Ryder gave her a small salute. He gave Jeremy a wink, and left.

CHAPTER
═ 9 ═

HE SHOOK HIS head and shook it again. He simply couldn't get over her feet. She'd obviously walked somewhere—certainly a farther distance than to the chamber pot—and it had been only a short time before, for the blood on the bandages was quite fresh.

Then he knew, of course. She'd seen or heard Sherman Cole arrive and she'd been terrified. She'd come down and doubtless listened at the door.

His jaw tightened when he remembered his words about her to Sherman Cole and the man's words about her. Ryder's had been the more damning because she'd come to trust him, at least with Jeremy. He'd given her a clout that was both unexpected and beyond cruel. Ryder realized he was standing in the middle of the entrance hall, simply standing there, doing nothing, looking at nothing in particular when James said, "Suh, you need something?"

"No, James. Was Miss Stanton-Greville downstairs a few moments ago?"

"Yes, suh, she was. In old Mr. Grayson's nightshirt, her hair all wild, that ancient nightshirt flapping around her poor bandaged feet."

"Thank you, James."

"Yes, suh. Ah, suh, will dat Thomas get his neck stretched out?"

"I hope so, I surely do."

Ryder walked out onto the veranda. He saw Emile riding up and waved him down.

"Camille Hall is running as smoothly as I can make it at the moment," Emile said as he dismounted his horse. "The inside smells revolting still but the slaves are working hard scrubbing away the soot and grime. I left Clayton, one of our bookkeepers, over there to meet with the Camille Hall bookkeepers and the head drivers. He's a sharp fellow and a good organizer. He will keep everyone working. I will return this afternoon to see what they've accomplished."

"No sign of Thomas?"

"Nary a shadow. I directed the grizzly job of getting Burgess buried. His body had simply been overlooked, if you can believe that. Jesus,

Ryder, it was a mess. At least it's done and over with. How are Jeremy and Sophie?"

"They're fine. Keep an eye out, Emile."

"Certainly. Where are you going?"

"To Camille Hall. Sophie and Jeremy need clothes." Emile frowned after him.

Clayton was a vigorous, harshly tanned, wiry little man who seemed to be moving even when he was standing still. He met Ryder at the door and began talking nonstop.

Ryder listened carefully to the man as he studied the great house, mentally noting what would have to be done, then dismissed Clayton and made his way upstairs. A giggling young girl with her hair wrapped in a colorful scarf showed him to Sophie's bedchamber. Her name, she pertly informed him with a sloe-eyed smile, was Dorsey. Sophie's bedchamber adjoined her uncle's. He looked over at that adjoining door and imagined it opening and Theo walking in, a whip in his hand.

He opened the armoire doors and saw at least half a dozen of the most garish gowns he'd ever beheld. All silks and satins, the colors too brilliant, all gowns much too old for her, gowns shrieking that she was a woman who knew men and would make a man scream with pleasure. There was nothing else hanging in the armoire save those utterly repulsive gowns.

In the drawers beneath, however, he found gowns that he could well imagine her wearing—soft pastels, light muslins. There were also her underthings—all well sewn and beautifully embroidered, but not what a whore would wear, all lawn, cotton, and linen, no silk, no satin. He shook out a nightgown and held it up. It was batiste, white, and looked as if it would be worn by a little girl.

He made a pile of clothing he would take back to Kimberly. He did the same thing in Jeremy's room.

All the clothes would be delivered in the early afternoon.

When he arrived back at Kimberly, hot, sweat making his shirt stick to his back, he couldn't believe his eyes.

There was Sherman Cole and with him were four men, all armed. Cole was yelling at Samuel to bring down the harlot. She was a murderess and he was here to take her back with him to Montego Bay.

Ryder rode his stallion through the men, stopping only at the first step to the veranda.

Cole whirled around. "You! It doesn't matter, sir, I will take her, and I have the men with me to do it."

Ryder waved a negligent hand to the four men, all of whom looked vastly uncomfortable, their faces flushed scarlet in the heat.

"Why don't you come in, Mr. Cole? I am sure there are some rather tasty buns for you to enjoy while we straighten out this confusion."

Cole shouted, "No! I want her, now!"

"I'm fatigued from this infernal heat," Ryder said, dismounting, and walking past Sherman Cole, "and from your infernal yelling. Either you accompany me inside or you can stand out here baying in the sun until you melt."

Samuel hurried after Ryder. Cole, taken aback yet again by this damned young man, followed more slowly. He could hear low conversation among the four men and wondered if the bastards were going to leave him here alone. None of them had wanted to come with him. Well, let them leave. He'd bring her back himself. Then he'd lock her in that room and he'd keep the key. She would be dependent on him for the very water she drank.

Ryder faced him in the salon and said without preamble, "You say Miss Stanton-Greville killed her uncle?"

"Yes, and this time I have enough proof. She shot him twice, one of my men found the derringer." He pulled it out of his pocket and dangled it in front of Ryder. "You'll see that it has two chambers. Both are empty."

"Interesting."

"Get her. It's obviously a woman's gun. Get her. I will take her back with me."

"Take her back where, Cole?"

The man's color was high and it went higher. "Why, there is a house we use to keep prisoners in. More a large room, really, but it will suffice for the likes of her."

Ryder could only shake his head. He should allow Cole to see her now—with her bruised face, bent over like an old woman because of her battered ribs, not to mention her bloody feet. Surely his ardor would cool at that sight. If he took her to this house, he would force her. Rape her endlessly. Ryder felt a knot in his gut and he rubbed his hand over his belly as he said easily, "I think not, Cole. Why don't you and your men ride back to Camille Hall. There's a nice fresh grave for you to dig up."

"What the devil are you talking about, sir?"

"Simply this, Cole. It seems that Theo Burgess wasn't buried immediately and thus Emile Grayson was able to examine the body before he saw him buried. It turns out Burgess wasn't shot. He was stabbed three times in the chest. Now, would you like to examine his body yourself? Emile did say that it was quite a messy job. You understand, of course.

The heat and all. No? Well, then, why not take yourself and your men off and find Thomas."

"But this derringer—"

"It's mine," Samuel Grayson said. "I appreciate your returning it. And you're quite right, sir, it is a lady's gun. It belonged to my wife."

Cole ignored him, his eyes hard on Ryder. "But what was she doing there?"

"I thought it was her home," Ryder said, an eyebrow climbing upward. "I will examine the body myself."

"Fine. A man called Clayton is there. He is a Kimberly bookkeeper but he is overseeing things at Camille Hall. He will doubtless provide your men with shovels. It won't be pleasant work, but I'm sure you know that. Good Lord, isn't this heat something? I might add that Emile was rather green when he returned after getting it done. Several more hours have passed. Ah well, how much more unpleasant can it get? Go now, Cole, I'm tired, and speaking with you tires me even more. Good luck with your digging. The result, I daresay, will be even less pleasant than the process."

Ryder turned away then and walked through the open doors onto the front veranda. He said nothing more, merely waited for Cole and his men to leave, which they did, Cole muttering threats under his breath.

"He was really stabbed?" Samuel asked.

"I have no idea. Emile didn't say."

"Are you saying that you just made that up?"

Ryder cocked an eyebrow at Samuel. "Why, yes. It makes for an interesting theory, doesn't it?"

"I'm still worried, Ryder. Cole is determined. He's a dangerous man, despite your contempt of him. We've just bought a little time, that's all. He wants her badly."

"She scorned him, you know. Struck him when he tried to kiss her."

"He isn't the kind of man to ever forget something like that." Samuel shook his head. "Something must be done and soon. Ah, that poor child."

"You mean Jeremy? I agree but he is young and adaptable. He will be just fine."

"No! I meant Sophia."

"Oh, her. I trust she's kept to her bed?"

"Yes."

Ryder said nothing more, merely walked back into the house and headed up the stairs.

When next he visited her, it was late afternoon. Sophie was wearing one of her nightgowns. She looked fresh and clean and very young. Her face was only faintly bruised now and she looked very bored. She frowned at him and said, "It is difficult to bathe and not get your feet wet."

"It's a sight I should have enjoyed witnessing. Perhaps you could bathe again this evening for my entertainment? I suppose that vicious snarl means I am to be denied. Well, it doesn't matter. I have come to talk to you."

"Talk, then."

"Feeling restive, are we?"

"I want to go home. I heard that one of your bookkeepers is overseeing things at home. That isn't right, Ryder. I should be there. Our people are perfectly capable of dealing with the problems themselves. I really must go home."

"Well, you can't just yet, so be quiet. As for Clayton, Emile says he's a diplomat so you needn't worry about lacerated sensibilities. Cole was here again after your lovely hide, but I told him that your uncle was just buried and it turns out he was stabbed, not shot."

She stared at him. "You're jesting."

"Who knows? It got Cole out of here. But I will tell you true. I think Thomas really did kill him and that he was the one you shot. Of course, that means it wasn't a mortal wound for he later spoke to Cole, giving his spurious evidence. But he's gone to ground now. I want to find him and toss him into the mangrove swamp. Yes, that's what I'll do."

"He won't return to Camille Hall. I really do want to go home, Ryder. There is so much to be done. There is no reason for Jeremy and me to remain here any longer. My ribs are much better now and my feet—well, I won't walk much, all right?"

"And just what would you do if Mr. Sherman Cole arrived with his men to remove you to Montego Bay?"

She paled. He remained unmoved.

"Actually," he said, looking beyond her right shoulder, "I've decided that we're all going back to England."

"You're mad!"

"Quite possibly. Jeremy needs schooling. He will go to Eton."

It was a dream come true, only Sophie didn't want it to come true this way, no, not through him. "No," she said. "I won't allow it."

"You have no choice at all," he said and smiled at her.

"I do have a choice. I won't be your mistress, Ryder, I won't."

"I don't recall having asked you. At least not in the past three days."

"I heard you! I heard what you said to Mr. Cole!"

"In that case, you must know that my ardor for your lovely self is quite in doubt now. After having examined you quite thoroughly I'm not sure at all that I am interested anymore. You are adequate for your environs, perhaps, but back in England? I don't know about that."

She picked up a heavy book of Shakespeare plays and flung it at him with all her might. He caught it square in his chest and grunted. Actually, she felt more pain in throwing the heavy tome at him than he felt at the blow. She paid it no mind. She threw a pitcher of water at him, a much easier shot, soaking the front of him.

There was nothing else to throw. She lay back against the pillows, panting and heaving, her forehead damp with perspiration. He hadn't moved, even to wipe the water from his face. "That's the second time you've attacked me," he said mildly. "What do you think I should do about it?"

"You should stop trying to take over my life."

"I want you to be well again."

"So do I!"

"Ah, but my reasons for wishing it are quite different from yours. I want you well and thus able to fight me. I want to hear you yowl when I've bested you, which I will do. I want to hear you curse me. I want you to hurl yourself at me again and again, because I know you, Sophie, I know you don't give up easily. When I have bested you, then you will get what you deserve."

"I wish you had never come here."

"Oh? And who should have come in my place? My little sister, Sinjun? I must admit that she would have found all this vastly amusing, but I'm not certain she would have dealt with you as well as I. She is very straightforward and honest, you see, utterly without guile. Or perhaps my pious younger brother, Tysen, who is right now at Oxford preparing himself for vicardom. He, I doubt not, will marry an equally pious girl who will be nauseatingly proper and good. Still and all, however, it's possible that Tysen would have been the recipient of one of your drowsy-eyed smiles and stuttered himself off the island and quite probably drowned. Now, as to the earl, why, my dear girl, he would have eaten you for breakfast. He has no patience, not like I have. He doesn't like games, either, not like I do. He doesn't indulge wholeheartedly in the sport women usually provide, not like I do. No, he would have put a stop to you immediately and walked away, dusting his hands. So, all in all, I think you were very lucky I came here, and I do promise you, Sophie, I swear it, that you will be bested by me, but in my own good time."

"A man's threats—always violence, always bragging and braying about the pain you will inflict."

"Oh no, I intend no pain."

"Very well, dominance. It's every bit as bad as physical violence. All men must know that they rule, even if it's just over a single woman."

"I believe we've been through similar charges before."

"Go to the devil, Ryder. You and all men are despicable! As for your repulsive family, I hope they all rot."

"Even Sinjun?"

"If she is like you, then yes, damn you."

Ryder wasn't used to explosions like this. He frowned at the newness of it, the abruptness of it, although since he'd met her, she'd knocked him off balance more times than he'd experienced in his life. But this—well, what could he expect? Her uncle had beaten her, probably countless times, out of the demented fun of doing it and to make her perform as he demanded. "You don't bore me," he said abruptly. "Actually, I find you quite amusing and I haven't even made—" He stopped cold in his tracks. No, he wasn't about to tell her that he hadn't taken her that night at the cottage when he'd drugged her. He had a clear flash in that instant of himself, staring down at her and how he'd wanted very much to touch her, to caress her, but he hadn't. He wasn't that cold-blooded.

"Well, Sophie, do you want to be my mistress for a time?"

"No."

"Ah, you find Oliver Susson more to your taste? Really, my dear, he's not at all a sterling specimen of manhood, although he is cooperative, which is a good thing for him. And that is the reason I haven't been up to see you earlier. I rode to Montego Bay to visit with Mr. Susson. Let us say that he now understands very clearly what he is to do. He will work to see that my guardianship is handled immediately. He apologized profusely for his ethical lapse and assured me that he would perform these duties without financial remuneration." Ryder paused for a reaction, but she held herself silent. She was well hidden from him, an act she was quite good at. He wanted to draw her, to bait her into fury, and thus continued in a mocking voice. "Naturally, the thought of losing you upset him dreadfully. He even went so far as to say that he would marry you, though he knew it would greatly affect his reputation in Jamaica. I thought there were actually tears in his eyes once he learned that he would never again enjoy you at the cottage."

"He never did enjoy me. He did, but not in the way you think."

"Oh? You say you were never at the cottage with him?"

"Yes, but I didn't—" She stopped. It was no good. She said abruptly, "All you have to do is look at my face and my ribs, Ryder, and know that I did nothing with any of these men willingly."

"Reluctant all the way, huh? Perhaps I believe you with a pathetic bastard like Sherman Cole. But with all the rest of them? I'm sorry, Sophie, but I do remember that first night with you and how you played the coquette to perfection. You didn't turn a hair when I pulled your gown to your waist and fondled your breasts. Oh no, you handled me with great skill—ah, the promises, the anticipation you built up in me. I positively festered with lust."

"Will you get me some bandages so I can wrap up my feet? I must get up, Ryder. I am so bored I want to scream and your conversation is rendering me nearly insensible."

So much for goading her into an excess of bile, he thought, and simply nodded. He himself wrapped up her feet, pleased that they looked better than they had that morning. Nice feet, he thought, narrow, highly arched. He said as he studied her toes, "When I finished my conversation with Mr. Susson, I checked on shipping schedules to England. There are several ships due in from England very soon now. We will have time to tie up all loose ends. I firmly intend for the three of us to be on the next ship back home."

"Sir, are you helping my sister again?"

Ryder slowly lowered her foot back onto the bed. He turned to see Jeremy standing in the doorway. He said under his breath, but Sophie heard him, "I really must remember to close that bloody door." He grinned at the boy. "Come in, Jeremy. Your sister is flushed from the heat and I was just trying to amuse her. She is bored, you know, and wants for diversions."

"You were holding her foot."

"Yes. She had a cramp in her toes but it is better now. As you can see I'm also bandaging her feet again. She is bored."

"I will read to her. Goodness, Sophie, whatever is the Shakespeare doing on the floor? You must be more careful. Some of the pages are twisted. Goodness, page four hundred and thirty is torn."

"You're right, Jeremy. She tore the second scene in *The Taming of the Shrew.*"

"Go away, Ryder," she said. "Just go away."

He did, whistling.

Sophie didn't know what had awakened her. At one moment she was dreaming deeply, and her mother was there with her, laughing and brushing her hair and talking about the future and all the fine young men who would want to marry her when they went to London upon her eighteenth birthday. The next moment, she was wide awake, jerking upright in bed, frozen still and listening.

The sound came again. Movement coming from outside.

Her heart began to pound, fast, shallow strokes. Slowly, she pulled off the single sheet covering her and eased out from beneath the mosquito netting. It was very late and very silent except for that other sound. It was a person and he was moving along the balcony outside, quietly but not quietly enough for her sharp ears.

She stepped onto the floor. Her feet were still bandaged but it had been two days since the fire at Camille Hall and the pain was nearly gone now. She walked slowly, tiptoeing to the open door and peering out. She heard nothing but the soft grating sound of a lone coqui. Then in the next instant, she saw a shadow, a long shadow, the shadow of a man, and he was moving stealthily around the side of the house.

She picked up the water pitcher beside her bed, the one she'd hurled two days before at Ryder, unceremoniously dumped the remaining water into the chamber pot, and walked out onto the balcony. There were no barriers. The balcony curved around the entire second floor of the house, a good eight feet deep with a twelve-foot overhang to protect from the sun. She crept after the man. Suddenly she was right behind him and she froze. He was silent, staring into a bedchamber.

It was Ryder's room.

She saw him raise a knife in his hand. God, it was Thomas and he was going to kill Ryder.

She waited until he stepped into the bedchamber then ran quickly after him, the thick bandages on her feet silencing them. She peered around the open doorway to see Thomas now standing by Ryder's bed. He had the knife raised. She saw a bulky bandage around his chest. She'd shot him, not her uncle. Ryder had been right.

But her aim hadn't been good enough, worse luck.

Slowly, he pulled back the mosquito netting.

Sophie screamed and screamed again, yelling like a banshee, shrieking like a mad voodoo priestess. She ran toward Thomas, the pitcher raised high.

Ryder awoke to see the silver flash of a blade over his body, a harsh scream echoing in his head. Jesus! He jerked away, rolling off the other side of the bed, but he tangled himself in the mosquito netting.

Sophie saw him roll quickly to the opposite side of the bed, but he didn't jerk the mosquito netting out of the way. He fell hard to the floor, tangled in the yards and yards of netting.

Thomas was running around the side of the bed, breathing hard, not even looking at her, intent upon getting to Ryder.

"Thomas!"

He jerked toward her then and she saw the hatred twisting his face.

"Thomas, I shot you, not Ryder! What's the matter, are you afraid of me? You miserable bastard, you *are* afraid of me, a girl, half your size.

Coward, murdering, sniveling coward! Why did you kill my uncle? Did he deceive you, cheat you?"

Thomas went berserk. He was trembling, making slashing downward and upward motions with the knife. "I know you shot me, you damned bitch! After I kill him I will deal with you. First I'm going to have me some fun with you and then I'll let you beg me not to kill you. On your knees, you little slut, on your knees in front of me begging and begging." He was stalking her, Ryder now forgotten.

Sophie didn't have time to question the wisdom of her attack. If Ryder didn't free himself quickly, she would very shortly be in grave difficulties. She moved behind a wicker chair, shoving it forward toward him.

Every nerve was tingling in her body. She felt dread, fear, and, oddly enough, excitement at the danger. Her eyes glittered as she looked at his hated face.

"You gutless coward!" she screamed at him, taunting him. Then just as quickly, she stepped to one side of the chair, looked beyond him, and yelled, "Yes, Ryder, kill him now!"

Thomas whirled about to face his new attacker, a man, and thus more of a threat.

It was a mistake.

Sophie rushed up behind him and struck the heavy pottery pitcher over his head. It cracked hard against his skull. Thomas groaned softly and slumped to the floor. The knife fell from his fingers and lay beside him, the long silver blade obscene in the pale light of the bedchamber.

Ryder pulled the mosquito netting off himself and slowly got to his feet. He walked over to Thomas, kneeled down, and felt the man's pulse. He was alive, just barely.

"You gave him a fine cosh," he said, still studying Thomas. "You did shoot him. Here, in the ribs. He must have still been in some pain." Ryder looked up at her then. She was standing there, silent as a stone, swathed in one of her voluminous white nightgowns, her hair loose down her back, her face as white as the Valenciennes lace at the collar of her gown. She was still holding the broken-off pitcher handle, clutching it like an amulet.

"Thank you, Sophie," he said, and slowly rose.

She drew in a sharp breath. He was naked and he didn't appear to be aware of it. He walked to a lamp and lit it. He turned to face her and at that moment, Samuel, Mary, Emile, Coco, James, and several other house slaves burst into the room. Coco promptly fainted. Emile caught her, luckily, and set her on Ryder's bed. "She's pregnant," he said and shrugged.

Ryder smiled and raised his hand. "It's all right. Thomas is the one on the floor. He came to kill me. At least I was first on his list. Sophie saved me."

"Ryder," Emile said on a strained laugh. "I'm delighted it's over and both of you are all right. Sophie saved you? She always was a daring girl, and anyone to attack someone dear to her got the brunt of her fury. But, my dear fellow, you are quite naked. This is the second time you've been thusly unattired."

"So I am," Ryder said, bemused. He walked over to a chair and shrugged into a dressing gown. "It's so bloody hot, you know. Sophie, are you all right?"

She still hadn't said a word. In fact, she hadn't moved an inch. He walked to her and gently touched his fingertips to her cheek. "Are you all right?"

"Sophie!"

It was Jeremy and he shoved and pushed his way into the room and ran clumsily to his sister.

She came alive then and held him against her. She stroked his tousled hair, saying very softly and calmly, "I'm fine, love, just fine, and so is Ryder. Thomas, however, isn't. That's grand, isn't it, Jeremy? No more villains to hurt us or anyone else. No more villains at all."

"Unfortunately the world abounds with villains," Ryder said. "But there is now one less. Emile, why don't the two of us tie this one up and take him to the mangrove swamp and leave him there for the crocodiles. I surely do like that notion."

"I do too," Emile said.

"We must notify Sherman Cole," Samuel said. "Surely now he will believe that Thomas murdered Burgess."

"I suppose you're right," Ryder said on a mournful sigh. "Perhaps Emile and I can take him into Montego Bay. Perhaps we can have a slight accident on the way, by the—"

"Mangrove swamp," Emile said, grinning.

"It's the middle of the night," Ryder said. "Let's tie him up and stuff him in some dark closet. Is there anyplace secure here, Samuel?"

"Yes, the icehouse."

Within five minutes Thomas was securely bound and carried out to the icehouse, a guard set over him. Finally Ryder's bedchamber was empty again but for Sophie and Jeremy. He was still holding her, clutching at her really, for she was all that was left of his world.

Ryder didn't think, he merely dropped to his haunches and said quietly, "It's all right, Jeremy. Truly. Sophie's safe. Now, my lad, why don't your sister and I take you back to bed?"

"A glass of milk first, Jeremy?"

The boy shook his head. "No, I'd throw it up. This was scary, Sophie, too scary. I'm tired of being scared."

"Me too, love, me too."

"I as well," Ryder said and ruffled the boy's hair when he stared at him, disbelieving.

It took a good thirty minutes to settle Jeremy. They both remained with him until he fell asleep. Ryder followed Sophie back to her bedchamber.

"Come outside and let's sit a while. Like Jeremy, I'm too excited to sleep just yet."

They sat in two wicker chairs, enveloped in silence, the terror fading slowly, very slowly.

"Thank you, Sophie."

"You're welcome."

"How did you know?"

"I just heard an odd sound, one that didn't belong to the night, and it woke me up. I saw this shadow and followed it. Then I knew it was Thomas and he was here to kill you."

"You reacted very quickly," Ryder said, and he sounded a bit annoyed. "I have never known a female to act so quickly and so competently. You didn't hesitate. You didn't swoon and give a pathetic little yell. You screamed your head off. You even had your weapon with you."

"As you recall, I had used that same pitcher before. I knew it was sound. You were tangled in the netting. What was I supposed to do? Let him gut you like a trapped fish? Also, a delicate feminine little whimper wouldn't have accomplished much. Besides, I was next and then possibly Jeremy."

"Yes, you were next," Ryder repeated slowly. "He would have succeeded if you hadn't been there. You know that, don't you? I am not a particularly light sleeper."

She shrugged as if she didn't give a good damn and it infuriated him, this strength in her, this bravado, that was or wasn't real—he didn't know and wondered if he'd ever know. He rose quickly to his feet and stared down at her. He was shocked at his own behavior. Never before in his life had he come face to face with a dog-in-the-manager attitude in himself. It was too much. She'd turned the world and all his experiences and beliefs inside out. "I am pleased that I am someone dear to you."

"What are you talking about?"

"Emile said you were ferocious when it came to protecting those dear to you."

"I told you, Ryder, he would have killed me after he'd taken care of you. I'm not stupid."

"How are your feet?"

"Fine. I'm nearly well."

"Good," he said, and jerked her to her feet. He pulled her against him before she had a chance to react. He grabbed her chin in his hand and held her still. He kissed her closed mouth, hard.

"I don't like this," he said against her mouth, his breath hot as the urgency that burned deep within him. "You are not as you should be. I cannot understand you. I won't put up with it anymore. Damn you, be a woman!"

He kissed her again. He felt her belly against him and his hands were wild down her back, caressing her, stroking down over her buttocks, pulling her upward hard against him.

She wrenched away from him. She didn't say a word. She just kept backing away from him, one step at a time, a single, small step, farther and farther away from him. She wiped the back of her hand across her mouth.

He knew such fury he was shaking with it. "After all the damned men you've had, you dare to wipe the taste of me off your mouth?"

She dropped her hand to her side and took another step backward.

"You go much farther and you'll end up in Samuel's bedchamber. You'll have to kick his housekeeper out of his bed, but I'm certain he'd be more than pleased to have you instead of Mary."

She shook her head, still silent.

"Damn you, say something!"

She turned on her heel and ran.

CHAPTER
═ 10 ═

THOMAS ESCAPED. No one was precisely certain how he'd managed to free himself from the icehouse, but there were two Kimberly slaves unconscious and bound in the bushes nearby. They'd been clobbered, but not killed, and that surprised Ryder. They hadn't seen a thing. Ryder suspected that some of Thomas's cohorts from Camille Hall had rescued him, and perhaps it was these cohorts who had kept him from killing the guards like one would swat flies. He was long gone, dammit. No crocodiles for him, dammit even more. Ryder sent out search parties. He sent word to Sherman Cole. Then he brooded about Sophie.

Ryder hated to brood. He'd done very little of it in his life for the very simple reason that he'd never felt the need to take himself apart from his fellow man and commit himself to brooding. It had always seemed to him to be a singularly boring way to pass the time. But now he felt the need and it was sharp and deep inside him. It was also unexpected and unwelcome and made him uncomfortable; nor did he particularly know how to do it properly.

Damn her for making him ponder and muse and agonize and absorb thoughts and feelings he didn't want or need.

He jumped to his feet, furious with himself and with her, and determined to end it once and for all.

She wasn't in her bedchamber—his former bedchamber, rather. She was dressed and sitting quietly in a chair on the balcony. Her eyes were closed, her hands folded in her lap. She looked to be asleep. She was wearing one of the pale blue muslin gowns he'd brought back from Camille Hall for her, a highnecked affair with lace that nearly touched her chin. He paused, just looking down at her for a very long time. Her hair was clean and pulled back with a pale blue ribbon at the nape of her neck. There were only the faintest bruises on her face now. She looked scrubbed, fresh, and immensely innocent, and too young.

Innocent, ha. But that was the crux of the matter, indeed it was, and he wouldn't stand for it anymore. He lightly touched his hand to her shoulder.

She opened her eyes slowly and stared up at him, her expression not changing. She didn't jump or exclaim.

She said only, "Ryder."

"Hello," he said, and he felt something odd and sweet touch him as she spoke his name. It made him angry and she felt it. She tensed beneath his hand. He pulled back, his hand dropping to his side, and took the chair opposite her.

"This is the second time we've sat here on this balcony like an old married couple reviewing the events of the day."

"Hardly," she said. She gave him a smile that didn't reach her eyes, a hard smile, and had he but realized it, a smile that cloaked an immense vulnerability. "If I didn't know better I would think you were agitated about something. Difficult to believe, I know. You, Ryder Sherbrooke, a man to whom the worries of the world are practically unknown. No, certainly that can't be it. You are not like normal people with normal concerns."

"I believe you have said quite enough. It always surprises me how you can go immediately on the attack with little or no buildup. Instantly, you are at the jugular, biting and nipping away. But you won't draw me this time or sidetrack me. That is always your purpose with me, isn't it? No, don't bother to deny it or bait me more. Now, I want to know something from you and I want the truth."

"Very well."

He sat forward, his hands clasped between his knees. "The truth, Sophie. I mean it."

"If you have to remind me, if you have to look as serious as an idol, I doubt you'll believe a truth when you hear it."

"Did you sleep with any of those men willingly? Did your uncle force you into being a harlot or were you a harlot before and your uncle merely molded you into doing what he wanted you to do and with whom?"

"No."

"Damn you, Sophie, don't you dare—"

She rose suddenly, her skirts swirling about her ankles, and he saw that she was barefoot. Still bandages, but no shoes. He didn't like that. It made him angrier.

"Answer my question, damn you!"

"Ask me a single question, then, and I will answer it." Her back was to him, her shoulders straight, and he knew that chin of hers was probably thrust up a good two inches.

"Very well. Did you sleep with any of those men willingly?"

"No."

"Not even Lord David Lochridge?"

"No."

"Had you slept with any men before your uncle coerced you into bedding those of his choosing?"

"No."

"I see," he said, but he didn't, not really. His brain wasn't functioning with its usual clarity—doubtless because of the brooding—and it was making him equal parts frustrated and furious. "Damn you, how old were you when you had your first man?"

She turned to face him then and she was still smiling that hard, cutting smile. "If you're to be believed, why then, the first man had me when I was nineteen. And that first man was you." She laughed at the infuriated expression on his face. "You see, Ryder, you refuse to believe me because you're a man and men must place women into very neat slots. A woman is innocent or she's not. There is no middle ground for a woman. A widow is all right, perhaps, but even then men assume that she will bed any number of them willingly, indeed, enthusiastically, because she's used to having sex and knows what it's all about.

"I have come to believe that once a woman has known a man intimately, she really isn't to be trusted after that. Goodness, if the man is her husband she just might cuckold him. Of course, a husband can't cuckold his wife. A husband can continue doing whatever he pleases. If he can't get a woman to willingly bed with him, why he simply buys a woman for the night. Or, like you—a rich man—he keeps mistresses. And the man remains utterly respectable. Indeed, his credit rises with both men and women. It is nonsense and not fair. I will tell you the truth again, Ryder. I have never been with a man intimately—"

"More of your unenlightened philosophy of life—how trippingly it flows from your mouth. You, Sophie, are more ignorant than a slug. You know nothing of men and women and what is important between them and how—"

She actually stamped one of her bandaged feet. "I never want to know! I sincerely doubt that there could be anything equal or fine or just between a man and a woman. I don't think you believe it either, Ryder. Don't you dare sneer at me. I will tell you again and it's the truth. I have never been intimate with a man, except you and you had to drug me and—"

"Damn you, I fondled and caressed your breasts and you allowed me to do it! You let me kiss you and you kissed me back expertly. You let me put my tongue in your mouth. By God, when you woke up on the beach and saw that I'd nearly stripped you and taken you then, what did you do? You smiled at me and teased me and invited me to be your lover. You promised you would dismiss the others. I would call that pretty damned intimate."

"—then you took me to the cottage, and I have no memory of that at all, as you well know. So, no, I'm no longer innocent, I suppose. I had assumed a man could tell if a woman was without experience and vice versa, but apparently it isn't so because you didn't apologize and admit that I had been a virgin when you took me."

Ryder rose very slowly. His face was red, the pulse in his throat was swelled and throbbing. He picked up his chair and hurled it with all his strength over the railing. A shout came from below. He gave her a look of utter loathing and strode off the balcony and out of the bedchamber.

Samuel Grayson found Ryder in the north canefield. He was speaking to one of the head drivers, a black man named Jonah who could snap a man's neck with one huge hand. Ryder wore a hat. His shirt was open nearly to his waist and his chest was shiny with sweat and darkened from the sun. Samuel set his jaw and rode to the two men.

Ryder finished his questions to Jonah, thanked him, then turned to give a salute to Samuel.

"A good man," Samuel said, looking after Jonah.

"Yes. I would certainly like to have him on my side during a fight. Thinking of him as an enemy makes my blood curdle."

"I must speak with you, Ryder."

Ryder took off his hat, fanned his face, then rubbed his sleeve over his forehead. "Let's go find some shade. Perhaps to the beach, if that's all right with you, Samuel."

They rode to Monmouth Beach. Ryder was aware of a slight deepening of recognition inside him, a warming that somehow pulled and tugged at him, which was quite foolish, of course. It was just a beach, for God's sake, a place that was pleasant, nothing more. Certainly it had nothing to do with her. They dismounted and settled themselves beneath a coconut tree. The breeze was steady and cool. Ryder felt the sweat drying and it brought a very nice chill to his skin. He sighed with pleasure and leaned back bonelessly against the trunk.

Samuel said without preamble, "I want to marry Sophia Stanton-Greville. Then I will be the boy's guardian. Camille Hall is the very next property to Kimberly. Emile and I will be able to oversee all operations and ensure that the boy's inheritance is secure."

Good God, this was a shocker, but it shouldn't have been, not really. Ryder knew Samuel was infatuated with her, had known it from the beginning, and had found it, at first, somewhat amusing. It was no longer amusing. He heard himself say in a faraway voice, "I will shortly be

Jeremy's guardian. As for Sophie, who knows? But, Samuel, there is no need for you to do anything."

"But you don't really want to be the boy's guardian. I know you want to return to England as soon as possible. Your life is there. You're taking the boy and Sophie with you because you don't see any other choice. But there is now a choice. They both belong here, not in England. I know there is a house and some property in Cornwall, but surely it isn't as important as the plantation is here. I will hire a tutor for Jeremy. He will be educated and someday he will assume his inheritance. Sophia will have security, a family, people around her who care about her."

Ryder felt suddenly very cold. He turned away from Samuel, suddenly afraid of what his expression might give away. He stared out over the sea. Where the devil had all his carefree laughter gone? "I see," he said at last. "You have thought a lot about this. I suppose you are one of these people who care for Miss Stanton-Greville."

"Yes."

"You also realize you're old enough to be her father."

"I naturally realize that as well and it concerns me. I had wanted Emile to marry her for their ages are closer, but he believes her a whore. He respects her at least now, for she did save your life, and that is something. Still, he looks at her with a sneer and in that assessing way a man looks at a woman he thinks just might want to bed him—the way you look at her. I want to protect her. I want to care for her. Once I marry her, Emile will keep his opinions to himself. Indeed, he might come to change them for they are quite wrong. She is a good girl, a wholesome girl. She has been maligned and her uncle is the only one at fault. I'm glad the man is dead."

"She plays the whore to perfection."

"If that is true, it is her uncle's doing. Everything she has done he's made her do. But he could not have made her agree to sleep with all those men."

"You believe, then, that all the men have simply lied about bedding her at the cottage?"

"They must have."

"Emile said she was a hellion."

"I don't think she could have survived had she not been strong-willed, had she not been able to endure. She has protected her brother to the best of her ability. I have wondered about the gossip, indeed, have listened to all the men who have claimed to have been her lover. She couldn't do such a thing; it's that simple. It isn't in her nature."

"But wouldn't she do anything to protect Jeremy?"

"Almost anything, yes, but not degrade herself, not that. She didn't hesitate to save your life either. If that makes her a hellion, why then, it is a good thing, at least I would imagine you believe it to be."

"Yes, she did save me, didn't she? Listen to me, Samuel, you must also realize that if you marry her neither of you will be received by the families here, or, even if you are received, she will be snubbed. She is already ostracized."

"I intend to change all that," Samuel said. "I will claim to all that she came to my marriage bed a virgin. I will tell the truth about her uncle."

"The only result to that assertion would be laughter. Be sensible, Samuel. No one will ever change their opinion."

"I will try, I must."

"When I spoke to Oliver Susson today he also said he would marry her."

"I wouldn't allow Oliver to get near her."

"If you want to shelter her from all the men she's entertained—forced to by her uncle or not—you would end up spending your lives as hermits. The list of men visiting that damned cottage of hers is long, Samuel."

"You are wrong, Ryder. I will change opinions. My word is respected here."

"No," Ryder said.

"Excuse me?"

"I said no. You won't marry her."

Samuel felt stirrings of anger at the young man. Even though he was Kimberly Hall's owner, Ryder Sherbrooke had no right to dictate personal matters to him. His reasons for his actions were sound. He rose slowly to his feet. "You have no say in the matter, Ryder. It is my decision, not yours."

Ryder smiled. "Actually, Samuel, it is Sophie's decision and she will say no."

"Why? Because you ruined her and thus she wouldn't want to shame me by accepting me as her husband? Don't look so bloody surprised. I knew very well you wanted her, that you wanted to dominate her, to bring her to her knees, if you will. You made it a test of manhood. Ah, yes, you behaved just like a new hound in the pack. You had to prove your virility and power with this woman, to yourself and to others. It was a competition. You had to show the world that you could have her, and in having her make her say that the others weren't important to her, just you. I'm not blind. Also, I was standing beneath the balcony a short time ago, and I heard what she said and your accusations as well. I heard her telling you that she'd been innocent until you'd taken her to the cottage.

"You have ruined Miss Stanton-Greville and you have made no move to remedy the situation. The only remedy that would occur to you would be to make her your mistress, and she a young lady of excellent birth and breeding. She is also a young lady of principles. Have you even given a thought to the possibility that you could have gotten her with child? Of course you haven't. Well, I care about her and I will marry her and if she is pregnant, then she won't birth a bastard. Damn you, keep that supercilious eyebrow of yours down! Can you swear to me that when you took her at the cottage she wasn't a virgin?"

Ryder said very quietly, "No, I can't swear."

"What you refuse to admit is that you breached her maidenhead, that you took a virgin. She is no harlot, and well you know it. I have told you what I intend. I have given you that much courtesy. At least I'm offering the poor girl a choice, which is more than you've thought to do."

Ryder picked up a small pebble and flung it toward the water. It bounced in the surf. "Just how do you plan to protect her when Sherman Cole comes to arrest her so that he can hang her for murdering her uncle?"

Samuel Grayson looked away from Ryder, out over the sea. "So you believe it better for you to take her away from here along with Jeremy? She would be your mistress, that, or she would be completely alone with no money, no friends, no way to support herself? That is some solution, I warrant!

"God save us all from men who think the world is theirs to command and women there for their selfish pleasures. I have also observed your notion of honor, sir; it burrows deep into your pride, into the years upon years of privilege and wealth you and your family have enjoyed. But the other? The worth of a single girl? Her honor? Her reputation? There is none, there is only your domination of her and her surrender to you, this competition you and all young men revel in. And then you walk away, thinking no more about the girl and what you've done to her. No, it will be done my way. If Sherman Cole arrests Sophie, why then, I don't know. But by God I will think of something. Good day." Samuel strode away from him, striking his riding crop against his thigh in his agitation.

Ryder stared after the man. He felt as if he'd just been verbally thrashed by his father. His father had been better at it as he recalled, but Samuel wasn't bad. He snorted as he watched Samuel mount his horse.

He leaned back against the tree trunk again and closed his eyes. Of course he didn't see the entire world as his to command, just a small bit of it perhaps. So what was wrong with that? He wasn't selfish; he wasn't greedy. He took but he didn't take too much. He didn't hurt people. And he did give, certainly he did. Jane could tell anyone that as well as his sister, Sinjun.

Was he such an unfeeling, selfish bastard? Had his aims been all that ignoble? Was he really the leader of the hounds? No, all that nonsense about proving his virility was just that, nonsense. He was himself and he wasn't all that bad, not at all. He was honorable because it was bred into him, Samuel was right about that, so what was the matter with it? But he felt guilty nonetheless and he felt a fraud, dammit, which wasn't fair.

"Well, hell," he said to a incredibly huge green turtle who was making a sluggish trail toward the water's edge. "Well, hell," he said again.

Samuel Grayson looked at Sophie with bleak eyes. Ryder had been right. She'd refused him without hesitation, but very nicely. She looked tired and somehow defeated. He hated it but didn't know what to do about it.

She tried to smile at him, but there were tears in her eyes. "You know I cannot," she said again, for he had remained silent. It seemed he'd used up all his words on Ryder Sherbrooke.

He said finally, his voice tired as his soul, "No, I don't understand. This shame of yours, it is nonsense. I am not a randy young man with expectations of purity, Sophia. I would that you reconsider."

Again, without hesitation, she said, "No, I'm sorry, Samuel." His name felt odd on her lips, for he'd been Mr. Grayson to her the entire four years she'd lived on Jamaica, but when a man proposed, she supposed it wouldn't be polite to treat him like your father.

"I apologize if this embarrasses you, Sophie, but I know about what Ryder did to you. I know this is your shame. I am sorry for it."

"He told you?"

"No, certainly not. But he knows that I know. Is it possible you are with child?"

She paled and clutched a chair back. She was shaking her head violently even as she whispered, "Oh no, I couldn't be, it wouldn't be fair. Oh Lord, what am I to do?"

"You can marry me and be safe. I don't care if you are pregnant with his child."

She marveled at the goodness in him, the genuine caring for her, and knew regardless that she couldn't marry him, not ever. "No, I would never do that, never."

Samuel sighed. "Ryder was right."

She stiffened. "What do you mean?"

"He said you would refuse me because he'd bedded you."

She laughed, actually laughed, and Samuel stared at her dumbfounded. "Well," she managed at last, "at least he believes me to have some honor. Me, the whore of Jamaica! Ah, but it is too much."

Ryder heard that laughter and found himself walking swiftly toward it.

It was strained and he felt the wildness of it to the very depths of him, a barely contained fierceness. It scared him to his toes. He quickly opened the door of the drawing room only to draw up in some embarrassment. He didn't know who he'd expected to be with her, but not Samuel Grayson. Good God, Samuel had said something to bring that on?

"Oh," he said. "Samuel, Sophie. Excuse me."

"No, Ryder, it isn't necessary," Samuel said. "You were right. She won't have me. Now, I must needs see to some work. No, stay here, I will be off. I believe I will ride into Montego Bay and see what Sherman Cole is up to. Perhaps Thomas has been caught." Ryder didn't say a word until Samuel had closed the door after him.

Ryder felt a spurt of relief so profound that he trembled with it. He didn't want to accept the relief because accepting made him so furious with himself that he wanted to howl. He looked at her standing there in one of her modest muslin gowns, her feet bare as an urchin's, no bandages now, and he said, "I assume all those sweet girlish gowns I brought over from Camille Hall for you were from your precottage days?"

Her eyes narrowed. Her hands fisted at her sides. Then she smiled at him, one of those drowsy-eyed smiles, and when she spoke, her voice was soft and mocking, and his body reacted before he could stop it. "Ah, Ryder, certainly they're from before. Boring little confections, aren't they? Could you ever doubt it? But what was I to do? You left all my other gowns at Camille Hall. Why don't you pretend that I'm wearing a bright scarlet satin cut nearly to my waist and come here and fondle me again? Be bold, Ryder, be a man and rip the gown right off me. Wouldn't you enjoy that? A real man asserting his strength and power. Goodness, it makes me shudder just to think about it. You could bend me back over your right arm. Really, don't I deserve a reward for saving your poor Mr. Grayson from a fate worse than death?"

He didn't move. Then he cursed. Then he shouted at her, "Stop that damned act!"

"Act? You mean you don't think I'm a harlot anymore?"

"Yes, no. I don't know, curse you."

"Did dear Samuel begin to change your mind?"

"No."

Just as suddenly as she'd assumed the polished harlot role, she became more vulnerable than he could bear. Because she couldn't control it, and she didn't want him to see that vulnerability, she whirled about and walked quickly to the veranda. But he had seen it and followed on her heels. She was wringing her hands as she said in a terrified whisper he barely heard, "What if I am pregnant?"

He did not pretend to misunderstand her. "Did you never think of that with all the other men? Did you always take precautions with them?"

"No."

More of her verbal confusion. He should have told her that if she were pregnant, it certainly wasn't with his seed. And if she were, just by chance, as innocent as she claimed to be, why then, they should be speaking of a possible religious birth.

He should tell her that he hadn't taken her. He should, really, but he didn't. Because if he did tell her she just might marry Samuel Grayson, and he knew he couldn't allow that to happen.

"When was your last monthly flow?"

She jerked with shock. He watched, fascinated, as she forced herself back into control. She looked him straight in the face, didn't say a word, then turned and walked quickly away.

He frowned after her. Her look had been one of utter scorn; she'd needed no words, for her expression had been quite enough. He should teach her how to sneer. She would do it well.

When Samuel Grayson returned to Kimberly four hours later, he was sweating profusely and he looked frantic. He said to both Emile and Ryder without preamble, "Sherman Cole is digging up Burgess's body tomorrow morning. It's the talk of Montego Bay. Thomas is still at large. Cole says that after he arrests Sophie, he will offer money to Thomas to come out of hiding and testify against her. He says he doesn't believe the story of Thomas coming here to murder you, Ryder. He also claims you were lying about Burgess being shot. I heard he is paying a lot of money to three men to dig Burgess up and examine him. He says he will arrest her immediately, try her, and hang her, all within the week. He says that none of us can stop it."

"So," Emile said, "the end is near. No matter what I think of her personally, I don't wish to see her hung."

His father snorted in disgust. "You blind young puppy! Well, Ryder, soon you won't have to worry about her. Soon it will be just Jeremy." He turned to his son. "I need you to be at Camille Hall when Cole goes there tomorrow morning. We must have warning. Go tell Sophie to stay close to the house."

After Emile had left the salon, Samuel said, "Now there is no choice. I will tell you, Ryder. There is the *Harbinger*, a big stout barkentine, in port right now. It is returning to England with the morning tide. Sophia and Jeremy must be on that ship."

"Yes," Ryder said. "They must." He grinned, splaying his hands in front of him. "I know, I know. I cannot send her to England with no protection. No money. No one to look after her."

"You cannot as yet leave Jamaica."

"I know, not until all this guardianship business is completed. There's Sherman Cole to be dealt with, of course, as well as that mangy bastard, Thomas, to be found."

"Then what will you do?"

"It appears my choices have just dwindled alarmingly. Get the vicar over here and I will wed her. She and Jeremy will be aboard that ship even as Sherman Cole is over digging at Camille Hall. Once they reach England, she and Jeremy will go to Northcliffe Hall, to my family. They will take care of them."

"And when you return to England, Ryder?"

"Don't push, old man. You've got your way. You've saved the girl, using me to do it."

"She will make you a fine wife."

Ryder cursed him and left to go find his soon-to-be bride.

Marriage! It was a truly appalling thought, but there was no hope for it. He thought of his brother, the earl, and prayed that his own recent marriage was shaping up, but in truth he'd had grave doubts when he'd left England, despite the pluckiness of Douglas's new bride. All because he'd come to Jamaica he would find himself leg-shackled. His life had been progressing just as he'd ordered it up.

He sighed. He might as well get it over with. He found her in the late afternoon at Monmouth Beach. Her mare, Opal, was grazing nearby on swamp grass. She was seated in the shade of an Indian almond tree, staring out over the water, her legs crossed, tomboy style.

He loosed his own horse, then strode to her, stood over her, his hands on his hips, and said, "I rode to Camille Hall. They said you had been there, overseeing the indoor work. You shouldn't have gone back there yet. You're not well enough."

She didn't look up. "Nonsense," she said.

He leaned down and jerked up the skirt of her riding habit. "Then why aren't you wearing shoes?"

She slapped her petticoats and skirt back down. "Go to the devil, Ryder. Camille Hall belongs to Jeremy now. He is still there. In truth I became overtired and came here to rest a bit. Now, what do you want? More truths from the resident harlot's mouth?"

"No."

"Then what do you want?"

He looked at her with acute dislike. He shook his head and said, "As of thirty minutes ago, you and I have no choice in the way we must now proceed. You will come back to Kimberly with me. You have much to do before tomorrow morning."

"What the devil are you talking about?" she asked with a cold indifference that nearly made his eyes cross with rage.

"Look at me, damn you!"

She sighed and looked up. "Your language is foul. You're also standing with your back against the sun and I can't really see your face. Forget your display of manliness and sit down, Ryder."

He did and crossed his legs, like hers. "You will listen to me now, Sophie. I dislike you speaking to me like that. That was no manliness display; I was just standing there, like anyone would just stand there."

She nearly smiled. She began to sift sand through her fingers. He truly didn't perceive the natural arrogance that was deep within him. All wish to smile vanished as he continued, saying, "Now, there is no other solution. I have thought and thought, but it does no good. I have argued with myself. I have brooded, a pastime I abhor. I have presented myself with all the reasons why it is the height of foolishness, the very depths of idiocy, but nothing has worked. Very well, then, I will have to marry you."

She stared at him. "You're mad."

"Yes. However, I will do it. I can't seem to find another choice for myself. I will marry you. You and Jeremy will be aboard a ship leaving for England early tomorrow morning. You will wed me this evening. When you reach England, you and Jeremy will journey to my family at Northcliffe Hall, and they will take care of you until I come home."

"You're doing this because you're afraid I'm with child? Your child?"

"No. Sherman Cole is digging up your uncle tomorrow. Then he will arrest you. He's even offered money to Thomas to come out of hiding to testify against you. Therefore you will marry me, and you and Jeremy will be long gone by the time Cole is rubbing his fat hands together contemplating having you completely in his power. No, don't say anything. You have to leave Jamaica. Ah, do you want to know what you're getting in a husband? You won't have a title because I'm the second son, as you know. However, I am rich enough even for you, I imagine. Hell, now that I own Kimberly Hall, I daresay I can give you whatever your heart desires."

"Excellent. All right, my heart desires that I will be Jeremy's guardian and that it will be I who will see he receives a gentleman's education."

"Don't do this, there is no time for further games on your part. We will wed. It will be done. Be quiet. I'm not jesting about Cole and his intentions."

She jumped to her feet. "I can't believe this. Are you certain? But—" She stared down at him, silent now. She turned and picked up her skirts and ran down the beach.

"Sophie! Come back here! Your damned feet!"

She ran faster. He, fool that he was, was worried because her damned feet weren't yet completely healed. He ran after her, and because he was stronger, his legs longer and unhampered by petticoats and skirts, he caught her quickly. He grabbed her arm and jerked her around to face him. He pulled her up against him and kissed her hard.

She struggled and jerked and tugged, but even when he released her mouth, he didn't let her go. "Do you prefer the hangman to marriage with me?"

She shook her head.

"Ah, but before the hangman you would doubtless have Sherman Cole slavering all over you when he rapes you."

"You don't have to say anything more."

"Good, because I was growing a bit impatient."

"This is absurd. I am very ordinary, Ryder. I am common. I have no secrets, nothing to interest you. I'm not ignorant because I have read a lot, a pastime I know gentlemen consider frivolous in women, mayhap even harmful for their brains. Believe me, I am nothing at all, merely a back-water colonial with no pretensions to anything. Why do you feel responsible for me? It is not your fault that my uncle is dead."

"Shut up." He kissed her again but she was struggling frantically against him, and he didn't want to risk hurting her ribs. He contented himself with merely holding her. He felt the heat of her, felt her breasts heaving against his chest, and he closed his eyes a moment.

"Do you forget how much you dislike me, Ryder? You think me a horrible woman. You scorn me and what you believe I am. Why are you doing this?"

He looked over her shoulder at the jagged black rocks that jutted out into the sea. "I have to. Call it my honor. Call it an attack of scruples. Samuel said I'd ruined you. Perhaps you are even now carrying my child. Now, in addition to your ruination and a possible babe, there is the matter of saving your neck. Now, come back with me. We both have a lot to do."

She fell into step beside him. She stared blindly ahead of her. She didn't believe that life could change so drastically and so very quickly.

She looked at his profile, pure and clean and strong. He would be her husband.

She shivered.

CHAPTER
═11═

THE VICAR, MR. Jacob Mathers, was a wizened little man with a shock of white hair sticking up like a rooster's comb. He knew all the gossip, naturally, but to his credit he took no part in it. Truth be told, he was more a listening man, particularly if he had a glass of rum punch in his hand. He listened and listened even more, and then disregarded the most of it. He had been a close friend of Samuel Grayson's for over twenty years, and thus, when an invitation to dinner arrived, he accepted gladly. After dinner was over and he learned what his other duty was to be, he blinked once, looked at Samuel for guidance and received a smile and a nod. If this was what Samuel believed was right, then Jacob would do it.

He would marry these two disparate people. When Ryder Sherbrooke had told him with a smile that he also wanted him to accept Kimberly Hall hospitality until the following afternoon, he readily agreed. He knew all about Sophia Stanton-Greville's reputation and that Sherman Cole wanted to arrest her very badly, for what reason he imagined he already knew. Human failings were, after all, his primary business. However, he wasn't a stupid man nor an unkind one, and curiosity wasn't necessarily a good thing. In this instance, he didn't really want to know all the ins and outs.

Everyone arranged themselves. Mr. Mathers had a remarkably deep voice, mellifluous and soothing, perhaps more so than usual because of the three glasses of rum punch he'd drunk at dinner. Soon, he was near the end of the brief ceremony. He was relieved that the young lady hadn't fainted. She was very pale, her eyes dark and blank, and her responses were barely above a whisper. As for Ryder Sherbrooke, the young man looked every inch the English aristocrat. He stood tall and straight; his voice was strong and steady. If he felt the same terror his bride felt, he was hiding it very well.

Ryder was wondering what Sophie was thinking. He knew well enough that she hadn't wanted to marry him. It was only the thought of being hung that had turned the tide. Not a very enlivening judgment for the groom. He doubted now that even if she'd believed she was pregnant with his child, she would have accepted him. Well, it would soon be done. He realized with something of a shock that he wanted it to be done. He wanted her as his wife. He wanted her safe, her and Jeremy.

He squeezed her hand when she whispered a very faint, "I do." Her refusal, his thinking continued as he looked down at her, must denote some sort of honor, some sort of honesty. Nor did she seem to want him, but that made sense to him given her experiences. He would soon change her mind about that. He wasn't a clod and she would be his wife. He thought of all the women he'd enjoyed since he'd come to manhood, how he'd pleasured them and teased them and laughed with them. And now, he must tie himself to the one woman who didn't want him. She was marrying him because she had no choice. At least they were even on that, he thought. He would never have considered marriage with her, despite the fact that she did, on occasion, give as good as she got. No, his honor demanded it, nothing more.

Sophie was pleased that she'd gotten her response out of her mouth. However, she was disgusted that she had sounded like a bleating goat, but the truth of the matter was, even though he was saving her, and she was well aware of what he was saving her from, he scared her to death.

Once he had her as his wife, he would be free to do anything he pleased with her. She knew that; her uncle had told her that often enough. She didn't believe he would beat her, no, Ryder wasn't that kind of man. What scared her was having him take her body, have it as his right, however and whenever he pleased. On the other hand, he'd already had her, and thus he'd seen her body, just as she'd seen his. Surely he hadn't hurt her. She'd felt nothing the next morning, not a bit of pain or discomfort. No, he hadn't hurt her.

And it would just be for one night.

She was scared. She fingered the soft muslin gown Coco had sewn for her throughout the afternoon. It was lovely and it was snowy white. That made her smile. "You'll look like a virgin sacrifice," he'd said when she'd shown him the nearly completed gown.

She wished the vicar would just be done with it. She felt sick to her stomach. She was terrified, not only of Ryder, but of Sherman Cole. She wondered if she and Jeremy truly would be aboard the ship tomorrow and be safe, once and for all.

She remembered when Ryder had come to fetch her for dinner. He'd come into the room, all elegant and handsome as the devil's right hand, and he'd just smiled at her.

"You're beautiful, you know that?"

She merely shrugged. "Passable, I would say."

"No, beautiful. Are you ready? The vicar is here. We'll have dinner

first, then the ceremony. I'm sorry about you not having anyone from
Camille Hall, but we can't risk it."

"You don't have to do this, Ryder."

"Be quiet," he said quite pleasantly, offered her his arm, and walked
beside her down the wide staircase.

Ryder felt her quiver when he said his vows. "Don't," Ryder said quietly. "Don't stiffen up on me. Trust me, Sophie. It will be over soon and
then nothing bad will ever touch you again."

She didn't believe him but it didn't seem to be the thing to say to him
now that he would be her husband. She saw Jeremy smiling just like he'd
been offered the world. Ryder had won him over with an ease that astounded her.

It was over. There were congratulations. Samuel looked delighted and
immensely relieved. Then he turned to Sophie, hugged her against him,
and said quietly, "It will be fine for you now, my dear. I have always believed that things happen for a reason. You and Jeremy were meant to
leave Jamaica and return to England. You will trust your new husband.
Once he realizes the right way, he embraces it without hesitation. Yes,
Sophia, trust him, for he's a very good man."

She looked over at her new husband. He was hugging Jeremy against
him and the boy was chattering faster than a magpie and Ryder was
laughing and nodding.

Suddenly, without warning, all the happy chatter began to die away.
Ryder looked up to see Sherman Cole standing in the doorway of the
salon.

Sophie wanted to sink into the mangrove swamp. She didn't move.
She watched Ryder stride over to Cole.

"What a pleasure, Mr. Cole. However, you weren't invited. What do
you want now?"

Sherman Cole looked around the room. He stared at Sophie, standing
there like a pale statue, in her wedding gown, her white wedding gown.
He saw Samuel standing there beside her, her arm in his, and he said,
"Good God, you think to protect the little slut by marrying her off? Has
that fool Grayson really married her? He actually married the little tart?"

Ryder sighed. "Did I not warn you before? You are slow of wit, sir, and
an unspeakable embarrassment."

"But he can't be married to her! Look here, Samuel, it will make no
difference! She murdered her poor uncle. I will come for her tomorrow,
once we've examined Burgess's body. You will have only one night with
her, no more, so be certain you enjoy it! And then it will be my turn, that
is to say, I will see that justice is well done and—"

Ryder hit him cleanly in the jaw. Sherman Cole went down in a graceless heap. Ryder grabbed the man beneath his arms and heaved and tugged until he'd managed to drag him behind a chair. His legs still stuck out. He pulled the chair out a bit more and shoved Cole completely behind it. Then he moved the chair back in place. He looked over at Sophie, grinned, and rubbed his hands together.

"That was fun," he said when he rejoined her. "Emile, when he rouses himself, why don't you see him back to Montego Bay. I like the notion that he believes Sophie is married to your father. He will remain unworried and quite pleased with himself."

"Now," Samuel said, "let us go into the dining room. I want to toast both of you with that champagne James unearthed for you."

She remained still and pale. Ryder frowned down at her. "Stop it," he said, and when she didn't, he pulled her against him and kissed her. Not hard, but very lightly, his mouth barely touching hers, gently pressing, but not demanding. Then he said into her mouth, "I am your husband. I will protect you. Cole won't touch you."

She was afraid. She didn't move. When he finally released her, he wasn't frowning, but he still looked thoughtful. She hadn't kissed him back, but then again, she'd just had another unpleasant shock.

"You know something, Sophie, I did indeed protect you this time. On the other hand, to be completely honest, I wanted very much to hit him, so I can't be certain that my motives were all that pure. But let's be kind and assume they were. Now, can I believe that you would likewise protect me?"

"I already did."

He grinned at her. "Yes, you were a marvel. Will you continue to be my Amazon? Will you continue to protect me?"

"You aren't Jeremy."

"No, I'm not. I'm your husband and, in the future scheme of things, I'm more important."

"Yes," she said on a sigh. "I will protect you, Ryder."

"Good."

Ryder looked back over his shoulder once. He saw Cole's feet sticking out from beneath the chair. What the devil had the man wanted? It was a long ride to and from Montego Bay. Had he merely come to gloat? To terrify Sophie? To try to intimidate the rest of them?

Ryder forgot Cole. Tonight he would have her. Very soon now. No more than three more hours and he would have her naked and in his arms and in his bed. He would have to sate himself on her to make up for the weeks they would be separated.

He was humming as he walked beside her into the dining room. He seated Sophie on his right hand then took the master's chair. He lifted her hand and kissed her fingers. She didn't move.

"Emile will take Cole away," he said. "Perhaps he'll find out how and what Cole found out and why he came here tonight."

"I wish I could have hit him," she said.

He was pleased. "Would you really? Well, perhaps I can find him again and bring him back to you. Show me your fist."

She did and he neatly tucked her thumb under. "Whenever you hit someone, don't let your thumb stick out. You could get it broken. That's it."

"You bruised your knuckles."

"Ah, but don't you see? One must weigh the bruises against the fun of it. Now, my dear, you're a new bride. Raise your glass and lightly touch it to mine. Yes, that's right. Now smile. Good."

She sipped the champagne. It was wonderful, cool and tart.

She took another longer drink.

Conversation at the table was brisk. As each new bottle of champagne was uncorked, the laughter and noise increased. The vicar recounted a jest about a saint who was accidentally sent to hell. He told it with all the enthusiasm of a devout sinner.

Ryder laughed until he looked at his wife. "You're too damned quiet. You ate almost no dinner."

"I didn't want this to happen," she said, eyes down on the plate with its slice of pineapple cake.

"It's happened. Get used to it. Accept it."

"I suppose there's nothing else to do," she said, and took another drink of her champagne.

"Are you planning to drink yourself insensible?"

"No, I don't think that's possible."

"Oh, it is, believe me. Young men do the most ridiculous things, you know, like drinking themselves into unconsciousness, singing at the top of their lungs even while they're falling flat on their faces under a table."

He was smiling at her charmingly, laughing, seducing her with the best weapons in his arsenal. It wasn't working.

"You're tired, Sophie?"

"Yes," she said, then realized the import of her words and actually jerked back in her chair.

"How are your ribs?"

"They hurt dreadfully as do my feet and—"

"You're a very bad liar. You didn't use to be, but you are now, now that I know you."

"You don't know me, Ryder. You truly don't."

"I will come to know you. It is something I want very badly. It's unfortunate we will be separated. I will give you a letter to present to my brother the earl once you arrive at Northcliffe Hall. Also I will give you sufficient funds so that you and Jeremy can rent a carriage at Southampton and several guards. Promise me you will hire guards."

She promised.

He was looking at the swell of her breasts above the soft lace over her bosom. "You're thin at the moment, but I don't mind. I'll fatten you up."

"Since I am with child, that will most certainly happen."

Lies, Ryder thought. It was damned difficult to keep up with them. Still, he said easily, "The child, as I've told you, isn't necessarily a foregone conclusion. It's possible that you're pregnant. I hope that if you aren't pregnant you won't be too disappointed."

"I don't feel well. I must be pregnant."

That was interesting, he thought. He sat back in his chair, twirling the stem of his champagne glass between his long fingers. "You know, Sophie, there's no reason for you to be embarrassed around me. No, please don't waste my time or yours denying it. I told you I know women. Please strive to remember that you're not a virgin since I took you. And I did look my fill at you. I even kissed that very cute birthmark of yours behind your left knee. So, you see, there is no need at all for embarrassment."

"That's true, I guess, but still—"

"Still what?"

"I wasn't really there when you did all those things to me."

"You will simply have to trust me."

"Trust you the way you trusted me?"

"All the past lurid machinations are over, all the druggings are over, though I still admit to a burgeoning of rage when I think of you and your uncle stripping me and offering me up to that other girl. What was her name, by the way?"

"Dahlia. She looked at you and said you were a treat."

When Ryder grinned she quickly added, "But not enough of a treat for my uncle not to pay her."

"Did you watch me with her, Sophie?"

"Just for a moment because my uncle said I had to, that you were the kind of man to share intimacies with his mistress and thus I had to be prepared to be intimate in my speech back to you, but I couldn't bear it, and left the cottage."

"It was a very nasty game. Now, my dear wife, you and I are going upstairs."

Not ten minutes later, she was staring at him across the bedchamber. He'd shut and locked the door. Then he was striding confidently toward her, smiling, looking at her with the victor's gleam in his blue eyes.

She did look like a virgin sacrifice, he thought, staring at her. He supposed it was at that moment he accepted the fact that she was indeed a virgin, that all her supposed lovers had enjoyed Dahlia, that Samuel had been right when he'd said that she simply wouldn't play the whore, no matter the cost.

He wondered briefly if he should tell her that she was still a virgin, and that he'd told her a magnificent lie to prevent her from marrying Samuel Grayson. Even as a silent thought, it didn't sound all that promising as a way to bring her around. It made him sound like a bastard, truth be told. No, no, he'd keep it to himself. He had all the time in the world to tell her whatever he wanted to tell her. The truth could wait a bit longer.

He took her in his arms. He didn't kiss her, just said as he looked down at her, "I know you have seen some of what men and women do together in bed. I know from firsthand experience that you know how to seduce a man, how to tease him until he's hard as a stone and willing to say anything, promise anything, to you. However, I know you've never experienced any of it, even with me, because of the odd circumstances. We are going very slowly, Sophie. I don't want you to hark back to the repugnant experiences you've had. They're not important now. Only you and I are important. Do you understand me?"

"I don't want this, Ryder. I need time."

"You will have all the time you wish after tonight, at least seven weeks of it. I'm not like those other pawing cretins. I will please you, I will make you forget all their annoying habits."

His hands were on her back, lightly stroking up and down, slowly, soothing, as if she were a child, as if she were a wary animal to be tamed. She saw Lord David, felt his hands on her, his mouth on hers. And Oliver Susson and Charles Grammond, and Dickey Mason, another man her uncle had ruined with her help. There were two others, one of them now dead, the other a drunkard who'd left Jamaica in disgrace. Dear God, it was too much. She hated it. She hated herself and she hated him for forcing her into this marriage. She pulled away from him suddenly, taking him by surprise, and he let her go.

She walked quickly to the balcony, not turning to face him until she was to the railing.

When she turned back, he was where she'd left him, standing in the middle of the room, only now he was taking off his coat. She froze, watching him. Next came his cravat. Then he was unfastening his shirt and vest. Then he sat down on a wicker chair and pulled off his boots. When he rose again, his hands on the buttons of his britches, she yelled, "No! What are you doing? Stop it!"

"Why?" he said. "I can't offend your maiden's sensibilities. Good

God, woman, you've seen me naked. Not only have you seen me naked, you've seen my sex swelled. You've seen my eyes glazed with lust. There's nothing new for you. Didn't you see all the other men as well?"

She stared at him, unmoving. He was soon naked, and as he had been before, his sex was swelled, but he made no move toward her. Instead, he held out his hand. "Come here, Sophie. It's time we began our married life together."

"I don't feel well," she said.

"Very well," he said more to himself than to her, and walked toward her.

Her wedding gown defeated her. She tried to duck around him but the skirts tangled between her legs and she couldn't move quickly enough. She tripped on the lace hem and felt the material rip beneath her left arm. She hadn't meant to hurt the gown. It was so beautiful, she hadn't meant it. Ryder's impatient voice brought her back to another misery.

"No more fighting me, Sophie. It's done. You're my wife. No more, do you hear me? We've only tonight and I want to consummate this damned marriage."

"Let me go."

"Not on your life. I'm going to undress you, Sophie. You will not fight me. You took a vow to obey me and it's time you took that vow seriously."

She raised her head and looked at him straightly. "From my uncle's domination to yours. I want to be free, don't you understand? A man is born with the taste of freedom in his mouth, but the chances that a woman can ever gain freedom are remote. It's just as I knew it would be. You're no different from the others. All of you are animals, selfish and brutal."

"I'm quite different from the others. I'm your husband until the day I stick my spoon in the wall."

She was standing stiff as a pole, watching him.

He had, suddenly, the most awful presentiment that she would never come to want him. No, that was absurd. He wouldn't allow it.

He sighed. "All right. Sit down. Let's talk for a little while."

She sat and he saw the relief flood her face, damn her. "Now, do you have more proclamations of men's dishonesty and general brutishness?"

She didn't look at him. She said at last, "I suppose it is stupid of me. You already took me and looked your fill at me and I suppose you didn't hurt me because the next morning I felt nothing. But you see, I didn't know you were looking at me, I didn't know anything." She raised her head and looked at him straightly. "It is difficult, Ryder."

"I'll make it easier. All you have to do is trust me. Now, about your freedom. I shan't lock you up, Sophie, if you believe that's what men do to their wives. For the most part I imagine you will do precisely as you please. If by freedom you mean you can't sail to the ends of the earth by yourself, that's quite true and the reasons are obvious. You are a woman and thus weaker than a man. You could be hurt. But in the future who knows? Perhaps we will visit faraway places together."

It wasn't at all what she'd meant by freedom but it didn't matter now. It was moot.

"I won't ever hurt you, Sophie, or beat you or threaten you. I think men who do are utter bastards. Your uncle was a conscienceless villain. He wasn't normal; he was twisted. I'm not like that. None of my friends are like that. I will never hurt you."

"I have no reason to believe you."

"You have no reason to disbelieve me." Ryder rose and offered her his hand. "Come inside. It's time to go to bed. I'll help you with the gown."

No choice, she thought. No more choices at all. She went with him. Soon her gown was open on her back and he was gently easing it down. He dropped a light kiss on her shoulder and felt her flinch.

"Take the gown off now. I assume you will want to keep it since it's your wedding gown. Doubtless you can repair that rip. It doesn't look too bad to me. Do you have space in your valise for it?"

"Yes."

She wanted to mend the gown now, truth be told. The night stretched out before her in a terrifying long number of minutes. But even Sophie knew from the look on Ryder's face that she'd pushed him far enough. She saw her uncle's face in its stead, the fury darkening his eyes when she'd pushed him. She remembered the pain of his fists, the rippling of her flesh when they struck. She was soon standing only in her chemise and stockings.

"You didn't wear slippers at your own wedding," he said, bemused. "I had thought you were taller. Let's get those stockings off, I want to look at your feet."

She sat on the edge of the bed wearing only her white muslin chemise, Ryder on his haunches in front of her, completely oblivious of the fact he didn't have any clothes on.

"Your feet are healing nicely," he said. "There are only a couple of cuts that still look tender. On board ship, don't wear slippers unless you have to and be careful of the decks, you could get splinters. Now let me look at your ribs."

He took her hand and drew her upright. He bent down to take the hem of her chemise in his hands. He stopped cold. He wanted to howl and laugh at the same time at the damnable irony. It was his wedding night and he'd been done in.

There was blood on her chemise.

"You don't feel well, Sophie?"

"Not very well. I'm not lying to you, Ryder. My stomach is cramping a bit."

"No wonder," he said and sighed very deeply. "I'm sorry if this disappoints you, but you're not pregnant."

She gasped as she looked down at herself. She turned white.

"No need to be embarrassed. Have you cloths?"

She shook her head.

"All right. I'll send Coco to you. Would you like some laudanum? Is the cramping bad?"

"No. Yes."

Fifteen minutes later Ryder stood beside the bed, wearing a dressing gown, looking down at his wife's pale face. Despite the heat she'd pulled the sheet up to her nose. He'd forced the laudanum down her throat, saying in a very irritated voice, "I swear not to ravish you whilst you're unconscious." To which she'd replied in an equally irritated voice, "Why not? You did before."

That had stopped him cold. He looked down at her now. "So much for the vaunted Sherbrooke luck," he said more to himself than to her, and lifted the sheet. He eased in beside her. "No, Sophie, don't have a fit and don't squirm around so much, you might fall on the floor. I won't force you to have me tonight. Hush now. The laudanum should be taking effect soon. That's right, just close your eyes and breathe deeply. Would you like me to rub your belly?"

He didn't expect an answer and he didn't get one. A short time later he heard her breathing evenly into sleep.

He took her hand in his.

The sky was beginning to lighten into morning. Ryder stood on deck of the *Harbinger* beside Sophie. "Don't forget to give my brother the letter," he said for the third time. "And don't worry. He will take good care of you and Jeremy. My mother could be a bit of a problem, but she's unaccountable. If she chooses not to be charming to you, simply ignore her, all right? You'll have quite an ally in Alex, I doubt not. Have you put the money I gave you in a safe place?"

"Yes, Ryder."

"Does your belly feel all right this morning?"

"Yes."

"You promise to hire two guards at Southampton?"

"Yes."

He frowned at her. "You think I'm treating you like a child, don't you?"

"Yes."

"Look, Sophie, I've never had a wife before, never really had any responsibilities of this sort before except of course for the chil—" He broke that off and shook his head at himself. He couldn't seem to keep his tongue quiet in his mouth around her. He would tell her about the children, but in his own time, in his own way. She was looking at him, an eyebrow lifted in silent question, but he merely shook his head, and continued. "In any case, you and Jeremy are mine now and I want to make certain you will be all right."

"We will be fine. Don't worry. Are you sure your family won't toss us out on our ears?"

"I won't lie to you. They will be very surprised. I hadn't planned to marry, at least for a very long time. I would appreciate it, Sophie, if you would try to make my family believe you are at least a bit fond of me, that you don't look upon me as a ravening beast."

Captain Mallory appeared at Ryder's elbow. There was a wide grin on his broad, ugly face. " 'Tis time for you to remove yourself, Mr. Sherbrooke. Your bride will be fine. Give her another hug and a kiss and get off my ship."

He smiled down at Sophie. "Can I have a kiss?"

She raised her face, her lips pursed. He lightly touched his fingertip to her lips, pressing slightly, then he kissed her very gently, with very little pressure. He felt a shudder in her but didn't know if it was from fear, nervousness, or wonderful lust. Somehow he doubted the latter.

"You will be careful," he said yet again, patted her cheek, walked over to Jeremy, hugged the boy tightly, ruffled his hair, and said, "Keep her spirits up, Jeremy. I'll return to England as soon as all this nonsense is taken care of. Be a good boy. Another thing. I'm quite fond of you so you will be careful of yourself as well."

He strode down the gangplank. He watched it hauled onto the ship's deck. He watched the sun rise full in the sky now and stood very still listening to Captain Mallory shouting his orders. He waved a final time to his bride and his new brother-in-law.

He continued to wait on the dock until the ship was gone from view. He turned then, smiling. She was safe now, completely safe. He whistled as he mounted his horse to return to Kimberly Hall.

At one o'clock that afternoon Sherman Cole arrived. Ryder smiled as he watched the man dismount and walk toward the veranda where he sat, a glass of lemonade in his hand. Samuel and Emile came out of the house and Ryder felt the relief radiating from them.

"What an unexpected surprise," Ryder said, and yawned deeply. He didn't rise. "Have you come to bring more discord, make more threats?"

"Damn you to hell, Sherbrooke!"

Ryder's eyebrow went up. "I beg your pardon? I truly didn't strike you that hard, though you deserved it."

"I was certain you'd lied, I would have wagered all I possessed that you had lied, damn you. And you did, of course, to protect that little slut."

"Where are all your bully boys?" Emile asked quickly before Ryder could rise from his chair and flatten Sherman Cole again.

"They're looking for Thomas."

"I wager you'll have to pay him quite a bit of money once you catch up to him. He probably won't trust you. You'll have to convince him that you want him to help you hang Miss Stanton-Greville."

"Pay him! Ha, I will hang the bastard! He lied to me, he made a fool of me."

Now this was the wrong play, Ryder thought, blank-brained. This is a comedy, not a tragedy.

"What do you mean?" Samuel asked.

"Burgess wasn't shot, nor was he stabbed, as Sherbrooke here said. He was garroted. Dammit, she couldn't have killed him, she doesn't have the strength."

He turned away, stomped to his horse, mounted, and rode away, never once looking back.

Ryder didn't move. "Dear God," he said at last, "I didn't have to marry her. I didn't have to ship her and Jeremy back to England. To be only twenty-five years old and be done in by irony."

"It's better done," Samuel said. "One never knows what Cole will do next."

But Ryder was immersed in contemplation of his fate. Well, perhaps it wouldn't be such a bad fate. One would have to see about that. He sighed and rose. He shook his head and said, "Garroted, the bastard was garroted."

He shook his head again. "I'll be damned," he said, and walked to the stables.

CHAPTER
═12═

The English Channel, seven weeks later

SOPHIE AND JEREMY stood side by side on deck, the fog-laden wind blowing into their faces, tightly holding the wooden railing because the water was choppy, the waves splashing high and rocking even the solid barkentine with their force. Jeremy was nearly squealing with excitement because he'd been the first to see the English shoreline through the thick fog bank. Gravesend, he'd shouted. As for Sophie, she wanted to shout hallelujahs as the English coast neared. She felt equal parts of anticipation and belly-deep fear as she watched the billowing fog bank just off port. Nearly home, but not really hers and Jeremy's home in Fowey, but Ryder's home—Northcliffe Hall.

The trip had been long and uneventful. Captain Mallory and his first mate, Mr. Mattison, both puff-chested Scotsmen who had nearly identical bald heads, had kept Jeremy and her entertained with the best tall tales they'd ever heard.

Sophie had tried to structure the days as best she could. She gave Jeremy French lessons an hour each morning. Captain Mallory tutored Jeremy in astronomy and navigation, the first mate taught him geography and gave him access to his collection of novels and plays that filled his small cabin to overflowing. Jeremy was nearly through the Restoration. As for Sophie, she too had nearly read her way through all the first mate's books as well. She occasionally wondered what she'd do when she turned the last page and closed the last book.

One afternoon several days before, Sophie and Jeremy were playing chess in their small cabin. A light rain splattered against the single porthole. The room was warm. Sophie played with verve and enthusiasm, but not much strategy. Jeremy, on the other hand, excelled in patience and tactics. He invariably beat her soundly, but it was slow torture, and Jeremy was heard to groan frequently.

She said after she'd moved her queen's bishop, "We will be home soon. Rather, we will arrive in Southampton."

"Yes, Ryder told me that a carriage would get us to Northcliffe Hall all in one day. He didn't want us to have to stop at an inn for the night because we're alone. He said I had to grow another foot at least before I could protect you properly." Jeremy smiled then and added, "Ryder's going to teach me how to fight."

"I'm delighted it pleases you so, but heed me, love, one doesn't necessarily need a man. I'm not a fool or helpless."

"Of course you're not like most girls," Jeremy said, not looking up at her, his entire attention now on the position of his pieces and his burgeoning strategy. "Ryder said you'd say something like that. He also said that he was responsible for both of us now and that was the end to it."

"Perhaps you would like to discuss some of the plays both of us have read."

Jeremy easily accepted her change of subject. "I was reading one of the Restoration plays and Mr. Mattison saw it. I thought he'd throw it overboard he was so upset. He turned red in the face and actually sputtered at me. Even the top of his head turned red. It was a remarkable sight."

Sophie chuckled. "Some of those plays are fairly racy. Perhaps you'd best show me what you plan to read before you read it."

Jeremy frowned as he looked up at his sister. "I've got to learn all about men and women sometime, Sophie. In the plays they act pretty silly and do the most outlandish things. As for the other part of it, it just seems strange to me."

"I think you're right about the strange part," Sophie said. She thought of Ryder and felt a pang of something—guilt? Anger? She wasn't certain. She did know, however, that she missed him—his wit, his outrageousness, the way he teased her until her eyes nearly crossed with rage. She looked up when Jeremy moved his queen's bishop pawn.

"Oh ho, it appears you want to trample my center." She moved her king's knight, a mindless move really, then sat back in her chair, her arms folded over her chest. "That should take care of your foolish hopes."

Jeremy said as he fiddled with a rook, "You're not very happy, Sophie. You miss Ryder, don't you? I know I do. He's a great brother-in-law. I'm glad you married him. I'm glad we left Jamaica, because we are English, you know. But still it's kind of scary." He finally released the rook and moved his queen's bishop instead. "Do you think his family will like us?"

"I pray so, Jeremy." Nor did she miss Jamaica. All the happiness she'd experienced on Jamaica could be weighed in her left hand.

"Well, I don't see why they wouldn't like us. We're nice and we know how to use our forks at the dinner table. You shouldn't have moved that knight. It was a bad move. I'm not just going to trample your center. I don't have to. Checkmate, Sophie."

"Why," she said aloud, "don't I ever learn?"

Sophie shook away the memory. She prayed every night that she and Jeremy wouldn't be shunted aside by Ryder's powerful brother, Douglas Sherbrooke. After that she simply stared off into space. She didn't know what to pray for. She couldn't begin to imagine her future. The wind whipped her hair into her eyes and she slapped it away.

Seven interminable weeks. It was nearly over. She wondered how much longer it would be before Ryder returned home. She would have to be a wife to him, whatever that would mean.

She immediately shied away from that.

Jeremy waved to Clancey, the third mate, a young man full of high spirits and liking for children. "Aye," he'd told Sophie at the beginning of the long voyage, "I was one of nine nippers, and there was only me ma to see to us. Don't ye worry about Jeremy here. He be a good lad. I'll see he don't go headfirst into the briny deep." Sophie liked him. He appeared utterly disinterested in her; some of the other sailors looked to be interested but they kept their distance, thanks to a frank discussion the captain had given them. "As the only woman on board, ma'am," he'd told her, "you will still be careful." And she had.

She was bored. She was also worried.

She made herself dizzy trying to structure the future for her and Jeremy.

Southampton at eight o'clock on a drizzly, foggy morning was an alien landscape with men yelling on the docks, drays and wagons of all sizes being loaded and unloaded. As it turned out, the first mate, Mr. Mattison, escorted them to the Outrigger Inn and hired a carriage and two outriders, just as Ryder had demanded.

Ryder had his way even here. She'd had no choice in the matter. She smiled up at Mr. Mattison and offered him her hand. "Thank you. You were kind to us. Good-bye."

Jeremy begged to ride on top of the carriage with the coachman, but Sophie said he couldn't until after the fog burned off and the sun came out.

The weather remained horrible.

Jeremy fidgeted until Sophie released him to ride with the coachman. It was after a lunch of codfish and strawberries that Sophie's stomach rebelled. Four hours later when the carriage pulled into the long winding drive of Northcliffe Hall, there was no one inside the carriage. Sophie and Jeremy sat huddled together against the drizzling rain, the driver pressed against Jeremy's other side.

An hour before Sophie had ceased to care. She felt trickles of rain snake down the back of her neck. She was shuddering from cold. There was gooseflesh on her arms.

"Goodness, Sophie, it's so big!"

She looked and swallowed. Northcliffe Hall was overwhelming, a huge Palladian mansion of three stories. She couldn't imagine real people living in that awesome structure. The two outriders, bored and wondering why the devil their escort had been needed in the first place—good hell, the girl had ridden on top like a serving wench—accepted payment from Sophie and took themselves off. As for the coachman, he scratched his head, stared from Sophie to Jeremy and back again and said, "Well, miss, this is the fancy cove's abode what ye wanted to come to. Northcliffe 'All. All right an' tight. Be ye sure this is where ye should be?"

Sophie wanted very much to say no, but she merely nodded, paid the man, and watched him bowl down the drive. She and Jeremy were left in front of the wide, deep stairs of the mansion, their two paltry valises sitting forlornly beside them on the gravel drive. Rain dripped off the end of her nose.

Had Sophie but had more than the hundred pounds Ryder had given her, she would have turned on her heel and left immediately. She would have walked to Fowey. She would have carried Jeremy to Fowey when he got tired of walking. But again she had no choice. She stood there for another minute, feeling more alone than she ever had before in her life, just staring up at the three-story mansion with ivy rich and green up the west side of it until Jeremy tugged on her sleeve.

"Sophie, I'm wetter than a wharf rat. Let's go in."

She shivered, picked up both their valises, and began climbing the deeply grooved marble steps. "That sounds like a verbal gift from Clancey. Contrive to forget it, Jeremy."

"Do you think they'll let us stay?" Jeremy whispered, his eyes large now with fright as they neared the incredibly huge double doors. There were large brass lion heads for doorknobs. The lions' mouths even had brass teeth. The doors looked more solid than a live oak tree.

"Of course," she said, and began another series of devout prayers.

There was an overhang just in front of the massive doors and Sophie pulled Jeremy out of the cold drizzle. She looked at the bellpull. There was no hope for it. The poor relations had arrived.

She pulled the bellcord with all her might. She jumped at the full-bodied ringing that seemed to reverberate throughout the mansion. They hadn't long to wait.

The door opened without a creak or a groan. A footman in dark blue and green livery stood before them. He was small and slender and he didn't say anything, just stared at them and blinked.

He was an older man, as bald as Captain Mallory and Mr. Mattison had been. He opened his mouth then and said, "Would you care to go to the servants' entrance?"

"No," Sophie said, and forced a smile. She could well imagine how the two of them looked.

"I saw you arrive, both of you sitting on top of the coach. Perhaps you're looking for employment? Then you must speak to Mrs. Peacham. As for the boy, I don't—"

"We are here to see the Earl of Northcliffe. You will show us to him immediately, if you please."

Her speech was upper class, no doubt about that, but there was a faint lilt to it, a sort of strange drawl that Jamieson couldn't identify. So she wanted the earl, did she? She and the boy looked like beggars. Wet beggars. He could tell the girl's gown was too short. Doubtless they wanted charity. The gall of these two. He drew himself up, ready to tell the minx what she could do with her demands when there came another man's voice. "What have we here, Jamieson?"

"Ah, Mr. Hollis, sir. These two just climbed off a carriage box. This one here's demanding to see the earl. I was just endeavoring to—"

Mr. Hollis looked at Sophie. She looked back at him. He smiled and stepped aside, ushering them in.

"Do come in, ma'am, and the lad too. Ah, the weather isn't what one would wish, is it? You are both wet and cold. Come with me. Jamieson, take the bags, please, and place them at the foot of the stairs."

"Who is he?" Jeremy asked behind his hand. "Is he the earl?"

"I don't know."

"This is all very strange, Sophie."

Their footsteps resounded in the immense entry hall. A huge chandelier hung overhead, its crystals glittering in the dim afternoon light. Italian black and white marble squares stretched in all directions. There were paintings on every wall, and even several suits of armor set on either side of a huge fireplace. Sophie remembered their snug Georgian house in Fowey. They'd had a chandelier there as well, only it wasn't as large as a room. When Ryder had spoken of his home, she'd never imagined anything like this. There were maids and more footmen, all looking at them, and, Sophie knew, whispering about them behind their hands.

She wanted to be sick. Her chin went up.

Mr. Hollis led them down a vast corridor into a small room that, luckily, had a blazing fire burning in the grate.

"I will inform the earl of your arrival. Now, may I give him your name, ma'am?"

"Yes," Sophie said. Suddenly, she grinned, for it really was too much.

"Please tell the earl that his sister-in-law and brother-in-law have arrived from Jamaica."

The man's dark eyes never registered anything but calm acceptance. If she wasn't mistaken, there was even a sudden gleaming in his eyes. "I see. Do remove your cloaks and dry yourselves. I am quite certain the earl will wish to see you immediately."

They were left alone in the small room. The draperies were drawn against the chill afternoon. It looked to be a lady's salon, with its feminine desk and pale green and yellow furnishings. There was a pile of books on the floor beside a comfortable wing chair. It was a lovely room and so unlike any room in Jamaica.

It was so bloody cold. She'd forgotten how very different England was from Jamaica. She helped Jeremy off with his cloak, then removed her own. They stood in front of the fireplace, hands extended to the flames.

"You did that well, Sophie. I was so scared I couldn't think of a word to say."

"They can't shoot us, at least I don't think they can. But what they will do—" She shrugged, saying no more. Her tongue felt as if it had a cramp in it.

The door flew open and in strode a young girl with thick, curly brownish-blond hair and the most beautiful blue eyes Sophie had ever seen. Actually, they were exactly the same color as Ryder's eyes; the girl's hair matched Ryder's as well. She looked exuberant, full of life—just as Ryder did—and she was grinning at them. "Ho! What's this? I saw you climb off that carriage. My, you're wet and doubtless miserable. I myself am so very tired of this blasted rain. Do forgive me, but I'm Sinjun, you know, the earl's sister. Who are you?"

Sophie had to grin back. There wasn't really a choice. This girl was exactly as Ryder had described her. She was tall, lanky, lovely really, and friendly as a puppy.

Sophie stepped toward her. "I am Sophia Stanton-Greville. Well no, that's no longer correct. I am Sophie Sherbrooke. I am Ryder's wife and this is Jeremy, my brother."

Sinjun could only stare at the wet, frowzy girl standing there in front of her in a girlish muslin gown that was too short for her, a gown that Ryder would have found utterly distasteful.

This was excessively odd.

"Oh dear, is it true? It's difficult to believe, you know. Ryder married! Imagine such a thing. It leaves the brain numb. I never thought he would take a wife because he absolutely adores so many ladies and—"

"I believe that is quite enough, Sinjun."

The earl, Sophie thought, and went very still. He didn't look at all like either Ryder or Sinjun. He was massively built, all lean and muscular, very tall, his shoulders broad as the front door, and dark as a Moor, his hair black as midnight, his eyes just as dark. He looked ruthless and mean and severe and she couldn't imagine him doing anything but tossing her and Jeremy out on their wet ears. He was looking at her, taking in every detail. Sophie knew what she and Jeremy looked like. It wasn't promising. Her chin went higher. She remembered Ryder telling her that his brother, the earl, would have demolished her in no time had he been the one to come to Jamaica. He wouldn't have enjoyed playing her games as Ryder had.

Then, quite suddenly, the earl smiled. It changed him utterly. Sophie heard Jeremy release a pent-up breath. "Forgive my sister here for bombarding you the moment you arrived. It wasn't well done of you, brat. Now, I am Douglas Sherbrooke, Ryder's brother. Welcome to Northcliffe Hall."

Sophie gave him a curtsy, saying quietly, "I am Sophia and this is my brother, Jeremy. We left Ryder on Jamaica to conclude business, but he will return here very soon. It is all very complicated." She paused, not another word swirling to the forefront of her brain, thrust her hand into her reticule and retrieved Ryder's letter. She thrust it at the earl.

He smiled at her quizzically as he took the letter, saying, "Please be seated. Sinjun, make yourself useful and have Mrs. Peacham send some tea and some cakes. Our guests look a bit tired."

"Yes, Douglas," Sinjun said, rubbing her hands together. "Wait until Alex hears about this, she's my other sister, you know. I just—"

"Go, brat!"

Sinjun went, but not before she winked at Sophie.

"Forgive my sister's impertinence," Douglas said as he opened the letter, "but no one has ever managed to curb her tongue."

"Her tongue is friendly. I didn't mind."

"Nor did I," said Jeremy.

"Actually, I don't either. Excuse me a moment," the earl said, and lowered his eyes to the letter.

Sophie didn't know what Ryder had written. She had wondered many times during the voyage, one time even going so far as to hold the envelope over a candle hoping to loosen the wax. She'd drawn it back. With her luck, if she did open it, it would show and the earl would believe her a sham. She pictured him pointing a long finger at her as she was dragged out the door. She stood there, stiff and miserable, waiting like a condemned prisoner in the dock. The earl read the letter through very slowly. When he looked at her there was a softening about his mouth. There was also a glittering in his dark eyes. He looked very human now. Sophie noted these changes with relief. She had learned to read men quite well in the past nearly two years.

"Ryder tells about some nasty business that has nearly been concluded satisfactorily."

Sophie hoped she wasn't the major part of the nasty business. "I see," she said, waiting, wary and very still.

"He also writes that I am to call you Sophie. He writes that Sophia sounds like a Russian princess who has ice water in her veins. He says you're warm and sweet."

"He wrote that?"

"My brother always gets to the kernel of the matter, Sophie. He doesn't waste time on trivialities. As for you, Jeremy, Ryder says you are the best of brother-in-laws and I am to immediately put you on a horse."

"Ryder really said that? But it is too bad of him, sir, for I am his *only* brother-in-law!"

"Yes, that is true as well. He requests that I look after the two of you until he comes home."

Both brother and sister merely stared at the Earl of Northcliffe. Douglas Sherbrooke realized fully that they'd been perfectly terrified of him. When Hollis had told him that his sister-in-law was waiting to see him, he'd laughed and wondered aloud at the gall of some of Ryder's women. "A child is with her, you say? Goodness, a boy about ten years old? It doesn't make sense, Hollis. Ryder isn't old enough to have fathered a boy that age!" But Hollis hadn't laughed with him. He'd looked utterly austere and said as he looked past Douglas's right shoulder, "Do not treat her badly, my lord. You are quite wrong. She is who she claims to be."

It was true they both looked like drowned urchins. It was even truer that Sophie wasn't a remarkable beauty, not like the women Ryder would normally rave about. But there was something lovely in the cast of her features, and he wasn't blind to the pride and stubbornness in her, or the character. His brother had married her. It was difficult to accept even with the evidence standing in front of him. It was difficult to accept even though Hollis had been convinced immediately. The earl shook himself and tried to find something to say. He was rescued by the entrance of Mrs. Peacham herself, the Sherbrooke housekeeper for twenty years.

"Master Ryder's wife, just imagine that! But you're not at all comfortable, are you, in those wet clothes? Oh, but aren't you a sweetling and just look at all that pretty hair! Goodness me, I'm Mrs. Peacham, and I'll take care of you and you'll not have to worry about a thing."

Sophie was overcome. She nodded. "I'm not all that wet now."

"Ah, and here is Hollis. You wish to meet the wife as well, Hollis?"

"Most assuredly, my lord. I am Hollis, ma'am. If you require anything at all, you have but to ask me."

Tea was dispensed. Mrs. Peacham and Hollis took themselves off. Sinjun was joyfully consuming scones and nudging Jeremy in his ribs as she pointed out the tastiest ones to him. He'd already moved closer to her.

Sophie took a bite of lemon cake. It was delicious. She looked nervously at the earl, who was thoughtfully studying her. The room was warm and pleasant. They'd been welcomed. They'd even been fed. Ryder had told his brother to call her Sophie. He'd told his brother to give Jeremy a horse. It was suddenly too much. Then, the earl smiled at her and offered her more tea.

Sophie burst into tears.

"Oh dear!"

"Sinjun," the earl said calmly, "I want you to take Jeremy to the stables and select a suitable mount for him. Go now. If it's still raining, why then, describe the horses to him."

Sinjun grabbed Jeremy's hand and nearly dragged him from the room. She said fiercely, leaning down to his ear, "Don't worry. Douglas will take care of your sister. I imagine she has had a very difficult time. She will be all right, Douglas will see to it. He's wonderful, you know."

Douglas waited a moment, then said to Ryder's weeping wife, "You have done very well. I believe I myself would have cracked under the pressure of coming here to a strange house filled with people you don't know, people who could make your life quite unpleasant. But you're here now and the people here accept you and welcome you and everything will be fine."

Sophie hiccuped and wiped the back of her hand across her eyes. The earl handed her a handkerchief and she blew her nose.

He moved back to lean against the very feminine desk, his legs crossed at the ankles, his arms crossed over his chest.

"Ryder stands the same way," Sophie said. "Only he does it to intimidate me. You look fine doing it."

Douglas smiled. "My brother tries to intimidate you? How peculiar of him. Usually Ryder has but to use his charm to receive any gift he wishes."

Sophie blew her nose again, then tucked the handkerchief into her sleeve. "That's what he kept telling me."

"Ryder had to remind you of his considerable charm? How very odd of him. Would you like to meet my wife now? By that time Mrs. Peacham will have prepared a room for Jeremy and aired your bedchamber. Later, if you wish, you can tell me more of what occurred on Jamaica. As I told you, Ryder wrote of important things, not the other superfluous things."

Sophie nodded and tried to swipe some of the wrinkles from her gown. She still looked wilted but she was nearly dry now. She caught a look of herself in a mirror in the hallway. She looked a fright. She made a distressed sound, her hand flying to a strand of hair that hung damply down the side of her face.

The earl said easily, "Don't mind that mirror. It lies always. My wife has remarked upon it. Even my wife's sister, Melissande, who is so beautiful it makes your teeth ache just to look at her, avoids that mirror. I regret that my wife can't come here to meet you. We must go to her. Also, you don't have a red nose. She does."

The Countess of Northcliffe was in bed, propped up with pillows. Her nose was indeed red, her eyes watery, and she was sniffling. Her hair was a marvelous shade of red and was braided loosely around a very pretty, pale face.

The introductions were made.

The countess stared at the girl who stood still as a Sherbrooke garden statue.

"As least you're wearing clothes," the countess said.

"I beg your pardon, my dear?"

"Oh, I was just thinking that Sophie is standing as still as our garden statues."

"And the statues, Sophie, are, unfortunately, quite bare of fig leaves and of shirts or trousers. My wife's mind has slipped a notch with this cold. It brought her low two days ago. She dislikes being kept in bed; she desires to be up and about, ordering all of us around mercilessly."

"He adores to tease me. Goodness, you've been crying. What happened? Douglas, weren't you kind to her?"

"No, Alex, I was vicious. I berated her for daring to come here. I told her she could sleep for two nights in the stables but then she would have to leave. However, I did give her my handkerchief."

"Well, it is true that Ryder actually marrying a wife is enough to overset one's thinking."

"He couldn't very well marry a monkey, Alex. I will bring up Jeremy later to see you. Keep your distance, Sophie, I don't wish Ryder to return home only to find his bride in bed with a red nose and a foul disposition."

The earl patted Sophie's arm, gave his wife a mock bow. "If my wife makes you uncomfortable, simply tell her to mind her own business. On the other hand, I have always found her utterly discreet and an excellent confidante. She also has an adequate sense of humor." He touched Sophie's arm once again, then took himself off.

"He is wonderful, is he not?" the countess remarked.

"That's what Sinjun said."

"It's true. Even when he behaves in a manner that provokes one to the point of madness and wanting to cosh him, he is still wonderful. I sound besotted, don't I? Well, I daresay it will go away in twenty or so years."

"I have wanted to cosh Ryder since the first moment I met him."

"Just excellent," said the countess and blew her nose. She then sneezed, lay back against her pillows and moaned. "I am so sorry not to be able to see to your comfort. But Douglas, you know, I'll wager at this very moment, he's ensuring that a maid will be assigned to you and that she will see to your clothes and that one of the footmen will see to your brother—Jeremy? Yes, a very nice name, yours as well. Please, sit down and tell me all about Ryder. That's right. Now you're more comfortable."

"He isn't wonderful!"

Alex merely looked at her new sister-in-law. "I see," she said slowly. "Do tell me more."

Sophie felt an ungrateful fool. She bowed her head and her hands fidgeted with her skirt. "I'm sorry. He is your brother-in-law and you must be fond of him. It's just that he married me only to save me from being hung. He didn't want to. He doesn't even like me. It all came about because he felt sorry for me. I do think he came to believe that I was indeed a virgin, at least before he drugged me and took me to the cottage and . . . and took off my clothes and did other things, except I don't remember because, as I said, he had drugged me."

Alex said not a word. Suddenly she felt miraculously better. She even sat up higher against her pillows. She didn't have to blow her nose. Her brain felt clear as a summer sky. Her silence was not uncomfortable. She smiled at Sophie, and Sophie, without a whimper, gave it up. "It's not that he's unkind or cruel or anything like that. Indeed, he saved me as many times as I saved him, no, more times, to be truthful. It's just that I am afraid of him and I didn't want to marry any man even though he said there was no reason to be embarrassed because he'd already done everything he'd wanted to me. He kept telling me to trust him but how could I given all that had happened?"

"I see," Alex said again. She waited, but Sophie said no more. Well, it didn't matter. This was fascinating and Alex didn't doubt that there would be more confidences very soon. She said quite easily, "This is now your home. I hope you will be happy here. There is only one person who could perhaps be a bit troublesome to your peace of mind and that is your mother-in-law, mine as well, more's the pity. But too much pleasantness would likely prove boring. She keeps me on my toes. She detests me, but I don't pay her much mind. She wanted Douglas to marry my sister, Melissande, but—Ah, but it's as complicated a tale as yours is, I fear. You and I will be able to entertain each other in both the tellings. In any case,

I won't be able to protect you for a couple of days. Lady Lydia just might take a liking to you, but I doubt it. Hers is not a particularly amiable disposition. Ah, here's Douglas. Oh, yes, Sophie, you are taller than I, but perhaps my maid can alter several of my gowns to fit you until we can bring a seamstress here."

"Oh no, I couldn't!"

But the countess said in the most imperious voice, "Don't be a ninny. The last thing we need is to have Lady Lydia see you in a gown like the one you're wearing, and she will forever relegate you to the underbelly of females."

Douglas laughed. "She's right, you know. After I have shown you to your bedchamber, you will return here and get yourself properly begowned. I will endeavor to keep my mother occupied until dinner." Even as he said the words, he sounded uncertain. Sophie could only stare at him, this man who looked as if he were master of the world. He walked to the bed, leaned down and kissed his wife's mouth, then said into her ear, "Many seams will need to be taken in, sweetheart. Your miraculous bosom is one of a kind, you know."

Sophie heard him. She stared some more, she couldn't help it. This stern man Ryder said would destroy her before breakfast was teasing his wife about her bosom? Perhaps, just perhaps, she didn't know men as well as she believed she did.

The earl straightened, gently ran his knuckles down his wife's cheek, then said to Sophie, "We will leave her to her misery for a while. You can return to take care of clothing in an hour, all right?"

Sophie nodded. There was nothing else to do.

CHAPTER
═══13═══

"WHAT IS GOING on here, Alexandra? I was told by Jerkins, who was told by Dora, who had overheard Mrs. Peacham talking to Hollis, that Ryder had married. Married! It is absurd. It can't, simply can't be true. It's one of his floozy women trying to pass herself off as a decent person and fool us. She wants money, her sort always does. I even heard there is a child involved. This is outside of too much. I'm here to assist you in removing her, Alexandra. You're sick and thus I am not surprised that the girl has taken you in. Good grief, is this she? She's in your bedchamber? She looks just as I thought she would—a slut, a fright, a sham. Get out, young woman, get out!"

The woman was actually shooing at her with her hands. Sophia stood still as the wing chair in front of the fireplace, staring at the woman, the distinctly unfriendly voice sounding in her ears, loud and imperious. She didn't have time to gather a response; she felt paralyzed.

"Oh dear," Alex said, and she suddenly looked very ill indeed. She even closed her eyes a moment.

Sophie stood in the middle of the room, wearing one of Alex's gowns. The gown came only to her ankles and it was frankly loose on the bosom, for Sophie didn't have Alex's magnificent endowment, as the earl had pointed out. What had the woman meant—one of Ryder's women?

Alex girded her mental loins and scooted higher on her pillows. "Dear Lydia, this is Sophie Sherbrooke, your new daughter-in-law. Sophie, this is Ryder's mother, Lady Lydia Sherbrooke."

"I don't believe it," said the dowager countess, hands on hips, voice flat and hard. "Just look at you! And that rag you have on, girl, it passes all bounds. It's ugly and cheap and you look quite the sham in it. No, you shan't take me in as has this other daughter-in-law of mine who shouldn't be either."

"Actually, ma'am, it's one of my gowns. We're having it altered for Sophie."

Lady Lydia wasn't at all daunted by this proof of her error, and not at all remorseful about the insult she'd just dished out to her daughter-in-law, for she usually dished out too many in the course of a day to remember more than a fraction of them. Her hands remained on her hips and her nostrils still quivered with indignation. She wasn't about to budge. She gave Sophie another long look, and said, "Well, the color is all wrong for her. Sallow, that's what it makes her, utterly sallow. Now, young woman, you dare to say you're married to my son. Well, you can't be. Ryder has always laughed when anyone mentioned marriage. He is content as he is with all his women. Therefore, you are a liar, an adventuress, doubtless a—"

"Sorry, Alex, I lost track of her, but I'm here now. Hello, Mother."

It was the earl, and he was actually out of breath. Sophie was tempted, but only for an instant, to laugh as she pictured this fiercesome man racing up the stairs and to this bedchamber to muzzle his mother.

"Ah, I see you've met Sophie. Her little brother is also here. Jeremy is with Sinjun, I believe."

As if recalling that he was the master, the earl strode like the lord he was into the room, giving Sophie a wink as he passed by her. He paused a moment and looked her up and down. He said to his wife, "You see, it is just as I said. You are quite unique. Now, Mother, would you like to welcome Sophie to Northcliffe Hall?"

The earl sat down on a very feminine chair that all but groaned under his weight, but his dark eyes were calm and deep on his mother's face, and if Sophie had been in the older woman's slippers, she would have stammered something quite inoffensive and slithered out of the room. She prayed she would never have to cross swords with this man. He was honed as the sharpest of knives.

"Well, what am I to think?" Lady Lydia said, her voice peevish. "Come, Douglas, don't tell me you believe her. Just look at her. Why, dear Ryder wouldn't look at her a second time."

"I imagine he had to, Mother, for they are married. You see, Ryder wrote me a letter introducing her and Jeremy. I would appreciate it if you would accord her one of your lovely smiles and welcome her here."

Sophie would have smiled like a fool if those quietly spoken, utterly calm words had been directed at her. Lady Lydia fidgeted a moment, then said stiff as a poker, "You are here. My son, who is also the earl and thus must be accorded respect and patience, has accepted you. We will see if you remain once my other son returns."

Back straight as a broom handle, Lady Lydia marched from the bedchamber.

The earl said to his pale-faced wife, "Have you been giving my mother lessons, my dear? That straight back of hers rivals yours at your most arrogant. Surely you must have instructed her."

"I wish you'd been faster," Alex said.

"Sorry, but as I said, she moves very rapidly when she wants to. The gown does make you look a bit sallow, Sophie. You must avoid shades of yellow. They look lovely on Alex, but you need pale pastels, I believe. Have you a soft pink, Alex?"

Alex owned three such soft pink gowns. Within fifteen minutes, the countess was tucked down for a nap, the maid had taken the pale pink gown away to alter, and Sophie was in her bedchamber, staring at the huge cherrywood armoire that held a goodly number of men's clothes. Ryder's clothes. She was in his bedchamber.

It simply hadn't occurred to her that she would be put in his bedchamber. To await him. What to do?

Ryder's bedchamber.

She walked over to the window that gave out onto the front drive. She saw Jeremy walking with his slow hitched gait beside Sinjun from the stables. She'd slowed her own step to match his. He was speaking with great animation, using his hands, just like his father, and Sinjun was looking down at him, smiling and nodding. Sophie felt a surge of gratitude. The sun had come out in the late afternoon and the beautiful grounds were lush and green, the flowers in bloom, not the suffocating sort of lush bloom on Jamaica, but nonetheless, it was beautiful. She wondered where the naked Greek statues were kept.

With Ryder living here, she would have imagined his windows looking over the statues. She found herself walking around the bedchamber, opening drawers in the dressers, seeing her underclothing next to his. It was disconcerting. It was frightening. She very quietly closed the dresser drawers. She lay on the bed and stared up at the ceiling.

It was a blustery day, cold with dampness heavy in the air. Sophie dismounted Lilah, the bay mare the earl had given her to ride, tethered her to the skinny branch of a yew bush, and walked to the edge of the cliff. Waves crashed on the rocks some fifty feet below. The beach was littered with driftwood, tangled seaweed, huge boulders, and very dark sand that looked wet and cold. She was shivering, and it surprised her still. She'd been cold ever since she and Jeremy set foot in England. She wrapped her arms over her chest and didn't move for a very long time. The savagery of the scene below held her silent. She stood there very quietly, rubbing her arms, her hair blowing about her face, soon free of its knot at the back of her neck.

This was the earl's thinking place, Sinjun had told her. However, her sister-in-law had added, a twinkle in her incredible Sherbrooke blue eyes, Douglas hadn't visited here very much at all since he'd married Alex and not at all since he'd decided to keep her as his wife. It was just as well; Sophie liked having the barren cliff and the churning water below all to herself. She'd spent hours here during the past week, escaping Lady Lydia's tongue and all the curious Northcliffe Hall eyes.

She sat down on a rock, arranging her riding skirt over her legs. Her mare suddenly whinnied and she looked up. It wasn't the earl riding toward her or even Sinjun, who came here quite often and simply sat at her feet, quiet and undemanding, but a man she'd met in the village several days before. His name, if she remembered aright, was Sir Robert Pickering. He was well into his thirties, married and a father of five daughters. He reminded Sophie of Lord David Lochridge, even to the assessing, very possessive way he'd looked at her when Alex had introduced them. She'd disliked him then, and his arrival here, on Sherbrooke land, made her dislike show on her face. She knew his sort, indeed she did, and she braced herself.

Sir Robert dismounted and strode to her. He stood over her, hands on hips, just smiling down at her.

"I was told I'd find you here. I trust you recall who I am? Certainly you do. All ladies remember gentlemen who look at them as I did you. You know, my dear girl, once Ryder returns you will be in dire straits, and he must return very soon now. Indeed, I expected him to come sooner. You must know he keeps many women and not one of them has he ever allowed to stay at Northcliffe Hall."

Oh yes, she knew his sort quite well. Sophie gave him a lazy look and yawned. "This is Sherbrooke land. I would that you leave now. And no, I don't remember your name at all. For the life of me I cannot imagine why I should."

She'd angered him a bit and it pleased her. She yawned again. He said, "My name is Sir Robert Pickering, and oh no, I shan't leave just yet. I wish to speak to you. I came here to find you. To come to an agreement, if you will. It is all the talk of the district, you know, how you, this simple maid from Jamaica, arrived with the little lame boy as your shill and pulled the wool over the Earl of Northcliffe's eyes. Of course, he is still so besotted with his new wife that it is no wonder he accepted you. It is even said that Lady Lydia avoids a room when you are in it. But your fun will soon be over. Who knows when Ryder will come back? As I said, it must be very soon. He won't allow you to remain, you know. You will be unmasked. He will not bed you in his home. He is discreet. He is very likely to be angry with you for your gall and impertinence. I think you are a quite pretty girl. Thus, I am willing to provide for you, and the little lame boy, but you must leave Northcliffe now. I will install you in a cottage I own some miles from here."

"I see," Sophie said, hating him so much her hands shook to shove him off the cliff. Sinjun had said on a giggle that he had a shocking reputation and all the ladies felt sorry for his wife, who, the poor woman, was continually with child. He was tolerated because his father had been a very popular man.

"Will you accept my offer, then?"

Sophie controlled her anger. She clearly saw his pretensions, his conceits, his fateful pride that would make him do and say very stupid things. She even smiled at him now.

"Tell me something, Sir Robert. Why are you so certain that I'm not married to Ryder Sherbrooke? Do you think I look like one of Ryder's women? Do I look like a girl who would be a man's mistress?"

"No, you do not and that pleases me. Actually, the half dozen or so women I know Ryder has kept are quite varied. Some are so beautiful they make a man's rod swell, others are simply pretty, but their bodies— all their bodies are magnificent. Now, as I already told you, Ryder has a reputation. He enjoys dozens of women. He would never tie himself to just one. Thus, you are one of his mistresses. There is no other way for it. Did I tell you I was one of her ladyship's confidants, just as my father was before me? No? Well, Lady Lydia would like to see you at Jericho. I enjoy obliging her. I will take action. Will you accept my offer?"

Sophie rose slowly. She dusted off her riding skirt. She smoothed out her gloves. As for her hair, she stuffed it as best she could under her riding hat. How very odd that it wasn't she who was regarded as the slut here, it was Ryder. She was only a slut by extension, for her husband couldn't be a husband and thus she had to be a liar. She gave him a remote look and said, "I would wager, Sir Robert, that you are the type of man to pin a maid against the stairs and fondle her."

He looked taken aback, then he nodded slowly at her, as if she'd just confirmed something he'd been thinking. He said, "I knew you would be brazen behind that demure façade of yours. There's just something about you, something that teases a man, that makes him want to throw up your skirts. A man looks at you and knows that you are well aware of what he wants of you. Your eyes, perhaps. You'd like that, wouldn't you? Like for me to take you right here."

"Your conceit is remarkable. If you come near me I will throw you over the cliff."

He laughed, moved quick as a snake, and grabbed her arm, jerking her against him. She felt no fear, just vast annoyance. Men, she thought, they were all the same, no matter what the country. She remarked the clump of hair on his jaw that his valet had missed while shaving his master. She smelled the pea soup on his breath. She waited, looking bored.

It enraged him. He crushed her against him and tried to find her mouth. But she eluded him. She knew he didn't understand, didn't accept that she wouldn't have him willingly. He grabbed her hair to hold her head still.

"You really shouldn't do this," Sophie said, still calm. "I won't allow much more."

"Ha," he said and managed to find her mouth. He touched her flesh, but that was all. Her hands were raised and fisted, her knee ready to come up and kick him in the groin. There was a furious yell behind him. Sophie felt him jerked like a mangy dog off her.

It was Ryder and he looked beyond angry. He looked vicious.

For a brief moment, she was so glad to see him she wanted to yell with it. He looked fit and tan and strong and she saw that his Sherbrooke blue eyes were alight with rage. She calmly watched him strike Sir Robert in the jaw with his fist. The man went down on his knees. Ryder reached for him again. Sophie laid her hand on his arm. "Don't, Ryder. He isn't worth bruising your knuckles and that is what would happen. He will already have to find an acceptable explanation for the wonderful bruise you've given him. Let him go. He is a worm, after all."

Ryder felt her words flow over him. He felt his rage lessen. His toes, however, still itched to kick the man in the ribs.

"Did the cretin hurt you?"

"Oh no. In fact—"

Sir Robert stumbled to his feet. His rage was directed at Sophie, not at Ryder, who'd struck him. It was, Sophie knew, the way men reacted. They always blamed the woman. She drew herself up and waited for his venom.

"She tried to seduce me, Ryder! Welcome home. I was here and she came and tried to seduce me!"

Ryder struck him again, and this time he grinned while he did it.

Sir Robert remained on the ground. "No one believes her tales, no one, particularly your mother. She claims to be your wife, Ryder, and everyone knows that's a patent falsehood. She wanted me, she's flirted shamelessly with all the men who've met her, she—"

Ryder knelt down, jerked him up by his collar, and said not two inches from his face, "She is my wife. Her name is Sophia Sherbrooke. You will tell all these randy men that if any of them come near her again, I will kick them into next week. As for you, Bobbie, you irritate her again and I'll kill you. You say anything about her and I'll kill you. Do you understand, Bobbie?"

Sir Robert nodded finally, and it was toward Sophie he shot a malignant look. He shook his head even as he backed away from Ryder toward his horse. "You are really married to her? To one single woman?"

"Did I not tell you she was my wife?"

Ryder said nothing more. He watched Sir Robert climb back onto his horse and kick the poor beast sharply in the sides. It wasn't until he was out of sight that Ryder turned to Sophie. She was standing there silently, the wind whipping her hair across her face, just looking at him, saying nothing. He smiled at her, reached out his hand and lightly touched his fingertips to her cheek. He wound a tress of hair between two fingers.

"It's been a very long time," he said, not moving himself. "They told me at the stable that you liked to come here. Hello, Sophie."

"Hello."

"Is this the first time Bobbie has bothered you?"

"Yes. I would have handled him, Ryder. There was no need for you to play knight to my damsel in distress."

His eyes narrowed. "I saw your knee ready to do him in. But I wanted to thrash him, Sophie. I am pleased you allowed me my fun. You understand that, don't you? You know men so well, after all."

"Yes."

"Why were you letting him kiss you?"

"He very nearly pulled my hair from my scalp."

Ryder shook himself. "This is bloody ridiculous. The last thing I want to talk about or think about is that damned lackwit Bobbie Bounder, as we called him when we were boys." He smiled down at her. "Come here."

She didn't move. She felt her heart begin to pound, slow, heavy beats. He came to her, pulled her into his arms and simply held her. "I missed you very much. And Jeremy. It's been a long time, Sophie." He lifted her face, his palm beneath her chin. He kissed her, his mouth warm and firm. She remained passive.

"Kiss me the way I know you can," he said against her lips.

"I can't," she said and tried to press her face against his neck.

"I am close to consummating our marriage right here, Sophie. It wouldn't be all that comfortable. Come, kiss me, you really must, you know, to hold me over until I can take you in our own bed tonight."

And it would happen, she knew. There was nothing she could do about it. She kissed him, kissed him with all the expertise she had garnered over the past two years. It didn't content him though. It aroused him until she thought he would fling up her skirts and press her against one of the boulders. He was breathing hard, his hands on her back, down to her hips, lifting her, and then she pushed at him. He stopped instantly.

He slowly lifted his head. He looked down at her, no expression on his face. "You are a tease. You are behaving just as you did on Jamaica. You have just spent several minutes making me wild. You have held back from me, controlled me. I had forgotten during the past eight weeks how very good you were at manipulation. I suppose I had rearranged my memories, had come to believe that since you were my wife, you would welcome me, you would treat me with some honor, some sign that you had come to accept me, even perhaps like me. But nothing has changed, has it, Sophie?"

"You took me by surprise."

He said something very crude and she flinched. "Don't tell me that shocks you? Dear God, you could probably outcurse me—no, no, this is absurd. I have just come home. I saw my brother and he told me that you were here, in his thinking place, that you came here quite a lot. And I saw Sinjun with Jeremy and he seemed very glad to see me. I suppose I was a fool to think you would extend the same courtesy to me. Look, it doesn't matter now. I won't annul our marriage. I'm an honorable man. I consented to wed you despite the fact that in the end, there was no reason for me to have to. Do you understand, Sophie? Your precious uncle wasn't shot or stabbed. Someone, Thomas probably, had garroted the bastard. I didn't have to marry you to keep you from the gallows."

"Garroted? I don't understand."

"Yes, he was. I made a grave mistake. If only I had paid more attention, but you see, his body wasn't a pleasant sight. I just assumed that you had shot him, but you hadn't. And I lied to save you, said that he'd been stabbed. The jest was on me, it certainly was. Garroted, the bastard was garroted."

"Is Thomas still free?"

"No. No, he's snug in that small dwelling Cole had planned on keeping you in. I didn't leave Jamaica until he'd been captured."

She turned away from him then and stared out over the sea. It wasn't the soft turquoise she was used to, it was savage and cold and very gray. "I thank you, Ryder. Your family has been quite nice to me and Jeremy. Now, though, since there is no reason for me not to return to Jamaica, I can. I will be responsible for Camille Hall and the plantation until Jeremy comes of age, I will—"

"Shut up, damn you!"

"You don't like me, Ryder. You can't possibly want to be my husband. I know about you now. You see, no one believed me to be your wife because everyone swore you would never wed. There were too many women hereabouts you enjoyed. It is odd. For the first time since Jamaica, I have been cut, not because I'm a tart, but because you are. I have found it vastly amusing save when Sir Robert tried to coerce me. If I could merely borrow some money from you, Jeremy and I could be on our way. Your life could return to what it was, to what you obviously enjoyed."

"I told you to shut up. You will go nowhere with Jeremy, my dear."

"Why? What do you mean?"

"I mean that I am his guardian. His legal guardian. You are nothing more than a female, his sister. I am responsible for the running of Camille Hall and the plantation. Emile is managing Camille Hall for me and Jeremy. Now, I should like to return to the hall and speak to my family. I wish to see if Douglas has accepted Alex as his wife."

"He has."

One of Ryder's eyebrows shot up. "Really? I understand that you were ever scarce there. You must be terribly observant to know my brother's feelings and be absent at the same time."

There was a distance between them that was growing even though they stood not two feet from each other. She couldn't blame him; but she couldn't blame herself either.

"Why?" she said at last. "Why, Ryder?"

"Why what?"

"Why don't you just let me go? Let me return to my home, resume my life."

"Ah, and what a life it would be. Even though your pretty neck would stay intact on your shoulders, you don't believe that all would be forgiven and forgotten, do you? You are the whore of Jamaica, my dear, and nothing will ever change that, even marriage to me. It's true. Everyone feels very sorry for me. You took advantage of my honorable nature and manipulated me into giving you my name. No, there is no going back for you, Sophie. There is only the present and that becomes the future soon enough. Now, I wish to return to the hall. Are you coming?"

He mounted his stallion, a magnificent barb she'd admired and fed whenever she'd been in the stables. His name was Genesis and she'd somehow known even before she'd been told that this was Ryder's horse. He looked down at her, arrogant, cold, aloof, and she hated it and accepted it.

"Tonight, as soon as it is politely possible to leave my family, you and I will adjourn to my bedchamber and I will take you and you will try your damnedest, Sophie, to act like a reasonable woman."

He said nothing more, merely gave her a small salute, wheeled Genesis around, and galloped away from her. She walked slowly to Lilah, climbed into the saddle, and rode after him.

CHAPTER
══14══

"My mother still resists believing me, but it is perversity on her part, no real conviction that you aren't actually my legal wife," Ryder said to Sophie as he tugged off his cravat. "She will get over it and treat you at least as nicely as she does Alex, which isn't very nice at all, but it will do for the present. You appear to get along well with Douglas and Alex. Of course you would like Sinjun. She's a nosy brat—Lord knows I'm the brunt of her nosiness—but all in all, she's an incredible girl."

Ryder turned to face her as he unbuttoned his white shirt. "Jeremy appears pleased to be here. I will decide soon if he will have a tutor or go to Eton for the fall term. Incidentally, I'm delighted Alex put you in my bedchamber. I've never shared it before. It's strange to see your gowns next to my shirts and britches in the armoire."

Sophie was standing by the front windows. She was doing her best to affect a casual pose. The evening hadn't been all that long for Ryder wanted her very badly. She knew that. Even as she'd walked beside him up the wide staircase, she'd known that if she looked at him, she would have seen the desire in his eyes. She knew well what desire looked like, both on a man's face and between his legs. What she didn't know was what to do about it. She felt incredibly weary, incredibly experienced and jaded. She didn't know what to do about that either.

He said again, "Don't misunderstand me, Sophie. It pleases me to see your gowns beside my clothes. Yes, Alex did well."

"Douglas put me in here. Alex was ill and in bed with a cold."

"Smart man, my brother. I also like the gowns Alex gave you. The pink is very pretty with your coloring. We'll see to some more new gowns for you soon enough."

She wanted to yell at him that she didn't want him to buy her gowns or anything else for that matter, but she remained still and silent.

Ryder sat down in what he had told her was his favorite wing chair. He tugged off his boots as he said, "My mother isn't always amiable, as I'm sure you've learned since you've been here. I had hoped she might change her colors just a bit, and perhaps she will. I don't want you to feel hurt. You should have seen what she did to Alex upon her arrival."

He flicked his wrists and both boots flew toward the huge bed in the center of the bedchamber, sliding smoothly underneath. Only one heel stuck out from beneath the duster cover. Sophie stared at that heel. He grinned at the boots. "I'm a bit off. I've been doing that since I was a boy. I always beat Douglas. It's in the wrist, you know."

He stood, his hands going to the buttons of his britches. She watched his long brown fingers on the buttons as he said, "How does it feel to be back in England?"

"It's cold," she said, still staring at his fingers. "I'd forgotten. Also, living in Jamaica for four years thinned my blood."

He smiled at her and pulled down his pants.

She closed her eyes, which was absurd really because she'd seen him naked, seen his sex swelled, seen him sprawled on the cottage bed with Dahlia over him. She swallowed.

"Sophie."

His voice was quiet, very warm and intimate. She opened her eyes. He was standing not three feet from her, quite naked and quite relaxed. He was smiling at her, his hand held to her. "You are my wife. Come here."

She didn't move.

"Should you like me to undress you? Is that why you've waited?"

"I should like a bath."

He blinked at her. "Very well. Let me ring."

He strode away from her and pulled on the silver-tasseled bellcord. He turned, then said as he climbed into the huge bed, "It is just as well. I have much more to say to you and we can have a pleasant chat while you bathe. If I touched you right now, I suspect we wouldn't say much until morning."

He wouldn't leave. She hadn't expected him to. He was behaving quite nicely, really, not lashing out at her, not condemning her, or calling her horrible names like her uncle had when she'd gone against his wishes.

It was another thirty minutes before Sophie was seated in front of the fireplace in the deep copper bathtub. She'd undressed in the shadows by the window and slipped on a dressing gown. However, to step into the tub, she'd had to take the damned thing off and she knew he was watching her. And she thought, I must accustom myself. He will do whatever he wishes to do to me for as long as I live. Then she shook her head at her thoughts, for nothing was right, nothing was as she'd expected it to be. He was acting so normal, so relaxed, as if they'd been here, in this bedchamber, chatting about everything and nothing for the past ten years.

He said nothing until she was soaping herself. "I like your hair wet around your shoulders and streaming over your breasts. I'm smiling, if you would but look at me once. I am happy to see you. I can't wait to get my hands on you, but I'm sure you recognize all the male signs—the lust-glazed eyes, the erratic speech, nonsense, most of it. I even like the way your legs are sticking up. The flesh behind your knees is very tender, by the by, and I will show you how much you will enjoy me touching and kissing you there. I must remember to kiss that small birthmark of yours too."

She lathered her hair with a vengeance. It would take a good hour to dry it.

"I can't wait to kiss you silly. Perhaps I can convince you to return my kiss. I will try my best." He sounded so sure of himself, so completely confident. She rubbed her scalp until it hurt. He also sounded amused.

"Shall I come and rub your back for you?"

"I wish you would go away," Sophie said, opening her eyes through a haze of soap. It stung and she gasped, ducking her head under the water.

"Very well," he said agreeably. "I will doze here in bed and wait for you. I really forgot everything I wanted to say to you. Why, I won't even think of you—my wife—all naked and wet and soft. You have five more minutes, Sophie, not a second more." He consulted the clock on the mantel as he spoke. Then he leaned his head back against the pillow and closed his eyes. He crossed his arms over his bare chest.

When he opened his eyes she was standing swathed in a voluminous white nightgown. Her hair was matted and tangled wet down her back. If she got any closer to the fireplace, she'd be standing atop the flames.

She was trying to dry her hair.

"Hold still," he said and rose. Ryder wasn't a randy boy. He was a man and he'd proved not only to himself but to her that he could be patient. He would continue to be patient. He took another towel from the chair beside the copper tub and pointed to his wing chair. "Sit down."

She sat like a prim schoolgirl on the edge of the chair, her hands in her lap. "Now, where are your comb and brush?"

He spent another fifteen minutes brushing her thick hair. He set the brush aside. He smiled down at her. "You look like a Madonna. You are quite lovely, Sophie. You please me. Your hair has so many varied shades in it. Yes, you're lovely. You would please me even more if you opened your eyes. I'm naked, 'tis true, but you've seen me on several occasions. Surely I don't displease you?"

She opened her eyes then and looked him straight in the face. "Please tell me the truth, Ryder. Did you truly believe I was pregnant?"

Their wedding and the subsequent damnable night were stark in his mind, but he managed an indifferent shrug. "I had no idea. You refused to

tell me the course of your monthly flow. It was possible you were pregnant, based upon my knowing nothing." He wondered if and when he
would tell her the truth. Ah, soon, he knew, for he hated lies. They were
always lying in wait to trip a man up. And Sophie was fast-witted. If he
didn't tell her, she would catch him and he didn't want the consequences
of that. Actually, though, she would know it was a lie soon enough.

Always his wit, she thought numbly. He drowned her in his damnable
wit, in the easy flow of his speech. Had she used to be like that? Had she
mocked him and teased him as he now did her? Memories flooded
through her. Ah yes, she'd done it with great skill, even to touching him
just so to make him mad with lust for her. But now she was a silent fool,
dull-tongued and stupid. Why couldn't she treat him as she had Sir
Robert? She sometimes wished she had herself back again but then she'd
realize she wasn't exactly certain who that self really was.

She felt his hands on her wrists. He pulled her upright and against him.
He said, his breath warm against her damp hair, "Now let me tell you how
we're going to spend the greater part of this wonderful evening. I will not
rush you. We must take time to learn each other. I will kiss you and—"

He paused, kissed her lightly on her mouth, then said, "No, let me just
show you. Do me a favor, Sophie. Forget all those damned men. Just forget them. They have nothing to do with us, with this. This is private, this
is us alone, a man and his wife together."

But she couldn't. She also knew she couldn't refuse him. He was her
husband; he had full and complete control over her, more control, in fact,
than her uncle had exercised, which had been unbearable. If he wanted to
strip her naked and tie her to the bed, why he could do it. She tried to be
calm. After all, she'd had weeks and weeks to come to grips with it. She'd
learned that much, surely she had. She wouldn't start screaming or become hysterical. She wasn't that way, and even if she had ever been that
way, her uncle Theo would have beaten it all out of her long ago.

When Ryder pulled her nightgown over her head, leaving her as naked
as he was, she drew back, hunching over, unable to stop herself. He
lightly touched his fingertips to her ribs. "No more bruises. Have you had
any more pain?"

She shook her head. "Good," he said and brought her against him
again.

For the first time he held her naked against him. His heart was pounding in deep, fast strokes. He wanted to come inside her this very instant
and bury himself in her, his wife. He wanted to hold very still, to feel her
around his sex, to feel the gentle tensing movements of her inner muscles.
But he wasn't stupid. She needed every bit of his expertise. Ah, that was
the rub. She was making it a damned serious business. Ryder had always

laughed before, for to him making love was a grand pastime filled with mirth and smacking kisses and shared moans and sighs. He wasn't laughing now; he didn't have a single jest in his head. It was going to be a grim business.

It would be enough, this expertise of his. He'd never failed with a woman before, never. He caressed her mouth, nibbled on her ear, found that very sensitive place in the hollow of her throat that made every woman he'd ever known squirm and moan when he'd caressed there with his tongue.

He told her how beautiful she was as he stroked his hands over her breasts, told her how much she pleased him, how much he wanted to touch her everywhere, with his hands and with his mouth. Her nipples were a dark pink and when he took one in his mouth he thought he'd spill his seed. The taste of her, her texture, were nothing he'd ever experienced before, which was surely false, but it seemed true to him now. He frowned even as he let the feelings settle deep within him.

He clasped his hands beneath her hips and lifted her onto her back on the bed. He came down over her, kissing her breasts, caressing and lifting them, wanting her desperately, more and more as each instant passed.

He slid his left hand over her belly, stilling a moment when he remembered the ugly bruises. God, he'd never forget them or the soul-deep rage he'd felt. She'd been hurt so badly. He slowed his hand, easing his fingers lower, until he was cupping her and he felt the stiffness of her body, despite her softness, and he pressed his fingers between her thighs. He found her woman's flesh and gently probed. He wanted to come into her now, this moment, for his need for her was so great that he trembled with it. Unlike the Ryder Sherbrooke before he'd met Sophie, he didn't want to lose his control. But it had been so very long that he'd wanted her, so very long that he'd been celibate, that he simply didn't know if he could hold himself under control.

Perhaps, he thought, staring down at her, just perhaps this was why he'd wanted to marry her. Perhaps he'd known that she would do this to him, that she would be like no other woman in his life. He closed his eyes as he eased his middle finger inside her. His breath hitched with the effort to keep control of himself. The feel of her around his finger, the softness of her, the heat of her, made him grit his teeth. She made a soft keening sound and he took it for burgeoning passion. It had to be. Sweet God, it had to be passion. How could she not want him when he was edging toward madness with need for her?

She was tight, her muscles squeezing his finger. He knew it would be over for him soon. He eased deeper until he touched her maidenhead. He smiled; he realized now he'd known he would find it. He widened her as best he could for he didn't want to hurt her too much.

He pulled her thighs wide and came down between them. He looked at her face. "Sophie, I'm coming inside you now. No, open your eyes. Remember, there's no reason for you to be embarrassed. We've already done this. There is nothing new here. Believe me. If you could try to relax, you just might enjoy it."

She looked at him as if he were mad. She closed her eyes against the urgency of his expression, then opened them again. No, she would bear all that he did to her. It wouldn't be bad. It would be over soon enough.

That damnable lie. He had believed it would help her to relax with him. It hadn't appeared to do anything of the sort. He knew he couldn't wait. He guided himself slowly inside her. He promised himself he would only come into her for a very short time and then he would ease out of her and give her his mouth. Yes, just a bit more, just until he knew she accepted him, for he wanted her to experience having him inside her before he brought her to pleasure. He said as he came deeper, "You are my wife," and there was wonder and satisfaction in his voice. "It is very odd for me, you know. I've never had a wife before, never thought to have one, but you are here with me and we are in my bed and I'm coming inside you. Please accept me, Sophie."

Accept him, she thought, holding herself as still as possible. She had no choice but to accept him. She waited, afraid, willing it to be over, willing him to make those ugly grunting noises the men made, the noises that soon meant they would be through, their sex shriveled, and shortly asleep and snoring.

She was a virgin and she was his wife and she would be his now. When his sex butted her maidenhead, he pushed forward as gently as he could. It held. He cursed, knowing he should withdraw from her. He tried, he really did, but he couldn't make himself pull out of her. He looked down at himself inside her. He shook and tried to pull away again. He couldn't. He leaned down and kissed her instead. His tongue was deep in her mouth when he groaned and thrust deep, tearing through her maidenhead until he was touching her womb and then it was simply too much. Even as he became aware that she was struggling against him, even as he tasted her tears in his mouth, he groaned again, feeling such swirling, utterly wild feelings, that he jerked frantically at the intensity of his release.

He stilled. She lay quiet beneath him. He was heavy on top of her, his breath still deep and fast, his body damp with sweat, his face on the pillow beside hers.

She hadn't expected the pain. Dahlia had never complained of pain, not that Sophie had ever asked her, but, on the other hand, Dahlia gave her opinions on everything with lazy abandon, comparing the men down to such details as the noises they made during their release. Sophie couldn't imagine that Dahlia would suffer pain willingly or in silence. Thus, this pain did surprise her and she burned deep inside with the stinging of it, and the alien fullness of him. She knew about a man's seed and knew it was in her as was the pain he'd inflicted upon her. How could a woman possibly enjoy this if it hurt so badly?

She'd known all about intimacies, known all about six men and their bodies and their needs, but she'd never realized that his sex entering her joined them in such a way. He was deep inside her still and she could feel him, feel every slick bit of him. If was as if he were trying to be a part of her but she wouldn't allow it. No, he was the different one and soon he would separate himself from her. She pressed her hips deeper into the mattress. She sucked in her breath, wishing he would just be done with her and leave her.

Ryder managed to balance himself on his elbows above her. He was actually smiling, a tender smile that confused her. "I'm sorry I hurt you. I won't hurt you ever again."

"Why did you hurt me this time?"

No more lies or evasions, he thought, and said simply, "This was your first time. You were a virgin just as I finally realized you would be. I had to get through your maidenhead. That's what hurt you."

She stared up at him, her eyes darkening as she finally understood. A lie, it had all been a lie, him taking her at the cottage, her possible pregnancy. "You bastard!" She heaved upward, trying to buck him off her.

"I know. I'm sorry for it." He clasped her wrists and pulled her arms over her head. He was heavy on top of her and she felt him growing inside her. It couldn't be, not this soon, no, she wouldn't allow it. She wanted, quite simply, to kill him.

"I am sorry I lied to you, Sophie. At first I meant it as simple punishment for what you'd done to me. Not very nice of me, I'll admit, but then again, what you and your uncle did to me wasn't any better. It gave me a power over you to have matched you at your same game. After, when I decided I would marry you, I used it against you. And I won."

"How can you believe that marrying me is winning? That is errant nonsense. I am nothing, less than nothing. I have no dowry, no reputation, no—"

"Damn you, you will be quiet."

Her eyes went a very dark gray at the anger in his voice; her face was as pale as the white sheets. "No matter your anger, you can't change what I have been, what I am. You haven't won a thing, Ryder."

"I will always win with you, Sophie. It's best you remember that."

Without warning, without any sound at all, she jerked her right arm free of his hold, and smashed her fist into his jaw. He saw the flash of movement but he wasn't fast enough, simply because he'd been laughing and bragging and telling her how omnipotent he was, in short, her master, the one man who would handle her always to his satisfaction.

Her fist hit him hard and he jerked back with the surprise and the flash of pain. She shoved at him, her legs striking him hard on his back, and he went over the side of the bed and landed with a loud thud on the wooden floor.

She lurched up and stared down at him.

He was laughing, lying there on his back, rubbing his jaw, and laughing. At her.

She scrambled off the other side of the bed, grabbed her nightgown and pulled it over her head. She was panting with fury, with fear, because she'd seen the blood on herself, but she knew it couldn't be her monthly flow. He'd hurt her, all right, hurt her so badly she was bleeding.

God, she hated him, hated herself, wished she could topple the bed over on top of him. It was rosewood and very heavy. She tried, but she couldn't lift it.

He stopped laughing, rose and shook his head. He stood on the other side of the bed now, just looking across at her. She couldn't help herself. She looked at his groin, at his flat belly and the thick mat of hair that surrounded his sex, at his legs that had pressed against hers. He wasn't fully aroused now and he was wet with her and with himself and there was blood too and she gasped.

Ryder looked down at himself then back at her face. He pulled back the covers and looked at the stains of blood on the sheet. "I won't seek retribution for that blow until after I've got you cleaned up."

"You come near me and I will break your back. You've hurt me quite enough, Ryder. No more. If I die from what you've done to me, so be it. I deserve it for being such a colossal fool, but you will stay away from me."

"I told you that the hurt is because this was your first time. As for the blood, that won't happen again either. Good God, if a woman bled every time she had a man, the species would cease to exist in a very short time. I'm not lying to you, Sophie. I do find it passing strange that you are ignorant of this. The bleeding signifies your passage into womanhood."

"That is sheer nonsense and you know it. I am nineteen years old, Ryder, very much a woman."

"Oh, I do agree, my dear wife, indeed I do. But my rending of your maidenhead now means you can bear a child. There will be some stretching for a while yet until you become used to me, but it won't hurt. Indeed, I've been told it's a very nice feeling."

"Yes," she said, "told by doubtless two dozen women!"

Acrimony? He wasn't certain. He prayed it was acrimony, a goodly dose of it. He walked around the end of the bed. She didn't back away from him as he'd imagined she would, instead, she flung herself at him and punched her fists into his belly, against his chest, tried to hit his face.

It was a silent battle and he became aware of that silence and wondered at it. Fighting was a loud business, at least in his experience—cursing, grunting, yelling. But she didn't make a bloody sound save for her harsh breathing. And he realized then, and said aloud, "You learned how to fight, to struggle, without a sound, didn't you? You knew that any sound could have awakened Jeremy and you couldn't allow that. Damn you, Sophie, it's different now. That mangy old bastard is well and truly dead. Damn you, yell at me when you fight me!"

She tried to kick him in the groin instead and he simply turned quickly to the side and her blow landed on his upper thigh. He ripped her nightgown off her and threw her onto her back. He brought his full weight over her.

She was heaving and jerking against him and he simply let her, holding her hands over her head. He didn't look at her heaving breasts, tried to ignore her legs thrashing against his, her belly tensing against his.

When she finally quieted, he said, "You didn't enjoy me touching you or kissing you at all, did you?"

She looked at him as if he'd lost his mind.

"No, that was a rather stupid question, wasn't it? We will change all that, Sophie. You are remembering the past year, aren't you? Those men, and what your uncle made you do. Dismiss it, Sophie, relegate it to a time that no longer matters, a time well gone, and forget it."

She realized then, in a flash of understanding, that she didn't doubt for an instant that he wouldn't hurt her no matter how much she tried to hurt him. Never would he raise his hand to her, never would he smash his fists into her ribs. She could probably shoot him and he wouldn't hurt her. She lay there simply looking up at him. Those blue eyes of his were blazing, brilliant as sunlight against a clear sky, yet somehow deep and calm. She said slowly, "You were a part of it. You were the biggest part of it. I knew everything would fail once you came, but my uncle wouldn't believe me. I tried to tell him you were different, because I knew, somehow I knew what you were, but he wouldn't listen. I didn't want to get near you but I did, and look what happened. How can I forget it?"

"In what way did you believe me different from the other men?"

She wished she hadn't said it but she had. "The others were so pleased with themselves, so filled with their pride and conceit, for they had gotten me, just a simple woman really, nothing more, but I was a prize, a possession, no matter how temporary, and it gave them stature and prestige in other men's eyes. You don't care what others think of you or what you do. You see things differently; you react differently."

He looked thoughtful. "Oh, don't get me wrong, Sophie. I wanted you, don't ever mistake that, but it was a game to me. I wanted to best you, to conquer you. Perhaps I wished to teach you a lesson, as I said, but things changed. I married you. Surely that isn't such a bad thing. You are safe with me, as is Jeremy. You are secure, you will never know fear again in your life. Now, you will forget the past. I am your present and your future. Can you feel me? I want you again but I will bathe you first and give you a while to ease. Will you continue to fight me?"

"Yes."

He sighed and rolled off her. He walked to a long, low dresser and pulled two cravats from a drawer. "I regret doing this for it will probably make you so angry you won't speak to me for a week, no matter that I'm your husband and you vowed to obey me."

She jerked off the bed and ran naked to the bed-chamber door. His hand slammed against the door above her head. "Are you quite witless, Sophie? You are splendidly naked, my dear. It is doubtful that any of my siblings or any of the servants are wandering the halls, but who knows? I prefer to keep all your female endowments just for my eyes. You are quite beautiful. Your legs are long and firm. You run well."

He took her hand and began to pull her back to the bed. She kicked him hard in the back of his leg and he felt the pain spurt through him and his grip loosened. She jerked away from him, and this time, she was at the door and through it before he could stop her. She ran down the long corridor, unaware really that she was naked and out of control. She simply ran until, quite suddenly, there was a shadow in front of her and she ran full tilt into it and it wasn't a shadow but a man and he was in a dressing gown. It was the earl, her brother-in-law, and his hands were wrapped about her bare upper arms and he was holding her gently yet firmly.

"Let me go!"

"You need some clothes," Douglas said, so stunned at the appearance of his new sister-in-law completely nude that he was surprised there were any words at all in his mouth.

"Please," she began, trying yet again to jerk away from his hold, looking back over her shoulder even as she struggled. Ryder was striding toward them, wearing a dressing gown, carrying another dressing gown over his arm. He looked furious.

Douglas saw the look on his brother's face in the dim light. He had no idea what was going on, but he felt the fear coming from her, and he felt a protectiveness that wasn't unlike what he felt toward his wife.

He eased his grip on her arms but didn't release her. He said quietly, "Your wife appears a bit distraught, Ryder."

"Yes," Ryder said when he reached them. He was dizzy with anger at her. And here was his brother, holding his wife, and she was naked. "Give her to me, Douglas."

Douglas knew there was no choice. He also knew Ryder wasn't a cruel man. He wouldn't hurt her, but he would give her a good dose of speech that could shrivel the stoutest of hearts.

He said quietly, "I trust everything will soon be all right?"

"Yes," Ryder said again. "Sophie, put this on. My brother doesn't need to see my wife."

Douglas released her. She was still, not moving when Ryder wrapped her in the dressing gown. It was soft, very soft from many washings; it smelled of him. She shuddered, but didn't move, didn't say anything. Everything had gone awry.

"Sleep well," Douglas said, his eyes resting a moment on his brother's face.

"Yes," Ryder said, took Sophie's hand, and led her back down the corridor.

Douglas stood there many minutes until they went into Ryder's bedchamber. What the devil was going on here?

Ryder didn't say a word. He just pulled her back to the bed. He took her squirming body and eased her down on her back. He pulled away the dressing gown. He reached for the cravats. He was over her again, straddling her, and he wrapped the cravats around her wrists, and secured them to the headboard.

"Now," he said, and moved off her again. He stood by the bed and looked down at her. She was pale and furious and still she made no sound.

"There is a lot of blood," he said and frowned. "I am sorry I hurt you, Sophie. Now hold still and let me bathe you."

She held still because she was too tired to fight him further. She tugged once at her wrists but his knots were secure. Why hadn't he said anything yet about her flight and capture by his brother? She felt him hold her legs apart and closed her eyes tightly. He was looking at her and she felt the wet cloth stroke over her. She hated it, this knowing he had of her, this power he had over her. He looked at her and he saw a woman's body that belonged to him.

When he was done he was silent for a moment, then, "Sophie, look at me."

She opened her eyes. He didn't like the message in them.

"What you did was foolish. I do not appreciate your showing my brother your body. I don't understand why—but it doesn't matter right now. You're tired; you're not yourself. Would you like to sleep now?"

"Yes."

He untied her wrists but didn't release them. He massaged them gently and thoroughly. And when he saw her looking about, he said, "No, no nightgown. Just the two of us together."

The bed could hold six people side by side and still he held her tightly against him. The strong beat of his heart sounded beneath her palm, the prickle of hair against her legs.

As for Ryder, he closed his eyes and sighed. "I like the feel of you against me. You're warm and soft. I locked the door. I do hope you don't snore too loudly."

"I do. I sound like a pig."

"How would you know? I know that I'm the first man ever to have you, the first man to hold you naked against him. If you are not delicate and soft in your sleep, I shan't tell you. I don't want to hurt your feelings."

She snorted and he kissed her hair.

He lay back and closed his eyes. Damnation. He hadn't given her any pleasure, not a dollop, not a blessed whit. He hadn't done anything particularly well with her, and that was unusual for him because he was well used to giving as much pleasure as he got. He hadn't with her. He would have to teach her to forget all the ugliness of the past months, including his own part in it, which could prove a formidable task. But he had to. He had to teach her how to love and how to make love. He felt her breasts against his chest, very soft breasts. He saw also in his mind's eye the look on Douglas's face. He must have heard them arguing and he'd come to investigate. Still, he'd held his tongue. He'd been gentle with Sophie.

Damnation.

He slept.

CHAPTER
══15══

RYDER AWOKE IN the middle of the night. Sophie was warm and soft against him. He was hard. He hurt and he wanted her, then, at that very instant. It seemed he'd wanted her forever. He wasn't completely full-witted and thus rolled her over onto her back, kissing her mouth even as he arranged her for himself, and came fully into her, hard and deep.

She cried out.

Ryder froze, but the madness prodded at him, and all his fine and honorable vows about her pleasure escaped his brain from one instant to the next. He was more awake than before but it made no difference. It was intense and powerful, this lust of his, and he thrust deeply into her, then pulled nearly out of her, heaving with the strain of it, the savage pleasure, again and again until suddenly he stilled. Then it dug at him again, this urgency for her, this frenzy to have her, to make her a part of him, to bind her to him. But he wanted to slow down, to make it last beyond the moment he knew was left to him. He held her tightly to him and rolled over, pulling her on top of him. He forced her upright and pulled her knees under her and against his flanks. She was riding him now, and she splayed her fingers over his chest to hold herself up. He thrust upward, holding her waist, then sliding his hands to her hips to lift her and bring her down on him, to show her what to do. All women enjoyed riding the man once in a while; they could set their own rhythm. They drove him mad with lust and they laughed as they did it, until like him, they moaned and flung their heads back. But Sophie wasn't moving; nor was she moaning. She held him deep inside her and he was forcing her to hold him, more deeply than the first time. Her breasts were thrust forward, beautiful and white and he gasped and pressed her further down on him. He couldn't see her face clearly in the dim light. And he wanted to. Then he heard her sob. He twisted about until he could see her face more clearly. Her eyes were closed and tears were rolling down her cheeks.

Sweet Lord, was he hurting her? He hadn't thought, hadn't realized, that this way of making love was deep, very deep and she was unused to a man, not just a man, but to him, her husband. Quickly, he lifted her off him and onto her back once again. When he rolled over onto her, he came into her again, not so deeply this time.

He wanted to pull out of her, to kiss her and soothe her, to tell her that he hadn't meant to go so strongly into her before she was ready to take him, but suddenly she moved, twisting to the side, and it sent him right over the edge.

It was a repetition of the first time, and he was furious with himself once he'd regained his wits. Again, he was balancing on his elbows over her and he felt the force of her sobs against his body, felt her heart against his, and he didn't like what he'd done.

"Go to sleep," he said and rolled off her.

She did eventually, but he listened to those soft, gasping cries of hers for more minutes than he could bear.

He awoke the following morning at the streaming of sunlight through the front windows. He felt her weight against him and smiled until he remembered the fiasco of the previous night. He'd been a clod, not once but twice, a selfish clod, a fool, a half-wit. He didn't understand it, and he didn't like himself for it.

Well, it was done. He would make it up to her. He would exercise more patience than he ever had in his life. On the other hand, he hadn't ever needed patience with a woman; a smile, a jest, a caress, and most had come to him. He knew the experiences in his life hadn't demanded much of anything that he couldn't readily and willingly give. Ah, his life had been filled with laughter and hour upon hour of pleasure and reckless freedom—the pounding strength of his stallion beneath him and the utter yielding of all the women he'd known and loved and held. His life had held no responsibilities he hadn't asked for. And that included his children, all seven of them. No, they were a joy, not a responsibility. It was true. His life had been fashioned by a benign deity. Now everything had changed. The woman he'd brought into his life, the woman he'd chosen for himself, didn't want him. There didn't seem to be laughter in her, no spontaneous joy, no wildness that came from deep within, and burst forth freely and gladly.

There was darkness in her. He understood at least some of this darkness for he'd seen it himself, he'd seen the results of it. Hell, he was the victim of it as well as she was. As for himself, the patches of pain and uncertainty that had come as they must to every man had been few. He'd been lucky and he knew it and he thought about it now, starkly. Everything was different and he perforce must also be different because of what he had done and of what she was and what he wanted her to become and be to him.

She still slept. He eased up until he was on his elbow and could look down at her. Her hair was tangled about her head, wild on the pillow, her face blotchy from her crying and she looked beautiful to him. This girl who wasn't really a beauty, not like some of the ladies he'd known so well, no she wasn't a diamond like Alex's incredibly lovely sister, Melissande, but she was impossibly beautiful to him, impossibly and inexplicably dear. He lightly ran a fingertip over her eyebrow. Slowly, she opened her eyes. She didn't move, didn't make a sound, merely looked up at him. He felt the tension building in her but ignored it.

"Good morning," he said and kissed her mouth.

She froze. He watched her eyes darken, then become carefully blank. He wouldn't tolerate it, this withdrawal from him. "Stop that, damn you. I won't hurt you again, I swear it."

"Men always hurt women."

"I admit that your experience hasn't shown you much of the other side of things. Men included."

"You hurt me two times last night. And you will do it again and again because you are the man and stronger than I am and you have the control and power and you can force me to do anything you wish to do."

"All that? Perhaps I should consider announcing my godhood." The studied lightness gave him a moment to think. The good Lord knew he needed many such moments now, with her, with this wife of his.

She shoved at him but couldn't budge him. She was panting now, and he could practically feel her urgency to get away from him. It was unnerving. It was frightening. "No, Ryder, I don't believe you. You will force me whenever you want a woman. You are lying to me. All men lie to get what they want."

He let her go and rose to stand by the bed. "You will learn to believe me, to trust me."

She was now on the far side of the bed. She simply stared at him and he saw all her fear of him in her eyes, a damned irrational fear, and in that moment he wanted to throw her out of the window.

The irony of it didn't escape him. He wondered what the hell he was going to do now. He rang for bathwater. Once he'd dressed, he left the bedchamber, left her alone and silent, lying in bed, the covers drawn to her chin.

Sinjun said to the breakfast table at large, "I saw the Virgin Bride last night. She probably came to visit Sophie and got the wrong bedchamber. Just think," she added, turning toward her sister-in-law, "you just might get a visit from the family ghost too. She won't hurt you. She just wants to welcome you to the Sherbrooke family. She's been around for ever so long and all the past earls have written about her."

"Be quiet about that damned ghost," this earl said. "There is no ghost, Sophie. The brat has a very active imagination. Ignore her."

"A real ghost? You're not jesting?" Jeremy whispered so that just Sinjun heard him. He wasn't about to disagree with the Earl of Northcliffe.

"Yes, I'll tell you all about her. Later, when we go riding."

"I've never seen her," Ryder said, setting down his coffee cup. He took a bite of egg, looked at his wife, and winked at her. "Perhaps she'll visit us. Would you like that?"

"A ghost. Yes, I would. Who is she?"

"A young lady whose husband was killed before they could consummate their marriage," Ryder said. "Sixteenth century, I believe. She has long, very blond hair and all the filmy trappings, so Sinjun tells us. Evidently she appears only to the women of the family."

Alex opened her mouth then shut it.

"The Earls of Northcliffe write about her, as I said," Sinjun said. "It is too bad of Douglas—he refuses to hear about her, and more than that, he swears he won't pen a word about her."

The earl harrumphed and gave a stern look to his wife, who was now studiously separating the kippers on her plate. He said to the table at large, "We must have a ball or something equally formal so that Sophie can be introduced to the neighborhood. In the meanwhile Alex will take you about, Sophie, to meet our more illustrious neighbors."

"Will Tony and Melissande come?"

"Doubtless they will, Sinjun," Alex said. She continued to Sophie, "Melissande is my sister. She's incredibly beautiful and she married Tony Parrish, Viscount Rathmore. He is Douglas and Ryder's first cousin. You will enjoy both of them. Perhaps Tysen can come from Oxford as well. He is the youngest of the brothers and plans to be a vicar."

The dowager countess said sharply, "She cannot go to a ball dressed in Alex's castoffs, Douglas."

"No, I quite agree. We will have that seamstress in from Rye. You know, Alex, the one who fitted you up."

Lady Lydia said to no one in particular, "Ah, dear Melissande. How I wanted her for my daughter, but Douglas wouldn't oblige me. I did have hope for you, Ryder, but Tony was impossible about the entire matter."

"Tony is married to her, ma'am," Alexandra said easily. "Besides, Tony is always impossible. It's part of his charm. You will like him immensely, Sophie, as he will you. As for Melissande, well, she is also many times vastly amusing."

Sophie stared down at the congealed eggs on her plate. All these people she didn't know and didn't care about, no more than they cared about her. Like all the men on Jamaica, Tony would probably look at her and decide she was a loose tart. She picked up a scone and nibbled on it. Conversation flowed around her. She vaguely heard more insults tossed in her general direction from her mother-in-law.

She suddenly felt him looking at her. She raised her head to see Ryder simply staring at her, his fork halfway to his mouth. What was wrong? Was there butter on her chin?

He grinned. "You look beautiful this morning, Sophie, but a bit pale. I want color in my wife's cheeks. After breakfast, change into your riding habit and I will show you this favorite place of mine. Unlike Douglas, I don't spend a lot of time striding over cliffs that could crumble beneath me. No, this is another sort of place. You will like it."

Sophie didn't imagine that she would like it at all. He likely wanted to take her to a private place and come inside her again. She hurt inside. The muscles in her thighs pulled and ached. She didn't want him near her. She said nothing.

She wanted to spend some time with Jeremy, but before she could open her mouth, Sinjun and Jeremy had risen together from the table. Sophie watched her little brother place his hand in Sinjun's and smile up at her. The two of them left the room together.

Ryder said very gently, "Sinjun is a new treat. You, my dear, are an old tale. I am pleased they do well together. You and I will fascinate Jeremy later."

She disliked his knowing what was in her mind; she disliked his logic, his reasonableness. Few men she'd ever known had been very reasonable. Ryder hadn't been reasonable either on Jamaica. He'd been cynical, utterly ruthless, and calculating as the devil. This was another side of him she didn't like, didn't want to see or to recognize.

Ryder said to his brother, "While Sophie changes into her riding clothes, would you like to join me in the estate room? I need to speak with you."

Lady Lydia took only one parting shot. "I say, my dear boy, should you like to invite the Harvestons to your ball?"

Since neither dear boy knew who it was their mother was addressing, both merely nodded, Douglas wincing and Ryder wanting to curse.

"The Harvestons, of course, have three beautiful daughters," Lady Lydia said. "They are just returned from a visit to American relatives in Boston." She added, a sapient eye on Sophie, "I don't like this at all."

"I don't either, ma'am," Sophie said, tossed her napkin on her plate, and pushed back her chair before Jamieson, a footman, could assist her. What her mother-in-law had meant, of course, was that she didn't like Sophie, who was a nobody, in her mind.

"Take your time changing, Sophie," Alex called after her. "Douglas and Ryder probably have a lot to discuss. It's been a long time and they're very close, you know."

In the estate room, Douglas was sitting behind his desk, watching his brother pace the length of the room. They were silent for moments.

"She's a charming girl," Douglas said.

"Yes, she is."

"She doesn't behave at all like a bride. She spent most of her time before you arrived alone. She is also unhappy."

Ryder paused in his pacing long enough to curse.

"I had believed her homesick at first, but that isn't it at all."

"No."

"Last night—it surprised me. Quite took me aback. I was on my way to the kitchen to fetch Alex some milk when I saw her flying down the corridor, her face pale as her skin. You don't have to tell me anything, Ryder. But I would help if I could. Is it because of something you've done that she is unhappy? Did she find out about all of your women? Did you hurt her? Is she jealous?"

"It is because of a lot of things. Thank you for taking such good care of her until I came home. I do wish Mother would control what comes out of her mouth, but I suppose it isn't to be expected."

"No. She will come around eventually. If she becomes too outrageous I will simply threaten to move her to the dower house."

"An excellent threat."

"Exactly."

The brothers grinned at each other. Douglas said, "I was vastly surprised when your wife and her brother arrived on the doorstep. Hollis knew immediately, curse his damned hide, knew the very instant he saw her that she was quality and that she belonged here. There is another thing. At first she avoided me. I couldn't figure out why. I was polite, I was solicitous, I tried to make her welcome. Then I realized she didn't trust me. She didn't trust me as a man. That I found very curious, inexplicable really. Why is she unhappy, Ryder?"

"She's afraid of me. She was probably afraid of you too."

There was utter silence. Douglas said, clearly disbelieving, "That's utterly absurd. Why would your wife be afraid of me? I did nothing untoward. Nor have I ever known a woman to be remotely afraid of you. Why, they pursue you, they won't let you alone. All of them want to get you out of your britches."

"Things change."

"Would you like to tell me what happened in Jamaica? No, no, not about Uncle Brandon leaving you Kimberly Hall and the fiasco surrounding all that, but why exactly Sophie Stanton-Greville doesn't want to be here with you as your wife, why she ran out of your bedchamber, seemingly terrified."

"It isn't a very uplifting story, Douglas. There have been many men in her life and none of them were nice." God, he thought, what an asinine thing to say. "That is," he amended carefully, "the circumstances of Sophie and all these men weren't very nice."

"I understand perfectly. No, no, you don't have to strain yourself to be more equivocal. If you need me, Ryder, I'm here."

"Thank you, Douglas."

"The boy is delightful. Was he born with the clubfoot?"

"Yes, he was. He rides very well. Do you think he would survive at Eton?"

"Let's give him a while longer to adjust, I think."

"She hates sex. She hates me touching her."

Douglas simply looked at his brother.

"Damnation, but it's very complicated," Ryder said, and plowed his fingers through his hair, making it stand on end. "I shouldn't speak so personally about my wife. The thing is she doesn't want me, never did want me. I manipulated her into marrying me. Can you imagine that? Me being the one to want to marry? Me, forcing a woman to marry me? But I did it and I'm not sorry for it. She didn't want to marry any man."

Douglas waited, saying nothing, until finally, "This is passing strange. If you wish to speak more about it, I'm always here. Now, I must tell you—Emily had twins. Unfortunately neither of them survived. She is looking forward to seeing you. She said something Hollis didn't completely understand, something about it being better this way because it wasn't fair, that she hadn't wanted to do this to you."

"I will see her as soon as I can."

"Do you understand what she meant?"

Ryder simply shrugged and looked out the window.

Douglas picked up a singularly beautiful black onyx paperweight and tossed it from one hand to the other. "I suppose you've decided what to do about all your women and your children."

"Yes, I've given it a lot of thought. There wasn't much else to do coming home."

"What, no available ladies on board ship?"

Ryder gave him an austere look.

"Just remember, Ryder, your life before you married Sophie was yours and you were free to do whatever pleased you. As was mine."

Ryder gave his brother a crooked smile. "I doubt she'd even care if I paraded a hundred women in front of her nose. She'd probably beg them to keep me away from her."

"One never knows about a wife, even one who appears to want to slit one's throat. Sophie just might surprise you, that is, if she does find out about all the other women."

"Ha."

Douglas pulled a sheet of foolscap out of the drawer of his desk. "Your most recent tally is seven children." He stopped, and stared at his brother. "You know all that. You've evidently decided what you will do about it."

"Yes, I have. I'm a married man now. There will be no other women."

The earl sat back in his chair. "I'm pleased you've decided to be faithful to your wife. Keeping a herd this size content would tax even the strongest man. Fidelity does have its advantages."

"I agree," Ryder said, then appeared startled at what he'd said. "I can't believe that I agree, but I do. Wanting only one woman is a startling revelation. But I want Sophie and only Sophie. Good Lord, it's rather unbelievable, I know, but there it is."

"For what it's worth, I've also discovered that a wife is very precious. A wife is beyond anything I had ever imagined in my life."

"Alex is a good sort. I'm relieved you worked things out."

"Oh, we did and therein lies a tale. Some long night this winter I'll tell you about it. It certainly would be more enlivening than writing about that damned ghost, the Virgin Bride." The earl rose. "I would say, old man, that you have quite a task ahead of you. On the other hand, nothing of true importance should come easily."

"I already appreciate her, if that's what you're getting at. It's odd but I truly do. She's important to me, more important than you can begin to imagine. You told me once that I thrived on challenges, the higher the stakes, the better I did. I won't lose this one, Douglas. I can't."

"You love her, then."

"You spout nonsense, Douglas. Love—a notion that makes me want to puke. No, pray don't go on and on about how much you adore and worship Alex—I see quite clearly that you're besotted with her. But love? Don't get me wrong. I like Sophie, certainly. I want her and she makes me feel things I've never felt before. I want her to be happy. I want her to realize that for whatever reason, she is important to me. There's nothing more to it than that and, indeed, that's quite enough. She's got me for life."

Douglas simply looked at his brother, a very black eyebrow arched upward a good inch.

"You haven't seen her as I did on Jamaica. You think her unhappy, a quiet mouse, no doubt. She's a hellion, Douglas. I wanted to tame her, wanted to make her submit to me." He shook his head and began pacing again. "I wish the hellion would come back." He grinned. "She was a handful and a more mouthy chit you'd never meet."

Douglas still just looked at his brother.

Sophie was smiling like an idiot, she couldn't help it. Her own mare, Opal, was here at Northcliffe, brought back from Jamaica by Ryder. She leaned over and patted her mare's long neck.

"Ah, I have missed you," she said, and threw back her head, letting her mare gallop ahead. She'd thanked Ryder, too shocked at what he'd done to really show him how much she appreciated it. He wasn't acting like himself again. It was disturbing, this kindness of his, this seemingly endless understanding and gentleness.

Ryder had shrugged and said only, "She would have eaten her head off if I'd left her at Camille Hall. She was fat and lazy and gave me these woeful looks every time I saw her. She neighed all the time I was around and soon it sounded remarkably like your name. What was I to do?"

And she'd said only, once again, "Thank you."

Ryder rode beside her, pleased at her pleasure, knowing that he'd surprised her but good. She owed him. He wondered how she would proceed to repay him, for repay him she would. He knew her well enough to know that she'd see this as a debt.

When she sent her mare into a gallop, he let her go ahead of him down the narrow country lane that bordered the northern boundaries of Northcliffe land. He slowed his own stallion, Genesis, a raw-boned barb who was black as sin and had the endurance of twenty Portuguese mules.

He began whistling. He was home, the day was glorious, warm, the sun bright overhead, and he'd pleased his wife. Things were looking up. He knew what he was going to do about his women and the solution was sound. As for his children, it was simply a matter of telling Sophie about them at the right time. He missed them. He would go see them all tomorrow. He'd brought back gifts for all of them.

Sophie rounded a narrow bend in the road and pulled over under the shade of an immense oak tree, old as the chalk cliffs just some miles to the south. She drew in a deep breath and realized she felt good. Ryder was behaving in a very civilized manner. Except for the previous night. That was reminiscent of the arrogant, utterly ruthless man she'd known on Jamaica. Perhaps today he'd realize that she didn't want him to touch her again, perhaps he'd simply be nice to her and remain civilized. She frowned.

She waited for him for some ten minutes, then turned to see if he were coming around the curve. There was no sign of him.

She fidgeted a moment longer, then wheeled Opal around and urged her back down the road. She felt a spurt of alarm. Could he have been hurt?

She saw Ryder. He wasn't at all hurt. There was a woman on a bay mare pulled to a halt next to him. They were in the middle of the road and they looked to be in intimate conversation. She saw the woman stretch out her hand and lightly touch Ryder's sleeve. She saw Ryder smile, even from here, she saw his white teeth in that utterly devastating smile of his. He then leaned closer to the woman.

Something in her moved and twisted. Something in her rebelled and boiled. Her jaw clenched. Her gloved hands fisted on Opal's reins.

Without thought, she jabbed her boots into Opal's fat sides and sent her straight toward her husband and the hussy who looked ready to leap onto his horse's back and onto his lap.

Ryder looked up and saw Sophie galloping *ventre à terre* straight at him. The look on her face was grim and pale. Jesus, she looked fit to kill. He grinned like a fool. He'd at first been uneasy when Sara had flagged him down. Now, seeing his wife ride toward him angry as a wasp, he was glad Sara had come. Anger bespoke feelings other than indifference.

Sara was speaking to him. She hadn't yet seen the madwoman bearing down on them. She was asking in that soft, gentle way of hers if he wouldn't like to kiss her. She leaned toward him and he felt her sweet mouth on his cheek, her gloved hand on his chin, trying to turn him toward her. He opened his mouth to tell her to stop, then shut it again. No, let Sophie see another lady kissing him. Her mouth was smooth and fresh but he felt nothing but anticipation to see what Sophie would do. His wife was on them then, and he had to jerk his stallion back so she wouldn't slam into them. As for Sara, she looked at the woman and actually paled.

"Just who the devil are you?"

It was Sophie's voice and Ryder hadn't heard that tone for more than two months. It was cold and angry and arrogant and he loved it. There was fire in her eyes.

"Damn you, keep away from my husband!"

"Your *what?*" Poor Sara was trying to make her mare back up but the beast was eyeing Opal with fascination and refused to move.

"You heard me! What are you saying to him? Why did you touch him? How dare you kiss him! Keep your blasted fingers and hands to yourself—and your miserable hussy mouth!"

Sara blinked. She turned from the woman to Ryder, who was lazily sitting his stallion, his eyes on the woman's face. He was smiling. His eyes were gleaming. He looked arrogant, naturally, Ryder was the most arrogant beast she'd ever known, but there was no cynical glimmer in his blue eyes, no, just pleasure and she didn't understand it. Goodness, if his eyes had been dark, they would have looked wicked. "She is your wife, Ryder?"

He turned to Sara then and nodded. "I was about to tell you but she rode down on us like one of the damned Greek Furies. Sophie, draw in your claws. This is Sara Clockwell and she is a friend of mine. Sara, my wife, Sophie."

It was at that instant that Sophie realized what she'd done. She'd acted like a shrew, a jealous, possessive termagant. She'd yelled and cursed and insulted this woman. And Ryder loved it. He looked very smug and satisfied and she'd just given him more fodder than a five-acre wheatfield needed. She felt humiliated; she felt exposed and very uncertain of herself and what she was and why she'd behaved as she had.

She nodded to the woman, silent as the grave now, a very lovely young woman with large breasts and an uncertain smile on a wide mouth. She said to her husband, her voice stiff as a fence post, "I am sorry to disturb your conversation with your *friend*. Since you haven't seen each other for quite a few months, I will leave you alone to renew yourselves." She wheeled Opal around and rode away fast as the wind.

Ryder merely smiled after her, the wickedness alive and thriving in his eyes. Douglas had been right about Sophie surprising him. It was beyond wonderful. Sweet heavens, he felt a surge of hope.

"Your wife, Ryder?"

He didn't hear hurt in her voice, just utter disbelief. He turned to look at Sara's bewildered face. "Yes, she is. I met her on Jamaica and wed her there. We have been separated until just yesterday. She's a hellion, isn't she? She speaks her mind openly. Forgive her but she is possessive of me. I like that, you know." He rubbed his hands together in pleasure.

"You . . . you like that?" Sara managed, still trying to grasp this beyond-odd situation. "You have never wanted a woman to be possessive. Why, Beatrice told me that—" Her voice broke off and she blushed.

Ryder's left eyebrow shot up. "You and Bea? Come, tell me the truth, Sara."

"Bea told me that you hated any sort of clinging or orders or demands from a woman. She said you hated for a woman to be serious, to bedevil you, to . . . well, she did also say that you were honorable and a woman could trust you. She said you were lighthearted and fun, that you only enjoyed women in your bed. She said you were always generous with pleasure and I told her I knew that for a fact."

Ryder was silent for a long moment. So his mistresses discussed him, did they? It made him feel rather strange. Of course men discussed their mistresses, but that was the way of things. But women discussing him?

He said finally, his voice very quiet, "Bea was wrong. Sophie is strong-willed and I fancy my days of freedom with other ladies are well over."

"You don't mind, truly?"

He grinned at her.

"But I wanted to see you, to tell you that—"

"That what, Sara?"

She said on a rush, "That I am going to marry David Dabbs. He's a farmer near Swinley."

"Congratulations. Then, I take it, you have no more use for me?"

She shook her head uncertainly, and decided it was her best course to essay a laugh. Sara had never been able to laugh when she was supposed to. But it hadn't seemed to bother Ryder. He'd always adored her breasts and her ears, he'd tell her in the next breath, even as he pumped into her, soft little ears that tasted like plums and peaches. She hadn't understood him, but she'd had more pleasure with him than she expected to share with the dour David. But a husband was a husband, and they lasted until they died, they had no choice in the matter, and now even Ryder was one. It was amazing; it was unbelievable, but he looked quite pleased about it. And this wife of his was possessive.

Only now he was frowning.

"You must go after her, Ryder. She is angry that she saw us together. She is angry that I was kissing you and that you were, well—there it is."

Ryder turned to grin at her. She sounded pleased that his wife was jealous of her. He enjoyed her show of vanity. Perhaps one day, Sophie would be just a bit transparent so that he wouldn't have to flay his mind to constantly outguess her. He leaned over and kissed Sara's cheek. "I wish you luck with your David, Sara. Good-bye."

Ryder didn't ride after his wife. He turned Genesis back toward Northcliffe. A wife should have to stew in her jealous juices once in a while. He certainly had no intention of apologizing to her for Sara or any of the others. Ah, what was she doing now?

He was whistling as he dug his heels into his stallion's sides.

CHAPTER
═16═

SOPHIE RETURNED TO the hall an hour later. She felt like a fool. She wanted to kick herself. She didn't, quite simply, understand why she'd done it. She left Opal with a huge bucket of oats in the stable, spoke with the head stable lad, McCallum, a man who was crusty and likable and looked at her just like he would a horse, then walked toward the mansion. She stopped suddenly, disbelieving, shading her eyes from the bright sun. No, it couldn't be true. Not again. There, standing on the deep-set front steps, was a young woman, a very pretty young woman with very black hair. Ryder was standing on the step above her. She was leaning into him and her hand was on his right arm. He was speaking quietly to her and she was nodding. Sophie's stomach churned and her jaw locked for the second time that afternoon. All rational thought fled her brain.

She shrieked, waving her fist at her husband, "You damnable rotter!" She picked up her skirts and ran toward them, unable to stop either her feet or the words that flew out of her mouth. "How dare you! Get away from my husband. If you try to kiss him, I'll break your arm!"

Tess Stockley froze. Then, because she wasn't stupid, she took a quick step back. "My God, who is she, Ryder? She looks like a madwoman. I don't understand . . . is she another one of your women? This is very strange, Ryder. Why is she so angry? Surely she knows she's just one of your women."

Ryder didn't reply. He was watching Sophie dash toward them, her hands holding up her skirts so that she could run without fear of tripping. He was enjoying the view of her ankles and the look of utter outrage on her face. Her hair was coming loose from its thick bun and thick tendrils were straggling down about her face. Her charming borrowed riding hat fell to the dirt.

A madwoman indeed—his madwoman. What marvelous timing. His Sherbrooke luck had returned. He crossed his arms over his chest, his heart speeding up in anticipation. Normally his women didn't come to Northcliffe Hall, but Tess had worried because he'd been so long in coming home. Bea had told her to stop her fretting because Ryder was like a cat, he always landed on his feet. But she'd come anyway, and she'd been near to tears when she'd seen him safe, and she was so happy to see him . . . then this strange girl was screaming at them.

Ryder's jaws ached from smiling so widely. He yelled out, "Hello, Sophie. Did you stable Opal? Did you feed her? You wish to say something to Tess? She's a friend of mine, you know. Do come and meet her. We were just talking of Jamaica and sea travel and—"

"You miserable bounder! Another one? How many women do you have? Are they all young and beautiful? By all that's sinful, you should be hung and shot and disemboweled! Why, I should—" Her voice swallowed itself. She paled. She shook her head and the bun fell to thick strands of hair, tangling down her back. "Oh no," she said, unable to believe herself. "I didn't just say that, did I?" She picked up her skirts again and ran away from the mansion toward the Greek statue-infested gardens. She just might enjoy those nude statues, Ryder thought, staring after her. Had she already seen them? He must remember to ask her. He thought of making love to her beneath a woefully bad marble rendition of Zeus seducing some swan or other.

He turned back to Tess, who was gazing with incredulous astonishment upon the fleeing Sophie. He said, smiling like a besotted fool, "She's my wife. Her name is Sophie Sherbrooke, and she's very possessive of me. You must keep your distance from her."

"Your *what*?"

Ryder knew a moment of irritation. Was his marrying such a bloody shock? Such a cause for disbelief?

"My wife, dammit. Now, Tess, since I am a married man, I must tell you that I cannot see you again. However . . ." He paused then smiled. "We have had much enjoyment together, you and I. But now it must stop. Do you think perhaps you would like to wed in the near future?"

She stared at him as if he had two heads. "But you love women, Bea says you need a variety, and—"

"What is Bea, your mother superior? Does she invite all of you over for tea parties to pour advice down your gullets? No, don't answer that. Sophie is my wife. Now, my dear, if you should perhaps like to consider getting yourself leg-shackled soon, why then, let me tell you about this very nice man in Southampton. He is the first mate on a barkentine, a solid man, quite admirable, really. Quite a manly man I should say, arms thick as an oak trunk."

Tess looked at him for a very long time. She said finally, "A girl should marry, I suppose. Sara says that husbands can belch and snore, but they'll stay because they have to. What is his name?"

Ryder told her. She was interested.

He felt very good as he walked into the huge entrance hall. He would have given a great deal of guineas to have been present at one of his mistresses' tea parties.

It was nearly midnight. Ryder rubbed the grit in his eyes with the heel of his hand and reviewed yet again the list he'd compiled during the voyage home. He was pleased. He leaned back in his chair and closed his eyes for a moment.

He pictured Sophie in their bed, probably still awake, probably afraid that he'd come to her and force her again and she'd be more vulnerable if she were asleep. But he hadn't gone to her and he wouldn't for a while yet. He'd keep her guessing. He had her there for he was as unpredictable as she was, his dear heart, and he knew it drove her quite mad. He'd said not a word about her behavior earlier in the afternoon. Not a single word. If there had been a knowing gleam in his eyes whenever he looked at her, well, that couldn't be helped. He'd been exquisitely polite. She'd gotten herself all puffed up, he recognized the signs, and for once she was completely transparent to him, and he'd simply sidestepped her with the ease of long and successful practice. He was well versed in the ways of women. And even Sophie, hide it as best she could, was still a woman. The presence of his talkative family was an unquestioned aid. He'd sent her to bed with a nod and a pat on the cheek. She'd looked three parts furious with him and another three parts bewildered. It was promising.

He shook himself and penned down another name on the foolscap. Joseph Beefly. Miserable last name, but the man was nice and steady, and a girl could do much worse for a husband. He did have a bit of a paunch, but on the other hand he didn't drink too much and he didn't abuse women. His breath wasn't offensive and he bathed often enough. He rather thought that Emily would do well with Joseph. As Sara had said, Tess her echo, a husband, after all, was a husband, and had to, perforce, stay put. Ryder paused for a moment to stare pensively into the wispy flame cast out by the single candle at his left elbow.

The list he'd compiled was impressive and he'd managed to add a couple more names. Alongside each woman's name he listed at least four men's names. It was a good thing he'd lived here all his life. He knew nearly everyone within a fifty-mile radius. So many men, thank the good Lord. Choice was important. The good Lord knew, too, that not all the women would want husbands. But he wanted to be certain each of them was well taken care of. He would naturally provide them all with dowries if they wished to wed. Those who didn't—well, they would get dowries too. He wondered if he should also compile a list of possible protectors to be found in London. No, it was too crass, far too crude for a polished sort like him.

He thought of his children then and smiled. They were a constant in his life and would always remain so. He didn't doubt for a moment that there would be more. Lord, he missed them. He anticipated the following day with pleasure.

Finally, having tired of his list and of making Sophie writhe in uncertainty, he rose and stretched. He blew out the candle. He knew every inch of Northcliffe and had no need to light his way.

Sophie wasn't asleep. She was sitting up in bed, staring toward the far corner of the bedchamber. Ryder quickly lit a candle and quietly approached the bed. At first she didn't pay him any heed. Then she turned and he saw that her face was pale, her eyes dilated, and she blinked into the candlelight.

He frowned down at her. "What's the matter? Did you have a nightmare?"

She shook her head. He stared a moment at all that tousled thick hair that fell onto her face and over her shoulders. She ran her tongue over her lips. Her hands fisted at the covers at her waist. "I think I just met your Virgin Bride."

"Excuse me?"

"The Virgin Bride—the Sherbrooke ghost. I guess Sinjun was right, she wanted to welcome me to your blasted family. Maybe."

"Bosh. You had a strange dream, nothing more."

Sophie just shook her head. She'd been afraid at first, very afraid, but then the young woman, a ghost presumably, had merely looked at her, and she would have sworn that she spoke, but she knew she hadn't because she'd been looking at her face and her lips hadn't moved. But she knew she heard her soft voice clearly saying softly, but with absolute conviction, "Don't worry. Even when they come it will be all right."

"Who?" Sophie had said aloud. "Please, what do you mean?" The young woman had shimmered in the dim light that hadn't really been there, just shimmered and retreated, quickly, yet there hadn't been any real movement, nothing jerky, just the quiet grace of the still air. She'd seen her clearly yet the bedchamber was dark, too dark to make out the details she knew she'd seen. Then she was simply gone, her hand stretched out toward Sophie, just as Ryder had come into the room.

"Sophie, there's no such thing as the damned Virgin Bride. It's a simple legend. Sinjun is a fanciful girl—it wouldn't surprise me if she occasionally plays the blighted young lady just to tease us. No, you dreamed her up."

"No I didn't. She spoke to me, Ryder, only she didn't, not really, but I heard her, and the words were very clear."

He was caught, he couldn't deny it. He set the candle on the tabletop beside the bed and sat down beside her, not touching her. "What were the words she didn't really say?"

"She said that I wasn't to worry, that even when they come it will be all right."

He frowned at that. Such a message was unexpected. He'd rather thought the words would hark to some sort of secret treasure or some such. Perhaps that Sophie would bear twins and they would grow up to wed English royalty.

"What the hell does that mean? Who are 'they,' for God's sake?"

"I asked her but she just disappeared. Then you came in. I think you chased her away."

"Nonsense."

Sophie turned to him, frowning, then realized that she was in her nightgown and he was sitting next to her, fully dressed, thank God, but still. He was here, sitting on the bed, and he was her husband. She forgot the ghost and the message. She forgot her lamentable behavior of the afternoon. She even forgot, for the moment, those two very lovely young women. She very slowly began to move away from him until she was on the edge of the other side of the bed.

Ryder pretended not to notice. He rose, stretched, and began to take off his clothes.

She wouldn't watch him this time, she wouldn't. She said, "What have you been doing? It's quite late."

"Ah, just a bit of this and that."

"You were with one of your legion of women, weren't you?"

"Legion? No more than a small battalion. I'm only one man, Sophie, no matter how much you stand in awe of my strength and vigor."

"I don't care. Your claims to such prowess is absurd. You are jesting with me, mocking me, and I don't like it. Keep a hundred women, nay, five hundred. It matters not to me."

"Are you certain about that, Sophie? You saw only two today and you went really quite charmingly mad."

She looked at him. He was naked. He was just standing there on the other side of the bed, quite without a stitch of clothing on. He was tall and lean and very nicely formed, she would give him that. She looked furtively toward the bedchamber door.

"No, no more races down the corridor. I prefer to be the only man to see you wearing only your beautiful hide."

"It was very embarrassing. It was difficult to face your brother today."

"I imagine that it was. However, perhaps Douglas is excessively my-opic. Now, just to clear the air between us, I know that you've wanted to box my ears all evening. Please feel free to box metaphorically, to express your heartfelt rage, to expound freely on your woman's ire."

"You would like that, wouldn't you? You would enjoy me squawking like a fool so it would make you feel important. Men like to have women fighting over them, they like to be the center of everything. Well, I will tell you, Ryder Sherbrooke, I felt nothing! Absolutely nothing, less than nothing. It was merely that I felt angry for your brother. It must be be-yond embarrassing for the earl to have all these women hanging about Northcliffe Hall, hanging on your arm and whispering nonsense into your ears and kissing you."

"Really? That sounds very rehearsed to me. Not bad, don't misunder-stand me. Just practiced, perhaps a dozen times." He scratched his belly and her eyes followed every movement of his long fingers. He wasn't all that hairy, but the thick light brown hair at his groin . . . she managed to look back to his face. He knew she'd been looking at him, he knew, but he said only, "Goodness, so you wish me to believe that all your curses at me were in defense of my poor beleaguered brother's sensibilities?"

Sophie knew she was digging a hole that would eventually reach to China if she didn't stop now. She tightened her lips until it hurt. She just shook her head.

"It pleases me that you've found a bit of control. But, my dear wife, if you wish to continue to rant, please do, I don't mind."

"Go to the devil," she said, then concentrated on keeping her mouth shut.

Ryder raised his arms and stretched. She was looking at him again and he knew it, and his sex swelled quite predictably, there was nothing he could do about it. She stared at him for a very long time, then jerked, as if finally realizing what she was doing. She looked away, toward the win-dows.

"You quite terrified both Sara and Tess," he said, dumping a bit of oil into the fire. "They couldn't accept at first that I would enjoy a posses-sive, quite jealous wife."

She managed not to take the bait.

He smiled at the back of her head as he stepped to the bed. He pulled back the covers and climbed in.

She felt the bed give and knew if she were going to run it had to be now.

"Don't, Sophie."

"Don't what, you wretched bounder?"

"Try to run again. I locked the bedchamber door."

This was ridiculous. She knew it and so did he. She closed her eyes a moment, then slowly she turned to face him. "Ryder," she said, "I don't want you to force me again. Please don't shame me or make me beg you."

"Lie down, Sophie. On your back."

She shook her head.

"Now, if you please. If you're good to me, I will tell you a story. Would you like that?"

"No," she said, but she lay down.

"Good." He leaned over her, looking down, studying her face. A beautiful face to him. He touched his fingertip to the tip of her nose. "I'm very glad you're here," he said.

"Why?"

"Because you're you and I managed quite by a wonderful stroke of luck to find you and I even had the good sense to marry you."

"That's absurd. I'm nothing, when will you admit it? You were simply caught up in a series of very strange happenings. You felt sorry for me, finally, nothing more. Your mother despises me. I don't belong here. Please, Ryder—"

"I was thinking about that," he said slowly, and his fingers continued to lightly touch her jaw, her nose, her mouth. "About not belonging here. You're right."

She froze, a blaze of unexpected pain going through her.

"No, no, you misunderstand. This isn't your home. Alex is the mistress here, though I imagine she must fight my mother to gain what she wishes, the poor girl. No, this isn't your home. I have a home, Sophie, in the Cotswolds, not far from Strawberry Hill. That's where my cousin, Tony Parrish, and his wife, Melissande, live."

"You have a home?"

"I've never lived there. It's called Chadwyck House. I visit it three or four times a year. There is a good deal of farm acreage and there are some twenty tenant families living there. I have a steward—a fellow named Allen Dubust—who deals with the daily affairs." He paused, frowning a moment. "I'm beginning to believe that a man should deal with his own affairs. What do you say, Sophie? Shall we go to Chadwyck House? Would you like to be the mistress of your own home?"

Her eyes had lightened. He wasn't mistaken about that. There was pleasure there that temporarily had tamped down her fear of him.

"Yes," she said only. She opened her mouth but he lightly touched his fingers over her lips.

"No, my dear, I know you would like to ask me all sorts of questions to keep me from making love to you. We will speak more of Chadwyck House afterward."

"I want you to stop reading my mind before I have a chance to do it properly for myself."

"I have this affinity for you. I can't seem to help myself. Now, Sophie, I want you to do me a favor."

She stared up at him, frozen and wary.

"I am your husband. I won't ever hurt you. I have your best interests at heart. Nod your head if you at least understand what I've said."

She nodded.

"Good, a healthy start. I want to make something else very clear to you. I will make love to you every night. I want you to become used to me, to trust me. I want to erase all the other men, I want you to simply dismiss all the meanness and violence of your uncle from your mind. I want you to think only of me, of us."

"It is very difficult."

"I know, but today you were a hellion again, a possessive wench, the savage Amazon who saved my hide in Jamaica from Thomas's knife. So I have hope. Now, let's get that nightgown off you. I want no clothes between us, Sophie, not at night, not when we're alone. I want to look at you. I want to feel your breasts in my hands."

"Ryder, I really don't want—"

"I don't give a good damn, Sophie, so stop your bleating. Tonight, perhaps you will allow yourself to have some pleasure. I'm going to kiss you, every sweet inch of you. I will never give up on you, so you might as well accustom yourself to coming about to meet me halfway."

He kept talking, nonsense really, some of it quite amusing, and he would have given anything for a simple smile from her. But she just lay there, silent and withdrawn. She didn't fight him, but she held herself stiff, her hands fisted at her sides. Ryder wanted to nibble on her toes, he wanted to taste the soft flesh between her thighs, but the woman who lay on her back beneath him wasn't about to give an inch. Oddly enough, he wasn't unduly disturbed: he hadn't lied to her. He would never give up. She didn't realize it yet but they would be together until they shucked off their mortal coils. "I see I will have to wait a while longer to kiss every white inch of you." He did kiss her breasts, enjoying the taste of her, the texture of her flesh, and his hands were on her belly, and then lower, his fingers finding her and lightly stroking her. She tried to pull away. He stopped. It was a beginning.

Ryder wasn't about to enter her until she could take him without pain. He'd promised her and he wouldn't break his promise. No more savaging her as he'd done the previous night. He simply drew away from her, patted her cheek, and told her to stay put. He fetched a jar of cream from the night table beside the bed.

"What is that?" Her eyes never left his fingers, which were dipping into that jar.

"You will see. Hush."

He pushed her back down onto her back and held her there, his hand on her belly, pressing her thighs open with his legs, while he eased his slick finger inside her. He closed his eyes a moment at the feel of her. Dear God, he wanted her. He smoothed in the cream slowly and gently, his finger going more deeply into her, and then he inserted a second finger to widen her. It was almost more than he could bear. She was trembling and trying to pull away from him, but he held her still.

"Stop, damn you!" She tried to bring her legs together, but succeeded only in pushing his finger deeper inside her.

"Shush, sweetheart. No, I will use cream on you until you let me love you properly. Don't you like my finger sliding inside you, Sophie?"

"No."

"I like it very much. I will do it every time we make love. Get used to it. Ah, you're more yielding, Sophie. Can you feel it? You're softening for me though your active brain doesn't like it."

When he'd widened her, when he had made her soft and ready, he came over her. Very slowly, he came into her, controlling his entry, watching her face in the candlelight. There was no pain, he knew it, and he knew that she wouldn't ever be able to throw that up at him again. He also knew that he wouldn't be able to bring her to pleasure this time either. What was important was that her body begin to recognize him, that when he touched her, she would eventually respond without her mind trying to dismiss him.

He would have her yet. Patience was all he needed. He stroked deeply into her now, then pulled nearly out of her. He continued slowly, every feeling in him attuned to her. It suddenly occurred to him that he was behaving quite differently with Sophie than he had with every other woman in his male life. Before, when he'd come into a woman, he'd known almost instant irreversible lust. He couldn't have stopped if a tidal wave had swamped him. But not with Sophie. She was at the center of all his feelings. His body, his mind, both were focused entirely on her. He would do anything to bring her around and he didn't care how long it took him to succeed. He would win. His own body would wait. Another novel occurrence, and one Douglas would doubtless disbelieve.

He remembered his brother's joke about having his valet sew his britches shut because Ryder couldn't stop once he'd begun, he couldn't make himself withdraw from a woman. With Sophie it was different, simply because he was different.

He wished he could make her laugh. He lightly caressed his fingers over her belly, down, to find her again. He teased her soft woman's flesh, nothing more, just teased and stroked. Soon she would respond to him. And he kissed her and didn't stop kissing her.

He found his release eventually, but he didn't yell like a wild man. He moaned his pleasure into her mouth, holding her close to him, letting her feel the movement of his sex deep inside her, letting her feel the heat of his body.

He was amazed at himself and pleased. It was a start. She was lying there, but this time there were no tears. If he wasn't mistaken, she looked surprised. Exactly about what, he wasn't sure. He continued kissing her until he eased off her. Then he pulled her against him, stroked her hair, massaged her scalp, and said quietly, "Now I will keep my promise. Remember? I said I would tell you a story if you were good to me. You did well, Sophie. You will do better the next time and the next time after that. Now, this story is about a one-legged pirate who found himself marooned with three lusty women. The first woman's name was Belle and she was a strapping girl, all breasts and wide hips. Well, she fell instantly in love with him—of course he was the only man she'd seen in a good three months. She flung him onto the beach and ripped off his clothes. But then the second woman came along—her name was Goosie—and she saw that wooden leg and knew this was the man for her. Her favorite hobby was carving wood into ships and such. She'd carved up a good dozen palm trees during those long three months. So the two women were arguing and shouting at each other and the pirate was lying there quite naked and grinning like an ape at his good fortune, when the other woman—her name was Brassy—came along. You wouldn't believe what she did."

Sophie gave out a loud snort, then settled into snoring.

"Very well, you don't as yet appreciate my stories. Tomorrow night I'll continue with my tale, and you'll learn what Belle and Goosie and Brassy all did to this poor one-legged pirate."

He kissed her forehead, and whispered against her damp flesh, "Perhaps tomorrow night you might like to put the cream on your hand and slick it over me. What do you think?"

She said quite clearly, "No. I would rather cosh your thick head and heave you and all your damned women into the sea."

"On the other hand," he continued, pleased as a rooster turned free in the hen yard, "perhaps tomorrow night we won't need the cream. I'm an optimist, and I'm your husband."

"How many women do you have? How many mistresses?"

"More than three, at least I did. They're all in the past now."

She stiffened.

"That was the first thing I heard when I arrived in Montego Bay. You had three lovers. Well, I have known more women than you were reputed to have known men. I won't lie about that. It was before I'd met you and wanted you and married you."

"I don't care if you keep them all."

It was such an obvious lie that he merely leaned down and kissed the tip of her nose.

"You're beautiful," he said.

"You're the one who is myopic, not your damned brother."

"Ah, a bit of vinegar, a dab of testiness. Let's get some sleep. I fancy that I will wake you up early in the morning. You'll be all sweet and warm with sleep, Sophie, and I'll come inside you, and it will be slow and gentle and you will enjoy it. At least a bit."

She said not a word. Ryder didn't despair.

When he awoke the next morning and reached for her, she was gone. Well, hell, he thought. He wouldn't tell her of his fond plans again.

"Alex," Ryder said to his sister-in-law the following morning at the breakfast table. "I would appreciate you taking Sophie around to meet our neighbors. As for a ball, let's wait a while for that."

"Ah, so you realize this girl won't do well with all our illustrious friends."

Ryder merely smiled at his mother. She had come armed to the breakfast table, and she'd fired her opening salvo immediately. "No, not at all," Ryder said easily. "On Friday, Sophie and I are going to our own home, to Chadwyck House."

There was instant pandemonium at the table.

"You can't mean it!"

"Goodness, Ryder, you just got home! This is your home!"

And from Douglas, nothing, merely a smile, nearly hidden as he slowly sipped his coffee.

Alex said slowly, her voice instantly quieting the voices, "That gives us two days, Sophie. There is also the matter of clothes for you. We don't have much time."

It was at that instant that Sophie realized Jeremy wasn't smiling. He was staring down at his plate.

Again, Ryder, the bounder, seemed to know exactly what was going on. He knew exactly what to do. He said easily, "Well, Jeremy, I hope you don't mind staying for a couple of weeks here at Northcliffe Hall. I know Sinjun can be the very devil, a veritable nodcock, but if you think you can abide her for a while, then you may remain here."

Jeremy shot a guilty look at his sister. Sophie forced a smile. "It's up to you, Jeremy."

"Sinjun's going to take me to Branderleigh Farm to buy a pony," he burst out, half guilt, half unmistakable excitement.

And that was that. Sophie found out from Sinjun that Ryder was paying for the pony.

During that day and the next two days, while Sophie was meeting all their neighbors, and being fitted for new clothes, Ryder was visiting his former lovers. Of course they all already knew he was married. Bea had called a meeting. Three of the five women were interested in marrying. He presented the names on his list and left them each to ponder the good points of each man. Emily was still in bed, recovering from childbirth, but she would mend and he even made her smile twice. The other two wanted to go try their luck in London. He gave them money and wished them luck. As for Bea, he simply shook his head when she opened the door of her cottage to him just after luncheon.

"Busy Bea," he said, and hugged her. "I swear you would do me in if you weren't so fond of me."

"Good thing for you that I am, Master Ryder!"

She loved to call him master, it was one of her favorite fantasies. Bea had great common sense and the most unusual preferences of any woman he'd ever known.

"I hear you've visited all your women and presented them with possible husbands."

Ryder rolled his eyes as he followed her into her small pristine drawing room. "Would you care to peruse the list for yourself?"

"Oh, not me, sir. I'm off to London to make my fortune, just like Laura and Molly. Actually, I think I'll ask Emily to come with me. The last thing she needs to do is fall into a decline. That's when a female is most vulnerable. I'll make certain she doesn't fall into the clutches of another despotic man. It's a boardinghouse I'm thinking about, Master Ryder, all my own. I've saved enough money, you know. You're a generous man, but still a man. I will remain my own woman and I will find another lover as polished as you are."

She ground to a halt and he picked up her hand and brought it to his lips. "There are no other men to be found who are as polished as I am."

She laughed and punched his arm.

"Now, my dear, I don't want you owning just any boardinghouse, no, I want you to buy a property in a very good section of London. I will give you the name of the Sherbrooke solicitor in London and he will see to it for you. Also, you will get a boardinghouse dowry from me."

"You will miss me, Ryder."

"Oh yes. I most certainly will. Wish me luck with my new wife, Bea."

"You need luck with a woman?"

"More than you know. I've met my match."

As Ryder rode away from Bea's cottage, he wondered if perhaps Sophie would enjoy playing slave girl to his master. Perhaps he could bring her around to it by November. Yes, the days would be shorter then and it would be chilly outside. It would mean long hours in front of the fireplace. He pictured her wearing soft veils, her hair long down her back, teasing him, and he would have her dance for him, like Salome. It would lead to laughter, this kind of play, and to passion. Then he wondered what the ghost had meant by "when they come . . ."

CHAPTER
═══ 17 ═══

RYDER'S LAST STOP of the afternoon was at Jane Jasper's spacious three-story house just outside of the small village of Hadleigh Dale that lay seven miles east of Northcliffe Hall. The house and drive were surrounded by oak and lime trees, thick and green now. He heard his children yelling and laughing before he saw them. He smiled in anticipation as he turned Genesis onto the short drive and dug his heels into his stallion's sides.

Jane and her three helpers, all young women with immense energy and goodwill, all of whom he'd selected himself, were standing in the front yard watching the children play. There were four boys and three girls, all between the ages of four and ten. They were well clothed, clean, loud, and Ryder felt such pleasure at the sight of them that he wanted to shout.

He saw Oliver standing a bit off to the side, a tall, thin boy of ten, leaning on his crutches, but there was a grin on his face as he shouted advice to Jaime, all of six years old and full of male bravado, on how to smash the grit out of Tom, a cherub-faced little boy who could curse more fluently than a Southampton sailor. John, the peacemaker at only eight, a barking spaniel nipping at his heels, was trying to keep them from coming to blows.

Jaime spotted Ryder first and let out a yell. The instant Ryder dropped Genesis's reins and turned, he was nearly brought to the ground by flying arms and legs, and three dogs all leaping and barking madly.

They were all shouting, laughing, all of them talking at once, telling him what they'd done during his absence, all except Jenny, of course, who hung back, her thumb in her mouth. Her mop of dark brown curls shadowing her small face, her ribbon long gone. Ryder gave his full attention to the children, trying to answer all of them at once. He grinned at Jane over Melissa's small head as the little girl took her turn and hugged her skinny arms around his neck until he yelled with imagined pain, making all the children shout with laughter. He was listening to Jaime's near brush with a sunken log while learning how to swim when

Jane and her helpers brought out glasses of lemonade and plates of cakes and scones. He sat in their midst, drinking his lemonade, tossing bits of scone to the dogs, listening to their stories, their arguments, all in all, enjoying himself immensely. Jenny sat quietly, two children away from him, slowly and methodically eating a small lemon cake.

After Ryder had distributed all their presents and stepped back to witness them attack the wrapped packages with ill-disguised greed, he walked over to Jenny. She raised her small face, and her blue eyes— Sherbrooke blue eyes, light as the blue of a summer day—were wide and not quite so blank as he remembered. She smiled and he saw joy in her expression, he knew he wasn't mistaken.

"My little love," he said and kneeled down in front of her. He pulled her thumb from her mouth, ran his fingers through her soft hair, and then, very gently, brought her against his chest. The little girl sighed softly, and her arms crept around his neck. He kissed her hair, then closed his eyes, breathing in the sweet child scent of her. God, he loved her, this child of his loins and of his heart.

"She does better, Ryder. She is learning. She is more a part of things, she is more aware."

He didn't release his daughter as he looked up to see Jane standing just behind her.

"She misses you dreadfully whenever you're gone for any length of time, even more this time, which is a very good sign. She asked about you every single day."

"Papa."

Ryder froze. Jane smiled. "That is her surprise for you. She's been practicing. She has said 'papa' for the past two weeks, each time I've showed her that small painting of you."

"Papa."

For a moment, he felt his throat close. Then he buried his face against her neck and felt her soft mouth against his face and she said again in a very satisfied voice, "Papa."

"I've brought you a present, pumpkin."

Her eyes lit up when he pulled the brightly wrapped package from his coat pocket.

Inside was a gold locket. Ryder showed her how to open the locket. On one side was a miniature painting of her and on the other a painting of her mother, who had died birthing her. Ryder remembered the birth, remembered his fear and the endless pain. He also remembered his joy when the small girl child finally came from her dead mother's body, and she was alive. Not completely whole, but alive, and that was all that had mattered to him.

Jane fastened the locket around Jenny's neck and immediately Jenny ran off to show her prize to Amy, a little girl of six who smiled a lot more now than she had five months ago. He heard Jenny yell, "Papa give! Papa give!"

"You're doing very well with her, Jane. You're doing well with all the children. God, I've missed them. I see Oliver's leg is much better. What does Dr. Simons say?"

"The bone is mending and he doubts Ollie will have a limp. He's a very lucky little boy. As for Jaime, the burn marks on his legs and back are completely healed. He's a smart one, Ryder. He reads every book you send over. He spends every shilling of his allowance on even more books. He is well known to Mr. Meyers, who owns the bookshop in the village. As for Melissa, she's got quite a talent with watercolors. Amy wants to be an Italian soprano, God forbid."

Ryder nodded and smiled. He followed Jane to the wide porch and the two of them sat down, watching the children. He listened carefully as she told him of each child's progress, of each child's needs.

He couldn't seem to take his eyes off Jenny, who was now proudly displaying her locket to Melissa, who'd gotten a French doll and wasn't in the least jealous. Ryder knew the children understood that Jenny was his real child, but he doubted it meant much to them, even to Oliver, who sometimes seemed to Ryder to be older than he was.

"I hear you married," Jane said abruptly, her eyes searching his face, and he knew she hoped it was a false rumor.

He smiled. "Yes, I did. Her name is Sophie."

"It's a surprise. To me. To your other women as well, I imagine."

"You're wrong about that. Bea has a very busy tongue. I have visited with all of them."

She arched a thick black brow.

"I'm married now, Jane." His voice was austere as a vicar's and she marveled at it.

"And the children?"

"What do you mean?"

She looked off toward a small knot of boys, craned her neck and her ears, then shouted, "Tom, stop saying that horrible word! Oh Lord, where do they hear such things? Don't curse! Particularly at John—you know he hates it."

Ryder, who knew Jane's worth, wasn't at all surprised when Tom shut his mouth, shrugged with a show of sublime indifference to keep his male pride intact, then turned to throw a ball to Oliver, who hit it expertly with one of his crutches. John, yelling, ran after the ball.

"What does your new wife think about the children?"

"I haven't told her."

"I don't suppose you've told your brother or your family yet either."

Her voice was tart but he just grinned at her. "It's none of their business," he said easily. "My sister knows, has known for a long time now. She keeps quiet though, for the most part. She refers to the children as my Beloved Ones."

"How did she find out?"

"The brat followed me here once, well over a year ago, and watched from the branches of that oak tree over there. Sinjun's smart. She will also keep her mouth shut." Ryder shrugged. "But as for the others, I've always felt that it's my business and mine alone, and that's how I will continue to feel. There is no reason for them to know. At least now since I'm married and made it clear to my brother that I will be the most faithful of husbands, I won't have to endure any more of his quarterly bastard meetings."

"Are you really certain about all this, Ryder? Fidelity just because you're married? It's not the way of your class, I understand."

"Perhaps that is true for many, but not for me. Ah, Jane, the earl has more faith in me than you appear to. He knows I will be faithful to my wife because he is besotted with his own and is firmly in the constancy corner. Thus, no more children, at least the way he looks at things. Poor fellow."

"At last you can quit your damned playacting."

"Now, Jane, not all of it is playacting."

"Ha, do I ever know that. Sara told me about a woman she'd met in the village. The woman knew who she was, asked how you were, and then proceeded to tell Sara that she'd first met you when you were sixteen. Then she gave Sara this vacuous smile. Just when did you begin, Ryder?"

Ryder frowned. "You will find no pot filled with gold at the end of that rainbow, Jane. Forget her, forget all of them. As for my wife, she will come around to believing me a faithful hound soon enough, I daresay. But not just yet. Actually, she's already met Sara and Tess, quite by accident." Ryder looked off toward the very green rolling hills in the distance, smiling. "She stews quite nicely. Sharp tongue in her mouth that I quite like. A wealth of curses that even Tom would appreciate. Hopefully I'll hear more out of her in the near future."

Jane gave him an odd look, saying slowly, "So, you don't see any reason for your family to change their opinion of you?"

"No reason at all. Why should I? They are all quite fond of me."

"You are purposely being perverse, Ryder. I don't understand you. You enjoy the reputation of a Lothario? You like being known as a womanizer, a satyr?"

"Haven't I earned it?"

"Yes, but that's not what I mean."

"I enjoy women, I always have. It's no secret. I know women, how they think, how they tend to feel about things. Ah, yes, Jane, even you. No, no, don't call me cynical again. But the children, well, that's quite different, as you well know. I have a feeling that what you really want to ask me is if I will forget about them now that I have my own family."

"You wouldn't do that precisely, but perhaps you wouldn't come to see them as much as you do now, which would be understandable, of course. It's just that I would hate to see them hurt."

"The children are my responsibility, and I love them. Nothing will change. I am taking my wife to the Cotswolds to my house there on the morrow. If there is any emergency, simply send a messenger to me there. It's quite near to Lower Slaughter, and only a day and a half away. Oh, incidentally, my wife has a little brother who's lame. Isn't that rather an odd coincidence?"

Jane just shook her head at him. If she were ten years younger, she herself would have very much enjoyed frolicking in Ryder Sherbrooke's bed. He had a way about him that drew women, a manner that had nothing to do with his good looks and well-formed body, a way that assured a woman he wouldn't ever be selfish or unheeding of her needs or of her wishes. As it was, they'd been friends since he was twenty years old, a young man wild as a storm wind, a young man who hated cruelty toward children even more than he loved making a woman scream with delight. Jane had been thirty at the time, filled with sorrow at the death of both her children in a fire, and frankly uncaring about her future. Ryder had, quite simply, saved her. He'd given her a year-old baby— Jaime—to care for. A baby, he'd told her in an unemotional voice, he'd happened to find dumped in a pile of garbage in an alley. He'd just chanced to hear a mewling sound and found him. A year later, he'd brought her Jenny, his own child. It was the first time she'd seen a sorrow to match her own.

She watched him as he rose, dusted off his britches, and went off to play with the children. She wanted to meet this wife of his.

Sophie was standing straight and still while Mrs. Plack, the seamstress from Rye, fitted a riding habit to her. It was a pale green wool with gold braid on the shoulders and Sophie agreed with Alex that it was very smart indeed.

But she couldn't help but fret about the cost of all the gowns and underthings and bonnets and slippers and now three—goodness, *three!*—riding habits. She fretted out loud. Alex merely shook her head and said, "Your husband's orders, my dear Sophie. Stop worrying. When I was first married to Douglas, he didn't want to buy me even a handkerchief. No, no more out of you. I have a feeling that all this largesse frightens you, that it represents something of a debt you will owe to Ryder, and that debt is growing with each article of clothing. Am I right?"

Sophie said not another word.

"Are you getting tired, Sophie?" Alex asked after another hour had passed.

Sophie shook her head for Mrs. Plack was working so hard, trying so much to please.

"Well, I am. Mrs. Plack is very nearly through with you. The clothes that aren't finished by the time you and Ryder leave for Chadwyck House I will have sent immediately to you."

"It is absurd," the Dowager Countess of Northcliffe said from the doorway.

Alex winked at Sophie. "What, ma'am?"

"That Ryder is taking this girl to Chadwyck House."

"This girl is his wife, ma'am."

"Just look at that shade of green. It makes her look quite bilious. Just how much of my son's money are you spending? I will have to tell him that you are greedy and that is why you married him."

Sophie said not a word, but she did close her eyes. She thought she heard Mrs. Plack snort.

"I think it goes charmingly with her complexion," said Alex.

"Ha," the dowager said. "You have no taste in colors either. 'Tis Douglas who selects all your clothes."

"You're right," Alex said easily. "I'm very lucky that Douglas is so splendid."

"Humph," the dowager said. "You don't fool me, miss, you weren't speaking about clothes."

"Well, Douglas is splendid when it comes to clothes as well. Except that he wants my necklines to touch my chin. He accuses me of flaunting if I can't touch my tongue to the top of my collar."

Sophie giggled.

The dowager looked aghast; she opened her mouth, then closed it again. However, she was made of stern stuff, and said after only four more seconds had passed, "I wonder why Ryder isn't here. Doesn't this girl consider him splendid?"

"Oh yes," Alex said quickly. "It's just there is so much to be done before they leave for Chadwyck House. Ah, ma'am, her name is Sophie, you know."

It was another five minutes before the dowager took herself off with nary a conciliatory word out of her mouth.

Alex rolled her eyes yet again, then rubbed her fingertips over her temples. "I never had a headache in my life until I met my mother-in-law."

It was another half hour before Mrs. Plack was finished. She was quite pleased with the sum of money Master Ryder was paying her and was effusive in her thanks to Sophie.

Once they were alone, Alex jumped to her feet and rubbed her hands together. "Now, Sophie, why don't we go to the estate room and steal some of Douglas's brandy?"

Sophie stared at her sister-in-law. "Every time I think I'm beginning to know you, you say something I don't expect."

"That's what Douglas says."

"He's right," Sophie said. "Let's go."

It was the earl who found two giggling ladies sprawled out on the Aubusson carpet in the middle of the estate room an hour later, a depleted bottle of his prized French brandy on the floor between them. Alex was lying on her back, hugging her sides, laughing her head off. Sophie was on her stomach, twirling her hair around a finger, saying, "No, no, Alex, it's quite true. I'm not lying. The pirate really had only one leg and all three of the women wanted him, each for her own reason."

"But Goosie? You're making that name up, Sophie! You say she wanted to carve his wooden leg into a ship? That she'd already carved up a dozen palm trees?"

"Ah," the earl said, coming down to his haunches, "so Ryder told you about the one-legged pirate and his adventure on the island, hmmm?"

Sophie was drunk. If she hadn't been, she would have been so embarrassed she wouldn't have been able to face him for a good year. As it was, both she and Alex burst into fresh laughter, Sophie saying on a strangled breath, "So you know the story, do you? Tell us the ending, Douglas. Ryder didn't tell me yet and Alex really wants to know."

"Do you want to know?" Douglas asked his wife, who was now lying flat on her back, grinning up at him like a fool.

"Ryder made up those names—Goosie, indeed! And Brassy—'tis too ridiculous."

Douglas raised his hand. "No, it's true, I promise." Douglas eyed the brandy bottle, then grinned down at his wife, leaning down to kiss her mouth. "No hope for it, I guess." He picked up Alex's snifter, filled it with brandy, and downed it. He set the bottle down, arranged himself cross-legged, and said, "Now, as to the story—Goosie was a very popular lady. Actually, she was the first one to escape off the island. She'd only begun to carve up the pirate's wooden leg. All she managed to carve was what looked like a keel. She went to St. Thomas with a crew of Dutchmen who were all blond and couldn't understand a word she said. But the captain, ah, he wasn't Dutch, he was a Dane and, of course, blond, but he understood the universal language, and that is one language that Goosie spoke quite fluently." He leaned down and kissed his wife again.

"You mean French, Douglas?"

"No, no, Alex," Ryder said from the doorway, "my brother is talking about love."

Sophie stared at her husband, stared at the brandy bottle, then flopped over on her back, and closed her eyes. She moaned.

"May I join the party?" Ryder asked.

"You said you'd be busy all day," Sophie said, her eyes still tightly closed.

"I was. It's after five o'clock now."

"Here," Douglas said, and handed his brother the nearly empty brandy bottle.

But Ryder had no intention of getting drunk. Therein lay disaster for a randy man. He'd watched and listened from the doorway for a good ten minutes and had been charmed. Sophie was drunk. He'd heard her laugh, a sweet, merry sound that warmed him to his very toes. Hell, all of them were going to feel vile tomorrow, but that was many hours away. The hours Ryder wanted were those just ahead. He tilted up the bottle and pretended to drink the rest of the brandy, then carried the bottle over to the sideboard and fetched another.

"Tell us what happened to the one-legged pirate," Alex said. "Douglas doesn't know, I'm sure of it. I want to know about Brassy. Douglas keeps avoiding it and going on to other stories."

"Actually, Brassy's story is shown in the gardens."

"What are you talking about?" Sophie said, still not looking at him.

"There are statues hidden deep in the garden. Haven't you yet seen them, Sophie? They were brought over by our very own uncle Brandon—you know, the fellow who left me Kimberly Hall. Let's go and I'll show you. Then you can come back and tell Alex."

"An excellent idea," the earl said, coming up on one elbow. Ryder saw that his brother wasn't at all drunk. What he was, the fraud, was enjoying himself immensely. He was running his fingers lightly over his wife's arm, then up her shoulder. He watched his brother's fingers lightly caress Alex's ear. Douglas was a cunning bastard, no doubt about it. Ryder grinned at him, then reached out his hand to take Sophie's. He pulled her to her feet, jerking hard at the last minute, and she came flying against him and he held her against his chest for a moment, before touching his fingertips to her chin, kissing her, then releasing her.

Sophie looked profoundly worried, and said even as she was weaving slightly, "Statues, Ryder? A statue of Brassy? How is that possible? Why Brassy and not Goosie?"

"You will see," Ryder said. "Douglas, take good care of your wife," he added, and led Sophie from the estate room. As he closed the door, he heard Alex giggle.

"I suppose this drinking orgy was brought on by something awesomely miserable?"

"Your mother," Sophie said.

"I quite understand."

"You will really show me Brassy?"

"I will show you whatever you want to see," he said.

When he led her onto the narrow paths of the garden, trees planted so closely together that there was a thick green canopy over their heads, she said, "This is beautiful. I didn't know about that turn back there. Why is this hidden?"

"You'll see," Ryder said.

He watched her look at the first statue—entwined statues, actually. The woman was sitting on the man's thighs, her back arched, her marble hair hanging loose, and his hands were on her hips, frozen in place, half lifting her off his sex.

Sophie gasped. "This is just awful."

But she didn't sound as if she thought it awful. She sounded very interested. She was weaving a bit again and he put his arm around her and brought her close to his side. "He's inside her, Sophie, as you can see. Not a bad life for a statue. Frozen for all eternity in the throes of pleasure."

"That looks difficult."

"Nonsense. Would you like to try that or see some other statues? There's a good deal of variety."

She nodded, looked surprised that she'd nodded, then slipped her hand in his. Ryder felt a surge of lust that was wonderfully familiar, but he also felt a deep tenderness that made him frown. What he was doing was dishonest. He was taking advantage of her drunken state. Who cared?

He led her to the next exhibition, this one very nearly hidden behind a half-dozen yew bushes. Sophie gasped but she never looked away.

"You would prefer this way, Sophie? It's a bit difficult for a woman to find pleasure in this position, but I think I could manage it. Also, with a woman on her hands and knees, the man is very deep inside her. Ah, but his hands are free to roam, it's just that—" He broke off. "Let me show you."

She looked up at him, her eyes blurry, her voice sounding uncertain. "I don't think so, Ryder. I should like to see more. I would like to make my own selection, if you don't mind."

"No," he said, awed by his discovery of a very different wife, "I don't mind a bit."

He showed her all the other groupings. When they came to the one with the man between the woman's raised thighs, his head thrown back, his mouth yelling his release, she stopped cold and simply stared, saying nothing.

"You are a traditionalist then?"

She thought about that for a moment, then suddenly, she paled and swallowed convulsively. "Ryder," she said, "this isn't good." She pulled away from him, fell to her knees, and vomited.

"Well, hell," Ryder said.

Sophie wanted to die. Her mouth felt as if it were filled with foul-tasting cotton, her head pounded, and even the beating of her heart made her shudder.

Ryder had carried her back to the house and put her to bed. He met his brother in the upstairs corridor, and the two of them had laughed then sobered quickly.

"Is Alex in as bad shape as my wife?"

"Probably worse. I have the remedy. My only problem is getting Alex to drink it."

"We could trade wives if you liked just long enough to get the potion down their respective throats."

So it was that Ryder found Alex lying on her back, her arm over her eyes, not moving at all.

"Don't worry, Alex, it's just me, Ryder. Now, I'm going to raise your head and you're going to down every bit of this potion. You will feel like trouncing Douglas within the hour, I promise you."

Alex looked at her brother-in-law, so surprised that it wasn't her husband that she opened her mouth and drank.

It wasn't quite so simple for Douglas, but Sophie was very nearly beyond embarrassment with him, and thus only moaned once before drinking the vile potion.

The brothers met in the corridor. Douglas said, "Sophie's asleep now and will probably stay that way until tomorrow. Sorry, Ryder, you will just have to contain your lust tonight. Now, tell me how you're going to travel to Chadwyck House and what I can do to help you."

On a very foggy Friday morning, the Sherbrooke family was gathered outside the mansion to see off Ryder and Sophie. Ryder moved away from his wife when she held Jeremy against her.

"I will miss you, love," she said for the first time. "Be a good boy, won't you? Your pony is wonderful and you must remember to take good care of him."

"His name is George, Sophie." Jeremy suffered all her advice because she was his sister, and he loved her, but at the end of it, he was beginning to squirm. Ryder saved him by lifting him up and saying, "Cosh Sinjun over the head every once in a while. She needs it. We will see you soon, Jeremy." He lowered the boy, shook his hand, and then assisted his wife into the carriage.

Three carriages bowled down the long drive. The second one held Tinker, Ryder's dour valet, and a young girl he'd insisted Sophie hire to train as her maid. She was painfully shy and her name was Cory.

The third carriage held mountains of luggage, most of it Ryder's.

"This is very difficult," Douglas said, staring after the carriages. He turned to smile at Jeremy, who had surreptitiously wiped a tear from his eye. "Ryder will take very good care of your sister, my boy. Don't worry. We'll all be together again soon."

As for Sophie, she didn't want Ryder near her, much less taking care of her. All she could think about were those utterly dreadful statues and staring at them and wanting Ryder to do all those things to her. It was beyond embarrassing and he knew exactly what she was thinking and how she was feeling.

"You're a bounder," she said aloud.

"And you are a traditionalist," he said, "despite everything you know about men. But you will want eventually to experiment with my poor man's body. You needn't worry that I'll forget any of the interesting positions of the statues in the garden."

"I wasn't thinking about those horrible statues. I hate it when you know what I'm thinking."

"Ah, perversity. Thank God I'm your husband. Otherwise you would spend all your time with me in the agony of mortification."

"I'm no more with child than I was in Jamaica."

Ryder wanted to cry, but he didn't. He grinned at her, patted her gloved hand, and said, "Perhaps there is something to having a harem. No need to have to put things off, you know."

* * *

Chadwyck House lay only five miles to the east of Strawberry Hill, the seat of the Viscount Rathmore, and very nearly in the middle between Lower Slaughter and Mortimer Coombe. Ryder had no idea if Tony Parrish and his beyond beautiful bride, Melissande, were still at Strawberry Hill or if Tony had taken Melissande to London. He really didn't care. They reached the Chadwyck House grounds by late afternoon.

"Have you ever before been to the Cotswolds, Sophie?"

"No. It's very beautiful."

"You're in for a treat. Just wait until October. The leaves are brilliant, the air crisp, and you want to cry it is so lovely."

But all thoughts of crying for loveliness fled Ryder's mind when the carriages bowled to a stop in front of Chadwyck House. He hadn't been here in close to a year he realized with a start. Eleven and a half months. And this had happened in that short period of time?

The graceful Tudor manor house with its diamond-paned windows, several of them broken, looked as if it had been left to molder. Ivy climbed to the second story of the house; the grass and weeds covered everything, even sprouting through the cracked stone front steps. The stables looked deserted, field implements lay rusted and unused next to the stable.

Sophie frowned. "I don't understand," she said finally.

"Nor do I."

He jumped from the carriage, then assisted her down.

He heard Tinker say, "Good Gawd, what the hell happened here?"

"I'll find Allen Dubust and find out," Ryder said. Sophie looked at him. She realized in that moment that she hadn't seen him this angry since Jamaica, since he'd found her beaten.

"Stay here," he said shortly, and strode up the cracked front steps. He pounded on the oak double front doors.

He pounded again.

Finally, very slowly, one of the doors opened just a crack and an old wizened face peered out.

"Master Ryder! Lawdie, Lawdie! The good Lord finally answered my prayers!"

"Mrs. Smithers, what's happened here? Where is Allen Dubust? What the devil is going on?"

"Lawdie, Lawdie," Mrs. Smithers said, then pulled both doors open wide.

"Sophie, come on in. Tinker, bring Cory, and oversee the luggage. I don't think there's much help coming out of here."

The interior of the house was a mess. Ryder started to curse, then no-

ticed that Mrs. Smithers was leaning on two broomsticks roughly fashioned as crutches.

"Tell me what's happened," he said. He saw Sophie from the corner of
his eye and added, "This is my wife, Mrs. Sherbrooke. Sophie, this is
Mrs. Smithers. She's been here forever. She will tell us what happened."

What happened was that Allen Dubust had thrown Mrs. Smithers
down the stairs after dismissing all the other servants because she'd refused to believe him and threatened him with the local magistrate. "I told
him he were a rotten sort and I always knew it and I wouldn't leave and
he couldn't make me. I told him I'd tell everyone what he did. He didn't
like that. He picked me up and threw me down the stairs." He'd stripped
the house, taken all the money, sold off land he had no authority to sell,
and left the district. "He told me, he did, that he'd been telling everyone
that you had sold Chadwyck House." Unfortunately, Mrs. Smithers
hadn't seen a blessed soul, because, after all, the house was vacant, and
since she couldn't walk, there was no way she could get to the village to
tell anyone what had happened. She'd barely managed to get to the front
doors.

Sophie said, "I will have Tinker ride immediately back to Lower
Slaughter and fetch a doctor for you, Mrs. Smithers."

"But the house!" Mrs. Smithers wailed and looked for the world as
though she would burst into tears.

Sophie patted her bent old shoulder and said gently, "It's just a house.
We'll fix it up again. You'll see. It's you we're worried about. You've
done very well. Don't you agree, Ryder?"

He looked at his wife. Jesus, he thought, she'd certainly changed from
the frightened, wary girl who'd lived in his brother's house. He cleared
his throat and said, "Everything will be put to rights. You first of all, Mrs.
Smithers. I'm proud of you and I thank you."

Two hours later, Mrs. Smithers was tucked into bed, heavily dosed
with laudanum, her broken leg properly set by an aghast Dr. Pringle, who
just kept shaking his head. "I just don't believe she managed to survive,"
he said over and over again. "That old woman just wouldn't give up."

Once the doctor had left, Ryder and Sophie stood facing each other in
the filthy entrance hall.

"I couldn't have manufactured a more excellent nightmare," he said.
"I'm sorry, Sophie."

To his surprise, Sophie grinned. "Let's go to the kitchen and see if
there's anything to eat."

There wasn't, not a scrap. But there were rats, big ones, who had enjoyed themselves for the past three weeks.

Sophie frowned, and said to a shrieking Cory, "Do be quiet. You're hurting the master's ears. Now, I want you to go stay with Mrs. Smithers. Mr. Sherbrooke and I are going to Lower Slaughter and hire help, and buy food."

"Yes," Ryder said, staring at his wife. "Ah, Tinker, please help the coachman with the horses and the luggage."

He rubbed his hands together. "Nothing like a challenge, is there?"

CHAPTER
══18══

THERE WAS NO bed.

Ryder just stood in the doorway of the great master bedchamber and stared blankly about the bare room. He'd avoided looking into the bedchamber earlier because he'd always hated this room. Damned dark and the ceilings were too low. The thick dark gold draperies still covered the long windows, draperies so ugly and shiny with age that Ryder wished Dubust had taken them as well, curse his hide.

No damned bed. It was too much. Sophie was exhausted, he was still so furious he hadn't allowed himself to feel weariness, and Mrs. Smithers was sound asleep, snoring loudly, after consuming a feast of food. She was in the sewing room, which had been quickly converted for her. Cory would sleep in the room with her. Dubust, the discriminating bastard, hadn't touched any of the servants' furniture.

He turned to see Sophie standing right behind him, linens on her arms. She said as she gazed about the room, "Oh dear. I'm so sorry, Ryder."

"According to the good doctor, Dubust simply told everyone that all furnishings were being sent to Northcliffe Hall. I still can't believe it. Damnation, Sophie, it's all my fault." She shifted the linens and he quickly took them from her.

"We will have to sleep on blankets, I suppose. You're so tired, sweetheart, I'll stop my ranting until morning. All right?"

"I don't particularly like this bedchamber, Ryder."

"I don't either, never have, for that matter. Let's go downstairs. Mrs. Smithers said Dubust slept in here, acted as though he were the prince of the castle. Damn, how could I have been such an irresponsible idiot?"

"If I didn't know firsthand just how awful the consequences, I'd suggest that we try to find a bottle of brandy."

He was forced to smile down at her. "You don't have to down an entire bottle, you know. There is a concept known as moderation."

"Ah, the concept of moderation—as in you and the very modest number of women you have in your herd?"

Was that acrimony he heard? He grinned down at her like a fool.

"Herd? Did you hear Douglas say something? No? Well, let me tell you that I have only one mare now and she appears a real goer, glossy coat, good shoulders and flanks, lots of endurance, thank God. She'll need all the strength she can get with an idiot for a husband and an empty house. Come, Sophie, before you fall on your face, let's build ourselves a nest. Thank God, Dubust didn't take all the blankets and pillows."

"No, he just wanted all the furniture. So many beautiful things, Mrs. Smithers kept telling me over and over, most of it from that damned second George, she said, not the crazy third George."

Ryder burst into laughter. "She's right. Let's go find a place to stretch out our exhausted bones."

It wasn't long before they were lying side by side, as comfortable as three blankets could make them. "Well, at least we've gotten things started," Sophie said. Without thought, she reached out her left hand and found Ryder's. For an instant, he stilled, then brought her hand to his lips and lightly kissed her wrist and palm.

"Yes," he said. "But it won't be easy, sweetheart. Damnation, I should be whipped."

"I have to admit it has in the past seemed to me to be an excellent thing to do to you, but not for this. This isn't your fault."

"And just whose fault is it? Mrs. Smithers's? Dr. Pringle's?"

"All right, so your judgment of Mr. Dubust wasn't correct. I wish you would stop flailing yourself, Ryder."

But he couldn't, at least not to himself. Irresponsible fool, that's what he was, and he knew it and despised himself for it. He'd already planned to change things, had already thought about it a good deal because he was now married and a husband, for God's sake, but he'd been too late.

Sophie was right. Flailing himself didn't help a thing at the moment. They'd at least gotten things started. Whilst they'd been in Lower Slaughter, they'd managed to find two women who had worked before at Chadwyck House who were perfectly willing to come back on the morrow. But for now, there was merely filth and more filth. They slept in the Blue Salon, on the floor near the floor-to-ceiling windows— "Hell," Ryder said, "we can call this the Black Salon if we want to. The good Lord knows there isn't a patch of blue left."

He cursed luridly.

"So much for your first night at my wonderful house," he said, and punched his pillow. He then pulled her closer to his side. "I'm sorry, Sophie. This is all a damned bloody mess and I've dropped you right in the middle of it."

She didn't answer. Not that he expected her to, because he was so furious, so ashamed that he'd let himself be such a lazy, worthless clod that such a thing could happen, that he wanted to rant, and so he did. "I'll find the fellow. It shouldn't be difficult. All the furnishings were catalogued, a fact I doubt our Mr. Dubust knew about. But Uncle Brandon was a great one for detail, indeed so much detail, I think he died finally from choking on it. In any case, we'll track all the things down, then I'll find Dubust and cut off his . . . well, the fellow will end up in a bad way, I swear it."

Ryder paused a moment, then realized that his bride was fast asleep. He kissed her forehead.

Life, he thought as he eased into sleep himself, was occasionally irritating and made one face up to what one was. On the other hand, life did bring some pleasant surprises, like the wonderful soft one who was nestled in the crook of his arm. Her palm was lying over his heart.

The next few days were beyond anything Sophie had ever experienced. She felt like a general directing her troops, that is, when she wasn't spending her time on the front line side by side with them. She spent her days immersed in dirt, bone tired by mid-afternoon, and having more fun than she could ever remember. What she was doing meant something. She felt wonderful. She felt worthy for the first time in a very long while.

Her hair was bound up in a dirty bandanna, smudges on her face, her gown too short and just as dirty as her bandanna, when Doris, a very fat good-natured woman, yelled from the front entrance hall, "Mrs. Sherbrooke! There's a gentleman here."

Sophie barely had time to set her broom aside when she came face to face with a very handsome man who had something of the look of the Sherbrookes. She said, her hand thrust out, "You must be Tony Parrish."

"Guilty, ma'am. And you are my cousin's new wife." He turned then and called out, "Come in, love, and dredge up all your wondrous charm. Our new cousin doubtless needs it."

When Melissande Parrish, Lady Rathmore, floated on fairy-slippered feet into the entrance hall looking like a princess stepping into a slum, Sophie could do nothing but stare at the incredible vision. She had never seen a more beautiful woman in her life.

"You're Alex's sister?"

"Oh yes. I'm Melissande, you know, and you must be Sophie. You're a surprise to every Sherbrooke in England, so Tony tells me. No one ever thought that Ryder would . . . that is, Ryder is so very much in demand with the ladies, but Tony believes he won't see his other mistresses now and—"

"I believe that's enough abuse of the topic, love," Tony Parrish said, and leaned down and kissed his wife full on the mouth, much to Sophie's astonishment.

Melissande blushed and said, "You shouldn't have begun that in the carriage, my lord, and now you will—" She broke off, shook herself, and said to Sophie, "My husband is a dreadful tease, you know. Now, I see no place to sit. It is very strange. Whatever shall we do?"

Sophie was stymied. In that moment, Ryder strode into the house, looking so beautiful in black Hessians, buckskins, and white shirt open at his throat and wild and male that she wanted, in that brief instant, to hurl herself into his arms. He'd changed so very much in the past three days. Or, she thought, her brow puckering, perhaps it was she who had changed, but just a bit, just a tiny little bit. No, he was just Ryder and she didn't feel a blessed thing toward him. He had a very nice smile, his teeth white, his face so very expressive, his light blue eyes crinkling at the corners with pleasure. There was something different about him. It took another moment for Sophie to figure out what it was. He was clearly in charge here. It hadn't been that he'd lived in his brother's shadow, no, not that, but here, at Chadwyck House, he was the master and he fitted the role very well. And I, Sophie thought, am the mistress.

The cousins shook hands, slapped each other on the back, and insulted each other's manhood in high good humor. Sophie felt herself stiffening as she waited for Ryder to turn to the beautiful woman at Tony's side. She was waiting for him to metaphorically fall at the fairy slippers of the gloriously beautiful Melissande.

He didn't.

He smiled down at her, a social, quite impersonal smile, and said, "Welcome to Chadwyck House, cousin. I told Tony to keep his distance else I'd put him to work."

"I'm not such a sluggard," Tony said. "Behold two willing slaves to do your bidding."

"We're not going to London until next week," Melissande said, looking around her and shuddering. "Until then Tony insists that we help out. However, it is much worse than I'd imagined. I've never been dirty before and I think that grime beneath one's fingernails is quite disgusting."

Artless, Sophie thought, achingly beautiful and artless. She tucked her fingers into a fist because her fingernails were black with blackening from the grate.

"You won't do a thing," she said to Melissande. "At least not in that gown." Sophie looked at her husband, a question in her eyes, but Ryder was looking at Tony, who, in turn, was grinning at his wife, saying, "You've been sweaty, very sweaty. Ah, I do remember a time in the Northcliffe gardens—you remember, don't you, sweetheart?—beneath that statue of Venus trying to cover her bosom with a very small hand— that you got really quite grimy and you didn't give a good damn."

Melissande punched him in the arm.

"Some things never change," Ryder said, shaking his head at his cousin. "Then again, some things change so much that it leaves a poor mortal nearly speechless."

"Ah," said Tony, "that is a state my dear wife hasn't yet quite achieved. But she draws ever nearer."

Melissande said, puzzlement in her voice, "You appear pretty, Sophie, even though you are wearing that horrid thing around your head and your gown is beyond awful. But you're not beautiful. It is all very odd, you know. I simply don't understand it."

Sophie blinked.

"There is simply no accounting for a man's preferences," Ryder said easily. "I daresay it is a lack in my man's character. She means," Ryder said in his wife's ear, "that it's incomprehensible to her that I, a manly man by all accounts, would prefer you to her."

"I can see why she would feel that way," Sophie said. She smiled at the vision. "You are very beautiful."

"Yes, I know, but Tony prefers that I try to turn aside such compliments, that I treat them as if they were as insubstantial as snowflakes, that is his metaphor, you know. That is the correct term, I believe. But I have no doubt at all that your compliment is terribly sincere and, after all, you're not a gentleman, thus it can be accepted gracefully, don't you agree, Tony?"

Tony Parrish, Viscount Rathmore, looked perfectly serious. "Such logic is irrefutable, my love." He said to Ryder, "All right, tell me what I can do. Incidentally, I brought six men over to help and four women."

Sophie felt like hugging her new cousin. More help, bless his kind heart. She gave him a dazzling smile that made him cock his head at her. "I see," he said slowly. "Yes, Ryder, perhaps I do see."

Four days later, Chadwyck House was spotlessly clean, and completely empty save for a big bed in the salon and the furnishings in the servants' quarters. Mrs. Smithers was cackling with pleasure, still eating like a stoat. She was delighted that the master had come home to stay and was cursing Allen Dubust for a bounder.

As for Allen Dubust, he'd been caught in a pub in Bristol, his pockets lined with the sale of all Chadwyck House furnishings, all ready to board a ship bound for America in a matter of hours. He had rent money as well from all the farming tenants. It was actually Uncle Albert Sherbrooke who saw him first and Aunt Mildred who screamed him down, offering three guineas to a group of young toughs to bring the lout down and hold him on the ground.

The furnishings were coming home. The rent money was coming home. Dubust was going to spend many years in Newgate, rotting. Mrs. Smithers cackled endlessly with that news. All would be well. Ryder felt profoundly lucky. He'd been stupid and irresponsible and he'd been saved despite it all. The wondrous Sherbrooke luck was with him still.

All the tenant farmers made their appearance and it was quite a surprise to Ryder that he actually enjoyed spending time with each of them, speaking of their needs, their profits, their willingness to set everything to rights again.

He realized with something of a start that he was a happy man, despite the havoc he himself had brought about because he'd been an absent landlord. He was setting everything to rights. He wrote his brother, detailing all that had happened, and Sophie's first bout with Melissande, who was, truth be told, developing into a quite acceptable female. She had even offered to oversee the polishing of some new silverware that Tony had presented to them from Mr. Millsom's warehouse in Liverpool.

It was a Tuesday afternoon, the sky overcast, the air chill. The gently rolling hills were serene and so lovely that Sophie wished she had more time simply to ride about and look. As it was, she had to ride into Lower Slaughter to the draperers. There was so much still to do and she loved it. She was humming to herself, thinking about Jeremy and wondering when he could come to live with them.

There, in the middle of the road, she came face to face with Lord David Lochridge. They stared at each other.

"Good God," he said. "It is you, Sophia Stanton-Greville. No, no, you married that Sherbrooke fellow, didn't you?"

Sophie felt sick to her stomach. She could only nod at him.

Lord David's eyes narrowed. "You did marry him, didn't you? Or are you his current mistress?"

"No," she said.

He laughed, and it was a nasty sound. "Would you like to know something else, my dear Sophia? Charles Grammond lives very near to Upper Slaughter. He'd gone to the colonies, to Virginia, I was told, but he hated it and moved here. He has a great-aunt who helps support him and that prune-faced wife of his and those four wretched children who are of no account at all. He's very much on the straight and narrow now, else the great-aunt will cut him out of her will. Isn't that a pleasant surprise for you? Two of your former lovers here, your neighbors."

"I must go," Sophie said, tightening her fists on Opal's reins.

"But not too far. We have much to discuss, don't we, Sophie? I will, of course, speak to Charles. I do wonder what he'll have to say. You see, I'm engaged to marry a local girl who's so rich it will take even me a good ten years to go through her fortune. Ah, yes, we must talk and make decisions. I do expect you to keep your mouth shut in the meanwhile, my girl, else you will be very sorry, both you and that husband of yours."

It was in that instant that Sophie remembered what the ghost had said—not really said, but told her so clearly in her mind—something about when they came it would be all right. Was this what the ghost meant? If so, how could it be all right? Nothing could ever again be all right.

She'd left the West Indies and come to a new life, a new life that had such promise until now.

She silently watched David Lochridge ride away from her. She did her errands. The draperer, Mr. Mulligan, shook his head when she left his shop. Poor Mr. Sherbrooke had wed himself to a half-witted female. It was a pity.

When she returned to Chadwyck House, she went upstairs to the master bedchamber that she and Ryder had changed completely. The walls were painted a soft pale yellow. There was a lovely pale cream and blue Aubusson carpet on the floor. She went to the now sparkling-clean window and stared out over the newly scythed east lawn. So beautiful. It looked like a Garden of Eden. It was her home. But not for much longer. Slowly, very slowly, she eased down to her knees. She bent over, her face in her hands, and she sobbed.

Mrs. Chivers, the newly installed housekeeper, saw her, managed to keep her mouth shut, and searched out the master. Ryder, not knowing what to expect, and firmly believing that Mrs. Chivers had misinterpreted Sophie's actions, still came to her immediately. He stopped cold in the doorway, staring at his wife. He felt a coursing of sheer fear.

He strode to her, nearly yelling, "Sophie, what the hell is wrong with you?"

She whipped about, staring at him. Oh God, what to tell him? That everything was over now? That the Sherbrooke name was on the verge of being ruined and that she was responsible? Oh God, Ryder had temporarily lost his furniture but she had brought utter devastation on his family.

She tried to get a hold of herself. He dropped to his haunches beside her and she felt his hands close over her upper arms. Slowly and very gently, he turned her to face him. Her face was without color, her eyes swollen from crying.

"No, no, don't cry," he said and pressed her cheek against his shoulder. "There is one very good thing about marriage, Sophie. You're not alone. There's another person to help you, no matter what the problem, no matter what the hurt. Talk to me, sweetheart, please."

She shook her head against his chest.

Ryder frowned over her head. It was she who had kept his spirits buoyed since they'd arrived here. It was she who'd directed the servants, who had overseen the meals, who had herself swept and cleaned and dusted and smiled through it all. She'd been happy, dammit. He knew it. What the hell had happened?

Her crying stopped. She hiccuped. He felt the soft movement of her breasts against his chest and felt instant and overwhelming lust. Her monthly flow had ended several days before but she'd been so tired, so utterly exhausted at the end of each day, that he'd simply held her at night.

But now, he wanted her. Very much.

"Talk to me, Sophie," he said again.

She straightened and leaned back, still held in the loose circle of his arms. "My knees hurt."

"We have a bed. Come, let's sit down."

She eyed that bed, knew that he wanted her, she wasn't blind. His sex was swelled against his trousers. She saw Lord David naked and stroking his sex, she felt again how he'd kissed her, stabbing his tongue into her mouth before she'd managed to distract him, and how he always stripped off his clothes at the cottage and showed her his body and his sex and how big he was and how he was going to take her.

And Charles Grammond, middle-aged, his belly sagging, not a bad man really, pathetically grateful when she'd first told him she would take him as her lover, and then how he'd changed, catching her in the middle of the day to force her against a tree and she'd had to hit him with her riding crop and he'd only laughed and pulled his sex from his britches and told her he wanted his sex in her mouth and she could do it now. And, dear God, she'd helped to ruin him even as she'd told him what a wonderful lover he was. And he pranced about, so pleased with himself, bragging about his virility—didn't he have four living children to prove it?

Now both of them were here. Both of them believed her a whore. Both of them would take great delight in ruining her. She clearly remembered the looks both men would give her whenever they saw her, and what they said to her in their lewd whispers, how they spoke about the nights they'd spent with her and what they'd done to her and she'd done to them. . . .

She jerked away from Ryder. He stared at her, his head cocked to one side in question.

She bounded to her feet, turned, grabbed up her skirts, and ran from the bedchamber.

He stared after her. He'd seen the blankness on her face when she'd looked at the bed, followed by the myriad facial expressions he knew were from her damned memories of Jamaica, and all when she'd seen his sex swelled against his britches.

He had hoped, prayed, that she was coming around to trusting him. His jaw tightened. He wouldn't let this continue, he couldn't.

He bided his time for the remainder of the day. There was always so much to be done that there wasn't any particular discomfort between them, even during dinner when they were alone. That night, at ten o'clock, Ryder stepped into their bedchamber, and saw that Sophie wasn't in bed. She was seated in a wing chair in front of the fireplace, her legs tucked beneath her, a book in her lap.

"I finished my work," he said.

The book, a collection of essays by John Locke, slipped off her lap. She made no move to retrieve it.

Ryder leaned down and picked it up. "Where the devil did you find this?"

"Your Mr. Dubust left it."

"I don't blame him. Listen to this: 'Latin I look upon as absolutely necessary to a gentleman.' What an appalling notion. I imagine that my youngest brother, Tysen—the future cleric—is now quite fluent in Latin. He says that his congregation will glean his meaning from his intonation, that the words aren't important, that God didn't mean for common folk to really understand in any case, only to gain the holy essence—whatever that may be—which will come from him, naturally."

"Your brother really said that?"

"He tried, but he hasn't the facility to be as fluent as I am."

"Nor has he your modesty, I doubt."

"Good," Ryder said, tossing the book back into her lap, "a bit of vinegar. Now, Sophie, it's time for you to come with me over to that bed. I know you had a bath earlier so that excuse went out with the bath-water."

"I don't want to, Ryder."

She was twisting her hands. It was amazing, his strong Sophie, the woman who had directed a score of servants during the past week, humming while she worked, was wringing her hands like a helpless twit.

"Nor do you want to tell me why you were crying this afternoon?"

"No. It isn't important, truly. It was just that . . . I lost some silverware."

Ryder only shook his head at her. He stripped off his clothes then came back to stand in front of the drowsing fire, naked, to gaze down at the orange embers.

She stared at him, she couldn't help it. He stretched out his hand to her.

"Come along now, sweetheart. I'm going to try my damnedest to give you some pleasure tonight. And if I fail you tonight, why then, there will be tomorrow night and the night after that."

She shook her head even as he was jerking her to her feet. He picked her up in his arms, carried her to the bed, and gently laid her on her back. He quickly unfastened the sash on her dressing gown.

He ignored the stiffness of her body, the pallor of her face, the damned wariness he saw in her eyes. He stripped off her nightgown, then straightened and stared down at her.

"No, don't cover yourself."

She turned her face away from him, and fisted her hands at her sides.

"You're beautiful, Sophie, not a dream princess like Melissande, certainly, but as she pointed out, you're pretty nonetheless. I'll keep you. Now I'm going to . . . no, let me just show you."

He came down beside her, lying on his side, and very gently he stroked his fingertips over her jaw, her lips, her nose, then smoothed her eyebrows. He simply looked at her and touched her face.

She looked up at him then.

"Ryder," she said, "I know that you want to take me. You don't have to play about with me as you're doing now. Please, just get it over with. I won't fight you. I know that it will do no good. I'm tired and want it over with."

He laughed.

"Ah, all those other damned men. 'Take you' . . . what a wonderful way to say 'making love.' Well, let me tell you something, Mrs. Sherbrooke, you're my wife. I want to play with you until you're yelling with pleasure. I want you to enjoy yourself. I want you to laugh and kiss me back and play with me. No, you can't begin to understand that, can you? But you will come to understand."

He leaned down and kissed her mouth, very gently, his own mouth light as moth's wings. He continued kissing her until he finally felt her ease beneath him. "Do you know how wonderful you taste to me? How much I enjoying kissing you?"

"It isn't bad," she admitted, sounding a bit worried. Even as she parted her lips to speak, he gently slipped his tongue inside her mouth and touched hers.

She started, becoming stiff as a bed slat.

Ryder was again in firm control of himself, just as he'd been before. Everything in him was focused on her, on her reactions, her shifts of expressions, the lightness or darkness of her gray eyes. All that he wanted was for her to become one with him, to replace all her memories with him—his laughter, his sheer joy in life, his pleasure in her.

He simply continued what he was doing. There was all the time in the world. The night was long. He figured she didn't have a chance.

He talked to her, distracting her from the memories he knew crept into her mind whilst he touched her. He told her how much he admired her breasts, that they were as white as fresh snow and as round as her belly would be when she was carrying his child. Ah, and her belly, he spanned his fingers to her pelvic bones and told her she should easily carry their children, as many as she wished to bear, and then he began to caress her, his fingers light and caressing her warm belly. When his fingers lightly touched her woman's soft flesh, she lurched up in bed and scrambled away from him.

He was so startled that she escaped him. He watched her blankly dash naked across the bare floor to the windows on the eastern side of the bedchamber. She stood there, her back to him, her head bowed.

He went to her, frowning, but said nothing, merely placed his hands on her shoulders and pulled her gently back against him.

"Now, what is all this about?"

"I feel so dirty."

Good Lord, he thought, staring at the back of her head, the dam had finally burst. About time too. He said slowly, "Finally you tell me the truth. It's about time, Sophie. Now we will deal with it."

She was silent.

"Somehow I don't believe it was my fingers between your thighs that brought this on, but it helped, didn't it? It made you remember—did you see one of the men doing that to Dahlia? Did one of the men force himself on you in that way?" He waited, but she said nothing. "All right then. You're not built as I am, Sophie. For you to reach a woman's pleasure, you must know caresses there between your thighs. There is no reason for you to feel dirty or ashamed or anything else except excitement and anticipation."

"It's not that entirely."

"Ah," he said, and felt a wrenching in his gut. As for his sex, all desire was long gone. "So some of those men touched you there? Fondled you there? Is that what this is all about? You would still have me battle memories, bloody ghosts?"

Ghosts, ha! she thought, shaking unconsciously.

"Sophie, talk to me."

"I'm sorry, Ryder."

He shook her then. "Damn you, woman, stop bleating like a twit sheep! You were a hellion when I met you and now you become a pathetic scrap on me. Stop it, dammit!"

She screamed at him, "All right, damn you, all right!" She jerked away, looked frantically around the bedchamber for something to hit him with, didn't see anything, and dashed from the bedchamber.

"You're naked!"

"Go to the devil!"

He was grabbing for his dressing gown when she ran back into the bedchamber. She was carrying a broom. She rushed at him, like a horseless knight in a joust, and he couldn't help himself, he laughed. He hugged his belly he laughed so hard, at least until she hit him on the head. Then hit him again and again, cursing at him all the while.

The pain of the sharp bristles finally got through to him as well as the sharp throbbing over his left temple, and he grabbed the broom handle. But she was strong, bloody strong with determination and rage.

It took a good deal of strength on his part to get it away from her without hurting her.

He tossed it aside, and grabbed her, pulling her roughly up against him. He kissed her hard. His hands were on her buttocks, bringing her up to fit intimately against him. She arched her back and tried to bite him.

"The good Lord knows I'm glad you're back," he said, and kissed her hard again. He threw her over his shoulder and carried her to the bed.

"You feel dirty, do you? Well, my dear wife, let's just see how you will feel when I get done with you."

CHAPTER
══ 19 ══

SHE FOUGHT HIM, kicking, twisting, panting with effort. She shrieked at him, called him every name she'd ever heard hurled at another in Jamaica.

He only laughed and held her down.

When he was kissing her belly, she yanked viciously at his hair. It was then that Ryder just sighed, stripped off one of the pillowcases, and tied her hands above her head to one of the huge carved bedposts.

She could still hurt him with her legs but he could bear that. He went back to his pleasurable task. He kissed her white belly, slipping his tongue into her navel while his hands were stroking her inner things. He paused then, and looked at her. "You will like this, Sophie." He dipped down, suddenly, and lifted her hips. He covered her with his mouth and she screamed, a high wailing sound that moved him not one whit.

He gently eased his middle finger inside her. Ah, he thought, she was damp. But still so very small. Well, it wouldn't matter once she'd come to pleasure.

And she was loosening and opening, feeling something near to pain deep inside her, low in her belly, and it held her, made her want, and despite herself, despite her screaming curses at him, she was raising her hips to bring herself closer to him. His finger was deep inside her, moving in and out, and his mouth found a rhythm that drove her wild.

She knew something was coming, she wanted it desperately, and she still wanted to curse him for what he was doing to her. Then she moaned, jerking so violently he nearly dropped her, and she froze, but just for an instant.

Ryder raised his head from her for just a moment. "Still feel dirty, Sophie?"

She yelled at him even as her hips jerked and heaved, "You damned bounder, you bastard, you—"

"Just another moment, sweetheart, and you'll understand. Keep cursing, it makes me want you to scream with pleasure all the more."

She was crying now, her breath short and gasping, and he knew she didn't understand that she was close, very close, and in the next instant, he pushed her, his finger deep, his mouth just as deep. He felt her legs stiffen, then felt the heaving contractions, the spasms that lifted her back off the bed.

He kept her there, locked into the climax, forcing the pleasure to continue, not to stop, but to go on and on until she was crying from the power of it, the finality of it, her acceptance of it. When finally she grew soft and yielding in his hands, he pulled her thighs wide apart and came into her, deep and hard.

He felt the sweet aftershocks of her climax and it was more than enough. He found his own release in the very next instant and he yelled his pleasure, not at his own climax, which was incredibly powerful, but at hers, at what he had finally given her.

She was slick with sweat, her breath deep and fast, and he lay on top of her, his sex still deep inside her, and he gently laid his palm on her heart.

He kissed her slack mouth. He simply looked down at her until she finally opened her eyes.

Shock, dazed shock.

He kissed her again, and she tasted herself and she simply couldn't believe what had happened, couldn't believe that she'd lost herself so completely, that even as she'd hated him and cursed him and wanted to kill him, her body had exploded into ferocious pleasure, and she'd wanted it, oh yes, she'd wanted it more than anything. And he'd watched her, and felt the wild spasms and known, known what he was doing to her, known how he was controlling her, known exactly what she was feeling. He kissed her again, then came up on his elbows.

"Your heart is finally slowing."

She looked at his chin but felt the warmth of his chest against her breast, against her heart. He would mock her now, she thought, he would blare his triumph over her, he would grind her under and proclaim his mastery. She stiffened, waiting, knowing what would come.

He gently pushed the hair off her forehead, hair damp with the wildness of her pleasure, and he said very slowly, his voice deep and rough, "I love you, Sophie Sherbrooke. I never thought such a thing existed, but evidently it does. I love you and I will love you until I cock up my toes and pass to the hereafter and I will still love you even as I float about in eternity. And I will continue to force you to pleasure until you accept my love and take me into your heart as well as into your body."

He suddenly looked startled. She felt him hard within her once again and, to her horror, she squirmed.

He didn't laugh, didn't mock her. He threw back his head, closed his eyes, and groaned. "Do you have any idea how you feel to me? Come with me again, Sophie, all right? Just let yourself go, forget all the past, those damned ghosts, just think of me and how I feel deep inside you. Just think about what my fingers are going to do to you, and my tongue—"

She didn't want to fall apart again, but there didn't seem to be much choice. In but an instant of time, she forgot about choice anyway. When he told her to wrap her legs around his flanks, she did so willingly and quickly, hugging him hard, lifting her hips to bring him deeper, and he groaned and she felt a burgeoning of those same feelings, those frantic barbaric feelings that stripped off everything except that wrenching pleasure that was so great it was nearly pain, but it wasn't, it was within her and within him and somehow it made them as one. His hand was between their bodies, stroking her, caressing her, and then his mouth was against hers, his tongue deep inside her mouth just as his sex was inside her body. And she was howling and bucking in her frenzy, and he encouraged her, telling her what to do, telling her what she made him feel. Then, just as he plunged so deep he touched her womb, she convulsed with pleasure and screamed.

Ryder was with her, holding her tightly against him, kissing her nose, her cheek, her eyebrows, her ears. He told her again and again that he loved her.

"Am I too heavy?"

He wasn't, not really, but her wrists were cramping, not because of how tightly he'd fastened the pillowcases, but because she'd jerked and twisted so violently, wanting more of him, more of herself.

"Can you untie my hands?"

He raised himself with effort, ducked his head down again and kissed her, grinning as he did so. "I can't get enough of you, Sophie."

"I don't mind kissing you," she said as he untied her wrists. He pulled out of her and came down onto his side. He rubbed her wrists, frowning at the redness. "I didn't mean to tie them so tightly. I'm sorry."

"It wasn't that," she said, not looking at him. "It was the other."

"What other?"

She looked at him straight in his blue eyes. "How you made me feel. I was an animal."

"Ah, another condemnation perhaps? Based on your wonderful objective experience? I hate to tell you this, Sophia, but we are both animals, carnal as hell, and so wonderful that I pray you'll go wild and ferocious on me every night." He paused, frowning. "Perhaps every morning as well. Ah, and there's the hour just after luncheon, you know, when you're just a bit tired and—"

She laughed.

Ryder was so surprised that he simply stared down at her. He kissed her again and six more times.

She kissed him back, but her body felt so languid she doubted she could have roused herself even if Mrs. Chivers had shouted fire. She felt beyond herself; she didn't understand. She didn't know what to think. And she had laughed.

She said, "Do you really love me?"

"Yes."

"You didn't just say it because you were inside me and your lust . . . well, you know what I mean."

"Yes, I know what you mean. Now, I'm not inside you. You've exhausted me twice. I'm limp and nearly expired. My wits have gone begging. I have no sensation below my heart. And I love you."

"You never said that before."

"I didn't realize I loved you before. Things have changed and I don't mind telling you that I'm quite pleased about it. No, Sophie, don't feel that you have to fill in the silence."

"You're the master here."

He said easily, accepting her words, understanding them, "Yes, I am. You want to know something? It feels good, damned good. I never felt I was needed at Northcliffe Hall and of course I wasn't. It was and is Douglas's home and his responsibility as the Earl of Northcliffe. But Chadwyck House, it's mine, Sophie, it's ours, and our children will grow up here, and this will be their home and, why, I might even wear a smock and become a farmer on Wednesdays and Fridays. What do you think?"

"I think you would look beautiful in a smock and hobnail boots."

"Ah," he said, and kissed her mouth. "Dear God, but I love kissing you."

Tell him, she thought, tell him, but she was afraid to, afraid he would search out both Lord David and Charles Grammond and threaten them or kill them, she didn't know which. But she knew there would be an awful scandal and she couldn't do it to him, to the Sherbrooke family, to Jeremy, to herself.

She kissed him back, urgently, wanting only to bury her misery, to forget it for just another instant, just one more moment, and she succeeded. He caressed her, and when he came into her again, she cried out in her climax, and Ryder thought he would die from the pleasure of it. When they slept, Ryder dreamed of his children and knew, even in his dream, that he would have to tell her about them very soon now and pray that she would understand.

Ryder didn't tell Sophie anything; he had no chance to. She was still sound asleep when he left the house the following morning, from exhaustion, from his exhausting her.

The following afternoon, when he was in the north field with three of his tenant farmers, a carriage pulled up in front of Chadwyck House. The Earl of Northcliffe, Alex, Jeremy, and Sinjun spilled out.

The earl simply stood there, his wife's hand in his, and stared at the house and grounds.

"You've done very well," he said to Sophie, who didn't look like a waif today but was actually wearing a gown that Mrs. Plack had made for her. Her hair was a bit mussed because she'd been polishing the crystals on a chandelier in what she now thought of as her own room, which was set at the back of the house, its doors giving onto the garden.

"Hello," she said, then turned to Jeremy, holding open her arms. He limped to her and hugged her, saying as fast as he could talk, "It's wonderful, Sophie! Oh goodness, I've missed you. Look, Sinjun, just look at the stables, certainly big enough for George and—"

"Who's George?"

"My pony, he's a barb and all black with two white socks and fast as the wind, Sophie."

"As in the second George or the crazy third George?"

Douglas laughed. "Actually, this George is a tradesman in Hadleigh who bears a remarkable resemblance to Jeremy's pony."

Alex said, "You've done marvels. We were so shocked to hear about what that wretched Dubust had done."

"The furniture will be back in the next few days. Alas, I have only three chairs and one table downstairs."

"Perfectly adequate," the earl said, then frowned as he looked around. "Where's Ryder?"

"He's with some of the tenant farmers."

Douglas stared at her. "Tenant farmers," he repeated blankly. "What is he doing?"

"I think they're talking about crop rotation. Evidently Mr. Dubust was more than just a criminal. He wouldn't allow the farmers new implements and discouraged letting fields lie fallow as they must, you know."

"Yes," Douglas said slowly, "yes, I know. And Ryder is dealing with this?"

"Not only is he dealing with it, he quite likes it."

Sinjun said to her brother, "Can Jeremy and I go find Ryder? It is late, Douglas, and he should be finished with all his rotations soon now. Please?"

"Go along, brat."

"Walk north," Sophie called after them. "See the trail just by the stables?"

An hour later, Ryder, Jeremy, and Sinjun strolled into the drawing room that held only three chairs. Ryder walked over to his wife and kissed her. "Look who found me. And I wasn't even wearing my hobnails or my smock."

Sophie felt a deep surge of pleasure at the sight of him and could only nod.

Ryder grinned at her, and lightly caressed his knuckles over her cheek. "No, Douglas, don't say anything, if you please. Things change, all right? To show me proper respect, call me Master Ryder or Farmer Ryder. I begin to think that I must design a new plow, one with style, one that will be made by an artisan as famous as Hoby or Weston. What do you think?"

"I think you're mad, Ryder, utterly mad and very happy."

"And what do you think of our home?"

"That it is a home and you've made it thus in a very short time."

"I must give Sophie credit for accomplishing a bit, a very little bit, but I don't wish to make her feel useless."

Sophie squawked and flew at him. Ryder, laughing, his blue eyes as light as the afternoon sky, gathered her against him and held her and then swung her about.

The earl looked at his wife, who was smiling at them.

The Earl and Countess of Northcliffe didn't mind at all sleeping on piles of blankets in a guest room. Indeed, if Ryder were any expert on the matter, and he most assuredly was, he knew that his brother and sister-in-law quite enjoyed themselves. His brother was a man of a creative nature.

The earl and countess remained for only a day and a half, for they were on a visit to the Duke and Duchess of Portsmouth. As for Sinjun and Jeremy, they were to stay for a long visit. Sinjun's goal, she said, giggling, was to see Ryder in his farmer's smock.

Not an hour after the earl and countess had left, Sinjun found her brother in a rather ardent embrace with his wife. She cleared her throat. Ryder looked up and frowned at her. "Go away, Sinjun. You're only fifteen and you shouldn't be witnessing all this excess of affection."

"Ha," Sinjun said. "You should see Douglas and Alex when they think no one's looking. You wouldn't believe what I've seen him doing, and Alex always throws her head back and makes these funny little noises and—"

"Be quiet, brat. Now, this had better be urgent or I'll tan your backside."

"I've got to speak to you, Ryder. Alone."

This was a very serious Sinjun, and Sophie, having regained her equilibrium, merely nodded, and took herself off.

Ryder crossed his arms over his chest and leaned against the mantel. "I'm too late."

"Too late for what?"

Sinjun, to her brother's absolute astonishment, turned red and wrung her hands. "They're nearly here. I rode as fast as I could back here to warn you. Oh, Ryder, I'm sorry, but there was nothing I could do. I know how you feel about Douglas or any of the rest of the family knowing how wonderful you are, but—"

Ryder had a peculiar feeling in the pit of his stomach. "What are you talking about?"

"The children should be here in no more than two minutes from now."

"You have two minutes, then, to explain all this to me."

"I took Jeremy over to Hadleigh to meet Jane and the children. All right, you can tan my bottom later for that, but Ryder, he fit right in and much enjoyed himself. He and Oliver are the best of friends. Oh dear, there's only one minute left. Jane came down with the measles. She immediately sent me a message saying the children had to leave so they wouldn't become ill; then Laura, one of her helpers, sent me a message at Northcliffe and she didn't know what to do. So I told her and Jane to send all the children here. What else should I have done, Ryder? Told Douglas?"

Ryder looked off into the distance. "Well, that solves one problem, doesn't it? Is that the sound of carriage wheels I hear? Probably. Who paid for all this, Sinjun?"

"I did. It took nearly all my savings, but I managed. I didn't want the children to travel by stage, so I hired four carriages, three for them and one for all the luggage, and I managed to secure four rooms at the Golden Calf Inn in Reading."

Ryder grinned at his sister. He patted her cheek. "You did well. Let's go meet all my brood. Good God, I hope none of them have come down with the measles. It can be quite nasty."

"What about Sophie?"

"Sophie isn't a fool," he said, but to Sinjun's fond and alert ears, his voice sounded very odd.

When he and Sinjun arrived on the front steps of Chadwyck House, there were Sophie and Jeremy assisting child after child from the carriages. Only Laura Bracken had come with them because the other two helpers had come down with the measles along with Jane. Laura, bless her heart, was exhausted. The children, luckily, were all well.

It was Jaime who first spotted Ryder. He let out a yell and rushed at him. Ryder swung the boy up in his arms and tossed him into the air, then hugged him tightly against his chest. The other children were on him in the next moment, and there was pandemonium for the next five minutes.

Sophie saw the little girl standing off to one side, her thumb in her mouth. She didn't understand any of this but, oddly enough, she was content to wait and see. It wasn't perhaps so strange with the children hanging on to his arms, legs, and neck that he wouldn't look at her.

Sinjun grabbed her arm. "I swear this isn't what you think, Sophie."

Sophie said easily, "No, I doubt it is. That boy over there must be all of eleven or twelve years old. Surely Ryder couldn't have fathered him. No, I'm learning that with Ryder nothing is as it appears to be."

"They are his children, his Beloved Ones," Sinjun said, desperate now, "but not really, all except for Jenny. Ryder saved each of them at different times, you know. He loves children and hates cruelty toward them, and—"

Ryder, dragging four children and holding two others, came down the steps, grinning hugely, but not at Sophie. He looked over her left shoulder as he said simply, "These are my children." He introduced all of them to his wife. Sophie smiled and spoke to each of them. A moment later, she realized with a shock that Ryder was embarrassed.

Then he got a huge smile on his face as he looked over at the little girl who was standing alone, watching silently.

"Now, all you wild savages, I want you to go with Jeremy and Sinjun to the kitchen. We don't have any furniture yet, but you can sit on the kitchen floor and Mrs. Chivers and Cook will make sure you have scones and biscuits and lemonade. Go now, and later I'll tell you all about my adventures and why the house doesn't have any beds for you."

"And I'll tell you more stories about the Virgin Bride," Sinjun said. "Who knows, maybe she's followed Ryder and Sophie here."

Amy shrieked with excited terror.

Ryder simply took Sophie's hand and led her over to the little girl. Sophie stood still, watching her husband go down on his knees. He opened his arms and the little girl came to him. He held her close, kissing her hair, stroking her back, and she heard him saying over and over, "Ah, Jenny, I've missed you, little love. Now, would you like to meet Sophie? She's not as pretty as you, but she is nice and she makes me smile. Just maybe she'll make you smile as well."

He looked up at his wife and she knew that this was his child, and that the little girl wasn't like the other children. There was a look of near desperation on his face and she realized that he was worried that she would snub the little girl.

"You should have some faith in me," she said as she came down to her knees beside her husband and held out her hand, making no move toward the little girl, who was huddled against her father's chest. "Hello, Jenny. That's a lovely dress you're wearing, much nicer than mine. I'm very glad to meet you and I'm very glad you're here. Your father has missed you very much. How old are you?"

Ryder raised her right hand, folded down her thumb and said very slowly, "One."

Jenny said, "One."

Ryder folded down the next finger and said, "Two."

When he reached her little finger, he only bent it in half and said, "There now, I'm four and a half years old."

"Yes, Papa."

There was such pride and love on his face. Another Ryder, no, another side to him. She said now, "Such a big girl you are and just look at that lovely locket. May I see it?"

Jenny very slowly stretched out her hand, and her fingertips lightly, tentatively touched Sophie's palm. She held out the locket and Sophie opened it. "Ah, what lovely paintings. You and your mama? Yes, I can see that you're as pretty as she is. You have your father's beautiful eyes though."

"Papa," Jenny said, and threw her arms around Ryder's neck again and buried her face in his neck.

"It's her new word," Ryder said, immensely pleased.

"Now, little love, my old bones are creaking. Let me heave you up— you're such a great big girl, Sophie's right about that—and let's go into the house. You'd like some lemonade, wouldn't you?"

Pandemonium reigned in the kitchen. Mrs. Chivers looked as if she'd just been dumped willy-nilly into Bedlam, but she was smiling, thank the good Lord. Cook, a Mrs. Bedlock, was running to and fro from the pantry. It was Sinjun, though, who was in charge of the brood. Each child was finally seated on the floor with a plate filled with goodies.

"There won't be anything left to eat," Mrs. Chivers said, staring from one child to the other. "I have three grandchildren and they all eat like it's their last meal."

"Then we'd best send Mrs. Bedlock to Lower Slaughter to buy out the town," Sophie said. Ryder looked at his wife, still didn't meet her eyes, and she would have sworn that he blushed.

He neatly managed to avoid her for the next several hours. It wasn't difficult because each of the children wanted his attention. He showed them the east wing, told them about Mr. Dubust, making the man a villain fit to rule the world, but his aunt, dear Mildred, had shrieked him down and now he would pay for his crimes.

Sophie merely bided her time and made decisions as to where the children would sleep.

At last she managed to corner him as he tried to slip past her out of the house. "Oh no you don't, Ryder. I want to talk to you and it's now or I will make you very sorry."

That ruffled his manly feathers and he said sharply, "Oh, and just how do you plan to do that? Tie me down and have your way with my body?"

She grinned at him. "Come along. We're going for a walk."

Sophie walked beside her husband in the apple orchard just behind the house. It was private, with not a single child hiding behind a tree. Sinjun was with the children, playing mediator, mother, and nursemaid. Ryder was silent. Sophie started humming.

Suddenly she laughed. "You're embarrassed! I couldn't believe it, you were actually embarrassed. You couldn't meet my eyes. Is it because I never, even for one instant, believed all those children to be yours! Ah, if that is it, why then, what a blow to your manhood."

"Go to the devil, Sophie."

"No, that isn't it at all. I had hoped to enrage you out of your damned silence. No, you were and are embarrassed because you don't want any one to know that you're not a care-for-nothing rakehell. You enjoy being the *homme terrible* and this, my dear, truly ruins that devil-may-care image."

"Maybe it doesn't. What the hell do you know? Did that wretched Sinjun speak to you?"

"Yes, at first she was desperate because she was afraid I'd get a gun and shoot you. Then later I pinned her against the wall and forced her to spill out the truth—you know, during all those hours when you assiduously avoided me. She told me she'd hoped you would have spoken to me before this, but that you were very reticent about your Beloved Ones, that you didn't consider the children to be anyone's business, even your family's. That it was your damned money and you could do whatever you wanted to do with it. Sinjun also said that Uncle Brandon probably was whirling about in his grave at your philanthropy, but that maybe he wouldn't spend so much time in hell because of the good cause you were putting his money to."

"She appears to have spilled her innards. I'll wager she even sang out about the quarterly bastard meetings, didn't she, curse her eyes?"

Sophie looked perfectly blank.

"Then forget it. God, the chit finally kept her mouth shut about something that is none of her business."

"Not on your benighted life will I forget it. Bastard meetings? What's that? Tell me this instant."

Ryder cursed and Sophie just laughed. "That won't get you out of it. Now, what's a bastard meeting?"

"Oh hell. Douglas and I had a meeting every quarter to count up bastards, so as not to lose any by accident, you know. He believed all the children were my bastards."

"I do wonder what he will say when he finds out the truth."

"He won't," Ryder said, his voice sharp. "It's not any of his damned business."

She arched an eyebrow at him. "You are so good, so kind, so wondrously chivalrous, why, I think I will cry."

"You could better consider keeping your mouth closed. It's not as if I don't much enjoy women," he said now, clearly irritated with her calm acceptance. "Dammit, Sophie, I have given five—five!—women their congé! I even made up a list of possible husbands for each of them. I will provide dowries for the three who wish to wed, and the other two are going to London and I am providing for them too. I am a lover in demand, and they are all saddened unto profound depression that I will no longer pleasure them."

She laughed. "Ah, Ryder, you are amazing, you know that? Truly amazing. You brag about your women and keep mum about your children. You know, I would never expect a man of your character to not take care when you climbed into a woman's bed. I'm very surprised that your brother knows you so little."

He sobered. "Don't blame Douglas. He only came home from the army less than a year ago. He believed what I told him, and as I told you, I am known for my prowess with women, far and wide, so my promised fidelity to you shakes him profoundly. He believes in true love because of it. Before, he merely accepted that lust ruled my head. As for him, he has a little girl nearly Jenny's age."

"Well, he is sure to suspect something is amiss with his opinions of you when he and Alex return to find a houseful of children."

Ryder cursed. "Damn Jane and her cursed measles!"

"It is fortunate that Chadwyck House is so very large. I fancy the east wing will accommodate all of them quite nicely. Indeed, I've already seen to their rooms—while you were ignoring me. Now, tell me about Jane. Do you think she would like to live here?"

"I don't know. Jane much enjoys her independence."

"Well, it's early yet. We will see. Doubtless she and I can work out something."

His face grew tight. A frown gathered on his brow. His lips thinned. Sophia looked on, fascinated. He kicked a pebble from his path. "You know, damn your so agreeable little hide, you could show a bit of jealousy. As my wife it would be thoroughly appropriate. I dislike your cursed understanding, your damned unctuous acceptance. It is fine, in its place, but its place isn't here, it isn't now. Damn you, Sophie, stop being so bloody tolerant."

"I've already attacked you with a broom. I am unable to jerk up one of the apple trees and cosh you with the trunk. However, if you insist on punishment, upon vituperation from a jealous wife, well then, you will have it."

She threw herself at him, hooking her foot behind his calf, and he went down, Sophie sprawled on top of him. She grabbed his hair to hold him still, then kissed him, every bit of his face, from his hairline to his earlobes.

"You sweetheart," she said, and kept kissing him. She pressed her belly against his and he moaned. She raised her head, looked at an apple tree just to her left and said, "Goodness, do you think we have enough bedding for all the children?"

"I am going to beat you, Sophie Sherbrooke."

"I hope you didn't give so much money to all your former mistresses that we won't have enough to buy food for all those little mouths. Goodness, did you go into debt with all the gowns Mrs. Plack made for me? Three riding habits, Ryder, three! How it is possible for there to be a more generous, a more giving, a more magnanimous man in the whole world? Or at least in the whole Cotswolds?"

He grabbed his arms around her back and rolled over on top of her. "Now you listen to me, you damned thorn in my flesh. I refuse to accept your sweet kisses just because you've decided I'm not the scoundrel you believed me to be. Ha! Half of what you say is sarcasm and you don't cloak it well. You don't even try. You rub my nose in it. Now you think I'm this benevolent philanthropist, this saintly creature, and even said so in that mocking voice of yours. The whole idea makes me want to puke. Damn you, I'm barely a nice man; I am barely to be tolerated. Don't you dare continue your kisses and your good humor just because now you think I'm different and bloody worthy."

"All right," she said easily, and clasped her arms around his back. "You're still the same. I think you're a bastard, a bounder, a man without conscience, a clothhead who has no caring for anyone save himself and his own pleasures and—"

"Damn you, I'm not a bad man either. Ah, that's it, Sophie. No more of your agile tongue, that I—fool that I am—called forth myself. To think I begged you to give me back the hellion I married. No more. I will not let you have the upper hand any longer. You do too well when I deign to let you have it. No, now I'm going to take the reins back and you're going to moan, not speak your damned banalities that enrage me."

"But, Ryder, you were embarrassed because your good deeds literally came home to haunt you."

He jerked up her gown, tore her shift, unfastened his britches, and plunged into her.

She couldn't believe that her body was warm and more than ready, truth be told, and she accepted him, craved him, the full length of him, and she lifted her hips to take more of him.

"Now do you feel dirty, damn you?"

She bit his shoulder, then licked the spot and moaned into his neck. He felt her hands pressing against his lower back, then against his buttocks, lifting her own hips even as she did so and he said again, "Do you feel dirty?"

"No." Then she cried out, and he took her cries into his warm mouth and took his own release.

"Do you still feel embarrassed?" she whispered against his throat.

"You're lucky I am an understanding and giving man," Ryder said.

"Yes, even to me, your wife."

"You will cease your taunts, Sophie."

"All right," she said, and kissed him full on his mouth.

It was at that moment, just when Ryder was ever so willing to resume their lovemaking, that Jeremy's voice came loud and clear. "Ryder! Sophie! Where are you? Melissa cut her hand and is yelling for you."

"What can one do?" Ryder laughed and rose, hauling Sophie up with him.

CHAPTER
═══ 20 ═══

MRS. CHIVERS BROUGHT Sophie the plain envelope with only her name in straight block letters printed on the outside.

"The Meyers boy delivered it, ma'am," Mrs. Chivers said in a matter-of-fact voice. "Quite plain he is, looks just like his father."

"Thank you." Sophie's hand was shaking as she took the envelope, but Mrs. Chivers didn't notice. She walked quickly into the small back parlor that she'd appropriated for her own use, shut the door, and leaned back against it, just staring down at that envelope.

The contents weren't all that disturbing on the surface. She read:

You will meet me this afternoon at three o'clock beneath the old elm tree at the fork of the road that divides Lower Slaughter from Upper Slaughter. Don't be late and it would be wise not to tell your husband anything. I wouldn't want to have to kill him.

It was signed with a simple "DL."

David Lochridge. Lord David.

Sophie walked away from the door and to her small desk. She sat down and placed the letter in the middle of the desktop and continued to stare at it. She didn't move, just stared and wondered what the devil she was going to do.

She had only two hours to decide.

"Sophie! Are you in here?"

The door was flung open and there was Sinjun, looking as beautiful and windblown as Ryder did when he galloped in from the fields. Her blue eyes sparkled, just as did Ryder's, with the simple pleasure of being alive.

Her expression stiffened in an instant.

"What's the matter? What happened?"

She was also as perceptive as her brother. "Nothing is the matter, Sinjun." Sophie rose. Slowly, very slowly, she folded the letter and slipped it into the envelope. What to do with it?

"I came to fetch you to luncheon. Unless, of course, you don't want to be part of the madhouse, which it will doubtless be. Ryder claimed he had a headache and was going to muck out stalls in the stable. I think Jane is probably right. She always says that adults should only dine with adults. Children only with children and guards."

Sophie smiled brightly. "Then we should continue with Jane's procedure. Have Mrs. Chivers tell Cook that the children will luncheon in the breakfast room. How many guards did Jane have?"

Sinjun laughed. "At least five."

"Good. See to it, please. Also, call in Ryder from the stables." And she laughed, she actually could laugh.

Sinjun left the room without demur and Sophie quickly put the envelope into the top drawer of her desk, way in the back, beneath some other papers.

Ryder returned quickly enough when he heard of the new arrangement from his sister. He and Sophie and Sinjun were the only ones who sat down to luncheon in the huge dining room. It was blessedly calm.

"This room is far too dark," Sinjun said as she forked a healthy bite of ham into her mouth.

"Yes," Sophie said, not raising her head. She made small piles of her food on her plate and proceeded to push the piles around.

"If you're sickening of something you'd best speak up," Ryder said sharply.

She dredged up a smile for her husband. "I'm fine, just a bit tired. Jenny had a nightmare last night, as you know. I had a difficult time going back to sleep."

Ryder frowned at her but held his peace. Actually, she'd fallen back to sleep instantly. It had been he who had worried about the nightmare for a good hour.

What the devil was wrong with her? Was she regretting welcoming the children here? Were they tormenting her? She wasn't used to bedlam and that's what seven children were. Or maybe she was backsliding again. She'd made love to him sweetly the previous night, but who knew?

Sinjun, bless her oblivious heart, continued with her monologue about the refurbishing of the dining room.

Ryder took his leave after luncheon. He kissed Sophie lightly on her mouth, ran his fingertips over her eyebrows, studied her face, but saw nothing he could interpret. There was so much to be done, so many decisions to be made. He had to see Tom Lynch in ten minutes, a farmer of intelligence and sound common sense. Ryder sighed and took his leave and hoped doing nothing was what she needed right now.

As for Sinjun, she was quick to absent herself, saying only that she was going to play with the children.

At precisely three o'clock, Sophie pulled Opal to a halt beneath the elm tree, whose trunk was so thick and gnarly that it looked far older than the surrounding hills, probably older than all the goblins that supposedly lived burrowed under those hills.

She hadn't long to wait. Lord David rode up looking as arrogant and self-assured as he always had. An angel's face with a devil's heart.

She didn't say anything, merely waited.

"You lied to me," he said in a very pleasant voice.

"What a novel thing to say, considering the man who's saying it."

"You told me you had the pox. You said you wouldn't be my mistress anymore because you didn't want to infect me. You lied. You don't have the pox else you wouldn't have married Ryder Sherbrooke. You just wanted to be rid of me."

"That's true."

"But that's absurd! Truly ridiculous. You not want me anymore?"

"It's true nonetheless."

"Ah, so you wanted Ryder Sherbrooke, and you knew you had to get rid of me else he could have found out about me, and if he had, why then, he would never have believed that you preferred him over me. Yes, if he'd known about me, he would have realized that you knew what a real man was like and wouldn't be taken in by the likes of him."

Sophie stared at him, wondering silently at the workings of his mind. "You think like no one I know," she said finally. "Besides, why do you care now? You told me you were going to wed an heiress. I can't imagine that you would want your betrothed to know about what you believe happened between us on Jamaica. Surely you cannot believe that I would say anything. You want this marriage to go forth, do you not?"

"I spoke to Charles Grammond. We've come to a decision."

She felt a frisson of uncertainty for the first time. Lord David was possessed of a mind that ran in only one direction; it was probably the key to his success at gambling. He couldn't be diverted or sidetracked or brought about to see another point of view. His voice had lowered, deepened, and in that instant, she saw him naked, standing in front of her, and he was laughing and drinking the rum punch, becoming sodden, becoming ready for Dahlia, thank God.

"What do you want, David?"

His back straightened and he threw back his head like a little king. "I am Lord David to a whore like you."

"What you are is a pathetic, corrupt, filthy-minded little bastard."

He raised his arm then lowered it. "No, I wouldn't want to bruise that

lovely face of yours. Your husband would surely notice and Ryder Sherbrooke is a man I won't wish to have as an enemy."

Sophie supposed that she, as a woman, would never be accounted as
an enemy worthy of notice. Well, she would tell him the truth and let him
stew on it.

"I will tell you something else, *Lord* David. I never slept with you.
Such a thought frankly turns my stomach. I never slept with any of the
men. It was Dahlia, a girl you perhaps met in Montego Bay, always
Dahlia at the cottage who came to see to you after you'd drunk yourself
silly."

He looked startled, then laughed. "Don't tell me that is the tale you
tried to pass off on Ryder Sherbrooke."

"It was all my uncle's idea. He forced me to pretend to take you all for
lovers so he could gain what he wanted for himself. The rum punch all of
you drank with great enthusiasm was, quite simply, drugged. You being
the way you are, most men being the way they are, why, it was very easy."

"Oh? And what did your uncle want from me?"

"He wanted you to ruin Charles Grammond so he would have to sell
his plantation, which he did, to my uncle. Then, after you'd done what he
wished you to do, he told me to dismiss you. The pox infection was his
idea and it worked quite well. I remember you turned positively white
with fear."

"You're lying. You will tell me no more lies. Your uncle was a gentleman who was distraught over your whoring ways. No one believed that
you didn't murder him, even when Cole had it said about that your uncle
was garroted by Thomas. And that damned Sherbrooke helped you escape Jamaica and punishment. Now you're blaming him! Jesus, a lady
wouldn't even know what the pox is. You're no lady. You're nothing but
a cheap little whore and both Charles and I have decided that we enjoyed
you enough so that we'll continue our little trysts."

"As I said, you're pathetic and if you think I would ever allow you near
me—"

"I'm near you now and I fully plan to get nearer."

"Ah, rape?"

He merely shrugged. "Your husband isn't a stupid man, but just maybe
he is where women are concerned. I don't pretend to fathom why the hell
he married you when he could have simply taken you until he was bored
with you. Oh no, Sophia, if you screamed rape to him, he would probably kill you, because once a whore always a whore."

"You make no sense, *Lord* David. You said you didn't want my husband for an enemy. He married me. He loves me. He wouldn't kill me, he
would believe me, not you. He would kill you."

THE BRIDES TRILOGY 491

"Are you so ignorant of your husband's nature? Of his reputation? Like you, he must have a great deal of variety. You loved sex, God, you started on your career when you were barely eighteen. You want sex still, I doubt it not. You can't stay faithful to one man, even to Ryder Sherbrooke, who, I've heard, has bedded every woman who resides in Kent. Now he's in the Cotswolds and no woman will be safe from him. You'll see. He'll parade his mistresses under your nose and laugh. Well, my dear, Charles and I are going to allow you to continue with your ways just as he will with his."

He dug his heels into his stallion's sides, and came up close to her. He reached out his arms to her. Sophie raised her riding crop and brought it down hard on his arm. He yowled, jerking back.

"You're utterly mad!"

His face flushed with rage, but before he could do anything, the silence was broken by what sounded like a pack of wild dogs, all howling in anger, growling deeply and viciously, bounding ready to attack, and to kill. Wild dogs in the Cotswolds?

"What the bloody hell!"

Sophie pulled Opal back from him. An arrow came flying through the air to land in Lord David's upper arm, just nicking it actually, but certainly ruining his superfine riding jacket. He screamed more in anger than in pain. He had no weapon. He had no way to defend himself against an unseen enemy.

"You brought someone, you perfidious bitch! This isn't over, you'll see!"

He wheeled his stallion about and was soon lost to her sight. Sophie just sat there, trying to breathe deeply. It was no surprise to her when the underbrush surrounding the road spilled out seven children, Jeremy, and Sinjun, all of them oddly silent after their sterling performance. Sinjun carried the bow. It had been she who had shot Lord David. Sophie climbed down from Opal's broad back.

Jeremy came to her and enfolded her in his arms.

"He's a bad man from Jamaica," the boy said. "I told Sinjun who he was."

"You did well." She raised her head. All the children, from four-year-old Jenny to ten-year-old Oliver, stood silent, all in a line, watching her. She wondered how they had known, then decided she didn't want to know. She tried to smile but it was difficult. She said finally, "I was in trouble. Thank you all for your help. I truly believed a pack of wild dogs had somehow come along. You were splendid. I'm very proud of all of you."

Sinjun said quietly, "I didn't think you wanted Ryder to know just yet.

We will figure out what to do, Sophie. You're not alone anymore. But Jeremy doesn't understand everything that happened on Jamaica. You need to tell me more."

"Yes, I will. Now, listen to me, all of you. I know that you all dearly love Ryder. But I beg you not to tell him of this. The bad man is as mean as a snake, he isn't honorable or good like Ryder. He wouldn't fight him fairly. I don't want Ryder hurt. Please don't say anything to him. All right?"

Amy said, "What's a hore?"

Tom slapped his hand over the little girl's mouth. "That's not a nice word. Don't say it again."

Amy, affronted, yelled back at Tom, "You say horrible words to Jaime all because Ollie said you grew up on the docks. You—"

Oliver got into the argument, waving one of his crutches about, and then Jenny said in a very carrying voice, "I want to go pull up my dress and visit Mrs. Nature."

Sophie felt something loosen inside her. She laughed, really laughed, and soon the children joined her, and it was Sinjun who carried Jenny off into the underbrush to visit Mrs. Nature.

Sophie realized on the way back to Chadwyck House that none of the children had promised her not to tell Ryder.

Jane and her two helpers were nearly recovered and would come to Chadwyck House within the next two weeks.

Sophie, who knew all about Jane now, realized that the woman wouldn't be happy living in another woman's household. There would be no problem. They would simply build another house in the small knoll that stood not one hundred yards from the main house. Ryder agreed and work would begin soon.

To Sophie's astonishment, Melissande decided after only one visit to Bedlam House, as Ryder had christened it, that perhaps having a child wasn't such a bad idea after all. All the children, even Jenny, told her over and over again how very beautiful she was. They were afraid to touch her for fear of somehow hurting her perfection. As for Melissande's husband, Tony, he groaned and said there was no hope for it. He was immediately taking her to London. "I can tolerate—just barely—some nodcock fool young man telling her that her eyebrows are like an artist's brush strokes, but all this nonsense from a pack of children? No, Sophie, it is too much. I will go into a decline if I have to hear much more."

Tony sighed deeply. Ryder laughed. Melissande beamed at all the children, patting every single head. She promised each of them a special sweetmeat on her next visit.

* * *

Ryder strode toward the house one afternoon, tired from a long day in the fields, speaking to many of his farmers. He'd also met with architects and arranged for artisans and workers for the new house. He'd also heard gossip about his gaggle of "bastards," and he'd gotten a good laugh from that. Just wait, he thought, just wait until there were a good fifteen children. Then what would the busybodies say? He wasn't at all surprised to realize that eventually, there would very probably be at least fifteen children, perhaps more.

It was a hot day, far too hot for this time of year, nearly Michaelmas now. He heard the children before he saw them. Always, they were ready for him. They had set up some kind of signal system. In another minute, many of them were there, escorting him to the house, all of them talking at once, even Jenny. She was talking like a magpie now and he realized it was his influence that had brought the rapid progress. He wouldn't let her out of his sight after this. He quickly forgot his fatigue; he laughed and listened to each of them and all of them at once, and silently thanked the good Lord yet again that none of them had come down with the measles.

And each night there was Sophie beside him, accepting him now, and he knew she enjoyed his body, knew that she looked forward to their time alone so she could touch him as much as she wished to, and accept his touches. Only last night, he had actually made her laugh when he was deep inside her. He felt good. He couldn't imagine the stars aligning themselves in a more propitious stance.

He was whistling until he found two letters in the top drawer of her desk. Sophie was in Lower Slaughter, three children and Laura and Sophie's maid, Cory, with her, buying cloth to make clothing. The seamstresses of Lower Slaughter—all three of them—were in alt because of the sudden manna from business heaven that showed no sign of ever diminishing. It was during Sophie's jaunt that Mrs. Chivers had complained to Ryder that the butcher was cheating them royally, and here they were, not royalty at all, and he really should do something about it and not spend all his time with those dirty farmers. And so he was looking in Sophie's desk for the butcher bills. And he found the letters from David Lochridge.

The second letter was even dated and the date was yesterday. He read:

I have made up my mind. You will become my mistress again. Charles Grammond will deal with you himself. I intend to enjoy myself again as I did on Jamaica. Come to the old Tolliver shack on the north side of your husband's property at three o'clock Thursday or you will regret it.

Signed merely "DL."

The damned bastard.

And damn Sophie's beautiful gray eyes. She'd said nothing; he'd known something was wrong. Indeed the previous evening, she'd wanted him urgently, too urgently, as if she wanted to keep something unpleasant at bay. But he hadn't questioned her; he'd merely given her what she'd wanted, what she'd appeared to need; he'd allowed her to escape this for the time she'd exploded into her climax.

She'd unmanned him with her silence.

He crumpled the letter in his fist, unaware that he'd even done it.

"Papa."

He looked up blankly. There was Jenny, standing in the doorway, looking from his face to the wad of paper fisted tightly in his hand.

Ryder forced himself to toss the crumpled paper back onto Sophie's desk. "Hello, pumpkin. Come here and let me hug you. It's been more than an hour since I've seen you—far too long."

Jenny raced to him and he raised her high in his arms and kissed her nose. "What is it you wish, little love?"

"Can you teach me to shoot a bow and arrow like Sinjun so I can shoot that bad man?"

He froze tighter than a spigot in January.

"Certainly," he said. "Tell me about it, all right?"

And she did. He would have laughed at all the children playing at being wolves if he hadn't been so angry. God, but they'd done well. Routed the bastard. And Sinjun, shooting him through the upper arm. Well done of her.

He'd strangle his sister once he got his hands on her.

Then he'd strangle his wife.

"Jenny! Where are you, pumpkin? Jenn—" Sinjun came through the doorway, stopped short, and immediately said, "Oh dear. Hello, Ryder. Whatever are you doing here? This is Sophie's room and—"

Ryder merely stared at his sister, words, for the moment, failing him.

Sinjun sighed. "I suppose Jenny said something?"

"You're not stupid, Sinjun. You are very quick to perceive when your perfidy has been discovered. It's a relief. I detest boring explanations. Yes. Jenny wants me to teach her how to shoot a bow and arrow so that she can shoot the bad man."

"Oh dear. I'm sorry, Ryder, but—"

He was controlled now. He said to Jenny as he disengaged her thin arms from about his neck, "Now, love, I want you to go with Sinjun.

She's going to give you a biscuit and some lemonade. Papa must do some work now. All right?"

"Papa," Jenny said, and went immediately to Sinjun.

"Go," Ryder said to his sister. "This time, you will keep your mouth shut—to my wife."

"All right," Sinjun said, and her voice was very small, so small in fact, so diffident and timorous, that Ryder nearly smiled.

At two-thirty on Thursday, Ryder calmly pulled his horse to a halt some thirty yards away from the Tolliver shack. He tethered him next to some goat weed to keep him quiet.

He felt a mix of anticipation, rage, and excitement all coming together inside him. He wanted to see David Lochridge. He wanted, quite simply, to pound him into the ground.

He waited in the thick elm trees that bordered the shack, whistling behind his teeth, his excitement building and building. He wondered when Sophie would arrive. He wondered when Lochridge would get here.

However, it simply never occurred to him that another person would put in an appearance here, of all places. He was frozen in silent shock when an older woman pulled an old-fashioned gig to a halt in front of the shack not five minutes later. She was plump, wearing a stylish gown, a bonnet far too young for her, for she was in her mid-forties, he guessed, and she looked somewhat familiar, but that couldn't be. Good God, was she here for some sort of tryst? Was this shack used for illicit affairs?

He didn't move. He watched the woman climb down from the gig, and lead the old cob around to the back of the cottage, out of sight.

What the devil was going on?

Sophie and Lord David Lochridge arrived at the same time, from different directions. Both Ryder and the other woman were well out of sight.

Ryder watched as Sophie dismounted Opal, turned and said very clearly, her voice as calm as the eye of a storm, "I am here to tell you one last time, *Lord* David, that I will have nothing to do with you."

"Ah, you're still being the tease," he said, but Ryder saw him looking around. For more wolves? His eyes fell on the riding crop she held in her right hand.

"No, I'm not teasing you. When I saw you last I told you the truth. All that happened on Jamaica was my uncle's doing and I was never with you intimately at the cottage, with you or with any of the other men. Now, if you don't choose to believe me, why then, I guess I will just have to shoot you."

Ryder's eyes widened. She drew a small derringer from her pocket and pointed it at his chest.

Lord David laughed. "Ah, a lady with a little gun. Come, my dear, we both know you haven't the nerve to do anything with that toy, much less pull the trigger."

"I thought you said I murdered my uncle. If you believe that then how can you possibly believe that I wouldn't or couldn't pull the trigger on you?"

Lord David was in a quandary. He eyed her closely. He fidgeted; he cursed. Finally, he said, "Come, let's talk about this. There's no reason for violence. I'm merely offering you my body. It is for your pleasure, just as I pleasured you on Jamaica. Why are you being so unreasonable?"

"Unreasonable, am I? And what about dear Charles Grammond? Does he wish to continue your silly fictions as well? Will I have to face him down as I am you?"

"Charles isn't my problem. He will do what he wishes to do."

Sophie was now the one who looked thoughtful. "It would seem to me," she said at last, "that we are at something of an impasse. You wish to wed an heiress; Charles Grammond must be discreet or his aunt will kick him out and leave him no money in her will. That is what you told me, isn't it? All right, then, I won't kill you if you will cease all this damnable nonsense. Go away, David. Just go away and marry your poor heiress. I wish I could warn her about you but I realize that I can't, not without hurting my husband and his family. There will be no scandal for either of us. Do you agree?"

In that moment, Lord David raised his chin and whistled. In the next instant, an older man came up behind Sophie, grabbed her arms, and wrested the derringer from her.

"Ah, Charles, your timing is of the best, as usual."

"Yes," said Charles. "I've got you, Sophie. You're beautiful. I'd forgotten, but now that I've got you again, why David and I will share you, just as before."

Sophie turned and screamed in his face, "You fool! You idiot! Don't believe David, he's a fraud, a bounder, he fleeced you out of all your money so that you lost your plantation on Jamaica!"

Good Lord, Ryder thought, staring at the man. It was Charles Grammond, one of Sophie's other lovers. Still he didn't move. He would have time to act. Besides, Sophie deserved to be frightened, just for a bit, for her perfidy.

But he realized he couldn't let her be frightened, not for an instant, not if he were there and could put an end to all of it. He stepped forward, but was forestalled by that other woman.

She came stomping forward around the side of the shack, there was no other way to describe it. Her cheeks were red, her bosom heaving. She was very angry.

"You let her go, Charles!"

The man stared at the vision coming toward him. He said in the most pitiful voice Ryder had ever heard, "Ah, Almeria. How come you to be here?"

"Let her go, you old fool. Are you all right, Sophia?"

"Yes, ma'am," Sophie said, staring at Almeria Grammond. Charles released her and she took two quick steps away from him. She was rubbing her arms.

Lord David looked flummoxed when Almeria Grammond turned on him. "As for you, you wretched cheat, I personally will see to it that this poor girl you intend to marry cries off. I will not have you for a neighbor!"

Ryder laughed, he couldn't help it. His excitement, his anticipation of at the very least breaking David Lochridge's face, had degenerated into farce, worthy of Nell Gwen and the Restoration stage.

He stepped forward. All eyes turned toward him. "A full complement now," he said, his voice as bland as the goat weed his stallion was reluctantly chewing. "Save, perhaps, for Lord David's betrothed."

"This is impossible," Lord David said. He was markedly pale and his long thin fingers were clenching and unclenching. "This should not be happening."

"One would think so," Ryder agreed easily. "You are Mrs. Grammond, I take it. I'm Ryder Sherbrooke, Sophia's husband. How do you do, ma'am?"

She gave him a slight curtsy, then looked at him more closely. Sophie watched, fascinated, as Mrs. Grammond's color rose again, only this time it was from the pleasure of Ryder's attention. Goodness, it appeared that a woman had to be on death's door before she was immune to him. Then she actually stammered. "A—a pleasure, Mr. Sherbrooke. Do forgive my husband. He is a nodcock. He has never had much sense, else Lord David wouldn't have ruined him. He won't bother your poor wife further."

"But how did you know?" Charles Grammond finally said, staring in utter horror at his wife.

She bestowed upon him a look of tolerant scorn. "I always read any letters you receive. Most of them are from tradesmen and you have no notion of how to deal with tradesmen. I do. Your aunt and I have discussed this in great detail and have come to an understanding. However, when I found this letter from the little lordling here, the cheating weasel who ruined us, I realized what had happened. Naturally, he couldn't prevent telling you all about the supposedly nonsensical tale Sophia had told him about her innocence and her uncle's guilt.

"I knew Theo Burgess when he was young. Even as a young man, he was a pious little fake. He was the kind of man who preaches goodness to all mankind on Sunday and cheats his bookkeeper out of a groat on Monday. Goodness, it was all very clear to me. In addition, of course, I followed you one night to that cottage and saw this other girl. You are such a fool, Charles. I won't allow your stupidity to prevent me and the children from living as we ought. You will now apologize to Mrs. Sherbrooke and to Mr. Sherbrooke and take yourself home. I will deal fully with you later."

Charles Grammond said, "I apologize, Sophia, Mr. Sherbrooke." He then looked at Lord David and frowned. "Surely you will no longer insist that she's a whore."

"She is, damn her!"

Ah, at last, Ryder thought, rubbed his hands together, and strode to Lord David, who had put up his hands in the stance of a prizefighter. Ryder laughed for the sheer joy of it, and knocked him flat.

Mrs. Grammond clapped her plump hands together.

Sophie, still stunned, simply stood there like a mute idiot.

Lord David came up on his elbows and shook his head. "I'm quite good at fighting. You knocked me down. It shouldn't have happened. Who taught you?"

"Stand up and we'll see if you can't improve," Ryder said and offered him a hand.

Lord David wasn't, however, a complete fool. He stayed on the ground. He said to Charles Grammond even as he was turning to leave as his wife had told him to, "You can't allow your wife to tell Agnes—the heiress's bloody name is Agnes!—about all this! Her father would ruin me. He would see that I was run out of the county."

Charles Grammond never slowed. He disappeared into the elm trees. His wife, however, turned to the felled Lord David.

"You're a poltroon, sir. However, I will make you a bargain. I won't say a word to your betrothed's father if you return all the money you cheated my husband out of on Jamaica."

Lord David turned white. "Madam, I haven't a sou. Why do you think I'm marrying this awful female named Agnes?"

"That, my lord, is your affair," said Mrs. Grammond, and she actually sniffed. "I expect to hear from you within three days, no more, else you will surely regret it. And don't think you can threaten to ruin the Sherbrookes with your nasty little stories. Both my husband and I will make certain everyone knows you're a liar.

"Now, Mr. Sherbrooke, Mrs. Sherbrooke, I do hope these two fools haven't overly upset you. There will be no more threats or problems from either of them. Good day to you both." She gave Ryder the sweetest smile imaginable, nodded briskly to Sophie, kicked dust in Lord David's face, and marched around the shack to where her gig was stationed like a waiting army.

Ryder laughed. He couldn't help it.

Sophia said in a wondering voice, "The Virgin Bride was right. She said when they came it would work out all right."

"There is no bloody ghost," Ryder said. "Just stop it. It was a lurid excuse for a nightmare that you hadn't yet had." He turned to Lord David, who was now sitting cross-legged in the dirt, shaking his head as he stared at his dusty boots. "As for you, you will keep your mouth shut. Unlike Mrs. Grammond, I won't content myself with ruining you. I'll kill you. Do you understand me?"

Lord David sighed deeply, and nodded. He was clearly distracted. He said on another deep sigh, "I wonder if I can convince the chit to elope with me. It's the only way I can get the money in three days."

Sophie and Ryder just looked at each other.

EPILOGUE

Chadwyck House
January 1804

RYDER LEANED DOWN and kissed the nape of her neck, her flesh warm and soft against his mouth. She sighed and said nothing, merely leaned her head back against his belly. He kissed her forehead, then moved to her ears, his hands lightly encircling her throat, caressing her jawline with his thumbs. She sighed again and tried to turn to face him, but he held her still.

"You taste so bloody good," he said, and kissed her neck one more time. He ran his hands down her arms, then sighed himself, and released her. "No time, dammit, to show you what other uses one can make of a desktop." He eyed the very feminine writing desk, adding, "We will take great care if ever we make use of this feeble-looking thing. Perhaps I could simply have you lean against it—"

"Ryder!"

He gave another long-suffering sigh and came over to repose himself against the writing table, crossing his arms over his chest. "I'm testing its strength," he said. "For future reference." He looked down at the list of numbers. "What are you doing?"

"Adding up the accounts for Brandon House. Soon, my dear, next week, I think, we will have an exodus. Jane and I are planning a party. Jane's impatient."

"It's not that Jane complains, exactly," he said. "But she is looking forward to moving into her new house. The children as well."

"I will miss them."

"The little heathens will be only a hundred yards distant. Whenever you want madness, it's just a short walk away."

"How is little Garrick?"

Ryder immediately sobered. His eyes narrowed and his jaw tightened. Sophie patted his fisted hand. "He's safe now."

"Yes, he is. Dammit, Sophie, how could that bastard treat a four-year-old child like that?"

"There are many more like him, more's the pity, children sold as apprentices to such brutes as that chimney cleaner, Mr. Ducking. But you saved Garrick, and now he will learn that life can be more than pain and tears. He smiled at me this morning. He and Jenny are becoming great friends. I love you, Ryder."

His jaw loosened, and he smiled. "Yes, and well you should love me very much, woman, since I give you my poor man's body every night for your diversions."

"You make me sound unnatural in my appetites."

"Your appetites are wonderful. Have you yet started your monthly flow?"

His bald speech still could disconcert her, leaving her tongue-tied. She gave him a bemused smile and shook her head.

He leaned forward and caressed her belly with the palm of his hand. "Perhaps our son or daughter is beginning?"

"Perhaps," she said, and she stared at his mouth. He'd taught her over the months to enjoy kissing as much as he did.

"Stop that, Sophie. There is no time, unfortunately." Still, he leaned over and quickly kissed her soft mouth. He would never forget the night when he was nipping at her bottom lip as he was telling her the story of the farmer who fell in love with his prize pig, when all of a sudden, she giggled, and bit his chin, and said she fancied a prize bull.

It was the first time their lovemaking had been filled with laughter and silliness and nonsense. He looked fondly at her mouth, shrugged, and kissed her again.

"My brother, Alex, and Sinjun will be here very soon now."

"Yes," she said, breathless now.

"Damn him."

She blinked. "Ah, this dog-in-the manger attitude of yours, Ryder, you really must stop it. Allow poor Douglas to enjoy himself, to feel useful."

"He doesn't have to take my children away."

"He has given Oliver a tremendous opportunity, admit it. Someday he will be the earl's assistant steward, perhaps eventually even his steward or his secretary. Oliver will make something of himself. He will be properly educated. Douglas is very fond of him."

"Damn him."

Sophie just grinned at her husband. "I shall never forget when Douglas and Alex walked in, completely unexpected, and all the children were shrieking and playing and eating and yelling in the entrance hall because it was raining outside, and Douglas just stood there as calm as a preacher, and said, 'I have surely come to the wrong house.'"

Ryder remained stubbornly silent. He tapped his fingertips on the desktop.

"Douglas did take your revelations well, Ryder. He accepted what he saw as your lack of confidence in him, though I know it hurt him. He didn't yell at you, as I know he wanted to."

"That was because Amy had climbed up his leg and he was forced to pick her up and she was telling him that he was pretty."

"Your family is very proud of you."

"I never wanted their pride. Don't you understand? It's something I just do because it's important to me, it means something, and there's nothing saintly about it, Sophie. It costs me nothing, really. I would that every Sherbrooke would shut his and her respective mouth. It becomes excessive, and downright embarrassing."

"Your mother doesn't embarrass you."

"No, she refuses to speak to me for dirtying my hands with slum brats. It's a refreshing attitude from a family member, and so I've told her. She didn't laugh when I encouraged her to maintain her censure. Now, who is that letter from over there?"

"From Jeremy. It just arrived an hour ago. He is well and enjoying his studies." She picked up the two pages to look at them again.

Ryder grabbed them and began to read. Soon he was nodding and smiling. "Good. He thrashed that wretched little bully, old Tommy Mullard's son. Tommy was always a coward, big mouth and all threats, until one simply slammed one's fist into his lard belly. You see, Sophie, I was right to teach Jeremy how to fight mean and dirty. I even taught him how to kick with his lame foot. Lord, did he ever become good. Sinjun even played his adversary, poor girl. She had many bruises on her shins before he left for school. And don't be fooled, boys at school can be cruel. It's encouraged, unfortunately, you know, the old theory of toughening up our young aristocrats, making real little stiff-lipped soldiers out of them. But Jeremy is holding his own. It helps that he's the best rider at Eton." Ryder rubbed his hands together, such was his pleasure.

Sophie thought she would burst with love for him at that moment. He was a remarkable man, but the hint of someone actually saying it, giving him even a modicum of praise, made him turn red with embarrassment, and defensive to the point of yelling. She said only, "It also helps that he's part of the Sherbrooke family."

"Of course," Ryder said, and continued reading.

He had barely finished the letter when the door burst open and Sinjun came dashing in. The room seemed to lighten with her presence.

"My dear," Sophie said and quickly rose to give her sister-in-law a hug.

"Ah, Douglas and Alex are right behind me. I raced ahead so I could see you first. You both look wonderful. Is that a letter from Jeremy? I got one three days ago. He told me all about how he beat the stuffing out of this dolt bully, and—"

"Enough, brat! Hello, you two."

The Earl of Northcliffe strode into the room, his wife on his arm. "You won't believe what I have to tell you, Ryder. Oliver has quite impressed my steward and all my tenants. I took him around and introduced him to everyone, and you wouldn't believe his questions—intelligent and thoughtful, all of them. Jesus, I was so proud of him. And now he has no limp at all. Oh, hello, Sophie. You look well. Here's Alex."

Sophie could only laugh as she watched the shifting and myriad expressions on her husband's face.

"Oh, another thing," Douglas said before Ryder could vent his spleen, if venting were indeed what he had in mind, "Alex is pregnant. We will have a babe in May. What do you think about that?"

No one had time to think about anything. Alex turned suddenly very white, gasped, and looked helplessly up at her husband. "I can't believe you did this to me. I'm going to be sick."

She ran from the room. Douglas shook his head. "I hope she misses that beautiful Aubusson carpet," he said, and turned to run after her.

Ryder and Sophie looked at each other. Sinjun stared after her departed brother and sister-in-law. "Goodness, I don't know if I wish to ever have a babe. Alex is always being sick at the most inopportune times. I think I would prefer having another Bedlam House, like yours and Sophie's, Ryder."

"It's Brandon House," Ryder said. "After dear departed Uncle Brandon. Sophie says that it will speed his way from the depths of hell. She thinks he might even gain purgatory, but only if we use his money and not the money we earn ourselves."

"Alex is pregnant," Sophie said, bemused. "Just fancy that."

"It happens, you know, particularly when one and one's wife perform all the proper rituals. Oh yes, Sophie might be pregnant too," Ryder said, turning to his sister.

"That leaves only Tysen," Sinjun said. "Oh dear, he plans to marry that girl you can't stand, Ryder, you know, the one with two names—Melinda Beatrice—and no bosom. Then there's only me left."

"You have all the time in the world, brat."

They heard the unmistakable sounds of someone being vilely ill. "Yes," Sinjun said fervently, "I do have all the time in the world, thank God. Do you know that just last week Alex got ill right in front of Hollis. He never turned a hair. He said in that royal way of his, 'My lady, I do believe you should carry a handkerchief in the future.' He gave her his. Then he instructed that a covered chamber pot be placed in every room. He conducted Alex on a tour to show her where each one was located. Oh, congratulations, Sophie. You feel all right, don't you?"

"Of course. I won't get sick on your slippers. Thank you, Sinjun. But we don't know yet if it's true or not. Ryder is just being optimistic."

"Not optimistic. Her monthly flow is late, by four whole days."

"Ryder! Sinjun isn't yet sixteen!"

Sinjun only shrugged and looked very world-weary. "I have three brothers, Sophie, and two of them are outrageous. I can't be shocked, I don't think."

"As for you," Sophie said, turning back to face her husband, "You will mind your tongue in front of your sister."

"But I was going to tell her the story about the eccentric Mr. Hootle of Bristol who wed every woman who would have him. He had this compulsion, you see, and every time a woman smiled at him, he lost all judgment, and dropped down to his knees to propose."

"That," Sophie said with approval, "is quite a proper tale. You may continue. One hopes it becomes more edifying."

"Then one day when he was on his knees, one of his other wives came upon him and his soon-to-be-betrothed. The two women compared what they knew and were not pleased. They took him away to a small room, took all his clothes and locked him in. Then they sent in all these other women, two at a time, all naked as sin, to prance and parade in front of him, and the poor man was tied down so he couldn't fall to his knees and propose or do anything else—"

"Enough! You are dreadful." Sophie fell against him, laughing and kissing his chin.

Ryder looked fondly at the writing desk behind him. Sinjun sighed. "Well, I see I shan't get any more sensible conversation from either of you. I shall go see Jane and the children."

When the door closed, Ryder said to his wife, "I saw the Virgin Bride last night."

Sophie stared at him. "You saw the ghost? Truly? But gentlemen don't believe in her, that's what Douglas and you are always saying."

"I was wrong," Ryder said. "She floated in our bedchamber last night, visiting, I imagine, for she supposedly never strays from Northcliffe Hall. Anyway, she smiled down at me, and said something, but not really, you know, but I heard her words clear and calm in my mind."

"Yes, that was exactly how it was with me. What did she tell you?"

"She said, even as she glittered and shimmered all over me, that we had the possibility of having fourteen children. She said it was all a matter of me stiffening my resolve if we were to have these children in this lifetime."

"You are going to suffer for that, Ryder, you surely are."

"You promise?" He kissed his wife, and knew such pleasure that he wanted to yell with it. He released her, and locked the door. He methodically stoked the fire, then turned back to his wife. "The Virgin Bride must know what she's about. The good Lord knows you women believe every supposed word she doesn't say. Very well then. Let's get to it, madam."

'The Heiress Bride

PROLOGUE

Vere Castle, 1807
Near Loch Leven, Fife Peninsula, Scotland

HE STOOD STARING out the narrow window down into the courtyard of his castle. It was April, but spring wasn't much in evidence yet save for the wildly blooming heather that poked through the patches of fog to dazzle the eye with a rainbow of vivid purples. Scottish heather, like his people, would burst through rock itself to bloom. This morning, fog hung thick over the stone ramparts; thick and gray and wet. He could hear his people clearly through his window two stories up in the north circular tower—old Marthe clucking to the chickens as she tossed them grain, Burnie yelling at the top of his lungs at young Ostle, a new stable lad who was also his nephew. He heard bowlegged Crocker yelling at his dog, George II, threatening that he'd kick the shiftless bugger, but everyone knew that Crocker would kill anyone who even said a cross word to George. The morning sounded no different from any he'd heard since he was a child. Everything was normal.

Only it wasn't.

He turned away from the window and walked to the small stone fireplace, splaying his hands to the flames. This was his private study. Even his brother, Malcolm, when alive, had kept away from this particular room. It was warm in the room despite the sluggish fire, for thick wool tapestries woven by his great-grandmother were hung on every wall to keep away the damp and chill. There was also a beautiful old Aubusson carpet that covered most of the worn stones on the floor, and he wondered how his wastrel father or his damned brother had overlooked the carpet; it was worth a good deal of money, he imagined, and could have provided at least a week's worth of gaming or wenching or a bit of both. So the carpet was left, and the tapestries, but little else of value. Over the fireplace on a nearly rotted tapestry was the coat of arms of the Kinrosses: *Wounded But Unconquered.*

He was nearly mortally wounded. He was in very deep trouble and the only way out of it was to marry an heiress, and quickly. He didn't want to. He would rather swallow one of Aunt Arleth's tonics than marry.

But he had no choice. The debts incurred by both his father and his now-dead elder brother had left him bowed to his knees and nearly beyond desperate. He was the only one to be responsible, no one else. He was the new earl of Ashburnham, the seventh bloody earl, and he was up to his peer's neck in financial woes.

All would be lost if he didn't act quickly. His people would starve or be forced to emigrate. His home would continue to decay and his family would know nothing but genteel poverty. He knew he couldn't allow that. He stared down at his hands, still stretched toward the fire. Strong hands he had, but were they strong enough to save the Kinross clan from the gut-wrenching poverty that had been his grandfather's plight after 1746? Ah, but his grandfather had been a wily man, quickly adjusting to a new reality, quickly ingratiating himself with the few powerful earls left in Scotland. He'd also been smart, not disdaining the smell of the factories; and he'd invested the few groats he could get his gnarly hands on in iron and cloth factories springing up in the north of England. He'd been successful beyond his wildest dreams. But he'd died like all men must. Luckily for him he died old and quite pleased with himself, not realizing that his son was a rotter and would bring Vere Castle back to its knees.

Hell, what was a wife anyway, he mused, particularly an English wife? He could, if he wished, simply lock her in one of the musty rooms and toss away the key. He could beat her if he found her proud and unbending. In short, he could do anything he pleased to a damned wife. Perhaps he would be lucky and she'd be as malleable as a sheep, as witless as a cow, as bland as the castle goats who were at their happiest chewing on old boots. Whatever she would be, he would deal with it. He had no choice.

Colin Kinross, seventh earl of Ashburnham, strode from the study room at the top of the north tower. The next morning he was on his way to London to find a bride with a dowry as great as Aladdin's treasure.

CHAPTER
═══ 1 ═══

London, 1807

SINJUN SAW HIM the first time on a Wednesday night in the middle of
May at a rout given by the Duke and Duchess of Portmaine. He was a
good thirty feet from her across the massive ballroom, partially obscured
by a lush palm tree, but it didn't matter. She saw him quite clearly enough
and she couldn't look away. She craned her neck around two dowagers
when he walked gracefully to a knot of ladies, bowed over a young one's
hand, and led her in a cotillion. He was tall; she could see that because
the lady came only to his shoulder. Unless, of course, the young lady was
a dwarf, and Sinjun doubted that. No, he was tall, much taller than was
she, the saints be praised.

She continued to stare at him, not knowing why she was doing it and
not caring in the least, until she felt a hand on her forearm. She didn't
want to look away from him, not now. She shook the hand away and
walked off, her eyes still on him. She heard a woman's voice from behind
her but didn't turn around. He was smiling down at his partner now, and
she felt something deep and strong move within her. She walked closer,
circling the dance floor, drawing nearer. He was no more than ten feet
away now and she saw that he was magnificent, as tall as her brother
Douglas, and as massively built, his hair blacker than Douglas's, ink-
black and thick, and his eyes—good Lord, a man shouldn't have eyes like
that. They were a rich dark blue, a blue deeper than the sapphire necklace
Douglas had given Alex for her birthday. If only she were close enough
to touch him, to set her fingers lightly upon the cleft in his chin, to sift
through that shining hair of his. She knew in that moment that she would
be perfectly content to look at him for the rest of her life. Surely that was
a mad thought, but it was nonetheless true. He was well built; she wasn't
ignorant about things like that, not with two outrageous older brothers.
Yes, he had an athlete's body, strong and hard and tough, and he was
young, probably younger than Ryder, who had just turned twenty-nine. A
small, insistent voice told her that she was being a silly twit, to open her

eyes, to stop this infatuated nonsense, for after all, he was just a man, a man like any other man, and in all good likelihood he was cursed with a troll's character to go along with his magnificent looks. That, or worse: He was a complete bore, or no brain worth speaking of, or he had rotted teeth. But no, that wasn't true, for he just threw his head back and laughed deeply, showing beautiful, even, white teeth, and indeed, that laugh bespoke great intelligence to her discerning brain, a rich, deep laugh, just like his eyes, and weren't they intelligent? Ah, but he could be a drunkard or a gamester, or a rake or any number of other exceptionable things.

She didn't care. She just kept staring. A great hunger welled up in her, a hunger that spread into a great coalition of hungers she didn't understand, but she knew that he had put them there, deep inside her. Finally the cotillion ended and he bowed over the young lady's hand, delivered her back into the bosom of her chaperon, and went to join a small group of gentlemen. They greeted him with loud and merry voices. So he was a man popular with other men, just like Douglas and Ryder, her brothers. The group went off toward the card room, much to Sinjun's disappointment.

Someone patted her bare arm again.

"Sinjun?"

She sighed even as she turned to her sister-in-law Alex. "Yes?"

"Are you all right? You've been standing there as still as one of the Northcliffe Greek statues for the longest time. Before, I called to you, but you didn't seem to even see me."

"Oh yes, I'm quite all right," she said, and looked back to where she'd last seen him. Then she heard a man laugh and knew it was his laugh, pure and resonant. It filled her with warmth and excitement, and made that something deep inside her move again, move powerfully. She felt it to her toes.

No man could be the ideal of perfection that she'd bestowed upon him at first sight. No, it was quite impossible. She wasn't stupid or naive or a silly little debutante, not with two brothers so flagrantly brazen in their behavior and speech. He was probably a troll, at least on the inside.

"Sinjun, what the devil is wrong with you? Are you sickening with something?"

She drew a deep breath and decided to keep her mouth shut, which was quite unlike her. But this was too new, too uncertain. She grinned hugely. "Alex, I quite like her grace, the Duchess of Portmaine. Brandy is her nickname and she begged me not to call her that horrid name Brandella. Isn't that exceedingly clever to shorten Brandella in such a manner?" Sinjun leaned down close to her sister-in-law's ear. "And would you just look at her grace's bosom—is it possible that she is more impressive than you? Of course, she is a bit older than you, I expect."

Douglas Sherbrooke, not stifling his laugh, said, "Good Lord, do you think that age is a factor, Sinjun? A lady's years adding to her endowments? My God, by the time Alex is sixty, she wouldn't be able to walk upright. But this calls for a closer study of the duchess. On the other hand, I must point out, Sinjun, as your eldest brother, that it is most inappropriate for you to remark upon her grace's assets and Alex's lack thereof."

Sinjun laughed at her brother's words and the look on his wife's face as he continued to Alex in a mournful voice, "I had thought you the most nobly endowed lady in all of England. Perhaps it is only in southern England that you hold that distinction. Perhaps it is only within the immediate vicinity of Northcliffe Hall that you lord it over other less worthy bosoms. Perhaps I have been taken in, perhaps I have been duped."

His fond wife punched his arm. "I suggest that you keep your eyes and thoughts at home, where they belong, my lord, and leave the duchess and her endowments to the duke."

"Just so," the earl said, then turned to his sister, who looked suddenly different to his critical and fond eye. She hadn't looked at all different earlier in the evening, but she did now. She looked abstracted, yes, that was it, which was odd, very odd indeed. Sinjun was usually as clear as a summer pond, her thoughts and feelings clearly writ on her expressive face; but now he didn't have the slightest idea what was in her mind. It bothered him. It was like a hard kick from a horse he'd just turned his back on. He suddenly felt as if he didn't know this tall, quite lovely young lady, not at all. He tried for neutrality. "So, brat, are you having a good time? This last cotillion is the only dance you haven't danced the entire evening."

"She is nineteen, Douglas," Alex said. "Surely you must soon stop calling her brat."

"Even when she continues to play the Virgin Bride to torment my sleep?"

Whilst the two of them argued over the luckless sixteenth-century ghost of Northcliffe Hall, Sinjun had time to think and decide what to say. When they finished, she sidestepped her brother neatly, saying only, "No ghosting about for me, at least in London, Douglas. Oh dear, there is Lord Castlebaum with his fond mama. I had forgotten that he has the next country dance. He sweats dreadfully, Douglas, and his hands are wet—"

"I know. He's also a very nice young man. But Sinjun," he continued quickly, raising his hand to still her, "it doesn't matter if he were a very dry saint. You don't have to marry him. Accept his sweat and his niceness and simply try to enjoy yourself. Remember, you are here in London to have fun, nothing more, just to enjoy yourself. Don't listen to Mother."

Sinjun couldn't hide her sigh. "Mother," she repeated. "It's difficult, Douglas. She says I must hie myself to the altar or I shall be on the wretched shelf. This shelf is the dreaded Spinster Shelf, and she always says it in capital letters. She continues to list out all the shelf's incumbent horrors, including becoming Alex's drudge once Mother has cast off her mortal coil. She even remarked that I was getting long in the tooth. When I looked at my teeth in the mirror, I swear one of my molars had lengthened just a bit."

"Don't listen to her. I am the head of the Sherbrooke family. You will enjoy yourself; you will laugh and flirt to your heart's content. If you don't find a gentleman to please you, it doesn't matter."

His voice was austere and very lordly, and Sinjun was forced to smile. "I'm also nineteen, and that, apparently, is nearing a disastrous age for a girl to be yet unwed, and completely unacceptable for a girl not to have even one beau. She even points to Alex being eighteen when she wed you. Then she says that Sophie was lucky to have coerced Ryder into marriage, because she was nearly twenty and likely to be a lifetime spinster. Taking in Ryder, she claims, was the smartest thing Sophie ever managed. It is also my second Season. Mother says I must keep my mouth shut because gentlemen don't like ladies who know more than they do. She says it drives them to the brandy bottle and to gaming hells."

Douglas said something crude and quite inelegant.

Sinjun laughed, but it was a sham laugh. "Well, one never knows, does one?"

"All I know is that Mother says a lot, too much."

But even as Douglas spoke, clearly harassed, she saw the man in her mind's eye and she smiled, this one real, filling her eyes with warmth and dreams. She realized that her sister-in-law Alex was looking at her closely, and that her expression was puzzled. But she said only, "Feel free to speak to me anytime you wish to, Sinjun."

"Perhaps soon. Ah, here's Lord Castlebaum, wet hands and all. But he does dance very well. Perhaps I shall discuss shelves with him. I will see both of you later."

She stepped on Lord Castlebaum's toes three times in an attempt to find the man again. Later she began to think that her eyes must have lied, that no man could be so immensely glorious to behold. But she dreamed of him that night. They were together, and he was laughing and standing close to her, touching his fingertips to her cheek, and she knew she wanted him and she was leaning toward him, wanting to touch him, and it was there in her gaze, all the wanting she had for him, and he saw it and knew it as well. The scenes softened and slowed, melding together into vague colors and intertwining bodies, and she awoke near to dawn, her heart pounding, perspiration lying heavy on her skin, and a moan in her throat. Her body felt languid and slow. There was a strange ache deep in her belly. She knew she'd dreamed the mystery of lovemaking, but only in blurred images. She had yet to solve the mystery, yet to know him, yet to be intertwined with him. She wished she'd discovered his name, for to be that intimate with a nameless man wasn't something she could accept.

She saw him the second time at a musicale at the Ranleagh town house on Carlysle Square three nights later. A very large soprano from Milan thumped the piano with her fist as her Viennese accompanist tried to keep his fingers on the trembling keys and mark a strong beat at the same time. Sinjun was soon bored and twitching with restlessness. Then, quite suddenly, she felt something strange sweep over her and knew, simply knew, that he had come into the room. She turned slightly in her chair and there he was. She sucked in her breath at the sight of him. He had just divested himself of a black cloak and was speaking quietly to another gentleman. He looked even more splendid to her than he had at the Portmaine ball. He was dressed all in black with a very white batiste shirt. His thick hair was brushed back, a bit long for current fashion, perhaps, but to her, perfection itself. He was seated at a diagonal from her, and if she kept her profile toward the bellowing soprano, she could look at him as much as she wanted. The moment he was seated, he grew instantly still. She watched him remain perfectly still, even as the soprano pumped up her lungs and gained a ringing high C. A man with courage and fortitude as well, she thought, nodding to herself. A man with manners and good breeding.

Her fingers itched to touch that cleft in his chin. She saw that his jaw was strong and well defined, that his nose was elegant and thin and that his mouth made her want to . . . no, she had to get hold of herself. The dream images mixed in her mind for a moment and she knew herself well lost. Goodness, it was quite likely that he was already wed, or betrothed. She managed a show of outward calm until there was, at last, an adjournment to the supper room.

She said in an offhand manner to Lord Clinton, a friend of Douglas's from the Four Horse Club, who had escorted her to dinner, "Who is that man over there, Thomas? The tall one with the very black hair? You see him, he's with those three other men who aren't nearly as tall as he is or nearly as impressive."

Thomas Mannerly, Lord Clinton, squinted in the direction she was pointing. He was myopic, but the man in question did stand out, no question about that. The man was very tall and too well built for his own good, the bastard. "Ah, that's Colin Kinross. He's new to London. He's the earl of Ashburnham, and a Scot." The last was said with a hint of disdain.

"Why is he here, in London?"

Thomas stared at the lovely girl at his side, nearly as tall as he was, and that was surely a bit off-putting, but he didn't have to marry her, just keep an experienced eye on her. He said now, carefully, as he brushed some invisible lint from the sleeve of his black coat, "Why do you care, Sinjun?" At her silence, he stiffened. "My God, he hasn't offended you in any way, has he? Those damned Scots, they're barbarians, even when they're educated in England, as he was."

"Oh no, no. I just asked out of curiosity. The lobster patties are quite good, don't you think?"

He agreed, and Sinjun thought: *At last I know his name*. At last. She wanted to shout her victory. At last. Thomas Mannerly happened to look at her just then and he sucked in his breath at the most beautiful smile he'd ever seen in his life. He forgot the lobster patty on his plate. He said something to her, something polished and just a bit intimate, and was chagrined when she didn't appear to have even heard him. She was, if he wasn't mistaken, staring at that damned Scot.

Sinjun was fretting within five minutes. She had to know more than just his name and the fact that he was a Scottish nobleman and why Thomas Mannerly had sounded a bit stiff about that. She didn't have much opportunity to find out more about Colin Kinross that night, but she didn't despair. It would soon be time to act.

Douglas Sherbrooke, earl of Northcliffe, was happily ensconced in his favorite leather chair in the library, reading the *London Gazette*, when he chanced to look up to see his sister standing in the doorway. Why the devil was she just standing there? She would normally come caroling in, speaking and laughing even before she had his attention, and her laughter would make him smile, it was so carefree and lovely and innocent. And she would lean down and kiss him on the cheek and hug him hard. But she wasn't laughing now. Why the hell was she looking so damned diffident? As if she'd done something unbelievably awful? Sinjun didn't have a shy bone in her body, not from the moment he'd first picked her up out of her cradle and she'd grabbed his ear and twisted it until he'd yowled. He folded the paper on his lap. He frowned. "What do you want, brat? No, you're too advanced in age for brat anymore. My dear, then. Come in, come in. What is the matter with you? Alex said there was something on your mind. Out with it. I don't like the way you're acting. It isn't like you at all. It makes me nervous."

Sinjun came slowly into the library. It was very late, nearly midnight. Douglas waved her to the seat opposite his. It was odd, she thought, as she approached. She had always believed Douglas and Ryder were the two most handsome men in the entire world. But she'd been wrong. Neither of them came close to Colin Kinross.

"Sinjun, you are behaving quite strangely, not at all like yourself. Are you ill? Has Mother been tormenting you again?"

She shook her head and said, "Yes, but she always does, saying it's for my own good."

"I will speak to her again."

"Douglas."

She stopped, and he blinked to see that she was staring down at her toes and she was actually plucking at her muslin skirt.

"My God," he said slowly, the light dawning finally, "you've met a man."

"No, I haven't."

"Sinjun, I know you haven't overspent your allowance. You're so tight with your purse strings that you'll be richer than I am in a matter of years. Mother picks at you, but most of it bounces off. You pay her no mind, truth be told. Alex and I love you within the bounds of common sense, and we've tried to make you as comfortable as we can. Ryder and Sophie will be arriving in a week or so—"

"I do know his name, but I haven't met him!"

"Ah," said Douglas. He sat back, grinning up at her, steepling his fingers. "And his name is?"

"Colin Kinross, and he's the earl of Ashburnham. He's a Scot."

Douglas frowned. For a moment he'd hoped it just might be Thomas Mannerly she liked. No such luck.

"Do you know him? Is he married? Betrothed? Is he a gamester? Has he killed men in duels? Is he a womanizer?"

"You would have to be different, wouldn't you, Sinjun? A Scot! No, I don't know him. If you haven't even met the man, then why are you so damned interested?"

"I don't know." She paused, and looked extraordinarily vulnerable. She shrugged, trying for a glimmer of her old self, and gave him a crooked smile. "It's just there."

"All right," Douglas said, eyeing her closely. "I'll find out all about this Colin Kinross."

"You won't say anything to anyone, will you?"

"I will to Alex but no one else."

"You don't mind that he's a Scot, do you?"

"No, why should I?"

"Thomas Mannerly had a touch of scorn in his voice, called him a barbarian, that kind of thing."

"Thomas had a father who believed to the soles of his viscount's feet that a true gentleman must be born breathing the fine, just air of England. It appears that Thomas has adopted his departed sire's absurdities."

"Thank you, Douglas." Sinjun leaned down and kissed his cheek.

As he watched her leave the library, a thoughtful frown settled on his forehead. He tapped his fingers slowly together. The only thing he had against a Scot was that if she married one, she would live very far away from her family.

He followed his sister upstairs not long thereafter. He walked into the bedchamber to see Alex brushing her hair, seated at her dressing table. He met her eyes in the mirror, smiled, and began to take off his clothes.

Her brush stilled. She put it down and turned to face him.

"You will watch me all the way to my bare hide?"

She just smiled and nodded.

"You are staring, Alex. Are you concerned that I have gained flesh? You wish to see that everything is still lean and all my parts are in good working order?"

She just smiled more widely, and this time she just shook her head and said, "Oh no. I suspect you are quite perfect. You were last night and this morning and—" She giggled.

When he was quite naked, he walked over to her, picked her up in his arms, and carried her to their bed.

When he was able to speak coherently again, he stretched out beside his wife and said, "Our Sinjun is in love."

"So that's why she's been behaving so oddly," Alex said on a huge yawn and came up on her elbow beside her husband.

"His name is Colin Kinross."

"Oh dear."

"What is it?"

"Someone pointed him out to me the other evening at the musicale. He looks very forceful, Douglas, and stubborn."

"All this from just a viewing of the man?"

"He's quite tall, perhaps even taller than you. That's good, because Sinjun is very tall for a woman. Ruthless, that's what I meant to say. He looks quite capable of doing anything at all to get what he wants."

"Alex, you can't tell all that about a man just by looking at him. Now, I will take away your clothes for two days if you don't stop speaking nonsense."

"I don't know anything about him, Douglas."

"He's tall and he's tough-looking. He's ruthless. A fine place for me to start."

"Yes, and you'll see I'm right." She laughed, her breath warm and soft against his shoulder. "My father despises the Scots. I hope you don't feel that way."

"No, I don't. Sinjun hasn't yet met him, she told me."

"She will, very soon, I doubt not. She's very resourceful, you know."

"In the meantime I'll endeavor to find out all I can about our Scottish gentleman. Ruthless, hmm?"

The next evening Sinjun felt like dancing in her bedchamber. Douglas was taking her and Alexandra to the Drury Lane Theatre to see *Macbeth* performed. Surely as a Scot and a Kinross, with scores of cousins named Mac Something, he would also be there. It was opening night. Surely, oh surely he would be there. But what if he accompanied another lady? What if he . . . She stopped herself. She had spent an hour on her appearance, and her maid, Doris, had merely nodded, smiling slyly. "You look beautiful, my lady," she had said as she lovingly threaded a light blue velvet ribbon through Sinjun's hair. "Just the same color as your eyes."

She did look well enough, Sinjun supposed, as she studied herself one last time in the mirror. Her gown was a dark blue silk with a lighter blue overskirt. The sleeves were short and puffed out, and there was a matching pale blue velvet sash bound beneath her breasts. She looked tall and slender and fashionably pale. There was just a hint of cleavage, no more, because Douglas felt strongly about things like that. Yes, she looked just fine.

Sinjun didn't see him until the intermission. The lobby of the Drury Lane Theatre was crowded with the glittering *ton*, who gossiped and laughed and whose jewels were worth enough to feed a dozen English villages for a year. The lobby was also very hot. Some unfortunate patrons were splattered with dripping wax from the hundreds of lit candles in the chandeliers overhead. Douglas took himself off to fetch champagne for Alex and Sinjun. A friend of Alex's came up, and thus Sinjun was free to search in every corner of the vast room for her Scot, as she now thought of him. To her delight and speechless excitement and horror, she saw him standing not eight feet behind her, speaking to Lord Brassley, a friend of Ryder's. Brass, as he was called, was a rake and kindhearted, a man who commendably kept his wife in more luxury than his mistresses.

Her heart speeded up. She turned completely to face him and began to walk forward. She bumped into a portly gentleman and automatically apologized. She simply kept walking toward him. She wasn't more than three feet away when she heard him laugh, then say quite clearly to Lord

Brassley, "Good Lord, Brass, what the devil am I to do? It's damned painful—I've never in my life seen such a gaggle of disasters, all of them in little knots or herds, giggling and simpering and flapping and staring. It isn't fair, no it isn't. I must needs wed myself to an heiress or lose everything I own, thanks to my scoundrel of a father and brother, and all those females I've met who fit the groat requirements scare me to my toes."

"Ah, my dear fellow, but there are other females who aren't disasters," said Lord Brassley, laughing. "Females you don't have to marry, just enjoy. You simply amuse yourself with them. They will relax you, Colin, and you certainly could use some relaxation." He slapped Colin Kinross on his shoulder. "As for the heiress, be patient, my boy, be patient!"

"Ha, patience! Every day that goes by brings me closer to the brink. As for those other females, hell, they would also want to spend all the groats I don't have, and expect that in my undying gratitude I would shower them with endless baubles. No, I have no time for distractions, Brass. No, I must find myself an heiress and one that is reasonably toothsome."

His voice was deep and soft and filled with humor and a goodly dose of sarcasm. Lord Brassley laughed, hailed a friend, and took himself off. Without further hesitation, Sinjun walked to him, stood there right in front of him until his beautiful dark blue eyes finally came to rest on her face and a black brow rose in question. She thrust out her hand and said quite clearly, "I'm an heiress."

CHAPTER
══ 2 ══

COLIN KINROSS, seventh earl of Ashburnham, stared at the young woman standing in front of him, her hand outstretched toward him, staring at him with utter sincerity and, if he wasn't mistaken, a goodly dollop of excitement. He felt knocked off his pins, as Philip would say, and stalled for time to get his brain back in working order. "Forgive me. What did you say?"

Without hesitation, Sinjun said again, her voice strong and clear, "I'm an heiress. You said you needed to marry an heiress."

He said slowly, his voice light and insincere, still stalling for mental reinforcements, "And you are reasonably toothsome."

"I'm pleased you think so."

He stared at her outstretched hand, still there, and automatically shook it. He should have raised her hand to his lips, but there that hand was, stuck out there like a man's, and so he shook it. A strong hand, he thought, slender fingers, very white, competent. He released her hand.

"Congratulations," he said, "on being an heiress. And on being toothsome. Ah, do forgive me, ma'am. I'm Ashburnham, you know."

She simply smiled at him, her heart in her eyes. His voice was wonderful, deep and smiling, much more beguiling than either of her brothers'. They didn't come close to this marvelous man. "Yes, I know. I'm Sinjun Sherbrooke."

"An odd name you have, a man's nickname."

"I suppose. My brother Ryder christened me that when he tried to burn me at the stake when I was nine years old. My real name is Joan, and he wanted me to be Saint Joan but it became Sinjun for Saint John, and so . . . there it is."

"I like Joan. I prefer it. It is feminine." Colin ran his fingers through his hair, realizing that what he'd said was ridiculous and not at all to the point, whatever that was. "This has taken me aback, truly. I don't know who you are, and you don't know who I am. I really don't understand why you've done this."

Those light blue eyes shone up at him as guileless as a summer day as she said clearly, "I saw you at the Portmaine ball and then at the Ranleagh musicale. I'm an heiress. You need to marry an heiress. If you are not a troll—your character, of course—why then, perhaps you could see your way clear to marrying me."

Colin Kinross, Ashburnham or simply Ash to his friends, could only stare at the girl who couldn't seem to look away from his face. "This is quite the oddest thing that has ever happened to me," he said, a baffling understatement. "Except for that time at Oxford when the don's wife wanted me to make love to her with her husband teaching Latin in the other room to one of my friends. She even wanted the door cracked open so she could see her husband whilst she was making love to me."

"Did you?"

"Did I what? Oh, make love to her?" He coughed, recalling himself. "I don't remember," he said, suddenly frowning, his voice austere. "Besides, it is an incident better forgotten."

Sinjun sighed. "My brothers would have confided in me, but you don't know me, so I can't expect you to be more forthcoming yet. I know I'm not beautiful, but I am passable. I'm in my second Season without even a betrothed, or even a remotely attached gentleman to my name, but I am rich, and I'm a kind person."

"I can't accept all of your assessment."

"Perhaps you have already found a lady to meet your groat requirements."

He grinned at that. "Plain speaking, huh? No, I haven't, as I suspect you already know, having overheard my whining plaints to Brass. Actually, you are quite the loveliest young lady I have met. You're tall. I don't have to get a painful crick in my neck speaking to you."

"Yes, and I can't help it. As to my loveliness, certainly my brothers think so, but you, my lord? This is my second Season, as I said, and I didn't wish to have it, for there is so much sheer boredom about, but then I saw you."

She stopped talking but didn't stop staring at him. He was startled at the hunger in those quite lovely light blue eyes of hers. This was really beyond anything in his experience. He felt bowled over, off kilter, and really quite stupid. The vaunted control he was known for was gone. It was disconcerting.

"Come over here, out of the crush. Yes, that's better. Listen, this is difficult. It is also a highly unusual situation. Perhaps I could call on you tomorrow? I see a young lady walking toward us, and she looks quite purposeful."

She gave him a dazzling smile. "Oh yes, I should quite like that." She gave him the Sherbrooke town house address on Putnam Place. "That is Alex, my sister-in-law."

"What is your complete name?"

"Everyone calls me Sinjun."

"Yes, but I don't like it. I prefer Joan."

"All right. It's Lady Joan, actually, for my father was an earl. Lady Joan Elaine Winthrop Sherbrooke."

"I will call on you in the morning. Would you like to ride with me?"

She nodded, looking at his white teeth and his beautiful mouth. Unconsciously, she leaned toward him. Colin sucked in his breath and quickly backed away. Good Lord, the chit was as brazen as a Turkish gong. So she'd fallen for him the first time she'd seen him. Ha! He would take her riding tomorrow, discover why she was playing this insane jest, and perhaps kiss her and fondle her just a bit to teach her a lesson. Damned impertinent chit—and she was a Sassenach to boot, which made sense since he was in London. Still, he believed Sassenach young ladies to be more reticent, more modest. But not this young lady.

"Until tomorrow, then," he said, and was gone before Alex could bear down on them.

Colin searched out Brass and unceremoniously plucked him out of the theater. "No, don't complain. I'm taking you outside, away from all these female distractions, and you're going to tell me what the devil is going on here. I think you're probably behind this absurd jest, and I want to know why you set that girl on me. The gall of her still has my head spinning."

Alex watched the man, Colin Kinross, pull Brass from the huge lobby. She looked back at Sinjun to see that she was also staring after him. She correctly assumed that Sinjun's thoughts about the man weren't nearly as prosaic as her own.

"He is an interesting-looking gentleman," Alex said, getting the ball rolling.

"Interesting? Don't be ridiculous, Alex. That's utterly inadequate. He's beautiful, perfectly beautiful. Didn't you see his eyes? And the way he smiles and speaks, it—"

"Yes, my dear. Come along now. The intermission is over and Douglas is getting testy."

Alex bided her time, but it was difficult. The moment they arrived back at the Sherbrooke town house, she kissed Sinjun good night and grabbed her husband's hand, dragging him into their bedchamber.

"You want me that badly?" Douglas asked, staring at her with some amusement.

"Sinjun met Colin Kinross. I saw her speaking to him. I fear she's been rather forward, Douglas."

Douglas looked down at his hands. He then lifted a branch of candles and carried it to the table beside their bed. He studied it for a while, in meditative silence, then shrugged. "We will leave it be until tomorrow. Sinjun isn't stupid, nor is she a silly twit. Ryder and I raised her properly. She would never ever jump her fences too quickly."

At ten o'clock the following morning, Sinjun was ready to jump. She was waiting on the front steps of the Sherbrooke town house, dressed in a dark blue riding habit, looking as fine as a pence, so Doris had told her firmly, and she was lightly slapping her riding crop against her boot.

Where was he? Hadn't he believed her? Had he just realized that she wasn't to his taste and didn't intend to come?

Just before she was on the edge of incoherence, she saw him cantering up, astride a magnificent black barb. He pulled up when he saw her, leaned down just a bit, and gave her a lazy smile.

"Aren't I to be allowed in your house?"

"I don't think so. It's too soon."

All right, he thought, he would accept that for the moment. "Where is your horse?"

"Follow me." She walked around the back of the house to the stables. Her mare, Fanny, was standing placidly, calmly accepting the caresses bestowed on her neck by a doting Henry, one of the stable lads. She waved him away and mounted by herself. She arranged her skirts, knew in her heart that she wasn't physically capable of presenting a finer picture, and prayed. She gave him a tentative smile. "It's early. Shall we go to the park?"

He nodded and pulled alongside her. She didn't say a word. He frowned as he neatly guided his stallion around a dray filled with kegs of beer and three clerks dressed in funereal black. The streets were crowded with hawkers, shopkeepers, wagons of all sorts, ragged children from the back streets. He stayed close, saying nothing, keeping a look out for any danger. There was danger everywhere, naturally, but he realized that she could deal with most anything that could happen. If she couldn't, why then, he was a man, and he could. Whatever else she was, she was an excellent rider.

When they reached the park, he said as they turned into the north gate, "Let's gallop for a bit. I know a lady shouldn't so indulge herself, but it is early, as you said."

They raced to the end of the long outward trail and his stallion, strong as Douglas's horse, beat Fanny soundly. She was laughing when she pulled her mare.

"You ride well," Colin said.

"As do you."

Colin patted his stallion's neck. "I asked Lord Brassley who you were. Unfortunately he didn't see you speaking to me. I described you, but to be frank, ma'am, he couldn't imagine any lady, particularly Lady Joan Sherbrooke, speaking to me as you did."

She rubbed the soft leather of her York riding gloves. "How did you describe me?"

She'd gotten to him again, but he refused to let her see it. He shrugged and said, "Well, I said you were reasonably toothsome in a blond sort of way, that you were tall and had quite lovely blue eyes, and your teeth were white and very straight. I had to tell him that you were brazen to your toenails."

She was silent for a moment, looking over his left shoulder. "I suppose that's fair enough. But he didn't recognize me? How very odd. He's a friend of my brother's. He is also a rake but good-hearted, so Ryder says. I fear he still tends to see me as a ten-year-old who was always begging a present off him. He had to escort me once to Almack's last Season, and Douglas told me in no uncertain terms that Brass wasn't blessed with an adaptable intellect. I was to remain quiet and soft-spoken and on no account to speak of anything that lay between the covers of books to him. Douglas said it would make him bolt."

Colin chewed this over. He simply didn't know what to think. She looked like a lady, and Brass had said that Lady Joan Sherbrooke was a cute little chit, adored by her brothers, perhaps a bit out of the ordinary from some stories he'd heard, but he'd never noticed anything pert about her himself. He'd then lowered his voice, whispering that she knew too much about things in *books*, at least he'd heard that from some matrons who were gossiping about her, their tones utterly disapproving, and she was indeed tall. But then again, she'd been waiting on the front steps of the town house for him to arrive, certainly not what the young lady of the house would do, would she? Wouldn't an English young lady be waiting in the drawing room, a cup of tea in her hand? Brass had also insisted that Joan Sherbrooke's hair was a plain regular brown, nothing out of the ordinary, but it wasn't. In the early sunlight it was at least a dozen colors, from the palest blond to a dark ash.

Oh, to hell with it. He didn't understand, and he wasn't at all certain he believed her. More likely, she was looking for a protector. Perhaps she was the lady's maid to this Lady Joan Sherbrooke, or a cousin. He should just tell her that he had no money and all she could expect from him would be a fun roll in the hay, no more, no less.

"I have taken you by surprise," Sinjun said, watching the myriad expressions flit over his face. On the heels of her calmly reasoned understatement, she said in a rush, "You're the most beautiful man I have ever seen in my life, but it's not that, not really. I wanted you to know that it wasn't only your face that drew me to you, it was . . . well, just . . . oh goodness, I don't know."

"Me, beautiful?" Colin could only stare at her. "A man isn't beautiful, that is nonsense. Please, just tell me what you want and I shall do my best to see that you get it. I can't be your protector, I'm sorry. Even if I were the randiest goat in all of London, it would do me no good. I have no money."

"I don't want a protector, if by that you mean you would take me on as a mistress."

"Yes," he said slowly, fascinated now. "That is what I meant."

"I can't be a mistress. Even if I wanted to be, it wouldn't help you. Surely my brother wouldn't release my dowry if you didn't wed me. I suspect he wouldn't be pleased if I did become your mistress. He is very old-fashioned about some things."

"Then why are you doing this? Pray, tell me. Did one of my benighted friends put you up to this? Are you the mistress of Lord Brassley? Or Henry Tompkins? Or Lord Clinton?"

"Oh no, no one put me up to anything."

"Not everyone likes the fact that I'm a Scot. Even though I went to school with a good many of the men here in London, they think it just fine to drink with me and sport with me, but not for me to wed their sisters."

"I think you could be a Moroccan and I would still feel as I do."

He could but stare at her. The soft blue feather of her riding hat—a ridiculously small confection of nonsense—curled about her face, framing it charmingly. Her riding habit, a darker blue, darker than her eyes, he saw, fit her to perfection, and it wasn't flirtatious, that habit, no, it was stylish and showed off her high breasts and narrow waist and . . . He cursed, fluently and low.

"You sound just like my brothers, but usually they're laughing before they get to the end of their curses."

He started to say something but realized that she was staring at his mouth. No, she couldn't be a lady. She was a damned jest, paid for by one of his friends. "Enough!" he bellowed. "This is all an act, it has to be. You can't want to marry me, just like that, and proceed to announce it in the most brazen way imaginable!" He turned suddenly in his saddle and jerked her against him. He pulled her out of her sidesaddle and over his thighs. He held her still until both horses quieted, not that he had to do anything, because she didn't fight him, not at all. She immediately pressed her breasts against him. No, she couldn't be a lady, no way in hell.

He forced her against his left arm and lifted her chin with his gloved fingertips. He kissed her hard, his tongue probing against her closed lips. He raised his head, anger in his voice. "Damn you, open your mouth like you're supposed to."

"All right," she said, and opened her mouth.

At the sight of her open mouth, Colin couldn't help himself. He laughed. "Bloody hell, you look like you're about to sing an opera like that vile soprano from Milan. Oh, damnation!" He set her again onto Fanny's back. Fanny, displeased, pranced to the side, but Sinjun, even a Sinjun who was nearly incoherent with pleasure and excitement and amusement, managed to bring her easily under control.

"All right. I will accept that you are a lady. I will . . . no, I cannot accept that you saw me at the Portmaines' ball and decided you wanted to marry me."

"Well, I wasn't precisely certain I wanted to marry you then, at that moment, just that I thought I could look at you for the rest of my life."

He was disarmed immediately. "Before I see you again—if I see you again—I would that you cloak yourself in a bit of guile. Not a tremendous amount, mind you, but enough so that you don't leave me slack-jawed, with nothing to say when you announce something utterly outrageous."

"I'll try," Sinjun said. She looked away from him for a moment, across the wide expanse of thick green grass, to the riding trails that intersected the park. "Do you think perhaps I could be maybe pretty enough for you? Oh, I know all the other about toothsomeness was just a jest. I wouldn't want you to be ashamed of me, to be embarrassed if I did become your wife."

She met his eyes as she spoke. He just shook his head. "Stop it, do you hear me? For God's sake, you're quite lovely, as you must certainly know."

"People will tell any number of lies, offer more Spanish coin than would fill a cask if they believed one an heiress. I'm not stupid."

He dismounted his stallion, hooked the reins about his hand, and strode to beneath a full-leafed oak tree. "Come here. We must talk before I willingly incarcerate myself in Bedlam."

Ah, to stand close to him, Sinjun thought, as she obeyed him with alacrity.

She looked up at that cleft in his chin, and without thought, she raised her hand, stripped off the glove, and her fingertip traced the cleft. He stood completely motionless.

"I will make you an excellent wife. Do you promise you don't have a troll's character?"

"I like animals and I don't shoot them for sport. I have five cats, excellent ratters, all of them, and at night they have the hearth all to themselves. If ever it is really cold in the dead of winter, they sleep with me, but not often, because I tend to thrash about and crush them. If you mean, would I beat you, the answer is no."

"You're obviously very strong. I'm pleased you don't hurt those who are weaker. Do you also care about people? Are you kind? Do you feel responsible for those people who are your dependents?"

He couldn't look away from her. It was very distressing, but he said, "Yes, I suppose so."

He thought of his huge castle, only half of it really a castle, and that one not medieval by any means but built by a Kinross earl in the late seventeenth century. He loved the castle with its towers and its crenellated battlements and its parapets and deep embrasures. Ah, but it was so drafty in some parts, so dilapidated, that one could catch an inflammation of the lung just standing in one spot for ten minutes. So much had to be done to bring the entire castle back up to snuff. And all the outbuildings and the stables, the crofts and the drainage system. And the depleted herds of sheep and cattle, and his crofters, so many of them, poor and dispirited because they had nothing, not even enough seeds to plant for crops to feed themselves, and the bloody future was so grim and hopeless if he didn't do something. . . .

He looked away from her, toward the line of immense town houses that lined the far side of Hyde Park. "My inheritance was sorely depleted by my father and polished off by my brother, the sixth earl, before he died. I need a lot of money or my family will be reduced to genteel poverty, and many of my dependents will be forced to emigrate, that or starve. I live in a huge old castle set at the eastern side of Loch Leven, beautiful really, not far to the northwest of Edinburgh, on the Fife Peninsula. But still, you would see it as a savage land, despite all its arable land and gentle rolling hills. You're English and you'd see only the barren heights and crevices, and savage, rocky crags and hidden glens with torrents of rushing water bursting through them, water so cold your lips turn blue just to drink it. It's usually not all that cold in the winter months, but the days are short and the winds occasionally heavy. In the spring the heather covers the hills with purple, and the rhododendron spreads over every crofter's hut and even climbs the walls of my drafty castle, in all shades of pink and red and magenta."

He shook himself. He was prosing on like an idiot poet about Scotland and his part of it, as if he were parading his credentials for her inspection, and she was looking up at him, her expression rapt, taking in every word and watching his mouth. It was absurd. He wouldn't, couldn't, accept it.

He said abruptly, "Listen, it's true. My lands have the possibility of wealth because of all the arable acres, and I have ideas how to help my crofters improve their lot and thus improve my own in the process. No, we're not like the Highlands that must even now import sheep to survive. It's called enclosing, and it's a pernicious practice, for all the men and women who have lived on their plots of land for generations are being systematically disinherited. They're leaving Scotland or coming to England to work in the new factories. So I must have money, Joan, and there is no other way for me to save my inheritance except by marrying it."

"I understand. Come home with me and speak to my brother Douglas. He's the earl of Northcliffe, you know. We will ask him exactly what my dowry is. It's bound to be very generous. I heard him saying to my mother once that she should stop her picking at me for being on the shelf. Since I was an heiress, he said, I could marry anyone I wanted, even if I was fifty years old and had no teeth."

He looked at her helplessly. "Why me?"

"I haven't the foggiest notion, but there it is."

"I could stab you in your bed."

Her eyes darkened and he felt a surge of lust so great it rocked him on his heels.

"I said stab, not tup."

"What does tup mean?"

"It means . . . oh, damnation, where is that wretched guile I asked you to fetch up? Tup is a crude word, forgive me for saying it."

"Oh, you mean lovemaking, then."

"Yes, that is what I mean, only I was referring to it in a more basic way, what it usually is between men and women, not the high-blown romantic nonsense that females must call lovemaking."

"You are cynical, then. I suppose I can't expect you to be perfect in every way. My two brothers make love, they don't tup. Perhaps I can teach you all about it. But first, of course, you will have to show me the way of such things. It wouldn't do for you to continue to shout with laughter when I open my mouth for you to kiss me."

Colin turned away from her. He felt marooned on a very insubstantial island, one that kept shifting beneath his boots. He hated losing control. He'd lost control over his inheritance, and that was enough to try any man. He didn't want to lose control with a woman to boot, but she kept thrusting and parrying, being utterly outrageous and taking it for granted that it was just fine, that it was normal, almost that it was expected. No Scottish girl would ever behave like this supposedly refined English lady. It was absurd. He felt like a damned fool. "I won't promise you love. I cannot. It will never be. I don't believe in love, and I have very good reasons. I have years of reasons."

"That's what my brother Douglas said about his bride, Alexandra. But he changed, you know. She kept after him until he converted himself, and now I do believe that he would gladly lie down in the middle of a mud puddle and let her tread across him."

"He's a bloody fool."

"Perhaps. But he's a very happy bloody fool."

"I won't speak of this further. You are driving me into the bloody boughs and down again. No, be quiet. I'm taking you home. I must think. And so must you. I'm just a man, do you understand me? Just a man, no more, no less. If I married you, it would be for your groats, not for your lovely eyes or your probably very nice body."

Sinjun just nodded and asked very quietly, "Do you really think I have a nice body?"

He cursed, gave her a boot up, and climbed back into his own saddle. "No," he said, feeling more harassed than he'd ever felt in his life. "No, just be quiet."

Sinjun was in no hurry to return to the Sherbrooke town house, but Colin was. She paid him no heed when they arrived, merely guided Fanny to the stables at the back of the mansion. He was forced to follow.

"Henry, do see to the horses, please. This is his lordship, Lord Ashburnham."

Henry tugged on the bright red curl that dipped onto his forehead. He looked very interested in him, Colin saw, and wondered at it. Surely this outrageous girl had dozens of men panting around her, if for nothing more than to see what she would say next. Lord, her brother must have to warn every man who came through the front door about her excessive candor.

Sinjun skipped up the front steps and opened the door. She stood aside to wave him into the entrance hall. It wasn't the size of the Italian black-and-white marble entrance hall at Northcliffe, but it was of noble proportions nonetheless. White marble with pale blue veins stretched to the pale blue walls, most of them covered with paintings of past Sherbrookes.

Sinjun closed the door and looked around to see if Drinnen, the butler, or any of his minions were anywhere to be seen. There was no one. She turned back to Colin and gave him a brilliant smile and a very conspiratorial one, truth be told. He frowned. She took two steps and stopped, toe to toe with him.

"I'm glad you came in. Now you believe I'm who I said I am. That's good, though the thought of being your mistress does interest me. The concept, you understand. Should you like to speak to my brother now?"

"I shouldn't have come in. I've thought about it all the way back from the park, and it can't be happening, not like this. I'm not used to having a girl chase me down like a fox in the hunt, it isn't natural, it isn't—"

Sinjun merely smiled up at him, put her arms around his neck, and brought him down to her mouth. "I'll open my mouth but not so much this time. Is this right?"

It was more than right. Colin stared for a very brief instant at that soft, open mouth and pulled her tightly against him. He forgot that he was in the entrance hall of the Sherbrooke town house. He forgot that there must be servants about, abounding in hidden places. He forgot all about the Sherbrooke ancestors staring down on them.

He kissed her, his tongue lightly tracing over her lips, then slowly going into her mouth. It was wonderful, and he felt her lurch against him and knew that she felt wonder as well. He kissed her more deeply and she responded freely, fully, and he forgot everything. He hadn't bedded a woman for a month, but he knew even so that this effect she had on him wasn't usual. His hands swept down her back, touching her, learning the feel of her, and he cupped her buttocks, lifting her tightly against his belly.

She moaned softly into his mouth.

"My God! What the hell is going on here!"

Those words pierced through the fog in Colin's brain at the same time he was literally dragged away from her, spun around, and struck with blinding ferocity in the jaw. He went down like a stone on the white marble. He grabbed his jaw, shook his head, and stared up at the man who looked ready to kill him.

"Douglas! Don't you dare. This is Colin Kinross, and we're going to be married!"

"Like hell you are! Did you see— No, dear God, a man who hasn't even had the breeding to speak to me, and here he is making love to you in the entrance hall! His hands were on your damned butt. My God, Sinjun, how could you allow a man to do that? Go upstairs, young lady. Obey me. I will see to this bastard, and then I will see to you."

Sinjun had never seen her brother so angry, but she really didn't care if he swung from the chandelier in his rage. She calmly stepped in front of him even as he was ready to advance on Colin again. "Oh, no you don't, Douglas. Just stop it. Colin can't hit you back because he's in your house, and it's at my invitation. I won't allow you to hit him again. It wouldn't be honorable."

"Like hell!" Douglas shouted.

Sinjun wasn't aware that Colin was now standing behind her until he said, "He's right, Joan. I shouldn't have gotten so carried away, here, in his house. Forgive me. However, my lord, I can't allow you to hit me again."

Douglas was beside himself. "You have won yourself a beating for that, you damned bastard."

He flung Sinjun aside and hurled himself at Colin. The two men grappled, pushing and pulling and grunting, fairly evenly matched. Sinjun heard one groan from a fist to someone's stomach. It was enough. She heard a cry from Alex, who was now dashing down the stairs. The servants were gathering, wide-eyed, huddled beneath the stairs and in the doorway to the dining room.

"Stop it!"

Sinjun's voice didn't result in a truce. If anything, they went at it all the harder. She was furious, at her brother and at Colin. Men! Couldn't they just talk things out? Why did they have to revert to being little boys? She yelled at Alex, "Just stay there, I'll handle this. Oh my, yes, and with great pleasure."

She pulled a long, stout walking stick from the rosewood stand in the corner next to the front door, lifted it, and struck Douglas hard on his shoulder. Then she brought it down equally hard on Colin's right arm.

"That's enough, you bloody fools!"

The two men fell apart from each other, panting. Douglas was holding his shoulder, Colin his right arm.

"How dare you, Sinjun!"

But Douglas didn't wait for an answer, just growled and turned back to the man who'd had the damned gall to caress his little sister's buttocks in the middle of the entrance hall. And to stick his tongue in her mouth, the damned bastard. In her mouth!

Sinjun just started swinging. Not hard, just enough to get their attention. She heard Alex yelling, "Just stop it, Douglas!" Then Alex struck her husband with her own walking stick hard against his back.

Just as suddenly, Douglas realized what he was doing. He stopped cold. There was his small wife and his flushed sister whirling walking sticks about like mad dervishes.

He drew a deep breath, looked over at the damned Scottish ravisher, and said, "They'll kill us. We have to either go to a boxing saloon or put our fists in our pockets."

Colin was looking at the tall young lady who had proposed marriage to him. She'd struck her brother to protect him. It was amazing. Now she had moved toward him so that she was standing between them, that walking stick held firmly in her strong hands. It was more than amazing. It was also humiliating.

"Fists in pockets, if you please, my lord," Colin said.

"Good," Sinjun said. "Alex, what do you think? Shall we put the sticks away or keep them just in case the gentlemen here lose their breeding and tempers again?"

Alex, frowning ferociously, didn't answer. She dropped the stick and sent her fist into her husband's belly. Douglas, too surprised to do anything but grunt, looked at his wife, then over at Sinjun, and sighed. "All right, fists in pockets."

"Civilization is not a bad thing," Sinjun said. "To cement the truce, we'll have some tea. But first, Colin, you must come with me for a moment. There is blood on your lip. I will clean it off for you."

Alex said, "And you're a mess, Douglas. Your knuckles are raw and you've ripped your shirt, the one I made especially for you on your birthday. But you didn't think of that, did you, when you dove headfirst into these absurd fisticuffs? Oh goodness, there's some of Colin's blood on the collar. I doubt even Mrs. Jarvis's best potions will get that out. Sinjun, we will all meet in ten minutes in the drawing room." She looked around, saw Drinnen standing there looking drawn and white, and said calmly, "If you please, disperse the staff, Drinnen. And bring tea and scones to the drawing room. His lordship here is Scottish and doubtless will be very critical. Be certain the scones are up to snuff."

And it was done. By two women. Colin followed Joan Sherbrooke without a word. From the corner of his eye, he saw the earl likewise trailing in the wake of his very small wife, that lady's shoulders back, her chin high as a general's.

Colin Kinross, seventh earl of Ashburnham, felt as if he'd been trapped in a bizarre dream. It wasn't a nightmare, but it was beyond passing strange. He looked at the mass of loose brownish-blond hair that streamed down her back, pulled loose of pins during their skirmish. He didn't know what had happened to her riding hat. Thick hair, quite lovely really. She was toothsome, no doubt about that, and kissing her had been more enjoyable than anything he could remember.

But this interference, he couldn't tolerate it. The fight was between two men. Ladies had no say. No, he couldn't, wouldn't, tolerate such interference from her again.

CHAPTER
≡≡3≡≡

"ENOUGH OF THIS, Joan. I will not be led around like a damned goat."

Sinjun turned at the irritated voice of the man she had decided irrevocably she would marry and smiled. She patted his arm. "I myself don't like to be led around, either, particularly in a strange house. I don't mean that the house is strange, just that it is unknown to you. Walk beside me, then we'll both be leading."

"It has nothing to do with the strangeness of the damned house. Or my strangeness or anyone else's strangeness." But nonetheless, he fell into step beside her, feeling like an idiot.

She led him into the nether regions of the large house, down a passageway and through a door into a huge kitchen that was cozy and warm and smelled of cinnamon and nutmeg and sweet bread baking in old stone ovens. He sniffed scones and his mouth watered. He'd been too long from home. "Sit down here at the table, my lord."

He gave her a very irritated look. "For God's sake, with all that's happened in less than twenty-four hours, I think you can call me Colin."

She gave him a dazzling smile. If he hadn't felt so irritated he might have grabbed her and kissed her again. As it was, he just sat in that damned wooden chair like a docile dog and let her dab a damp cloth against his mouth. It burned like the devil but he kept still.

"I would have preferred to take you to my bedchamber," Sinjun said, pausing a moment to view her handiwork, "but Douglas would probably have immediately canceled the truce. He is, at times, unaccountable."

He grunted.

"As it is, you get to meet Cook, Mrs. Potter by name, and she makes the best scones you will ever eat in England. Dear Mrs. Potter, this is Lord Ashburnham."

Colin nodded to the immense woman all garbed in white, including her apron, holding a long-handled bread paddle. She gave him a suspicious stare. He stared at the paddle and the meaty hand holding it.

"Who was that small woman?"

"Douglas's wife, Alexandra. She loves him dearly and would give her life for him."

Colin grew very still. An odd concept that, and he wasn't certain he could even begin to believe it. He reached up his hand and grabbed her wrist, drawing it down. He pulled slightly and soon she was leaning down to him, not three inches from his face. "Do you believe in such loyalty?"

"Yes."

"You struck your brother, true, but then you turned and struck me harder."

"I did try to be fair, but in the heat of battle, so to speak, it's difficult to mete out an exact equality of blows."

He had to smile, which he did.

"If you don't release me, I think Mrs. Potter is going to hit you with the bread paddle."

He let her go. She finished patting the cut on his lip. "Hot tea will burn a bit, but it will taste good, too. Now, onward to the drawing room. You must deal with Douglas, since he is the head of the Sherbrooke family."

I don't believe this is happening to me, Colin thought as he strode beside the tall girl with her coltish walk and her tumbled hair. She began to whistle, just like a boy. He started, then just shook his head. He said aloud, "This really isn't what I expected. I didn't know you existed until last night, and now here I am in your house and your brother attacked me and I've even been in your kitchen."

"Douglas firmly believed you deserved it. He didn't know you then. All he saw was this very handsome man holding me up with his hands."

"That's not all I was doing with my hands."

Instead of blushing like an English heiress maiden should, she stared at his mouth and said in a very wistful voice, "I know. It was very nice, although it was startling. No one has ever done that to me before. I quite liked it."

"You must keep your mouth shut, Joan. The guile I spoke of, it's a useful thing. You must protect yourself."

"I can and I do, though there is seldom the need. How old are you, Colin?"

He sighed and let it go. "I'm twenty-seven. My birthday is in August."

"I thought you were about Ryder's age. He's one of my brothers. You will meet him soon. He's quite outrageous and funny and charming and quite the philanthropist. He used to hate anyone knowing how kind and good he was because he liked his wicked rake's image. As to my youngest brother, Tysen the Holiness we call him, I will protect you from his vicaring, which is what Douglas calls his prosing on and on about good deeds and the many paths to hell and such. But he is my brother and

I love him despite his narrow vision of things; and then there is his wife, Melinda Beatrice. Ryder said two names were too many, and besides she has no bosom."

Colin could only stare at this outpouring. "I've never met a family like yours before."

"No," Sinjun said comfortably, "I expect not. My brothers and sisters-in-law are wonderful. All except Melinda Beatrice, and she's really a bore, to peel the bark off the tree. Do you know they've been married four years and have three children? My brothers are forever twitting Tysen about unvicarlike potency and lack of control and overloading Noah's ark with all his offspring."

They had reached the drawing room. Colin turned to her and smiled. "I won't attack your brother, I promise. Hands in pockets."

"Thank you. I also hope that my mother keeps herself absent until after you've left. I must deal with her gently but firmly, and that will require having Douglas on my side first."

When he remained quiet, Sinjun turned and asked, "Do you want to marry me, Colin?"

He looked thoughtful. "I want to meet your mother first. It is said that daughters become the very image of their mothers."

Sinjun, aghast, poked him in the arm. "Oh dear," she said. "Oh dear." When he laughed, she poked him again and dragged him into the drawing room.

She said to her grim-faced brother and a smiling Alex, "Now we shall do things properly. This is Colin Kinross, the earl of Ashburnham. He is twenty-seven years old and he is considering marrying me, Douglas, so you see it was all right for him to take, er, liberties with my person."

"He was caressing your bottom, dammit! A man only does that to his wife."

"Douglas!"

"Well, he was caressing her, Alex. Was I to stand there watching the bounder seduce my little sister?"

"No, of course not. I apologize for not quite understanding the situation. Drubbing him was exactly the proper thing to do. Ah, here's Drinnen with tea. Do come in. Sinjun, you and Colin please sit over here on the sofa."

Colin Kinross looked at the earl of Northcliffe. He saw a man some five or so years older than he was, an athlete, no dandied-up fop like many of their contemporaries. "I apologize for taking liberties with Joan. I suppose that since I have, it would only be honorable for me to marry her."

"I don't believe any of this," Douglas said. "And you call her Joan! Only Mother calls her that. It's repellent."

"I don't care for the mannish nickname."

Douglas just stared at him.

"I assure you I don't care," Sinjun said, then smiled grandly. "He can call me anything he wishes to. Now, I thought if one put one's mind to it, this courtship and marriage business wouldn't be all that difficult. You see, I was right. It's grand to get things moving properly. What would you like in your tea, Colin?"

"Just a moment," Douglas said. "There is nothing simple about any of this, Sinjun. I want you to listen to me." But he turned to Colin. "I have found out, sir, that you are on the hunt for an heiress. You haven't been at all discreet about it. You doubtless know very well that Sinjun here will be quite rich upon her marriage."

"So she tells me. She came up to me and announced she was an heiress. She wanted me to speak to you to find out exactly what she's worth."

"She *what?*"

Sinjun only smiled at her brother. "It's true, Douglas. I knew he needed a wife with money, and so I told him I was perfect for him. Groats and toothsomeness all in one female person. To make it even grander, he catches all the other Sherbrookes in the family net as well as me."

Alex laughed, she couldn't help it. "I hope, Colin, that you can control this minx. She tackled me once in the immense entranceway of North-cliffe Hall, in front of everyone, and held me down until Douglas could be released from the room I'd locked him in. You must be careful, for she's really quite very determined once she sets her course."

She went into peals of laughter, and Sinjun grinned. Douglas looked wooden as a church pew, and Colin looked as if he were indeed in Bedlam and the inmates were ganging up on him.

"I'll tell you all about it later," Sinjun said, and lightly patted his biscuit-colored coat sleeve. She made the mistake of looking at his face and felt her own color rise at her very interesting thoughts.

"Stop it, Joan," he said low, through his teeth. "You're a danger to yourself. Just stop it. Do you want your brother to attack me again?"

"Listen, all of you just cease and desist for a minute." Douglas rose and began pacing the drawing room. He was also carrying his teacup and sloshed tea onto his hand. He grimaced, set the cup down, and resumed his pacing. "You saw him for the first time five days ago, Sinjun. *Five days!* You can't possibly know that you'd be content with this man—he's a bloody stranger."

"He said he wouldn't beat me. He said he was kind and felt responsible for his dependents. When it's really cold he lets his cats sleep with him. What else should I know, Douglas?"

"You might want to know if he cares for anything other than your money, my girl!"

"If he doesn't now, he will come to care for me. I'm not a bad person, Douglas. You like me."

Colin rose to stand his full height. "Joan, you will cease to answer for me as if I were a half-wit and not even here."

"Very well," Sinjun said, and primly folded her hands in her lap.

"Damnation, my lord, I don't have a bloody word to say to you! This isn't . . ." Words failed Douglas. He stomped to the door and turned to say over his shoulder, "I will speak to you again, Colin Kinross, this time next week. *Seven days!* Seven additional days, do you understand me? You're to keep away from my sister. One week, mind, no sooner. And keep your damned hands off my sister before you leave her in ten minutes!"

He slammed the door shut behind him. Alex rose then and grinned at them. "I fancy I will anoint his troubled brow with rosewater. It will soothe him." She giggled and followed her husband from the salon. She said at the door, not turning, "Keep your hands off him, Sinjun, do you hear me? Men have no tolerance in matters of affection. You mustn't drive him over the brink. Even in only ten minutes, gentlemen can forget every proper behavior they ever learned."

Were all the Sherbrookes—even those not born Sherbrookes—quite mad?

"I am pleased to have accorded your sister-in-law so much amusement," Colin said, and there was more irritation in his voice than there was tea in his cup. "If you want me to keep my hands off you, then stop staring at my mouth."

"I can't help it. You're so very beautiful. Oh dear, all we have are ten minutes."

Colin jumped to his feet, and he took up Douglas's pacing. "This is all immensely unlikely, Joan," he said, pivoting to walk toward the marble fireplace. "And in the future I will speak for myself." And just what would he say? Damnation. He paused, looking down into the empty grate. It was pale pink Italian marble, expensive and fashioned by masters. Then he pictured in his mind the huge blackened fireplace in the great hall of Vere Castle that could hold an entire cow. Old and filthy, the bricks cracking, the mortar falling out in chunks. Jesus, even the magnificent painting of a pastoral scene over the Italian marble mantel was old and reeked of solid wealth and an acceptance of great privilege. Wealth and privilege of many generations. He thought of the winding narrow stairs that climbed to the second-floor north tower, so dangerous now because of wood rot from the cold wind seeping through the gaps in the outer stone. He drew a deep breath. He could save Vere Castle. He could save his people. He could replenish the sheep. He could even plant crops, since he'd learned all about crop rotation. He could buy grain. He turned to his future wife and said, "I will accept your belief that I'm beautiful. A man, I suppose, wants to be thought reasonably acceptable to the woman he marries."

"More than acceptable," Sinjun said, and felt her heart thump wildly in her breast. He'd accepted her. Finally. She wanted to kick her heels in the air.

He sighed then and plowed his fingers through his hair, making it stand on end. He stopped cold when she said in a marveling voice, "I didn't ever think I would fall in love. No gentleman has ever made me think there was anything to this love business. I found some of them amusing, but nothing more than that. Others were stupid and rude and had no chins. Some thought me a bluestocking, and all because I'm not ignorant. I couldn't imagine having any of them kissing me. Goodness, if any of them had even touched my bottom, I should have shrieked and killed them. But with you . . . it's different. I understand that you don't love me. Please believe me that it doesn't matter. I will do my best to make you care for me. Now, there is nothing more I can say other than I will try to make you a good wife. Would you like to eat one of Mrs. Potter's scones, or would you like to leave and go somewhere private to brood?"

"Brood," he said. "There is so much you don't know about me. You might very well change your mind."

She gave him a long, thoughtful look. She said quite calmly and with great finality, "You will care for me, will you not, if we marry?"

"I will protect you with my life. It would be my responsibility."

"You would give me respect?"

"If you deserve it."

"Very well, then. You can tell me anything you wish to after the ceremony. Not before. And know now that nothing you say to me will change how I feel about you. It's just that I don't want anything untoward and unimportant coming to Douglas's ears before we're married."

He would wed her. He desperately needed the money, and he liked her, despite her outlandishness. It was frightening, this openness of hers, this truth that knew no tempering. Well, he could teach her to moderate her tongue. He knew he wouldn't find it at all difficult to bed her. Yes, he would wed her. But he would wait the week her brother had demanded. But it had to be soon after that. The situation back home was growing worse by the day. She would do just fine. And she'd presented herself to him on a wondrous silver plate. Only a fool would look such a gift-heiress in the mouth. Colin Kinross wasn't a fool.

He strode over to her, pulled her to her feet, and just looked down at her silently. Then he kissed her lightly on her closed mouth. He wanted more but forced himself not to take any more from her, even though he imagined he could ease her down to the floor this very minute and take her without much fuss. But he didn't. He would keep himself within safe bounds. He said, "I would like to see you again, despite your brother's edict. Would you like to go riding tomorrow? We'll be discreet."

"I would love to. Douglas will never know. Oh, Colin?"

He turned.

"Will you teach me how to speak Scottish?"

"Aye, and 'twill be my pleasure, lassie." His voice was lilting and smooth as honey. "Ye'll be my sweetheart, dinna ye ken?"

"I've never been a sweetheart before. It sounds grand."

All he could do was shake his head at her.

Douglas said to his wife, "I've discovered nothing ill about Ashburn-ham. He is liked and respected. He attended Eton and Oxford. He has many men friends in society. The only thing any of them can say is that he must marry an heiress." Douglas, in a habit that was becoming more pronounced, plowed his fingers through his hair again. He continued his pacing as his wife watched him from her dressing table. It was still early in the evening, three nights from the week Douglas had demanded. Both of them knew that Sinjun had met Colin the day after the historic brawl, but neither wanted to make an issue of it. As far as Douglas knew, Sinjun hadn't seen him since. But who could know with Sinjun? She was damnably resourceful.

"How long has he been the earl of Ashburnham?"

"Just six months. His brother was a wastrel, as was his father. Together they ran the estate into the ground. He has a huge barn of an old castle that will require vast sums to bring it back to what it was. Then there are the crops, the sheep, the poverty of his people—crofters, they're called in Scotland."

"So," Alex said slowly, "when he became the earl and discovered the true state of his affairs, he made a decision, the only one he could make. You don't dislike him for that, do you, Douglas?"

"No. It's just that—"

"That what, my dear?"

"Sinjun doesn't know him. She's infatuated, that's all. She'll end up in Scotland, with no one to protect her, and what if—"

"Do you believe that Colin Kinross is an honorable man?"

"I have no idea. On the surface, I'd say yes. What goes on in his mind? In his heart?"

"Sinjun will wed him, Douglas. I only hope she doesn't seduce him before they're wed."

He sighed. "I hope so, too. Now I must go to speak with Mother. She is squawking again, driving her maid insane, demanding that the young man be brought to her. She is threatening to send Sinjun to Italy until she has forgotten this foreign bounder. The strange thing is that she doesn't at all mind that he is marrying her daughter for money. What she minds is that he is a Scot. She says all Scots are hard and mean-fisted and *Presbyterian*."

"Perhaps you should quote some Robert Burns poetry to her. It's really quite lovely."

"Ha! It's a foreign language and she'd have even more fits than she's having now. Damnation, I wish Sinjun weren't lying in her bed with a headache. She is never about when I need her."

"Shall I come with you?"

"If you were to do that, Mother would rage until we were both deaf. You still haven't won her over, my dear. I doubt not she will soon come around to blaming you for this debacle." Douglas sighed and left the room, mumbling about his damned sister and her equally damned headache.

Sinjun didn't have a headache. She had a plan and she was well into its execution. She had carefully molded a bolster into a reasonable human shape and covered it. Excellent. If there were no close inspection, the bolster would pass muster as a likely female. She patted her own pants leg, straightened her jacket, and pulled her felt hat more fully down over her forehead. She looked like a boy, no doubt about it. She turned and looked at her back in the long mirror. Just like a boy, even to her black boots. She whistled softly. Now all she had to do was climb down the elm tree into the garden. Then she was off.

Colin's lodgings were on the second floor of an old Georgian town house on Carlyon Street, only three streets away. It wasn't yet dark and she kept whistling to keep away any fears that might try to nibble at her, and to make anyone who saw her see only a boy, out for the evening. She saw two gentlemen in their swirling cloaks, laughing and smoking cheroots, but they paid her no heed. There was a ragged boy sweeping the path for anyone who passed, and she thanked him and gave him a pence. Sinjun found his lodging without problem and strolled to the front door as if she hadn't a care in the world. She pounded the huge eagle's-head knocker.

There wasn't a sound from within. She knocked again. She heard a giggle and a girl's high voice scolding, "Now, sir, don't you do that! No, no, not there, you mustn't. Now, we've a visitor. No, sir—" There were more giggles and when the door opened, Sinjun was face-to-face with one of the prettiest females she'd ever seen. The girl's neckline was low over very white, full breasts, and her pale hair was mussed and her eyes were bright with excitement and fun. She was grinning wickedly.

"And just who'd you be, my fine lad?" she said, striking a pose, one hand on her hip and her chest poked out.

The fine lad answered with a wide smile, "Who do you want me to be? Your father, perhaps? No, that isn't possible, is it? I would have to scold the gentleman who was making you laugh, and you wouldn't want that, would you?"

"Oh, you're a fine one, you are! All jests and games and a well-oiled tongue. You want to see someone here?"

Sinjun nodded. She saw a gentleman from the corner of her eye as he slipped into a door off the main corridor. "I'm here to see Lord Ashburnham. Is he in?"

The girl struck another pose, this one even more provocative, and giggled once again. "Aye, a pretty one, his lordship is. But he's poor, you know. Can't afford a nice girl, he can't, or a gentleman's man to help him. Talk is he's marrying an heiress, but he won't say boo about it. Probably the heiress is a stoat all dressed in fancy silk, poor man."

"Some heiresses can even whistle, I've heard," Sinjun said. "Now, his lordship's apartment is on the second floor, isn't it?"

"Yes," the girl said. "Hey, wait! I don't know if he's here or not. Haven't seen him for two days now. Tilly, one of the girls, went up to see if he wanted some fun—all willing to give it to him on the house, she was—but he wasn't there. Leastwise he didn't answer. And what man wouldn't answer when he heard Tilly calling out to him?"

Sinjun took the stairs two at a time, saying over her shoulder, "If he isn't there, perhaps I shall return and you and I can, er, have a cup of tea and a chat."

The girl giggled. "Ah, go along with you, my cute lad! Ah, 'tis you, sir, back again. Now, where were we? Ah, what naughtiness you are!"

Sinjun was still smiling when she reached the landing. It was a solid house with a wide hallway. Well maintained, the paint fresh, a gentleman's establishment. Were the pretty girls here all the time? She found Colin's door and knocked. There was nothing. She knocked again. Please, she thought, please let him be here. It had been too long. Four whole days without him. It was too much. They'd fooled Douglas that first morning, but Colin hadn't called on her since. She had to see him, to touch him, to smile at him.

Finally she heard a deep voice call out, "Whoever you are, go to hell."

It was Colin, but he sounded strange, his voice low and raw. Was he with someone? A girl like the one downstairs?

No, she wouldn't believe that. She knocked again.

"Damnation, go away!" The curse was followed by a hacking cough.

Sinjun felt a spurt of fear. She gripped the door handle, and to her immense relief it wasn't locked. She pushed the door open and walked into a small entrance hall. She looked to her right into a long, narrow drawing room that was well enough furnished, she supposed, but impersonal, without any individual character. It called up nothing of Colin. Nothing of anyone except perhaps a musty gentleman from the past century. She called out, "Colin? Where are you?"

She heard some cursing coming from beyond the drawing room. She hurried now, pushed the door open, and came face-to-face with her betrothed. He was sitting up in the middle of a rumpled bed, quite naked, the sheets drawn only to his waist. Sinjun stood there a moment, just gawking. Goodness, he was big, and there was black hair all over his chest, and he looked strong and muscular and lean and she couldn't stop staring at his chest and his arms and his shoulders, yes, even his throat. There were black whiskers on his face, his eyes were bloodshot, and his hair was standing on end. He looked quite wonderful.

"Joan! What the hell are you doing here? Are you out of your damned mind? Are you—"

His voice was a croak. Sinjun was across the room to him in a moment to stand by the side of the bed. "What's wrong?" Even as she asked him, she realized he was shaking. And she'd been standing there staring at him like a half-witted fool. "Oh goodness." She pushed him back down and pulled the covers up to his chin. "No, no, just hold still and tell me what's wrong."

Colin lay flat on his back, looking up at Joan, who was trying to look like a boy, which was ridiculous. But perhaps it was the fever; perhaps she wasn't really here, perhaps he'd just conjured her up.

He said tentatively, frowning, "Joan?"

"Yes, love, I'm here. What's wrong?" She sat beside him and laid her palm on his forehead. He was hot to the touch.

"I can't be your love," he said. "It's much too soon. Damnation, I'm tired or something, and weak as a day-old pup. Why are you pretending to be a boy? It's silly. You have a woman's hips and long legs that aren't at all remotely like a boy's."

It was an interesting avenue of conversation, but Sinjun was too scared to be sidetracked. "You have a fever. Have you been vomiting?"

He shook his head, then closed his eyes. "Have you no damned sensibilities?"

"Your head hurts?"

"Yes."

"How long have you felt bad?"

"Two days now. I don't feel bad, I'm just tired."

"Why didn't you send for a doctor? For me?"

"I don't need anyone. It's just a passing fever, nothing more. I was out in the rain, at a boxing match on Tyburn Hill. I'm just tired."

"We'll see," she said. Men, she thought, as she leaned down and pressed her cheek to his. They couldn't bring themselves to admit to any weakness. She drew back. The heat was incredible. His eyes flew open, but she said as she gently laid her fingertip on his lips, "No, don't move. I will see to everything now. When did you last eat?"

He looked as irritated as his voice sounded. "I don't remember. It isn't important. I'm not hungry. Just go away, Joan. It's vastly improper for you to be here."

"Would you leave me if you found me sick and alone?"

"It's altogether different, and you know it. For God's sake, I'm bare-assed."

"Bare-assed," she repeated, smiling at him. "My brothers have never said that before. No, no, don't frown at me or curse at me anymore. Just lie down and I will see to things."

"No, dammit, just go away!"

"I will, and I will soon be back with help. Lie down and keep warm, Colin. Now, would you like some water?"

His eyes lit up and he nodded.

Once he'd drunk his fill, she said matter-of-factly, "Do you need to relieve yourself?"

He looked ready to spit. "Go away."

"All right." She leaned down and kissed his mouth and was gone in the next moment.

Colin pulled the covers to his nose. His thoughts were vague. The room blurred. When he opened his eyes again, he was alone. Had she really been here? He wasn't so thirsty anymore, so someone must have come in. Lord, he was cold and he couldn't seem to stop shivering. His head pounded and his thoughts grew vaguer. He was ill, more wretched than he'd been when he'd cracked two ribs in a satisfying fight just two months before his brother had gotten himself killed and Colin had inherited a title he'd wanted only because he hated the destruction of his home.

He closed his eyes and saw Joan dressed like a boy and she was smiling down at him. Unaccountable girl. She would be back, of that he had no doubts—that is, if she'd ever been here in the first place.

An hour later he received a shock when not only Joan returned, but her brother Douglas with her. He saw that she was still wearing boys' clothes. Didn't her brother discipline her? Wasn't she given any guidance on how a young lady of quality was to behave?

Colin stared at the earl, who was staring back at him. He was unable to find a single word to say. Douglas said calmly, "You're coming back to Sherbrooke House. You're ill, I can see that, and my sister doesn't want to marry a man who's nearly dead."

"So you were really here," he said to Sinjun.

"Yes, and now all will be well. I'll take excellent care of you."

"Dammit, I'm only tired, not ill. You're making too much of this, and I just want to be left alone and—"

"Do be quiet," Douglas said.

And Colin, because he felt worse than a half-starved mongrel, shut his mouth.

And that, he thought, too ill to care, was that.

"Sinjun, get out of here. The man's naked and you aren't to stay about and embarrass him. Send in Henry and Boggs to help me get him into clothing."

"I can dress myself," Colin said, and Douglas, seeing the fever burning bright and hot in his eyes, agreed.

He didn't do it well, but he managed to dress himself quickly. However, the ride to the Sherbrooke town house was a nightmare Colin would just as soon not have lived through. He passed out when Henry and Boggs were helping him up the wide stairway.

It wasn't until they were in the guest bedchamber that Douglas discovered the jagged four-inch-long knife wound at the top of Colin's right thigh.

CHAPTER
══ 4 ══

"YOU MUST GET SOME REST, Sinjun. It's nearly one o'clock in the morning."

Sinjun didn't wish to look away from his still face, but she forced herself to glance up at her sister-in-law. "I'm resting, Alex. It's just that I must be here if he wakes up. He's always so thirsty, you know."

Alex said calmly, "He's a strong man. He won't die. I'm not worried about him now. I don't want you to lose your health."

"Do you promise, Alex?"

"Yes, I promise. His breathing is a bit easier, I can hear it. The doctor said he would survive this. He will."

"I still don't want to leave him. He's had horrible nightmares."

Alex handed Sinjun a cup of tea and sat beside her.

"What sort of nightmares?"

"I'm not sure. He's frightened and he's confused. Whether it's real or just the fever, I don't know."

Colin heard her voice. It was pitched low and it was calm, but the underlying worry was there, thick and deep. He wanted to open his eyes and look at her, but he couldn't. It was that simple. He was deep within himself, and he was afraid; she'd been right about that. He'd seen Fiona again, and she was lying there at the base of the cliff, quite dead, her body sprawled on the jagged rocks. He was standing there looking down at her. Fear welled up in him and he wanted to get away from it, but it pursued him, overwhelmed him, and he was dying of the fear and the terror of what he couldn't or wouldn't remember, and the god-awful uncertainty. Had he killed her? No, dammit, he hadn't killed his wife, he hadn't. Even this nightmare couldn't make him believe that he had. Someone had brought him here, perhaps Fiona herself, and she'd fallen, but he hadn't killed her. He knew it deep down. He'd backed away from the cliff edge very slowly, one step, then another. He felt dizzy and strangely detached from himself. He'd led men back there, to where he'd found her, and no one had asked him what had happened, how it was that Fiona was lying there thirty feet below, her neck broken.

Ah, but there was talk, endless talk, and that talk was more devastating than an outright accusation, for it swirled around him, always out of his reach, those damned whispers and innuendos; and it ate at him because he knew he could shout his innocence, but how could he explain how he'd come to be there on the cliff edge himself? That he didn't know, didn't remember. He'd just come to himself and he'd been there. There was no reasoning he could grasp, nothing. The only person he'd told everything he remembered had been Fiona's father, the laird of the MacPherson clan, and he'd believed him. But it wasn't enough, never enough, for he couldn't remember and it preyed on him, brought him down when he slept, when he was at his weakest, this guilt that wasn't really guilt. But he still felt the nightmares to be a penance he was obligated to pay.

He was thrashing now, moaning deep in his throat. The knife wound in his thigh burned and gnawed at him. Sinjun was on her feet in an instant, gently holding him still, her hands on his shoulders. "Hush, Colin. It's all right. They're just nightmares, nothing more than nightmares. Just phantoms to plague you. Nothing more. That's right, listen to me. I won't lie to you. Come closer, yes, here's some water, it will make you feel better."

She tipped the water glass slightly and he swallowed. She held the glass until he turned his head away. She dabbed the water from his chin, saying quietly to her sister-in-law, "I put some laudanum in the water. It should help him into a deeper sleep, away from the nightmares."

Alex said nothing. She knew no one could pull her away from Douglas were he ill. Thus, she just patted Sinjun's arm and left the bedchamber.

Douglas was awake. He pulled Alex against him and held her close. "How is he?"

"Very ill. He's having nightmares. It's awful, Douglas."

"Couldn't you get Sinjun to leave him to Finkle for the rest of the night?"

"No. Finkle would fall asleep and probably wake poor Colin up with his snoring. You told me about the times when you were campaigning that Finkle would wake you up with his noises even after you'd been in battle for twelve hours and exhausted. No, let Finkle see to Colin during the day. Sinjun is young and strong. She needs to be with him. Let her."

Douglas sighed. "Life is bloody unexpected. I forbade him to enter the house, knowing deep in my brain that the two of them would naturally see each other. Damnation, he could have died if Sinjun hadn't taken matters into her own hands and gone to his lodgings. It's my bloody fault. She doesn't know about the knifing, does she?"

"No. Now, if you continue to blame yourself, Douglas, for something that could never be remotely your fault, I shall write to Ryder and urge him to come here immediately and bash you into the ground."

"Ha! Ryder wouldn't do that. Besides, I'm bigger than he is. I'd thrash him into a lump."

"Ah, but then you'd have to deal with Sophie."

"A terrifying thought."

"I hope you don't mind that she and Ryder can't come to London just now. With two of the children hurt in that fall from the hayloft, they wouldn't much enjoy it; they'd be too worried. Also, the twins are quite happy there with their cousin and all the other children."

"I miss the little heathens," Douglas said fondly.

"All twelve of the children plus our two and Ryder and Sophie's one?"

"Two at a time is preferable. I like the notion of trading children around. They never quite have time enough to roll you up so you'll do whatever they want."

"You're right about that. Ah, but my dear, with Colin so ill and the wedding to be seen to, it is better, I suppose, that we leave the boys with their aunt and uncle."

"I think Sinjun will want to marry Colin just as soon as possible. If that's so, then Ryder and Sophie won't be here."

"I'm too tired to think more on the situation. Let's get some sleep."

Douglas felt a soft hand stroke down his chest and smiled into the darkness. "Ah, I thought you were tired. You have regained your vigor? Am I to be rewarded?"

"If you promise not to shout too loudly and awaken your mother again." Alex shuddered, remembering the one night she and Douglas had enjoyed themselves immoderately, and his mother had burst into the room, thinking Alex had killed her beloved son. The memory still made her stiff with mortification.

"I'll stuff a handkerchief in my mouth."

He was whole-witted at last, but so weak he couldn't seem to raise himself so he could use the chamber pot. It was damnable. At least the fever was gone and the pain in his leg was tolerable. He'd been a fool not to see a doctor when it had happened, but he simply wasn't used to having some quack dose him, for God's sake, for whatever reason. Never had he seen Dr. Childress, the Kinross physician for over thirty years, for anything more than childhood illnesses. He was young and strong and healthy as a stoat. A simple little knife cut and here he was flat on his back, sick with fever and out of his head.

He watched with half-closed eyes as Joan came into the room. He was testy and hungry. He didn't want her there. He needed a man to help him.

"Ah, good, you're awake," Sinjun said, giving him a smile that lit up the bedchamber. "How do you feel?"

He grunted.

"Should you like me to shave you? I shaved Tysen's head once while Ryder held him down. Not more than ten years ago. I could try, and I would be very careful."

"No."

"The strangest thing, Colin, there's a man downstairs who claims he's your cousin."

That brought him bolt upright in the bed. The covers fell to his belly and he could but stare at her. Which cousin? None of his cousins knew he was here, did they? Ah, MacDuff did.

"That's not possible," he said, and fell back to the pillows. Sinjun was looking at the line the covers made below his waist. She swallowed. He was so beautiful, all hard and long, black hair covering his chest, ah, but it narrowed to a soft black trail and disappeared beneath the covers. He was too thin, she could see his ribs, but that would change.

"You must stay warm," she said, and pulled the covers up to his shoulders, even though she wanted to pull them to his feet and look at him for six hours at least.

"Joan, you're not jesting? MacDuff is here?"

She blinked. "MacDuff? He didn't give me his name, just said he was your favorite cousin. MacDuff, as in Shakespeare's MacDuff?"

"Yes. As boys, we all called him MacCud—"

"As in a Scottish cow?"

He grinned. "That's it. His real name is Francis Little, absurd for someone of his height, breadth, and width, so we chose MacDuff for him when we were boys. As I recall, he threatened to smash us in the dirt if we didn't stop calling him MacCud and change it to MacDuff."

"It fits him better than Francis Little, which isn't at all right for a man with a chest the width of a tree trunk. MacDuff! That's very clever, Colin. I imagine you devised that name. You know, he's got the reddest hair and no freckles. His eyes are as blue as a summer sky—"

"His eyes are just the same shade as yours. Stop your rhapsodizing about my bloody giant of a cousin. Bring him up."

"No," Sinjun said. "Not until you've eaten your breakfast. Ah, here's Finkle right now. He'll assist you with other matters as well. I will be back in a few minutes and help you eat."

"I don't need your help."

"Certainly not, but you will enjoy my company, won't you?"

He just looked at her. She smiled at him, kissed his closed mouth lightly, and nearly danced from the room.

She turned at the doorway. "Should you like to marry me tomorrow?"

He gave her a look that held irritation rather than shock, and said, "You would have a memorable wedding night. I would be lying dead to the world at your side and that would be it."

"I shouldn't mind. We have the rest of our lives together."

"I refuse to wed you until I can bed you properly." It was a stupid thing for him to say, he realized. He needed to wed her in the next hour, if it were possible. Time was growing short. He desperately needed her money.

Sinjun sat back, watching the two cousins talk. They were speaking quietly, so she couldn't understand them, nor did she really want to eavesdrop, something at which she was really quite accomplished. With three older brothers, she'd learned at a very young age that most information kept from her, wicked or otherwise, was best discovered through a keyhole. She looked out the window down into the enclosed garden. It was a cool day, but the sky was clear and blue and the flowers and plants in the garden were in full bloom. She heard Colin laugh and looked up, smiling. MacDuff—surely that nickname was stranger than her own nickname, Sinjun—seemed a pleasant man, and more important, very fond of Colin. Even sitting by the bed he looked huge, not fat, no, not at all, just huge like a giant. His laugh was huge, too, shaking his entire body. She liked him. She had no qualms about MacDuff because she'd told him that if he tired Colin, she would personally boot him out.

He'd looked down at her from his vast elevation and grinned. "You're no coward, I see, just a bit stupid to take this mongrel into your home. Nay, I'll close my trap when the time comes so as not to tire out the poor lad."

In perfect accord, she'd taken him in to see Colin.

Even now he was rising and saying to Colin, "It's time you rested, old man. No, no arguments. I have promised Sinjun and I have a mighty fear of her."

"Her name is Joan. She isn't a man."

MacDuff raised a violent red eyebrow. "A bit irritable, are we? A bit of a green color about the gills? I will see you in the morning, Ash. Do what Sinjun tells you to do. She's invited me to the wedding, you know."

And MacDuff the tree trunk was gone.

"He has no Scottish accent, just as you don't."

"MacDuff, despite his nickname, prefers the English side of his family. My father and his mother were brother and sister. His mother married an Englishman from York, a very wealthy ironmonger. Both of us were educated in England, but he went more deeply into it than I did. I used to think he would cut all ties with Scotland if he weren't tied to it so closely, at least that's what he always said. But now I believe he's changed his mind, because during the past few years he's lived most of the time in Edinburgh."

"You're tired, Colin. I want to hear all about this, but later, my dear."

"You're a nag."

He sounded sour, which pleased her. He was mending.

"No, not a nag. One rides a nag," she said, patting the covers at his shoulders.

He stared at her. "Your sexual innuendos aren't at all the thing for a virgin."

He realized she had no idea what he was talking about and snorted at her. "Just go away, Joan."

"All right. Forgive me, Colin. You're tired and must rest."

She turned at the door. "Would you like to marry me the day after tomorrow?"

"Perhaps if I can walk tomorrow I shall be able to ride the day after tomorrow."

She cocked her head to one side in question, and when he just continued to look sour, she smiled and left him.

Colin lay back and closed his eyes. He was worried, very worried, and so angry he wanted to spit. MacDuff had come to tell him that the MacPhersons were moving on Kinross lands. They'd heard about his financial ruin, knew he was out of Scotland, and had thus taken advantage. They were, according to MacDuff, freely raiding Kinross land and sheep. They were vultures, normally incompetent and content to whine about all their misfortunes— all brought on by themselves. They'd even killed several crofters who'd tried to save their homes from pillage. His people were doing what they could, but there was no leader there for them. Colin had never felt more helpless in his entire life. Here he was, lying in this lovely damned bed in this beautiful house, weak as a day-old foal, and useless to himself and to his family and his people.

Marrying Joan Sherbrooke was the most important thing he could accomplish. It wouldn't have mattered if she'd had rabbit teeth, so long as her guineas were shining and numerous. Nothing mattered except smashing the cowardly MacPhersons and saving Vere Castle and all the other Kinross properties. He had to move quickly. He tried to rise, gritted his teeth at the wash of pain through his thigh, and fell back again. Colin's head began to pound. The next time Joan asked him to wed her, he'd ask that the preacher be brought in the next five minutes.

Douglas Sherbrooke very carefully folded the letter and slid it back into its envelope.

He began to pace the length of the library, then stopped, pulled the letter from the envelope, and read it through again. The big block letters were in black ink and carefully printed. He read:

Lord Northcliffe,

Colin Kinross murdered his wife. He will wed your sister and then do away with her. Doubt it not. He is ruthless and would do anything to get what he wants. The only thing he wants now is money.

It was the sort of thing that Douglas hated. An anonymous accusation that left one furious and disbelieving because it was anonymous, but still planted a seed of doubt despite what one felt about the one being accused. The letter had been delivered just an hour before by a small urchin, who simply told Drinnen that a cove bid 'im to deliver this letter to the lordship o' this fancy 'ouse.

Drinnen didn't ask the lad to describe the cove. A pity. He assumed it had been a man. He paced again, now crumpling the letter in his hand.

Colin was mending rapidly. Sinjun was already dancing about, wanting to marry him by the end of the week. Jesus, it was already Tuesday.

What to do?

He knew deep in his gut that Sinjun wouldn't care if the wretched letter accused Colin of murdering an entire regiment. She wouldn't believe it. She would never believe it. She'd go to war with her entire family before she'd believe it.

Damnation. He knew he couldn't ignore it, and thus, when Alex and Sinjun left the house to fetch Sinjun's wedding gown from Madame Jordan's, he didn't put it off. He strode up to Colin's bedchamber.

Colin was wearing one of his own dressing gowns, thanks to Finkle and several footmen, who had returned to his lodgings and packed all his clothing and brought his two trunks here. He was standing beside the bed, looking toward the door.

"Do you need some assistance?" Douglas asked as he stepped into the room.

"No, thank you. I'm endeavoring to prove that I can walk across this room and back three times without falling on my nose."

Douglas laughed. "How many times have you done it?"

"Twice, at five-minute intervals. This third time looks to be the death of me though."

"Sit down, Colin. I must speak to you."

Colin sat gingerly in a wing chair near the fireplace. He stretched his leg out in front of him, wincing as he did so. He began to gently massage the leg. "You didn't tell Joan, did you?"

"No, only my wife, although I don't know why you care if Sinjun knows or not."

"It would infuriate her and worry her and she wouldn't stand for it. She would probably hire a Bow Street Runner and the two of them would go haring off to track down the man who did it. She would probably place an advertisement in the *Gazette* for information leading to his capture. She could hurt herself. She obviously needs to be protected, more from herself than anything else."

Douglas could but stare at him. "You've known her such a short time and yet . . ." He shook his head. "That's exactly what she'd do. I sometimes feel the good Lord doesn't know what she plans to do until she does it. She's very creative, you know."

"No, but I suspect I'll learn."

"You have yet to tell me how you got knifed in the thigh."

Colin didn't meet Douglas's eyes. "It was a little bully who wanted to rob me. I knocked the man down and he pulled a knife from his boot. My thigh was as high as he could reach."

"Did you kill him?"

"No, but I probably should have, the damned blighter. He wouldn't have gotten much from me had he succeeded in picking my pocket. I had no more than two guineas with me at the most."

"I got a letter just a while ago, accusing you of murdering your wife."

Colin became very still. It was as if, Douglas thought, he had pulled inside himself, away from pain or perhaps guilt? He didn't know. Colin looked beyond Douglas's left shoulder toward the fireplace.

"It wasn't signed. The person who wrote it sent a boy around with it. I don't like letters like this. They're poisonous and they leave one feeling foul."

Colin said nothing.

"No one knew you'd already been married."

"No. I didn't think it was anyone's affair."

"When did she die?"

"Shortly before my brother died, some six and a half months ago."

"How?"

Colin felt his guts twist and knot. "She fell off a cliff and broke her neck."

"Did you push her?"

Colin was silent, a hard silence both deep and angry.

"Were you arguing with her? Did she fall accidentally?"

"I didn't murder my wife. I won't murder your sister. I gather the writer of the letter warned you about that."

"Oh yes."

"Will you tell Joan?"

Douglas blinked. He still couldn't accustom himself to Colin's calling Sinjun Joan. "I must. It would be preferable, naturally, if you told her, perhaps gave her explanations that you've not given to me."

Colin said nothing. He was stiff, wary.

Douglas rose. "I'm sorry," he said. "She is my sister and I love her dearly. I must protect her. It is only fair that she know about this. I do feel, however, that before the two of you marry, this must be resolved. That is something I must demand."

Colin remained silent. He didn't look up until Douglas had quietly closed the door behind him. He leaned his head back and closed his eyes. He rubbed his thigh; the stitches itched and the flesh was pink. He was healing nicely.

But was he healing quickly enough?

Who, for God's sake? Who could have done this? The MacPhersons were the only ones who came to mind, and it was a powerful motive they had, if they were indeed responsible. His first wife, Fiona Dahling MacPherson, had been the laird's eldest daughter. But old Latham had supposedly absolved him, at least he had at the time of Fiona's death. Of course her brother hadn't, but the laird had kept Robert in line. During the past several months Colin had heard that the laird wasn't right in the head, that his health was failing rapidly, which was only to be expected, since the man was as old as the Gaelic rocks at Limner. Ah, yes, the letter had to be from the MacPhersons, the wretched cowards, there was no one else.

The damned letter paled into insignificance. He had to marry Joan, and quickly, or all would be lost. He closed his eyes.

He forced himself to rest. Several hours later Colin rose from the chair and walked the length of the bedchamber, two times, then three. He was gaining strength, thank God. He just prayed it was quickly enough.

It was during dinner that evening, Joan eating her own dinner beside him, that he made up his mind. He looked up from the fork bite of ham to realize that she was speaking.

". . . Please don't misunderstand me, the wedding gown is lovely, truly, but it's all such a fuss, Colin. My mother would probably display you like some sort of trophy, she's so pleased that I'm finally to be yanked off the Spinster Shelf. Oh, I do hate the trappings of it all. How I should simply like to whisk you away from here so we can begin our lives together. All this other nonsense is just that, nonsense."

His jaw dropped. Relief flooded him. Manna from heaven, all of it flowing from her mouth. He'd floundered and thought and thought some more, rejecting one idea after another, and here she was, giving herself to him, without reservation.

"I'm not yet very strong," he said, concentrating on chewing the ham.

"You will be strong enough by Friday. Perhaps even sooner. Ah, if only you could be well right this minute."

Colin drew a deep breath. "I must tell you something, Joan. No, please, listen to me. It's very important. Your brother will forbid the marriage. He has told me he will, that he must, to protect you."

Sinjun just looked at him, the peas on her fork, hovering above her plate. She waited, slowly ate the peas, then drank some of her wine. She continued to wait, saying nothing.

"Oh, the hell with it! Your brother believes that I killed someone. He will tell you about it if I don't. He must protect you, as I said. He wants everything resolved before we marry. Unfortunately, there is no way to resolve any of it, ever. I didn't tell him that, but it's true. We won't marry, Joan, I'm sorry. Your brother won't allow it and I must go along with his wishes."

"Who did you supposedly kill?"

"My first wife."

Without hesitation, Sinjun said, "How utterly absurd. Not that you are so young and already once wed, but that you would hurt her or anyone for that matter, and certainly not your wife. Nonsense. How did he hear such a ridiculous thing?"

"An anonymous letter."

"There, you see. Someone is jealous of you; that, or someone simply has taken you into dislike because you are so handsome and have cut such a dash in London. I will speak to Douglas and set him straight on this."

"No."

She heard the determination in that one word. She said nothing. She waited. Patience was difficult, but for once she managed it.

She was rewarded after an interminable wait when he said slowly, looking right into her eyes, "If you want to marry me, we will have to leave, tonight. We will go to Scotland and marry over the anvil, but not in Gretna Green, for that would be the first place your brother would go. It will be done, and your brother will not be able to do a thing about it. We will stop at the Kinross house in Edinburgh and have a proper wedding." There, he'd done it. Dishonor filled him. But what else could he do? There was no damned choice, and she had offered herself to him on the proverbial platter.

Sinjun was silent for a very long time. When she spoke finally, he nearly fell back against the pillow with relief. "I wasn't weighing your suggestion, Colin, I was planning. We can do it. My only concern is that you aren't at your full strength just yet, but no matter. I will take care of everything. We will leave at midnight." She rose and shook out her skirts. She looked every bit as determined as her brother had. "This will hurt my brother, but it is my life and I must choose to do what I believe is best for me. Oh goodness, there is much to be done! Don't worry. You must rest and regain your strength." She leaned down and kissed him. He had no chance to respond, for she was already striding toward the door, her steps so long that the material of her gown pulled across her buttocks and thighs. She turned, her hand on the doorknob. "Douglas isn't stupid. He will know immediately what we've done. I will plan an alternate route. We must throw him off. It's a good thing that I'm tightfisted. I have a good two hundred pounds of my own. After we're wed, Douglas will have no choice but to give you my dowry, and you won't have to worry about losing everything anymore. He must do it quickly—we will make him understand that—I know that you must have the money very soon. I'm truly sorry about that letter, Colin. Some people are the very devil." With that, she was gone. He could swear he heard her whistling.

It was all right. He'd won; against all odds, he'd won, and he was doing only what she wanted, after all. She'd been the one to push it, not he. Ah, but the guilt was there, deep and roiling inside him. Even having known Joan only a short time, Colin had no doubt that she would have them off exactly at the time she'd determined, in a very comfortable carriage that her brother would have a devil of a time tracing. He wouldn't be surprised if she even had matching grays pulling the carriage. He closed his eyes, then opened them. He had to eat everything on his plate. He had to become strong again, and very soon.

My brothers will kill me, she thought as the closed carriage bowled through the dark night toward the Reading road. Colin was sleeping beside her, exhausted. She leaned over and lightly kissed his cheek. He didn't stir. She tucked the blankets more closely around him. He was quiet, his breathing deep and even. Excellent, no nightmares. It still surprised her that the illness had so weakened him. But it didn't matter now. He would be well again, very soon, particularly since she would be the one to see to him.

She loved him so much she hurt with it. No one would ever come between them. No one would ever harm him again. It is my life, she thought, not Douglas's or Ryder's or anyone else's. Yes, it's my life, and I love him and trust him and he is already my husband, my mate in my heart.

She thought of her mother and how she'd managed to grind poor Finkle under just that afternoon, and sailed into Colin's bedchamber like the Queen's flagship. Colin had grinned as he'd told her that her mother had stood there, eyeing him for the longest time, and then she'd said, "Well, young man, I understand you want to marry my daughter for her dowry."

Colin smiled at Joan's mother and said, "Your daughter resembles you greatly. She's lucky, as am I. I must marry for money, ma'am, I have no choice in the matter. However, your daughter is beyond anything I could have expected. I will take good care of her."

"You speak with a honeyed tongue, sir, and it is entirely acceptable to me that you continue doing so. Now, pay attention to me. Joan is a hoyden. You will have to find some way to control her pranks, for she is quite good at them; indeed, she is known far and wide for them. Her brothers have always applauded her escapades, for they are imbeciles when it comes to proper feminine propriety. It is thus your responsibility now. She also reads. Yes, I am being truthful to you, I feel I must. She *reads*"— the dowager drew a deep, steadying breath—"even treatises and tomes that should rightfully be covered with dust. I am not responsible for this failing. It is again her brothers who haven't shown her the correct way to comport herself."

"She truly reads, my lady? Tomes and such?"

"That is correct. She has never bothered even to hide her books beneath her chair when a gentleman visits. It is provoking and I try to scold her, but she only laughs. What could I do? There, I have told you the truth. Joan may suffer for it if you decide her character is too malformed for you to wed her."

"It will be my problem, my lady, as you said. I will ensure that she reads only those things I deem appropriate for a young wife."

The dowager countess beamed at him. "This is excellent. I am further pleased that you don't speak like a Scottish heathen."

"No, ma'am. I was educated in England. My father believed that all Scottish nobility should speak the King's English."

"Ah, your father was a wise man. You're an earl, I understand. A seventh earl, which means that your title goes back a goodly way. I don't approve of newcomers to the peerage. They're upstarts and believe themselves to be equal to the rest of us, which, of course, they're not."

He nodded, his serious expression never faltering. The interrogation had continued until Sinjun had flown into the room, gasped, then said firmly, "Is he not handsome and terribly clever, Mother?"

"I suspect he'll do, Joan," the dowager countess said as she turned to face her daughter. "He has come to rescue you from a spinster's fate, thank the good Lord. Were he ugly or deformed or obnoxious of character, I should have to refuse him—though it would be a close thing, since you grow older by the day, and thus fewer gentlemen want you for their wife— but our consequence would demand it. Yes, this is a good thing. He is handsome, although too dark. He resembles Douglas. Odd that neither you nor Alexandra seems to mind. Now, Joan, you will not allow him or yourself to fall into slovenly Scottish ways once you return to that *place*. I am glad you brought him here to the house. I shall visit him every day and teach him about the Sherbrookes and his duty to you and to our family."

"I should be charmed, ma'am," Colin said.

That had gone off splendidly, Sinjun thought, calming her breath. She'd been scared to death when Finkle had told her that her mother had descended upon Colin. She saw that Colin was grinning at his own cleverness, and she leaned down and kissed him. "You did well with her. Thank you."

"I outlasted her, that's all. And I heaped her coffers with Spanish coin. She likes Spanish coin."

"It's true. Neither Douglas nor Ryder is much in the habit of flattering her. She misses it. You did well, Colin."

She wanted to kiss him now, but she feared to awaken him. There would be time, all the time in the world. By the time they reached Scotland, by way of the Lake District, she would not be a virgin any longer, she was planning on that. A girl couldn't elope with a gentleman and emerge unscathed. She would ensure that she was very well scathed indeed. Their marriage, once in Scotland, would be a mere formality.

Sinjun slipped her hand beneath the blanket and closed her fingers around his hand, a strong hand, lean and powerful. She thought of his wife, a woman now dead. She'd asked him nothing more about it, and she wouldn't. If he wished to tell her more about his first wife and how she had died, he would. Sinjun wondered what her name was.

She also wondered if she would ever tell him that her brother had spoken to her of the letter long before she'd gone to his room. She'd even read it, twice. She'd argued only briefly with Douglas, knowing well he was worried about her, and knowing as well that she must argue with him, else he would be suspicious. Oh yes, she'd agreed with him, yielding to his demand that the marriage be postponed until the charge of murder could be resolved. All the while she was determined to elope with Colin that very night. Perhaps Colin would find out that it had been she who had maneuvered him into making his elopement suggestion, perhaps sometime in the misty future.

It was a pity that she must hold her tongue when it itched to be nothing more than truthful, but she knew men abhorred the notion that they could be manipulated. The thought of a woman managing them sent them into a rage. She would spare his male pride, at least until he was completely well again. And perhaps until he came to care for her. For a moment, the thought of telling him the truth made the misty future look on the dark and gloomy side.

CHAPTER
=== 5 ===

"WE ARE ONLY GOING as far as Chipping Norton, to the White Hart," Sinjun told Colin when he stirred. "We will be there in another hour. How do you feel?"

"Bloody tired, dammit."

She patted his arm. "You didn't say that with much heat, Colin, which means you're probably a good deal more than tired; you're exhausted, what with all our hurrying and sneaking about. But you'll get your strength back more and more each day. Don't worry. We won't be to Scotland for another six days as best as I can figure it. You will have plenty of time to mend."

Because it was dark inside the carriage Sinjun couldn't see the irritation in his eyes, and it was there, for he felt helpless, unmanned, like a small child in the care of a nanny, only this nanny was just nineteen years old. He grunted.

"Why in God's name did you pick the White Hart?"

She giggled. An unexpected sound from a nanny, Colin thought with surprise. "It was because of the stories I heard Ryder and Douglas telling Tysen, and he was appalled, naturally, since he was studying to be a man of the cloth. Of course Ryder and Douglas were laughing their heads off."

"And none of them had any idea that you—the infant daughter of the house—were eavesdropping."

"Oh no," she said, waving her hand airily as she smiled. "No idea at all. I got quite good at it by the time I was seven years old. I have this feeling you know all about the White Hart and how the young gentlemen at Oxford spent many evenings there with their light-o'-loves."

Colin was silent.

"Are you remembering your own assignations?"

"Yes, as a matter of fact. The wife of one of my dons used to meet me there. Her name was Matilda, and she was so blond her hair was nearly white. Then there was the barmaid at the Flaming Dolphin in Oxford. She was a wild one, insatiable I remember, loved the feather ticks at the White

Hart. Then there was Cerisse—a made-up name, but who cared? Ah, all that red hair."

"Perhaps we shall have the same bedchamber or bedchambers. Perhaps we should simply hire the entire inn, to cover all the possibilities, so to speak. A symbolic gesture of your sown wild oats."

"You're a very inappropriate virgin, Joan."

She looked at him closely. The moon had finally come from behind thick dark clouds, and she could at last see his face. He was pale, she could see that, and looked dreadfully pulled. The fever must have been more devastating than she'd thought to have left him so very weak. "You don't have to worry about merely sleeping next to me tonight, Colin. You can even snore if it pleases you to do so. I don't mind being a virgin until you have all your strength back."

"Good, because that's what you're going to remain." He felt the rawness in his thigh and wondered why he yet cared that she shouldn't know about it. It didn't really matter, not now.

"Unless, of course," she said, leaning closer to him, her voice dropping to what she hoped was a seductive whisper, and wasn't at all, "you would like to tell me how to go about accomplishing what it is that should be done. My brothers always accused me of being a dreadfully fast learner. Would you like that?"

He wanted to laugh, but ended by groaning.

Sinjun was forced to assume that was a no, and sighed.

The White Hart stood in the middle of the small marketing town of Chipping Norton, comfortably set in the Cotswolds. It was a fine, very picturesque Tudor inn, so old and rustic Sinjun felt charmed at the same time she was praying for it not to fall down around their ears. So this was where many of the young men came for their trysts. It did look rather romantic, she thought, and sighed again.

There wasn't a soul to be seen, for it was three o'clock in the morning. Still, Sinjun was far too excited to be tired. She'd managed to escape her brother, and that was no mean feat. Sinjun was out of the carriage in a trice, giving orders to the driver, a man of few words, bless him, and big pockets to hold more guineas than she'd planned to pay him. But she wasn't at all worried. If she ran out of money, she'd simply sell her pearl necklace. Nothing was more important than Colin and getting herself safely wedded to him. She turned to help him down from the carriage.

"You'll be in bed in a trice. I'll go in if you'd like to wait here, Colin, and—"

"Hush," he said. "I will deal with our ostler. He's a dirty old lecher, and I don't want him getting the wrong idea. Damn, I wish you had a wedding ring. Keep your gloves on. You are my wife and I will see to things."

"All right." She beamed at him, then frowned. "Oh dear, do you need money?"

"I have money."

Nevertheless, Sinjun dug into her reticule and pulled out a sheaf of pound notes. "Here. I would feel better if you keep it." She gave him a sunny smile.

"Let's get this over with before I fall on my face. Oh yes, keep your mouth shut."

It was as they walked across the quiet, dark courtyard that Sinjun noticed how badly he was limping. She opened her mouth and then closed it again.

Ten minutes later Sinjun opened the door to a small bedchamber set under the dark eaves and stepped back for Colin to enter first. "I think the ostler believes we lied," she said, not at all concerned. "But you did very well with him. I think he's afraid of you. You're a nobleman, and thus quite unpredictable."

"Aye, he probably did think I lied, the fat old carp." Colin looked toward the bed and nearly moaned with the pleasure that awaited him. He felt her hands on his cloak and stilled. "I doubt he'd recognize a husband and wife if he attended their wedding."

"Let me help you." She did, efficient as a nanny, and it irritated him, but he held still, just looking at that bed. He wanted to sleep for a week. "If you will sit down I'll pull off your boots."

That was soon done. She'd had enough practice with her brothers. Sinjun stepped back. "Shall I do more?"

"No," he said. "Just turn your back."

She obligingly did as he bade, removing her own shoes and stockings, hanging up her cloak and his in the small armoire provided. She turned back when she heard the bed creak. He was lying on his back, his eyes closed, the covers drawn up to his bare chest. His arms were at his sides, on top of the blanket.

"This is all very odd," she said, chagrined that her voice sounded so much like a maiden's, all skinny and scared.

He didn't answer her and she was emboldened to continue. "You see," she said slowly, "it's true that I am rather outspoken, I guess you'd say, but my brothers have always encouraged me to speak my mind. So it was the same with you. But now, well, it feels strange, being in this room with you, and I know you don't have your clothes on and I'm supposed to climb in on the other side of that bed and—"

Her monologue was interrupted by a low rumbling snore.

Sinjun had to laugh at herself. All her soulful meanderings, only for her and the armoire and a sleeping man. She walked quietly to the bedside and looked down at him. He was hers, she thought, all hers, and no one would take him away from her, not even Douglas, no one. Murdered his wife! What arrant nonsense. Lightly, she stroked her fingertips over his brow. He was cool to the touch. The fever was long gone but he was still so very weak. She frowned, then leaned over and kissed his cheek.

Sinjun had never slept with anyone before in her nineteen years, particularly a man who was large and snoring, a man who was so perfect to her that she wanted to spend the rest of the night looking at him and kissing him and touching him. Still, it was strange. Well, she would get used to it. Douglas and Alex always slept in the same bed, as did Ryder and Sophie. It was the way married people did things. Well, except perhaps for her parents; and truth be told, she wouldn't have wanted to sleep in the same bed with her mother, either. She crawled in next to him, and even from nearly a foot away, she could feel the heat from his body.

She lay on her back and stretched out her hand to find his. Instead her hand found his side. He was naked, his flesh smooth and warm. She didn't want to leave that part of him, but she did. It wouldn't be fair to take advantage of him when he was asleep. She laced her fingers through his. Surprisingly, she was asleep very shortly.

Sinjun awoke with a start. Sunlight was pouring through the narrow diamond-paned window. It certainly wasn't the crack of dawn. On the other hand, to get strong again, Colin had to sleep, and a bed was preferable to the jostling he got in the carriage. She lay there a moment, aware that he was beside her, still sleeping soundly. He hadn't moved, but then neither had she. She realized then that the covers weren't tucked up about his neck, where they were supposed to be. Slowly, knowing she shouldn't but unable not to, she turned and looked at him. He'd kicked the covers off and they were tangled around his feet. As for the rest of him, he was there in the bright sunlight for her to see. She'd never before seen a naked man, and she found him as beautiful as she thought she would. But too thin. She stared at his belly and his groin, and at his sex nestled in the thick hair. His legs were long and thick and covered with black hair. He was beyond beautiful; he was magnificent, even his feet. When she finally forced her eyes away from his groin—a difficult task, for she was frankly fascinated—she blinked at the white bandage around his right thigh.

Of course the fever alone hadn't been responsible for his continued illness. She remembered that damned limp of his the previous night. He'd been hurt somehow.

Anger and worry flooded her. She'd been a fool not to suspect that some other injury was at work here. Why the devil hadn't he told her?

Damnation. She scrambled off the bed and pulled on her dressing gown.

"You wretched man," she said under her breath, but it wasn't under enough. "I'm your wife and you should trust me."

"You're not my wife yet and why are you bleating at me?"

His jaw was a stubble of black whiskers, his hair was mussed, but his eyes were alert, such a deep blue that she forgot to speak for a moment, content just to stare at him.

Colin realized that he was naked and said calmly, "Please pull the covers over me, Joan."

"Not until you tell me what happened to you. What is this bandage for?"

"The reason I was so ill was because I was knifed, and like a fool, I didn't see a physician. I didn't want you to know because I could just see you tearing London apart with your bare hands to find the villain and bring me his head on a platter. Now we're out of London so it doesn't matter. You're safe from yourself."

Sinjun simply looked at him. He had a point. She would have been greatly incensed, no doubt about that. She smiled down at him. "Does the bandage need to be changed?"

"Yes, I suppose so. The stitches need to come out tomorrow or the next day."

"All right," she said. "I'll do it. The good Lord knows I've had enough practice with all of Ryder's children."

"Your brother? How many children does he have?"

"I call them his Beloved Ones. Ryder saves children from dreadful situations and brings them to live in Brandon House. There are about a dozen children there right now, but one never knows when another will arrive, or when one will leave to go to a family Ryder has carefully selected. Sometimes it makes you cry, Colin, to see a little one battered by a cruel drunken father or just left in an alley by a gin-soaked mother."

"I see. Get yourself dressed, but first cover me up."

She did, reluctantly, and he found he was chuckling. Never in his life had he met any female like her. Her interest in his body was embarrassing it was so blatant.

Sinjun solved the privacy problem with a blanket hung over an open armoire door. She didn't stop talking to Colin while she dressed. While she was eating her breakfast, she watched him shave. She volunteered to help him bathe, but that treat was denied her. Again, she was ordered to pack their things, her back turned to him. He did, however, allow her to look at his thigh. The wound was healing nicely. Sinjun lightly pressed the flesh around the stitches. "Thank God," she said, "I was so afraid."

"I'm fine now. It's just a matter of building back my strength."

"This is all very strange."

He eyed her, the flamboyant girl who didn't seem to have a fear of anything or anyone, who looked at the world as if it were hers to rearrange and reshape just as she wished. Life, in his brief experience, had a way of knocking that out of one. He found himself rather hoping it wouldn't be knocked out of her for a good long time. She was strong, no fluttering miss, and for that he was grateful. A fluttering English miss would never survive Vere Castle and all its denizens, of that he was sure. Just then he saw a hint of panic in her eyes, and it was that small sign of vulnerability that kept him quiet. She would find out quickly enough.

Then she was laughing and smiling again, even at Mr. Mole, the ostler of the White Hart. When he made a leering comment to her as they were leaving, she merely turned to him and frowned. "It is a pity, sir," she said, "that you must needs be so disagreeable and show so little breeding. My husband and I stopped here only because he is ill. I assure you that we will never come here again, unless he is ill again, which is unlikely because—"

Colin laughed and took her hand.

He soon became markedly silent, and Sinjun left him to his thoughts. He continued silent through the day and the evening and into the next day. He was preoccupied, frankly absent from her, and she decided to allow him the peace to work out whatever was bothering him. What bothered her most was that he had ordered two bedchambers for them, without explanation. She'd left it alone.

It was late the following afternoon, as the carriage bowled toward Grantham, that he turned to face her in the carriage and dropped the boot. "I have given this a lot of thought, Joan. This is difficult for me, but I must do it, to absolve myself of a veritable little bit of my guilt. I abused your brother's hospitality by slipping out like a thief in the night with his sister. No, no, keep quiet. Let me finish. In short, I cannot justify what I've done, no matter how hard I try to rationalize it. However, there is one thing I can do that will hold some honor, that will help me live with myself. I won't take your virginity until our wedding night."

"*What?* You mean I've left you to yourself, been silent as a punch bowl, and over the past day and a half all you've come up with is that bit of arrant nonsense? Colin, listen, you don't know my brothers! We must, that is, you must make me your wife and this very night, else—"

"Enough! You make it seem like I'm going to torture you, for God's sake, rather than preserve your damned innocence. It isn't nonsense, arrant or otherwise. I won't dishonor you in that way; I won't dishonor your family in that way. I was raised to hold honor dear. It's in my blood, in my heritage, generation upon generation of it, even through all the killings, the savage battles, there was honor somewhere lurking about. I must marry quickly to save my family and my holdings, you know that well enough, and to protect them from the damned raiding and lying MacPhersons, but one thing I don't have to do is be a rutting stoat on an innocent girl who isn't yet my wife."

"Who are the MacPhersons?"

"Damnation, I didn't mean to mention them. Forget them."

"But what if Douglas catches us?"

"I will handle it when and if it happens."

"I understand about honor, I truly do, Colin, but somehow it's more than that, isn't it? Do you dislike me so much? I know I'm too tall and perhaps too skinny for your tastes, but —"

"No, you're not too tall or too skinny. Just leave it be, Joan. My mind is made up. I won't take your virginity until we're wed, and that's that."

"I see, my lord. Well, my lord, my mind is also made up. I fully intend for my virginity to be but a memory by the time we reach Scotland. I don't think it reasonable to think that you can simply *handle* Douglas if he catches us. You don't know my brother. I might think I'm clever, all my machinations to evade him, trying alternate routes and all that, but he's as cunning as a snake. No, my virginity is more than just a marital thing, Colin. It's necessary that you rid me of it quickly. I feel very strongly about this, so it's not just that's that. Now, just whose mind is it that will carry the day?"

She wished he'd yell as Douglas and Ryder did, but he didn't, saying only, very calmly, very coldly, "Mine, naturally. I'm the man. I will be your husband and you will obey me. You can begin obeying me now. It will doubtless be good for your character."

"No one has ever spoken to me like that except my mother, and she I could always ignore."

"You won't ignore me. Don't be childish about this. Trust me."

"You're as autocratic as Douglas, damn you, even though you haven't yelled."

"Then you should realize your only choice is to shut your mouth."

"Take out your own stitches," she said, utterly infuriated with him, and turned to look out the window.

"A spoiled English twit. I might have known. I'm disappointed but not surprised. You can back out of this, my dear, you surely can, with all your English virtue still intact. You're not only outspoken, you're a termagant if you don't get your way, a hoyden, and perhaps even bordering on an overbearing shrew. I begin to think your groats aren't worth all the suffering."

"What suffering, you beetle-brained clod? Just because I disagree with you, it doesn't make me a termagant or a shrew or anything else horrible you just called me."

"You want to back out of this? Fine, have the man turn the carriage around."

"No, damn you, that would be too easy. I will marry you and teach you what it is to trust someone and confide in someone, to compromise with someone."

"I'm not used to trusting a woman. I already told you that I liked you, but anything else was out of the question. Believe it. Now, I'm so tired my eyes are crossing. You will be my wife. Act like a lady, if you please."

"As in fold my hands in my lap and twiddle my thumbs?"

"Yes, a good start. And keep your mouth closed."

She could only stare at him. It was as if he were trying to drive her away, but she knew he couldn't want her to back out of the marriage. It was male perversity. Besides, she also had no choice but to marry him. She wanted to yell that it was too late for her, far too late. She'd given him her heart. But she wasn't about to let him become a tyrant, and groveling at his feet with such a confession would surely make him into a veritable Genghis Khan, given his present attitude. Oh yes, she knew all about tyrants, even though Douglas assumed the tyrant mantle now very rarely. Ah, but she remembered those early days when he'd first wed Alexandra. She gave Colin a sideways look but held her peace. She became silent as a stone. Colin slept until they arrived at the Golden Fleece Inn in Grantham late that evening.

Sinjun assumed that Colin did take out his own stitches, for he again procured two bedchambers, bade her a dutiful good night before her door, and left her. The next morning he hired a horse, merely telling her shortly at breakfast that he was bored with riding inside the damned carriage. Ha! He was bored with riding with her. He rode outside the carriage for the entire day. If his leg bothered him, he gave no sign of it. In York, Sinjun hired a horse, with a look daring him to object, but he only shrugged, as if to say, it's your money. If you insist upon wasting it, it doesn't surprise me. She was glad now that he'd decided not to go to the Lake District, though she'd argued vehemently with him at the time. He wanted to get home more quickly, and even her warnings of Douglas with three guns and a sword hadn't dissuaded him. She thought, as the wind whipped through her hair, that Lake Windermere was too romantic a spot to share with him. This endless gallop north with the silent man riding just ahead of her wasn't at all the way she'd imagined her elopement to Scotland to be.

The morning they rode ahead of the carriage across the border into Scotland, Colin reined in and called out, "Stop a moment, Joan. I would speak to you."

They were in the Cheviot Hills, low, rangy mounds that were mostly bare, stretching as far as she could see. It was beautiful and lonely as the devil and not a soul was to be seen, not a single dwelling. The air was warm and soft, the smell of heather strong. She said to him, "I'm pleased you remember how to speak, given how long it's been."

"Hold your tongue. It defies belief that you are angry with me just because I wouldn't bed you, and here you are a young lady of quality."

"That isn't the point—"

"Then you're still holding your sulk that we didn't go to the Lake District, a ridiculous ploy that wouldn't fool an idiot."

"No, I'm not angry about that. All right, what do you want, Colin?"

"First of all, do you still want to marry me?"

"If I refuse, will you force me because you must marry me because you need my money?"

"Probably. I would think about it, perhaps."

"Excellent. I won't marry you. I refuse. I will see you in hell first. Now force me."

He smiled at her, the first time in four days. He actually smiled. "You aren't boring, I'll give you that. Your outrageousness even occasionally pleases me. Very well, we'll marry tomorrow afternoon when we reach Edinburgh. I have a house on Abbotsford Crescent, old and creaky as the devil and needs money poured into it, but not as badly as Vere Castle. We will stop there and I will try to have a preacher wed us. Then we will ride to Vere Castle the following day."

"All right," she said, "but I will tell you again, Colin, and you really should believe me. Douglas is dangerous and smart; he could be anywhere waiting for you. He conducted all sorts of dangerous missions against the French. I tell you, we should wed immediately and—"

"That is, we will ride to Vere Castle unless you're too sore to ride. Then I will prop you up in the carriage."

"I don't know what you're talking about."

"I'm talking about taking you—our wedding night—until you're raw with it."

"You're being purposefully crude, Colin, purposefully nasty and unkind."

"Perhaps, but you're in Scotland now, and you will soon be my wife, and you will learn that you owe me your loyalty and your obedience."

"You were one way when we first met. Then, when you were ill, you were really quite nice, albeit irritable because you hate weakness. Now you're just being a fool. I will marry you and every time you're a fool in the future, I'll do something to you to make you regret it." There, she thought, that was setting things straight. She loved him to distraction—a fact she knew well that he knew, and thus his outlandish behavior toward her—but she wouldn't allow his character flaws or his outmoded notions of husbands and wives to interfere with what she insisted that he be.

He laughed. It was a strong, deep laugh, a laugh of a man who knew his own worth and knew it to be above that of the girl who rode beside him. He was well again and strong of body and ready to take on the world—with her groats. "I look forward to your attempts. But be warned, Joan, Scottish men are masters in their own homes, and they beat their wives, just as your honorable and kind Englishmen occasionally do."

"That is absurd! No man I know would ever raise a finger against his wife."

"You have been protected. You will learn." He started to tell her that he could easily lock her in a musty room in his castle, but he kept quiet. They weren't yet married. He gave her a look, then a salute, and kicked his horse in his sides to gallop ahead of her.

They arrived at the Kinross house on Abbotsford Crescent at three o'clock the following afternoon. It had been drizzling lightly for the past hour, but Sinjun was too excited to be bothered about the trickles of water down her neck. They'd ridden the Royal Mile, as fine as Bond Street, Sinjun gawking all the way at the fine gentlemen and ladies who looked just as they did in London, and all the equally fine shops. Then they turned off to the left onto Abbotsford Crescent. Kinross House was in the middle of the crescent, a tall, skinny house of red aged brick, quite lovely really, with its three chimney stacks and its gray slate roof. There were small windows, each leaded, and she guessed the house to be at least two hundred years old. "It's beautiful, Colin," she said as she slipped off her mare's back. "Is there a stable for our horses?"

They cared for their own mounts, then paid the driver and removed their trunks and valises. Sinjun couldn't stop talking she was so excited. She kept tossing her head toward the castle that stood atop its hill, exclaiming that she'd seen paintings of it, but to actually see it all shrouded in gray mist, the power of it, how substantial and lasting it was, left her nearly speechless. And Colin only smiled at her, amused at her enthusiasm, for he was tired, the rain was dismal, something he'd grown up with, and the castle, indeed, was a fortress to be reckoned with, but it was just there, brooding over the city, and who really thought about it?

The door was opened by Angus, an old retainer who had been a servant to the Kinross family his entire life. "My lord," he said. "Dear me and dear all of us. Oh Gawd. Aye, the young lassie is wi' ye, I see. More's the pity, aye, sech a pity."

Colin grew very still. He was afraid to know, but he asked nonetheless, "How do you know about my young lassie, Angus?"

"Och, dear and begorra," said Angus, pulling on the long straight strands of white hair that fell on each side of his round face.

"I hope you don't mind that I invited myself in. Your man here didn't want to let me over the threshold, but I insisted," Douglas said as he came up behind Angus. He was smiling through his teeth. "You damned bastard, do come in. As for you, Sinjun, you will feel the flat of my hand soon enough."

Sinjun looked at her furious brother and smiled. It was difficult, but she managed it, for she wasn't at all surprised to see him. Ah, but Colin was, she saw. She'd warned him, damn his stubborn hide. She stepped forward. "Hello, Douglas, do forgive me for giving you such a worry but I was afraid you would be intractable. You have that tendency, you know. Welcome to our home. Yes, Douglas, I'm a married lady, married in *all* ways, I might add, so you can forget any notions about annulment. I would appreciate your not trying to kill him, for I'm too young to be a widow."

"Blessed hell! The damned devil you say!" And there was her brother Ryder, standing at Douglas's elbow, and he looked fit to kill, flushed to his eyebrows, unlike Douglas, who never stirred when his anger was deep and burning, just remained cold-stone still and yelled. "Is this the fortune-hunting bastard who stole you from Douglas?"

"Yes, that's him," Douglas said through still-gritted teeth. "Blessed hell, your *husband!* Damn you, Sinjun, there's been no time. Ryder and I have ridden like the very devil. You're lying, Sinjun, tell me you're lying, and we will leave right now, right this instant, and return to London."

Colin stepped into his own house and raised his hands. "Be quiet, all of you! Joan, step aside. If your brothers want to kill me, they will, regardless of your trying to protect me by flapping your petticoats at them. Angus, go see to some refreshment. My wife is thirsty, as am I. Gentlemen, either kill me now or come into the drawing room."

This all seemed very familiar, and Sinjun was forced to smile. "There are no umbrella stands about," she said, but Douglas wasn't to be drawn. He was stiff and cold and looked severe as an executioner.

"Ryder, this is my husband, Colin Kinross. As you can see, he shouts as loudly as you and Douglas do, and he looks a bit like Douglas, only he's more handsome, much wittier, and of a more reasonable nature."

"Bosh!"

"How do you know, Ryder? This is the first time you've ever met him. Colin, this is my brother Ryder."

"It's certainly going to be interesting," Colin said.

Ryder studied him closely, all the while yelling, "I can tell by the look of him that he's none of those things. He's about as reasonable as

Douglas here, no more, certainly. Damnation, Sinjun, you've been a perfect idiot, my girl. Let me tell you—"

"Go into the drawing room, Ryder. You can tell me all you wish to there." Sinjun turned to Colin and raised a brow.

"This way," he said, and led them across the narrow entrance hall that smelled musty and clogged the nostrils with dust, through a single door into a room that could kindly be called elegantly shabby.

"Oh dear," Sinjun said, eyeing the room. "It's proportions are quite nice, Colin, but we must get a new carpet, new draperies—goodness, those must be eighty years old! And just look at those chairs—the fabric is rotting right off them."

"Be quiet!"

"Oh, Douglas, I'm sorry. You aren't interested in all my housewifely plans, are you? Please sit down. As I said, welcome to my new home. Colin tells me the house is all of two hundred years old."

Douglas looked at Colin. "Are you well yet?"

"Yes."

"You swear you're fully and completely healed and back to your strength?"

"Yes."

"Good, damn you!" Douglas leaped on him, his hands going for his throat. Colin, no fool, was ready for him. They went down to the floor, dust billowing up from the faded carpet, and rolled, Douglas on top, then Colin, each kicking the other with his legs, each rolling the other over.

Sinjun looked at Ryder, whose lovely blue eyes were narrowed and filled with fury. "We must stop this. It happened before. It would be a very bad melodrama were it not so dangerous. Will you help me? It is absurd. You're all supposed to be civilized gentlemen."

"Forget civilization. If by any wild chance your *husband* just happens to knock Douglas out, it's my turn."

Sinjun shouted, "Blessed hell! Stop it!"

There was no discernible effect.

She looked wildly around for a weapon. No blessed umbrella stand or any other piece of dilapidated furniture she could use to bash Douglas's head.

Then she saw just the thing. She calmly picked up a small hassock nearly hidden behind a sofa and swung it with all her might, striking Douglas's back. He roared, jerking about and staring at his sister, who now had the hassock raised over her head.

"Get off him, Douglas, or I swear I'll break your stubborn head."

"Ryder, take care of our idiot sister whilst I kill this mangy bastard."

But it wasn't to be. The panting, the cursing, the grunts were all abruptly stopped by the obscenely loud report of a gun. In the closed room it sounded like a cannon.

Angus stood in the open doorway, an old blunderbuss smoking in his hands. There was a huge hole in the ceiling of the drawing room.

Sinjun dropped the hassock with a loud thud. She looked at the hole, smoking and blackening the ceiling all around it, and said to Douglas, "Is my dowry large enough to repair even that?"

CHAPTER
══ 6 ══

ANGUS STOOD QUIETLY in the corner of the drawing room, holding the blunderbuss close, eyes still watchful, even after he'd announced, "Forgive me, my lords, but her ladyship here bain't much of a Kinross yet, and thus if someone must have his neck shot through, it will be one of ye even though yer her brothers. Ye also be Sassenach toffs, an' that makes me finger itch like th' divil."

And that was that, Ryder thought, after he'd figured out the essence, which wasn't at all good as far as he and Douglas were concerned.

Now Colin and Sinjun sat side by side on the worn pale blue brocade sofa, Ryder and Douglas on equally worn chairs facing them. There was no rug between them. Silence was the news of the day.

"We were married in Gretna Green," Sinjun announced.

"The devil you were," Douglas said. "Even you, Sinjun, wouldn't be that stupid. You would think that I would go there immediately, and thus you would go elsewhere."

"No, you're wrong. After I thought that, I realized that you wouldn't go there, that you would come to Edinburgh instead and quickly find Colin's house. You see, I know you very well, Douglas."

"This has nothing to do with anything," Ryder said. "You're coming home with us, brat."

Colin raised a black eyebrow. "Brat? You're calling her brat and she's Lady Ashburnham, my wife?"

Sinjun said to him as she patted his hand in what she hoped was a wifely gesture, "It takes my brothers time to change and adapt to things. Ryder will come about, just give him a year or so."

"I am not amused, Sinjun!"

"No, neither am I. I am married. Colin is my husband. It was doubtless the damned MacPhersons who wrote the anonymous letter to Douglas claiming Colin killed his wife. They're coward and liars and they're out to destroy him, and what better way to go about it than to begin by ruining his nuptials with me?"

Colin stared at her. She was frightening. He'd mentioned the MacPhersons but one time, yet she'd put it all together. Of course, he hadn't really spoken to her for nearly three days. She'd had a lot of hours to think and sort through things. Thank God she didn't know the full extent of it—yet.

A very fat woman came into the room. She was wearing a huge red apron that went from right beneath the massive bosom of her black gown to her knees. She was smiling widely. "Och, ye're here, me lord. It's home ye be at last. And this sweet little lassie be yer wife?" She curtsied, using her apron.

"Hello. What is your name?"

"Agnes, me lady. I'm here wi' Angus. I do what he doesn't, which be most of everything. Look at the hole in the ceiling! My Angus always was excellent at his work. Be any of ye hungry?"

There was a chorus of yeas and Agnes took herself off. Angus hadn't moved from his spot in the corner, blunderbuss still held firmly against his chest.

It was at that moment Colin realized that he'd been silent as the grave. He cleared his throat. It was his home, after all. "Gentlemen, would you care for a brandy?"

Ryder nodded and Douglas clenched his fists again and said, "Yes. Good smuggled French brandy?"

"Naturally."

Well, that was something, Sinjun thought, relaxing just a bit. Men who drank together couldn't smash each other, not with brandy snifters in their hands. Of course, they could throw the snifters, but she'd never seen either Ryder or Douglas do that.

"How are Sophie and all my nephews, and the children?"

"They're all well except for Amy and Teddy, who were fighting in the hayloft and a bale of hay rolled off its stack and knocked both of them out and down to the ground. No broken bones, thank God."

"I expect Jane lambasted them but good." Jane was the directress of Brandon House, or Bedlam House, as Sinjun called the lovely large three-story house that lay but one hundred yards from Chadwyck House, the residence of Ryder, Sophie, and their young son, Grayson.

"Oh yes, Jane had a rare fit, threatened to pull ears and dish out bread and water after they recovered from all their bruises. I think that's what she did do, adding just a dollop of jam to their bread. Then Sophie kissed them both and yelled at them as well."

"And then what did you do, Ryder?"

"I just hugged them and said if they were ever so stupid again, I would be very upset with them."

"A dire threat," Sinjun said, and laughed. She rose and walked to

Ryder, leaned down, and hugged him close. "I've missed you so very much."

"Blessed hell, brat, I'm exhausted. Douglas dragged me out of bed—and Sophie was so warm, it was damned difficult to leave her—and he forced me to ride like the devil himself were snapping at our heels. He said he would outfox you, bragged, he did, but you won, didn't you?"

"Here is your brandy, my lord."

"I'm not a lord, Kinross. I'm a second son. I'm only an honorable, and that strikes me as a mite ridiculous. Just call me Ryder. You are my brother-in-law, at least until Douglas decides whether or not he will kill you. Take heart, though. Not many years ago Douglas gave a good deal of thought to killing our cousin Tony Parrish—called him a rotten sod—but in the end he gave it up."

Angus relaxed a bit.

"That situation is nothing like this one, Ryder."

Angus snapped back to attention.

"True, but Sinjun is married to the fellow, Douglas, no way around that. You know she's never one to do things half-measure."

Douglas cursed foully.

Angus relaxed a mite, for curses were a wise man's way to relieve his spleen.

Colin strolled to Douglas and handed him a brandy. "How long do the two of you plan to stay? Don't get me wrong. You're welcome as my brothers-in-law to remain as long as you wish, but there are few furnishings here and thus it wouldn't be very comfortable for you."

"Who are the MacPhersons?" Douglas asked.

Colin said calmly enough, "They are a clan who have feuded with my clan for several generations. Indeed it all started around 1748, after the Battle of Culloden. There was bad blood there because the laird of the MacPhersons stole my grandfather's favorite stallion. The feuding finally stopped when I married the current laird's daughter, Fiona Dahling MacPherson. When she died so mysteriously some six months ago, her father seemed not to blame me. However, the eldest brother, Robert, is vicious, unreasonable, greedy, and utterly unscrupulous. When my cousin visited me in London, he told me the MacPhersons, led by that bastard Robert MacPherson, had already raided my lands and killed two of my people. Joan is correct. It is very likely one of them penned that letter. The only thing is, I can't imagine how they knew where I was or how any of the sniveling cowards had the cunning to come up with such a plot."

"Why the hell do you call her Joan?" Ryder said.

Colin blinked. "It's her name."

"Hasn't been for years. Her name is Sinjun."

"It's a man's nickname. I don't like it. She is Joan."

"Dear God, Douglas, he sounds just like Mother."

"True," Douglas said. "Sinjun will bring him around. Back to the MacPhersons. I don't want my sister in any danger. I won't allow it."

"She may be your sister," Colin said very quietly, "but she is my wife. She will go where I go and she will do as I bid her. I will keep her from harm, you needn't worry." He turned to Sinjun. His eyes glinted in the soft afternoon light but his expression remained utterly impassive, as did his voice. "Isn't that right, my dear?"

"Yes," she said without hesitation. "Shortly, we will travel northward to Vere Castle. I will take very good care of Colin, neither of you need worry."

"It isn't that poaching bastard I'm worried about," Douglas yelled at her. "I'm worried about you, dammit."

"That's very nice of you, Douglas, and understandable, since you're fond of me."

"I'd like to take a strap to your bottom."

"Only I will take straps to her in the future," Colin said firmly. "She doesn't believe that now, but she will learn."

"Sounds to me," Ryder said very slowly, looking back and forth between the two of them, "yes, it does seem that you just might have met your match, Sinjun."

"Oh yes," she said, purposefully misunderstanding her brother. "He is my match, my mate for life. I was waiting for him and at last he found me." She walked over to her soon-to-be-husband, who was standing by the mantel holding a brandy snifter. She put her arms around his chest, leaned up, and kissed his mouth. Douglas growled and Ryder, dear blessed Ryder, laughed.

"All right, you're no longer a brat," Ryder said. "I would like another brandy, Colin, if you please. Sinjun, do remove your arms from him, it might save him from further pummeling by Douglas."

"This isn't settled yet," Douglas said. "I'm very upset with you, Sinjun. You could have trusted me, you could have spoken to me. Instead you just stole out of the house like a damned thief."

"But Douglas, I understood your position, truly, and I respected it. But the fact was and is that Colin is innocent of any wrongdoing, and what's more, he had instant need of my money and simply couldn't wait for some sort of resolution that probably would never come. I was rather concerned about that, since both you and my money would still be in London. But that's not the case now, thank God. I am glad you came—albeit you weren't happy when you arrived—so that you and Colin can work it all out."

"Joan," Colin said very quietly, "one doesn't speak about settlements in such a way. Certainly not in front of ladies, and not in the drawing room, under such oddly unconventional conditions."

"You mean because there's a hole in the ceiling?"

"You know very well what I mean."

"But why ever not? It's my dowry, and you're my husband. Let's get on with it."

Douglas laughed, he couldn't help himself.

"I think," Ryder said, "that this means your hide just might remain on your body, Colin. Sinjun, take yourself off and the gentlemen will deal with all the money matters."

"Good. Don't forget Great-Aunt Margaret's inheritance to me, Douglas. You told me once it was an impressive number of groats and all invested on the 'Change."

"We're as good as married, Colin."

He turned to face her in the dark-cornered earl's suite at the end of an equally dark and quite dismal corridor on the second floor of Kinross House. There was but one branch of candles lit and he was holding it. He set it down on a battered surface that had once held all his father's shaving objects.

He just shook his head. "I know we must pretend that we are, and I intend to do so until your brothers leave. I will sleep with you in that bed, and as you can see, it's large enough for a regiment. You will keep your hands to yourself, Joan, else I'll be displeased with you."

"I simply don't believe this, Colin. I do hope you aren't the sort of person who makes a decision, then sticks to it whether it's good or miserably bad."

"I'm right in this decision."

"You're ridiculous."

"A wife shouldn't be so disrespectful to her husband."

"You're not my husband yet, damn you! What you are is the most stubborn, the most obstinate—"

"There's a screen in the corner. You may change behind it."

When they were lying side by side in the mammoth bed, Sinjun staring up at the dark bed hangings, which smelled moldy, he said to her, "I like your brothers. They're honorable and quite fit as friends. As relatives, they're superlative."

"So nice of you to say so."

"Don't sulk, Joan."

"I'm not sulking, I'm cold. It's damp in this dreadful room."

He wasn't cold, but then again he was rarely cold. But he knew that if he pulled her into his arms, he would make love to her, and he wouldn't break his vow, particularly with her brothers here under his roof, flesh-and-blood reminders of his perfidy.

He leaned up and grabbed his bedrobe that he'd tossed at the foot of the bed. "Here, put this on. It will wrap around you twice and keep you very warm."

"I am overcome with your generosity and reasonableness."

"Go to sleep."

"Certainly, my lord. Whatever you wish, whatever you demand, whatever you—"

He began snoring.

"I wonder why Douglas didn't demand to see our marriage lines. That isn't like him not to be thorough."

"He just might, mightn't he? Shall we wed tomorrow, whilst your brothers are visiting the Castle? It turns out Douglas has a friend who's a major there, and he wants Ryder to meet him."

"That would be just excellent," Sinjun said. "Colin?"

"What now?"

"Would you just hold my hand?"

He did, and felt very warm fingers. So she was on the verge of freezing to death, was she? He imagined that his soon-to-be-wife would do just about anything to gain what she wanted. He would have to watch her carefully. "I hope you enjoy my dressing gown."

"Oh yes, it's soft and smells like you."

He said nothing to that.

"Wearing it, I can fancy you're touching me everywhere."

At ten o'clock in the morning the following day, Colin and Sinjun were wed by a Presbyterian preacher who had been friends with Colin's uncle Teddy—not his father, Colin explained to her, because his father had been all that was sinful and a rotter. Reverend MacCauley, an ancient relic, was blessed with more hair than any old man should have, but best of all, he was fast with his lines and pronouncements and dictums, the latter being the most important consideration. When they emerged as Lord and Lady Ashburnham, Sinjun gave a skipping little step. " 'Tis done, at last. Now, shall I volunteer to show my brothers our marriage lines?"

"No. Stop, I want to kiss you."

She became still as a stone. "Ah," he said, gently taking her chin in the palm of his hand and raising her face. "You're no longer hell-bent on being bedded, are you? It was all an act. But why?" He stiffened then, his fingers tightening a bit on her chin. "I see now. Even last night you were worried that Douglas and Ryder just might discover that we weren't yet wed. You wanted to protect me, didn't you? You wanted to get your dowry into my hands."

"No," she said. "Not entirely. I could look at you naked until I die. Even your feet are lovely."

"You're always taking me off-stride, Joan. I like it sometimes. Also, just being naked isn't the same thing. What will you do when you're lying on your back in bed naked and I'm standing over you, ready to come to you?"

"I don't know. Close my eyes, I suppose. It sounds rather alarming, though, but not repellent, at least not with you."

He grinned. "I should like to do something about this right this minute. At least within the next hour, at the most. But your brothers are here and I don't think Douglas would take it kindly were I to throw you over my shoulder and haul you upstairs. Tonight then, Joan. Tonight."

"Yes," she said, and stood on her tiptoes, her lips slightly parted. He kissed her lightly, as he would an aunt, and released her.

Abbotsford Crescent was only a fifteen-minute walk from Reverend MacCauley's residence. Colin had stopped Sinjun and was pointing out an old monument from James IV's reign when suddenly, without warning, there was a pinging sound and a shard of rock shot up to strike Sinjun, slicing her cheek. She'd moved in front of Colin and bent over to look at those age-blurred words just a moment before. She jumped now with the shock of it, and slapped her hand to her face. "What was that?"

"Oh hell," Colin shouted, and pushed her to the ground, covering her with his body. Passersby stared at them, hurrying their step, but one man ran over to them.

"A man shot at ye," he said, spitting in the next instant in disgust. "I saw him, standing over there by the milliner's shop, he was. Are ye all right, missis?"

Colin helped Sinjun to her feet. Her hand was pressed to her cheek and blood oozed between her fingers. He cursed.

"Ah, the lassie's hurt. Come along to my house, 'tis just over there, on Clackbourn Street."

"No, sir, thank you very much. We live just in Abbotsford Crescent."

Sinjun stood there numb as a frozen toe, listening to them exchange names and addresses. Colin would come by and speak to the man later. *Someone had shot at her.* It was incredible. It was unbelievable. She still felt no pain in her face, but she felt the wet, sticky blood. She didn't want to see it, so she just kept her palm and fingers pressed tightly to her cheek.

Colin turned back to her, frowning. Without a word, he picked her up in his arms. "Just relax and rest your head against my shoulder."

She did.

Unfortunately for both of them, Ryder and Douglas had just returned when Colin walked in with her. There was no way to hide the blood still seeping from between her fingers, and thus there was pandemonium and flying accusations and questions and yelling, until Sinjun calmly said, "That's quite enough, Douglas, Ryder. I fell, that's all, I just fell like a clumsy clod and cut my face. Stupid, I know, but at least Colin was there with me and carried me home. Now, if you will both just be quiet, I should like to see how much damage there is."

Of course the brothers weren't at all quiet. Sinjun was carried to the kitchen, just as she had once taken Colin to see to his cut lip in the London Sherbrooke kitchen, a fact that wasn't lost on him, she saw. She was set down on a chair and told to hold still.

Douglas automatically demanded warm water and some soap, but it was Colin who firmly removed the soft cloth from his hand and said, "Take your hand away, Joan, and let me see how bad it is."

She closed her eyes and didn't make a sound when he touched the damp cloth to her flesh, wiping away all the blood. The shard of rock had grazed her, and not deeply, thank the good Lord. It looked like a simple scratch, and for that he was grateful, what with her two brothers hovering over him, watching his every move, ready, he supposed, to fling him aside if he didn't do things as they would have done them.

"It's not bad at all," Colin said.

Ryder moved him aside. "An odd cut, Sinjun, but I don't think you'll be scarred. What do you think, Douglas?"

"It doesn't look like a simple scratch; rather, it looks like something sliced across your cheek with great force. How did you do it, did you say, Sinjun? You really didn't expect me to believe this is from a fall?"

Sinjun, without hesitation, collapsed against Colin and moaned. "It hurts so much. I'm sorry, Douglas, but it does hurt."

"It's all right," her husband said quickly, "I'll see to it."

While Colin was dabbing some alcohol on the cut, Douglas was frowning.

Sinjun didn't like that frown at all. "I don't feel well. I daresay I'll be ill very soon. My stomach is turning over."

"It's only a small cut," Douglas said, his frown deepening. "Something that wouldn't even slow you down."

"True," Colin said, "but sometimes a sudden injury knocks the body off its bearings. I do hope she won't retch." It sounded like a threat, and Sinjun said, "My stomach is settling even as you spoke, Colin."

"Good. Look, Douglas, she's very tired, as I imagine you can understand."

There was dead and utter silence. Both brothers stared from their new brother-in-law to their little sister—their little *virgin* sister, their former little virgin sister. It was a huge pill to swallow. It was difficult. Finally Douglas said on a loud sigh, "Yes, I suppose so. Go to bed, Sinjun. We will see you later."

"I won't bandage the cut, Joan. It will heal faster."

She gave her husband a brave smile, yet a smile so pathetic and wretched that Ryder began to frown.

"I don't like this at all," he said to the kitchen at large. "You have no more guile than a pot of daisies, Sinjun, and you're a wretched actress and—" It was then that Agnes walked in and Sinjun closed her eyes in relief. The three men were given to know in short order that they were all next to useless and they'd gotten blood on the kitchen table. And here was the poor little missis, all hurt and them carrying on like three roosters with only one hen.

Ten minutes later Sinjun was lying on the bed in the earl's suite, two blankets pulled over her.

Colin sat down beside her. He looked thoughtful. "Your brothers suspect your retching and moaning was an act. Was that an act?"

"Yes, I had to do something quickly. I wanted to faint, but neither of them would have believed that. I'm sorry, Colin, but I did as best I could. We can't have them know the truth. They'd never leave here, else they'd cosh you on the head and steal me. I couldn't allow that."

He laughed even though he was amazed. "You're apologizing because you got shot and tried to pull the wool over your brothers' eyes. Don't worry, I'll maintain the charade. Rest whilst I speak to them, all right?"

"If you kiss me."

He did, another light, disgustingly brotherlike kiss.

Sinjun wasn't sleeping when Colin came into their bedchamber. She was scared, excited, and at the moment she was holding her breath. He strode to the bed and stood there, staring down at her, the branch of candles raised high in his hand.

"You're turning blue. Breathe."

Her breath came out in a whoosh. "I forgot to for the longest time."

"How does your cheek feel?"

"It's fine, just throbs a bit. I thought dinner went off smoothly, don't you?"

"As well as can be expected with each of your brothers taking turns studying your cheek. At least Agnes sets an excellent table."

"Is all my money in your hands now?"

He thought it a rather odd way of putting it, but merely nodded. "Douglas has written me a letter of credit. In addition, we will visit the manager of the Bank of Scotland tomorrow. He will have his man of business send me all the information I will need for any future financial transactions and the status of all your investments. All is done. Thank you, Joan."

"Was I as much an heiress as you hoped I'd be?"

"I'd say you were more than an adequate heiress. What with your inheritance from Great-Aunt Margaret, you are one of the plumpest-in-the-pocket young ladies in England."

"What are you going to do now, Colin?"

He set the branch of candles down and sat beside her. "Are you cold?"

She shook her head and said, "Yes."

He lightly touched his fingertips close to the now-red slash across her smooth flesh. "I'm very sorry about this. We must talk about it, you know. I hope the bullet was meant for me and you were in the way at the last moment."

"Well, I certainly don't hope that! I don't want anyone trying to shoot you. On the other hand, I don't particularly want to be shot, either." She fell silent, from one instant to the next, silence, and she was still as a stone, frowning.

"What is it?"

"The knife wound in your thigh. What if it wasn't just a robber? What if it was another attempt on your life?"

He merely shook his head. "No, don't go so far afield for blame. London is a nasty place, truth be told, and I wasn't in a very prime location at the time it happened. No, it was just a little bully trying to line his pockets and I was his mark, nothing more. Now, would you like to be made love to? This is your wedding night, after all."

That certainly gave her thoughts a new direction, Colin thought, looking down at his bride of one day. She was wearing a virginal white lawn nightgown that very nearly touched her chin it was so high. Her long, tousled hair was loose to the middle of her back, with several tresses over her shoulder. He lifted a handful of hair and brought it to his face. Soft and thick and the scent of jasmine, if he wasn't mistaken. "So many different shades," he said, quite aware that she was leery about the entire business now, since there was no more need for bravado and self-sacrifice in order to save him. He knew if he'd allowed it, she would have very likely stripped off her clothes, stretched him out on his back, and done the deed herself. And all to protect him and give him her money. She was sweet and guileless and determined and smarter than she should be. He would have to deal strictly with her, this wife of his, else she would take him over, and he would never allow that. Somehow, though, he couldn't quite see himself locking her in a musty tower room.

He was lucky to have found her, no doubt about that. Then he thought about that bullet hitting the rock and the shard slicing her cheek. What if the bullet had hit her? What if the rock shard had struck her eye? He drew back from those thoughts. It hadn't happened. He intended to take measures to protect her, beginning the moment her brothers left on the morrow. They would leave shortly thereafter for Vere Castle. That was the one place in Scotland he could be sure she was safe.

He leaned down and kissed her mouth. She started, then opened her lips, just slightly, but he didn't take her invitation. He continued to kiss her lightly, his tongue stroking her bottom lip but not entering. He continued to kiss her until he felt her begin to relax. He wasn't about to touch her yet. He just held that thick tress of hair in his hand and rubbed it against his face.

He raised his head a bit and said, "You're quite pretty, Joan, quite pretty indeed. I would like to see the rest of you now."

"Isn't my face enough for the moment?"

"I should like to see more of the picture." He should have lit a fire in the blackened fireplace, he realized. He would have liked to stretch her out on her back and look his fill at her, but she'd freeze, and that would never do. Instead, he helped her lift the nightgown over her head, then he gently pressed her again onto her back and drew the covers to just beneath her breasts. He wanted to see and touch and kiss her breasts.

"Now, let me look at you."

Sinjun didn't like this. She covered her breasts with her hands, realized how ridiculous her action was and dropped her arms to her sides. He was completely dressed and here she was like a white lump just lying here. She wasn't in control, he was. She didn't like it one bit.

He straightened and looked at her breasts, not touching them, just looking. "Very nice," he said, a vast understatement. He was surprised that they were so full. She walked like a boy, a coltish walk that was free of the coquette, free of any feminine swaying and teasing. Ah, but her breasts were very nice indeed, high and full and the nipples a soft deep pink.

"Colin?"

"Is that little thin voice actually coming from the woman who wanted to rip my breeches off and have her way with me the instant we left London?"

"Yes, but I don't like this. This is different. The motives are no longer there for getting it done. What's more, you're looking at me—"

"As I recall, you did the same to me, only the covers were down around my ankles. You looked your fill, did you not, and you were fully dressed?"

"Not at first. I was in my nightgown at first."

"But you wouldn't cover me until you'd looked your fill."

"It wasn't enough, Colin. I could have looked for a good deal many more hours."

He had no smart reply to that. He leaned down, not touching her with his hands, and gently took her nipple in his mouth.

He thought she'd try to fling him off her, but she only quivered a bit, then became still as a stone.

"What are you doing, Colin? Surely that—"

He blew warm breath over her and she gasped.

"This is my prelude," he said, and lowered his head again to his pleasant task. Her scent filled his nostrils and he strengthened his pressure on her soft flesh.

"Oh dear, Colin, that feels quite strange."

"Yes, I trust it is also enjoyable."

"I don't know. Perhaps. No, not really . . . oh goodness."

He very gently lifted her breast in the palm of his hand, pushing her firmly against his mouth. When he raised his head to look at her face, he also saw the darkness of his flesh against the white of hers. So different they were.

Perhaps having a wife wasn't going to be such a disaster after all. He wanted to come inside her now, this instant, but he knew he would have to wait. He knew that women needed encouragement, particularly stroking between their thighs, and he knew also that he wanted to taste her, to learn the textures of her soft flesh against his mouth and his tongue.

Enough was enough. It was time to expand upon his prelude. He rose quickly to stand beside the bed. He was quiet a moment, just staring down at this new bride of his, the bride he hadn't wanted, the bride who had saved him and his family for generations to come. He took off his clothes, calm and controlled, just smiling down at her, seeing the anticipation, the banked excitement in her incredible blue eyes—Sherbrooke blue eyes he'd heard them called in London. But he also saw the wariness there; her eyes were following his every move. He shrugged out of his shirt, then sat down to pull off his boots. He didn't turn around when he stripped down his britches; indeed, he never looked away from her. He straightened when he was naked and smiled at her, his arms at his sides. "Look your fill, my dear."

Sinjun looked and she kept looking. Then she shook her head as she said, clearly appalled, "This will never work, Colin. It can't."

"What can't work?" He followed her eyes and looked down at himself. He was fully aroused, something of a surprise since he hadn't really gotten things started yet; he was also a large man, and although in his experience women usually grew quite excited at the sight of him, he imagined that a virgin wouldn't be quite so enthusiastic, at least not at first.

"That," Sinjun said, pointing unnecessarily at him.

"It will be all right, you will see. Could you try to trust me?"

Her throat worked. She couldn't seem to get the words out. She just kept staring at him. "All right," she whispered, pulled the covers to her chin, and slid over to the far side of the bed. "But I don't think trust has much to do with it."

He waited a moment, then said, "Do you have any idea of how all this will work?"

"Oh yes, certainly. I'm not stupid or ignorant, but what I thought can't be right. You're too big and even though I trust you it can't be the way I thought it would be. It's utterly impossible. Surely you can see that."

"Well, no, I can't," he said, and, still smiling at her, he walked to the bed.

CHAPTER
═ 7 ═

SHE'D BEEN SUCH A TEASE, so certain of herself, utterly outrageous in her speech, trying to get him to bed her, yet in truth she was terrified. It amused him, this virginal fear of hers, given all the invitations she'd forced down his throat. He looked down at her, aware that she was trying to shift away from him.

He lifted the covers and climbed in beside her. He came down over her, and her breasts pressed against his chest. She sucked in her breath at the same moment he sucked in his. "This is very nice, Joan," he said, and kissed her even as he rubbed himself against her breasts.

"You feel furry, and it sort of tickles. It's very strange, Colin."

"And you feel soft and warm, like silk slowly rubbing against one's flesh."

His tongue entered her mouth at the same time his hand moved flat and smooth over her belly to curve around her.

His fingers rested there, not moving, just touching her to feel the heat of her and for her to feel the heat of him. Then he merely pressed down, giving her the weight of his hand against her flesh. She quivered, he felt it, and it pleased him. He was also harder than a stone; it was unnerving, nearly painful, and it was also driving him witless.

Sinjun was looking at him when he kissed her. His eyes were closed and his thick black lashes were against his lean cheeks. He was utterly beautiful, and this was what she wanted, what she'd wanted since she'd decided to have him, but goodness, there was so much of him, surely too much of him, much too much, and it couldn't be pleasant, not remotely pleasant. Ah, but his hand and his fingers, resting there, just lightly pressing against her, and it was such a private place, this part of her, yet it felt right for him to have this intimacy with her, perhaps. Perhaps not. This wasn't unpleasant, certainly not, and perhaps he would content himself with this. She rather prayed that he would. Then he opened his eyes.

"Any closer and your eyes will cross," Colin said, and laughed, a rather painful sound because he'd grown even harder than a stone in the past minute, nearly gone beyond anything he could remember except when he'd been a boy and so randy he'd been in constant need; and he wanted to come inside her this moment, this very instant, deep and deeper still, and . . .

"Please," she said, and wrapped her arms around his neck. "Please teach me how to kiss, Colin. I do like kissing. I could kiss you forever."

"There's much more than kissing, but we'll begin there and always come back to it. Just open your mouth to me and give me your tongue."

She did, and when her tongue searched his out, she felt his fingers sliding down, rubbing lightly against her flesh, and she squirmed at the strange sensations it brought to her, so deep inside her, so very low, and she moaned into his mouth, startling both of them.

He lifted his hand and looked at her face at the same time. Her disappointment was clear for him to see. He smiled, albeit painfully. "You like that. Shall I continue?"

"Perhaps it would be all right."

He laughed as he kissed her again, but her moan when he eased his finger inside her made him forget everything but the pounding need he felt, a need that was growing beyond him, beyond his control.

She was very small, this bride of his, and he knew he had to keep control of himself. He wanted to give her pleasure, but he doubted it would be possible this first time. Perhaps it was better just to get this first time over with, and quickly. She was easing around his finger, her warm flesh accommodating him now, and he moved deeper. Yes, she was softening for him and the moistness of her made him picture his sex deep inside her and he nearly went over the edge with lust.

He moaned and shuddered and moaned again, and Sinjun, momentarily loosening herself from the feelings he was building in her belly, snapped her eyes open. "Colin? What's wrong? Did I hurt you?"

"Yes, and it's wonderful. Joan, I must come into you now. You're eased for me, truly, but it will be tight. Trust me. I'll go very slowly, but come into you I must. This first time must be done or there couldn't be a second time, which will be wonderful for you, you'll see, just trust me."

Every pleasant feeling evaporated in the flash of an instant. Sinjun stared at him, now between her legs, raising her knees, positioning her for himself. He was too big, far too big, it was unimaginable. "No," she said, panicked now, as she pressed her fists against his hairy chest. "Please, Colin, I have changed my mind. I should like to wait, perhaps Christmas might be a nice—"

He came into her and she yelled, pressing her hips into the feather mattress, but he only grasped her hips in his hands and pushed deeper and deeper still. She tried to hold herself still, to keep her cries deep in her throat, but it was difficult. She closed her eyes against him and against the pain, but it became only more rending. Then she felt him stop inside her and he was breathing hard, his voice trembling when he said, "Your maidenhead, I've got to get through it. Don't scream. Sweet Jesus, I'm sorry, sweetheart." He pushed forward even before he stopped speaking, and she yelled, loud and hoarse, and he brought his hand down quickly over her mouth, muffling her cries, and he was touching her womb and she hated it, hated the pain and the rawness of it, the alien invasion of her body, but he wasn't hurt, oh no, he was a wild man, driving into her then pulling out, again and again until suddenly he was rigid over her, his back arched, stiff as a board, and she opened her eyes and stared up at him to see that his eyes were closed, his head thrown back, his throat working against what seemed to her to be a raging cataclysm.

He moaned, then yelled, muted because of her brothers, she assumed, then he fell forward on her. She felt him then inside her, the wetness of him, his man's seed, and she felt . . . she didn't know what she felt. The pain he'd inflicted in her body, yes that, certainly, but more than the throbbing pain, the rawness. He'd lied, telling her to trust him, and like a twit she had, at least a little bit, until he'd forced himself into her.

She felt betrayed.

He was breathing hard, his face beside hers on the pillow. His body was heavy on hers. She felt the sheen of sweat on him and on her.

It was difficult for her to speak calmly, because she wanted to strike him and scream at him, but she managed it. "I didn't like that, Colin. It was awful."

His heart was drumming in his ears. He was breathing so hard he thought he would burst with it. He felt as if he'd been flattened, and every minute of his flattening had been wondrous, beyond anything he could have imagined . . . And she didn't like it? It was awful? No, it couldn't be true. He shook his head. He must have misunderstood her.

He calmed his breathing. It took him a good deal of time. She remained quiet, not moving beneath him, and he imagined that he was heavy on her, but he didn't move. He was still inside her, not so deep now, but the feel of her flesh made him shudder with pleasure and need. Finally he managed to raise himself on his elbows. He stared down at his wife.

Unconsciously, he pushed forward and high into her, breaching her deeply, and she winced, gritting her teeth. He stopped immediately.

"I'm sorry," he said, but he wasn't, not for what had happened, because he had enjoyed it more than he ever had in his life. "Your virginity, it's past now, and there won't be any more pain."

Her calm was cracking. "You lied to me, Colin. You said it would work. You told me to trust you."

"Naturally, I'm your husband. It did work, can't you feel me? I'm supposed to be inside you. I'm supposed to spill my seed in your womb. It will be easier next time. Perhaps you will even enjoy it. You did somewhat this time, didn't you?"

"I don't remember."

She didn't damn remember? Ah, but he wanted her again. It surprised him and dismayed him. Surely he wasn't a rutting savage to maul his innocent bride yet again. No, he wasn't. He groaned, feeling her tight and hot around him. It was too much, it was more than a man with few wits left could handle. He stiffened above her and drove deep into her once more.

She yelled at the shock and pain of it. She hit him with her fists, shoving against him, trying to throw him off her, but it only sent him deeper and he just kept driving, feeling her flesh convulse around him, driving him and pushing him, and he couldn't stop himself. He heard her cries but he didn't slow, he couldn't, and again he climaxed, raw groans ripping from his throat.

He was flat on top of her again, breathing hard, wondering what the devil had come over him.

"How many times will you do that?"

"I think I've stopped for a while. Joan, you're not crying, are you? No, tell me you're not crying. I'll hold very still now, I promise."

Her voice came steadier, which relieved him, until he heard her say, "I do care for you a lot, Colin, but it will be difficult to bear this often. It wasn't pleasant. I know we had to do it so that Douglas couldn't take me back to London with him and annual the marriage. But now that you've done it, will you have to do it often?"

He wanted to tell her that he could easily take her again, a third time, perhaps a fourth, but he held his tongue. He'd hurt her, and she had no idea of what pleasure could be. "I'm sorry," he said, and slowly forced himself to pull out of her. He felt the pulling of her flesh, heard her whimper.

"I'm sorry," he said again, and disliked himself for apologizing like a damned parrot.

"I don't understand though."

"What don't you understand?"

"I always thought that Douglas and Alex—that's his wife, you know. Well, I always believed that she much enjoyed staying with him in the same bed. And Ryder and Sophie, too, but now . . . perhaps it's just kissing they enjoy, and the other, they must bear it, they choose to bear it because they love their husbands. But it's difficult, Colin. I didn't realize what it would be like."

"I told you that when I take you again you will enjoy it. I promise you that."

She clearly didn't believe him, not that he could blame her, for hadn't he just lost himself again, slamming into her when he knew it would hurt her? "I'm sorry," he said for yet a third time. "I will make it up to you."

She lay there, sprawled on her back when he rose to stand beside the bed. There was his seed and her virgin's blood on her thighs and on the white sheets. He leaned over her, and Sinjun, fearing the worst, yelled at the top of her lungs.

Then, in the next instant, there was a hammering on the bedchamber door and Douglas was yelling, "What's happening in there? Sinjun, what's wrong?"

"Move out of the way, Douglas, he's killing her!"

It was Ryder who flung open the door and burst into the bedchamber, Douglas on his heels.

There was appalled silence. They stood there, their dressing gowns flapping around their bare legs, staring at their new brother-in-law, who was standing naked by Sinjun, who was sprawled on her back on the bed, but that was just for a flash of an instant, for in the next, she grabbed the covers and pulled them to her neck. "Get out!" she screamed at her brothers, so filled with humiliation she thought she'd die of it. "How dare you! Damn you both, get out!"

"But Sinjun, we heard you yelling, screaming in pain—"

She got ahold of herself. She didn't think it was possible, but she did it. She even managed to smile at them, but it was wobbly and mean and utterly mortified. "Now, Douglas, I've heard Alex yelling her head off— many times, in fact. Can't I yell as well?"

"Yours wasn't pleasure yelling," Ryder said, his voice so cold she shivered at the sound of it. "Yours was pain yelling. What did this bastard do to you?"

"Dammit!" Colin roared. He grabbed his own discarded dressing gown and shrugged into it. "This is bloody ridiculous! Cannot I have privacy in my own house? Yes, she yelled, damn you both to the devil. What the hell do you expect? She was a bloody virgin and I had to get through her bloody maidenhead!"

Douglas looked at Ryder, then back at Colin. He roared in rage and yelled at the top of his lungs, "You cunning bastard, you despicable savage, I'll bloody well kill you this time, you lying sod!"

"Not again," Sinjun said.

"Yes, again, dammit!" Ryder now, and his jaw was working he was so angry. "You were a *virgin*, Sinjun? You, who have been married to this damned heathen for how long now? *Completely* married, you told us? In *all* ways, you said. Well then, just how the hell could you still be a virgin? This rutting stoat doesn't look like he'd wait for anything or anyone."

Sinjun pulled the covers around her and brought her legs over the side of the bed. Colin was looking like a dog ready for a good fight, bent forward, hands fisted, his eyes mean as a snake's. Her brothers were coming closer and closer, just as ready to spill blood.

"Stop it, all of you!" she yelled. Where was Angus with his damned blunderbuss? She jumped in front of her brothers. "No more, do you hear me? No more!" They were ignoring her, intent on bashing Colin. She spoke calmly now, colder than they'd ever heard her voice. "You will leave my bedchamber now, both of you, or I swear it, Douglas, Ryder, I will never speak to either of you again. I swear it."

"No, you can't mean that," Douglas said, paling.

"You can't know what you're saying," Ryder said, taking a step back. "We're your brothers, we love you, we—"

"I do mean it. Get out, both of you. We will speak of this in the morning. You have embarrassed me to my toes, both of you, and if—" Her voice broke off and she burst into tears.

It was so utterly unexpected that both Douglas and Ryder rushed forward to her. Colin raised his hand and said quite calmly, "No, gentlemen. I will see to her. We will speak in the morning. Go away."

"But she's crying," Ryder said, clearly aghast. "Sinjun never cries."

"If you've made her cry, you bastard—"

"Douglas, leave us alone." Colin tightened his arms around his wife's back.

Ryder and Douglas backed off. They didn't want to, but they had no choice. Both left the bedchamber cursing.

Colin said nothing. He simply held her tightly against him, watching the door close finally.

"I should have locked the damned door," he said, filled with disgust for himself. "That will teach me to be more careful when my wife has two brothers who love her so much they'd kill anyone who broke her fingernail."

"They would have broken the door down. It would have made no difference. And you broke more than a fingernail."

"Why, she speaks," he said. "How grand. A bride who bursts into tears one minute and speaks calm as a clam the next." He shoved her away from him. Her eyes were wet with tears, but none had spilled over. It didn't slow him though. He grabbed her shoulders, squeezing tight, and shook her. "I will tell you this once, Joan, and I don't expect to have to repeat myself. This is my house. You are my wife. Damn you, I am a man, not some sort of sniveling hound for you to protect by shoving me behind your damned skirts. Do you understand me, madam?"

She tried to pull free of him, but he held on tightly. She wanted to strike him herself, hard. She snarled like an animal at him, "Blessed hell, they would have killed you! They would have bashed you to the floor. And if you would open your eyes, you would notice that a skirt isn't what I'm wearing."

"Don't you dare try to distract me. You will never again jump in front of me. Do you understand me, madam? For God's sake, there could be real danger, possibly, and you could be hurt. This is Scotland, a land vastly different from that gentleman's paradise to the south. There is always the chance of violence here. I won't tolerate your foolish behavior, ever again. Do you understand me?"

"You're not a sniveling hound, you're a bloody stupid fool! You're raging about like a bull, Colin, and it's absurd! I merely pretended to cry, just to stop them, and it did. Whatever was wrong with that?"

"Enough!" He slammed his palm against his forehead. "It is too much, dammit! Get into bed, Joan, you're shivering."

"No, I shan't. You'll do those horrible things to me again. I don't like it, Colin. I don't want you to do that again. I don't trust you."

He could only stand there, in the middle of the dim bedchamber, with its too-dark walls, shabby furnishings, frayed draperies. And here was his bride telling him he wasn't to bed her again. It was enough. It was too much. And she'd had the gall to interfere again between him and her brothers. He was enraged. He was quite beyond logical and calm thought. He was on her in an instant, ripping the covers off her. He picked her up and threw her on the bed.

"Stay there!"

He untwisted the covers and tossed them over her. "Get yourself warm."

"You won't stick yourself in me again, Colin, I shan't allow it. It was horrible and you won't do it. Damn you, get away from me!"

It sent him right over the edge. First her brothers and now her, giving him orders, and she was his wife, and it was time to begin as he meant to go along. He felt himself hardening, and it was enough. He slammed down on top of her. He immediately clapped his hand over her mouth, then shoved her legs apart. She fought him in earnest this time, but it didn't help. He was between her legs, spreading them wider until he was satisfied, and then he came into her, slower this time, and since she was slick with his seed and with herself, he moved quickly to seal himself deep inside her. When he moved, it didn't hurt quite so much, but enough, because her flesh was raw. This time she didn't cry out. The last thing she wanted was for her brothers to burst into their bedchamber again, for he still hadn't locked the door. She suffered him, closing her eyes, her hands at her sides now, fisted. She turned her face away, pressing it against the mattress, and lay still. He wasn't violent with her, nor was he at all rough. He moved deep then eased out, once, twice, three times, and yet again. It didn't last long. He tried to kiss her, but she kept her head turned to the side. She heard his breathing quicken, felt his body pulse and shudder with his exertions. When he released his seed, he groaned deep in his throat. When it was over, he didn't fall on her as he'd done before. He pulled out of her immediately. She nearly cried out. She felt raw, so bruised by him she wondered if she would be able to walk. She knew he was standing beside the bed, looking at her, but she didn't care. What did it matter that her legs were sprawled? That she was naked and lying there? It didn't matter now, nothing did. If he wished, he could take her again, and there was naught she could do about it. Let him look. She didn't care. He said nothing; she could still hear his breathing, harsh and fast.

"I'm all sticky and I want to bathe."

He stilled himself. Jesus, he could just imagine how wet and sticky she was. He'd spilled his seed in her three times. He sighed, drawing on his control, dampening his guilt, willing his anger at the absurd situation to quiescence. "Just lie still. I'll get you some water and a cloth."

Sinjun didn't move. She closed her eyes. This was her wedding night and it was a shambles, painful and embarrassing, and then Douglas's and Ryder's bursting in. She turned her back to Colin and pulled her legs to her chest. She wished she were the Sinjun she'd been just a month before. Everything had been simple and straightforward to that Sinjun; that Sinjun knew about fun and humor and had dreamed about love. She had looked upon Colin and seen her dream come true. Ah, and what a dream it was to this Sinjun: a mess, a girl who didn't know a blessed thing. Everything had gone awry.

She cried, for the first time in three years.

Colin stood by the bed. He felt like the damned rutting bastard Douglas had accused him of being. He felt helpless. Her sobs weren't delicate and feminine, they were hoarse and ugly and immensely real.

"Well, hell," he said, climbed into the bed, and cupped his body around hers. Her tears lessened. She began to hiccup. He kissed the back of her neck. She stiffened. "Please, Colin, don't hurt me again. Surely I don't deserve any more of your punishment."

He closed his eyes against her words, words she meant, no doubt about that. And it was his fault, because he'd been too rough with her, had moved too quickly, good Lord, he'd taken her three times, and that third time hadn't been well done of him. The second time was not all that well done, either, but at least that second time was perfectly understandable. But he had punished her with the third, pure and simple. No, he'd not behaved as he should have. "I won't come inside you again," he said. "Besides I can't. I have no more seed to spill in you. Go to sleep."

Surprisingly, Sinjun closed her eyes and did just that. She slept long and deep. It was Colin who woke her up the next morning as he turned her on her back. She shivered at the sudden cool air on her skin and opened her eyes. He was standing over her, holding a damp cloth.

"Hold still and let me bathe you."

"Oh no." She jerked away from him, rolling over until she was on the far side of the mammoth bed. "No, Colin, I will see to myself. Please, go away now."

He stood there, frowning at her, holding the cloth in his outstretched hand, feeling like a fool. "Very well," he said at last. He tossed the cloth to her, hearing it slap against her wrist. "Angus is bringing up buckets of hot water for your bath. Get it done quickly, for I, too, wish to bathe, and you don't seem at all interested in sharing the tub with me, more's the pity, though I am now your husband, something you wanted more than anything, if you would be honest with yourself, marriage and my man's body, but not in that order, not at first."

"You're angry," she said as she pulled the covers to her nose. She was utterly confused. "This is very odd, Colin, since it is you who hurt me. How can you dare be angry?"

"I'm angry at this damnable situation." There was a knock on the door. "Don't move," he said over his shoulder. "Keep yourself wrapped in the covers."

It was Angus, not her brothers brandishing swords, and he was carrying two steaming buckets of water.

Once they were poured into the porcelain tub, he looked up and said, "Do you fancy walking naked over here and climbing in?"

She didn't fancy it at all. She shook her head. "You may go first."

He stripped off his dressing gown, climbed into the tub, leaned back, and let his knees stick up. Sinjun would have laughed if she hadn't felt so miserable. She didn't want to get out of the bed. She didn't want to face her brothers.

They said not a word. Both Douglas and Ryder seemed determined that there be no more fights, no more arguments with Colin. They actually seemed to understand that they'd embarrassed her to her very toes. It embarrassed her even more to know that they must have discussed the situation and had decided upon a course of behavior. To be talked about, even by her brothers, was almost more than she could bear.

After a second cup of coffee, Ryder said, "Douglas and I are leaving this morning, Sinjun. We're both sorry that we've intruded and made you uncomfortable. However, should you ever need us, you need but write or send a messenger to Douglas or to me. We will come to you immediately. We will do anything you wish us to do."

"Thank you," she said. Suddenly she wished they wouldn't leave her, wouldn't promise not to interfere again. They always had. They loved her. Even last night—it was because they loved her.

When they took their leave an hour later, she felt hollow inside. She felt utterly alone and, for the first time, truly afraid of what she'd done. She threw herself into Douglas's arms, hugging him tight. "Please take care. Give my love to Alex."

"I will."

"And to the twins. They are destroying Ryder's home with their exuberance, he told me. It must be wonderful. I miss all the children so much."

"Yes, I know, love. I miss them, too. It's fortunate both Ryder and Sophie adore children, even those who are destructive little heathens. I've closed up the London house. Alex and the boys will be at Northcliffe Hall when I return. Don't worry about Mother. I will see to it that when she writes you, it will be pleasant, and not endless carping."

When Ryder gathered her against him, he said, "Yes, I shall kiss Sophie for you and hug and pet all the little heathens. And I'll miss you like the very devil, Sinjun."

"Don't forget Grayson, Ryder. He's so beautiful, and I miss him dreadfully."

"He's the picture of Sophie, only with Sherbrooke blue eyes and the Sherbrooke stubborn-as-hell chin."

"Yes, and I love him dearly."

"Shush. Don't cry, love. I understand a bit how you must feel, for Sophie had to leave her home in Jamaica to come to England, and I know she was sometimes heartsick. At the very least she was cold here. But Colin is your husband and he will take care of you."

"Yes, I know."

But she didn't sound like she knew it, Ryder thought. Oh hell, what were they to do? She was married to the man. Ah, but to leave her here alone . . . he didn't like it. But Douglas had insisted that they'd interfered enough. "Sometimes at the beginning of a marriage, things aren't quite as straightforward as one would wish them to be." She just looked at him, her expression remote, and he floundered on. "That is, occasionally there are slight problems. But any problems are resolved with time, Sinjun. You must be patient, that's all."

He had no idea if what he'd said made any sense to her situation, but the pain in her eyes smote him. He didn't want to leave her in this damned foreign land with this damned husband she'd only just met.

Colin stood apart from the three of them, watching and frowning. He felt jealous, oddly enough, and he recognized it for what it was. The three of them were so very close. He and his older brother, Malcolm, had always been at each other's throats. And their father had just laughed and sided with his brother, because he'd been the future laird, the future earl, and it was his opinion that counted, his words that were believed, his wishes that were important, his never-ending gambling debts and wenching expenses that must be paid. Then Colin had refused to join with Napoléon, knowing that his father was skirting disaster with his damnable beliefs, beliefs that weren't really all that strongly held, no, they were beliefs that it amused his father to hold, nothing more. And his brother shared the beliefs as well, to taunt him, to try to make him leave Scotland, but he wouldn't go. He wanted a commission in the English army, but naturally his father refused to buy it for him. No, his father had other plans for him. He'd been used to end the feud with the MacPhersons. He'd wedded Fiona Dahling MacPherson when he was twenty years old. It had ended the feud—until a month ago. Until something had happened that had set Robert MacPherson off.

"Is something wrong, Colin?"

It was Douglas speaking, and Colin quickly brought himself away from his miserable memories. "No, certainly not. I will take care of your sister. Don't worry."

"You will also bring her to visit her family early next fall. Is it possible, do you think?"

Colin thought for a moment, then nodded. "You have now given me the means to recover myself, my home, and my lands. There is much for me to do. However, all should be in good order by the fall."

"All the money was rightfully Sinjun's, not mine. I'm glad it will be put to good use. I personally hate to see an estate fall into ruin."

"Perhaps," Colin said slowly, looking toward the two magnificent Arabian stallions who were blowing and snorting, one held by Angus and the other by a clearly frightened stable lad, "you would wish to come and visit us sometime in the future. After, of course, Vere Castle has been refurbished a bit. The drive to the castle is very beautiful, all tree-lined, and now, in the early summer, the leaves form a canopy overhead."

"No doubt we would be pleased to," Douglas said. "Ryder can bring all the children."

"I like children," Colin said. "Vere Castle is a large place, surely there are enough rooms to house all of you."

Then Douglas and Ryder were gone, with one last wave, riding down the cobblestoned street, their great coats billowing out behind them.

Sinjun stood there on the street, watching them, feeling more miserable than she could remember. She wouldn't allow that misery to remain clogged in her heart and in her mind; no matter this sex business, she was married to Colin. Ryder was right. She must be patient. After all, she adored her husband, despite what he'd done to her. She would deal with it. There was much to be done. She wasn't one to lie down and moan her distress. Of course, in the past there never had been much distress to consider moaning about.

She turned then and smiled at her husband, not really much of a smile, but an honest effort at one. "I should like another cup of tea. Would you?"

"Yes, Joan, I believe I would." He fell into step beside her. "I like your brothers."

She was silent a moment, then said with desperate cheerfulness, "Yes, I rather do, too."

"I know you will miss them. We'll see them soon, I promise you."

"Yes, you promise."

He gave her a quick look but said nothing.

CHAPTER
=== 8 ===

THE DOCK ON THE FIRTH OF FORTH was a nasty place, smelling of fish in all stages of rot, unwashed bodies of yelling stevedores, and other odors she couldn't, thankfully, identify. It was filled with so many carts and drays and boats of every size in the water that it was difficult to see why they hadn't all crashed into each other. In that moment, two drays did collide, tipping an oak barrel off the end of one of the drays. It bounced hard on the cobblestones and then rolled, picking up more speed, until it slammed into an iron railing, cracking wide open. Rich dark ale spilled out, filling the air with its pungent smell. Sinjun smiled and sniffed. She supposed the London docks were much the same, but she'd never been to see them. Colin took her elbow, saying nothing, and directed her to a ferry that looked to be on its last legs, had it been a horse. It was a long, narrow barge with unpainted wooden railings, and its name was *Forth Star*, surely an ambitious title for such a scrawny boat. The horses were already on board, standing very close to the people, and not happy about it. The ferry was owned by an old man who had the foulest mouth Sinjun had ever heard. He cursed at the people, at the animals, at all the valises and trunks. He even yelled at the opposite bank of the Forth. Sinjun regretted that she could only understand just a bit of what he said. She did see Colin wince several times when the old man got bitten in the shoulder by a horse and yelled his displeasure to all within three miles.

When the ferry got under way, Sinjun watched with horrified eyes, knowing it had to run into other boats. One ship from Holland came within scraping distance. Another from Spain was so close the sailors were leaning over the sides with long poles to push any boat away that came too close. Nothing seemed to bother Colin—natural, she supposed, because he was, after all, a Scot, and none of this was new to him. Even the horses started blowing loudly in the salty clean air. Thank God it was a beautiful day, warm and balmy, the sun high in a cloud-strewn sky. As they neared the other side of the Forth, she saw that the Fife Peninsula seemed from here to look every bit as English as Sussex. The green was

soft and pure and deep, and the hills were rolling and gentle. It was
lovely, and Sinjun felt a stirring of enthusiasm. At that moment, the *Forth
Star* hit another small barge. The two captains howled at each other, the
horses whinnied, and the people shook their fists. Sinjun tried not to
laugh as she yelled at the other captain herself.

The ferry crossed at the narrowest point, called the Queensferry Nar-
rows, not a beautiful spot, for the water looked thick and dirty and swirled
about the barge. Ah, but looking toward the east, to the North Sea, was
beautiful.

Colin said unexpectedly, "At this point the Forth is a long tidal estu-
ary. The river itself begins nearly all the way to the western sea. It's a
mighty river there, deep and so blue it makes you want to cry. Then it nar-
rows and meanders over a flat peaty wilderness to Stirling."

Sinjun breathed in deeply. She nodded at his offering, then turned back
to lean her elbows on the railing. She was afraid of missing something.
She also didn't particularly wish to speak to her husband.

"If you turn about you can see the Castle. It is clear today and the view
is rather spectacular."

Sinjun obligingly turned and looked. "I thought it more mysterious,
more ethereal perhaps, last evening, when it was shrouded halfway up in
fog. Every once in a while you could hear the soldiers yelling and it seemed
like ghost voices coming out of the gray mist. Wonderfully gothic."

Colin grunted at that and turned back to look down at the swirling waters. "You will have to accustom yourself to the mists. Even in summer
we can go weeks at a time without the sun. But it is warm and it stays
light enough to read even at midnight."

Sinjun brightened at that. "You have a well-stocked library, Colin, at
Vere Castle?"

"The library is a mess, as is most everything else. My brother didn't
particularly care, and since his death I haven't had time to see to things.
You will have to go through it and see if there is anything that interests
you. I also have a library of sorts in my tower room."

"Perhaps you have some novels?" Her hopeful voice made him smile.
"Very few, I'm afraid," he said. "Remember, you're deep in Presbyterian
country. Hellfire would surely await anyone so ill-advised as to read a
novel. Try to imagine John Knox enjoying a Mrs. Radcliffe novel. It boggles the mind."

"Well, hopefully Alex will send me all my books when she sends us
our trunks."

"If your brother didn't order all our things burned first."

"A possibility," Sinjun said. "When Douglas is angry, he can do the
most awesome things."

Sinjun hoped the trunks would arrive soon. She was perilously close to having very little to wear. Even her blue riding habit, of which she was inordinately fond, was looking sadly distressed. She swiped the dust off her sleeve as she looked at her fellow passengers. Most were country people, dressed in rough homespun woolens of dull colors, and clogs and open leather vests. There was one aristocratic fellow with very high shirt points who looked a bit green from the swaying of the barge. There was another man who looked to be a prosperous merchant, who kept spitting over the side of the barge, his teeth as brown as his spittle. And the speech, it wasn't English, even though Sinjun could understand most of it. It was filled with slurring and lilting sounds that were melodic and coarse all at the same time.

Sinjun didn't say anything else to her husband. At least he was trying to be pleasant, as was she. But she didn't want to be pleasant. She wanted to hit him. She looked at his profile, drawn to look at him really because he was so beautiful. His black hair was blowing in the gentle breeze. His chin was up and his eyes were closed in that moment, as if he were reaffirming that he was a Scot and he was home. A sea gull flew perilously close, squawking in his face. He threw back his head and laughed deeply.

She wasn't home. She stuck her chin up as high as his was. She breathed in the sea air, the nearly overpowering smell of fish and people and horses. She looked at the terns and the gulls and the oystercatchers. They were all putting on a grand show, hoping for scraps from the passengers.

"We will ride to Vere Castle today," Colin said. "It will take us about three hours, no more. The sun is shining and thus it will be pleasant. Ah, do you think you will be able to do it?"

"Certainly. It's strange you would ask. You know I'm an excellent rider."

"Yes, but that was before. I mean, you're not too sore, are you?"

She turned slowly to face him. "You sound very pleased with yourself. How odd."

"I'm not at all pleased. I'm concerned. You're obviously hearing what you want to hear, not what's there."

"There is a wealth of conceit in your tone. All right, Colin, what if I said I was too sore? What would you do? Hire a litter, perhaps? Put a sign around my neck reading that I was unable to ride because I'd been plowed too much—like an overused barley field?"

"An analogy that is perhaps amusing but nothing more. No, if you were too sore, I would carry you before me. You would rest on my thighs and ease the pain you perhaps might be feeling."

"I would prefer to ride by myself, thank you, Colin."

"As you wish, Joan."

"I would also prefer that we had not yet left Edinburgh."

"You have already expressed yourself at some length on that subject. I've told you why we left so quickly. There is danger and I don't want you exposed to it. I am taking you to Vere Castle. I will return to Edinburgh. There is much that both of us need to do."

"I don't really want to be left alone in a castle with people I don't know, Colin."

"Since you are the mistress, what should it matter? If something displeases you, you may discuss changing it with me when I return. You may even make lists, and I will certainly review them."

"I sound like your child, not your wife. If a servant displeases me, do I dismiss the servant or just add it to the list so that the master—"

"I'm the laird."

". . . so that the laird may review it like a judge and issue forth a decision?"

"You are the countess of Ashburnham."

"Ah, and what does that entail, other than making lists and learning how to plead my cases before you?"

"You are being purposefully annoying, Joan. Look at that bird, it's a dunlin. On your English coast you call them sandpipers."

"How knowledgeable you are. Did you know they get a black stripe on their bellies when they wish to mate? No? Well, they certainly didn't do all that well with your education at Oxford, did they? But perhaps some of it was your fault. You spent far too much time tupping all your ladies at the inn in Chipping Norton."

"Your memory is lamentable. Tupping is crude. You won't use it again. Your tongue also runs too smoothly, Joan, so smoothly that you are in danger of being tossed overboard."

She continued, not hesitating, "Now, let me present my only item to you—the judging laird. I wish to remain with you. I'm your wife, despite everything."

"What do you mean, despite everything? Are you referring to your less than wonderful experience in our marriage bed? All right, so you weren't that pleased with the result of our union. You are small and I was too enthusiastic. I shouldn't have forced it that third time. I have apologized to you several times. I have told you it will get better. Can you not trust me?"

"No. You will remain as you are, and that is too rough and too big."

"A bit salty of tongue now, aren't you?"

"Oh, go to the devil, Colin!"

"Have you looked at your face, Joan? 'Tis still red from the stone that slashed across it. That was a bullet. You could have been hurt, killed even. You will stay at Vere Castle until I have seen that it will stop and that you will be in no more danger."

"But I didn't even get to visit Edinburgh Castle!"

"Since you will live in Scotland for the rest of your life, I daresay that you will see the Castle as often as you wish."

"The MacPhersons live in Edinburgh?"

"No, they are some fifteen miles from my lands, but the old laird is there, I was told. They've a comfortable house near the Parliament Building. I must see him. There are also, as I've already told you several times, many things for me to see to. Bankers and builders to speak to. New furnishings to consider. Sheep to buy and have transported to Vere and—"

He fell silent when she simply turned away from him. Damn him, as if she didn't care about new furnishings, new stock for the land, new plans for building. But no, he was excluding her. She'd already given him all her arguments. None seemed to matter.

She sat down on a valise. It collapsed under her weight and she remained seated on a smashed-down valise, and tucked her legs under her. She said nothing more to her husband. At least he hadn't attacked her again before they'd left Kinross House. She was sore, very sore, but she would never admit it to him. She would ride and she wouldn't say a word, not if it killed her, which she hoped it wouldn't.

An hour later they had debarked from the *Forth Star* and were on their way to Kinross land and Vere Castle, their valises strapped on the backs of their saddles.

"Perhaps later in the summer we can travel into the Highlands. The scenery is dramatic. It is like going from a calm lake into a stormy sea, everything is churned about, its civilized trappings stripped away. You will like it."

"Yes," Sinjun said, her voice abrupt. She hurt from the horse's gait. She was an excellent rider but the pain was something out of her experience, and no matter how she shifted her position, the saddle seemed to grind into her.

Colin looked over at her. She was staring straight between her horse's ears, her chin high, as it had been now for the past two days. She was wearing the same dark blue riding habit she'd worn since she'd begun riding beside him during their elopement, a beautiful, starkly fashioned outfit that suited her, for she was tall and elegant, this wife of his, and pale-skinned, her hair tucked neatly beneath the matching blue velvet riding hat, the ostrich feather curling gently around her right cheek. It was dusty and looked a bit worse for wear, but still, he liked it. Now that he had money, he would be able to buy her lovely things. He thought of her long white legs, the sleek muscles of her thighs, and his guts knotted.

"We will stop for lunch at an inn near Lanark. You can have your first real taste of our local dishes. Agnes at Kinross House has always fancied herself above all our native dishes. Her mother was Yorkshire-bred, you know, and thus it is English beef and boiled potatoes for her, quite good but not Scottish. Perhaps you can try some broonies."

He was trying, she'd give him that, but she didn't care at the moment. She simply hurt too much. "How far is the inn?"

"Two miles or so."

Two miles! She didn't think she would make another two feet. The road was well worn, wide, surrounded by rolling hills and more larch and pine trees than she could begin to count. There were farms and carefully tilled lands, reminding her of England, and grazing cattle. They were riding northward through the Fife Peninsula that lay between the Firth of Forth and the Firth of Tay, Colin had told her earlier, a region protected from the Highlanders from the north and the English invaders from the south, which had thus been the historical cradle for religion and authority. Again, she recognized that the land was beautiful, and again, she simply didn't care.

"Over there are some strange-looking hills—they're basalt thrown up by old volcanoes. They become quite thick soon and they cover a lot of land and go quite high. There are even lochs scattered in amongst them. There is some good fishing to be had in many of them. We haven't time today, but soon we'll ride to the coast. It's rugged, strewn with rocks, and the North Sea batters against the land with the fury of an enraged giant. There's a string of tiny fishing villages, many of which are very picturesque. I'll take you climbing up West Lomond, the highest point. It's shaped like a bell, and the view from the top is spectacular."

"Your lectures are very edifying, Colin. However, I should prefer hearing about Vere Castle—this dumping ground you're taking me to."

"West Lomond is just southwest of Auchtermuchty."

Sinjun yawned.

His jaw tightened. "I am rather trying to entertain you, Joan, to teach you something of your new country. Your continued sarcasm doesn't sit well with me. Don't make me regret our alliance."

She twisted about in her sidesaddle to stare at him. "Why not? You have certainly made me regret it." She saw the anger build in his eyes, and she felt her own anger building apace. She urged her horse forward into a gallop, away from him. She regretted it instantly, for she slammed up and down on the saddle. The pain rocketed through her. She bit her lip. She felt tears sting her eyes, but she didn't slow down.

The Plucked Goose—surely an odd name for an inn—lay in a small village at the base of some of those damned steep basalt hills. The large, freshly painted sign that swung from its chains was of a large goose with a small head and a long neck and utterly bare of feathers. The inn was quite new, which surprised Sinjun, who thought every inn in England and Scotland must go back at least to Elizabeth I, and the yard was clean. She heard Scottish coming from every window and door in the inn, but this was a different accent, and despite her misery she smiled.

She pulled her horse to a halt and just sat there for a moment, trying to calm her body from its assault. She looked over to see Colin standing beside her, his hands outstretched to lift her down. Normally she would have simply laughed and jumped from her horse. Not today. She allowed the courtesy. He eased her down the length of his body as he lowered her. And when she was finally on her feet, he said, "I've missed you," and he leaned down to kiss her.

He felt her stiffen and released her. They were, after all, in the public yard of a very public inn. The innkeeper's wife, Girtha by name, who welcomed Colin as if he were her long-lost nephew, exclaimed how thin he was and how pretty Sinjun was, how sleek their horses looked even though they were obviously rented hacks, commented on how the blue of Sinjun's riding habit matched her eyes, all without taking a breath.

The taproom in the inn was dark and cool and smelled of ale and beer, very pleasant really. There were only a half dozen locals drinking there, and they were quietly talking, paying the earl and countess no heed.

Colin ordered broonies for himself and for Sinjun. When they came, he watched as she bit into the oatmeal gingerbread. They were wonderful, and she nodded her enthusiasm to the hovering innkeeper's wife.

"Now," he said, "let's have some haggis."

"I know what's in it. I asked Agnes. It doesn't sound very appetizing, Colin."

"You will accustom yourself. Everyone around you will eat it and enjoy it. Our children will be weaned on it. Thus, I suggest you try it now."

Their *children!* She stared at him, her mouth open. Children! Good God, they'd been married less than a week.

He grinned at her, understanding her reaction. "I worked you too hard, very true, but I did spill my seed in you three times, Joan. It's possible you are already carrying my child."

"No," she said very firmly. "No, I am too young. Besides, I'm not at all certain I want to do it yet. When poor Alex was pregnant she vomited all the time, at least at first. She would suddenly turn white and simply be sick. Hollis, our butler, had a sick pan placed discreetly in every room at

Northcliffe Hall." She looked pained at the memories and shook her head again. "No, I won't do it, Colin. No, not yet."

"I fear you have no choice in the matter. It is many times the result of lovemaking and—"

That got her attention. She dropped her fork and stared at him. "Love-making. What an odd way to refer to what you did to me. Surely there is something else more appropriate to call it. Like your infamous tupping."

"There are many words that are used to refer to the sex act," he said in a pedantic voice, ignoring her sarcasm. "However, in my experience, ladies prefer poetry and euphemisms, so lovemaking is the more accepted form of reference. Now, you will lower your voice, madam. If you haven't noticed, there are people around us and they may be savages in your aristocratic English eyes, but they are my people and not at all deaf."

"I didn't ever say that. You're being—"

"I'm being realistic. You could be pregnant and you'd best face up to it."

Sinjun swallowed. "No," she said. "I won't allow it."

"Here, have some haggis."

It was a bagged mess of livers and heart and beef suet and oatmeal all served up with potatoes and rutabagas. Sinjun took one look at the bloated sheep stomach it was served in and wanted to run.

"You didn't order it from the innkeeper's wife," she said slowly, just staring at that foreign-looking stretched hot bag filled with things she'd just as soon never see in her life. "There hasn't been time."

"I didn't have to. It's the main dish served here and has been since the inn opened five years ago. Eat." So saying, he cut into the skin and forked down a goodly bite.

"No, I can't. Give me time, Colin."

He smiled at her. "Very well. Would you like to try some clapshot? It's a dish from the Orkneys, supposedly coming to us from the Vikings. All vegetables. It's usually served with haggis, but eat it by itself and see if it settles nicely in your belly."

She was grateful. The rutabagas were nasty things, but she could shove them to the sides of the plate. The potatoes were good, and the hint of nutmeg and cream made it quite tasty. There was no more conversation between her and Colin.

Sinjun spent the next hour and a half in a daze of pain. She didn't notice the damned countryside, even though Colin kept up a stream of travel commentary. She was nearly to the point of telling him she couldn't ride another yard, another foot even, when he said, "Pull up, Joan. Yon is Vere Castle."

There was a wealth of pride and affection in his voice. She craned up in her saddle. Before her, sprawled out over an entire low hillock, was an edifice that was the size of Northcliffe Hall. There all similarities ended. The west end was a true fairy-tale castle, with crenellated walls, round towers, and cone-topped roofs that rose three stories. It was a castle from a children's storybook. It needed but flags flying from all the towers, a drawbridge, a moat, and a knight in silver armor. It wasn't massive, like Northcliffe Hall, but it was magical. It was connected to a Tudor home by a two-story stone building that resembled a long arm with a fist at each end. A fairy castle at one end and a Tudor manor at the other—in this modern day two such disparate styles should have been a jest, but in reality the whole was magnificent. It was now her home.

"The family lives primarily in the Tudor section, although the castle part is the newest, built back at the turn of the seventeenth century. That earl, though, didn't have quite enough money to do it right, thus it is rotting at a faster pace than the Tudor section, which is nearly one hundred and fifty years older. Still, I love it. I spend much of my time there, in the north tower. When we entertain, it's always in the castle."

Sinjun stared. "I hadn't expected this," she said slowly. "It's massive and all its parts, well, they're so different from each other."

"Of course there are different parts. The original Tudor hall dates back to the beginning of the sixteenth century. It has a fireplace large enough to roast a large cow. In the Tudor wing there's a minstrel's gallery that would rival the one at your Castle Braith in Yorkshire. Oh, I understand. You expected something of a hovel, something low and squalid and probably smelly, since Scots, of course, have their animals living with them. Something not nearly as impressive as your wondrous Northcliffe Hall. It isn't stately, but it's real and it's large, and it's mine." He fidgeted a moment. "The crofters many times have their animals in their houses with them during the winter. That is true, but we don't at Vere Castle."

"You know, Colin," she said mildly, looking at him squarely, "if I indeed were expecting a ratty hovel, why, then, wouldn't that prove how much I wanted to marry you?"

He looked nonplussed at that. He opened his mouth, then closed it. She turned away from him but not before he saw, for the first time, the utter weariness and pain in her eyes that she'd kept hidden from him. At least this was something tangible, something he could get his teeth into. "Sweet Lord," he bellowed, "why the devil didn't you say anything to me?" He sounded utterly furious, which he was. "You're in pain, aren't you? Yes, you are, and you didn't say a damned word to me. Your stubbornness passes all bounds, Joan, and I won't have it, do you understand me?"

"Oh, be quiet. I'm fine. I wish to—"

"Just shut up, Joan. Not too sore, are you? You look ready to fall down and expire. Are you bleeding? Have you managed to rub yourself raw?"

She knew she wasn't going to stay on her horse's back for another moment. She simply couldn't. She pulled her leg free and slid off her horse's back. She leaned against the horse until she could get control of herself. When she had control, she said, "I will walk to your castle, Colin. It's a beautiful day. I wish to smell the daisies."

"There aren't any damned daisies."

"I will smell the crocuses, then."

"You will just stop it, Joan." He looked enraged. He cursed, then he dismounted.

"Stay away from me!"

He drew up three feet from her. "Is this the girl who wanted me to kiss her in the entrance hall of her brother's home in London? Is this the girl who walked up to me at the theater, thrust out her hand, and informed me she was an heiress? Is this the girl who kept insisting that I bed her immediately? Even in the carriage? Where is she, I ask you?"

Sinjun didn't answer. She didn't care. She turned away from him and took a step. She felt pain grind through her. She stumbled.

"Oh damnation, just hold still and be quiet."

He grabbed her arm and turned her to face him. He saw that damned pain again in her eyes and it struck him silent. Gently now, he drew her against him, supporting her with his arms around her waist. "Just rest a moment," he said against her hair. "Just rest and then allow me to hold you. I'm sorry, Joan." He pressed her face against his shoulder. She breathed in the scent of him.

She didn't say a word.

She arrived at her new home in the arms of her husband atop his horse, just like a fairy princess being brought to her prince's castle. However, unlike that fairy princess, Sinjun was wrinkled and dusty and painfully aware that she looked a wreck.

"Shush, don't stiffen up on me," he said in a low voice, his breath warm on her cheek. "I don't believe that you're frightened, not you, a Sherbrooke of Northcliffe Hall. My family and my people will all welcome you. You will be their mistress."

She was quiet. They rode beneath the incredible canopy of green formed by the tree branches meeting across the drive. As they drew nearer, there were men and women and children and all sorts of animals appearing along the road to welcome Colin home. There was great cheering. Some of the men threw their caps into the air, women waved their aprons. Several mangy dogs yapped and jumped about Colin's horse, who took it all in stride. There was a goat chewing on a length of rope, not appearing to care that the master was once again gracing them with his presence.

"Everyone knows you're my bride, my heiress bride, here to save my hide and my castle and keep my people from starvation or emigration. They are probably cheering God's beneficence rather than us. Though you did find me. I should perhaps let that be known. Then you would be soundly cheered. MacDuff should still be here. I wanted you to have a warm welcome."

"Thank you, Colin. That's kind of you."

"Will you be able to walk?"

"Certainly."

He smiled over her head at the utter arrogance in her voice. She had guts. She would need them.

Sinjun awoke with a start to pale evening light. For a moment she was confused, then memory righted and she closed her eyes against it. It seemed impossible, but it wasn't. Colin hadn't told her. He'd conveniently remained silent on what she considered to be a very important part of her life here at Vere Castle, as his wife. She shook her head, blanking out incredulity and anger at him for his damnable silence, and stared about the huge bedchamber, the laird's bedchamber, with a gigantic bed set up upon a dais, a bed that would hold six men lying side by side. The room was wainscoted with dark oak, beautiful really, but the dull, very dusty burgundy draperies that were all pulled nearly closed made the room as somber as a monk's cell. The furniture was old, and she recognized the Tudor style of the huge armoire that dominated one entire corner of the room.

She still didn't move, just looked about her. She thought of the list of things to be done that was already forming in her mind. So much to be done. Ah, but where to begin? She didn't want to think about her reception as the countess of Ashburnham, but she had to.

Colin had kept his arm about her waist as he led her through the gigantic oak front door into the large square first floor. He kept his arm around her even when all the servants appeared, all of them staring at her, all of them doubtless seeing it as a very romantic gesture. The minstrel's gallery rose on three sides on the second floor, the railing old and ornate. A quite large chandelier hung down from the third story. There were high-backed Tudor chairs against the walls, and little else. She saw all of this in a haze, listening to Colin as he introduced one person after another. She hurt, but she wasn't a coward or a weak-kneed miss. She smiled and repeated names. But she couldn't remember a one after the repetition came out of her mouth.

"This is my aunt Arleth, my mother's younger sister. Arleth, my wife, Joan."

An older, sharp-chinned face came into view and Sinjun smiled and took the woman's hand, bidding her hello.

"And this is—was—my sister-in-law, Serena."

Ah, a very pretty young woman, not many years older than Sinjun, and she smiled nicely.

"And these are my children. Philip, Dahling, come here and say hello to your new mama."

It was at that point that Sinjun simply stopped cold in her tracks. She stared at her husband, but he said nothing more. She thought she couldn't have understood him properly. But there, walking slowly toward her, their faces sullen, their eyes narrowed with suspicion, were two children. A boy, about six years old, and a little girl, four, perhaps five.

"Say hello to Joan. She's my new wife and your new stepmother." Colin's voice was deep and commanding. She would have answered if he'd spoken to her in that tone. He'd made no move toward his own children.

"Hello, Joan," the boy said, then added, "My name's Philip."

"I'm Dahling," said the little girl.

Sinjun tried to smile, tried to be pleasant. She loved children, she truly did, but to be a stepmother without any warning? She looked again at Colin, but he was smiling down at the little girl. Then he picked her up and she wound her arms around his neck and said, "Welcome home, Papa."

Papa! It couldn't be true, but it was. Sinjun managed to get out, "Are you really darling? All the time?"

"Of course, what else could I be?"

Colin said, "Her name's actually Fiona, like her mother. There was confusion, so everyone started calling her Dahling, her second name." He then spelled it for her.

"Hello, Dahling, Philip. I'm pleased to meet both of you."

"You're very tall," Philip said, the image of his father, except for cool gray eyes that were staring at her hard.

"You're all rumpled," Dahling said. "There's an ugly scar on your face."

Sinjun laughed. You could always count on children for unadorned candor. "That's true. Your father and I rode all the way from Edinburgh—indeed, nearly all the way from York. We're both in need of a good bath."

"Cousin MacDuff said you were nice and we were to be polite to you."

"It sounds like a good idea to me," Sinjun said.

"Enough, children," Aunt Arleth said, coming up to them. "Excuse them, er—"

"Oh, please call me Sinjun."

"No, call her Joan."

Serena looked from one to the other. It was at that moment that Sinjun wished with all her heart that she were standing on the cliffs next to Northcliffe Hall, looking out over the English channel, the sea wind ruffling her hair. She hurt between her legs, hurt very badly. She looked at Colin and said calmly, "I'm afraid I don't feel very well."

He was quick, she'd give him that. He picked her up and, without another word to anyone, carried her up a wide staircase, down a wide, very long corridor that was dark and smelled musty. It seemed to Sinjun that he'd marched a mile with her in his arms before he entered a huge bedchamber and put her down on the bed. He then started to pull up her riding skirts.

She batted at his hands, yelling, "No!"

"Joan, let me see the damage. For heaven's sake, I'm your husband. I've already seen everything you have to offer."

"Go away. I'm not very fond of you at the moment, Colin. Please, just go away."

"As you will. Shall I have some hot water sent up?"

"Yes, thank you. Go away."

He did. Not ten minutes later a young girl peeked in the room. "My name's Emma," she announced. "I've brung yer water, m'lady."

"Thank you, Emma." She excused the maid as quickly as she could.

She was indeed a mess, her flesh raw and very sore from all the riding she'd done today. She cleaned herself up, then crawled into the bed, staying close to the edge. She felt out of place, she felt fury at Colin for his excruciatingly important omission. She was a stepmother to two children who, it appeared, couldn't bear the sight of her. To her relief, she'd fallen asleep quickly and deeply.

But now she was awake. She would have to get up. She would have to face Colin, his aunt, his sister-in-law who wasn't anymore, and the two children, his children. She didn't want to. She wondered what Colin had said to everyone. Certainly not the truth. Now they would believe her a weakling, an English weakling. She was on the point of getting out of the bed when the door opened and a small face appeared.

It was Dahling.

CHAPTER
═══9═══

"YOU'RE AWAKE."

"Yes, I am," Sinjun said, turning to see Dahling peering into the room. "I was about to get up and get dressed."

"Why did you get undressed? Papa wouldn't tell us what was wrong with you."

"I was just tired. It was a long trip from London. Your papa wanted to get home quickly to you and Philip. Is there something you wanted?"

Dahling sidled into the room. Sinjun saw that she was wearing a heavy woolen gown that was too short for her, and stout boots that looked too small and very scuffed. Surely the child must be uncomfortable in such clothing.

"I wanted to see if you were as ugly as I thought."

Precocious little devil, Sinjun thought, reminded of Amy, one of Ryder's children, a little girl who was an imp and brazen as a brass gong, hiding, Ryder knew, a fear that was deep, very deep. "Well then, come closer. You must be fair, you know. Yes, climb up here on the bed and sit really close to me. Fairness is very important in life."

When the little girl reached the dais, Sinjun reached down and lifted her beneath her arms and up onto the bed. "There, now make a study of me."

"You talk all funny, like Aunt Arleth. She's always yelling at Philip and me not to speak like everyone else does, except Papa."

"You speak very well," Sinjun said, holding very still, for the little girl was now running her hands over her face. Her fingers lightly touched the red mark on her cheek. "What is this?"

"I was hurt when your father and I were in Edinburgh. A flying rock. It's nothing, and the mark should go away soon."

"You're not too ugly, but just a little bit ugly."

"Thank you for relieving me of such a major curse and leaving me with just a minor one. You're not ugly, either."

"Me? *Ugly?* I'm a Great Beauty, just like my mama. Everyone says so."

"Oh? Let me see." Sinjun then did exactly what Dahling had done to her. She ran her fingers over the little girl's face, pausing here and there, saying nothing.

Dahling began to fidget. "I *am* a Great Beauty. If I'm not now, I will be when I'm grown up."

"You also have the look of your father. He's very handsome, so that's all right. You have his eyes. Beautiful dark blue eyes he has, and so do you. Mine are also beautiful, don't you think so? They're called Sherbrooke blue. That's my family name."

Dahling chewed on her bottom lip. "I suppose so," she said at last. "But that doesn't mean you're not still a little bit ugly."

"You have your father's dark hair. That's also nice. Don't you like my hair? It's called Sherbrooke chestnut."

"Maybe it's all right. It's very curly. Mine isn't. Aunt Arleth just shakes her head and says I must bear with it."

"But you're still a Great Beauty?"

"Oh yes, Papa told me so," Dahling said with complete conviction.

"You believe everything your papa tells you?"

The little girl cocked her head to one side. "He's my pa. He loves me, but sometimes he doesn't see me or Philip, now that he's the laird of the Kinross clan. It's a very important job. He's very important and everybody needs him. He doesn't have much time for *bairns*—children."

"You don't have your father's nose. Yours is turned up on the end. Is that like your mother's?"

"I don't know. I'll ask Aunt Serena. She's Mama's younger sister. She takes care of me when the governesses all leave, but she doesn't like to. She'd rather be out picking flowers and wearing flowing gowns like a girl waiting for a prince to come."

Sinjun felt a sinking at that artless news. "Governesses? You and Philip have had more than one?"

"Oh yes, we never like them, you see. They're all English—like you— and ugly, and we make them leave. That, or they didn't like Mama, and she'd make them leave. Mama didn't like other ladies around."

"I see," Sinjun said, but didn't. "How many governesses have you had since your mama went to heaven?"

The little girl said very proudly, "Two. But mind you, it's only been seven months. We can make you leave, too, if we want."

"You think so, do you? No, don't answer that. Now, my dear, I must attire myself for dinner. Should you like to help me, or would you like me to help you?"

Dahling frowned. "What's wrong with me?"

"Do you dine in the nursery or with the family?"

"Papa decides. He decides everything now that he's laird. Aunt Arleth doesn't like it. I've seen her eyes turn red sometimes she's so angry at him. Papa says that sometimes we're the very devil and he doesn't want us around when he's eating his soup."

"Well, why don't you dine with us this evening, to celebrate my being here. Do you have another gown?"

"I don't like you and I don't want to celebrate. You're not my mama. I'll tell Philip that we'll make you leave."

"Do you have another gown?"

"Aye, but not new. It's short, just like this one. Papa says we don't have any groats for fripteries—"

"Fripperies."

"Yes, that's it. Aunt Arleth says I grow too fast and Papa mustn't waste his groats on me. She says she's not surprised that we're poor, since he should never have been the laird in the first place."

"Hmmm. Your papa now has sufficient groats for new dresses. We'll ask him."

"They're your groats. I heard Cousin MacDuff talking to Aunt Arleth about how you were a great heiress and that's why Papa married you. She sniffed and said it was proper that he had sacrificed himself. She said it was the first decent thing he'd done in his life."

Good grief, Sinjun thought, momentarily stunned. Aunt Arleth sounded like a thoroughly nasty old bird. She said, calmly enough, even with a smile hovering, "That's right. The poor boy is very noble and pragmatic. So you shouldn't want to send me away, because I'm here for a higher purpose than your governesses."

"Aunt Serena said that Papa had your money now and that maybe you'd go to heaven, like my mama."

"Dahling! Shut your mouth!"

Colin strode into the bedchamber, his eyes on the little girl, who was gazing at him with adoration and now some perturbation, because he hadn't sounded pleased with her. Sinjun stared at him. He looked stern and forbidding, striding into the room, the laird, the master, the earl, and he looked harassed.

"She was just giving me the family news, Colin," Sinjun said mildly. "Surely you want me to know what Aunt Arleth and Auntie Serena think of me. I have also decided that you're right and Dahling just might be a Great Beauty. Lord knows she's precocious. But she does need some new gowns. More than enough reason, don't you think, that I accompany you back to Edinburgh?"

"No. Dahling, go to your aunt Serena. You'll be dining with us at the big table tonight. Go now."

Dahling scooted off the bed, looked back at Sinjun, shook her head, and skipped from the room.

"What was she telling you?"

"Just children talk, Colin, about everything and about nothing. As I told you, I quite like children and I'm with them a lot, what with my three nephews and all of Ryder's Beloved Ones. Why the devil didn't you tell me about them?"

She saw then that Colin could be just like Douglas and Ryder and Tysen. She supposed that it was a trait all men shared. When they were clearly in the wrong, or when a topic wasn't to their liking or made them uncomfortable, why then, they simply ignored it. He said now, "What did she say?"

However, living with three brothers had taught her perseverance. "Why didn't you tell me?"

He raked his fingers through his black hair, making it stand on end. "Damnation, Joan, it doesn't matter now."

Sinjun leaned back against the pillows, pulling the covers over her more securely. "I can see your point of view, Colin. Actually, I can see it quite clearly. You were afraid I wouldn't want you for a husband if you'd told me I'd be the proud stepmother of two children who chase away every governess that you or your wife ever hired. Isn't that right?"

"Yes. No. Maybe. I don't know, dammit."

"Are there any more little surprises you've got waiting for me? Perhaps a mistress in one of those castle towers, who has long golden hair and unrolls it out of the window to pull you up? How about a couple of illegitimate children wandering about? Or perhaps a mad uncle locked away in the Tudor section in a priest hole?"

"Do you have a gown to wear this evening?"

"Yes, but I'll need Emma to press it for me. I do have only one, Colin. Are there any more surprises?"

"I'll get Emma, and no, there aren't, except . . . how did you know about Great-Uncle Maximilian? He is mad, true, and he does howl at the full moon every month, but who could have told you? Normally he's content to quote Rabbie Burns and drink gin."

"I will assume you're jesting."

"Yes, damn you, I am. But the children, that's different. They're just children, Joan, and they're smart little beasts, and they're mine. I hope you won't take them into dislike and abuse them just because you're angry at me for not telling you about them."

"As in throw rocks at them?"

"I'm serious."

"Perhaps, then, I can throw rocks at you?"

"If you're well enough to throw rocks, why then, you're well enough for me to take you again tonight." He felt instant guilt, because she actually paled at his words. "Oh, stop it! I'm not a damned savage."

"I'm relieved. How many governesses have Philip and Dahling enjoyed, say, in the past two years?"

"I don't know. Not more than three, maybe four. Fiona didn't like one of them, so the children weren't responsible. The last one was a fainting ninny and she had no guts."

"No guts, huh? All right, please tell Emma to press my gown for me. I will have it for her when I have unpacked my valise."

"She will do that for you."

"No, I prefer to."

"How do you feel?"

"Fine. There's no dressing screen in this room. I trust you will fetch one."

"Why? You're my wife and I'm your husband."

"It isn't proper for me to dress and undress in front of you. Besides, I will need assistance. Where is the countess's bedchamber?"

"Through that door," he said, and pointed to a door that she could barely see because it was built into the wainscoting.

"Is that where your former wife slept?"

"Joan, what's wrong with you? It doesn't matter, none of it. She's dead. You're my wife and—"

"Since you have my groats, you can send me to heaven with Dahling's mama. You say that bullet in Edinburgh was intended for you. Perhaps it wasn't, Colin."

He picked up a pillow and threw it at her. It hit her smack in the face.

"Don't you ever speak like that again, do you hear me? Damn you, you're my bloody countess!"

"All right. I was just angry with you and that's why I was nasty. Forgive me."

"I will, this time. Kindly moderate your insults in the future, and stop carping at me. Now, you must hurry. Dinner is served in forty-five minutes. I'll get Emma."

He left her without another word.

Well, Sinjun thought, smoothing her hand over the pillow he'd thrown at her, his reaction was interesting. Perhaps he did care for her a bit.

Cousin MacDuff was the first family member she encountered when she came downstairs. He was standing at the foot of the staircase, a brandy snifter in his hand, looking very pensive. He looked even more massive than she remembered. His violent red hair was pomaded down, and his clothes were quite natty, black britches, white linen, white silk stockings.

She was nearly upon him before he noticed her presence. "Joan! Hello and welcome to Vere Castle. Forgive me for not being here when you arrived."

"Hello, MacDuff. Please call me Sinjun. Only Colin persists in this Joan business."

"You'll bring him about, I daresay."

"You think so, do you?"

"Yes. He told me about your reception in Edinburgh—your brothers being there and all." He paused and looked upward at the minstrel's gallery, all in gloom now, frowning a bit. "I should like to have seen it. It sounds like you had quite a bit of fun. Did Angus really shoot a hole in the drawing room ceiling?"

"A very big hole. It made everything quite black and smelly."

"I'm always on the short end of adventures. It doesn't seem fair, since I'm so big, does it? I could champion any number of lovely young ladies just by frowning at the opponents. They would scatter to the winds, I daresay, were I to wave one of my gigantic fists at them. Colin also told me about the shot." He paused and studied her face, touching the mark with his blunt, large fingers. "There won't be a scar, thank the good Lord. Don't worry, Colin will bring the culprit to justice. What do you think of your new home?"

Sinjun looked at the dusty oak wainscoting, the dull and dirty stair railings that were so beautifully carved. "I think it's magic. I also think a lot of dirty hands have touched the railings and a lot of other hands have been idle."

"No one has done much of anything since Fiona and Colin's brother died."

"Including simple housekeeping?"

"So it would appear." MacDuff looked around the large first floor. "You're right. I hadn't noticed. But you know, things have been like this since Colin's mother died some five years ago. It's good you're here, Sinjun. You can see that all is brought back up to snuff."

"Her name is Joan."

"Your one refrain, Colin?" His voice was amiable. He shook his cousin's hand, making Colin wince.

"Joan is her name."

"Well, I prefer Sinjun. Now, let's go into the drawing room, shall we? Doubtless your bride would like a sherry."

"Yes, I would," Sinjun said, and looked at her husband and swallowed. He was beautiful in black evening garb and pristine white linen. He was immaculate and so handsome she wanted to hurl herself into his arms. She wanted to kiss his mouth, his earlobe, the pulse in his neck.

"Good evening, Joan."

"Hello, Colin."

He arched a black brow at the interested tone of her voice, but said nothing, merely bowed.

Aunt Arleth was the only one in the dark and dour drawing room, sitting near a sluggishly burning peat fire. She was dressed in unrelieved black, a beautiful cameo at her throat. She was very thin, her hair black and luxuriant, pulled up in an elegant twist, white wings sweeping back at her temples. She had once been quite pretty. Now she looked annoyed, her mouth thin, her pointed chin up. Aunt Arleth rose and said without preamble, "The children are eating with Dulcie in the nursery. My nerves are overset, nephew, what with the arrival of this Young Person, whom you had to carry upstairs, with everyone looking. I don't want the children at my table tonight."

Colin merely smiled. "I, on the other hand, have missed my children." He motioned to a footman, who was wearing a very ragged livery of dark blue and faded white. "Fetch the children, please, Rory."

There was a hiss of anger, and Sinjun turned to Aunt Arleth and said, "Please, ma'am, it is I who wish to have them at the dinner table. They're now my responsibility and I should like to get to know them."

"I have never believed children should be allowed to eat with the adults."

"Yes, Aunt, we know your feelings. Indulge me for this evening. Joan, some sherry? Aunt, what would you like?"

Aunt Arleth accepted her sherry, sat down, and became markedly silent. Serena came into the drawing room at that moment, looking like a princess in a very formal gown of pale pink silk, her lovely dark brown hair threaded through with matching pink ribbon. She was smiling, her eyes bright and very gray and staring directly at Colin. Oh dear, Sinjun thought, and accepted her sherry from MacDuff. What, she wondered, was it going to be like when Colin left? Serena then nodded to Sinjun and gave her a smile that said quite clearly that she knew she was beautiful and Sinjun must know it as well.

Sinjun smiled at her, willing to try, and to her surprise Serena smiled back. It seemed a genuine smile, and Sinjun prayed it was, but she wasn't stupid. There were deep waters in Vere Castle, very deep. Then the children were ushered in by Dulcie, the nursery maid, a young girl with merry dark eyes and a lovely smile and a very big bosom.

Both children were beautiful. Philip, the image of his father, stood tall and proud and scared. His eyes darted from his father to Sinjun and back again. He made no move toward anyone, nor did he say anything. Dahling, on the other hand, walked over to her father in her too-short gown and a pair of slippers that had certainly seen better days, and said, "Dulcie said if we weren't good at the dinner table and made you yell at us, the ghost of Pearlin' Jane would get us."

"Och, what a bairn!" Dulcie exclaimed, throwing up her hands and laughing. "Yer a wee nit, ye are, my lass!"

"Thank you, Dulcie," Aunt Arleth said, clearly dismissing the girl. "You may return to fetch them in an hour, no longer, mind."

"Aye, ma'am," Dulcie said in a squashed voice as she curtsied.

"I don't like you filling the child's mind with those absurd ghost stories."

"No, ma'am."

"There are many who have seen Pearlin' Jane," MacDuff said mildly. He turned to Sinjun. "She's our most famous ghost, a young lady who was supposedly betrayed and heartlessly murdered by our great-grandfather."

"Nonsense," said Aunt Arleth. "I've never seen her. Your great-grandfather wouldn't have hurt a gnat."

"Fiona saw her many times," Serena said quietly to Sinjun. "She told me that the first time she saw her in her white pearl-sewn gown, she nearly fainted with fright, but the ghost didn't try to harm her or scare her. She just sat there, atop the castle gate, her face as white as death itself, and stared at her."

"I fancy that was just about the time Fiona discovered Colin had a mistress."

Sinjun gasped. She stared at Aunt Arleth, not believing what the woman had said. It was outrageous; it was unbelievable. Now she said to Sinjun, her voice full of spite, "Don't be a ninny, girl! Men are men no matter where you are, and they all have mistresses, aye, and Fiona found out about that little slut he'd taken to his bed."

Sinjun looked swiftly at Colin, but there was only a sardonic look on his face. It was as if he were quite used to this sort of attack and didn't regard it. But Sinjun had no intention of ignoring it. She was infuriated. She said in a very loud and clear voice, "You will not speak of Colin again in that discreditable way. He would never break his vows, never. If you think he would, why then, you are either blind or stupid, or just plain mean. I won't tolerate it, ma'am. You live in my husband's house. You will treat him with the respect he deserves."

How to make an enemy in just a few short seconds, Sinjun thought. Aunt Arleth sucked in her breath but said nothing. Sinjun looked down at her clasped hands. There was utter silence.

Then Colin laughed, a deep, full, rich laugh that reverberated off the water-spotted wallpaper of the large drawing room. He said with very real humor, "Aunt Arleth, beware. Joan here must needs protect me. She won't allow any insult against me. She needs but a horse and some armor and she would go into a tourney to defend my honor. I suggest, ma'am, that you moderate your speech when around her. I have found that even when she is angry with me, she is still ferocious in her defense of me. Only she is allowed to cosh my head, no one else. It's odd, but it's true. Now, shall we all adjourn to the dining room? Philip, take Dahling's hand. Joan, allow me to show you the way."

"She needs to be taught manners," Aunt Arleth said under her breath, but of course not under enough.

"My groats are on you," MacDuff said in her ear as Colin seated her in the countess's chair down the long expanse of mahogany dining table. It was Aunt Arleth's chair, Sinjun knew that. She held her breath, but Aunt Arleth merely paused a moment, then shrugged. She seated herself in a chair held by Colin, on his left hand. No upset, no uproar, for which Sinjun was grateful. The children were placed in the middle, MacDuff on one side, Serena on the other.

"I wish to propose a toast," Colin said, and rose to his feet. He lifted his wineglass. "To the new countess of Ashburnham."

"Hear! Hear!" MacDuff shouted.

"Yes, indeed," said Serena warmly.

The children looked from their father to their new stepmother. Philip said very clearly, "You're not our mother even though Father has had to make you the countess to save us from ruin."

Aunt Arleth smiled maliciously at Sinjun.

"No, I'm not your mother. If you hadn't noticed, Philip, I'm far too young to be your mother. Goodness, I'm only nineteen. It was a strange thing for you to say, you know."

"Even when you're old you won't be our mother."

Sinjun only smiled at the boy. "Perhaps not. Soon my mare, Fanny, should arrive. She's a great goer, Philip. Do you ride?"

"Of course," he said in a scornful voice. "I'm a Kinross and someday I will be the laird. Even Dahling rides, and she's just a little nit."

"Excellent. Perhaps both of you will show me some of the countryside on the morrow."

"They have their lessons," said Aunt Arleth. "I must teach them, since the governesses won't stay. It's Serena's duty, but she shirks it."

Colin said mildly, "Joan is a treat, Aunt. Let the children attend her. No matter their snits, she is their stepmother and is here to stay. They must get to know her." He then bent a very stern eye on his son. "You won't torment her, do you understand me, Philip?"

"Yes," Sinjun agreed in high good humor, "no snakes in my bed, no slimy moss dredged up from a swamp for me to sit on or clutch in my hand in the dark."

"We have better things than that," Dahling said.

"The slime is an interesting thought," Philip said, and Sinjun recognized that intense contemplative look. She'd seen it a number of times on every child's face she'd ever known.

"Eat your potatoes," Colin said. "Forget slime."

There was haggis for dinner, and Sinjun wondered if she would fade away and become another resident ghost through lack of food. At least there were several removes, so she managed to eat enough to satisfy her. She listened to Colin and MacDuff discuss several business ventures and problems with local people. She drifted a bit, for there was still pain between her thighs, dull and throbbing now, but still there. She jerked her head up when she heard Colin say, "I'll be leaving in the morning to return to Edinburgh. There is much to be done."

"Now that you have her money?" Aunt Arleth said.

"Yes," Colin said. "Now that I have her money I can begin to solve all the miserable problems left by my father and brother."

"Your father was a great man," said Arleth. "None of it was his fault."

Colin opened his mouth, then merely smiled and shook his head. He continued his conversation with MacDuff. Sinjun would have liked to throw her plate at his head. He truly was going to dump her here in this strange place, and without a by-your-leave. Wonderful, just wonderful. Two children who would do their best to make her life miserable, and two women who would probably just as soon see her jump from one of the crenellated towers as speak to her.

Serena said, "We must have a party for your wife, Colin. It will be expected. All our neighbors will be aghast to learn that you've married again so quickly—after all, it's only been seven months—but since you only did it for her money, it's best that they understand it as quickly as possible. Don't you agree, MacDuff?"

Cousin MacDuff said nothing, merely turned to Colin when he said, "When I return we will discuss it."

Sinjun forked down a bit of potatoes and gave her attention to her new home. It was far more pleasant than her dinner companions. The Tudor dining room was, somewhat to her surprise, utterly charming. It was long and narrow, with portraits covering nearly every inch of wall. The huge table and ornately carved chairs were heavy and dark and surprisingly comfortable. The draperies that ran the entire brace of long windows at the front of the room were old and shiny, but the quality was there and the color was superb. She fancied that she would match the same soft gold brocade.

"Vere Castle is the finest house in all the county."

She smiled toward Serena. "It's magical."

"It's also falling down about our ears," Aunt Arleth said. "I don't imagine that Colin has got you with child yet."

That was straight talking, Sinjun thought. She heard a fork clatter to a plate and looked up to see Colin staring at his aunt. It was a bit of impertinence, but since Colin had already spoken of it, Sinjun wasn't shocked as she had been at first.

"No," she said mildly.

"You will remember the children are here, Aunt."

"We don't want any of her children around," Philip said. "You won't allow it, will you, Papa? You have me and Dahling. You don't need more children."

"We wouldn't like them at all," Dahling said. "They'd be ugly, like her."

"Now, now," Sinjun said, laughing. "They could be quite beautiful, like your father. And, Dahling, you did admit that my Sherbrooke blue eyes were nice as well as my Sherbrooke chestnut hair."

"You made me," said Dahling, her lower lip jutting out.

"True. I twisted your arm and stuck pins in your nose. Already I'm such a wicked stepmother."

"Pearlin' Jane will get you," Dahling said as a last resort.

"I look forward to seeing her," Sinjun said. "I will see if she is as impressive as our own Virgin Bride."

"Virgin Bride?" MacDuff cocked his head to one side, his bushy red eyebrows hiked up a good inch.

"She's our resident ghost at Northcliffe Hall, a young lady of the sixteenth century who was just wedded when her groom was murdered before he could come to her."

Dahling's eyes were fixed on Sinjun's face. "She's real? You've seen her?"

"Oh yes. She appears to the ladies of the family, but I know for a fact that my brother the earl has seen her as well, though he refuses to admit it. She's quite beautiful, really, with very long pale hair and a flowing gown. She speaks to you but never out loud, it's in your mind you can hear her, I guess you'd say. She seems to want to keep the ladies of the house safe."

"Utter nonsense," said Colin.

"That's what Douglas says. But he has seen her, Alex told me so. He just can't bring himself to admit it out loud, because he fears people will think him hysterical and he will think himself hysterical as well. All the Northcliffe earls have written about her, but Douglas refuses to. A pity, really."

"I don't believe you," Philip said. "Virgin Bride, what a silly name!"

"Well, I don't believe you either. Pearlin' Jane is a pretty silly name, too. No, I shan't believe you until I've seen Pearlin' Jane for myself." As a challenge, it was excellent, Sinjun thought, looking at Philip from beneath her lashes. She wouldn't be at all surprised to have a rendition of Pearlin' Jane haunting her room once Colin had left.

"Children, you will leave now. Here's Dulcie."

Sinjun didn't want the children to leave. At least she'd gotten their interest. Philip gave his father a pathetic look, but Colin only shook his head and said, "I will be up later to tuck you up. Be good now and go with Dulcie. Joan, when you are finished, you may take Aunt Arleth and Serena into the drawing room. MacDuff and I have some more plans to discuss. We'll join you shortly."

"What a pity that you interest him so little that he must leave you."

Ah, Auntie, Sinjun thought, you'd best mind your tongue. She smiled lovingly at the woman and said, "I agree. If his marvelously great father hadn't been such a wastrel bastard, perhaps he wouldn't have to leave."

She heard Colin laugh from behind her. She had played her cards all wrong, she decided later. He would leave with no concern that she would have any problems with his relatives. If she had only had the foresight to burst into helpless tears, just maybe he would have remained—that, or taken her with him back to Edinburgh.

"I think Colin is quite the handsomest man in all of Scotland," Serena said.

"You're stupid and silly," Aunt Arleth said. "Just like your sister was."

Sinjun drew a deep breath and kept a smile pinned to her mouth.

It was after midnight when Colin came quietly into the laird's bedchamber. Joan was sleeping very close to the far edge of the bed, the covers pulled to her nose. He smiled, then stripped off his clothes. Naked, he walked to the bed and stepped onto the dais. Slowly, he eased the covers down. She stirred, batting at the covers with her hands, but she didn't awaken. Slowly, he eased up her long cotton nightgown. Easy and slow, he told himself. He'd gotten it up to her thighs when he was content to stop for a moment and look at her long white legs. Very nice legs, very nice indeed. He felt himself swell, but knew she couldn't accommodate him tonight. No, he wanted to see if he could accommodate her. He gently lifted her hips and pulled the nightgown to her waist. He moved the candle closer. Ah, but she was lovely. He stared at the chestnut hair that covered her woman's mound, her flat white belly that could even now have his child growing there. It was a heady thought. She tried to twist away from him, moaning a bit in her sleep. He eased her legs open, and she obligingly parted them more widely. Now, he thought. He bent her knees up and parted her flesh. He winced at the sight of that soft flesh roughened from the hard riding they'd done. He parted her with his fingers, wincing again at the redness. "I'm sorry," he said quietly, and wondered if he should try to give her pleasure. Why not? She needed to learn that it was possible to enjoy him. He leaned down and lightly touched his mouth to her white belly. She quivered; he felt the smooth muscles tighten at the touch of his mouth. He continued kissing her, light, nipping kisses, until he eased down between her legs and found her and blew his warm breath over her flesh. She squirmed. He smiled, pleased.

He parted her soft flesh and lightly touched her with his tongue. In the next instant, she screamed, jerking away from him, flinging her hands out to ward him off, pulling her nightgown down.

"Hello," he said, grinning up at her. "I love your taste, but I must have more of you to be certain. What do you think, Joan?"

CHAPTER
═10═

SINJUN OPENED HER MOUTH to yell again, then closed it. He was lying between her legs, his arms hooked around her thighs, his chin lightly resting on her belly. He was grinning at her.

"Well? Would you like me to do more?"

She got hold of herself, by a meager thread. It was difficult because she'd never imagined such . . .

She said aloud, "What you were doing—it was startling. It is very embarrassing. Are you certain such things are done?"

He leaned down and lightly kissed her again, then raised his head, pushed her legs more widely apart, and gave her a beautiful smile. "You do taste good, Joan. Yes, my dear, a man much enjoys kissing a woman between her legs."

"I feel very odd, Colin. Would you please let me go? I am not used to having my nightgown around my waist and anyone positioned precisely where you are. It is disconcerting. And you are a man, after all."

"If I continue to kiss and caress you here, you will enjoy it immensely."

"Oh no, how could that be true? Really, Colin, let me go now. Goodness, you're naked!"

"Yes. Don't be frightened. I have no intention of taking you again. Actually I wanted to see how badly you'd hurt yourself by riding today."

"I hurt *myself!* What gall! 'Twas *you* who hurt me."

He drew himself up between her legs and she saw that he was staring down at her and now his fingers were lightly stroking over her and she was so embarrassed she couldn't think of a word to say. "You're raw, I'm afraid. But you will heal. Just stay off a horse for a while." Then he kissed her belly, lowered himself over her, and settled himself comfortably. She felt his sex hard and pressed against her and tried to bring her legs together, foolish, of course because he was lying between them.

"Your breasts feel nice against my chest. What do you think?"

"I don't like this. I don't think you can control yourself. I don't want you to hurt me again."

"I'm a man, Joan, not a randy boy. I won't take you, I promise. Now, kiss me and I'll leave you alone."

She pursed her lips, but he just laughed and ran his tongue along her bottom lip. "Open your mouth. Don't you remember begging me to teach you to kiss? How could you have forgotten so quickly?"

"I haven't forgotten. I just don't want to do it right and have you become a ravening barbarian again."

"A good point." He kissed her again, lightly, then rolled off her. He watched her quickly jerk her nightgown down to her toes, then pull the covers over both of them and lie down on her back, all the world like a supine statue.

"If you like, you can give me pleasure, then."

He was balanced on his elbow, facing her. His eyes were dark, his cheeks flushed, and she knew it for what it was. A man's desire. "How is that possible? You promised, Colin, not to hurt me again."

"Oh, it's very possible. I was touching you and fondling you between your legs. You can do the same to me."

She looked at him as if he were mad, completely and utterly mad.

"It's done all the time between people who care about each other."

"I'm not quite certain I understand, Colin."

"My sex, Joan. You can kiss and caress my sex."

"Oh."

"On the other hand, perhaps it's better that I go to sleep now. I must leave early tomorrow morning."

"Really? You would like that? It would give you pleasure, Colin?"

He wasn't deaf to the utter bewilderment and disbelief in her voice, and said quickly, "It's all right. I do have to get some sleep."

"I'll try it, if you wish."

"What?"

"I'll kiss you there, if you wish."

He saw then that she wasn't at all repelled by the thought of him. On the contrary, she was quite intrigued by the notion, and he felt himself begin to shake. He wondered if he'd spill his seed if he allowed her mouth on him. His sex throbbed. No, best not to disgust her, because he couldn't be certain that he could control himself. He shook his head vehemently and said, "All right."

He lay on his back but did nothing more. Sinjun raised the covers and stared at him. He felt her staring at him and throbbed all the more. "Touch me."

Very slowly, she lowered the covers to his feet, then she simply stared at him for a very long time. She finally flattened her palm on his hard belly just at the instant before he believed he would yell with the need for her to touch him. "You're beautiful, Colin."

He couldn't help it. He moaned, even as he pressed upward. When her fingers lightly touched him, he quivered like a raw young boy.

He held himself rigid, his hands fisted at his sides. "Touch me, Joan. With your mouth."

She stared at him again, then lightly closed her hand around him. She eased down on her knees beside him, her hair cascading over his belly, but he didn't notice the beauty of it, the warmth of it, because he was focused on his sex and on her mouth. He felt her hot breath and nearly died from the intense pleasure. When she lightly nipped at him, he very nearly yelled.

"You're very different from me," she said, and caressed him; oh, it was tentative, but that made it all the more seductive. "I could never be as beautiful as you." He wanted to tell her that was nonsense, but he was silent, straining, wanting so much for her to take him into her mouth, but she didn't, not understanding, really, but she would learn, and he wanted her to do things at her own pace. She experimented and he squirmed and wanted to groan, but held his mouth shut, not wanting to frighten her.

When she finally took him into her mouth, he knew he couldn't control himself. The nearly painful sensations that rocketed through him shook him deeply. He had to stop this. He had no intention of shocking her or repelling her, and thus, even though he felt more frenzied, more urgent than he ever had in his life, he pulled her away.

She twisted about to look at him and her hair tumbled over his belly and chest. "Didn't I do it right?"

He looked into her beautiful Sherbrooke blue eyes and tried to smile— not much of a success that smile, but he tried. "I'm a man, Joan, and it's difficult for me. Now, no more questions. Settle here, against me, and let's go to sleep."

She nestled against him, her palm over his racing heart. She said nothing. Finally, his heart began to slow. She kissed his chest, then said, "I'll try to do things properly, Colin, and touching you with my hands and my mouth is quite nice, really, for you are so splendid. But this other business of your body—you are much too large, surely you must realize that. It won't work, you have already seen that it won't. I'm sorry, but there it is."

"You're a ninny who doesn't know anything." He kissed her nose, then squeezed her more tightly against him. "I should prefer it if you removed that ridiculous nightgown."

"No," she said after several thoughtful moments. "I don't think that's a good idea."

He sighed. "You're probably right."

"Colin?"

"Hmmm?"

"Will you bed other women when you return to Edinburgh?"

He was utterly silent. "Do you believe I took a mistress while my first wife was alive?"

"Certainly not!"

"Well then, why would you believe I would sleep with another woman whilst wedded to you?"

"Men do, I know, except for my brothers. They're faithful to their wives because they love them very much. I hope you are more like them than all those other men who have no honor. On the other hand, you don't love me. So it is a question."

"Will you seduce any men while I'm gone?"

She hit him in the belly, and he obligingly grunted. Then her hand smoothed over where she'd hit him, her fingers splaying downward to touch him, and then he did moan. "No," he said, his breath hard and deep. "Don't, please."

She drew her hand away, and he was both relieved and hated it.

"Why did your aunt Arleth say you'd taken a mistress while your wife was still alive?"

He didn't answer her but said instead, "She doesn't much care for me, as you will discover, since you're my wife and you now live here. I don't know why."

"One could believe her, you know," she said, "except it's obvious she doesn't know how you're made. I know how large you are, I know how a woman would look at you and want to run. That is, you're beautiful, Colin, but as I told you, that part of you that—"

"It's called my sex, Joan."

"Very well, your sex, Colin. What woman could possibly want to do that willingly? It would have to be your wife and thus she'd have to do it."

He laughed, he couldn't help it. "You will see. Yes, you will see."

"Are other men even larger than you?"

"How do I even attempt to answer that question? I'll sound like a conceited sod if I say no, certainly not, and I'd bludgeon my own male pride if I said yes. I haven't seen all that many naked men, actually, particularly when they're aroused. Nonetheless, you don't know anything about it. You will learn, however. Now, go to sleep."

She fell asleep before he did. His mind was filled with visions of Robert MacPherson, and the bastard was plotting his demise. He also thought about his very innocent wife, who had no qualms at all about asking him questions about his male parts with the utmost candor. It was amusing, really. He'd never met a girl like her in his life. Ah, and the feel of her mouth on him—it was enough to make a stoic man cry.

He really didn't want to leave her just yet, but there was no choice. He had so much to do, and he simply refused to put her at risk. She would be safe here. MacDuff had told him MacPherson was in Edinburgh, far from Vere Castle. Yes, she'd be safe here, and he would be able to track Robbie MacPherson down and make the ass see reason, that or kill him. At least he wouldn't have to worry that his wife would try to protect him and attack MacPherson herself.

When Sinjun went downstairs the following morning, Colin was already gone. She stared at Philpot, the Kinross butler, and said blankly, "He left already?"

"Aye, my lady, with the sun."

"Well, blessed hell," Sinjun said, and walked to the dining room.

Sinjun was staring up at the Kinross coat of arms above the huge fireplace in the medieval central section of the house. Three silver lions were painted on a shield of gold. Two larger lions were holding the shield upright, and a griffin flew atop. It said beneath the shield: *Wounded But Unconquered.*

She laughed. It was a wonderful motto and at the moment, with the soreness still in evidence between her thighs, it was even somewhat apt for her.

"Fiona always liked the Kinross coat of arms, but she never laughed that I remember."

Sinjun turned to face Serena. She smiled. "The motto just reminds me of something. I had thought to fetch Philip and Dahling after lunch. Do you know their schedule?"

"Aunt Arleth has the headache. Philip and Dahling are probably riding roughshod over Dulcie."

"Goodness, I wish I'd known. If you will excuse me, Serena, I'll go see to them."

"He won't ever love you, you know."

That was plain speaking, Sinjun thought, staring at the woman. "Why not? I'm not a bad person nor am I ugly, even though it pleases Dahling to think so."

"He loves another," Serena said, her voice verging on the dramatic. Sinjun nearly laughed. She pressed her hand against her breast and breathed, "Another?"

"He loves another," Serena said again, and walked like a graceful princess from the huge Tudor entrance hall.

Sinjun could only shake her head. She was waylaid on her way to the nursery by the housekeeper, Mrs. Seton, a lady with very dark eyes and thick dark eyebrows that very nearly met over her eyes. She was the wife of Mr. Seton, a very important man in the local kirk, Colin had mentioned to her, and also the Kinross steward. Sinjun gave her a bright smile.

"My lady, I understand—indeed, all understand—that we are no longer in Dire Straits."

"This is true. His lordship is in Edinburgh right now to pull us all out of the River Styx."

Mrs. Seton drew a deep breath. "Good. Vere Castle has been my home all my life. It's disgraceful, all this neglect."

Sinjun thought of Philip and Dahling and decided they could happily torment Dulcie for a little while longer. "Why don't I come to your rooms, Mrs. Seton, for a nice spot of tea? We can make a list of what we need."

A list. Then it had to be approved by Colin. What an absurdity. What did Colin know of bed linens or draperies or rents in chair fabrics or dishes and pans?

"Then you must tell me where we can go to replace all that we need."

She thought Mrs. Seton would burst into tears. Her thin cheeks filled out and turned quite pink with pleasure. "Oh aye, my lady, oh aye, indeed!"

"I also notice that the servants aren't garbed all that well. Is there a good seamstress in Kinross? The children need new clothes, as well."

"Oh aye, my lady! We'll go to Kinross—a small village just at the other end of the loch. Everything we'll need will be there right and tight. No need to go to Edinburgh or Dundee, good enough goods up here, ye'll see."

"Colin won't like you interfering like this. You have just arrived, you don't really belong here, and yet you're trying to take over. I won't have it."

Sinjun winked at Mrs. Seton before turning to Aunt Arleth. "I had thought you prostrate with the headache, ma'am."

Aunt Arleth's lips thinned. "I roused myself because I was afraid of what you might do."

"Do begin the list, Mrs. Seton. I shall join you in your sitting room shortly. Oh yes, I should like to inspect all the servants' rooms as well."

"Yes, my lady," Mrs. Seton said, and her departing walk was brisk with energy.

"Now, Aunt Arleth, what would you like to do?"

"Do? Whatever do you mean?"

"I mean, do you intend to keep sniping at me? Do you intend to continue in your unpleasant vein so that all are made miserable by your behavior?"

"You're a young girl! How dare you speak to me like that?"

"I am Colin's wife. I am the countess of Ashburnham. If I wish to tell you to go to the devil, Aunt Arleth, I am within my rights to tell you to."

Aunt Arleth looked so flushed Sinjun was momentarily concerned that she'd overdone her dose of honesty and the good lady would swoon at her feet with palpitations. But then the lady got herself well in hand. Aunt Arleth was made of sterner stuff, and Sinjun realized it fully when the lady said, "You are from a privileged, wealthy family. You are English. You don't understand what it's like to see everything rot around you. You haven't the least idea what it's like to see the crofters' children crying with hunger. And yet you come here and flaunt your money and expect all of us to fall at your feet."

"I don't believe I expected that at all," Sinjun said slowly. "What I expected was to be given a fair chance. You don't know me, ma'am. You are spouting generalities that rarely have anything to do with anyone. Please, can't we try to live in peace? Can you not just give me a chance?"

"You are very young."

"Yes, but I daresay that I will add to my age as the years progress."

"You are also too smart, young lady!"

"My brothers taught me well, ma'am."

"Colin doesn't belong here as the earl of Ashburnham. He is a younger son, and he refused to obey his father, refused to join with the Emperor."

"I'm very relieved that he didn't have anything to do with Napoléon. However, Colin did oblige his father. He stopped the feud with the MacPhersons by marrying Fiona. Isn't that true?"

"Aye, but then look what happened—he killed the bitch. Tossed her over the edge of that cliff, then pretended he didn't know what had happened, pretended he didn't remember. Oh aye, and now he's the laird and the MacPhersons are out for blood again."

"Colin didn't kill Fiona and you know it. Why do you so dislike him?"

"He did. There was no one else to have done it. She'd played him false, aye, with his own brother. That's a nice shock for you, isn't it, you ignorant little English twit. Well, it's true. Colin found out and killed her, and I wouldn't doubt it if he didn't also kill his brother, the beautiful boy, *my* beautiful clever boy, but that wretched Fiona flaunted herself to him and seduced him all unawares, and he couldn't help himself, and look what happened."

"Aunt Arleth, you are saying a good many things and all of them are quite confused."

"You stupid girl! Taken with Colin's good looks, weren't you? You couldn't wait to bed him, couldn't wait to have him make you a countess! All the girls want him, no sense at all, none of them, no more sense than you likely have and—"

"You said that Fiona didn't want him, and yet she was his wife."

"He didn't like her after a while. She wasn't pleased with how he treated her. She was difficult."

"All I know for certain is that Fiona wasn't a very good housekeeper. Just look, Aunt Arleth, everything is falling to bits and much of it has to do with a dusting cloth, or a mop and bucket—not my groats. Now I suggest that you calm yourself and have a cup of tea. I intend to set things aright here. You may either help me or I will simply go through you."

"I won't have it!"

"I'm speaking truthfully, ma'am. Will you cooperate with me or will I simply pretend you're not here?"

Goodness, she sounded firm and wonderfully in charge. Sinjun wanted to throw up she was so scared in that moment. Her first ultimatum. She'd pictured her mother as she'd spoken, and that had given her a goodly dose of confidence. No one ever gainsaid her mother.

Aunt Arleth shook her head and left the hall, her shoulders squared. Sinjun was rather relieved she couldn't see the good lady's face. She'd won; at least she could believe that she had.

Why, Sinjun wondered, staring at a thick, deep cobweb that was draped over the immense chandelier overhead, hadn't Mrs. Seton done any housekeeping? She seemed competent; she seemed eager. She got the answer to her question an hour later, once the Great List was done and each of them was sipping a cup of tea.

"Why, my lady, Miss MacGregor didn't allow it."

"Who is Miss MacGregor? Oh, Aunt Arleth."

"Aye. She said that if she saw anyone doing anything to make this pile of filthy rubble look cleaner, she would personally take a whip to them."

"But she just told me how much she hated how everything was going to rot and how the crofters' children were crying with hunger."

"What wickedness! Our crofters' children are never hungry! Och, if the laird had heard her say that, he'd have lost his wig right 'n tight!"

"How very odd. She's trying to sow dissension. Now, why would she want to do that? Surely it couldn't be just for my benefit." And Sinjun wondered about the other things she'd said. Were they lies, too? Very probably.

"After her sister, Lady Judith, died some five years ago—that was his lordship's mother—Miss MacGregor believed that the old laird would wed her, but he didn't. I believe he bedded her, but it wasn't marriage in the kirk he had in mind. Men, och! All alike they are, save for Mr. Seton, who has no interest at all in the desires of the flesh."

"I'm very sorry, Mrs. Seton."

"Aye, my lady, I am, too. In any case, Miss MacGregor was very angry, and as time passed she became more and more bitter. Petty, I guess ye'd say, with all of us. Ah, but she loved and pet Malcolm—the Kinross laird for such a short time, he was—and she treated him like a little prince. Malcolm even preferred her to his own mother, he did, because she spoiled him into rottenness and his mother swatted his hands but good when he was naughty. He'd run to Miss MacGregor and whine. Och, it wasn't good for his character, needless to say. A wastrel he became, beggin' yer pardon, my lady, but a wastrel he was, truly, just like his pa. Then he died all unexpected like, and Master Colin became the Kinross laird. We've yet to see what he will do. At least he isn't a wastrel, and he's fair. Perhaps there is more, but I don't know of it. As to the state of the castle, why, gentlemen rarely notice the state of things, until the cobwebs fall into their soup an' wind about their spoon. O' course, my lady, Fiona didn't care. When finally I did mention it to the new laird, he said we had no money for anything."

"Well, now we have money, and we have the will to do something, and you and I will see to it. By the time his lordship returns, Vere Castle will look like it did in his mother's time."

"Och, 'tis a fine day indeed when his lordship found ye to buy him."

"I would prefer that you said that a bit more diplomatically, Mrs. Seton."

"Aye, my lady."

Sinjun left the housekeeper's room whistling, tickled with herself that she'd had the foresight to remove her still nearly two hundred pounds from Colin's keeping. She wondered what he'd think when he missed the money.

Sinjun lay in the huge laird's bed, aware that even though the sheets were clean and the covers well aired, there was still a clinging musty smell of a room left closed up too long.

Her first three days at Vere Castle had passed quickly. Goodness, there was so much to be done. Mrs. Seton had already hired a good dozen women and another six men to come and clean the castle. Sinjun herself planned to scour this room. If she'd waited as her husband had demanded, her list for him would have stretched to the North Sea. Naturally, she'd never had any intention of waiting. Mrs. Seton was a fount of local knowledge, and on the morrow Sinjun would ride to Kinross, a fishing town that boasted both a seamstress and a man who worked with wood, and every sort of shop one could wish for. She had visited Colin's room in the north tower and had been charmed and dismayed. The stairs reaching the room were dangerous, the wood rotted in many places. Treacherous. The room itself was moldy, and all his books were in danger of rotting if she didn't act soon. She intended it to be in perfect condition before her husband ever again ventured up to his tower room.

Mrs. Seton, Murdock the Stunted, who came only to Sinjun's armpit and was one of Colin's most trusted servants, who did a bit of everything, and Mr. Seton the Kinross steward—the abstinent steward—all had accompanied her. If the men believed she would let them deal with the carpenters alone, they soon learned their mistake.

Kinross-shire was a small, quite pretty country town, mainly a base for the fishermen for nearby Loch Leven. A narrow road clung to the northern edge of Loch Leven, and the horses they rode knew the path very well indeed. The water was startling in its blueness and the hills that rose from it were alternately lush and green or barren and rugged and looked impassable. Nearly every foot of land was tilled, and now, in early summer, the land was covered with barley, wheat, corn, and rye.

Mr. Seton had quickly pointed out the kirk when they entered Kinross, extolling the local minister's virtues and condemnation of all those who were ripe for the nether regions. He pointed to the old town cross that was still attached to the iron collars for wrongdoers. As for Murdock the Stunted—all of four feet three inches in height, with a great head of red hair—Sinjun saw that he avoided going anywhere near the kirk or that town cross with its iron collar.

She'd discovered quickly enough that she might be the countess of Ashburnham, but all the locals were leery of her ability to pay the bills, and she knew she had to hoard the two hundred pounds. After all, as old Toothless Gorm pointed out, the old laird had sold the Kinross Mill House, hadn't he? And now a demned ironmonger was living there and lording it over all the locals. It took Mrs. Seton at her most undiplomatic—aye, my lady's an heiress, just dripping groats, and the laird got her married to him right and tight!—to bring old Toothless Gorm and the others back to smiles and enthusiasm. They'd purchased materials for new clothes for the children, for the servants, and for Sinjun, new plates for the servants' hall, new linens, and the list went on and on—Colin's list that he would never see, and many items were now duly crossed off. What a day it had been, full and satisfying.

Sinjun now turned onto her side in the huge bed. She was tired but that didn't help her to sleep. She thought of Kinross Mill House. She'd asked

Murdock the Stunted to take her there. It was a lovely house with superb gardens planted in the seventeenth century and an old mill with its wheel still poised above the water of a rushing stream. She'd stood there, looking at the lovely fish ponds, the graceful statuary, the topiary, and the immensely beautiful rose gardens, and vowed that somehow she and Colin would bring Kinross Mill House back into the family. Their children and grandchildren deserved to have their heritage restored.

She missed Colin dreadfully. He, on the other hand, didn't appear to be in any hurry at all to return to her. She had come to realize that men had to have women, it was that simple. Not just kissing, but their sex had to come into a woman and they had to release their seed. She would have to suffer this to make him content with her. And it had doubtless been the three times that had hurt her so much, that followed by the hard riding the following day. If she could convince him that just once would be sufficient for his needs, she could bear that easily. Once a night? Once a week? These were things she didn't know. As for her brothers Douglas and Ryder, she wondered how often they made love to their wives. Why the devil hadn't she spoken to Alex and asked her some pointed questions? Ah, she knew why. She'd believed she'd known everything there was to know. She'd read all of Douglas's Greek plays, after all, and they weren't at all reticent about matters of the flesh.

Blessed hell. She pictured Alex and Douglas, always touching, those two, kissing ardently when they believed no one was looking. And Ryder and Sophie were much the same. Ryder laughing as he fondled Sophie, teasing her even as he was nibbling on her ear. She would like Colin to do those things as well. It was just the other. Why hadn't she asked Alex? And Alex was such a small woman, much slighter than Sinjun, and Douglas was as large as Colin. It didn't make sense that Alex could possibly tolerate it. Blessed hell.

She sighed and rolled onto her back. It was then she heard the noise. She cracked an eye open and stared off into the darkness in the direction of the noise. It was just a very low scratching sort of noise. She must have imagined it. It was a very old house. All old structures had strange, unexplained shudders and sounds. She closed her eyes and snuggled down.

The noise came again, a bit louder this time. Scratching, as if something were trapped in the wainscoting. A rat? She didn't like that thought.

It stopped yet again but Sinjun was tense, waiting for it to resume.

It did, louder now. There was another sound with the scratching. Behind it, sort of. It sounded like something dragging along the floor. Something like a chain, heavy and slow, dragging across a wooden floor but oddly muffled.

Sinjun bolted up in bed. This was absurd!

Then there was a moan, distinct, sharp, a human moan that made gooseflesh rise on her arms. Her heart pounded. She strained to see in the darkness.

She had to light the candle. She reached out toward the night table to grab the lucifer matches, but she knocked them to the floor instead.

The moans stopped suddenly, as did the scratching. But the chain, dragging slowly, was louder now, and it was coming closer, still muffled, but it was coming, closer. It was in the bedchamber now.

Sinjun knew such terror she very nearly screamed. But the scream stuck in her throat. There was now a flicker of a light coming from the far corner of the bedchamber. Just a flicker of very white light, almost like smoke, because it was thin and vague, too. She stared at that light and knew such fear she nearly swallowed her own tongue.

The moans came again, and suddenly the chain slapped hard against something or someone. There was a cry, as if it were indeed a person the chain had struck.

Oh Jesus, she thought. She couldn't just sit here trembling like a twit. She didn't want to, but she forced herself to slither off the bed. She fumbled to find the matches. They'd slid somewhere and she couldn't find them. She was on her hands and knees when the moan came again, sharp and loud and filled with pain.

She paused. Then, still on her hands and knees, she crawled toward the end of the dais. She kept close to the floor. When she reached the end of the dais, she peered about the edge. There in the far corner the light burned more brightly. And the look of it was so very strange, so floaty and vague, yet so white.

Suddenly there was a horrible scream. Sinjun nearly leaped to her feet to run from the bedchamber. The hair lifted off her neck. She was shaking with cold terror.

Just as suddenly, the light was gone. The corner of the room was perfectly black again. There were no more moans.

She waited, so cold now she was shaking from that and not fear. She waited and waited, nerves stretched to the limit.

Nothing. No more scratching, nothing more.

Slowly, Sinjun reached up and pulled the covers down to the floor. She wrapped herself in them and curled against the dais. Finally she fell asleep.

It was Mrs. Seton who found her the next morning. Sinjun cocked open an eye to see the lady standing over her, saying over and over, "Oh, och! Ye're hurt, my lady! Oh, och!"

Sinjun was sore and all stiff from her hours on the hard floor, but she wasn't hurt. "Mrs. Seton, ah, please help me up. Yes, thank you. I had this dream, you see, a hideous nightmare actually, and it frightened me so I curled up down here."

Mrs. Seton merely arched one of those tremendously thick black brows at her and assisted her to her feet.

"I'll be fine now. If Emma could fetch some water for a bath, I'll be downstairs soon."

Mrs. Seton nodded and walked toward the door of the bedchamber, only to draw up short and stare at the floor. "Och, what is this, pray?"

It was the far corner of the bedchamber.

"What is what?" Sinjun's voice sounded creaky and harsh.

"This," Mrs. Seton said, pointing to the floor. "It looks like some sort of ooze from the Cowal Swamp, all black and smelly and thick. "Och, there are even wee lumps of—" Her voice broke off and she stepped back. "My mither always said it takes a lang spoon tae sup wi' the devil."

Mrs. Seton, who normally spoke the loveliest English, had fallen into a very thick Scottish brogue.

She got hold of herself in short order, however, and said thoughtfully, "However did it get here? Goodness, the swamp isn't all that close to Vere Castle." She gave Sinjun an odd look, then shrugged. "No matter. I'll send someone to clean up the mess."

Sinjun didn't want to see the mess up close, but she did. It was disgusting, as if something or someone had ladled out some of the filth onto the floor—that . . . or dragged it in, perhaps with a chain.

It was really quite well done of them, she thought as she stepped into her bath. Really quite well done.

CHAPTER
=11=

SINJUN MADE HER WAY around four local men yelling at one another in a language that wasn't at all English. They'd lowered the huge chandelier, replaced the dangerously rusted chain, and were now cleaning off the years of filth before the women began to wash all the crystal.

She spoke to them, smiled, and continued on her way to the smaller dining room, which was called the Laird's Inbetween Room. She drew to a halt to see Aunt Arleth berating a serving woman who was on her hands and knees in the massive Tudor entrance hall, scrubbing the marble squares.

"I won't have it, Annie! Get up and get out of here!"

"What is the problem?" Sinjun asked calmly.

Aunt Arleth whirled on her. "I don't approve of this, any of it, my girl. Now look what she's doing! Those squares have been as they were for years upon years."

"Yes, and so filthy, poor Annie must have pads on her knees she's been scrubbing so long."

"I told you that you didn't belong, young lady, and I meant it. And now you have the gall to spend the laird's money for this sort of nonsense."

"Oh no," Sinjun said, smiling. "It's all my money, I promise you."

"I think it looks nice, Aunt."

Serena, looking even more like a princess who'd lost her bearings than the last time Sinjun had seen her, floated down the wide staircase and into the entrance hall wearing a soft pale blue silk gown.

"What would you know? You, who do nothing but take and take. Just look at you! You're daft!"

"Look at what, Aunt? I look beautiful. Mirrors don't lie. You're old, so I understand that you would be jealous. Now, dear Joan, how may I be of service?"

"Well, that is very kind of you, Serena. Why don't you come into the Laird's Inbetween Room now and we'll discuss it over breakfast."

"Oh, I don't wish breakfast now. I believe I will pick some purple thistle, it's the emblem of Scotland, you know."

"No, I didn't know."

"Oh yes. It seems that some Vikings came ashore to rape and plunder, but one of them stepped on a bed of thistles and cried out in pain. It alerted all the native Gaels, and they were able to escape the enemy."

"Silly nonsense," said Aunt Arleth. She added under her breath, "Why don't you go sit under a rowan tree?"

"That is unkind, Aunt. Even if I did, nothing would happen. I become stronger by the day. I'm a witch, you know, Joan, but a good witch. I will speak to you later, Joan."

She floated through the massive front doors, humming softly to herself.

"What's a rowan tree?" Sinjun asked.

She heard Annie suck in her breath.

"Just never you mind."

"Very well. You will kindly leave Annie alone, Aunt Arleth. Should you like to have breakfast with me?"

"I will rid this place of you," Aunt Arleth said in the meanest voice Sinjun had ever heard. Then she turned on her heel and walked quickly from the entrance hall, not outside, as Serena had done, but upstairs. Now what was upstairs for her to ruin? Nothing, Sinjun thought, relieved.

"When you're tired, Annie, please stretch your legs and go to the kitchen. Cook has made big urns of coffee and tea for everyone, and I do believe there's also a grand tray of broonies." Sinjun rolled her tongue as she said the name of those tasty little oatmeal gingerbread biscuits.

"Thankee, m'lady."

Sinjun smiled, hearing the carpenters working on the stairs. After all the main stairs were repaired, the railings sound again, they would continue to repair the stairs that surrounded the minstrel's gallery. Then it was onward to the stairs in the north tower. All was proceeding apace. Sinjun felt quite pleased with herself.

She went into the Laird's Inbetween Room and was delighted to see Dulcie seated between Philip and Dahling.

"Good morning, Dulcie, children."

Dulcie said, "Good morning to ye, m'lady. Philip, dinna frown like that, it'll put creases in yer forehead fer all yer lifetime, ye ken? Dahling, stop smearing yer eggs on th' tablecloth!"

Another normal breakfast, Sinjun thought, remembering the breakfasts with all of Ryder's children. Bedlam, sheer and utter bedlam.

She served herself from the sideboard and sat down in Colin's chair, since it was closest to the children.

"That's Papa's chair."

"Yes, and it's a very nicely carved chair. It's even big enough for him."

"You don't belong there."

"You don't belong *here*," Dahling added.

"But I'm your father's wife. Where do I belong if not here, at Vere Castle?"

That stumped Dahling, but not Philip.

"Now that Papa has your money, you could go to a convent."

"Master Philip!"

"But I'm not Catholic, Philip. What would I do there? I don't know anything about crucifixes or matins or confessions."

"What's matins?"

"Prayers said at midnight or at dawn, Dahling."

"Oh. Go to France and be the queen."

"That's quite good, Dahling, but unfortunately there isn't a queen of France at the moment, there's just Empress Josephine, Napoléon's wife."

Both children were at an impasse. "This is delicious porridge. The fresh oatmeal makes all the difference. I love it with brown sugar."

"It's better with a knob of butter," Philip said.

"Oh, really? Then I will try it with a knob of butter tomorrow." She took the last spoonful, sighed with pleasure, took a sip of her coffee, and announced, "I have worked very hard for the past three days. This morning I have decided to reward myself, and you will be the rewards. You will go riding with me and show me around."

"My tummy hurts," Dahling said, grabbed her middle, and began to groan.

"Then 'tis buckbean ye be needing, Dahling."

"I'll ride with you," Philip said. Sinjun caught the evil wink he gave to his sister.

It took Philip less than two hours to get her lost in the Lomond Hills. It took Sinjun another three hours to find her way back to the castle. However, the morning wasn't a waste by any means. She'd met five crofters' families and drunk five different ciders. She found one man who could write—Freskin was his name—and thus he had a quill and some foolscap. She began to list all their names and what needed to be done in repairs. They had little grain, and nothing could keep the fear from Freskin's wife's face when he said it. They needed a cow and a couple of sheep; ah, but it was grain that was most important.

If any of the men, women, or children believed it a pitiful state of affairs for her that she was here only because of her healthy stock of groats, they were polite enough not to say so. Sinjun began to understand more and more of the local dialect. It was either that or drown in lilting sounds.

A sweetie wife, she learned, meant a gossip. Freskin's wife was certainly a sweetie.

Since the day was beautiful, she let her mare canter over the soft rolling hills and through the forests of larch, pine, birch, and fir. She drank from her cupped hands from Loch Leven. The water was so cold it made her lips tingle. She let her horse wander through a clump of fir trees and nearly stumbled into a peat bog. She held her mare to a walk over the harsh barren moors of the eastern hills. All in all, when she returned to Vere Castle she was tired and had quite enjoyed herself.

She paused atop the rise she and Colin had halted at such a short time before. Vere Castle still looked magical, perhaps even more so now that she felt a part of it. She reminded herself to purchase some material to make pennants to fly from those four castle towers. Perhaps she could even find a lovely young girl with golden hair to sit in one of the tower windows and plait and unplait her hair.

She was singing when she espied Philip surely on the lookout for her, near the massive Tudor front doors.

"Why, Master Philip, what a fine chase you led me! Goodness, you did best me, didn't you? You just wait until I take you with me to visit my home in southern England. I'll get you lost in the maple woods. But I will leave a trail of bread crumbs for you to follow home."

"I knew you'd come back."

"Yes, naturally. I live here."

Philip kicked a pebble with a very worn shoe. "I'll do better next time."

She didn't pretend to misunderstand him. She grinned and ruffled his beautiful thick black hair—his father's hair. "I have no doubt you will try to do better, but listen, Philip. I am here to stay, you know. Best accustom yourself, don't you think?"

"Dahling's right. You are ugly."

Sinjun was lying in her bed, wide awake, staring up at the black ceiling. It had been well over a week now, and still no word from Colin. She was worried; no, she was angry. The Tudor rooms were all immaculate and nearly all her two hundred pounds were gone. She was tempted to go to Edinburgh, not just to track down her husband but to get more funds. The people who were working for her surely deserved money for their efforts, not promises.

The carpenters were ready to move on to Colin's north tower. Perhaps she should wait; perhaps she should allow him to oversee the work. No, damn him. He didn't deserve the fun. She turned on her side, then flopped again onto her back and sighed.

She'd had her first visitors today, a local viscount and his wife, and they had come to see the heiress who'd saved the laird's hide.

She chanced to hear Aunt Arleth say, " 'Tis a mighty burden for all of us, Louisa. She might be an heiress, but she's most ill-bred and has no respect for her betters. She pays me no heed at all, ordering everyone about, she does."

Sir Hector MacBean had been looking about him with growing appreciation and no little astonishment. "I fancy her orders have accomplished a great deal, Arleth. The place smells positively clean. Louisa, just look up at the chandelier. I vow I used to fear walking beneath that monstrosity. Now it sparkles and it looks to have a new chain holding it up."

And that, Sinjun thought, arranging the skirts of the only gown left to her, was her cue to enter, which she did, all smiles.

The visit had gone off nicely. Philpot, attired in his new uniform of stark black and white, served Cook's clootie dumplings, surely the most delicious dish in all the world. He was as regal as King George III on one of his better days, and just as frigidly polite.

Aunt Arleth looked ready to spit. Sinjun had offered her a clootie dumpling, saying, "The custard sauce Cook makes defies description. Isn't it delicious, Aunt?"

Aunt Arleth was stuck. She could but nod.

The MacBeans were pleasant and appeared sincerely fond of Colin. When they were on the point of leaving, Lady Louisa smiled at Sinjun, patted her arm, and said in a low voice, "You seem a very competent girl. There is much here at Vere Castle that is odd, and all those damnable rumors, of course, but I fancy that you will bring things aright and ignore the talk, for it is nonsense naturally."

Whatever that meant, Sinjun thought, thanking the woman.

She remained on the front steps to wave them away. Aunt Arleth said, "You think you're so much better than the rest of us. Well, I daresay that Louisa saw through you. She will tell everyone that you are a mushroom, a no-account upstart that—"

"Aunt Arleth, I'm the daughter of an earl. If that makes me a mushroom, then you have need of further education. You will cease your diatribes. I have much to do." She turned, not giving Arleth a chance to say more. "Dahling! Come here, sweeting, we have a gown to fit on you."

The night before there had been a snake in Sinjun's bed: long and black and slithering frantically about, trying to hide. She'd blinked, then smiled. Wrapping it gently around her arm, she had carried the poor snake downstairs and let it escape into the overgrown gardens.

She wondered what they would do this night. She hadn't long to wait. It turned out to be a repeat of the first hoary ghost performance. They were quite talented actually, and Sinjun, smiling into the darkness, said aloud in a quavery voice, "Oh dear, not you again. Leave me, O Spirit, please leave me."

The spirit departed shortly thereafter, and Sinjun would have sworn she heard a soft giggle.

Colin called out her name even as he strode up the well-indented stone steps of the castle.

"Joan!"

It was Philip and Dahling who greeted him, Dahling flinging her arms about his leg, crying that Sinjun was mean and nasty and ugly and utterly cruel.

As for Philip, he kept still. Colin hugged both his children and asked them where Joan was.

"Joan?" Philip said blankly. "Oh, her. She's everywhere at once. She does everything. She won't let anyone rest. It's provoking, Papa."

Then Aunt Arleth was there, hissing as close to his ear as she could get that the *girl* he'd had to marry was giving *everyone* orders and ruining *everything*, and what was he going to do about it? It lacked but Serena, and she made her entrance in the next minute.

She smiled at him sweetly, went up on her tiptoes, and kissed him on the mouth. He was startled and drew back. Her smile didn't falter.

"I am glad you're back," she said in her soft voice, and his eyebrow arched upward a good inch.

"All of you—Dahling, let go of my leg now; Philip, take your sister away from here. Where? Anywhere, I don't care. Arleth, a moment, please. Where's Joan?"

"I'm here, Colin."

He looked up to see her coming down the wide staircase. She was wearing a new gown, a very simple muslin of soft pale yellow, not at all stylish, a gown such as a country maid would wear, but, somehow, on Joan it looked smart as could be. He'd missed her. He'd thought of her more than he'd liked and had come home before he'd accomplished all he'd needed to in order to see her. Yes, he thought, she looked very nice indeed, and he couldn't wait to strip off that gown and kiss her and plunge into her. Then he sniffed, and his pleasant fantasy vanished. Beeswax and lemon. Images of his mother rose to his mind and he stiffened, for that was surely impossible.

Then he looked around and what he saw made him blink.

Everything was spotless, not that he'd ever noticed that it had been particularly dirty before. But now he remembered, oh yes, he remembered.

The chandelier looked to be new, the marble floor was so clean he could see his reflection. He didn't say anything. He was stunned. He walked into the drawing room, then into the Laird's Inbetween Room. There were new draperies that appeared nearly the same as the old but weren't, and there were what couldn't be new carpets, yet their blues and reds shone vivid in the afternoon sunlight.

"It's nice to see you, too, Colin."

He looked at his wife, saw that her lips were pursed, and he said low, "I see you have been busy, Joan."

"Oh yes, we all have. You will notice the draperies, Colin. They are new but I copied the same fabric. Can you believe the warehouse in Dundee still carried the same fabric? It's a pattern from nearly fifty years ago! Is it not wonderful?"

"I liked the draperies as they were."

"Oh? You mean you liked dust and years upon years of grime dripping onto the floor?"

"Those carpets look odd."

"Assuredly so. They are clean. They no longer send up clouds of dust when you walk across them."

He opened his mouth but she forestalled him, raising her hand. "Let me guess—you preferred them as they were."

"Yes. As I said, you have been busy, have done things I did not approve."

"Should I perchance have lazed about on a chaise, reading novels that you don't have in that moth-eaten chamber you call a library, eating broonies?"

He realized they were standing three feet apart, but he made no move to close the distance. He was in the right and he had to make her understand, make her apologize. "You should have waited for me. I specifically asked you to make your lists for my review and then we—"

"Papa, she is cruel and nasty to Philip and me! She even made me stay in my room one morning and it was a lovely day."

"Even my children, Joan?" Colin looked down at his daughter. "Go to Dulcie. I wish to speak to your stepmother."

"We don't want her here! You will tell her not to beat us anymore?"

Sinjun stared at the little girl, then gave a shout of laughter. "That is really quite good, Dahling. A front shot of the cannon. Quite good."

"Go, Dahling. I will see to Joan. Ah, Aunt Arleth, you are here, too? Please leave now and close the door. I'm speaking to my wife."

"You will tell her to stop ruining everything, will you not, Colin? After all, 'tis you who are the laird, the husband, and the lord, not this girl here. It isn't she who is in charge at Vere Castle, it is you. You will see that she—"

"Send her to a convent!" Dahling yelled, then disappeared from the doorway.

Arleth merely nodded and took her leave. She closed the door behind her very softly. They were alone in the middle of the beautifully clean and scrubbed Kinross drawing room. Even the battered old furniture had a fine patina to it, but Sinjun wasn't paying any attention to all her accomplishments at the moment. All her attention was on her husband. Surely he wouldn't believe Dahling's dramatic performance, surely . . .

"Did you strike my children?"

She stared at him, and he was beautiful and her pulse speeded up just at the mere sight of him, but now he seemed a stranger, a beautiful stranger, and she wanted to hit him.

"Did you, Joan?"

It was absurd, ridiculous. She had to stop it and stop it now. She quickly walked to him, laced her fingers behind his neck, and rose to her tiptoes. "I missed you dreadfully," she said, and kissed him. His lips were firm and warm. He didn't open his mouth.

He grasped her arms in his hands and drew them down. "I have been gone for nearly three weeks. I came back only to see you, to assure myself that you were safe, that the damned MacPhersons hadn't tried anything. I couldn't find that damned Robbie MacPherson in Edinburgh. He's avoiding me, curse his coward's hide. Of course, I would have been told if something had happened, but I wanted to come myself and see for myself. You are quite the queen of the castle, aren't you? You have made yourself quickly in charge and done whatever it was you wished to do. You had no care for my opinions. You ignored my wishes. You ignored me."

She felt his words wash over her. She wasn't used to words that hurt so very much. She looked at him now and said simply, "I have done what I believed best."

"You are too young, then, to be trusted to know."

"It's absurd and you know it, Colin. Ah, here is Serena, doubtless here to kiss you again. Do you wish to continue your sermon with Serena present? I can call the children and Aunt Arleth again if you like. Perhaps they can harmonize in a chorus, singing of my sins to you. No? Very well then, if you wish, you may come to your tower room. You might as well relieve yourself of all your bile now."

She turned on her heel and strode away, just like a young man, he thought, his jaw tightening, almost no female sway to those hips of hers, yet he knew the feel of her, and his hands fisted at his sides. He followed her, saying, "It would have been nice had you made an effort to befriend my children. I see they still think you're an interloper. I see that you dislike them as much as they dislike you."

She didn't turn about to face him, merely said over her shoulder, "Louder, Colin. Children tend to behave in the ways of their parents, you know."

He shut his mouth. He kept on her heels all the way to the north tower. He could smell the beeswax and the lemon here and knew that she'd had the gall to do as she pleased to his room—the only room that was truly his and only his—as well as to the rest of the castle. He speeded up. When he saw the repaired tower stairs, he said, "I didn't wish to have them repaired in this way. What the devil have you done?"

She was three steps above him when she turned. "Oh, what would you have authorized, Colin? Perhaps you wished to have the stairs placed diagonally? Or perhaps skipping every other stair, with a dungeon below for those who were not careful walkers?"

"You had no right to interfere with what is mine. I told you not to."

He said nothing more, pressing past her on the narrow stairs. He opened the brass-studded door of his tower room, and the fresh smells that assailed him were more than he could bear. He stopped in the middle of the circular room, staring at the vase of summer roses set on his desk. Roses, for God's sake, his mother's favorite flower, and the smell mingled with the tart scent of lemon.

He closed his eyes a moment. "You have overstepped yourself, madam."

"Oh? You prefer filth, then? You prefer that your books continue to rot? They were quite close to it, you know. Naturally, the shelves upon which they sat had worm rot and beetles and God knows what else. It was a close thing."

He turned then to face her, furious and feeling utterly impotent. She was right, damn her, he was being a dog in the manger, but he'd wanted to oversee things, it was his home, his rags and his tatters, his responsibility. But no, she'd set herself up as the arbitrator of everything, and done just as she'd wished to do and without any direction or permission from him. He could not forgive it. He'd exiled himself to protect her, and she'd done him in, taken over, all without a by-your-leave. He continued to wax eloquent in his mind, then blurted out, a new outrage coming to the fore, "I despise lemon and beeswax! The smell of roses makes me want to puke."

"But Mrs. Seton said your mother—"

"Don't you dare speak about my mother!"

"Very well, I won't."

"You came into my room, the only private room in this entire pile of rubble that has belonged to me since I was bloody well born. You came in here and you changed it to suit you."

"I changed nothing, if you would but cease being an unreasonable boor and look about you. The roses, yes, but nothing else, and they're not a change, just a mere temporary addition. You think you would prefer that the tapestries your great-great-grandmother wove lose all their magnificent colors in years upon years of filth and fray until they turn to dust? And the stones, Colin, you could have easily broken your leg had they not been replaced and reset. I did nothing differently. You will even notice that the damned stones match. And the carpet, dear God, that beautiful Aubusson carpet, at least now you can see the vibrant colors in it."

"It was up to me to have it done."

He was dogged, she'd give him that. Once the bone was in his mouth, he wasn't about to let go of it. She drew on her depleted control. "Well, it cost little to replace the stones. Why didn't you do it, then?"

"What I did or didn't do is my affair. I don't have to explain any of my actions to you. This is my house, my castle. What you have done is wrong."

"I am your wife. Vere Castle is also my home. It's my responsibility."

"You are only what I allow you to be."

"By all that's fair, you're being an idiot! I've waited and waited for you to return home. Nearly three weeks and not a single bloody word from you. Well, my lord, you seem to forget that you also have responsibilities—such as your children."

"My children! They appear to dislike you as much as they did when you first met them, and there's probably an excellent reason for it. You did raise your hand to them, didn't you? You probably saw yourself as taking my place—what with you having all the damned money—and you decided that a man would stride about and give everyone orders and buffet children who didn't immediately conform to what it was you wanted."

Sinjun was careful not to touch the first-edition Shakespeare. She chose instead a thick tome written by some obscure sixteenth-century churchman and hurled it at him.

It struck him solidly in the chest. He grunted, stepping back. He stared at her, not believing that she would hurl a book at him. Had she had a sword available to her, she probably would have tried to run him through.

He'd looked forward to coming home, be it just for a day or two, had looked forward to seeing his bride, and she'd thrown a book at him. He'd seen himself seated at the grand dining table, she as his bride in her place, his children, well scrubbed—doubtless by her own soft hands—smiling and laughing, happy as little clams with their new stepmother. He rubbed his palm over his chest, staring at her still. His pleasant fantasy vanished.

Damn her, but he was in the right of it. Because she was the heiress, she'd thrust herself into his role and made herself the master of his home. He wouldn't tolerate it.

"I believe I'll lock you in the laird's bedchamber. You can cause no more discord there."

She stared at him. The day was warm and his beautiful black hair was windblown. His face was tanned, his eyes such a deep blue, a treacherous blue, she thought, hard now with his anger and his dislike for her. She said slowly, "Just because I've tried to become a Kinross you would punish me?"

"A true Kinross wife wouldn't force everyone to obey her commands. She would be sensitive to others' feelings. She would obey her husband. Just because you're the heiress, you cannot behave as if you are also the laird. I won't have it."

She walked away from him quickly, saying nothing more. He started forward, only to stop. She went through the narrow open door and he heard her light step going quickly down the circular stairs, the newly repaired circular stairs.

"Well, damn," he said.

Sinjun walked straight to the stables. She wished desperately that Fanny were here, but nothing had yet arrived from Northcliffe Hall, not her trunks or her mare. Murdock the Stunted was there. When he saw her face, pale and set, her eyes wide with something he didn't understand, he quickly saddled the mare she'd been riding, a rawboned bay whose name was Carrot.

Sinjun wasn't wearing a riding habit. She didn't care. She saw that Murdock hadn't put a sidesaddle on the mare. She didn't care about that, either. She grabbed a shock of the horse's mane and swung herself up. Her skirts were at her knees, showing her white silk stockings and her black slippers.

She was out of sight of the castle quickly.

"Good. She's gone."

Colin stared at Aunt Arleth. "What do you mean?"

"I mean she rode away from here and the hussy wasn't even wearing a riding habit. Her gown was hiked up showing her stockings. I watched her from the dining room windows."

"Will you be able to keep her money, Colin?"

This was from Serena, who was flitting about the entrance hall, looking at herself in every shiny surface she passed.

He had no time to answer, for at that moment Murdock the Stunted appeared in the doorway, his frayed red cap in his gnarled hands.

"I be a mite worried, milor' " was all he said.

Colin cursed, long and fluently. Murdock looked upon him with grave disapproval. Aunt Arleth opened her mouth to round on Murdock, but she didn't have time. Colin was out the front doors.

He cursed all the way to the stables. His own stallion, Gulliver, was blown. He took Old Cumber, a gentle ancient fellow who'd known more feud fights than most men who lived here.

"Which way did she ride?"

"Toward the western end of the loch."

He didn't find her, not a trace, not a single damned track. He spent two hours searching, alternately cursing her, then so worried that one of the MacPhersons had stolen her that he shook. He found himself doubting that Latham MacPherson, the old laird, had truly managed to forbid any further raids on Kinross land. Hell, it was quite possible Robbie MacPherson had left his father's side—that is, if he'd ever gone to it in the first place. He sweated. Finally, as the sun was beginning to set, he returned to the castle. Her mare, Carrot, was munching on hay.

Murdock the Stunted merely shrugged, but he didn't meet the laird's eyes. "She came in a good hour ago, milor'. Quiet she were, but all right an' tight."

"I see," Colin said, and flicked his riding crop angrily against his thigh.

He wasn't overly surprised to find the laird's bedchamber not only empty but as sparkling clean as the rest of the castle. It was still as dark as before, but not nearly so dreary now. He hated to admit it. When he went downstairs for dinner, bathed and dressed in formal evening attire, he decided he would hold his tongue. He didn't want another scene in front of the entire family.

He saw her standing beside the empty fireplace, wearing the same gown, holding a glass of sherry. Aunt Arleth was holding forth about something doubtless unpleasant, Serena was seated on a settee looking dreamily off into space, and the children were there, sitting side by side on a love seat, Dulcie standing like a big-bosomed pixie guard behind them.

Sinjun looked up to see him striding into the room. Damn, but he was splendid. She didn't want to take his place, the stupid lout. How could he be so blind? She wanted her own place, not his, she wanted to be beside him, laughing with him, working with him, kissing him and feeling his body with her hands.

"Good evening," Colin said to all assembled.

"Papa, she said we couldn't have any dinner, but since you're here she had to give in."

Dulcie gasped and grabbed Dahling's arm. "Ye're a wicked wee mite, ye are, Dahling Kinross!"

"A veritable witch, I see," Colin said.

"You overdid that one a bit, Dahling," Sinjun said, smiling toward her stepdaughter, "but it was a worthy try. I will give you dramatic lessons. You mustn't ever overdo a role, you know, that's the cardinal rule of the theater."

"I should like to tread the boards," Serena said. "That is the correct way the English say it, isn't it, Joan?"

"That's exactly the way. You already walk so gracefully it's as if you float. The rest would be easy for you."

"All of this is nonsense," Aunt Arleth said, standing. "What are your intentions, Colin?"

"To dine, Aunt Arleth. Joan, here's Philpot to announce our dinner. Give me your arm."

She didn't want to, particularly, but everyone was watching and she had no choice. She tensed as he patted her hand, preparing for battle. "Oh, my dear, not here. When I tell you what I expect from you it will be from behind a locked door in my bedchamber—the laird's bedchamber— the laird's very clean bedchamber."

CHAPTER
═12═

COLIN WAS GOOD TO HIS WORD. He gently shoved Sinjun into the laird's bedchamber, then closed and locked the door. He watched her even as he slipped the key into his vest pocket. He watched her walk to the center of the vast room and stop, rubbing her arms with her hands.

"Should you like me to light a fire?"

She shook her head.

"Perhaps it would be a good idea. You will shortly be naked, after all, and I won't wish to have you shivering from cold. I want you shivering just from me."

So this was a man's punishment, she thought, looking back at him now. He was completely in control, his size alone gave him that, and he looked mean and determined and oddly angry. She'd said nothing to draw forth that anger, at least not at the dining table. He was probably smelling the dreaded beeswax and lemon again.

But Sinjun had been blessed with two singularly unmanageable, obstinate, very intelligent brothers, who had taught her a lot about men and their strange outlooks and unaccountable behaviors.

Here was Colin acting like the sultan, and she was here to be his slave girl. The image pleased her. It would have pleased her more were he laughing and teasing her. Ah yes, veils, dozens of veils in all colors, and she would dance for him and . . .

"What the devil are you smiling about?"

"Veils."

"Joan, have you lost your wits?"

"Oh no, I was just seeing you as the head sultan and me your slave girl for the night, and I was wearing veils and dancing for you."

He paused, at a loss. She was unexpected; what she thought and said were unanticipated. Even when she said something that he could possibly expect, at the edge of his brain it still shook him that she could speak so clearly and candidly and without guile. He didn't like it.

"I think that a charming and apt idea. However, tonight you will simply dance for me naked. I will clap my hands for you if you need accompaniment. I will fetch you some veils when I return to Edinburgh. Then we can try it again, conforming more to your vision."

"Ah, so it is your intention to leave in the morning, then? Before dawn, I daresay. Whilst I'm still asleep, naturally. I understand, Colin. The last thing you want is to face a pathetic wife who just might beg you not to leave her here again, not to leave her stuck in your home, on your lands, in your damned foreign country. Do you think perhaps I could change your mind about leaving? No, I didn't think so. Oh yes, I mustn't forget the pleasant relatives you have immured me with. Aunt Arleth is a treat. She hates you, she hates me; as far as I can tell the only ones she loved were your brother and your father, who played her false, at least in her mind. As for Serena, I have no idea if she is of this world or of the fairies. She's daft, but pleasantly so. The children—why, I will simply continue to beat them whenever it suits my fancy."

"I don't wish to argue with you any more this night. Just know, Joan, that you will do absolutely nothing more whilst I'm gone. Nothing. You will try to present a pleasant face to all my people and to my children. That is what I expect of you, my wife."

"Go to the devil, Colin."

He watched her chin go up and felt his blood quicken, felt his damned blood rush from his brain to his groin. This girl, who'd worshiped him so ardently in London, who'd begged for his man's body all the way to Scotland, ah, why she'd become a termagant. There was no ardent devotion in her Sherbrooke-blue eyes at the moment. There was a good deal of fire, and oddly it looked cold as the moon. It also excited him.

He took a step toward her. She stood her ground. She wasn't about to let him chase her around the laird's bedchamber, although she'd heard Alex shrieking once when Douglas was chasing her. And then the shrieks had stopped and Sinjun had known that what they were doing was wonderful. But this wouldn't be wonderful.

"I will let you kiss me, Colin. I much enjoy that. I already told you."

"Oh yes, I will kiss you."

"If you wish I will also kiss you."

"Yes, I expect you to kiss me back."

"No, I mean I will kiss your sex and caress you, if you wish. It was enjoyable that first time to hear you moan and see your body tighten and jerk and all because of what I was doing to you."

He stopped dead in his tracks at that. He swallowed. He also hardened considerably. He easily pictured her above him, touching him with her mouth and her hands. He could still feel her hair spread over his belly.

"No," he said, "I don't want you to do that," and felt his body nearly revolt.

"Why not? You liked it. I don't know why you made me stop so quickly that first time. I was just learning how to do it. I could continue on and on tonight. I don't wish to have you do the other thing to me. We have already decided that you will not. You are too large."

"I told you that you didn't know anything. For a girl who's so intelligent, so very well educated, your ignorance in this matter is laughable. I will make love to you, Joan, and I will come inside you the way I am supposed to, the way men and women have come together since the moment God set them in Eden."

"Very well, I see you are quite set on this. I was just testing the waters. I'm willing to compromise with you, Colin. I will be able to endure one time, I think. It shouldn't be so bad. But more than one time I cannot allow. It would be cruel of you to insist."

He laughed, he couldn't help himself. God, he'd missed her, and he hadn't wanted to, damn her Sassenach hide. No, he'd wanted to take other women, but he hadn't, though several ladies had issued invitations that only a blind man would have missed. No, he hadn't touched another woman, and he'd thought about her, those long white legs of hers, but most of all her absolute honesty. He cursed. He didn't believe for a minute that she would ever lay a finger in anger on a child, any child, even Dahling at her most irritating.

"No, we'll do it right. I have endured abstinence. I'm not meant for celibacy. At least no more of it. I will take you as many times as it pleases me to do so, and you will enjoy it, Joan. You will trust me."

She didn't move an inch, didn't twitch. "You force me to bare my soul, so to speak, to mortify myself, which I don't like to do." She drew a deep breath and stared him right in the eye. "I'm not pregnant, Colin."

"It is just as well that you aren't. You and I need more time together before you bear my children. We need more understanding between us. You must needs learn your role in my house and what I expect from you."

"No, I mean I'm not pregnant right now."

He felt an earthquake of frustration. He felt all the blood in his groin whoosh back to his brain. If there had been a full moon, he'd have howled and run like a crazy man over the Lomond moors.

He looked at her with a thread of hope. "You mean you didn't discover you weren't pregnant last week, say?"

"No, right now. Right this very minute as we speak."

"Perhaps you are nearing the end of it?"

"No."

Did he expect her to tell him the truth? As a matter of fact, he did.

"Well, blessed hell," he said.

"That's my brothers' favorite curse," she said, "all except for Tysen, who's the clergyman."

"I must have heard your dear brothers say it enough. It always preceded their attacking me."

"They love me," she said simply. She waited. He didn't say a word, didn't even look as though he wanted to, but simply lacked the proper words or the ability. "Yes," she said, "blessed hell."

"Come here and I will kiss you."

It wouldn't solve anything, but it would be pleasant, of that she had no doubt. She walked to him with no hesitation. "I would like that. Thank you, Colin."

For a Colin kiss, it wasn't his best, she thought, wishing he would kiss her as he had on their wedding night. He gently set her away from him but kept his hands on her upper arms. He breathed in the sweet scent of her. He felt the softness of her flesh beneath his fingers.

She said, her eyes never leaving his mouth, "Edinburgh is but a half day from here."

"Yes, I know."

"You could come home every few days, Colin."

"Yes, but I won't, not until everything is handled to my satisfaction."

"Where is Robert MacPherson? Have you spoken to the old laird?"

"I have no idea where Robert MacPherson is right now. Perhaps he followed me back here. I don't know. But it seems most likely that he will remain in Edinburgh, to try to get to me there. He hasn't tried anything so far. I have met with old Latham, his father, and he doesn't understand why Robbie is acting like such a cowardly sod. He's put out the word for his son to see him, but to date hasn't shown himself. He says that Robbie told him I had no proof of anything and he himself would admit nothing to his father. We will see. He will have to come to me sooner or later."

"Why don't you just kill him?"

Colin blinked down at her. "You're a woman," he said slowly. "Women are supposed to be gentle, to despise violence and war. You want me to kill him?"

She looked thoughtful, then nodded. "Yes, I suppose you must. He sounds unbalanced, a bit like Aunt Arleth. I don't wish to live in fear of his hurting or killing you. Yes, I think you should kill him, but cleverly, of course."

He could find no words.

"I could write my brothers and ask them how best to proceed."

"No," he said quickly, "oh no, don't do that. Listen, it's possible he hasn't had anything to do with the trouble. I don't believe that myself, but it's possible. After all, you were the one hurt in Edinburgh. Robbie is a good shot. It's difficult to believe he missed."

"You're forgetting London. And I should say that trouble is a passionless word for trying to kill someone, Colin."

"I can't be certain. It is likely, but not certain."

"So you will remain in Edinburgh until he either kills you or you manage to kill him in the act of trying to kill you?"

He gave her a lopsided grin. "I expect that's about it."

"Sometimes I think gentlemen are too soft."

"I shouldn't wish to hang."

"Oh, you're much too smart to have anyone think you'd done it. Aren't you?"

"I don't know. I've never before killed anyone with any kind of premeditation."

He released her and watched her walk to one of the huge overstuffed leather chairs. She stood behind it. "Nor have I. I wish you would consider it, though. Now, Colin, I wish you would apologize to me for your distressing behavior today."

He stiffened up like the fireplace poker. "You and I had a bargain. You didn't keep to your end of it. You disobeyed me."

"And if I weren't indisposed at the moment, you would punish me for it."

"Lovemaking isn't punishment, damn you!"

"Ha! I'm your wife and I'm in a very certain position to know that it is! It's painful, humiliating, and isn't at all pleasant except for the man, who could doubtless rut a goat and still enjoy himself!"

He cursed, nothing original from what Sinjun could hear, but it showed a frayed state of mind. Not being an unkind person, she said, "It's all right, Colin, I will forgive you even though you can't find it in yourself to apologize. I will continue to improve upon matters here, but I will tell you that I have spent all the two hundred pounds."

"Good, then you will be done with your damned meddling."

"Oh no, if you don't provide me with more funds, I shall simply smile and let Mrs. Seton continue reminding all the tradesmen how you, the fortune-hunting laird, managed to snag an heiress."

"Continue?"

"Oh yes, she much enjoys getting back her former consequence. She's even fond of me, since I'm the bottomless pit of groats. It was quite easy to win her over."

It was as if he were sinking in the treacherous Kelly peat bog with no hope of rescue. "I will speak to her and tell her to keep her tongue behind her teeth." It was a pitiful attempt to regain a semblance of control and he knew it. However, she didn't have to grin at him.

Colin sighed. "I came home to see you, truth be told. And my children, of course. I wish you would make a push to gain their affections."

"Children do things in their own good time. Philip and Dahling are no different. I'm quite pleased with our progress, actually."

"You are but nineteen, not ninety-nine! You don't know everything about children!"

"Of course I do. I have found them to be unpredictable and perverse and immensely creative. But bad feelings don't suit them, not really. We will see. It would help if you were to remain and assist them to see their new stepmother as a very charming person."

"I'm going to Clackmannanshire to oversee the purchase of sheep. The cattle are coming from Berwick. I will return home when that is taken care of and Robert MacPherson is either dead or I judge him innocent."

Sinjun gave him a long look. "There are several lists for you in the estate room, from the crofters I have visited. I trust you wish to see to them?"

He cursed again, but she said nothing more, simply went behind the musty Oriental screen and put on her nightgown.

He was gone the following morning before she awoke.

Sinjun smiled as she heard the huge clock downstairs strike twelve times. Ah, the stroke of midnight. It shouldn't be long now.

It wasn't. Not ten minutes later she heard the soft scraping sounds, like light-footed scurrying rats in the wainscoting. There were the familiar moans, the slapping of the chains.

Very slowly, she sat up in bed and counted to five. Finally she cried out, sounding so terrified she scared herself. "Oh, please stop, halt, I say! Oh, dear heavens, save me, save me!" Then she moaned herself. "I cannot bear it, I shall have to leave this haunted place. Ah, Pearlin' Jane, no, no."

Finally the sounds ceased.

She was grinning like a half-wit when she slipped out of bed an hour later.

Philip was twitching in his sleep. He was dreaming about a large fighting trout he'd caught in Loch Leven the previous week, when he'd gone with Murdock the Stunted. The trout grew as his dream lengthened. It got bigger and bigger and its mouth seemed now the size of an open door. Then Murdock the Stunted was touching him, telling him what a fine fisherman he was, his voice soft and softer still . . .

But it wasn't Murdock the Stunted's fingers or his voice. Suddenly the trout was gone and he was back in his own bed, but he wasn't alone. He felt it again, like soft fingers on the back of his neck, and he heard the soft voice saying, "You're a bright lad, Philip, so bright and so kind. Och, aye, a good lad." He lurched upright and there, beside his bed, hand still outstretched, was a dead lady.

She had long, nearly white hair and wore a flowing white gown. She was young and beautiful, but she looked ghastly. Her hand was but inches from him and that hand and all its dead fingers were whiter than her gown.

Philip swallowed, then yelled at the top of his lungs. He grabbed his covers and yanked them over his head. It was a nightmare, his brain had made the trout into a ghost, that was all, but he burrowed farther down into the feather mattress, clutching the covers over him like a lifeline.

There was the soft voice again. "Philip, I'm the Virgin Bride. Your new stepmother told you about me. I protect her, Philip. Your Pearlin' Jane is afraid of me. She doesn't like the way you and Dahling are trying to scare off Sinjun."

Just as suddenly the voice stopped. Philip didn't move. Since he couldn't breathe, he made a small tunnel beneath the bedclothes to the edge of the bed. He waited, his breath coming in huge gasps.

It wasn't until dawn that he eased his head out from under the covers. Dull morning light was seeping into his bedchamber. There was no sign of anything or anyone. Not a sign of the Virgin Bride.

Sinjun went about her usual duties, outwardly serene, smiling, wishing Aunt Arleth would drop into a deep well. Colin had been gone four days now, and she was so angry with him that she occasionally shook with it.

She was very tempted to go to Edinburgh. Or would he now be in Clackmannanshire or Berwick? Damned man.

Her trunks and Fanny her mare arrived late that morning, delivered by James, one of the head Northcliffe Hall stable lads, and three of his companions, stable lads all. She danced about like a child, so excited that she even kissed James and hugged the other stable lads. All was well at Northcliffe Hall, including her mother, the dowager countess, who was, nevertheless, according to James, a bit downpin because there was no one else about for her to improve upon. James delivered letters to Sinjun, saw Dulcie smiling at him as if he were a prince, and was more than delighted to spend the night at Vere Castle.

After she saw James and the stable lads off the next morning, their satchels filled with food for them and letters for her family, she went to the stables and saddled Fanny herself.

"She be a foine mare," said Murdock the Stunted. Young Ostle, all of twenty-two years old, agreed fervently. George II, a mongrel of indeterminate lineage, barked wildly at the scent of the new animal, and Crocker yelled at him in language so colorful Sinjun vowed to make him her teacher.

The day was warm, the sun bright overhead. Sinjun click-clicked Fanny onto the gravel drive, now widened and newly regraveled—with the assurance, naturally, that the laird would pay for it upon his return. She was smiling. She'd ordered other things done as well the same day that Colin had left again. Three of the crofters' huts were getting new roofs. She'd purchased seven goats and distributed them to all the crofters with children and babies. She'd sent Mr. Seton—never loath to impress his neighbors and the tradesmen with his importance—to Kinross to purchase more grain and sorely needed farming implements. A score of barrels and several dozen chickens had been duly distributed to the crofters. Ah, yes, she'd been busy, she'd meddled to her heart's content, and if Colin didn't return home soon, she fancied she would begin another wing to Vere Castle. She'd also set the local seamstress to work on pennants for the four Vere Castle towers. The Kinross tartan pattern was of red, dark forest green, and black. She wished she could see Colin garbed in a Highland kilt, but they'd been outlawed after Culloden in 1746. It was a pity, but the pennants would proudly fly the Kinross tartan.

Sinjun set Fanny into a gallop all the way to the very edge of Loch Leven and loosed the reins so her mare could drink the cold water. She looked toward the eastern moors that stretched up the sides of the Lomond Hills themselves. Barren and empty and immensely savage. Even at this distance she could see patches of purple heather, sprouting up between rocks and out of deep crevices in the land. And to the west, the land was verdant, rich and lush, and every acre of it tilled and flowering with growing wheat and barley and rye. A land of contradictions, a land of beauty so profound she felt it touch the deepest part of her. It was now her land, and there was no going back.

She patted Fanny's sleek neck. "I'm being a romantic and you're fat," she said, sniffing in the clear sweet air, the scent of honeysuckle and heather light and teasing. "Douglas has been letting you eat your head off in the stables, hasn't he? A good gallop is just what you need, my girl."

"I occasionally say that to my women."

Sinjun turned slowly in her saddle. A man was seated on a magnificent bay barb not six feet from her. Why hadn't Fanny whinnied?

"I wonder why my mare didn't alert me to your presence," she said aloud, straightening now and looking at him.

He frowned. A bit of fear would have pleased him. At least a show of surprise at his unexpected appearance. Perhaps her wits were slow and she hadn't understood his small jest.

"Your mare didn't alert you because she's drinking from the loch. The loch water is magical, 'tis said, and a mare will drink until her stomach bloats."

"Then I should stop her." Sinjun gently tugged the reins back, forcing Fanny's muzzle from the water. "Who are you, sir? A neighbor, perhaps?"

"I suppose I'm a neighbor. You are the new countess of Ashburnham." She nodded.

"You're quite lovely. I expected a rabbit-toothed hag, truth be told, since you're such a full-blooded heiress. Colin must believe he's the luckiest bastard alive."

"I'm pleased I'm not a hag, for Colin never would have wed me, regardless of the number and weight of my groats. As for his feelings of luck, I cannot attest to that."

He frowned at her. "Colin is a fool. He's not worthy of any woman's regard."

She looked at him more closely now as he spoke. He was tall, perhaps taller than Colin, though it was difficult to be certain, since he was sitting atop his stallion, his posture indolent, his expression amused, his clothing of the best quality and fitting him perfectly. And he was very slender, to the point of delicateness, but surely that was an absurd thought to apply to a man. He had a full head of very soft blond hair and his forehead was high and wide. If anything, his features were too refined, too soft, almost feminine. His complexion was fair, his eyes a pale blue, his jawline and his chin as soft and delicate as a woman's. This quite pretty man was vicious?

"Who are you?" she asked.

"I am Robert MacPherson."

"I suspected as much."

"Did you now? Well, that does make it easier, doesn't it? What has the bastard said about me?"

Sinjun shook her head. "Did you try to kill Colin in London?"

She saw that he hadn't; the surprise was too sharp in his eyes, his hands tightened too quickly and roughly on his stallion's reins. So it had evidently been a coincidence after all. He laughed as he flicked a fly from his stallion's neck. "Perhaps. I try to take advantage of opportunities when they present themselves."

"Why would you wish to kill Colin?"

"He's a murdering sod. He killed my sister. Broke her neck and threw her off a cliff. Isn't that an excellent reason?"

"Do you have proof of your accusation?"

He drew his stallion closer to the mare. The mare flung back her head, nervous, her eyes rolling at the stallion's scent.

"No closer, if you please." Sinjun calmed Fanny, crooning to her, ignoring Robert MacPherson.

"I don't understand why you aren't frightened of me. I now have you in my power. I can do as I please with you. Perhaps I will ravish you until your womb takes my seed. Perhaps you will bear a child and it will be mine."

She cocked her head to one side, studying him. "You sound like a very bad actor in an inferior play in Drury Lane. It is curious, I think."

Robert MacPherson was nonplussed. "What is curious, damn you?"

Sinjun's look was remote. "I had pictured you otherwise. Don't you find that is so often the case? You thought I would be a hag, but I'm not. I had thought you would look something like Colin, or perhaps Mac-Duff—you must know MacDuff, don't you?—but you don't. You are . . ." She stopped. *Pretty* wasn't a particularly politic thing for her to say. Nor was *graceful* or *elegant* or *quite lovely, really*.

"I am what?"

"You seem quite nice—a gentleman, despite your vicious words."

"I'm not at all nice."

"Did your sister resemble you?"

"Fiona? No, she was dark as a gypsy, but beautiful, aye, she was more beautiful than a sinner's dream, blue eyes the color of the loch in winter, and hair so black it was like the devil's own midnight. Why? You are jealous of a ghost?"

"I don't think so. But I am curious. You see, Aunt Arleth—that's Miss MacGregor—she says that Fiona fell in love with Malcolm and betrayed Colin, and that's why Colin killed her. I find that odd, since Colin is the most perfect man in the world. What woman could conceivably want another man, if he were her husband? Do you think it's possible?"

"Perfect man! He's a bastard, a murdering bastard! Damn you, Fiona loved only her bloody husband. She wanted only him from the time she was fifteen years old, no other, certainly not Malcolm, although he did want her. Our father pushed for Malcolm, since he would be the laird after his father's death, but she wouldn't hear of it. She nearly starved herself until our father gave in. She got Colin, but she wasn't happy for very long. All I remember now was that she was always accusing Colin of infidelity, she was so jealous of him. He couldn't look at another woman without Fiona shrieking at him, trying to claw his eyes out. He grew bored with her and her insane jealousy, even I understand that, but he had no right to rid himself of her. He had no right to hurl her over that damned cliff. And to claim that he had no memory of it. Absurd."

"This is all quite confusing, Mr. MacPherson. No one tells the same story. Also, I don't understand how Fiona could have possibly believed Colin to be unfaithful. He would never break his vows."

"What nonsense! Of course he broke his vows. He slept with women far and wide. Fiona was once filled with laughter and charm. Men couldn't keep their wits about them when she was near, and it pleased Colin's pride to have it so, but only at first. Her jealousy extended even to the servants at Vere Castle. That's when he bedded other women, to punish Fiona. But that doesn't mean he didn't also sleep with her. She would tell me how he'd take her in a frenzy, his need was so great for her. She was a witch, Fiona was, a jealous witch. Even while he despised her, he was filled with lust and desire for her. And she for him, more's the pity. But she's dead now, dead because he was tired of her and he found it expedient to kill her.

"I have had to wait for retribution because my father believed Colin innocent of the crime. But now he's an old man with an old man's failing wits. He still refuses to take action. His man tells me he sits and drools and dreams aloud of long-ago nights with his men, raiding the lowlands or fighting the Kinrosses. Ah, but it doesn't matter now, at least to me. I do as I please. Soon I will be laird.

"I've been watching Vere Castle for several days now. I know Colin is waiting for me in Edinburgh, waiting to confront me, perhaps even to try to kill me as he killed my sister. But I decided on another course. I came back here. At last you have come out alone. You will now come with me."

"Why?"

"You will be my prisoner, and thus Colin will be at my mercy. I will at last see justice done."

"I cannot tell you how difficult it is to take you seriously when you quote such atrocious lines."

He snarled with fury and raised his fist.

"I don't think so," Sinjun said, and quick as a streak of lightning, she slashed his face with her riding crop.

He yowled. His stallion, startled, reared back, unseating his rider. He fell off, landing on his side, but he was up in an instant.

Sinjun didn't wait to see what he would do. She forced Fanny to run straight at his stallion and, at the last moment, to swerve away. She grabbed the stallion's reins and pulled them over his head. She felt her arm nearly pulled from its socket as the stallion balked at being led, but finally he broke into a run, coming neck to neck with Fanny.

She heard Robert MacPherson yelling curses behind her. Unlike Douglas's stallion, Garth, this animal didn't respond at all to his master's voice. Thank God.

He was a very odd man, she thought.

CHAPTER
===13===

SINJUN SAID NOTHING about her encounter with Robert MacPherson to anyone. Who was there to tell, anyway? She could just imagine what Aunt Arleth would say. Blessed hell, she would probably clap her hands and cheer Robert MacPherson on. She would probably drug her and have her delivered to MacPherson in a gunnysack.

She'd released his stallion close to the border of MacPherson land and slapped its rump. She hoped that MacPherson had a very long walk ahead of him.

Colin must be fetched immediately from Edinburgh. On the heels of that thought, she shook her head. What she needed to do was think, then act, quickly.

But, she thought, as she changed from her riding habit to a soft muslin gown of dark green, if Colin were here, what would he do? Hunt MacPherson down? Challenge him to a duel? MacPherson was a weasel, a very pretty weasel. He'd shown his true colors in Edinburgh, when he'd tried to shoot Colin and gotten Sinjun instead. She touched her cheek, remembering the shard of rock slicing into her. It had healed now with no scar, not that it mattered much. No, she couldn't take chances with Colin's life. She knew he would behave with honor; he was that kind of man. She doubted MacPherson had much of that attribute in any significant quantity. She would simply have to do away with MacPherson herself. Yes, gentlemen were too nice in their notions; they were bound by concepts of behavior that had no practical use when it came to the sticking point. She had to do something, and she would do something. She wanted Colin safe and home with her and the children. It wasn't likely that he could learn to care for her if he never came home.

She walked quickly up the stairs of the north tower to Colin's chamber. She wanted a gun and he had an adequate collection kept there. She would not ride out again from Vere Castle without one. The door stood partially open. Puzzled, she quietly pushed the door open more widely.

Philip stood in front of his father's gun collection, his hand lifted to pull free an old dueling pistol that Sinjun doubted could still be fired with safety.

"Philip," she said very quietly.

He jumped and whirled about, his face deathly white.

"Oh, it's just you," he said, and his shoulders slumped in relief. "What are you doing here in my papa's room?"

"I might ask you the same thing. Why do you want that dueling pistol, Philip?"

"It's none of your affair! Besides, you're a stupid girl and you wouldn't understand!"

She arched an eyebrow at him and said, "You think so, do you? Well, if you wish to test your beliefs, why don't the two of us go to the gardens and have a bit of a competition?"

"You can shoot a gun?"

"Naturally. I was raised by my brothers, you know. I am also a champion with a longbow. Are you?"

"I don't believe you."

"There is no reason for you not to. Once I shot a very bad man in his arm and quite saved the day."

He turned away from her then and she saw that he was wringing his hands.

It hit her hard when she realized what was wrong. The Virgin Bride had scared him, truly scared him, and it was her fault. She'd never before played the ghost with a child. She hadn't thought, hadn't imagined that it would so terrify him. She drew a deep breath, feeling so guilty she bit her lip.

"What's wrong, Philip?"

"Nothing."

"Did I tell you that Pearlin' Jane has visited me several times since I've been here?"

He started, his face flooding with color. "Silly ghost, she doesn't exist. You made it up because you're a girl and you get scared of anything."

"Boys aren't scared of ghosts?"

He looked on the verge of a faint. But his chin—his father's chin—went up and he gave her an excellent sneer. "Certainly not!"

"Do you remember me talking about the Virgin Bride—she is the ghost that lives at Northcliffe Hall?"

"Yes, but I didn't believe you."

"Well, you should. She is there, truly. However—" Sinjun drew a very deep breath. "However, she isn't here at Vere Castle. As far as I know she's never traveled, though I imagine she'd find Scotland charming."

Philip made a grab for the dueling pistol, but Sinjun jerked his arm away. "No, Philip, she isn't here. Come with me, I have something to show you."

He followed her, wariness stiffening every line of his body.

"This is my papa's bedchamber."

"I know. Come in."

Sinjun dismissed Emma, who was dusting the heavy armoire. She waited until Emma had left the room, then she opened the armoire doors and burrowed in one of the corners and opened a small bandbox.

"Here, Philip."

She brought out the long wig and the white gown.

She thought he was going to collapse, but he just turned paler and backed away.

"No, it's just a costume. I made the wig out of raw wool and goat hair. You and Dahling tried to frighten me with your Pearlin' Jane performance, which, I must tell you, was quite excellent. You scared me half to death that first time. I decided to have a bit of revenge. I visited you during the night, after your last ghostly visit to me."

He stared at her. "You were the ghost who patted me on the neck and told me to leave Sinjun alone?"

"Yes." She wanted to tell him she was very sorry for having frightened him so desperately, but she could just imagine how a proud boy would take that.

"Why does Papa call you Joan?"

That made her blink, then chuckle. "He thinks Sinjun sounds too much like a man's nickname, which it is, but it is also my name and I quite like it and am quite used to it. Would you like to call me Sinjun?"

"Yes, it doesn't sound like a silly girl or an—"

"An evil stepmother?"

He nodded, his eyes still riveted on the wig and white gown.

"How did you know that it was Dahling and me and not Pearlin' Jane?"

"The swamp ooze. By itself, it would have been quite terrifying, but with the chains and the moaning and the scurrying behind the wainscoting, it was overdone, if you know what I mean. Also, that next morning, just to be sure, I asked Dulcie and she told me that you'd gone out with Crocker and your direction was the Cowal Swamp."

"Oh."

"You don't need that dueling pistol, Philip."

"If I did, I could use it, and I could beat you at any competition."

Little boys, she thought, marveling at him, were indeed splendid. Little boys became men who didn't seem to change at all in this regard. "Do you fence?"

That took him aback. "No, Papa hasn't yet taught me."

"Well, there is something both of us could learn together, then. Mac-Duff said that he would be coming back soon for a visit. If your papa isn't yet returned, perhaps he could give us a lesson."

"You can really shoot a crossbow?"

"Yes."

"There's an old armory up in the south tower. There are all sorts of weapons there, including crossbows and swords. Crocker keeps them up. It's his hobby."

"Would you like to learn to shoot a crossbow?"

He nodded slowly, his eyes going to that white wig and floaty gown. "I think Sinjun is all right. Joan sounds like a cocker spaniel."

"My sentiments exactly."

MacDuff arrived the following afternoon to find Sinjun and Philip in the apple orchard with crossbows two hundred years old and in perfect condition. Crocker was sitting on a fence whittling new arrows, his mongrel George II at his feet.

At the sight of the huge MacDuff, George II bounded up and barked maniacally.

"George, old boy, down!"

For a dog named after a king, he was singularly obedient. He sank back down at his master's feet and rested his head on his paws, his tail wagging as frantically as a flag in a strong wind.

Sinjun heard the dog bark but she didn't turn around. "Now, Philip, that's excellent form. That's right, right under your nose and keep your left arm perfectly straight and still. Yes, that's it."

The target was a straw-stuffed scarecrow that Sinjun had borrowed from the wheat field. It was only twenty paces distant.

"Now, very easy . . . that's it, easy."

He released the arrow and it sped toward the scarecrow, striking it squarely in the groin.

MacDuff yowled in feigned pain.

"Good shot," Sinjun said, and turned to face her cousin-in-law. "Mac-Duff! Goodness, it's about time you came back to visit. Your timing is quite perfect. Do you shoot?"

"Oh no, Sinjun, not me. I've never had to. I'm far too big and too ugly for any man or any three men to try to take me on." He held up a meaty fist and shook it at her. "This is all the protection I need, at least bullies think so."

"You're right," Sinjun said. "Did you see Philip's shot?"

"I certainly did. Where did you learn, Philip?"

"Sinjun," the boy said. "She's quite good. Show him, Sinjun."

She did, deftly targeting the scarecrow and releasing the arrow quickly, with no fuss. It struck the scarecrow right through the neck, the arrow coming out six inches through the back.

"My God," MacDuff said. "That was excellent. Your brothers taught you?"

"Oh yes, but they have no idea that I can now outshoot them. Perhaps they do but it would never occur to them to admit it."

"You're wise not to tell them," MacDuff advised. "They would be crushed, their male pride stomped underground."

"Men," Sinjun said. "What does it matter?"

"I don't know, but it does."

"Philip, why don't you tell Aunt Arleth that MacDuff is here. You will stay some time with us?"

"A couple of days only. I'm on my way to Edinburgh and just wanted to see if there was anything you needed."

Yes, I need my husband, she wanted to say, but said instead, "You were staying here in the neighborhood?"

"I have friends, the Ashcrofts, who live near Kinross."

"Well, I'm glad you're here, for even so short a time."

MacDuff merely nodded, watching Philip race back to the castle. He said, wearing a small smile, "I see you have quite won over Philip. How goes Dahling?"

"Ah, she's a tough little nut, but I believe I've found her weakness."

"She's only four and a half years old, Sinjun, and she already has a weakness?"

"Oh yes, she's quite horse mad. I took her out to see my mare, Fanny, and I thought she would burst the seams of her gown. It was love at first sight. I haven't yet let her ride Fanny. But when I do, that should quite drop her into my net."

"You're dangerous, Sinjun. So all goes well, then."

"I suppose all goes. How well or not is a matter of the time of day and the mood of the inmates here."

They walked together to the castle, Sinjun stopping every so often and frowning.

"What is the matter?"

"Oh, I'm just making a mental list of things that still need to be done. It's endless, really. The chickens need a new roof on their house, and the fencing there needs mending. I imagine we've lost many hens due to that. Ah, there's so much. Let me show you the new garden. Cook is all atwitter about it and the scullery maid, Jillie, is sheer magic with plants. She is now only a scullery maid half of the time and a gardener the other half.

Cook is happy, Jillie is radiant, and our meals are better by the day. All that remains is talking Cook into trying her hand at some English dishes."

"Good luck to you," MacDuff said, and laughed. He admired the garden, still stubby green sprouts just showing above rich dark earth. "Colin isn't happy," he said suddenly, coming to a halt near the cistern. He leaned his elbows on the worn stones and looked down.

"It's very deep," Sinjun said. "The water is sweet."

"Yes, I remember that it is. I see that you've put a new chain and that's a new bucket."

"Yes. Why isn't Colin happy?"

MacDuff lowered the bucket, letting it down slowly, listening closely until it finally hit the water. He raised it and took the wooden mug hanging from a hook and dipped it into the bucket. He drank.

"As good as I remember," he said, and wiped his mouth with the back of his hand.

"Why isn't Colin happy?"

"I believe he feels guilty."

"He should. I'm here and he's not and there is another thing—Robert MacPherson . . ." She broke off, wanting to kick herself. Colin would come riding home *ventre à terre* to protect her. MacPherson wouldn't care how he got to Colin and with Colin here, there were too many possibilities, including the safety of the children. No, she would have to deal with MacPherson. There was no other way as far as she could see, and she'd thought about it very hard, listing out pros and cons as Douglas had taught her to do when faced with any problem.

"What do you mean about MacPherson?"

She shrugged, looking guileless as a nun. "I just wondered what Colin was doing about the man."

"Nothing. He's gone to ground. Colin visits the old laird, and he's learned that Robert's been going behind his back with his people, trying to get the power. Distressing, but true. Colin's in a bit of a bind because, truth be told, he likes the old laird, despite Robert and Fiona."

"He will figure it out," she said shortly, looking out over the barley rows to the east. "It hasn't rained in three days. We need it."

"It will rain, it always does. This is paradise for growing. Colin is truly blessed with all the arable land. Here on the Fife Peninsula there are usually mild temperatures and ample rain. Much of Scotland is barren crags and empty moors and savage hills. Yes, Colin is very lucky to have Vere Castle. His ancestors, naturally, were lucky to be here and not in the Highlands or the borderlands."

"I doubt the first Kinrosses had their pick of where they wished to be in Scotland. Who are these Ashcrofts, MacDuff?"

He smiled. "Friends of my parents. It was a long-overdue visit."

"We're long overdue as well. I'm glad you're here."

"I wish to see all that you've done. Incidentally, what does Colin think of all your improvements?"

"Not much."

"I hope he hasn't hurt your feelings."

"He has. I fancy you know that."

"Perhaps. Try to understand, Sinjun. Since he was a little boy, Colin usually lost those things that were his. He learned secrecy. He learned to guard what was his. But even then he wasn't always successful. He was the second son, you see, and as such, anything that was his that his brother Malcolm wanted, why, it was taken away from him. I remember he had this small stash of items, nothing valuable, you understand, just things that were his and were important to him, things he didn't want taken away from him, and Malcolm would have, I never doubted it. Anything that was Colin's he wanted. Colin hid them in this small carved box in the trunk of an oak tree. He would go to the oak tree only when he knew Malcolm was somewhere else.

"Perhaps that explains why he still wishes to keep the doing of things here at Vere Castle to himself. You see, everything is now his and what is his, he protects. He guards jealously."

"I see," Sinjun said, but she didn't, not really. It made no sense. He was no longer a boy, he was a man.

"It has sorely chafed him that there was no money to bring the castle back into its former splendor. You have made a very big difference, Sinjun."

"Why does Aunt Arleth hate him so?"

"She's a strange old witch. The workings of her mind have eluded any meaningful analysis. Malcolm was her favorite, I don't know why. Perhaps because he'd be the future laird and she wanted him to look at her with lasting respect and affection. She treated Colin like he was a gypsy's get, of no importance at all. I remember she told Malcolm about Colin's love of poetry—he got that from his mother—and Malcolm told his father that he also loved poetry and he wanted Colin's book. He got it."

"But that wasn't fair!"

"Perhaps not, but the laird saw the Kinross future as being in Malcolm's hands, thus Malcolm wasn't thwarted in anything he wanted. It ruined his character. Naturally Aunt Arleth hated her sister for the simple reason that she wanted the earl for herself. The word is that she got him after her sister died, but only in her bed, not at the altar. Odd how life goes, isn't it?"

Sinjun shivered, not because wispy gray clouds had moved to block the afternoon sun, but because she'd never seen such behavior in her family. Her mother had always been a trial, but it hadn't mattered. It was even amusing now that she could think about it from a goodly distance and not have to live with it.

"But now Colin is the laird. He's a good man and I daresay he's found himself an excellent wife."

"That's true," she said, voice tart. "It's just a pity that he isn't here to enjoy his good fortune."

What to do?

Sinjun chewed over all alternatives she could think of during the next two days, always changing and honing down her list of pros and cons. There was no word from Colin. MacDuff was helpful and kind. He consented to give both her and Philip fencing lessons and both of them proved adept with foils. He complimented her continually on the state of the house, and her reply was only that soap and water were not expensive.

"Aye," he said, "but it takes fortitude to hold out against Aunt Arleth and all her plaints."

She herself studied Colin's gun collection, finally selecting a small pocket pistol with a silver butt cap and a double barrel, not more than fifteen years old, that would hide itself in the skirt pocket of her riding habit.

Now she had to rid herself of MacDuff and be available for Robert MacPherson to come upon. She'd decided on making herself bait. It was the cleanest, most straightforward way of getting him. She didn't doubt for a moment that he or one of his minions was watching Vere Castle. For that reason, she kept both Philip and Dahling close. They were never alone, and if they wondered at her firm stricture, they didn't voice it.

It was at breakfast the morning of MacDuff's departure that Dahling swallowed her porridge and said, "I've decided that you aren't ugly, Sinjun."

MacDuff stared at the little girl but Sinjun only laughed and said, "My thanks, Dahling. I have nearly broken my mirror in my anxiety."

"May I ride Fanny?"

"Ah, I understand now. The child is attempting a stratagem," MacDuff said.

"Would I be ugly again if I said no?"

Dahling looked undecided, but finally shook her small head. "No, you just wouldn't be a Great Beauty, like I will be."

"Well, in that case, why don't we compromise? I'll set you in front of me and we'll both ride Fanny."

The little girl beamed at that, and Sinjun, knowing quite well that the child had gotten exactly what she wanted, didn't mind a bit.

"So both children call you Sinjun now."

"Yes."

"I daresay that Colin will have to come around. Is there any message you wish me to deliver to him?"

Now she realized that she didn't want him around, not until she'd dealt with MacPherson, and only the good Lord knew how long that would take. She said only, "Tell him that the children and I miss him and that all goes well here. Oh yes, MacDuff. Tell him that I would never steal that box of his in the oak tree trunk."

MacDuff leaned down from his great height and lightly kissed her cheek. "I don't believe Colin has read any poetry since Malcolm took his book."

"I will think about that."

"Good-bye, Sinjun."

Sinjun marveled that MacDuff's horse, a hard-jawed hacker a good eighteen hands high, didn't groan when he swung onto his back. Indeed, the stallion even managed to rear on his hind legs. She remained on the deeply indented front stone steps until he was gone from her sight.

Now, she thought, now it was time to act.

But it was Philip who prevented her. He begged and begged to show her the Cowal Swamp. He even promised her, in a voice that offered a great treat, to let her bring some of the swamp ooze back for her own uses. And that, she thought, wondering how Aunt Arleth would react, convinced her.

Crocker accompanied them, and Sinjun noted that he was well armed, despite the fact there'd been no further violence. She wondered if Colin had told him to arm himself. Very likely. Crocker had said the MacPherson name but once, and he'd spat after he'd said it.

It was a good hour through some of the most beautifully savage moors Sinjun could have imagined. Then, quite suddenly, there was a peat bog that deepened and thickened into a sluggishly repellent swamp, with rotting vegetation hanging into the mucky shallow waters.

Crocker gave her a history that included any moving lumps that one could see rippling beneath the surface of the water. Sinjun wouldn't have placed a single toe into that swamp had her life depended on it. The odor was nasty, like sulfur and outhouses that hadn't been limed, both mixed together. It was hotter here, which seemed curious, but it was so. Hot and wet and smelly. Insects buzzed about, dining off the newcomers, until finally Sinjun called a halt. She swatted at a huge mosquito and said, "Enough, Crocker! Let's fill our buckets and leave this odious place."

It rained all the way back to Vere Castle, thick, sheeting rain that turned the afternoon to night very quickly. The temperature dropped dramatically. Sinjun took off her riding jacket and wrapped it around a shivering Philip. As for Crocker, his single cotton shirt was plastered to his stocky body.

Sinjun fretted about both of them, seeing to it that Crocker bathed in front of the fire in the kitchen and Philip in his bedchamber. He appeared to be fine at bedtime.

The following morning Dahling climbed onto Sinjun's bed, ready to ride Fanny.

"It's late, Sinjun. Come along, I'm all dressed."

Sinjun opened an eye and stared with blurry vision at the small girl sitting beside her.

"It's very late," Dahling said again.

"How late?" Her voice came out a croak, hoarse and raw. Sinjun blinked to clear her vision. A shaft of pain over her eyes nearly knocked her senseless. "Oh," she moaned and fell back against her pillow. "Oh no, Dahling, I'm ill. Don't come any closer."

But Dahling was leaning forward, her small palm on Sinjun's cheek. "You're hot, Sinjun, very hot."

A fever. It was all she needed to go with the pain in her head. She had to get up and get dressed. She had to see Philip and make her plans to get MacPherson, she had to . . .

She tried but couldn't make it. She was too weak. Every muscle, every fiber of bone and sinew and muscle ached horribly. Dahling, worried now, climbed off the bed. "I'll go get Dulcie. She'll know what to do."

But it wasn't Dulcie who came into the laird's bedchamber some ten minutes later; it was Aunt Arleth.

"Well, felled at last."

Sinjun managed to open her eyes. "Yes, it appears so."

"You sound like a frog. Crocker and Philip are quite well. I suppose one would expect an English miss to be the one to become ill."

"Yes. I should like some water, please."

"Thirsty, are you? Well, I'm not your servant. I'll have Emma fetched."

She left without a backward look or another word. Sinjun waited, her throat so sore that it hurt to breathe. Finally she fell into an uneasy sleep.

When she awoke Serena was standing beside her bed.

"Water, please."

"Certainly." Serena turned and left and Sinjun wanted to cry. Oh God, what was she going to do?

Unlike Aunt Arleth, Serena returned with a carafe of water and several glasses. She filled a glass and put it to Sinjun's lips.

"Drink slowly, now," she said, her voice soft and crooning. "Goodness but you don't look at all well. Your face is quite pale and your hair a ragged mess. Your nightgown looks sweaty. No, you don't look well at all. It came on you so quickly, too."

Sinjun didn't care if she looked like a goat. She drank and drank and drank. When she didn't want any more, she lay back, panting with the effort it had cost her.

"I can't get up, Serena."

"No, I can see that you are quite ill."

"Is there a physician nearby?"

"Oh yes, but he's old and infirm. He doesn't visit just anyone."

"Have him come here at once, Serena."

"I will speak to Aunt Arleth about it, Joan." And she left, floating out of the bedchamber in a rich silk gown of deep crimson that was so long it trailed the floor behind her like a train. Sinjun tried to call after her, but her voice came out a whisper.

"We haven't the money to pay any doctor."

It was Aunt Arleth. Sinjun felt light-headed now. It was difficult for her to focus on the woman. It was late afternoon, according to the clock that stood near the bed. She was thirsty again, terribly hungry, and she had to relieve herself.

"Fetch Emma or Dulcie for me."

"Oh no, Dulcie is quite occupied with the children. Goodness, it's so very warm in here, isn't it? You must needs have some fresh air."

Aunt Arleth shoved open the windows and tied back the pale gold brocade draperies. "There, that should cool your fever. Do get better, my dear girl. I will look in on you later."

She was gone again. Sinjun was alone. The room was getting colder by the minute.

She managed to relieve herself through sheer effort of will, and stumbled back into bed. She burrowed under the covers, her teeth chattering.

The following morning, Philip slipped into the room. He ran to the bed and looked at Sinjun. She was asleep, but she was also shivering. He put his palm on her forehead and jerked it back. She was burning with fever.

He realized then that it was very cold in the room. The windows were open. Aunt Arleth, he thought. He'd known she'd come to see Sinjun, for she'd told the rest of them that she had, and that Sinjun was very nearly well. She was still lying abed because she was English and thus slothful, enjoying ordering everyone about. She'd meant mischief, that was clear. His mind balked at pursuing that thought.

Philip closed the windows and united the draperies. He fetched more blankets from his own bedchamber and piled them on top of his stepmother.

"Thirsty," Sinjun whispered.

He held her head in the crook of his elbow and put the edge of the glass to her lips. She was so weak her head lolled against his arm. He felt a shaft of fear.

"You're not better," he said, and Sinjun dimly heard the fear in his voice.

"No. I'm glad you're here, Philip. You're here . . . I've missed you. Help me, Philip." Her voice trailed off and he knew that she was more unconscious than asleep this time.

Aunt Arleth had told them all to stay away from the laird's bedchamber. She didn't want any of them catching their stepmother's slight cold. She'd assured them that all was well, that their stepmother didn't want them to come see her.

It was more than a cold. Aunt Arleth had lied. Sinjun was very ill.

He stood there, staring down at her, wondering what to do.

"You disobedient little boy! Come out of here now! Do you hear me, Philip? Come here!"

Philip turned to face Aunt Arleth, who stood ramrod straight in the open doorway.

"Sinjun is very ill. You were wrong about her condition. She must have help."

"I've been giving her help. Has she said anything? If so, she's only trying to gain your sympathy, to turn you against me. You see? I'm here yet again to help her, you silly child. I don't want you to be near her, you might sicken as well."

"You said she was just lying about because she was lazy. How could I get sick from laziness?"

"She still has just a touch of fever, nothing much, but it is my responsibility in your father's absence to see that you're well taken care of. That means seeing to it that you don't become ill."

"Sinjun was taking care of both Dahling and me very well."

"She's a shallow chit, thoughtless and clearly negligent, or she never would have gone to that wretched swamp with you. Surely you see that she was just playing at being responsible. She cares naught for either you or Dahling. She cares naught for any of us. She merely enjoys telling us all what to do and flinging her wealth in our faces. Oh yes, she sees all of us as mere poor relations she must tolerate. Why do you think that your dear father isn't here in his own home? It's because of her; he can't bear her company because she rubs his nose in his own poverty and lords it over him. She doesn't belong here, she's a Sassenach. Come away now, Philip. I shan't tell you again."

"The windows were open, Aunt."

"Oh, for heaven's sake! She ordered me to open them. I told her it wasn't wise, but she just kept fretting and whining until finally I simply obliged her."

She was lying, he knew it, and he was suddenly very frightened. He didn't know what to do. He looked back at Sinjun and knew deep down that if something wasn't done she would die.

"Come away from her, Philip."

Slowly, he walked toward Aunt Arleth. He even nodded as he came up to her. He knew exactly what he was going to do.

He turned to watch Aunt Arleth place her hand on Sinjun's forehead and nod. "Ah yes, I knew it. Hardly any fever at all now. No need for a doctor."

Philip left the bedchamber.

CHAPTER
═14═

Northcliffe Hall
Near New Romney, England

ALEXANDRA SHERBROOKE, the countess of Northcliffe, was napping in the middle of a warm Wednesday afternoon. She was permitted this indulgence, her mother-in-law had assured her, even going so far as to pat her cheek with what could be termed affection, because she was carrying another child for Douglas—as if she were some sort of vessel for her husband's use, Alex had thought, but nonetheless had slipped off her gown and fallen quite easily to sleep.

She dreamed of Melissande, her incredibly beautiful sister, who had just borne a little girl who greatly resembled Alex, even endowed with Titian hair and gray eyes. It was justice, Douglas had told her, since their own twin boys were the very image of the glorious Melissande, a happenstance that still made Tony Parrish, Melissande's husband, grin like a smug bastard at Douglas. But in her dream something was wrong with Melissande. She was lying motionless on her back, her beautiful black hair spread like a silk fan against the white of the pillows. Her face was pale, faint blue shadows showing beneath her skin, and her breath was hoarse and low.

Suddenly, her hair wasn't black, it was chestnut, and drawn into a long thick braid. It wasn't Melissande's face now, either. No, it was Sinjun's.

Alex blinked, dragging herself from sleep. What a strange dream, she thought, as she closed her eyes again. She'd just written to her sister-in-law, so that was perhaps why she'd taken Melissande's place in her dream.

Alex quieted. Gently and easily, she dozed, but this time there wasn't a dream awaiting her, there was a soft voice, a woman's low voice, and it was near her ear, saying over and over, "Sinjun is ill . . . Sinjun is ill. She is in trouble. Help her, you must help her."

Alex frowned, then moaned. She awoke with a jerk. There beside her bed stood the Virgin Bride, calm and still, her white gown gently shimmering in the silent bedchamber, and she spoke again, but the words were in Alex's mind, not coming from the ghost's mouth, soft and quiet, but insistent. "Sinjun is ill . . . in trouble. Help her, help her."

"What's wrong? Please, tell me, what's wrong with Sinjun?"

"Help her," the soft voice said, pleading now. The beautiful young woman was clasping her hands in front of her. Odd how her fingers were long and so very slender, yet they seemed to be clear, the bones showing through as dark shadows. Her exquisite long hair was so blond that it shone nearly white in the afternoon sunlight. "Help her. There is much trouble for her."

"Yes, I will," Alex said, and rolled off the side of the bed to her feet. She saw the ghost nod, then gently retreat toward the corner of the countess's bedchamber. Alex watched her simply fade into a pale reflection of herself, lighter and lighter, until there was nothing there. Nothing at all.

Alex drew a deep breath. The ghost hadn't come to her in months and months, and the last time the ghost had smiled and told her that Farmer Elias's cow had survived the colic and could now give milk to the ailing baby in the house. And she'd been here when Alex had needed her, when she'd been screaming in labor with the twins, so torn with the agony that she didn't believe she would live through it. The Virgin Bride had come to her then and told her that she would be all right and she wasn't to doubt it for a moment. Alex would have sworn that a soft hand had touched her forehead, then her belly, and the pain had lessened. Of course, Douglas informed her that she'd simply been delirious. She never should have told him. He was so stubborn about it, and she knew why. Men couldn't bear to accept something they couldn't understand, something they couldn't grasp by the throat and look at and speak to and throttle if they didn't like it. The Virgin Bride couldn't be explained, thus she couldn't exist.

And now she'd come again to tell her that Sinjun was in trouble and ill. Alex felt a slight spasm of dizziness but it passed quickly. Her heart was pounding hard and she stopped, drawing deep breaths.

Douglas wasn't here. He'd had to return to London to meet with Lord Avery at the Foreign Office several days before.

Well, he would be of no use in any case. If she told him what the Virgin Bride had said, he'd sneer and laugh and be an ass about it. No, it was a good thing that he wasn't here because she knew that he wouldn't allow her to take any action—he'd gone so far as to swear her to near complete inaction during his absence—and she knew she had to.

Alex informed her household that she was going for a visit to her brother and sister-in-law in the Cotswolds. Hollis, their butler, stared at her as if she'd lost her wits instead of her breakfast, but her mother-in-law seemed overly pleased to see the back of her for a while.

Sophie had received her own visits from the Virgin Bride over the past five years. Together they would figure out what to do.

Vere Castle

Philip crept out of the castle at ten o'clock that night. He wasn't scared, not so much that he couldn't think, anyway. Any fear he did feel was overcome by his worry for Sinjun.

He made the stables without a single bark from George II, whom he saw just in time to scratch behind his mangy ears before the dog could howl the house down.

Philip didn't pause in the stables. The lads were asleep in their chambers off the tack room. He saddled his pony, Bracken, and quickly led him well down the drive before mounting.

He had a long ride ahead of him, but he was determined. He just prayed that he would be in time.

He'd wanted to tell Dulcie what he was going to do, but he knew deep down that she wouldn't be able to keep her mouth shut. He told her instead, as he was yawning deeply, all ready for his bed, to please look in on his stepmother, and give her water to drink and keep her covered with as many blankets as she could find.

Dulcie had promised. He prayed as he sent his pony into a gallop that Aunt Arleth wouldn't come upon Dulcie and dismiss her, or worse, hurt her.

There was a half-moon overhead and the dark rain clouds of the past three days had disappeared, replaced by soft white ones that did little to obscure the moon or stars. He could see quite well enough.

When he heard hoofbeats behind him, Philip thought his heart would burst through his chest. He quickly guided Bracken into the thick brush beside the road and clamped his fingers over the pony's nostrils to keep him from whinnying.

There were three men riding toward him. When they neared he heard them speaking clearly.

"Aye, 'tis a wee-witted lassie she be, but I'll hae her non' the less."

"Nay, she be fer me, ye louthead, her father promised me an' th' laird is fer th' banns."

A third man laughed aloud, a smug, triumphant laugh. He spat and said, "Well, yer both off the mark, ye are. Dinna ye ken, I already bedded wi' her, she's all mine. I'll tell th' laird, an' 'tis done. I'll tell ye something else, lads, her tits bain't be wee."

There were howls and yells and curses, and the horses were whinnying and plowing into each other. Philip stayed still as a stone, waiting,

praying that the strongest of the men would get the wee lassie and the
other two would go to the devil.

The fight lasted another ten minutes. Finally, Philip heard a loud curse
and then the loud report of a gun. Oh God, he thought, swallowing so
hard he nearly choked himself.

There was a yell, followed by a profound silence.

"Ye kilt Dingle, ye fool."

"Aye, he bedded wi' her, he deserved t' croak it."

The other man groaned, then shouted, "An' wot if she's got his seed 'n
her belly? Yer a stupid sod, Alfie, MacPherson'll have our guts fer his
breakfast."

"We'll nae say a word. 'Tis a bloody Kinross wot kilt him. Away, then!
Away!"

They left the third man there. Philip stood irresolute. Then he left
Bracken tied to a yew bush and quietly made his way back to the road.
The man was sprawled on his back, his arms and legs spread wide. There
was a huge red stain covering his chest. His eyes were wide with surprise,
his teeth still bared in a snarl. He was quite dead.

Philip threw up. Then he ran back to Bracken and sent him back onto
the road.

He'd recognized the man. It was a bully whose name was Dingle, and
he was one of the MacPhersons' meanest fighters.

His father had pointed him out once to Philip on a visit to Culross
Palace, telling him that the fellow was a cretin and an excellent example
of the caliber of MacPherson's men.

Philip rode until Bracken was winded and blowing hard. He fell asleep
astride his mare. It was Bracken who nudged him awake. Philip, not
knowing how much time had passed, panicked. But his pony couldn't
sustain a steady gallop and he was forced to slow. He saw more men and
several peasant women. What they were doing up and about in the middle of the night would remain a mystery. He avoided them, thought he
heard one of the men shouting after him.

He was on the ferry to Edinburgh at four o'clock in the morning, paying the ferryman every shilling he had taken from his father's strong-box
save one. He nestled down between two bags of grain for warmth. He
reached his father's house in Abbotsford Crescent just past six o'clock in
the morning. It had taken him a good hour to find the house, and he'd
nearly been in tears when, finally, he'd spotted it.

Angus opened the door, yawning deeply as he did so, and stared down
at the boy, mouth still agape.

"Oh och, 'tis ye, th' young master! By gawd, bain't this be a treat fer
th' laird. Who be wi' ye, laddie?"

"Quickly, my father, Angus. I must see my father." While Angus was gaping at him, trying to gather his wits together, Philip ducked around him and raced up the stairs. He didn't stop running until he reached the laird's bedchamber and flung open the doors, banging them loudly against the walls.

Colin came awake in an instant and bolted upright in bed. "Good God, Philip! What the devil are you doing here?"

"Papa, quickly, you must come home. It's Sinjun; she's very sick."

"Sinjun," Colin said blankly.

"Your wife, Papa, your *wife*. Quickly, come now." Philip was pulling back the covers, so frightened and relieved that he'd found his father that he was shaking with it.

"Joan is ill?"

"Not Joan, Papa, Sinjun. Please hurry. Aunt Arleth will let her die, I know it."

"Blessed hell, I don't believe this! Who came with you? What the devil happened?" But even as he spoke, Colin flung off the covers and jumped off the bed, naked and cold in the gray light of dawn.

"Speak to me, Philip!"

Philip watched his father pull on clothes, watched him splash water on his face, watched him wave Angus away when the old man appeared in the doorway.

He told him about the Cowal Swamp and the rain on the ride back to the castle and how Sinjun had taken off her riding coat and made him wear it. He told him about the cold room and the open windows and the lies Aunt Arleth had told them. He stopped then, stared with frightened eyes at his father, and started to cry, low deep sobs that brought Colin to his son instantly. He enfolded him in his arms and hugged him close. "It will be all right, Philip, you'll see. You've done very well indeed. We'll be home soon and Joan will be all right."

"Her name is Sinjun."

Colin forced his exhausted son to eat some hastily prepared porridge. Within a half hour, they were on horseback and off. He'd suggested that his son remain here because he was so weary, but Philip wouldn't hear of it. "I must see that she's all right," he said, and in that moment Colin saw the future man in the boy, and he was pleased.

Sinjun felt strangely peaceful. She was also incredibly tired, so very weary that she just wanted to sleep and sleep, perhaps forever. There was no more pain, just this sweet desire to release her mind from herself, to give in to the gentle lassitude that tugged persistently at her. She moaned softly, the sound of her voice odd in her ears, far away really, as if that sound came from someone else. Tired, she was so very tired. How could she be so tired and not sleep? Then she heard a man's voice, echoing in her head as if it came from a great distance, and wondered if it was her own voice she was hearing and if it was, why she was speaking. Surely there was no need to speak, not now, not forever. No, his voice was strong, deep, impatient, and commanding, surely a man's voice, a man who wasn't pleased about something. She'd heard that tone of voice enough times in her life from her brothers. But it wasn't Douglas or Ryder. It couldn't be. Now the man was speaking more closely to her, next to her ear, but she couldn't understand his words. They weren't important, surely not. She heard another man speaking as well, but his voice was old, softer, blurring at the edges of her mind, not intruding, bumping gently against her consciousness, then rolling away, harmless and indistinct.

The hard man's voice was retreating, at last. Soon she would be free of it. It was gone now and her head lolled to the side, her mind eased. She felt her breath slow and slow yet more.

"Damn you, wake up! I won't tell you again, Sinjun, wake up! You shan't give up like this. Wake up, you damned twit!"

The shouting brought her back with a lurch of pain. Douglas shouted like that but she knew it wasn't Douglas. No, he was far away. She felt as if she were teetering on the edge of something that was very close to her but still unseen; she was drawn to it, yet still wary of it. It was strangely seductive.

The man's voice came again, a loud, horribly grating voice that made her brain pound. She hated it, she wanted to scream at him to be quiet. She stepped back from the edge, so angry at the interference that she even opened her eyes, wanting to protest, to yell at the man. She opened her mouth but didn't make a sound. She was looking up at the most beautiful man she'd ever seen in her life. Her mind absorbed his image, his black hair and incredible dark blue eyes, and that cleft in his chin, and she managed to say in a raw whisper, "You are so beautiful," then she closed her eyes again, for she knew he must be an angel and she was here in heaven, and she wasn't alone, and for that she was grateful.

"Damn you, open your eyes! I'm not beautiful, you little twit. Good God, I haven't even shaved!"

"An angel doesn't curse," she said clearly, and once again forced her eyes open.

"I'm not an angel, I'm your bloody husband! Wake up, Sinjun, and do it now! I won't have any more of your lazing about! No more dramatics, do you hear me? Wake up, damn your Sherbrooke eyes. Come back to me and do it now, else I'll beat you."

"Bloody husband," she repeated slowly. "No, you're right, I must come back. I can't let Colin die. I don't want him to die, not ever. He has to be saved, and I'm the only one to do it. He's too honorable to save himself. He isn't ruthless and only I can save him."

"Then don't leave me! You can't save me if you die, you understand me?"

"Yes," she said, "I understand."

"Good. Now, I'm going to pick you up and I want you to drink. All right?"

She managed a nod. She felt a strong arm beneath her back and felt the cold glass touch her lips. She drank and drank and the water was ambrosia. It ran down her chin, soaking into her nightgown, but she was so very thirsty nothing mattered but the sweet water trickling down her throat.

"There, enough for now. Listen to me. I'm going to bathe you and get that fever down. Do you understand me? Your fever's too high and I've got to get it down. But you won't sleep again, do you understand me? Tell me you understand!"

She did, but then it escaped her. Her brain tripped off in another direction when she heard a woman's shrill voice say, "She worsened suddenly. I was just on the point of fetching that old fool Childress when you came, Colin. It isn't my fault she got sicker. She was nearly well before."

Sinjun moaned because she was afraid. She tried to pull away from that woman, tried to curl up in a ball and hide from her. The beautiful man who wasn't an angel said in a very calm voice, "Leave, Arleth. I don't want you inside this room again. Go now."

"She'll lie to you, the little bitch! I've known you all your life. You can't take her side against me!"

She heard his voice come again, but he was pulling away from her. Then there was blessed silence. She suddenly felt a cool wet cloth on her face and she tried to lean upward to bury her face in it, but there was his voice again, this time soothing and so gentle, telling her to lie still, that he would see to it that she felt better. "Trust me," he said, "trust me." And she did. He would keep the woman away from her.

She heard the other man, the one with the old voice, the soft voice, saying, "Keep that up, my lord. Wipe her down until the fever lessens. Every several hours, make her drink as much as she'll take."

She felt the cool air touch her skin. She vaguely realized that someone was taking off the sweaty nightgown, and she was thankful for it, for quite suddenly she felt the itchiness of her skin. She felt the wet cloth wipe over her breasts and ribs. But it didn't go deep enough. She was still so very hot, deeper inside, and the wonderful cold of the cloth didn't reach it. She tried to arch her back to bring the cloth closer.

She felt a man's hands on her arms, pushing her back down, and he was saying quietly now, that beautiful man, "Hush, I know it burns. I had a very bad fever once, as you well know, and I felt as if I were in flames on the inside, where nothing could reach, and I was burning from the inside out."

"Yes," she said.

"I'll keep doing this until that burning is gone, I promise you."

"Colin," she said, and she opened her eyes and smiled at him. "You're not an angel. You're my bloody husband. I'm so glad you're here."

"Yes," he said, and felt something powerful move inside him. "I won't leave you again, no matter what."

It seemed then she must make him understand. She tried to lift her hand to touch his face, to gain his attention, and her voice was hurtling from her throat, the words raw and ugly. "You must leave, it's safer for you. I didn't want you to come back until I'd taken care of him. He's a weasel and he would hurt you. I must protect you."

That made Colin frown. What the devil was she talking about? Who, for God's sake? She closed her eyes again and he continued to wipe her down, from her face to her toes. When he turned her onto her stomach, she moaned softly, then sprawled boneless on the sheets.

He continued rubbing her with the damp cloth until she was cool to the touch. He closed his eyes for a moment, praying for her and praying for himself, that God would find him ample enough in grace to listen to him. Finally the fever was down. "Please, God, please let her be all right," he said aloud in the silent bedchamber, a litany now.

He covered her when he heard the bedchamber door open.

"My lord?"

It was the physician. Colin turned, saying, "The fever is down."

"Excellent. It will rise again, doubtless, but you will handle it. Your son is sleeping on the floor outside the door. Your daughter is sitting beside him, sucking on her thumb and looking very worried."

"As soon as I've put my wife in a nightgown, I will see to my children. Thank you, Childress. Will you remain here at the castle?"

"Yes, my lord. If she will survive, we'll know by tomorrow."

"She will survive. She's tough. You will see. Besides, she has a powerful incentive—she's got to protect me."

And he laughed.

Sinjun heard the woman's voice and she knew deep sudden fear. She was afraid to move, afraid to open her eyes. The voice was vicious and mean.

It was Aunt Arleth.

"So you're not dead yet, you little slut. Well, we'll just have to see about that, won't we? No, no use you struggling, you're weak as a gnat. Your precious husband, the young fool, left you. Aye, left you to my tender mercies, and you'll get them, my girl, oh aye, you'll get them."

"Aunt Arleth," Sinjun said as she opened her eyes. "Why do you want me dead?"

Aunt Arleth continued speaking, her voice softer now, running on and on, the words melting together. "I must move quickly, quickly. He'll be back, doubt it not, the young fool. He doesn't want you, how could he? You're a Sassenach, not one of us. Aye, perhaps I must needs place this lovely soft pillow over your face. Yes, that will do it. That will send you away from here. No, you don't belong here, you're an outsider, a no-account. Yes, the pillow. No, that's too obvious. I must be more cunning. But I must act, else you might live to spite me. Aye, you'd make my life even more a misery, wouldn't you? I know your sort—vicious and mean and not to be trusted. Aye, and pushy, treating us all like worthless savages and taking over. I must do something or we're all lost. Even now you're planning to send me away."

"Aunt Arleth, why are you in here?"

She whirled about to see Philip standing in the open doorway, his hands fisted on his hips. "Papa told you to stay away from here. Get away from her, Aunt."

"Ah, you wretched little giblet. You ruined everything. You're a disgrace to me, Philip. I'm taking care of her. Why else would I be here? Go away, boy, just go away. You can go fetch your papa. Yes, go get the bloody laird."

"No, I will stay here. 'Tis you who will leave, Aunt. My papa isn't a bloody laird, he's *the* laird and he's the very best."

"Ha! Little you know what *he* is! Little you know how his mother— aye, my own sister and your grandmother—played her husband false and fell in with a kelpie, aye, a kelpie she called up from the devil himself to dwell in Loch Leven. He became a man in the form of her husband, but he wasn't her husband because it was me he loved, and he didn't look at her anymore. No, the man she fornicated with wasn't her husband, for the real laird was mine in all ways. Hers was this kelpie and he was one of Satan's minions, a false image, evil through and through, and the son she bore this false husband was Colin and he is as evil and bone-deep blighted as was his kelpie father."

Philip didn't begin to understand her. He prayed his father would come, and quickly, or Mrs. Seton or Crocker, anyone, anyone. Please God, bring someone. Aunt Arleth was agay wi' her wits, as Old Alger the barrel maker was wont to say.

Philip was afraid; he didn't see any of his fervent prayers being answered. Aunt Arleth was moving toward Sinjun. He dashed forward, hurling himself up onto the bed next to his stepmother, covering her body with his, trying to shield her from Aunt Arleth.

"Sinjun!" he shouted, grabbing her arms and shaking her. He shouted her name again, and this time she opened her eyes and stared up at him.

"Philip? Is that you? Is she gone yet?"

"No, she isn't, Sinjun. You must stay awake now. You must."

"Get out of here, boy!"

"Oh God," Sinjun whispered.

"And did you know, you silly boy, that her real husband—your grandfather—put a rowan cross over the door to keep her from entering? He knew she was fornicating with a kelpie. Ah, but Satan had sent a charm that protected her even from the rowan cross."

"Please go away, Aunt."

She drew herself up and slowly stared from the boy to the woman who lay on the bed, those damned covers to her chin. Her eyes were open and filled with fear. It pleased Arleth to see that fear.

"You fetched your pa. You filled his ears with lies, aye, you brought him back with lies, you made him feel guilt. He didn't want to come back, you know. He wants her to leave. He has her money, so why bother with the likes of her?"

"Please go away, Aunt."

"I heard you speaking of a rowan cross and kelpies. Hello, Aunt, Philip. How is Joan?"

Philip jumped at the sound of Serena's voice. She'd glided up silent as a ghost to stand beside him at the edge of the bed. "Her name is Sinjun. Take Aunt Arleth away from here, Serena."

"Why ever for, my dear boy? Now, about the rowan cross. They are nasty things, you know, Aunt. I detest them. Why would you speak of them? I'm a witch, true, but the rowan cross has no effect on me."

Philip wondered if he wasn't losing his wits. He wasn't afraid now. No matter what else Serena was, she wouldn't allow Aunt Arleth to hurt Sinjun.

"Go away, Serena, else I'll crown you with a rowan cross!"

"Oh no you won't, Aunt. You can't hurt me and well you know it. I'll always be too strong for you, and too good."

Aunt Arleth looked pale and furious, colder than the loch in January.

Then, to Philip's utter relief, his father strode into the room. He stopped short and frowned at his son, who was hovering on the bed next to Joan as if he were protecting her, for God's sake. Serena was looking vague and beautiful, like a fairy princess who had mistakenly stepped into Bedlam and didn't know what to do.

As for Aunt Arleth, there was no expression at all on her thin face. She was looking down at her pale hands, at the age spots that dotted the backs. "Colin?"

He smiled now and walked to the bed. Sinjun was awake and had her wits about her, finally. "Hello, Joan. You're back again. I'm pleased with you."

"What's a kelpie?"

"An evil being that lives in lochs and inland lakes. He can assume different forms. He gets his power from the devil. It's an interesting question. Why do you wish to know?"

"I don't know. The word just kept coming into my mind. Thank you. May I have some water?"

It was Philip who helped her to drink. "Hello to you," she said to him. "What's wrong, Philip? Do I look that horrid?"

The boy lightly touched his fingertips to her cheek. "Oh no, Sinjun, you look fine. You're better, aren't you?"

"Yes. You know something? I'm hungry." She looked at Aunt Arleth and said, "You dislike me and you wish me ill. I don't understand you. I've done nothing to harm you."

"This is my house, missy! I will—"

Colin said mildly, "No, Aunt Arleth. You will stay away. No more from you." He watched her leave the room, slowly, unwillingly, and he was afraid that her mind, tenuous at best, was losing its meager hold. He turned back to hear his wife say to Philip, "Get me the pocket pistol, Philip. It's in the pocket of my riding habit. Put it under my pillow."

Colin said nothing. He wanted to tell her not to be such a fool, but in truth he couldn't be at all certain that Arleth, from some misguided notion of loyalty, hadn't tried to hurt her.

He said now, seeing that his son was fairly itching to get the pistol for her, "I will speak to Mrs. Seton about some invalidish dishes for you, Joan."

"I remember you called me Sinjun."

"You wouldn't respond to your real name. I had no choice."

Sinjun closed her eyes. She felt beyond tired, her bones so weak she knew she couldn't lift the small pistol even to save herself. The fever was rising and she was shivering. She wanted some more water badly.

"Papa, you stay with Sinjun. I'll talk to Mrs. Seton. Here's the pistol, Sinjun. See, it's right under your pillow."

Colin gave her water to drink, then sat down beside her and watched her. She felt the flat of his hand on her forehead, then heard him curse quietly.

The heat became cold from one instant to the next and she knew that if she moved, her body would crack, just as ice would crack. She felt brittle; she knew that if she blew her breath out, she would see it, for the air was frigid in her lungs.

"I know," Colin said. He stripped off his clothes and climbed into bed beside her. He drew her against the length of him, pressing her even closer, trying to give her all his warmth. He felt the tremors, the convulsive shaking, and it hurt him, this pain of hers. He wanted to know many things, but now wasn't the time.

He held her close even when he began to sweat. When she finally slept, he still held her, his hands stroking up and down her back.

"I'm sorry I wasn't here," he whispered against her hair. "I'm so sorry." He was very aware of her breasts pressing against his chest, her thighs against his, and her belly . . . no, he wouldn't think of that. Oddly enough, even though he was hard, he felt more protectiveness toward her than lust. It was odd, but it was so. He wanted her well again. He wanted her yelling at him when he again took her to bed, only this time she wouldn't mind at all when he came into her. He would see to it that she welcomed him. He wouldn't be a clod.

The fever broke the following day.

Colin, more exhausted than he'd been in his life, smiled at the doctor. "I told you she'd survive. She's tough."

"Most odd," said Childress. "She's English."

"What she is, sir, is my wife. She's now a Scot."

That night one of the crofters came to the castle. MacPherson had stolen two cows and killed MacBain and his two sons. Colin felt such rage he shook with it.

"MacBain's wife said the brutes told her to tell ye that it was t' pay fer Dingle's life ye took."

"Dingle! Why, I haven't seen that miserable lout in longer than . . ." Colin cursed soundly. "I don't know when I last saw him. What is it, Philip? What's wrong? Is it Joan?"

"No, Papa, but I know all about Dingle."

When Colin heard the story he felt his guts knot at how close his son had come to disaster on his journey to Edinburgh. However, he managed to pat his son's shoulder, and retreat to his tower chamber.

He could see no hope for it. He wanted the feuding to stop. He would have to speak to MacPherson. But tell him what? That he truly couldn't remember a thing about Fiona's death or how he came to be unconscious by the cliff edge?

Sinjun was sleeping fitfully. There was a strange light at the edge of her mind, a soft, very white light that was soothing and clear, yet somehow shadowy and deep, filled with meanings buried in mysteries that she wanted very much to understand. She tried to speak but knew it wouldn't help her. She lay still, her mind and body calm, waiting. A flicker of darkness appeared in the white light, then faded only to glitter again, like candlelight flickering in a breeze. Then it seemed to grow stronger and shimmer in its own pale way. And then there was a female figure, a very ordinary young female figure, her expression good-natured, and she was all gowned in pearl-covered white material. So many pearls—never had Sinjun seen so many pearls. Surely the gown must be very heavy with all those pearls.

Pearlin' Jane, Sinjun thought, and smiled. She'd left the Virgin Bride to come to another ghost and now this one must needs make her acquaintance. She felt no fear at all. She'd not harmed this ghost nor had Colin. She waited.

The pearls glittered in a light that strengthened, growing stronger and brighter until Sinjun's eyes hurt from the intensity of the light. The pearls flashed and sparkled. The ghost did nothing at all, merely looked at her, her expression studious now, as if she didn't know what kind of person Sinjun was and wanted to.

"He tried to buy me off," she said at last, and it seemed to Sinjun that her lips moved. "He did indeed, the betraying fool, with naught but a single cheap pearl, but I knew what he was about. He'd kilt me, hadn't he? Not a brow he raised when he ran me down in his carriage, his lady love beside him, her nose in the air, like I was nothing more than a bit of trash beside the road. So I demanded enough pearls to cover my gown and then I would leave him alone."

That answered that question, Sinjun thought, and she thought again, *But you were already dead, weren't you?*

"Aye, dead as a mousie rotting in the wainscoting, but I took care of that demned blighter, aye, I did. Made his life a misery, I did, and his little wifey, aye, I tormented that bitch until she couldn't bear the sight of him. I see my portrait's gone again. Fetch it back; it goes between the two of theirs, always in the middle, between them, separating them in death as it did in life, that's where my portrait must hang. See that you do it. I don't know why it was taken down. Put it back up. I will trust you to see that it stays in its rightful place."

"All right. Please come again whenever you wish."

"I knew you wouldn't be afraid of me. 'Tis good you're here."

Sinjun slept deeply now, a healing sleep, and when she awoke late the following morning, she sat up in bed and stretched. She felt wonderful.

CHAPTER
═══ 15 ═══

PHILPOT OPENED THE DOORS and gaped. Two stylish ladies stood on the front steps, a traveling carriage with a high-nob crest on the side on the graveled drive behind them. The two magnificent bays in harness were blowing and stamping.

There were two outriders, who had pulled their horses to stand protectively on either side of each lady. The man driving the carriage was whistling, his whip upright on his leg, looking at Philpot with ill-concealed suspicion. Damned Sassenachs, Philpot thought, insular buggers, all of them.

The ladies themselves were in traveling gowns of the highest quality—Philpot might be the son of a Dundee baker but he knew excellence when he saw it. They were also dusty, a bit on the wrinkled side, and one lady, in a gray gown with military gold braiding on the shoulders, had red hair, not really absolutely red hair but dark red hair that wasn't all that dark. . . . He shook his head. She also had a spot of dirt on her nose. The other one was just as pretty and just as travel-worn. She was gowned in a deep forest-green traveling gown and her chestnut hair was thick and braided atop her head with a nonsensical little bonnet perched on top. Part of the thick braid had come loose and was hanging over her shoulder. They had traveled quickly. Philpot wondered how far they'd come in how short a time.

The lady with the red hair that wasn't really all that red, just sort of red, stepped up, a wide smile on her face. "This is Vere Castle, home of the earl of Ashburnham?"

"Aye, my lady. Might I inquire as to who you—"

There was a shriek from behind him and Philpot paled hearing the countess. Oh Gawd, had she fainted? He whirled about as quickly as his age and dignity permitted. She was leaning against a decorative suit of Elizabethan armor just behind him, pale as could be, staring at the two ladies.

"Alex? Sophie? Is that really you?"

The lady in green rushed forward. "Are you all right, Sinjun? Oh, please, my dear, tell me you're all right? We were so dreadfully worried about you."

"I think I am now, Sophie. But why are you here? Are Douglas and Ryder outside? Why—"

"You have been ill! I knew it. No matter now, Sinjun, Sophie and I are here to see that everything will be all right. You're not to worry about anything anymore."

The two ladies had swept past Philpot as they spoke, and quickly converged on the sickly countess and took turns hugging her and patting her pale cheeks and telling her how much they'd missed her.

Finally, after all the affections had been duly dispensed, Sinjun introduced them to Philpot, then said, "Do you know where the laird is?"

"Ye shouldn't be out of yer bed, m'lady," he said, sounding as disapproving as a bishop.

"Don't scold me, Philpot. I was sinking like a dead stone into the feather tick. Had I remained abed any longer I would have smothered myself. But you're right, I'm feeling a bit shaky. I'll sit down in just a moment. Please send for the laird. Tell him we have guests, my sisters-in-law, to be exact. We'll all be in the drawing room. Alex, Sophie, come with me."

Her ladyship tried to lead the way, but she faltered. Philpot jumped forward, but the two ladies were quicker. They all but carried her into the drawing room.

Sinjun was settled on the sofa, her feet put up, a cushion beneath them, another pillow behind her head.

"Are you warm enough, love?"

"Oh yes, Alex, I'm just fine, though I am much enjoying seeing the both of you hovering. Ah, you're really here, it's wonderful. I can't believe it. How?"

Alex looked at Sophie, then said simply, "The Virgin Bride sent us. She said you were ill."

"Douglas and Ryder?"

Sophie gave an elaborate shrug and didn't look one whit guilty. "Douglas was easy. He's in London, so Alex just left Northcliffe Hall to come visit me, bringing the twins with her. Ryder, however, presented more of a strategic difficulty. We had to wait until he went to the Ascot races with Tony, a three-day outing, thank heaven. I pleaded an indisposition, as did Alex. Then we left, simple as that." She paused a moment, then said, "I believe Ryder thinks I'm pregnant. He was giving me all these male possessive looks and tender pats on my stomach. It was difficult not to laugh. I wanted to ask him if he thought being with child was catching—since Alex is pregnant, you see."

Sinjun groaned. "They'll come," she said. "They'll come and try to kill Colin again."

"*Again?*" This from both Alex and Sophie together.

Sinjun groaned again, leaned her head back against the cushion, and said, "Yes, again. Alex knows about the first time. She herself coshed Douglas with a walking stick to help me break up their scuffle. There were two other times as well, both here in Scotland. Did you bring the boys?"

"No," Alex said. "Directress Jane of Brandon House is free to enjoy all three of them whilst we're gone. That is the title she selected, you know. She insists upon it whenever I introduce her to someone. The twins feel like they've arrived in heaven when they get there, what with Grayson and all the Beloved Ones. That's a total of fourteen children right now. But who knows—Ryder just might bring home another child from Ascot."

"Lucky Jane!"

"Oh yes," Sophie said serenely. "She is indeed. Grayson would kill any number of dragons for Jane. As for Alex's twins, Melissande will doubtless visit them nearly every day, since they look like her. She calls them her little mirrors. It very nearly renders Douglas incoherent with nausea. He will look at the boys, shake his head, gaze heavenward, and wonder aloud what he did to deserve the two most handsome male children in the world, which will undoubtedly ruin their characters and make them insufferable."

"Sit down, both of you. Now, my head is awhirl. The Virgin Bride came to you, Alex? She told you I was ill?"

Before she could answer, the door opened and Mrs. Seton, bearing a large silver tray, her dark eyes nearly crossed in her excitement, came into the drawing room. To a stranger she would have looked stiff and proper as a duchess, only Sinjun wasn't fooled for a minute.

"Thank you, Mrs. Seton," she said formally, maintaining Mrs. Seton's pose. "These two ladies are here to visit us awhile. They are my sisters-in-law, the countess of Northcliffe and Mrs. Ryder Sherbrooke."

"Charmed, my ladies," Mrs. Seton said, and gave them a curtsy that would have done justice to the Queen's drawing room. She lacked but a feather in her hair.

"I shall prepare Queen Mary's room and the Autumn Room," she added with more ceremony than Sinjun's mother would have deemed appropriate, and proffered another quite impressive curtsy. "The footmen are seeing to your valises. Emma will unpack for you."

"You are very kind, Mrs. Seton. Thank you."

"This is the laird's castle, my lady. Everything is done properly here."

"Yes, certainly," Sinjun said, and watched Mrs. Seton take herself out of the room. "Phew! I never knew Mrs. Seton had quite so much . . ."

"I don't know the word, either, but it was impressive," Alex said.

"Also we only have one footman, Rory, and he does everything in addition to any footing. However, Emma is an excellent girl and it is she who will take care of you. Now, back to the Virgin Bride."

Before Alex could say anything, the drawing room door opened again and Colin strode into the room like the master of his castle, looking at once belligerent and wary. He saw only two young ladies seated beside his wife, cups of tea in their elegant, albeit somewhat wrinkled, gloved hands. The one he recognized as Douglas's wife. Oh Lord, the bounder had to be here somewhere. He craned to see the rest of the room.

"Where are they? Are they armed this time? Pistols or foils? Are they hiding behind the sofa, Joan?"

Sinjun laughed, a weak laugh, but it made him smile.

"Good lord," Sophie said, and stared at her sister-in-law's husband. "You look like a bandit!"

Indeed, if a bandit were wearing naught but a white flowing shirt, unlaced at the top to show some of his hairy chest, and tight black knit breeches and black boots, his black hair windblown, his face tanned from the summer sun, then Colin was a bandit. Sophie happened to look at Sinjun. Her sister-in-law was staring at her husband with such wistful besottedness that it made Sophie lower her gaze.

Colin looked at his wife then, saw her pallor, and frowned. He strode to her, leaned down, and lightly pressed his palm to her forehead. "No fever, thank God. How are you? Why are you downstairs? Philpot was more concerned about telling me that you'd been tottering about than he was about our visitors. Welcome, ladies. Now, Joan, what the devil are you doing downstairs?"

"I was growing mold in bed," she said, and raised her hand to touch his jaw, the cleft in his chin. "I couldn't bear it any longer. Please, I'm fine, Colin. These are my sisters-in-law. You know Alex already. This is Sophie, Ryder's wife."

Colin was charming but cautious. "Ladies, a pleasure. Where are your husbands?" he asked as soon as could be, still standing, still wary.

"They'll be coming," Sinjun said. "But it will take a while, I hope, because Alex and Sophie are smart."

"Smarter than you were, I trust," he said. He turned to the ladies. "We arrived in my house in Edinburgh to find Douglas and Ryder already in residence, waiting to kill me. It was my manservant's blunderbuss that saved us."

"And put a big black hole in the drawing room ceiling."

"That was a sight," Colin said. "Actually, it still is. I haven't yet had it repaired."

Alex looked very interested. "Odd that Douglas didn't mention that. He did mention your house in Edinburgh, Colin, but no talk of violence. What was the other time they attacked you? He said nothing about another time, either."

Colin flushed, Alex was sure of it. Her curiosity rose to unprecedented heights. She happened to look at Sinjun and saw that she was utterly crimson, all the way to her hairline.

Sinjun said quickly, "Colin, they got together and came to me because of the Virgin Bride."

"Isn't that the ghost at Northcliffe Hall you were telling the children about?"

"Children?" Alex said blankly.

Colin flushed again as he was lifting a cup of tea. He moved about in his seat. "Yes," he said, "children."

"I have two wonderful children," Sinjun said smoothly. "Philip and Dahling. They are four and six, and delightful little heathens, just like all our others. I told Colin all about Ryder's Beloved Ones."

"You didn't mention the children in your letters, Sinjun," Sophie said, her voice reproachful.

"Well, no. You see—" She stalled. "Colin, the Virgin Bride came to Alex and told her I was ill. So she and Sophie came as quickly as they could get away, because they were worried about me."

"It was more than that," Alex said, allowing herself to be sidestepped. Another mystery. It was fascinating. "She also said you were in trouble."

"Oh dear," Sinjun said, and looked at her husband, who appeared sincerely puzzled. Douglas would have been sneering and carping on about idiot nonsense. Ryder would have been laughing his head off.

"There is no trouble," Colin said. "Well, maybe a bit, but nothing I can't handle. What the devil is going on here? I want the truth now, all of it."

"We have come for a visit," Alex said, giving him a fat smile. "A simple visit, that's all. We will oversee things until Sinjun is well enough to take over again. Isn't that right, Sophie?"

"Exactly," Sophie agreed, nodding as complacently as a maiden aunt as she ate her second scone. "We both have different household talents, you see, Colin, thus the both of us are necessary so that all may continue to run smoothly. Delicious tea, Sinjun."

Colin looked at her, one dark brow arched up a good inch. "Indeed," he said. "Joan is blessed in her relatives."

"Joan?" Sophie said, frowning. "Wherever did you get that, Colin?"

"I prefer it to her man's nickname."

"Oh. But—"

"It doesn't matter, Sophie," Sinjun said, adding quickly, "Thank you both for coming. I'm so glad you did." She added, without thinking, "It's been rather harrowing."

"What do you mean?" Sophie asked, licking a dollop of sweet raspberry jam from her finger.

Sinjun darted a look at her husband, saying quickly, "Later, Sophie, we will speak of it later."

Colin was frowning ferociously. "You will go back to bed, Joan. You look pale as my shirt and you're sweating like a Caerlaverock goat. I don't like it. Come along. I'll carry you up. I want you to stay in bed this time. I'll tell you when you can get up again." He didn't wait for her to reply, merely picked her up in his arms and carried her to the door. He said over his shoulder, "You may follow us, if you like, ladies. It will help you get the lay of the land."

And so Sophie and Alex, relieved that Sinjun was all right and confused to their eyebrows at the notion of children and harrowing things, silently followed their brother-in-law up the impossibly wide staircase.

"Think of it as an adventure," Alex said to Sophie behind her hand. "Would you look at the gentleman in that portrait! Goodness, he's naked!"

Colin smiled but didn't turn, merely said over his shoulder, "That's my great-great-grandfather, Granthan Kinross. The stories have it that he lost a wager with a neighbor, the result being that he had to have his portrait painted without his plaid. There is a judiciously placed yew bush in front of him, though."

"What was the wager?" Alex asked.

"The story goes that Granthan was a wild young man and much in demand with all the local ladies. He took it on as his mission in life to see that they were all happy. One neighbor said Granthan would never seduce his wife no matter what his blandishments, because of her unflagging virtue, and a bet was made. The wife, it turns out, was really a young man in disguise and Granthan did indeed lose the bet and his clothes for the painting."

Sophie laughed. "You're right, Alex. It's going to be a grand adventure."

That evening after dinner Sophie and Alex came to Sinjun's bedchamber and settled themselves by her bed. Colin let them be, adjourning himself to the children's nursery.

"No, don't ask about my health again. I'm fine, just bloody weak. I got sick from a good dousing in the rain, nothing more, nothing less, except that Aunt Arleth tried to kill me."

Sophie and Alex gaped at her.

"The devil you say," Alex said at last.

Sophie said, "She's a sour old thing—not at all happy to see us, I can tell you that!—but to try to kill you? Why?"

"She doesn't want me here, just my groats. Maybe not even my groats, I'm not certain. When I was ill, Colin was in Edinburgh. She opened windows, left me alone; all in all, she sent me to the edge of oblivion. Philip rode by himself throughout the night to fetch his father. He's a wonderful little boy. Later she tried again. I don't know if she was really serious, perhaps she's just unhinged. She speaks of many things but makes little sense. Now, what do you think of my children?"

"They were only allowed for a few minutes in the drawing room. They're the image of their father, which is to say that they're quite handsome. Dahling hid behind her father's leg, her thumb in her mouth, but Philip came to me and said he was glad we were here. He lowered his voice and told us to be careful for you. He didn't want you hurt again. You have quite a champion there, Sinjun. He will also break ladies' hearts one of these years."

"Just as his father, hopefully, won't break mine."

"Why should he?" Alex demanded. "You're everything a man could wish for in a wife."

"My heroine," Sinjun said fondly, patting her sister-in-law's hand.

"There are problems," Alex said. "You might as well tell us everything, Sinjun. I have this dreadful presentiment that the husbands will arrive here yelling and demanding our heads by dawn tomorrow morning."

"No," Sinjun said firmly. "We'll have more than two days of respite before the husbands descend. We must. You two did very well. It will take them time to get together and make their plans. Didn't you say Ryder was with Tony at Ascot?"

"Yes, but that won't matter," Sophie said. "I agree with Alex. Somehow they'll know and they'll get together. Tomorrow at dawn. And you know how they'll behave—Douglas will be enraged because Alex is pregnant and traveling without his godship's permission, and Ryder will want to skin my hide for keeping secrets from him."

Alex just laughed but didn't disagree. "No, don't worry about me, I feel grand. No more retching in indecorous places, thank God! At least I haven't retched in a day and a half. Talk, Sinjun."

"Sophie's right. We must move quickly. Lying here whilst you were all downstairs gave me the perfect plan. I just need a bit of time to get it into motion."

"Plan for what?" Sophie asked.

Sinjun began with the MacPhersons and moved to Pearlin' Jane, a ghost that both Sophie and Alex readily accepted.

"Do you think," Alex said thoughtfully when Sinjun paused in her recital, "that ghosts can somehow communicate with each other? How did the Virgin Bride know you were ill and in trouble? Did this Pearlin' Jane tell her?"

It was a question to which there was no answer. But Sinjun said, "Oh dear, I forgot to place Pearlin' Jane's portrait and the other two back in their places. She won't like it and I did promise."

"What is all that about, do you know?"

"Evidently Pearlin' Jane wanted all the pearls she could get from the benighted earl, a long-ago Kinross who'd seduced her and left her and then killed her, and she wanted her portrait painted—from her lover's memory, of course—and placed between his portrait and his wife's. Every time it was moved, something unpleasant happened to either the master or the mistress of Vere Castle. Oh, not being struck down by a bolt of errant lightning, but just something unpleasant, like becoming ill eating something bad. I don't want that to happen to me. I think Aunt Arleth moved all the portraits, hoping some affliction would strike me. I'm guessing, but it surely sounds like her."

"A thoroughly dreadful woman," Alex said. "We're here now so she doesn't dare try anything."

"I find Serena the odd duck," Sophie said as she dropped to her knees on the stone hearth and began to build up the fire. "So ethereal, in both her manner and her mode of dress. That gown she was wearing tonight was really quite lovely, not to mention very expensive. Now, that's a good question. If Colin didn't have any money, where did she get the gold for the gown? She was pleasant to us, don't misunderstand me, but vague, cryptic, you could say."

"I'd say she's daft," Alex said.

"Perhaps," Sophie said thoughtfully. "But you know, Sinjun, it's almost as if it's all an act. I don't think she's so out of touch with things as she wants you to believe."

"She did tell me that Colin doesn't love me, that he loves Another. She also likes to kiss him on the mouth when he doesn't expect it. But on the other hand, she seems to accept me. She is certainly strange." Sinjun shrugged and yawned. "As to the cost of her gowns, that's an excellent question. Why don't I ask her tomorrow?"

"Only if your husband allows you out of bed," Sophie said, and grinned at her.

"Oh dear, you do look tired, Sinjun."

"All I need is another good night's sleep," Sinjun said firmly. "Tomorrow I must set my plan into motion. Day after tomorrow—no later—we must act. Don't forget the husbands. They will come, no doubt about that."

"All right," Sophie said. "We'll pray you're right about them not being here until Friday. We'll breakfast with you tomorrow and you can tell us this plan of yours. All right?"

"What plan?" Colin asked from the doorway.

"He walks as quietly as Douglas does," Alex said. "It's provoking."

"Our plans for the day, naturally," Sophie said smoothly, rising from her position in front of the hearth and dusting off her skirt. "Dividing up the housekeeping chores, all that sort of thing. Things that would never interest a gentleman; you know, Colin, discussing Alex's pregnancy and how she feels, knitting blankets and tiny baby slippers—that sort of thing."

Colin appreciated her tactics. He said, a wolfish gleam in his dark blue eyes, "You think I have no interest in women's matters? Why, they're my matters, too. Goodness, as soon as I can manage it, Joan's belly will be swelling up with my child."

"Colin!"

"Yes, perhaps I'll even take up knitting and the two of us can sit in front of the fire, our needles clicking away, selecting names for our progeny."

Sophie said, ignoring him, "There, the fire is set now for several hours. Thank you for letting us visit you, Colin. Come along, Alex. Good night, Sinjun."

When the door was closed, Colin walked to the bed and sat down. He gave his wife a brooding stare. "They are as dangerous as their husbands. It is only their stratagems that differ. I don't trust them an inch. Nor you, for that matter. Now, you will tell me what's going on, Joan."

She yawned again, this one manufactured specifically for the occasion. "Nothing at all. Goodness, I feel I could sleep a week."

"Joan, you are to stay out of my affairs," he said quietly, too quietly.

"Certainly," she said, starting to pretend to another yawn and then changing her mind.

He raised a brow at that. "You said a lot of things when I came back from Edinburgh. There were no brakes on your tongue when you were so ill. You went on and on about protecting me, not that that's anything out of the ordinary or new, merely there is MacPherson. I'm ordering you, my dear wife, to keep to the castle. You will leave me to deal with that bastard."

"He is very pretty," she said without thinking, then realized what she'd done and gasped, her expression now perfectly horrified.

"So," Colin said, leaning closer to her now, his hands on the headboard of the huge bed, on each side of her face, "you have met Robbie, have you? When? Where?"

She tried to shrug but it was difficult, for his fingers were now lightly stroking her throat. She wondered if he would strangle her. "I was riding and met him at Loch Leven. He was a bit nasty and I left him, nothing more, Colin."

"You're lying," he said, and sighed, rising to stand beside the bed.

"Well, I did, ah, take his horse. Nothing more, I promise." She paused, then opened her mouth, but he forestalled her.

"You took his horse. Damnation, I never knew a woman could positively thrive on being so bloody meddlesome. No, don't add to your deceit, just promise me that you will stay safe in the castle."

"No," she said finally, "I can't promise you that."

"Then I will have to lock you in our bedchamber. I won't have you disobeying me, Joan. Robert MacPherson is a dangerous man. You had the cut on your cheek to prove it."

Sinjun felt only mildly concerned; after all, both Sophie and Alex were here. Amongst the three of them, they'd save Colin from any possible danger.

"I agree," she said. "He is dangerous. It's odd since he is so pretty."

"Perhaps that has something to do with his viciousness, but I'm just guessing. As he grew into manhood, his face didn't grow into hard lines, his features softened. He became more difficult, more severe and violent, inside and out. Now, wife, will you obey me?"

"In most things, Colin, you know that I do willingly. But in some things you must grant me leave to behave as I deem proper and right."

"Ah, yes, and one of the *some things* is our having sex together."

"That's right."

"You speak with such confidence. Is it because you know I am not enough of a bastard to take you whilst you're still weak from your illness?"

He had a point there and Sinjun was forced to nod.

He sighed, plowing his fingers through his hair. "Joan, I wasn't very kind to you when I came home before."

"You were a mean-spirited sod."

"I wouldn't go that far," he said, giving her a harassed look, "but I realize that at least now my children care a great deal for you. My small six-year-old son risked his life to come to me in Edinburgh."

"I know. It makes my blood run cold to think of it. He is a very brave boy."

"He is my son."

She smiled at that.

"Also Dahling—when she can be convinced to take her thumb out of her mouth—now sings your praises. Well, your mare's praises more than yours, actually." He sounded a bit baffled and, strangely to Sinjun, a bit put out.

"Will you also allow that it is my right and responsibility to be in charge of the household?"

"I suppose so. MacDuff said he had a message from you. It was something about you not stealing my box. What does that mean?"

"It means that I don't want to take anything away from you, like the box you hid in the oak tree to keep it safe from your brother's greed. I simply want to share what is ours. I'm not Malcolm nor am I your father."

He turned away from her. "MacDuff's mouth overworked itself, I see."

"He just wanted me to understand you. When is your birthday?"

"The last day of August. Why?"

She just shook her head and smiled. She wondered what poets he liked best. Then she yawned, a true yawn, and he said, "You will rest now. I doubt not that your two brothers will be on their wives' heels. You have my permission to protect me from those two. The wives, I see, didn't know about their husbands' bursting into our bedchamber."

"No, thank God."

"Perhaps I should tell them."

"Colin! Oh, you're jesting."

"Yes, I am. Another thing, do Douglas and Ryder know their wives are here?"

"Why, certainly they know."

"How could they let them come alone? No, I don't want to know the tale, it would likely grizzle my hair."

Colin stepped toward the fire and began to strip off his clothes. He was very aware that his wife was looking at him, he could *feel* her looking at him.

He said, "I think Alex is imprudent to have come here. It is a great many miles and it's early days yet. I wouldn't ever want you to risk losing a child with such foolishness. When you are pregnant you will do as I tell you."

Sinjun just smiled at his back, knowing she would do just as she pleased, and willed him to turn around and face her. She wanted to see him, all of him. He was naked now and she stared at the long line of his back, his buttocks, his legs. He was perfect, no doubt about that. She couldn't imagine another man in the world looking as he did.

"Colin?" Her voice sounded hoarse to herself.

"Yes?" he said slowly, turning to face her now, knowing, she thought, just knowing what she was thinking and wanting.

She swallowed. She stared and she wished he would remain there for another hour or so. Perhaps she could take up painting and he could agree to pose for her. She wondered if he would agree to such a ruse.

"Yes, Joan?"

"Will you sleep with me tonight? Hold me?"

"Oh yes. I know you enjoy that. It doesn't threaten you, does it? I will even kiss you and you do like that very very much."

He walked to the bed, knowing she wanted to look at him and allowing it. Her fascination amused him and, truthfully, pleased him inordinately. It was splendid for a wife to admire her husband, yes indeed. He heard her suck in her breath and frowned. He looked at himself. Under her gaze, his sex had aroused itself with predictable enthusiasm, and now she was afraid. Well, what did she expect—that he would shrivel?

Damnation. He wanted her to be well again, quickly. This nonsense of hers was irritating to his nerves.

"You will stay home now, Colin?"

"Yes, as I told you, since MacPherson is here now, causing more trouble, I must deal with him here. And I will, Joan—without any help from you. Also it appears I must protect you from Aunt Arleth."

"I appreciate that, Colin."

He climbed into bed with her and she willingly came into his arms. They lay on their sides, facing each other, their noses nearly touching.

"You still have your bloody nightgown on."

"Perhaps it best stay on."

"You're probably right, damn you." He kissed her mouth, then grinned. "Open up, Joan. You've forgotten what I taught you. No, not like a fish or an opera singer. That's right. Ah, yes. Give me your tongue."

He wanted her very much and if he wasn't mistaken she wasn't at all averse to his continuing with his mouth and with his hands, but he knew she was still weak, not at all up to snuff, and he didn't want her to become ill again. He kissed the tip of her nose and gently pressed her cheek down to his shoulder as he turned onto his back. It was damned difficult but he did it. He felt at the height of his nobility. She gave a small gasp of disappointment and tried to kiss him again.

"No, Joan, I don't wish to tire you. Hush, that's right. Just relax now. I'll hold you, that's all. Was Philip right? Did Aunt Arleth really try to kill you?"

Sinjun was nearly stuttering with lust. She was trembling against him, trying to control herself, but it wasn't easy. She had very little experience in turning off the spigot, so to speak. She wanted to kiss him until she couldn't breathe. She wanted her hands all over his body. She wanted to kiss his belly, his sex, take him into her mouth again. Ah, but it was difficult to simply stop, to simply forget that he was against her, his body hot and hard and fitted against hers so perfectly. She strained against him, unable to help herself. Her hand fisted over his belly. Slowly, very slowly, she flattened her hand over his stomach and felt the heat and hardness of him, and the crispy hair lower on his groin.

Colin closed his eyes and bit his lip. "No, Joan. Hold still, you must really, sweetheart. Move your hand before you make me very uncomfortable. Please, answer my question."

She realized then, vaguely, that he was also trying to control himself, and she supposed she appreciated his concern with her illness, but she would rather take her chances with another fever. Her fingers moved lower, just touching him now. He jerked away from her. He was bent on nobility. She sighed, then said, "She didn't come right out and force poison down my throat, but she wanted me to die, no doubt about that. She even opened the windows to assist me to my eternal reward. After you came, she found me alone once and spoke to me about how she would use a pillow to smother me. She then decided it wasn't the way to do it, it was too obvious. She said that I had ruined everything, that I would make her life even more miserable. There were so many things she said on that day, Colin, so many things she's said at other times, and things I've found out about during your absence." She told him about the kelpie ramblings, how she'd forced Mrs. Seton to keep the castle filthy, how Colin's father wasn't really his father, rather it was the kelpie demon, and the laird had loved her, Arleth, not her sister, who was a fool and evil. Colin asked many questions, but it was confusing. Finally, though, when she was too exhausted to speak another word, he said, kissing her left temple, "I will see to it that she is removed from Vere Castle. She is a danger to herself and to us. Lord knows what she could do to the children were her mind to snap in another direction. Odd that I've never before noticed her strangeness, just her dislike of me—obvious enough, of course—and I paid no heed to that.

"Sleep now. Please, move your hand upward. Yes, that's right. My chest is not such a dangerous place."

She smiled against his shoulder. Nothing could happen to her with him here. As to something happening to him, she would do what she had to do. He could rant and be as lordly and autocratic as he pleased, but it would make no difference. He had no chance against the three sisters-in-law.

No chance at all.

CHAPTER
═16═

DOUGLAS AND RYDER didn't appear at Vere Castle at the crack of dawn, much to the wives' combined relief and chagrin. At eight o'clock that morning, in the laird's bedchamber, Sophie finally voiced her worry. "But where are they? Do you think they've been hurt, Alex?"

"Oh, no, I don't believe so," Alex said, her brow lowering. "I'm beginning to think they're angry and not coming. It's a lesson. Douglas is tired of trying to have his way and only succeeding half the time, and thus he's punishing me with his absence."

Sinjun looked from one to the other and started to laugh. There were two identical expressions of outrage but she couldn't stop laughing. "I can't believe the two of you—you sound as if you want them to come this very instant."

"Oh no!"

"How absurd!"

Sinjun looked from one glum face to the other. "Did either of you brilliant sweetings bother to leave a note as to where you were bound?"

Alex looked at Sinjun as if she were a half-wit and gave her a disdainful shrug that would have done Douglas proud. "Why, naturally I told him where I was going! What kind of a person do you think I am? I would never want to worry Douglas."

"And what did you write to Douglas?"

"Ah . . . that I was off to see Sophie. Oh damn."

Sinjun turned a twinkling eye to Sophie, who was now frowning ferociously down at her pale green slippers. "And you? Did you tell Ryder where you and Alex were bound?"

Very slowly, eyes still firmly on her feet, Sophie shook her head. "I just wrote to him that we were going to do a bit of sightseeing in the Cotswolds and that I would write him to tell him when we would return."

"Oh, Sophie, you didn't!" Alex threw a pillow at her. "I can't believe you didn't tell him the truth. What were you thinking, for God's sake?"

"Well, Alex, you did no better!" Sophie rounded on her and threw the pillow back, striking her magnificent bosom. "You only told part of the truth because you were the first leg of the deception, so to speak. You didn't have to lie like I did."

"You should have realized that there was no need for a lie! You should have thought, but you didn't think, you—"

"Don't you dare call me stupid!"

"I didn't call you stupid, but if the glove fits—"

"That's enough from both of you," Sinjun said, trying desperately not to laugh. Alex's splendid bosom was heaving; Sophie was red in the face, her hands fisted at her sides.

It was Alex who said finally, her voice reeking of catastrophe, "What are we going to do?"

Sinjun didn't crack that smile; the laughter was no longer bubbling up in her throat. She said very firmly, "Ryder and Douglas will figure it out quickly enough. I know they will. If it makes you feel better, then both of you write letters to them right this instant and I will have one of our stable lads go to Edinburgh with them. I don't believe it's necessary, though."

"That will take forever!"

"It isn't necessary," Sinjun repeated. "Now, trust me. I promise that both husbands will be here before too much longer. Indeed, I still hold to Friday, no later. Would the two of you like to shake hands now and we'll get on with the business at hand?"

Sinjun realized she felt quite good as she watched her sisters-in-law continue to grumble at each other even as they hugged. Yes, she felt stronger than she had the day before. Not up to full snuff yet, but she was clear-headed and her brain was functioning quite well. She didn't feel wilted any longer.

They discussed their plan until Sinjun, at least, was pleased, and all the consequences she could think of were covered. Sophie and Alex didn't like the plan but Sinjun convinced them it was the only way. "Would you prefer that I just shoot him and toss his body in the loch?" she'd said, and that had shut down most of their objections. She'd written her letter the afternoon before and had Ostle brought to her. Him, she had sworn to secrecy. Pray God he would keep mum about what he'd done.

Sinjun looked from one sister-in-law to the other. "Now, we will act this morning. We can't take the chance that we'll have another day. You may not have faith in Douglas and Ryder, but I do."

Both Alex and Sophie had brought pocket pistols. Both knew how to shoot, not as well as Sinjun, but well enough. The sight of the pistols brought their feet firmly to the ground.

"The Virgin Bride said trouble, Sinjun," Alex said. "We're not stupid, no matter we didn't think of *everything*. Or *write* everything. Now, where's your pistol?"

Sinjun drew the small pistol from beneath her pillow. "I'm strong enough for us to do it this morning. I will ensure that Colin is off doing something else and not paying any attention to either of you or to me. I'll manage it somehow. Now come here and listen carefully."

Getting rid of Colin wasn't as easy as Sinjun had hoped it would be. Finally, at her wits' end, she played the invalid and began to cough pitiably, bending over and clutching at her ribs as she coughed and coughed. She had the headache, too, of course, a pounding pain over her left eye. Ah, and she could barely catch her breath. She did it well, her eyes even tearing as the raw scraping coughs came from her throat. She even managed some convincing shudders.

"Damn, I thought you were so much better," Colin said, his big hands rubbing up and down her back as he cradled her against him. It was he who insisted on riding himself for the physician Childress, but not before he gained both Alex's and Sophie's promises not to leave her. An easy promise to make and to keep. Talk about guilt, Sinjun was about ready to sink with it at his show of concern, but she knew she had to hold a steady course, they all did.

If men weren't so bloody intractable, she thought, but it was an absurd wish.

"I feel just excellent," Sinjun said in reply to Alex as she dressed quickly in one of her riding habits, a blue serge that was shiny with age and wear. "I'll probably be as weak as a sick goat later, but for now everything's fine. Don't worry, you two. We must take care of this before the husbands arrive. No, don't glare at each other. They will come, and soon."

"Where are you going?"

It was Philip. He strode into the bedchamber, paying no heed to either Sophie or Alex, and walked straight to Sinjun, stopping and staring at her, his hands on his hips, a stance just like his father's. "Where are you going?" he asked again. "You're wearing a riding habit, not a nightgown. Papa won't be pleased, Sinjun. Nor am I."

Sinjun wanted to ruffle his hair but restrained herself. She contented herself with giving him a small smile. "I'm just taking your two new aunts about the grounds. I feel quite good, Philip, and I will be careful. As soon as I tire I'll come back to bed."

"Where is Father?"

"He's doubtless with Mr. Seton going over accounts or perhaps visiting the crofters. He was gone for three weeks and there is much that requires his lordly attention. You didn't ask him?"

"I wasn't downstairs when he left. Dahling was throwing a tantrum and trying to bite Dulcie's leg. I had to protect Dulcie."

"Well, whilst I'm being an excellent hostess, why don't you keep watch on Aunt Arleth for me."

His eyes lit up. "Yes," he said. "I'll do that, but Sinjun, don't tire yourself, all right?"

"I promise." She watched Philip leave the bedchamber and felt the knife of guilt turning in her innards. "I hated doing that, but he's just as protective as his papa."

"You're a wonderful actress, Sinjun," Alex said as they slipped down the back servants' stairs. "I've never been that good."

"I hate it, but it had to be done," Sinjun said on a sigh. "Ah, the guilt. But I must keep Colin safe. He will know how important it is to me. He will understand, if, that is, he ever discovers what we did."

"Your optimism is built on sand, my dear," Sophie said. "He's a man. I shouldn't hold my breath were I you. Understanding isn't a virtue men necessarily cultivate, particularly if it relates to a wife."

"Sophie's right," Alex said. "If Colin does find out, and in my experience husbands usually discover *everything* you don't want them to know about, he will feel enraged and worried to his toes because you might have been hurt; and being a man, he would naturally blame you for worrying him. It all makes sense to them. Strange, but it does."

"A man can't accept that there is anything he can't do," Sophie continued. "If his wife succeeds where he can't, why, he'll be so furious he'll spit nails. And he'll blame her for succeeding."

"I know," Sinjun said on a deep sigh. "I'm married now and I realize well enough that Colin is no different from Douglas and Ryder. He shouts and yells and carries on until I want to cosh him. But surely he will understand that he's left me no choice but to do what I must."

"Ha," said Alex.

"Ha, ha," said Sophie.

"That is if he ever finds out."

"You're dreaming," said Alex.

"More a drunken fantasy," said Sophie.

The three ladies were lost in gloomy thoughts until they reached the stables. Sinjun spotted Ostle and ordered Fanny and two horses for the other ladies.

"I dinna like this, m'lady," he said once, and then again and once more. "It bain't be right."

"You will hold your tongue, Ostle," Sinjun said with such force that her sisters-in-law stared at her. "Now, you will ride to Edinburgh today as soon as we're gone and make the other inquiries. It's critical that you don't let anyone know what you're about. It's critical that you return as quickly as possible. And you must contrive to see me alone. Do you understand me, Ostle?"

He was miserably unhappy, but he nodded, the sweet guineas piled thick in his pocket, tipping the scales against telling the laird what was up.

Unfortunately, due to the depletion of the Kinross stables, there was only one other mare suitable for a lady to ride.

"Very well," Sinjun said after a moment. "I'll ride Argyll, Sophie will take Fanny, and Alex, I'm sorry, but you will have to ride Carrot."

Carrot, a very docile swaybacked mare of ten years, looked at Alex, blew loudly, and nodded her long head.

"We'll do," Alex said. A horsewoman of some renown, she was delighted.

"Er, m'lady, Argyll bain't be in a sporting mood t'day, nay, he bain't. His lordship was going t' ride him, saw that he was nastiness hisself, and rode Gulliver instead. Nay mere than ten minutes ago his lordship left."

Gulliver was the bay Colin kept in Edinburgh. Gulliver was the bay he rode back with Philip because he'd been so worried about her. She gulped and said, "Well, nasty or not, it's Argyll for me. Ten minutes, hmmm. Do hurry, Ostle, and don't worry, all will be well."

She'd never before ridden Colin's stallion—lord, she thought as she swung up on his broad back, he could outrace the rain in a storm. She prayed Colin wouldn't notice he was missing. But if he did, it wouldn't matter. He wouldn't know which direction they'd taken. Ostle wouldn't be here to question. She drew a deep breath and dug her heels into Argyll's muscled sides.

Short minutes later they were galloping smoothly down the long tree-lined drive of Kinross Castle, the summer air warm and soft on their faces, slivers of bright sunlight slicing through the dense canopy of green leaves overhead.

"It is so beautiful here," Sophie said, craning back to see the castle on its rise at the end of the long drive.

"Yes," said Sinjun, and gulped. "Colin said one of his ancestors—the one who is painted naked—planted all the trees. They're very lovely. Of course, there aren't any gardens like yours at Northcliffe, Alex."

"Perhaps not, but these trees. I shall do it at Northcliffe Hall," Alex said. "What do you think—pines and birches and oaks?"

Sinjun knew both of them were scared to death of her plan and scared for her. Alex was babbling about trees; Sophie was looking grim as a defeated general, staring straight between her Fanny's ears. Sinjun said nothing. She was set on her course. She directed them immediately off the narrow road. No tracks for Colin to follow if he happened to be in this exact spot and so inclined.

They rode steadily, not speaking now, staying close to Sinjun's stallion, Argyll, who seemed pleased as could be to have her on his back. Not a bit of trouble did he cause her, which was fortunate, because Sinjun didn't want to deplete her store of strength on a damned recalcitrant horse.

Sinjun called for them to halt in another mile. They were near the barren Craignure Moor. "The MacPherson castle—St. Monance—is but seven miles, over this desolate stretch, then into the Aviemore Hills. I know a short way around—I asked Ostle. We'll be there in an hour. Are both of you ready for this? Are you certain?"

"I don't like it at all, Sinjun," Sophie said, "and neither does Alex. There must be another way. It was easier to talk about and agree to than it is now, actually doing it. It's dangerous. Anything could happen."

Sinjun shook her head. "I've thought and thought. The last thing I want is to have him come across me or Colin by accident, or by design, for that matter. He's already tried to kill Colin once, and possibly twice; the second time I was hurt by mistake." Their breaths sucked, for she hadn't told them about the attempt in Edinburgh, and she continued inexorably, "No, I must be the one in control, the one with a plan. We will take him by surprise. I know there are problems with this, unknowns, if you will, but I couldn't think of anything else. It will work. You must trust me on this. Ostle will find out what we need to know in Edinburgh. It won't take many more days, probably two at the most. Even if the husbands do arrive, why, then I will simply sneak away and finish things off. Then let Colin yell and pound the furniture with his fists if he discovers what I've done. It won't matter. Indeed, I shall enjoy hearing him carry on because I know he'll now be safe. Now, my dears, let's go."

"Your husband will yell and pound the furniture and then he'll kill all of us."

"I will lie to him and he will know it, but how will he ever guess the truth?"

"What lie have you planned to tell him to explain your absence and ours?" Alex asked. She held up her hand. "You see, Sinjun, there's today and then yet another day to deal with, and perhaps even another and another after that. The scheduling of this is difficult, even without the husbands' interference. Now, what will you tell Colin?"

"Truth be told, I haven't the faintest idea now, but with Colin yelling at me, I doubt not that something wonderful will spring to mind. It always does. First things first. Let's go." Argyll galloped forward, spewing pebbles in his wake.

They rode hard and saw very few people. The deeper they rode into the

hills, the more difficult the going became. Purple heather sprang up thick
from between sharp-edged rocks, giving the landscape a savage beauty.

"You're certain this is a shorter route?" Alex asked.

Sinjun nodded. "Nearly there."

Actually, St. Monance Castle, home of the MacPherson clan, was set
at the very end of the Pilchy Loch, a narrow body of water that had grown
thinner during the past century. There were trees aplenty surrounding the
loch, sufficient arable land that Sinjun could see. Unlike Vere Castle, St.
Monance looked its age. Because it was summer, there were brilliant
flowers about, softening the ravages of time, but there were more weeds
than blossoms, and everything looked untended and uncared for. Everything looked weathered and poor. It was what Crocker had told her. The
weathered gray stone had crumbled or caved in at many places on the castle walls. Once there had been a moat, but now there were only tall weeds
and a swampy area that stank nearly as badly as the Cowal Swamp in the
warm morning air.

"This place desperately needs another heiress, Sinjun."

"From what I've learned, nearly every Scottish clan needs a huge ra-
tion of money, particularly the Highland clans. We're lucky here in Fife.
There is arable land aplenty, so there is no question about sheep being
brought up and the people shoved off their land, which is what is happening in the Highlands. Why the MacPhersons are poor, I don't know.
Goodness, I'm starting to babble like you, Alex." Sinjun drew a deep
breath. "I do hope that Robert MacPherson is here. Now, as you know, I
told him in my letter that I would be alone, and that I would be here this
morning. If he isn't here, well, then I've failed. Keep your fingers
crossed. Stay here and keep hidden. With any luck I'll have him with me
very soon. Now, I need the two of you to assure me that a man would just
look at me and become cross-eyed with lust."

"At least cross-eyed," Sophie said, and she meant it.

This was the part of the plan that both Sophie and Alex had serious
qualms about, but Sinjun seemed so very sure of herself. "Ostle swore he
delivered the letter," she said. They looked at each other but could think
of no more to say. They pulled to a halt in the midst of birch and fir trees
and prepared to wait. "If you aren't back with him within a half hour,
we're coming in to fetch you," Alex told her.

Sinjun rode directly to the front of the castle. Chickens and goats and
dogs scattered before Argyll. There were perhaps a dozen men and women
about outside, and they stopped their tasks to watch the lady ride up.

She saw two men look at her, then disappear through the great iron-
studded front doors. She pulled Argyll to a stop at the bottom stone step
and smiled at the people around her.

To her wondrous relief, Robert MacPherson appeared in the open doorway. He stood there and simply stared at her. Slowly, saying nothing, he strode down the deeply pitted stone steps, stopping when he was on eye level with her.

"So," he said, his arms crossed over his chest. "You came. My question, my lady, is why you would come to my lair all alone, and no fear in those beautiful eyes of yours?"

He was so pretty, she thought, each of his features so finely drawn, from the perfect arch of his fair eyebrows to the thin aristocratic nose. His eyes were just as beautiful as her Sherbrooke blue eyes, surely. She contented herself with simply staring at him for a few moments longer.

"Come ride with me," she said.

Robert MacPherson threw his head back and laughed. "You think me that witless? Doubtless your husband is over there, yon, in the birch trees, waiting with a dozen men to shoot me down."

"You weave that notion from cobwebs. You truly believe Colin Kinross so lacking in honor that he would send his own wife to fetch his enemy to him?"

"No," MacPherson said slowly, "Colin has too much pride to do that. It's not a question of honor. It's an arrogant man you married, my dear, overly proud and vicious. He would come himself, ride up to my door as you have done, and challenge me."

"So you are also saying he is fearless?"

"No, his unbridled vanity leads him into stupidity. He would probably die without understanding how it could happen. Have you come to challenge me?"

"You have misunderstood my letter, then? My trip here was for naught?"

"Oh no, I understood your every word, dear lady. I will say that your servant nearly relieved himself in his breeches he was so afraid. But not you. That interests me. But, truth be told, it doesn't seem plausible to me that you would want to see me. Our last encounter didn't leave me with the impression that you wished my company again. Indeed, our last encounter made me rather angry with you. It was a long walk."

"It was your own fault. You underestimated me because I am a woman. You were, frankly, a boor. You should not have tried to force yourself on me or threaten me. I don't take kindly to such things. I'm now offering you a chance to improve your manners and gain a new friend, perhaps."

"Ah, that is what fascinates me. Why?"

Sinjun leaned down in her saddle toward him. She said softly, her breath warm on his face, her eyes as blue as the cloudless sky, "You're too pretty for a man. It has teased me, this prettiness of yours. I want to see if you are a real man beneath those britches of yours, or a pretty boy prancing about in a man's body."

His eyes narrowed in fury. He grabbed her, but she gently raised her hand, the pistol not six inches from his face.

"I told you I didn't appreciate boors, sir. Now, will you prove yourself to me? What is it to be—a pretty boy or a man with a man's desires?"

Now she saw lust spring to life in his eyes, raw and deep. She'd practiced this so many times during the past day and she'd won, but it was terrifying.

"How do I know you won't take me into the woods and shoot me with that pretty little pistol?"

She smiled at him. "You don't."

He studied her face a moment longer. "You're a bit pale now. Perhaps you are a bit frightened?"

"A bit. After all, you could have your men hidden about to shoot me. But it would sorely hurt your reputation were you to kill a woman. On the other hand, who knows? And I have always thought life should be experienced to the fullest and if there are no risks, then why bother? Do you have men hidden about?"

"No. As you said, you're only a woman. You're also an Englishwoman, an earl's daughter. I've never met another woman like you. You fascinate me. Why did you marry Colin if you didn't want him? You've been married two months, isn't that right?"

"Perhaps you've also heard that of that time, we've spent very few days—and nights—together. He remains in Edinburgh and I am stuck here in that moldering castle of his. I'm bored, sir, and you appear to be something out of the ordinary. I knew you were different from Colin the moment I saw you. You are quite pretty, you know."

He gave her a brooding look, saying finally, "Come to the stable. I will get my horse and then, my dear, I will take you to this special place and show you that a man can have a pretty face and be endowed with splendid attributes as well."

"As splendid as Colin?"

He stiffened taut as a poker.

"I could say many things about my husband, but the fact is that he is every inch a man. It's just that he doesn't care about me, just my money."

"He is nothing," MacPherson said at last. "I will prove it to you shortly."

Sinjun sincerely doubted that could be true, but she held her tongue. She wanted him to come with her, not howl with fury and try to knock her from her horse. The last thing she wanted to do was to have to shoot him here on his own lands. It didn't seem the politic thing to do.

Ten minutes later Robert MacPherson was surrounded by three ladies on horseback, each of them pointing a pistol at him. He turned to Sinjun. "So, I see I was right."

"Not at all. Colin knows nothing about this. You see, Colin has much too much honor just to hunt you down like the wretch you are and do away with you. Thus, sir, we three have decided to remove the burden from his shoulders. I cannot allow you to try to harm him again. You really shouldn't have tried to kill him in London or in Edinburgh. You really shouldn't have burned our crofters' huts and killed our people.

"You will pay for your crimes and it will give me vast relief to have you long gone from here. Incidentally, my husband didn't kill your sister. If he wouldn't kill a vermin like you, why then, how can you possibly believe that he would ever harm a woman who was his wife?"

"She bored him. He was tired of her."

"Perhaps you have a point. After all, after only two meetings, you bore me quite beyond reason. However, even though I am tempted to toss you off a cliff, I won't, even though in addition to being a boor, you're a bully and a sneak and a man who knows no honor. I understand from Colin that your father is a good man and I wouldn't want to distress him overly. Enough of this. Alex, Sophie, I've said my piece. Shall we tie him to his horse?"

Colin was at first utterly confused, then so furious he wanted to spit and curse at the same time, something that wasn't easily accomplished.

He stood in front of his son and said in a voice so angry it sounded calm, far too calm, "You are telling me that your stepmother and your two aunts are out wandering about the estate?"

"That's what Sinjun told me, Papa. She said she felt wonderful and wanted to show them around. I asked her where you were and . . . she didn't tell me the truth, I guess."

"You bloody well mean she lied! Damn her eyes, I'll beat her, I'll lock her in my bedchamber, I'll—"

"My lord," Dr. Childress said, touching his age-spotted hand to Colin's sleeve. "What is amiss here? The countess isn't ill after all?"

"My wife," Colin said between his teeth, "pretended to be very ill, all to get me out of the way. Damnation! What is she up to?"

He was silent for several moments, then slapped his palm to his forehead. "How could I be so stupid?"

He turned on his heel and raced for Gulliver, who was chomping contentedly on some of Aunt Arleth's white roses beside the front steps.

Philip said to the doctor, "I fear my mother has enraged my father. I'd best go after him and protect her. Forgive us, sir." And Philip raced after his father.

Dr. Childress stood alone, bemused, listening to the boy's footsteps echo off the entrance hall stones. He'd known Colin since the moment he'd slipped from his mother's womb. He'd watched him grow straight and tall and proud. He'd watched his father and his older brother try to kill the spirit in him, and fail, thank the good Lord. He said aloud, his voice pensive, "I fear the young lady has unleashed a tiger."

The tiger pulled to a stop in the cover of some fir trees and stared toward St. Monance Castle. Gulliver was blowing hard, and as he watched the castle he gently patted his stallion's neck. "You're a good old fellow, aren't you, Gull? Well, you're in a damn sight better position than my wife, who isn't going to like the way her day proceeds after I get my hands on her. Another thing," he continued to his horse, "Ostle is gone, supposedly ill and back in his bed. I don't think that sounds at all believable. Another thing, that fool wife of mine had the gall to take Argyll." He shuddered even as he said those words to his horse. Gulliver paid no heed, just shook his head to get the flies off.

Colin couldn't make out anything unusual at St. Monance Castle. MacPherson folk were going about their tasks. There didn't seem to be anything out of the ordinary, no massing of men, no shouting, nothing at all unusual.

What had Joan and the wives planned to do? That stymied him. What was she plotting? Had she indeed come here?

He realized after another ten minutes of quite boring observations that he was wasting his time. Unless he intended to ride up to the big iron-studded doors of St. Monance and demand to know where his wife was, then sitting here like a blind fool would gain him naught. His fear and fury at his wife had made him act without thinking.

Where the devil was Joan? Where were the wives?

He drew a deep breath, turned Gulliver, and stared at his son, who was sitting there astride his pony, quiet as could be. Colin said nothing. He hadn't even heard Philip ride up. He was in bad shape. He shook his head. Together, father and son rode thoughtfully back to Vere Castle.

He supposed he wasn't overly surprised to see all three horses returned to the stables, in their stalls, eating their heads off. It was obvious to the meanest eye that they'd been ridden hard. Damn her eyes. Argyll looked up at him and stared, as if to say, "She really did it this time, my good man."

Colin grinned, but it wasn't an amused grin. He was ready to kill. What the devil had she done? And she'd ridden that damned horse, curse her eyes.

He strode to the house, his riding crop slashing against his thigh in rhythm to his walk.

He didn't say anything to anyone. He shook his head at Philip when he would say something, and took the stairs two and three at a time.

"Remember, Papa," Philip shouted after him. "Remember she's been ill!"

"She'll pray for a fever before I'm through with her," Colin shouted back over his shoulder.

He saw Aunt Arleth. She, in turn, saw his rage and smiled. It was obvious to Colin that she was devoutly praying that he would murder his wife. It was a thought, but he preferred torture and slow strangulation. Emma was coming out of one of the wives' bedchambers. She saw the earl and quickly dashed back inside.

"Smart of you," he said under his breath. He wanted to crash into the laird's bedchamber and start yelling. At the last minute he forced himself to calm. These ladies had to be handled carefully. They were used to men who yelled; yelling wouldn't yield the desired effect of making them fall in a faint and stutter and plead and stammer out the truth.

Very gently, his fingers nearly cramping with the effort to contain his ire, Colin opened the bedchamber door. Odd, but he wasn't at all surprised to see the two wives gowned as gloriously as society ladies all set for tea. They looked elegant, fresh, and beautiful; his wife was lying in bed, her hair soft and curling around her face, wearing a lovely lace-covered peignoir. She looked very young and elegant and innocent as a lamb. She was holding a book in her hand. All looked tranquil. It could have been an English drawing room in Putnam Square. There wasn't a hair out of place on any of their heads. There wasn't a wrinkle in any of their gowns. They were giving him inquiring looks, as if to say, "Goodness, a gentleman is here. How very strange. He came without an invitation. What should we do with him?"

Sinjun called out, her voice as sweet and innocent as her damned face, "Oh, Colin. I'm delighted you're back. Do forgive me for sending you on that quite useless errand to Dr. Childress, but I felt much better nearly the exact moment after you'd left. Strange, isn't it? I tried to call you back but you left too quickly. I'm just fine now, as you can see. Aren't you pleased?"

"What I see," Colin said mildly as he walked into the room, "is a quite perfect stage setting. My God, it would do any Drury Lane theater proud. The three of you are really quite good. I've always known that Joan could move quickly—indeed, accomplish incredible tasks in very little time, just witness our elopement—and now I see that you two aren't to be left in the dust. Even the color of your gowns and her peignoir complement each other. Remarkable. I applaud you."

Sinjun said nothing. The wives were silent, blank smiles firmly affixed to their faces, their hands steady in their laps.

He walked to Sinjun and sat beside her on the bed. He very lightly traced his fingertips over her cheek. She looked suddenly flushed as a very ripe apple. He was so furious he wanted to strangle her. He looked at her white neck wistfully. Her hair was soft and lovely, so very thick and curly. He ran his fingers through several strands. He remained silent, just looking at her, touching her face and hair.

Sinjun had believed he would storm into their bedchamber and yell and rant. But he hadn't and now she wasn't so sure. She waited, keeping quiet. There wasn't a word in her head in any case.

"How very lovely you look," he said after another few moments of silence. "Lovely and clean and there's not even a hint of horse smell on you."

"We only rode for a very little while. I did tire quickly."

"Yes, I imagine you did. Poor darling, are you certain you're better? I don't have to fear another relapse?"

"Oh no, Colin, I feel just grand. It's kind of you to be concerned for me."

"Yes, isn't it? Actually, what I want from you, Joan, what I want this very instant, is the truth. If you lie to me, I will know it and I will punish you."

"Punish me? Really, sir, such a threat isn't at all civilized."

"At this moment I'm not feeling at all civilized. I'm feeling quite savage. Speak to me, Joan. Now." His voice was so low and calm and quiet, yet his words . . . Oh dear, he couldn't be any more dangerous than Douglas or Ryder at their best, could he?

She darted a look toward Sophie and Alex, who both looked nailed to their chairs. Then Sophie, bless her, jumped to her feet. "Goodness, Colin, all we did was ride out a bit, nothing more. Then Sinjun felt a bit weak and we came back to the castle and put her to bed. Surely you aren't angry about that."

Colin said pleasantly, "You're lying, Sophie. Unfortunately, I'm not your husband so I can't beat you. But this simpleton here is my wife. She belongs to me. She is supposed to obey me; however, I've yet to experience that blessed phenomenon. She will have to learn that—"

Alex grabbed her stomach, groaned loudly, and jumped to her feet. "Oh dear! The baby—my stomach. Sophie, I'm going to be ill. Oh dear!"

It was a tableau worthy of Emma Hamilton, and Colin wasn't untouched by the talent to produce it. He began clapping. "Bravo," he said. "Ah, yes, bravo."

Alex fell to her knees and vomited on the newly cleaned Aubusson carpet.

CHAPTER
═17═

"SHE WAS ALWAYS THROWING UP when she was pregnant with the twins," Sinjun said, struggling to get out of bed. "The first three months kept everyone on their toes trying to keep basins near her. Poor Alex."

"No, stay put," Colin said to his wife. He strode over to Alex, who was clutching her sides now, nothing more in her belly, trying to catch her breath. He grasped his sister-in-law under her arms and pulled her upright. He took a look at her pale face and the sweaty strands of hair plastered to her forehead, and swung her into his arms. He said gently, "You're feeling miserable, aren't you? I'm sorry, but it will get better soon." Sighing, Alex lay her face against his shoulder.

"Get some water and dampen a towel, Sophie," Colin said, and laid Alex next to Sinjun on the bed.

"At least she didn't eat much breakfast," Sinjun said. "Poor Alex, are you all right?"

"No," Alex said, and groaned. "Stop calling me 'poor Alex.' It makes me feel like a gouty maiden aunt."

Sophie alerted the servants to the disaster and for the next few minutes pandemonium reigned. Emma stared wide-eyed at the mess, two other serving maids stacked behind her, gawking. Sophie brought a wet towel, Rory the footman behind her, craning to see into the bedchamber. Mrs. Seton trailed her with a basin of cool water.

"Here, drink this," Colin said, and lifted Alex slightly. She sipped at the water he'd poured into a glass from the carafe on the bedside table, promptly grabbed her stomach, and groaned again.

"I remember drinking water sometimes made her stomach cramp," Sinjun said. "Mrs. Seton, what we need is some hot tea."

"Poor little mite," said Mrs. Seton, and efficiently wiped Alex's face. "Aye, birthing isn't always an unafflicted joy."

Alex groaned again, and Sophie announced, "I wasn't sick for a minute."

"Shut up, Sophie," Alex said, teeth gritted. "First you don't have the good sense to tell Douglas where we are and now you're bragging about how wonderful you felt carrying Grayson when I want to die."

"Shush," Colin said, taking the cloth from Mrs. Seton and wiping Alex's clammy face. "You'll feel just the thing very soon, I promise."

There were suddenly loud footsteps in the corridor, coming closer and faster, as if a battalion of crusaders had just arrived to free the Holy Land. It needed but this, Colin thought, staring at Douglas Sherbrooke as he burst into the bedchamber, flinging the door so hard that it slammed against the wall. Ryder nearly rammed into Douglas's back, and there was Philpot, consternation writ plainly on his face, jumping up and down behind Ryder.

"My lord," Philpot yelled above the jumble of voices. "They truckled right ov'r me!"

"It's all right," Colin said on a sigh. He continued to wipe Alex's face. "Hello, Douglas, Ryder. Do come in. Philpot, they won't attempt violence in front of their wives. Ah, Emma, stop staring at the mess. Please clean it up. The rest of you—out!"

"I knew you'd come," Sinjun said, beaming at both of them. "But this is faster than I expected, even for you two."

Sophie was staring down at her slippers.

Alex just groaned and closed her eyes.

Douglas said dispassionately, as he strode to the bed and stood there, staring down at his wife, "So you were sick, were you? And on the beautiful carpet, I see. Well, Sinjun, it's your own fault. You know how Alex is. Blessed hell, she threw up on every carpet of value at Northcliffe Hall. Didn't you have the foresight to put a basin in every room? She even threw up on my favorite burgundy dressing gown."

"You deserved it," Alex said without opening her eyes.

Ryder wasn't at all dispassionate. He strode to his wife, grasped her arms, and shouted two inches from her face, "Damn you, look at me, Sophie!"

"I'm looking!"

"You left me! You vex me, woman; your gall has gone too far this time."

"My gall has never gone anywhere before! And you're here, Ryder, here with Douglas, just as we knew you'd be, although Alex was beginning to think that Douglas wouldn't come just to punish her with his absence."

"Yes, I'm here. I would never use absence as a punishment and neither would Douglas. Blessed hell, I was worried about you, nearly fretted myself out of my mind until I realized it was all a lie. You're not pregnant."

"I never said I was. You were strutting around all arrogant and pleased with yourself. I simply didn't gainsay you."

"I will beat you. Where is your bedchamber?"

"I shan't take you to my chamber. Alex is sick. Sinjun was sick but she's better now. Colin appears philosophical but I don't trust it. You and Douglas are as you always are. Sinjun knew you'd be here. But I don't know how you could be here since I didn't tell you where we were going."

"Yes," Alex said, "how did you know, Douglas?"

Douglas was looking at poor Emma, who was cleaning up the carpet. He turned to his wife and said, "You twit. You think I couldn't very quickly determine where you'd gone?"

"I told you I was going to see Sophie," Alex said, refusing to open her eyes.

"Och, here's a cup o' tea for her ladyship," Mrs. Seton said, and marched to the bed. She gave Douglas a severe look and he obligingly moved. She sat down and gently put the rim to Alex's lips. "Oh, that's good," Alex said, her head falling back on the pillow after three healthy sips.

"The two of you look quite remarkable in that bed, side by side," Ryder said.

"I want you to feel better," Douglas said to his wife. "I have quite a bit to say to you, madam."

"Oh, stow it, Douglas," Sinjun said, and immediately regretted opening her mouth, because her brother, frustrated because his wife was ill and thus immune from his displeasure for the moment, bent the full force of his anger on her. "So, little sister, you've been up to all sorts of nonsense again, haven't you? I can see you're well enough again for any sort of just deserts. I would personally enjoy taking your skirts up over your bottom, but you've a husband now and I must deny myself that pleasure. However, I must hope that he will do it. She is well enough now, isn't she, Colin?"

Colin smiled. "Yes, she certainly is well enough now."

"Good," Douglas said, rubbing his hands together. "I hope he won't suffer your pranks as I've had to over an interminable number of years."

"I daresay I won't suffer pranks at all."

Sophie interrupted. "Listen, Douglas, I want to know how you and Ryder knew to come here. Sinjun said you'd be here Friday, but that's just because she thinks you're both gods."

Alex moaned softly. Mrs. Seton reached in one of her large pockets and drew out a fat scone, wrapped in a napkin and bulging with raisins. "Try this, my lady, 'tis soft an' easy for the belly. 'Twill make ye settle, ye'll see."

Sinjun was staring at Douglas. He looked uncomfortable; he was actually flushing. He rose and strode across the bedchamber and back again. He was clearly agitated.

But it was Alex who was eyeing him with dawning comprehension as she chewed on her scone. "It was the Virgin Bride! She came to you and told you where we were. What else did she tell you?"

"That's utter nonsense!" Douglas shouted. "Nothing of the sort. That bloody damned ghost. She doesn't exist—"

"Naturally not," Sinjun said. "She's been dead for centuries. It's her ghost that hovers about."

"Shut your mouth, Sinjun. I merely applied a few mental processes— very few were necessary, given you two—and quickly realized that you would go haring off to Scotland."

Ryder was frowning at his brother. "You fetched me from Ascot. You told me we had to go get our wives, that they'd heard from Sinjun, and that she was ill and that there was trouble. I didn't think to question you then. I thought Alex had left you a letter, but obviously she hadn't. How did you know Sophie was involved? What's going on here, Douglas?"

Douglas plowed his fingers through his hair, standing it on end. He looked clearly harassed, defensive, and wary. "I just got this feeling, that's all. A simple feeling. We all have simple feelings from time to time, even you, Ryder. This bloody feeling came when I was sleeping in Alex's bed because Mother had insisted on having my mattress restuffed and pounded, God knows why. I like flat goose feathers. I just felt them then, during the night, these simple feelings when I was thinking about Alex, that's all. Simple feelings and simple deductions."

Colin had moved to stand by the fireplace, leaning negligently against the mantel, his arms crossed over his chest. He looked utterly unmoved by all the carping and ghost talk. He even appeared mildly amused to Sinjun's fond eye, at least she hoped he was amused. He'd be easier to deal with if he was amused. He said at last when there was a moment's break, "The carpet wasn't all that expensive. Don't worry about it, Alex. I think Emma's done an excellent job."

Alex cocked an eye open. "Thank you, Colin. You're very kind to a sick lady, unlike—"

"Don't even think about saying it," Douglas said. Mrs. Seton had left, albeit with a lagging step, and he had resumed his seat on the bed by his wife. "No, not a damned word. I am your husband and it is I who am kind to you, no other man, do you understand?"

Her eyes twinkled at him for the first time. "I understand. But Douglas, you must have seen the ghost and she told you where we'd gone."

"No, dammit!"

"What I don't understand," Sophie interrupted, "is why the Virgin

Bride would tell Douglas. Doesn't she think we're capable of dealing with the situation by ourselves?"

"Oh God," Sinjun said. "Sophie!"

Sophie clapped her hand over her mouth, darting an agonized look at Colin.

"So," Colin said, "there is a situation, not that I ever doubted it. It must involve MacPherson. I assume you took care of him once you'd gotten rid of me this morning. My dear wife, what have you done with him? Is he dead? Did the three of you draw lots to see who would kill him?"

"Never," Alex said.

"I would have liked to kill him," Sinjun said wistfully, "but I didn't think you'd approve. You're fond of his father. No, the bounder isn't dead. You do understand, don't you, Colin? I had to do something. I had to protect you. You're my husband. He would have snuck up on you, stuck a knife in your back; he's that sort of man. Or he would have sent some of his bullies, like he did in London when you got stabbed in the leg. He has no honor, no—"

Colin didn't move a muscle, but Sinjun saw the tic by his right eye. He said with superb calm, "This is all quite interesting, don't you agree, Douglas, Ryder? My wife, who is also your little sister, thinks I'm helpless as a motherless foal. She enjoys unmanning me. She believes me feeble, a fool, unable to see to the truth of things, unable to protect myself when appropriate. What do you think I should do to her?"

He didn't sound very amused now, Sinjun thought.

"You're her husband," Douglas said. "You will do whatever is necessary to keep her safe."

"I should like to know," Ryder said thoughtfully, disregarding Colin and Douglas and still clutching his wife's upper arms, "how you three all got together."

"The Virgin Bride visited Alex, naturally," Sophie said. "She normally only appears in the countess's bedchamber, as Douglas very well knows, except for that time when I first came to Northcliffe Hall. Then she welcomed me in your bedchamber, Ryder."

"Bosh," said Ryder. "You were anxious for me to make love to you, and when I didn't come to you quickly enough, your female brain decided upon something dramatic to relieve your anxiety. That or Sinjun played the Virgin Bride again. Alex's brain has done the same thing."

"But she does usually visit only the countess's bedchamber," Alex said. "As Douglas very well knows."

"That's not entirely true. Once—" Douglas stopped and cursed. "Listen, all of you. Enough is enough. For whatever combination of reasons, all of us are here. There is a situation. I should like to get it resolved.

Now, Sinjun, what have you done with this MacPherson fellow whom we don't yet know?"

"We manacled him and locked him in a deserted croft."

The three men stared at Sinjun, speechless for the first time in fifteen minutes. The chamber reeked with the blessed silence.

"We weren't overly cruel," Sinjun continued. "He has some length on the chain so he can walk about a bit and do private things as well. But the manacle was necessary. We couldn't risk his escaping."

"I see," Colin said slowly. "And is Robbie to starve to death?"

"Oh no," Alex said, eyes firmly on Colin, not on Douglas. "We're taking turns going to the croft to feed him. We didn't want you to suspect anything." She sighed. "I suppose it's all blasted to hell now."

Douglas's dark eyes twinkled, he couldn't help it. "No," he said, patting his wife's pale cheek, "no, it's not at all blasted anywhere." He rose. "Ryder, Colin, shall we handle this situation to our satisfaction now?"

Sinjun gasped. "No, we won't let you! Why don't all of you just go back home—"

"I am home," Colin said.

"You know what I mean. We don't need your interference. Everything is going splendidly. There is no more situation. I have everything in hand. All plans will . . . Oh damn, just go away, all of you."

"Where is the croft, Joan?"

"I shan't tell you. You'll just let him go and then he'll kill you and I'll be a widow even before I'm scarcely a wife, and it isn't fair."

"I fully intend that you become a full and complete and happy wife," Colin said, and was pleased when she closed her mouth. "Where is the croft?"

Sinjun just shook her head.

Douglas said, "All right, Alex, where is it?"

Alex batted her eyelashes and looked utterly helpless. She heaved a deep sigh, which sent her husband's eyes immediately to her glorious bosom. She fluttered her hands. "I don't remember, Douglas; you know how horrid I am with directions. It was all this way and then that way and only Sinjun knows. Sophie and I were hopelessly lost, weren't we, Sophie?"

"Hopelessly."

"I'm going to beat you now," Ryder said, and hauled his wife tightly against him. He leaned down to say something, but kissed her instead, full on her mouth. He raised his head and grinned. "Don't worry, Douglas, Colin. I can get anything at all out of her with enough time. She melts like a candle. It's really quite charming and—"

Sophie sent her fist into his belly.

He sucked in his breath but continued to grin. "Now, love, don't deny it, you know that you adore me, that you worship me and the very shadow of my footsteps. You're like a lovely rose that opens to the sun each morning."

"Gawd," Sinjun said, "you're a horrible poet, Ryder. Just be quiet and let Sophie alone."

Colin, frowning, said, "I would like to know what you three intended to do with MacPherson. Surely you don't want to have to feed him three times a day for the next thirty years?"

"No," Sinjun said. "We have a plan. If you would simply go away and drink brandy or something, all will be taken care of."

"What is the plan, Sinjun?" Douglas asked. He rose now to walk around to her side of the bed. She shook her head and stared at the middle button on his buff riding jacket.

"Sinjun," he said, leaning down over her, "I held you in my arms when you were born. You burped up milk on my shirt. I taught you how to ride. Ryder taught you how to tell jokes. We both taught you how to shoot and enjoy books. Without us, you would have grown up to be scarce anything at all. Now, tell us what your plan is."

She shook her head again.

"I can still whip you, brat."

"No, unfortunately you can't, Douglas," Colin said. "But I can and I firmly intend to. She swore to obey me when we were wedded but she hasn't yet gotten beyond the abstract to the concrete."

"How the devil could I obey you when you were in Edinburgh? Ignoring me, I might add. You were happy as a lark in that damned house with the black hole in the drawing room ceiling, weren't you?"

"Ah, a bit of anger, Joan? Perhaps you would like to tell everyone here why I have remained in Edinburgh?"

"Your reasons were absurd. I reject them. I spit upon them."

Colin sighed. "It's difficult. I wish to deal with you properly but I can't, not with your damned brothers hovering about. Douglas, Ryder, why don't you remove your wives from this bedchamber? Then I can question Joan suitably."

"No, I want Alex and Sophie to stay here! I'm hungry. It's time for lunch."

"Ah," Colin said. "And which of the wives is to take MacPherson his lunch?"

"Go to the devil, Colin."

Ryder laughed. "Well, we'll have our answer soon enough. Unless they wish MacPherson to starve, they will have to take him food sometime. Then we will know."

"Why did you remain in Edinburgh, Colin?" Douglas asked.

"To protect my wife," Colin said simply. "And my children. That morning when she had the cut on her cheek, it was from a bullet ricocheting off a rock and striking her. I couldn't allow her to remain in Edinburgh with me. I thought she would be safe here, and she was until MacPherson decided to leave Edinburgh and go to ground back here."

"What children?" Ryder asked, looking at his brother-in-law blankly.

"Not again," Sinjun said. "I have two stepchildren, Philip and Dahling. You will meet them shortly. They will adore you, Ryder, as all children do. They might not even run screaming from you, Douglas, if you would stop your scowling."

Douglas was giving Colin a brooding look. Finally he sighed. "There is much here to consider. I think I shall take my wife to bed—so she can rest, naturally—then I would like to meet my new niece and nephew."

"Come along, Sophie, you may accompany Alex. If I get you alone, I just might behave in a manner ill-suited to our blissful married state."

When Colin and Sinjun were alone, Colin shoved off the mantel and strode over to her. His expression was bland but his eyes, those beautiful dark blue eyes of his, were hot with anger. He sat on the bed beside her. He said nothing, merely leaned down over her, his face inches from hers. He looked into her eyes. Finally he said very quietly, "You have gone too far this time. I will tolerate no more insults from you, no more interference in my affairs. Where is MacPherson?"

"If I tell you he might be able to hurt you. Please, Colin, can't I continue with my plan?"

He leaned back a bit and crossed his arms over his chest. "Tell me this plan of yours."

"I am delivering Robert MacPherson up to the Royal Navy. I understand they aren't terribly discriminating about who is delivered up to them, whether or not the man wishes to be there or not, you understand."

"Oh yes, I understand." He looked away from her now. "It isn't a bad plan," he said mildly. "Which ship of the Royal Navy do you have in mind?"

"I sent Ostle to Leith to see which ships were available to us. There's bound to be at least one, don't you think?"

"Yes, if not right this minute, then not long from now. However, there is something you couldn't have known that makes it impractical."

"And what is that, pray?"

He grinned at the rancor in her voice. "The word clan comes from the Gaelic *clann* and means simply 'children.' So you see, the Clan MacPherson are really the children of MacPherson. If you eliminate one of the clan, or children, the others are bound to seek revenge and retribution. If you make the son of the laird disappear, the Kinross clan will be the prime suspects, and there will be violence. It will escalate with scarce any provocation at all. It's a vicious cycle. Do you understand?"

Sinjun nodded slowly. "I didn't realize. Oh dear, what shall I do now, Colin?"

"First, you will promise me that you will never again take matters into your own white hands. You will never again keep secrets from me. You will never again seek to protect me from any enemies."

"That's a lot to promise, Colin."

"You did it before and you lied to me. I will give you another chance, mainly because you're too weak for me to beat you with any sort of efficacy."

"I will promise if you will promise the same thing."

"I'll beat you despite your weakness."

"Do you want to?"

"Not really, perhaps fifteen minutes ago I would have thoroughly enjoyed it, but not now. Actually, it was strangulation I was thinking of. I would prefer now to strip that nightgown off you and kiss every inch of you."

"Oh."

"Oh," he repeated, mimicking her.

"I think I should like that, at least the kissing part."

"I will kiss you once you have told me where MacPherson is so I can deal with this."

Sinjun didn't know what to do. She was frightened for her husband and unfortunately it showed on her face. He said, "Don't even think it, Joan. Tell me the truth now and tell me all of it. Then you may give me your promise to keep yourself out of my affairs."

"He's in the croft that lies just on the western edge of Craignure Moor."

"An excellent hidey-hole. No one goes there. He should be quite enraged by now."

"He hasn't been there all that long, no more than three hours now."

"I will see you later," he said, and rose to stand beside the bed. "I wish you to rest and regain your strength. I've realized that keeping away from you wasn't a good idea. You're my wife. I will sleep with you tonight and every night for the rest of our lives."

"That would be nice," she said, then began twisting the covers in her long fingers. "I want to go with you, Colin. I want to see this through."

He looked at her for a very long time. "Remember I told you the message MacDuff brought to me in Edinburgh? That you had no intention of stealing my box? I looked at him as blankly as a cutpurse caught in the act, and he explained that he'd told you about my father and my brother. I wish he hadn't, but now it's done. I also realize, a bit perhaps, that you want to be important to Vere Castle and to me and to the children. Very well, Joan, you and I will go see Robert MacPherson."

"Thank you, Colin."

"Let's wait for another couple of hours. I should like him to be raw-brained with rage."

Sinjun grinned at him. To her deep pleasure, he smiled back at her. "I will come back to awaken you. Sleep now."

It was a very good start, she thought, watching him leave the bed-chamber. An excellent start. She hadn't the heart to tell him she was quite hungry, not at all sleepy.

It was close to ten o'clock at night. Sinjun was sitting in her husband's lap in a deep wing chair that sat facing the fireplace. She was wearing a nightgown and a pale blue dressing gown. Colin was still in his buckskins and white batiste shirt. The evening was cool. Colin had lit a fire and the warmth of it was soothing. Sinjun laid her face against her husband's shoulder, turning slightly every few moments to kiss his neck.

"The brothers and wives seem to be speaking to each other again," Colin said. "I would further say that if Sophie isn't with child right now, she soon will be. Ryder was looking at her all through dinner like a man starving."

"He always looks at her like that, even when he's furious with her."

"She's a lucky woman."

Sinjun looked up at his shadowed jaw. "Perhaps you could look at me like that sometimes."

"Perhaps," he said, and tightened his hold on her. "How do you feel?"

"Our adventure with Robert MacPherson didn't tire me out at all."

"Ah, so that's why you slept for two hours upon our return home?"

"Maybe a little bit," she conceded. "Do you think he'll draw off the at-tack now? Do you think you can believe him?"

Colin thought back to the hour he and Joan had spent in the dismal lit-tle croft with Robert MacPherson. They'd arrived in the middle of the af-ternoon and he'd allowed her to enter the croft first. She walked like a general leading her troops. He smiled at the back of her head. He was glad he'd brought her with him. Two months before he couldn't have imagined doing such a thing, but Joan was different; she'd made him see things differently.

Robert MacPherson was so furious he couldn't at first speak. He saw her coming through the door of the croft and he wanted to leap upon her and cuff her senseless. Then Colin came in behind her and he froze, frightened for the first time, but he refused to let the bastard see his fear.

"So," he said, spitting in the dirt floor in front of him, "it was a lie. You did know about this. You sent your damned wife to get me. You rotter, you damned slimy coward!"

"Oh no," Sinjun said quickly. "Colin has come to rescue you from me. I would have given you over to the Royal Navy and let you swab decks until you reformed or got kicked overboard and drowned, but Colin wouldn't allow it."

"You don't look very comfortable, Robbie," Colin said, stroking his jaw. MacPherson lunged forward, but only three feet. He was pulled to an ignominious halt by the chains.

"Get these things off me," he said, panting with rage.

"In good time," Colin said. "First I'd like to talk to you. A pity there are no chairs, Joan. You're looking just a bit white around your jawline. Sit on the packed dirt and lean back against the wall. That's right. Now, Robbie, you and I will discuss things."

"You bloody murderer! There's nothing to discuss! Go ahead and kill me. Aye, you do that, you murdering sod. My men will destroy Vere Castle and all your lands. Go ahead!"

"Why?"

"What the hell do you mean, why? You killed my sister. You killed poor Dingle."

"Oh no, Dingle was killed by another of your own men. As it happens, my son, Philip, witnessed the whole thing. It was a fight about a woman, naturally. Alfie killed him."

Robert MacPherson shook his head and said in disgust, "That damned chit! I told them—" He broke off and jerked forward once more against the chains. They held firm. "All right, I will give you that one. Still, you murdered my sister."

Sinjun opened her mouth, then closed it. This was up to Colin, and she realized that it was important that she keep still. MacPherson must know now that she loved her husband to distraction, must believe she'd lie for him without hesitation, all true naturally. It was difficult, but she kept quiet, and watched.

"Your sister died nearly eight months ago. Why didn't you act immediately against me?"

"I didn't believe you'd killed her then. My father was certain you were innocent and I believed him. But then I found out the truth."

"Ah," said Colin. "The truth. Could you tell me the source of this truth?"

MacPherson looked suddenly crafty. "Why should I? I have no reason to doubt the source. My father wouldn't either if he had an unconfused thought left in his pathetic brain."

"Your father was quite clear in his thinking the last time I visited him," Colin said. "Go back to Edinburgh and tell him. See if he agrees with you. My guess is that he will laugh at you. I think you're afraid to tell him, Robbie, afraid of his scorn at your damned credulity. Well? Answer me. No? I will tell you something else. I believe you prefer skulking about in the shadows, hiring your bully boys. I believe you prefer claiming your father is brain-soft and that is only because he won't agree with you about me. Thus, you want to toss him out with the rubbish. Tell him, Robbie. He's the MacPherson laird. He's your father. Trust him, for God's sake. Now, who told you I killed your sister?"

"I won't tell you."

"Then how can I allow you to leave here? I don't wish to die, nor do I wish to have to worry all the time about Joan's safety and my children's safety."

MacPherson looked at the chafed flesh on his wrists. Chained to the bloody wall like a damned criminal, and all by that ridiculous little chit who sat on the floor, watching him with her wide blue eyes. She'd tricked him; she'd made a fool. He pulled his eyes away from her. He stared at Colin Kinross, a man he'd known all his life, a man who was tall and lean and trustworthy, with a man's strong features, not pretty as he was, a man women adored and sought out. The man Fiona had loved despite her insane jealousy. No one doubted Colin's virility; oh yes, he'd heard the silly girls giggling about him, his endowments, his skills as a lover. No one questioned that he was less than a man. He felt the jealousy grind into him and looked away. He said, his voice low, "If I promise I won't attempt to harm either this girl here or your children, will you release me? Good God, man, Philip and Dahling are my nephew and niece, for God's sake! They're Fiona's children; I wouldn't hurt them."

"No, I believe that would be beyond even you, Robbie. However, that leaves Joan. She is my wife. She also has this unfortunate habit of trying to save me all the time. It's appealing when it isn't enraging."

"She should be beaten. She's only a bloody woman."

"I daresay you wouldn't feel that way were she always on the lookout to keep you safe. Who told you I killed Fiona?"

"I won't harm her, damn you!"

"But you will keep trying to hurt Colin, won't you?" Sinjun was on her feet now. She felt no charitable leanings toward MacPherson. Were it up to her, she'd leave him chained here until he rotted.

He saw her feelings on her face and grinned at her. Colin said, "Sit down, Joan. Keep out of this."

She subsided, but her brain was working furiously. Who had accused Colin of murder? Aunt Arleth? That seemed a distinct possibility. With him dead, she could do as she pleased. But it made no sense, not really. Aunt Arleth much appreciated the money Sinjun's dowry had brought to the laird. If I were dead, she would rejoice, Sinjun thought, but Colin? What if Aunt Arleth did hate him enough to want him dead, because she somehow believed he was responsible for his brother's death? Sinjun felt a headache begin to pound at her over her right temple. It was too much, all of it.

Colin jumped as a log rolled off, scattering embers out onto the hearth. He was pulled abruptly back from his memories of the afternoon with MacPherson. He hugged his wife closer as she said, nestling closer as she kissed her husband's throat yet again, "Do you believe him, Colin?" She kissed him again. He tasted warm and salty and utterly wonderful. She could kiss him until she cocked up her toes.

"I don't wish to speak of him anymore tonight."

"But you let him go! I'm frightened!"

"You'll be safe. He swore on his father's name."

"Ha! He is a little weasel, pretty but deadly."

"Hush, Joan. I want to kiss you now." He gently shifted her in his arms and brought his mouth to hers. He tasted of the sweet, darkly mysterious port he'd drunk with Ryder and Douglas after dinner. His mouth was firm and when his tongue came gently between her lips she felt a desire to lock her arms around his neck and never let him go. "That feels wonderful," she said into his mouth. His tongue touched hers and she squirmed a bit.

He raised his head and looked at her. "I've missed you. Tonight, Joan, you'll learn pleasure. Will you trust me and cease your babble about my being too large for you?"

"But you're still as large as you were, Colin. That can't change. I still don't see how it can be at all wonderful for me when you have to come inside me."

He just grinned down at her. "Trust me."

"I suppose I must, since I want to see your beautiful face every day until I die. You're very important to me, Colin. You must take good care of yourself. All right?"

"Yes, and I'll also take good care of you."

He kissed her again and yet again. He continued kissing her, lightly then more deeply, nipping at her lower lip, kissing her until she was gasping and pressing herself against him, her fingers wild in his hair and on his shoulders. He made no move to caress her breasts or touch her anywhere but her back and her arms. Kissing seemed to be the only thing on his mind. Sinjun was very happy about it, for about five minutes.

She wanted more. It was disconcerting, but she didn't mind at all. She felt that tugging sensation low in her belly, a sort of burning that was intense yet still vague and indistinct, but she knew there had to be more and she wanted it. She vaguely remembered those feelings now, oh yes, she'd had them before, but they'd vanished when he'd hurt her. She grabbed his hand and pulled it to her stomach. She pressed his palm against her belly. "I feel very strange," she said into his mouth, her breath warm, her voice hoarse. She began to kiss him wildly, without restraint, her hands in his hair, stroking his face and shoulders.

"Yes, I can feel that you do," he said. His fingers didn't move for the longest time, merely rested lightly on her stomach. But he continued to kiss her until she moaned into his mouth. Then his fingers slipped slowly downward. Sinjun sucked in her breath, waiting. She felt frantic, and very very warm. She felt as if there was something wonderful waiting for her, and it was close now, very close.

"Colin," she said, and moaned into his mouth.

"What would you like now, Joan?"

CHAPTER
≡18≡

COLIN HAD A STRATEGY and he had no intention of allowing himself to forget it or modify it. No, he had no intention of losing his control. No, tonight he was going to make his wife want him desperately, then he would see.

She was getting close and he was both delighted and immensely relieved.

He continued to kiss her. She was warm and soft and urgent and he wanted very much to cover her with his fingers, to ease inside of her, to feel her around him, to feel the softness and warmth of her. But he held off. No, let it build within her, this passion he would continue to inflame, until she was moaning with it, then yelling. He closed his eyes, trying to picture her face when her pleasure took her.

"I want—" she began, then touched her tongue to his and gasped.

"Yes, I'll give you that," he said, and deepened his kiss. His fingertips were lightly cupped over her, but not moving, not caressing her, just lying there.

Sinjun wondered what was happening. She remembered that he'd been a wild man before and he'd hurt her. She realized dimly that he was being very careful with her, very restrained. Did he believe her still weak from her illness?

No, he didn't want to scare her off again. She smiled against his wonderful mouth. She said quite without thought or hesitation, "I love you, Colin. I loved you from the first moment I saw you. I think you're the most remarkable man in Scotland."

He jerked at her words. He felt something move deep inside him, something he'd never felt before in his life, something hot and frantic, yet strangely gentle and tender. It scared the hell out of him. At first. Then he eased, allowing the feelings into himself, and her words. Yes, her words. He would think about it later. He kissed her again, tasting the sweetness of her mouth, and kissed her three more times before saying, "Only Scotland?"

"All right, perhaps in all of Britain."

"Kiss me, Joan."

Her mouth was red and swollen with his kisses, and yet again she leaned up against him without an instant's hesitation, and he saw the need in her beautiful eyes, felt the slight trembling of her mouth as his tongue slid between her lips.

When her tongue was warm in his mouth, his fingers suddenly dipped lower. His middle fingers pressed inward, hot as the devil against the light lawn of her nightgown. She thought she'd leap from his lap.

"Let's get you out of this damned thing," he said, feeling the soft material dampen beneath his fingers. He brought his fingers to her lips and gently pressed against them. "That's the taste of you, Joan. It's very nice, don't you think?"

She could but stare at him. Slowly, she nodded. He straightened her and pulled the gown over her head. He sat her there on his thighs, the firelight glowing behind her, her breasts in profile to him and her narrow waist and her flat belly. He'd never in his life seen a more beautifully made woman. And she was all his. His hands trembled and he flattened them to his thighs. No, he would hold control. He wouldn't frighten her, ever again. He would hold to his plan, but it was difficult, damned difficult.

He leaned his head against the chair back. The old leather creaked comfortably under the pressure. "What would you like me to do, Joan?"

"I want you to kiss me some more."

"Where?"

He heard her breath suck in sharply. "My breasts," she said, lightly stroking her fingers over his chin. "You're still clothed, Colin. That isn't fair."

"Forget fairness for the moment," he said, gently clasping her arms and pulling her against him. He wasn't about to let her see him naked. It would probably make her forget her passion. It would probably scare her out of her mind.

"I think your breasts can wait a bit," he said, and, still careful not to touch her anywhere that would make her tremble and shudder, he kissed her mouth, and again and then once more, his hands cupping her face, his fingers sliding through her hair, holding her head still for him. When she was squirming against his thighs, very lightly he cupped her left breast in his warm palm.

"Oh!"

"You're quite nice." His knuckles were rubbing lightly over her nipple. "Lie back against my arm."

She did, staring up at him. She watched him lean down even as his arm brought her upward, and when his mouth closed over her, she nearly yelled with the power of it. He smiled, tasting her sweet flesh, quivering himself, but experienced enough to keep it from her. His sex was hard as a stone and he wanted her very much, so much that he considered briefly just carrying her to the bed, spreading her thighs for him, and coming into her. Surely she was ready for him now. But no, he was a fool even to consider it for a moment.

He stopped himself and kissed her breast, fondling her with his fingers and his tongue until he knew she was very ready for him. His hand flattened on her belly and he felt the muscles tighten. "Now, I want you to close your eyes, sweetheart, and just picture in that lively mind of yours what my fingers are doing."

He didn't hold back now. His fingers found her quickly and he began a rhythm that was at once deep and gentle, light and urgent. She had no chance to object, no chance to feel embarrassed. All she could do was feel how her body was jerking, her legs clenching, then opening to him, and he saw those feelings clearly on her expressive face. She stared up at him, her eyes vague and bewildered. "Colin," she whispered and ran her tongue over her lower lip.

"Come along now, Joan. I want you to think about what my fingers are doing to you. I'm going to kiss you and I want you to let yourself go and cry out in my mouth."

At that moment, he eased his middle finger into her and nearly cried out himself at the wondrous feeling of her. He kissed her as if he would die without her and he wondered vaguely in those moments if it wasn't true. His fingers were on her swelled flesh again, stroking her, caressing her until she stiffened and pulled back. He looked at her face and smiled at her, painfully. "Yes, sweetheart. Come to me now."

She did, from one moment to the next, she was gasping, her legs stiff, such sensations pulsing through her that she couldn't begin to understand what was happening to her. Whatever it was, she prayed it would never stop. It was so strong and so deep and he was there, staring down at her, that smile in his eyes, and he was saying again and again, "Come to me, come to me . . ."

The feelings crested, flinging her into a world that was fresh and magical, a world that held her now and would never release her. She quieted. His fingers quieted, soothing her now, no longer inflaming her.

"Oh goodness," she whispered. "Oh goodness, Colin. That was wonderful."

"Yes," he said and there was both pain and immense pleasure in his voice and he never stopped looking at her, and now he leaned down and kissed her, softly, lightly. Ah, the bewilderment in her Sherbrooke blue eyes, and the vagueness and the excitement. It pleased him, pleased him to his soul.

Sinjun drew a deep breath. His pleasure, she thought. He hadn't received any pleasure from her. Would he hurt her now? Oh no, he wouldn't ever hurt her again. But his pleasure . . . Her heart slowed. Her eyes fluttered closed. To Colin's chagrin and amusement, she was asleep in the next moment.

He held her for a very long time in front of the warm fire, looking down at her, then into the dying flames, and wondering what this woman had done to him.

When Sinjun awoke the following morning, she was smiling. A silly smile, one that was absurdly content, one that held only one thought, and that thought was of her husband. Of Colin. God, she loved him. Suddenly she stilled and the smile slid off her face. She'd told him she loved him, loved him from the first moment she ever saw him, and he hadn't replied. But he'd given her such pleasure that she'd wondered even as she prayed it would never end if she would die from it.

She'd told him she loved him and he'd said naught.

Well, she'd been a fool, but she didn't care. It seemed ridiculous to her now that she would hold back anything from him. He cared for her, she knew that. Now he knew that she loved him. If it gave him power over her, then so be it. If he used the power to hurt her, so be that as well.

She was herself. She couldn't change. She was a wife, Colin's wife. God had given him to her; she would never hold back from him. He was, quite simply, the most important person in her life.

Still, when she entered the Laird's Inbetween Room some forty-five minutes later for her breakfast, she felt flushed and nervous and embarrassed. Colin was there, seated at his ease at the head of the table, a cup of coffee in his hand, a bowl of porridge in front of him, a curl of heat rising from it. The bowl sat on a beautiful white linen tablecloth she'd bought in Kinross.

Her brothers weren't there. Neither of the wives was there. The children weren't there. Neither Aunt Arleth nor Serena was there. There was a bloody castle full of people and they were alone.

"Everyone finished thirty minutes ago. I've been waiting for you to come down. I didn't think you would appreciate a full table."

Was that ever the truth, she thought, pinned a smile to her mouth, and walked in, head up.

He grinned at her like a wicked potentate. "I thought perhaps you'd want to speak to me about how I made you feel last night. In private, naturally. I thought perhaps you'd be disappointed because I only brought you to pleasure one time. I'm very sorry you fell asleep, Joan, but I was too much the gentleman to wake you and force you to climax yet again. You've been ill, after all, and I didn't want you to have to feel too much like a wife all at once."

"You're very kind, Colin," she said. She met his eyes and she flushed. He spoke as boldly as did her damned brothers. She never colored up like a silly chit when they were outrageous. She willed her tongue into action; her chin went up. "I'm not disappointed, husband, but I did worry about you. You were too kind. I told you, I would be your wife, but you didn't allow me to give you any respite."

" 'Respite,' " he repeated. "What a gloomy word to use for screaming, thumping sexual pleasure. 'Respite.' I must mention that to my friends and see what they think."

"I would that you not do that. It is a rather private matter. Very well, I will take back 'respite' and be more like my brothers. I'm sorry you didn't have any sexual screaming, Colin."

"That's better. What makes you think there was no pleasure for me? I watched you climax, Joan. I watched your eyes get bluer, if that's possible, then grow dim and vague and it was quite charming. Indeed, I felt your pleasure, for you were trembling beneath my fingers and moaning and when you made those cries in my mouth I assure you I wanted to howl with masculine pleasure. Along with you."

"But you didn't," she said, slipping into her chair.

He gave her a look that was completely unreadable to her and said as matter-of-factly as a fifty-year husband, "Should you like some porridge?"

"Just toast, I think."

He nodded and rose to serve her. "No, remain seated. I want you strong again."

He poured her coffee and set her toast in front of her. Then, without warning, he grasped her chin in his hand and lifted her face. He kissed her, long and hard, then very gently. When he released her, her eyes were vague and dazzled and she was leaning against him, her arms loose at her sides.

"Philip told me he would forgive you for lying to him if you asked him nicely," he said, and walked back to the end of the table. "It appears he understands you very well. He said that you would walk through fire to save me, thus a lie was nothing if it served your cause in serving me."

She stared at him. Philip was a smart boy. She continued to stare at

Colin, at his mouth. A word of affection would have been nice, she thought. Perhaps an endearment. Perhaps an acknowledgment that he was touched that she loved him. She tasted him on her own mouth. She just looked at him helplessly, all that she felt on her face.

He gave her a pained smile that vanished as quickly as it had appeared. "Eat, Joan." His expression remained unreadable, the sod.

She chewed on her toast, wondering why God, in his infinite wisdom, had created men to be so very different from women.

"I also wished to tell you that I intend to question Aunt Arleth this morning. If she was the source Robert MacPherson claims told him I killed Fiona, then I will get the truth out of her."

"Somehow I can't believe it was her. But she does cherish an amazing dislike for you. But then again, she heartily disliked Fiona. It was only your father and your brother she loved, if I understand what worked its way out of her mouth. Actually, Aunt Arleth makes little sense at the best of times. Remember all her talk about a kelpie being your father? She's very strange."

"It doesn't matter. Once I've either confirmed or rejected her part in this, she's leaving Vere Castle, her strangeness with her."

"She has no money, Colin."

"As I told you, she has family and I've already sent her brother a message. He and his family live near Pitlochry, in the central Highlands. They have no choice but to provide her a home. I'm sorry she behaved as she did toward you."

Nearly killed me dead, truth be told, Sinjun started to say, then stopped. It didn't matter now. She would soon be gone. She said, "If she wasn't Robert MacPherson's source, then who was?"

"I don't know, but I will find out. In the meantime, as you know, Robbie has promised to keep his men in control as well as himself. He's promised to speak to his father and to listen to him, really listen. Don't mistake me, Joan, if he attempts more violence against any of us or against any of our people, I will kill him. He knows it. Perhaps he will seek to be reasonable now."

"Serena is his sister. It makes more sense that she would have accused you to him."

He looked amused and vain as a very young man with his first compliment from a lady. "Oh no. Serena loves me. At least she's told me so countless times, and all those times since I married you. I'm also seeing that she returns to her father."

"Goodness, the castle will be bare! Please, Colin, it isn't necessary. Serena is an odd duck, perhaps daft, but harmless. If she tries to kiss you again, though, perhaps I will have to speak to her."

Colin laughed. "She doesn't realize how ferocious you are, how possessive of me you are. I should tell her that she isn't safe around you if she touches me again. She should request that I send her back to her father. Now that you're here for the children, there's no need for either of those ladies. Do you agree?"

"I quite agree," Sinjun said.

"Everything is happening now," he continued after a moment. "The sheep will be arriving within the next two days—not sheep to force our people off their lands, just enough to provide enough raw wool and milk. And the cattle, naturally, enough for all our people. I have also called a meeting of all my crofters and tenants. My proposition is that they will go from one croft to the next. I will furnish all the supplies and equipment we need. We will make all necessary repairs, from roofs to fences to bed frames. There will be no more want or uncertainty for the Kinross clan. Thank you, Joan."

"You're welcome," she said, and swallowed. He'd spoken to her like his partner. "Why are you telling me all this?"

He was silent for a moment. He took a spoonful of porridge and chewed thoughtfully. "It's your money that allows all this. It's only proper you know its disposition."

She felt a streak of disappointment, for his voice was cool and dismissive, but she managed to say calmly enough, "Tell me what to do. The household is shaping up quite nicely, but there is still much repair to be done. I also need gardeners."

"Yes, Alex has already filled my ears with what needs to be done outside. I shouldn't be surprised to find her out there weeding around the rosebushes. She was very impassioned about it. You will speak to Mr. Seton. He will bring men to you to interview. It will all take time, but time is something we now have. The creditors are no longer breathing down my neck. We are afloat; indeed, we are rowing smartly forward. We will make up that infamous list together quite soon. Now, Douglas and Ryder wish me to take them around and show them what we're doing. They wish to meet some of our people. Should you like to accompany us?"

She looked at her husband. He was including her. Did he finally understand she wouldn't steal his box and this was the proof of it? No, probably not. It was her money, as he'd said. He didn't want her to feel excluded. He was being kind. Blessed hell, but she hated kindness from him; kindness was a bloodless emotion.

"No, not this time," she said, tossing her napkin on her plate and rising. "I wish to visit with the children, particularly Philip. I owe him an apology, and since he is very much your son, I imagine he will make me grovel before absolving me."

Colin gave a shout of laughter.

"Also, the wives will want to know what's happened with MacPherson."

"I already told them everything at breakfast. Alex was arguing toe to toe with me when she turned green, grabbed her stomach, and sprinted from the room. Douglas sighed and hefted up the basin Mrs. Seton had given him and went after her. Ryder and Sophie were alternately laughing and yelling at each other. They were trying to look interested in all my projects, but failed woefully. Your brothers are charming, Joan, when they're not trying to kill me."

She grinned, picturing the scene without difficulty. "How did Aunt Arleth and Serena react? Guilty? Angry?"

"Aunt Arleth said not a word. Serena looked vague. It was Dahling who had all the questions. She wanted to know why you didn't take her to confront MacPherson since it was a ladies' battle. She then asked Serena why her brother was such a bad man. Serena said he hated his angel's face and thus he cultivated his devil's soul."

"It appears I must apologize to her as well. Are you certain Aunt Arleth didn't look guilty?"

"No, afraid not. Still, I will speak to her privately."

"I'm still afraid, Colin."

He rose and strode to the end of the table where she was standing. He stood there beside her, looking down at her. Then he opened his arms. "No one will ever hurt you again," he said, and pulled her up against his chest. "Dear God, you scared the very devil out of me."

She nuzzled her face into his throat. "Good," she said, as she kissed his chin. "You had a great deal of wickedness. A little less won't serve you ill."

He laughed, hugged her more tightly, and stood there, holding her. "Do you feel well today?"

"Much better. Just a bit on the weak side."

"That was from last night. You'll feel that way nearly every morning from now on."

She raised her face to kiss him.

"Papa, surely Sinjun doesn't like to have you pet her at the breakfast table."

Colin sighed, kissed her lightly on her chin, and released her. He looked down at his son, who stood in the doorway, hands on his hips, a stance just like his father's.

"What do you want, Philip? Joan was shortly to be on her way to find you. She is quite prepared to give you an abject apology. She is prepared to grovel, to cook you sugared almonds until your teeth rot out. She is quite ready for you to abuse her endlessly, since you are my son."

For a brief moment Philip managed to look severe, but then he said, "It's all right, Sinjun. I know you. I doubt you'll ever change." Then he turned immediately to his father. "Uncle Ryder asked me if I wanted to visit him and Aunt Sophie and all their children. He says there are more than a dozen now and I would quite enjoy myself. Brandon House is where they all live and it's right next to his house. Did you know that he saves children, Papa, from all sorts of terrible situations? He becomes their guardian and takes care of them and he loves them. He didn't say that but I could tell that he does and Uncle Douglas told me that he does. I think it embarrasses him when people think he's good. Uncle Ryder told me about his brother-in-law Jeremy, who's at Eton and lame and quite the best fighter he's seen in a long time. He said Jeremy can also ride like the wind. He said he'd teach me how to fight dirty if it was all right with you. He said I'm nearly the age Jeremy was when he taught him. Please, Papa, can I?"

"Uncle Ryder and Uncle Douglas," Colin mused aloud. "I'll tell you what, Philip. I'll fight dirty with your uncle Ryder and whoever wins will teach you, all right?"

Philip, no fool, said, "Perhaps it would be best if both you and Uncle Ryder taught me how to fight."

"He should be in the diplomatic service," Colin said to his wife, hugged his son to him, and continued. "The two uncles and I will discuss all this. You rest, Joan. I will see you later."

"Oh, Papa, Sinjun is teaching me how to shoot a bow and arrow. But there's still fencing. MacDuff gave us some beginning lessons, but then he had to leave. You can do that, can't you?"

"Joan was learning with you?"

"Yes, and I must continue. I can't let Philip get ahead of me."

"I didn't know you were so accomplished."

He sounded a bit miffed. She cocked her head to one side and grinned. "You sound just like Ryder and Douglas when I happen to outdo them at something. They taught me to shoot, to be an excellent archer, to ride like a veritable Diana, to swim like an—well, never mind. My point is they taught me all the manly sorts of things, but when I prove proficient, they act scandalized."

"They're unreasonable, naturally. A man enjoys having his wife don his britches and ride off to do battle with his enemies, leaving him to flounder about with nothing to say, nothing to do."

"I've decided it's not just a matter of wives. I think it's just that men must always feel that they are the ones in control."

"For all your daring, Joan, for all your bravery, for all your passion for my welfare, and your terrifyingly creative mind, you are still weaker than I. Any man, be he brilliant or a half-wit, could hurt you. That's why you have men. We really are useful creatures. It's our responsibility to protect our wives and our children."

"Ha! You know that's nonsense, Colin. This is no longer medieval times, when robbers roamed the land."

"Why are you arguing?" Philip asked, looking from her to his father. "Both of you are right. Boys, too, can prove worthwhile in a fight. Didn't I ride to fetch you, Papa, from Edinburgh? Without me, Joan would have been really ill."

They looked at each other over Philip's head. Sinjun grinned. Colin said, "You believe every family member should contribute his bit, eh? Everyone should have the chance to be a hero once in a while?"

"That would mean even Dahling would get her chance," Philip said, frowning. "What do you think, Sinjun?"

"I think your father has finally grasped the right straw."

"Now, Philip, if you will accept Joan's apology—"

"Her name is Sinjun, Papa. I accept, Sinjun. You'd do anything for Papa, so I suppose I shouldn't hold it against you."

"Thank you," she said humbly. She watched Colin's left eyebrow go up a good inch; she watched father and son leave the Laird's Inbetween Room, Colin leaning down to hear what Philip was saying.

She loved him so much it hurt.

Who the devil had told Robert MacPherson that Colin had murdered his wife?

The late afternoon was cool. The sky was clear—Sherbrooke blue, Sophie had remarked to her husband, then kissed him.

Colin had wanted to be alone, for just a little while. He frowned now at the water stain on the book he held in his hand. He could tell that the book had been carefully cleaned, its binding oiled, but the stain had been there a long time and would remain there. She'd cleaned it, of course. And all the other books as well. He'd known that she had, only he hadn't realized until now that she'd treated each book as a treasure in itself, carefully and with respect. He laid the book down and walked back to his desk. He sat back in his chair, his arms behind his head, and closed his eyes.

He was in his north tower room. He could smell the fresh heather and roses. And the lemon and beeswax. It smelled of his mother, and now he didn't feel anger at his wife, he felt profound gratitude. He fancied that before long when he smelled lemon and beeswax, it would be his wife he thought of, not his mother.

I love you.

Colin supposed he'd always known she loved him, though the notion of that sort of emotion upon meeting another person he couldn't easily credit. On the other hand, she'd taken his side from the very beginning. She'd never wavered in her belief in him. Even when they'd argued, he'd known that she'd die for him if it came to it.

It was humbling.

He was so damned lucky he couldn't believe it. He'd gotten his heiress. He'd also gotten a lady who was a wonderful mother to his children, a lady who was an excellent wife. Albeit stubborn; albeit much too impulsive.

Just when everything seemed at last to be coming out from behind that awful black cloud, there was an enemy still hidden. He wondered if he should have simply beat the name out of MacPherson. Probably. Joan wouldn't have held him back at the croft. She probably would have argued with him to hit MacPherson herself.

That made him grin. She was bloodthirsty when it came to his safety. He thought of Aunt Arleth, a woman who'd lost her grip on things, only he hadn't recognized it in time. Because of his blindness, Joan could have died. He clenched his teeth at the thought. It was quite true, Aunt Arleth had even admitted that the little slut would be better off dead. Then things would return to normal; then she would be in charge again.

But she hadn't told MacPherson anything. Colin sighed and opened his eyes when he heard footsteps coming up the tower stairs. He recognized the light step and leaned forward in his chair, his eyes fixed on the iron-studded door.

It was Joan, pink with exertion, her forehead damp with perspiration.

He rose immediately and went to her. "You're still not back to your Amazon self. Come and sit down for a moment and regain your breath."

She did as she was bid. "It's lowering to be puffing about over some simple stairs. Hello, Colin. I haven't seen you. Are you all right? I wanted to get away from everyone for a while. Did you, as well?"

"Yes, but I'm glad you're here."

She drew a deep breath. "I came for a reason."

"You want to know about Aunt Arleth."

"Perhaps, but not really. That is, there's something else, but I don't think it was Aunt Arleth or you would have hunted me out immediately. No, it's about something else entirely, but it can wait. I see you're holding a book."

He cocked one of those black eyebrows of his, then handed the book to her. "Thank you for trying to mend this book. It was my grandfather's. He used to read to me from it. It's Chesterfield's *Letters to His Son*. I was thinking it was time for me to read the letters on mythology and history to Philip, and I was right."

"Chesterfield's son was named Philip also. Isn't that curious? Douglas didn't introduce me to Chesterfield, but I found him very quickly. He was miserable with his wife and thus has a very low opinion of women, but Douglas said he'd never met me so he'd been deprived, thus I wasn't to pay him any attention. Ah, this is one of my favorites: 'Wear your learning, like your watch, in a private pocket. . . . Above all things, avoid speaking of yourself, if it be possible.' "

He could but stare at her. He wondered if she would continue to surprise him for the rest of their lives.

"My books from home are still in crates. There's been no time to unpack them." She looked at him then, and her expression was tentative. "Also I don't know where you would like me to put them."

Colin felt like a self-centered ass. If she hadn't been the kind of person she was, he would have completely terrorized her, ground her under. Even now she wasn't at all certain of his reception. About her damned books, for God's sake.

"You know," he said slowly, smiling at her, "there are dozens of rooms in the castle. You can use any of them you wish to. However, if you would like, I should be delighted to share this chamber with you."

She gave him a dazzling smile and jumped to her feet. "Oh, Colin, I love you so much." She leaped into his arms.

He held her, laughing and kissing her ear and her nose and smoothing her eyebrows with his fingertips. He whirled her about. "All this just for the offer of this benighted room and a few bookshelves?"

It was part of himself he was offering, something he'd held dear and very close so it wouldn't be taken from him, but she didn't point that out. He was offering it to her because he trusted her; he knew she would never take from him. "I came to see you for a specific reason," she said, her eyes brilliant. She kissed his chin.

"Yes, but you didn't tell me what it was."

"I came to make love to you, Colin."

"You mean you want me to make you scream with more pleasure?"

"No, I want to do it to you."

He was nonplussed. He was the man, dammit, he was the husband. It had been his plan to seduce her slowly, so when he finally came into her she wouldn't realize what had happened. Now here she was . . . No, he couldn't be certain what she meant.

"I think it's foolish to continue as we have. I have forced you to it and you have been very kind, very giving, too giving. I have been selfish. But now, I want to do everything with you."

"As in everything?"

"Oh yes."

CHAPTER
═19═

"BUT THIS ISN'T THE WAY it's supposed to be done," Colin said slowly, staring down at his wife, all visions of his future very gentle and tender seductions taking flight toward the window.

She just stroked his face with her fingertips, hugged him close, kissed his mouth a dozen times, his chin, his nose, tugged on his earlobe with her teeth. She said between kisses and bites, "I've been selfish and quite childish. I've been a coward. You're a man. You expected a woman when you married me. That's what you will have, right now. I don't care about any pain. It's not important. I want to give you what it is you must have. I will give myself to you as often as you wish, with no moaning or plaints."

"Ah, Joan, but the pain. I know you remember the pain. I have no wish to torture you. I don't wish to make you weep."

"I won't weep. I'll be strong. I was raised to be stoic by Douglas and Ryder. Ryder used to box my ears when he thought I was acting like a girl. I won't disappoint you, Colin, ever again." She drew a deep breath. "I swear it."

He gripped her forearms in his hands, slowly pulling her arms from about his neck. "I can't allow this sacrifice. It's too much to ask of you. Perhaps once a year you will allow me to come inside you—to create a child, nothing more." He sighed deeply and assumed the expression of a martyr. "I don't mind, truly. To give you pleasure night after night will suffice me. It must. I'm no monster to make you scream with pain."

"Oh, Colin, you're so noble, so very kind, but I have made up my mind. I've decided that I will do it right now. That way I should be fully recovered by dinner. Also, if I happen to cry out from the pain, there's no one near here to hear me. Now, I wish to undress you."

He could only stare at her, utterly amused, trying to keep the laughter well under hatches. "To believe you love me so much to offer yourself to me like this," he said, his voice thick with emotion. "Despite what you know will happen, you are still willing to open yourself to me. It moves me, Joan. It makes me realize how very strong and giving you are. It humbles me."

She was fumbling with the string on his shirt, tugging at the buttons on his britches. He laughed, slapping her hands away. "We'll do it together, all right?"

She nodded, not looking at him now, and proceeded to strip off her clothes.

She wanted to seduce him on the carpet? She wanted to ravish him right here? Upon brief reflection, he thought it was a grand idea.

Colin was tugging off his left boot when she was naked, standing in front of him, her hands at her sides. She was trying to give him a siren's smile, but failing woefully at it. She looked scared but determined. She looked like her namesake Joan of Arc on her way to martyrdom, elated that she was guarding her dignity even whilst she contemplated the flames. The foolish little twit.

When he was naked, he knew her eyes were on his belly and nowhere else. He wasn't fully aroused, so she shouldn't yet scream with fright.

He started to resume his role of the tender seducer, to end this damnable charade, when she jumped at him. His quick reflexes saved both of them. She was holding him in a strangle lock about his throat and kissing him until he was laughing.

Let her do it, he thought. He stroked his hands over her buttocks and hefted her legs around his waist.

"Oh," she said and kissed him until she had to stop for a breath.

"What do you want me to do now, Joan?"

"I want you flat on your back so I can kiss you. I don't want you to move, Colin."

He obliged her, easing both of them onto the Aubusson carpet. Late afternoon sunlight sent silver beams through the narrow windows into the chamber. The air was soft and warm. She was lying on top of him, her legs between his, his sex hard against her belly.

He saw the fear in her eyes when he moved inadvertently against her, but then she smiled at him and leaned back. "You're very beautiful, Colin. I'm the luckiest of wives."

"Er, thank you," he said, aware that his sex was responding to her more quickly than he'd thought possible. He was big and hard as a stone against her now. Still, she didn't hesitate. He heard her draw a deep breath.

"I don't want you to move, Colin. I want you to lie very still. I'm going to kiss you just like you kissed me. Is that all right?"

He choked, nearly swallowing his tongue. This was madness. He managed to nod.

She kissed his throat, his shoulders, his chest, her fingers soft and busy in the mouth's wake. She covered him with kisses. He thought he'd burst. He twitched. He raised his arms to pull her down.

"No, don't move, you promised."

He hadn't promised anything, he thought wildly. But he forced himself to stillness. He fisted his hands at his sides. This was what she wanted. She would learn, oh yes, she would soon learn.

When her warm mouth touched his belly, he heaved and shuddered.

"Joan," he said. This was pain, he thought, this was truly very real pain.

She looked up at him and grinned. "Do you feel like you made me feel? Urgent? As if there's a fire building up inside you, but you'd kill to make it even hotter?"

"Close enough."

She touched his sex with her hand. She stroked him. She was looking intently at him, then at her hand holding him. He was oddly embarrassed. He felt strange. Then she frowned slightly. "No," she said more to herself than to him. "I want more and I want to see how you taste." She took him in her mouth and he jerked and moaned and his chest heaved. He thought, quite simply, that he was going to die.

"Ah," she said, feeling his wonderful response to her, and set out to make him scream with pleasure.

He nearly did, so close did he come to his release. "Joan, no, sweetheart, you've got to stop. I'm different from you. I'll spill my seed if you continue. Then your sacrifice will have been in vain."

"Oh," she said, and drew back. "You must spill your seed inside me. That's the way of things. You're a man and that's what you want, I know. This you enjoy as well, but the other . . . that's what it must be. Very well."

Before he knew what she intended, she came up over him and straddled his hips.

"Oh no," he said as she tried to bring him into her. If he weren't hurting so much for her, he would have laughed. She wasn't near to ready to take him into her and yet, here she was, trying to impale herself.

She looked at him as he spoke, and he saw she was paler than a moment before; she was afraid of the coming pain.

He smiled, stroking his hands up and down her arms. "Not yet, Joan. Don't try to force me inside of you just yet. I'm not ready for you. Not even close. No, no, it's true. I must have more so that I will enjoy myself. I can't reach my full potential unless—" He stopped at her gasp.

She looked at his sex and then back at his face. She looked at him as if he were mad. "You mean to say there'll be even more of you? But you were moaning, Colin, and twitching. You're sweating. Surely there can't be that much more."

"But there is," he said, desperate now. "I'm a man and I've got to have more. Believe me. You must trust me in this. I'm the one with the experience. I must have more, else my pleasure won't be anything beyond the ordinary. It won't be worth the passage of moments it will take to bring me to it. You do want me to have more pleasure rather than less, don't you?"

"Of course. I promised you that I wouldn't be selfish about it. If you wish to increase in your size even more, if that's what makes you scream with pleasure, then so be it." She drew a deep breath. "What do you wish me to do now?"

He smiled painfully. "Roll over onto your back. No, no, I'm not taking charge, nothing like that. I just must show you what's necessary for you to do to make me scream with pleasure like I made you do last night."

She nodded, looking dubious, but did what he'd asked. She lay on her back, and she was looking at him coming over her and he saw that damned fear in her eyes again, but he couldn't blame her, his sex was hard as a stone, fully aroused. And she thought he'd get bigger?

He calmed himself. He wasn't about to let this wonderful surprise turn into another fiasco.

He lay between her legs as she had between his. He settled himself over her, balancing his weight on his elbows. "Now," he said. "Look at me, Joan. Yes, that's right. Now, I must have you kiss me some more. It's important, else I'll just have to pretend I'm enjoying myself. Surely you don't want me to feign enjoyment with you."

"Oh no," Sinjun said, finding no fault with his program. When she was kissing him, she could momentarily forget about that part of him pressing against her belly, huge and hot and it would hurt, impossible for it not to, but she was resolute, she wouldn't let him down this time. She wouldn't ever again let him down. He wanted her and she would have him in any way he wished.

Colin took his time. He kissed her, parting her lips, and slipped his tongue into her mouth. He kissed her until finally, blessed be to the kind heavens above, she moaned and squirmed beneath him. He smiled a bit painfully, then eased down her body to caress her breasts. She tasted wonderful and the feel of her sent him shuddering with need.

"You want me enough now, Colin?"

He ducked his head down at the sound of that strained little voice. "No, no, not just yet. I need more, Joan. It takes me time to grow into my need."

"Very well."

"Are you enjoying what I'm doing to you? That is, sweetheart, it's not necessary, but you might as well as long as I am."

"Oh yes, it feels quite nice."

Just you wait, sweetheart, he thought, as he moved down until his tongue was lightly caressing her white belly. He felt the deep clenching of her muscles, felt her quiver then, and he knew that she didn't know what he would do, but she was very interested, she was excited, she was nearly ready to have him topple her over the edge.

He gave her his mouth in the very next instant, and she yelled, her hands fisting in his hair.

He kissed her and caressed her with his mouth. His fingers eased into her and he thought he'd burst with the joy of it. She was ready for him. Very ready. He brought her to the edge, then quickly reared up over her, lifting her hips in his hands.

"Look at me, Joan."

She opened her eyes as he eased inside her. He saw her Sherbrooke blue eyes widen and he knew she was tensing, waiting for pain, but she would wait in vain. Yes, indeed. There would be no pain.

He kept easing into her, lifting her hips to take more of him. He felt her flesh stretching to accommodate him, but there was no pain, of that he was certain. Her warmth made him grit his teeth to keep his control.

"Colin?"

"What's the matter, doesn't that feel nice?"

"Oh blessed hell, yes. I don't understand. Why aren't I feeling that awful hurt again? I'm stretching to take you, I feel filled with you, but it doesn't hurt. It feels quite nice, actually."

He drove forward, seating himself to his hilt inside her. Then he came back down over her and began to kiss her. "Move against me, Joan, it will enhance my pleasure. It's what you want for me, isn't it?"

"Oh yes," she said, and moved in rhythm to him, jerkily at first, but then her body responded without her mind's interference. He kissed her and fondled her and moved in a fierce rhythm in and out of her. Finally, when he knew he couldn't keep his brain in charge any longer, he eased his hand between their bodies and found her.

He watched her face as his fingers caressed her.

She looked, quite simply, absolutely astounded.

"Colin," she said on a high thin wail.

"Yes, sweetheart. Let's meet this together, shall we?"

"I don't understand what's happening here—" she began, then threw her head back, her back arching, and cried out, her body convulsing around him, and he let himself go.

She was utterly still beneath him.

Colin finally slowed his breathing. He pressed his palm to her breast. Her heart was still galloping. He grinned. He wanted to dance.

"Easy now," he said, and feathered her lips with his.

Her breathing slowed. Her hand fluttered up, then dropped to her side. He rather wished she would hug him but decided he'd exhausted her. It was rather nice to do that to one's wife, particularly when she had fully expected to be impaled and ravaged.

"You were very brave, Joan," he said, serious as a man in the confessional. "I think you're wonderful to hide your pain from me, to make me believe you were enjoying yourself. I'm the luckiest of men to have such a giving and noble wife."

The next instant he was groaning and rubbing his arm. "Giving and noble and mean," he said. "Why did you hit me?"

"You lied to me, you damned man. No, damn you, don't raise one of your supercilious eyebrows at me. You lied to me. You agreed with me that the pain was horrible. You were laughing at me, knowing, and I hate you!"

He laughed aloud now, and felt himself coming out of her. He shut his mouth. He didn't want to leave her. Just thinking of himself in her, just feeling the softness of her, the heat of her, he swelled and eased more deeply.

"No, that was your nonsensical idea. Don't rewrite the past, Joan. I know our first time—"

"First time! You ravaged me three times!"

"Very well. It wasn't well done of me and I did apologize to you if you'll recall. Also, if your memory wasn't completely burned out in your recent pleasure storm, I told you that it wouldn't ever hurt again, but you refused to believe me. Now you know that I was telling you the truth. I told you this morning that men are useful creatures. We're good for protection—if you allow us to protect you—and we're useful at giving you pleasure. Now that you know all about pleasure, why then, should you like to do it again?"

She looked up at him. She looked ready to spit in his face. Her blue eyes were narrowed to slits. She said, "All right."

He loved her slowly and it lasted longer than three minutes this time, which pleased him. When she twisted and moaned, he closed his eyes against the soul-deep pleasure of it and let his own release take him.

"Admit it, Colin, you have been laughing at me, haven't you?" she said later as she shifted herself to her side.

"A bit, perhaps. Up my sleeve, for the most part. You were so sincere, so convinced that my body couldn't possibly fit with yours. Yes, it was amusing, when it wasn't painful. You see, I wanted you very much. Ah, perhaps I want you again. What do you think? No, wait, it will be the infamous three times again. Think carefully before you answer, Joan."

"All right," she said immediately, and arched up to kiss him.

They were late to dinner. They were more than late. Philpot and Rory were serving blueberry-and-currant tarts when they arrived. Philip and Dahling had already eaten and been duly removed by Dulcie back to the nursery.

Serena, the brothers, and the wives were there. Aunt Arleth was in her room and would remain there until her brother sent a carriage to fetch her home.

Douglas raised an eyebrow but kept his mouth shut. Sinjun wondered at his discretion until she saw his mouth was full with tart.

Ryder's mouth was full only of wickedness. He sat back in his chair, his hands clasped over his lean belly. His blue eyes gleamed with devilment. "Sinjun, I think you have a look on your pretty face that makes me want to kill Colin. You're my baby sister. You have no right to look that way, no right to do what you've quite obviously done with great abandon."

"Be quiet," Sophie said, and stuck the tines of her fork into the back of his hand.

"It's true," Douglas said, once he'd swallowed the tart, and prepared to launch his own salvo.

"Don't you get into it," Alex said. "She's a married lady. She's no longer ten years old."

"That's a fact," Colin said, grinning at his new relatives, kissed his wife's nose, and seated her in the countess's chair. "Actually that's two facts."

He strode to the head of the table, eased himself down, raised his wineglass, and said, "A toast. To my wife, a beautiful, quite challenging lady who's been mired in female confusion and wrong thinking to the point that—"

"Colin! You will be quiet!" Sinjun heaved her soup spoon at him. It fell short since the table was twelve feet long, clattering against a vase of daffodils.

Philpot cleared his throat loudly but no one paid him any heed.

Serena sighed, looked from Colin to Sinjun, and said, "Colin never looked at Fiona or at me like that. It's not just a man's lust he's taken care of, no, it's something beyond that. He looks like a cat who's eaten more cream than he deserves. I think he's very selfish. I hope he vomits up all that cream. I think you've quite ruined him, Joan. Philpot, would you please give me some tarts?"

Philpot, poker-faced, gently placed the plate of tarts in front of her.

"I'm relieved he's beyond lust now," Ryder said in great good humor to his sister. "You have a witches' brew, little sister? Perhaps you've been sharing that recipe with Sophie here? She is so greedy, so without pity for me, that it requires all my nobility to remain bravely standing in the face of her demands. Regard a man who's striving with all his might to provide her with another child. She won't leave me alone. She's after me constantly. I am safe from her only at the dinner table."

"Surely she will stab you again if you don't close your mouth," Alex said. "I just hope, Sophie, that when you're with child again, you will turn green and lose your breakfast just once."

"Oh no," Sophie said. "Not that, never that. Besides, I'm much too nice a person to have that happen. I think it's your husband, Alex. It's he who makes you sick."

All three wives were laughing.

Douglas was frowning at his sister-in-law.

Ryder puffed out his chest. "No, Sophie will never know a day's illness. I will simply forbid her to."

Alex just shook her head back and forth and said to Sophie, "Sometimes I forget what they're like. When I'm reminded, why, I realize that life is more than sweet, it's delicious. It's even better than those blueberry-and-currant tarts Douglas is gobbling down."

"Now that you've spoken the pure truth," Douglas said, "I beg you not to run out of here toward the basin Philpot set in the entrance hall."

"I would that we shift the subject a bit," Sinjun said.

"Yes," Ryder said, "now that Douglas and I see that you're pleased with this man, Sinjun, we will move on to other matters. Douglas and I have given this situation a good deal of thought, Colin. It seems to us that the person who told Robert MacPherson that you'd killed his sister is quite likely the same person who killed her himself."

"Or *her*self," Alex said.

"True. But why would anyone want Fiona dead?" Sinjun asked. "And to have Colin there, unconscious by the edge of the cliff, all ready to blame because he couldn't remember anything. It was a carefully thought-out plan. Serena, do you know of anyone who hated your sister that much? Someone who knew enough about potions and such to erase Colin's memory?"

Serena looked up from her tart, smiled vaguely at Sinjun, and said in her soft voice, "Fiona was a faithless bitch. I quite hated her myself. I also know enough about the effects of opium and henbane and the maella plant. I could have done it quite easily."

"Oh."

"Let's go another step," Douglas said. "Serena, who hated Colin?"

"His father. His brother. Aunt Arleth. Toward the end, Fiona hated him because she was so jealous of him and he didn't love her. She was even jealous of me, but I never touched you then, Colin. I was very careful."

Colin went very still. He slowly lowered his fork back onto his plate. He said mildly, belying the pain Sinjun knew he must feel at Serena's words, "My father didn't hate me, Serena. He merely had no use for me. My brother was the future laird. I wasn't important. I understood that as much as I realized it wasn't right or fair, as much as it hurt me. It would be like Joan and me having a son and disregarding him because Philip is the firstborn.

"As for my brother, why, Malcolm had no reason to hate me, either. He had everything. If there was any hate to be festered, why, I should be the one brimming with it. As for Aunt Arleth, she loved my father and hated her sister, my mother. She wanted my father to marry her after my mother died, but he didn't. It's true she dislikes me amazingly and believed my brother was a prince among men, but I doubt even she understands why. It was as if she feared me, perhaps, because I was also a son, a possible future earl."

"I don't hate you, Colin."

"Thank you, Serena. I truly don't know how Fiona felt about me before she died. I pray she didn't hate me. I never wished her ill."

"I would never hate you, Colin, never. I only wish I had been the heiress. Then you wouldn't have had to go to London and marry her."

"Ah, but I did and there's an end to it. And you, my dear, will go to Edinburgh to live with your father. You will go to parties and balls. You will meet many nice men. It is for the best, Serena."

"All adults say that when they wish to justify what they're doing to someone else."

"You're an adult," Sinjun said. "Surely you don't wish to remain here at Vere Castle."

"No, you're right. Since Colin won't make love to me now, I might as well leave." With those words, she rose from her chair, not waiting for Rory to assist her, and, oblivious of the stunned silence, wafted her way from the room.

"You have very odd relatives, Colin," Douglas said.

"What about your mother, Douglas, and how she treats me?"

"All right, Alex. Most families have strange members," Douglas said, grinning at his wife. "Serena . . . I don't know, Colin. She seems fey, if you know what I mean. Not daft, not really, just fey."

"Yes, as if both her feet weren't quite planted firmly on the grass.

She's always fancied the notion that she was a witch, and she's dabbled with her plants for many years now."

"But you don't believe she would kill her own sister. And drug you so you would take the blame?"

"No, I don't, Joan. But as Douglas says, Serena is odd. She always has been. Fiona adored her though, insisted that she live here with us, though I wasn't overly pleased about it."

"Did she try to kiss you in front of her sister?"

"No, Alex, she didn't. That began after her sister died. When I brought you back, she tried to waylay me behind every door."

"It would be nice to have some clarity here," Douglas said.

"Perhaps," Sinjun said, "we should call Dahling. She has opinions on everything and everyone."

"Joan," Colin said suddenly, frowning down the table at her, "you haven't eaten and it doesn't please me. I must insist that you regain your strength. Philpot, please serve her ladyship a noble plate."

At that, both brothers and both wives looked at each other, then burst into merry laughter. Colin blinked; then, to Sinjun's surprised delight, he flushed, again.

Colin, a celibate for too many weeks, had no difficulty in pleasing his wife yet another time before they slept. And Sinjun, laboring under mis-apprehensions for too many weeks and delighted with her newfound knowledge, was nothing loath.

They both slept deeply until suddenly, without warning, Sinjun was in-stantly awake, her eyes wide open to the darkness of their bedchamber.

There, shimmering in a soft light with her brocade gown weighted down with dozens and dozens of glistening pale cream pearls, was Pearlin' Jane, and she was upset, Sinjun knew it, deep down.

"Quickly, Aunt Arleth's room!"

The words were loud in Sinjun's mind, so loud she couldn't believe that Colin hadn't come roaring awake.

Then Pearlin' Jane was gone, vanished from one instant to the next. Not like the Virgin Bride, who gently eased out of view, slowly moving away until the shadows and she became one. No, Pearlin' Jane was there and then she wasn't.

Sinjun shook Colin even as she threw back the covers.

"Colin!" she shrieked at him as she pulled her discarded nightgown over her head.

He was awake and confused, but her urgency shook him. "What, Joan? What's the matter?"

"Hurry, it's Aunt Arleth!"

Sinjun ran from the bedchamber, not bothering with a candle. There was no time.

She shouted as she passed by each brother's door but she didn't slow. When she reached Aunt Arleth's room, she flung open the door. She stopped on the spot, frozen with horror. There was Aunt Arleth hanging from a rope fastened to the chandelier in the ceiling, her feet dangling at least a foot from the floor.

"No!"

"Oh God."

It was Colin, and he shoved her aside as he ran into the bedchamber. Quickly, he grasped Aunt Arleth's legs to push her up, relieving the pressure of the rope around her neck.

Within moments, Douglas, Ryder, Sophie, and Alex were crowding into the room.

Colin held her firmly against him, yelling over his shoulder, "Quickly, Douglas, Ryder, cut that damned rope. Perhaps we're not too late."

There was no knife to be found, so Douglas stood on a chair so he could reach the knot at the base of the chandelier. It took him several moments, moments that stretched longer than eternity, to untie the knot. Slowly, Colin eased Aunt Arleth down into his arms and carried her to her bed. He gently untied the knot about her throat and pulled it away.

He laid his fingers to the pulse in her throat. He slapped her face several times. He rubbed her arms, her legs, slapped her again, shook her. But there was nothing.

"She's dead," he said finally, straightening. "Dear God, she's dead."

Serena said from the doorway, "I knew she'd be dead. Your mother's kelpie lover came for Arleth because she told Joan about your origins. Oh yes, the kelpie was your father, Colin, and now Arleth is dead, as she deserves to be."

She turned and left the bedchamber, her pale nightgown floating around her as she walked. She paused and said over her shoulder, "I don't believe in that kelpie nonsense. I don't really know why I said it. But I'm not sorry she's dead. She was dangerous to you, Colin."

"Oh God," Alex said, and to her own astonishment, she crumpled where she stood.

CHAPTER
═20═

"SHE DIDN'T KILL HERSELF," Colin said.

"But the stool beside her," Sinjun said, "it was kicked over, as if she—" her voice simply stopped. She swallowed, her head lowered. Colin hugged her tightly to him.

"I know," he said quietly. "I know. If only we'd been just a few moments sooner, perhaps—"

Douglas rose and strode to the fireplace. He stood there, leaning against it, a cup of hastily prepared coffee in his hand. "No, she didn't kill herself. I'm positive of that. You see, I untied the knot that was at the base of the chandelier. She simply wouldn't have had the strength or the ability to fashion such a knot."

"Shouldn't we have Ostle fetch the magistrate?" Sinjun asked her husband.

"I am the magistrate. I agree with Douglas. I have only one question for you, Joan. How did you know to wake up and go to her room?"

"Pearlin' Jane woke me. She told me to hurry to Aunt Arleth's room. We went immediately, Colin, there was no hesitation. I wonder why she waited so long. Perhaps she didn't realize Aunt Arleth wouldn't survive, or perhaps she didn't want her to live; she wanted her punished for what she did to Fiona and to you, Colin, and to me. How can we possibly understand a ghost's motives?"

Douglas shoved away from the fireplace, his face red. "Dammit, Sinjun, enough of this bloody damned ghost talk! I won't have it, not here. At home I have to bear it because it's a damned tradition, but not here!"

On and on it went. Sinjun was so tired, so shocked into her tiredness that she simply sat there, listening but not really hearing everyone as they voiced their opinions. And being Sherbrookes and wives of Sherbrookes, they all had opinions and all their opinions were contrary to one another's.

At one point Sophie shuddered and stepped quickly back, bumping into a chair. Ryder, frowning, immediately went to her and brought her into the circle of his arms. He leaned down, pressing his forehead against his wife's. "It's all right, Sophie. Tell me what's wrong, love."

"The violence, Ryder, the horrible violence, the pain. It just brought it all back to me, all of Jamaica. I hate the memories, dear God how I hate them."

"I know, sweetheart. I'm sorry about this, but you're with me and you will remain with me and no one will ever hurt you again, ever. Forget your damned uncle, forget Jamaica." He rubbed her back, rocked her gently against him.

Douglas said, "Why don't you take Sophie to bed, Ryder. She's had quite enough. She looks as fatigued as the rest of us doubtless feel."

Ryder gave his brother a nod.

Some five minutes later, at four o'clock in the morning, Colin said, "Douglas is right. Everyone is exhausted. Enough for tonight. We will speak of this again tomorrow."

He held Sinjun close, his arms locked around her back, his face pressed against her temple.

"Who killed her, Colin?"

He felt her warm breath against his throat. "I don't know," he said, "blessed hell, I don't know. Maybe she was an accomplice in Fiona's death, just maybe . . . I don't know. Jesus, what a night. Let's get some rest."

The next morning there was surprisingly little conversation at the breakfast table. Colin had told Dulcie to keep Philip and Dahling with her, he wanted no horrific tales spun in front of their young faces.

Still, there wasn't much more to say.

Serena said nothing at all. She ate her porridge, chewed slowly, even nodded occasionally whilst she chewed, as if she were carrying on a private conversation with herself, which, Sinjun thought, she probably was. She would never understand Serena; she wondered if Serena understood herself.

As if at long last, Serena became aware that Sinjun was looking at her. She said, her voice as calm and serene as a warm starlit night, "A pity it wasn't you, Joan. Then Colin would have all your money and me. Yes, a pity. I like you, naturally, it's difficult not to. But it's still a pity." With those words that made Sinjun's blood freeze in her veins, Serena merely smiled at everyone and left the Laird's Inbetween Room.

"She's frightening," Sophie said, and shuddered.

"I think she's all talk," Alex said. "And I think she speaks that way for effect. She loves to shock. Sinjun, pull yourself together. It was just words, nothing more."

Colin said, "I will see that Serena returns to Edinburgh as soon as may be. In fact, it might be best if I sent Ostle with a message to Robert MacPherson. He could come for her himself. There's no reason to wait."

Robert MacPherson did come to Vere Castle, and with him were half a dozen of his men, all armed to the teeth.

"You'll notice Alfie isn't among my men. I hanged him for killing Dingle."

He dismounted, waved his men to do the same, and entered the castle, careful that the great doors remained open. "There is much improvement," he said, then nodded to Sinjun. "You're quite the housekeeper, aren't you?"

"Oh yes," she said, wondering why she hadn't shot him when she'd had the chance. She didn't trust him an inch, this pretty man with his evil heart.

"I will take Serena to Edinburgh now. I did promise you that I'd speak to my father, though I warn you, Colin, he's not as he should be in his mental parts."

"He was all that he should be when I last saw him," Colin said. "If you simply told me who it was who claimed I killed your sister, we would both save ourselves a lot of time."

"Oh no," Robert MacPherson said, casually flicking a speck of dust from his coat sleeve. "To tell you would lead to nothing. You would try to kill the person in a rage, and I would still be left with doubts. No, I will speak to my father. I will tell him about this person who accused you. I will listen to what he has to say. Ask no more, Colin."

"I wouldn't kill your damnable informant!"

"If you didn't, then your bloodthirsty wife would."

"I surely would," Sinjun said. "He's right about that, Colin."

Colin suddenly realized they were all standing in the entrance hall. He didn't want MacPherson in his home but he had come for Serena. He had to be somewhat civil, but that didn't mean taking him into the drawing room and giving him a cup of tea. They would remain in the entrance hall. Colin said, to break the uncomfortable silence, "You know the wives, do you not?"

"Oh yes, bloody savages those two. Ladies," Robert MacPherson added, and gave them each a deep bow. "And their husbands, I presume. I'm relieved that you both are here. These two charming females should be kept under lock and key."

He turned back to Colin. "Now, your letter said you wanted me to remove Serena. May I ask why, at this particular moment in time?"

"Aunt Arleth died last night. Hung in her room."

"Ah, I see. You lured me here to accuse me of murdering the old witch. Fortunate that I brought my men with me, isn't it?"

"Don't be a fool, Robbie. It was made to look like a suicide, but Douglas rightfully pointed out that Arleth wouldn't have had the strength to tie the rope knot so tightly to the chandelier. No, someone killed her, perhaps this information of yours was her accomplice. Perhaps he feared she'd talk and did away with her."

But Robert MacPherson just looked at him. He did move a bit closer to the open front doors, closer to his men on the steps outside, all of them at the ready.

"Dammit, Robbie, that means someone got into the castle and murdered her!"

"Perhaps she was strong enough with the bloody knot," he said. "Arleth was more robust than she appeared."

Colin gave it up. He fetched Serena. She looked at him as he walked beside her down the wide staircase as if he were her lover. She looked at him as if he were Romeo to her Juliet.

"I'm very relieved that she's leaving," Sophie whispered to Sinjun. "She frightens me, be it all an act or not, it doesn't matter."

"Me too," Sinjun said.

"Sister," Robert MacPherson said, nodded briefly at her, and motioned for his men to fetch the two valises from Colin.

"Hello, Robbie," Serena said. She stood on her tiptoes to kiss her brother on his mouth, "you're more beautiful today than you were even six months ago. I pity your wife. She will have to compete with you for beauty. When we go to Edinburgh, you must promise not to escort me anywhere."

He sucked in his breath, and for one horrible moment Sinjun was afraid that he would strike his sister. Then he smiled and said easily, "I will grow a beard."

"I'm pleased you are able to," Serena said. She turned to Colin, stroked her fingers over his cheeks, then rose onto her tiptoes and kissed him full on the mouth, just as she'd done her brother. "Good-bye, my love. A pity you prefer this one. A pity she is kind, but I am pleased that you married her because she was an heiress."

Without another word, Serena walked past her brother out the front doors.

Colin simply nodded to Robert MacPherson. He walked beside him outside. The day was overcast and chilly. He watched Serena mount a mare her brother had brought for her. He watched one of Robbie's men fasten her valises to the back of his saddle. He watched them all mount, watched them ride down the long tree-lined drive of Vere Castle.

"You will come to me once you've spoken to your father," Colin called after him.

"I will certainly do something," Robert MacPherson yelled back over his shoulder.

"Actually," Colin said to his wife as he turned back into the entrance hall, "I'm glad I married an heiress as well, particularly this heiress."

Sinjun grinned up at him, though it was difficult. He was trying to lighten everyone's mood, but it was tough going.

Sophie rubbed her hands together. "Now," she said, "we have a mystery to solve. Sinjun, I want to hear more about Pearlin' Jane. Why do you think she came to you and told you about Aunt Arleth?"

Douglas turned on his heel and left the castle. He said over his shoulder to Alex, who was standing there staring at him, "I'm going riding. I'll return when you're done chewing over this damnable ghost nonsense."

"Poor Douglas," Ryder said. "He's a man who must maintain his stand once he's taken it."

"I know," Alex said. "I can talk him around to just about anything, but not the Virgin Bride. Sophie's right. It's time to discuss this fully."

Colin said, "It would be simple if the castle were to be locked up tightly every night, but it isn't. Anyone who's remotely familiar with the castle could get in and go anywhere he pleased."

"That," Sinjun said, "is a great pity. I did fancy Serena, blast her eyes."

They talked and debated and argued until finally the children interrupted them, their faces pale because they'd heard of Aunt Arleth's death from the servants.

"Come here," Colin said. He gathered both children to him and hugged them. "It will be all right. We'll figure out what happened. I'm smart. Your uncles and aunts are smart. Your stepmother even occasionally comes to proper conclusions, once she's been nudged onto the suitable path. Everything will be all right."

He held them for a very long time. Then Dahling looked up at him and said, "Papa, let me go now. Sinjun needs me."

Dahling fell asleep in Sinjun's lap. Philip took up a stand at her side, her protector, she thought, and smiled at him with all the love she felt.

Aunt Arleth's body was removed by her brother, Ian MacGregor, the following afternoon. If he was surprised or upset by the news that she'd been murdered in her own bedchamber, he hid it well. It became clear very quickly that he simply wanted to leave Vere Castle as soon as possible. He didn't wish to involve himself. It was that simple. He had a wife and seven children, after all, he told them all in a pious manner that made Sinjun want to slap him. He had no time to spend here. He had to return home. He would bury Arleth, yes he would, but he would let Colin—as was only proper since she was dispatched in his home—solve the mystery of her death. She'd always been odd, she had. Always wanted what her sister had. Aye, a pity it was, but life was many times a pity.

He said to Sinjun as he prepared to leave, "I trust you won't get yourself killed like poor Fiona did, although I suppose it's not all that important now that Colin has married you and has your money in his pockets."

They watched him ride beside an open wagon that held Aunt Arleth in a casket covered with a black blanket.

"He's my uncle," Colin said more to himself than to anyone else. "He's my bloody uncle and I haven't seen him since I was five years old. He's married to his fourth wife. He has many more than seven children. It's seven children from this, his fourth wife. One wife dies from too many births in too short a time, and he immediately weds another and does the same thing. He's a paltry fellow."

There was no disagreement to this pronouncement.

"You have something of the look of him, Colin," Douglas said. "Odd that he is so very handsome and such a rotten man."

Sinjun turned to burrow against Colin's chest. "What are we going to do?"

"What truly disturbs me is that someone came into the castle and murdered Aunt Arleth. It couldn't have been Serena. At least I pray it wasn't."

"But I tell you Serena couldn't have managed it," Douglas said. "I even looked at her upper arms last night. Skinny arms, no muscle at all. Sinjun could have managed it, but not Serena."

Colin didn't find that observation to his liking. He gave Douglas a look, but the earl of Northcliffe only shrugged.

"It's true, Colin," Sinjun said. "I'm very strong."

"I know," Colin said, kissed Sinjun's forehead, and sighed.

Sinjun was sitting in a pile of straw, playing with some kittens whose mother, a stable cat called Tom, had delivered in the third stall, thankfully empty, some four weeks before. She heard Ostle speaking to Crocker. She heard Fanny snort in her stall two doors down, doubtless wanting some hay.

She was tired but also blessedly numb, although the fear was still waiting deep inside her to come out again. She'd left Colin speaking with Mr. Seton. Her brothers were with the crofters doing hard physical labor. "It calms my mental works," Ryder said when Sophie asked him why he was doing it.

"Douglas wanted to sweat as well," Alex had said. "It's frustration. It's been two days since Aunt Arleth's death."

Sinjun had left the two wives arguing even as they went about the castle checking every door for possible clues. She wanted some private peace of her own. The kittens soothed her. Even now, two small toms were climbing up her skirt to settle into her lap, purring while kneading her legs through her many petticoats.

She patted them absently. Ostle's voice was far away now, growing dimmer. Had he said something to her? No, surely not. And Crocker was hard to hear now as well. Fanny snorted again, but Sinjun only dimly heard her. She felt very relaxed. Soon she slept.

When she awoke, not much time had passed at all. The kittens were asleep in her lap. The sun was very high in the sky, shining fully through the big window in the stable.

MacDuff was on his haunches beside her.

She shook her head, smiling up at him. "Hello, what a wonderful surprise. Let me get up and greet you properly, MacDuff."

"Oh no, Sinjun, you needn't move right now. Have some consideration for the kittens. Cute little buggers, aren't they? No, just stay there, I'll join you."

"All right," she said, and yawned. "So much has happened, so very much. I just wanted to get away from everyone for a little while. Have you seen Colin? Do you know about Aunt Arleth? Are you here to help us?"

"Oh yes," he said. He leaned down very close to her. He gently lifted the sleeping kittens from her lap and placed them on an old blanket.

"Now," he said, and drew back his fist and slammed it into her jaw.

Colin looked around the drawing room. It was late afternoon and everyone was assembled for tea.

"Where's Joan?" he asked.

"I haven't seen her since just after lunch," Sophie said. "Nor has Alex, for we were together all afternoon."

"We were looking for clues, specifically which door the murderer entered to come into the castle. But we couldn't find any clues or a plausible entry."

Sophie threw a scone at her. "You are so stubborn, Alex! We did find the door. It's the small one off the kitchen, Colin. I know it had been forced, but Alex here claims that it was just normal use because it is so old."

"I will look at it," Colin said. "Thank you both for trying."

"Where the devil is Sinjun?" Ryder asked the drawing room at large.

It was a small son of one of Colin's crofters who delivered the letter.

"Don't move," Colin told the boy as he ripped open the envelope. He read it once and then again. He paled. Then he cursed.

He questioned the boy, but he could tell him nothing. It was a gentleman, the boy said, his hat pulled down over his eyes, and he wore a scarf that muffled him to his ears. He did look something familiar, but he didn't know, not really. He was on a horse and he never got down from the big brute.

Colin walked into the drawing room and handed the letter to Douglas.

"Good God, I don't believe this!"

There was pandemonium until finally, it was Ryder who read aloud:

Lord Ashburnham,

I have your heiress wife. I will kill her if you don't bring me fifty thousand pounds. I give you two days to fetch the money from Edinburgh. I suggest you leave immediately. I will be watching. When you return to Vere Castle with the money I will contact you again.

"Blessed hell," Alex said.

A few moments later Philpot came into the drawing room to announce that one of the lads had just found both Crocker and Ostle bound and gagged in the tack room. Neither man knew who had done it to them. Just talkin' they were, an' knocked all over their heads.

Colin turned to stride from the room.

"Where are you going?" Douglas asked, catching his arm.

"To Edinburgh, to get the damned money."

"Wait a moment, Colin," Ryder said slowly, stroking his long fingers over his jaw. "We must do a bit of thinking now. I do believe I have a plan. Come along."

Sophie flew to her feet. "Oh no you don't! We came here to help Sinjun and you shan't exclude us now!"

"No indeed!" Alex shouted, then clutched her belly and ran to the corner of the room, where Philpot had placed a basin.

MacDuff watched Colin ride from Vere Castle early the following morning, riding that huge brute stallion of his, Gulliver. Fast as the wind, that one was. He'd supposed that Colin would have left immediately, but then again, this marriage hadn't really been to Colin's liking. He'd married Joan Sherbrooke only to get his hands on her money. Why should he hurry? Why should he care overly if she was killed?

Of course, his honor would demand that he ransom her.

Colin rode alone. MacDuff rubbed his hands together. With luck, Colin would return to Vere Castle sometime tonight, money in hand. He'd decided to let them all gnaw on their fear for her, and not deliver the other letter until the following morning. But something urged him to bring it all to a close. There was no reason to draw it out.

He rather liked the notion that both her brothers and their wives were here at Vere Castle. He hoped they would try to interfere, that they would somehow try to fool him with some stupid plot, and come with Colin into the trap MacDuff had set for him. He would enjoy showing them up as inept English bastards. He was rather pleased they were here; he couldn't have planned it more to his liking.

The English losing soundly. That had a delicious irony to it and Mac-Duff was pleased. It dulled the ever-present pain in his chest.

He waited a while longer to see if either of Sinjun's brothers would leave the castle, but no one came through the great front doors. He waited another hour. Finally satisfied that nothing was afoot now, MacDuff mounted his horse and rode back to the small croft.

It was Jamie, the youngest of the crofter lads, who slipped into the side door off the kitchen, the infamous doorway Sophie swore was the one used by the murderer to get into the castle. He was only one of a dozen small boys who'd been stationed around the castle in a wide perimeter, well hidden, waiting and watching.

Colin was waiting there, seated at the kitchen table, a mug of thick black coffee in his hand.

" 'Tis a man, milor'. 'Tis yer cousin, th' giant wi' all th' red hair. Mac-Duff ye calls him."

Colin paled. Ryder's hand came down on his shoulder.

"Who is this MacDuff, Colin?"

"My cousin. Douglas met him in London. Dear God, Ryder, why? I don't understand any of it."

Ryder gave Jamie a guinea. Jamie, mouth agape, gasped and said, "Thank ye, milor', thank ye! Me ma'll bless yer soul, aye, she will."

Colin rose. "Now, Jamie, take us to the place you saw him."

Douglas slipped through that side door off the kitchen an hour later. His eyes glittered with ill-suppressed excitement. He looked up to see the same look in his wife's eyes. "We're two of a kind, aren't we?"

"Oh yes. And soon we'll have MacDuff. Remember him, Douglas? He was the very nice giant of a man who came to see Colin in London. Colin was knocked off kilter. He doesn't understand why MacDuff would do this."

"Dear God."

"I know. It's a shock. Colin and Ryder went with the lad who saw him to the place he is hiding."

"Soon we'll have Arleth's murderer as well as Fiona's. I do wonder what his motive was."

Alex just shook her head. "I don't know, Douglas. Neither does Colin. Of course, Sophie is claiming she would have suspected him instantly if only she'd been in London with us to meet him."

Douglas laughed.

When Douglas rode back to Vere Castle at seven o'clock that night, he knew MacDuff was watching him and from what vantage point. He was careful to keep his face averted from that dense copse of fir trees. He was careful to ensure that MacDuff got a good look at the bulging packet fastened to his saddle. He hoped MacDuff wouldn't notice that Gulliver wasn't sweating from his hard ride. Indeed, Gulliver had been running only about ten minutes. He was a terror, Douglas thought, wondering if Colin would sell him the horse.

Thirty minutes later, Philpot retrieved the letter that had been left on the front steps. He opened it and read it. He smiled.

MacDuff was whistling as he pulled his horse to a stop in front of the deserted croft that huddled beneath some low-lying fir branches just short of the eastern edge of the Cowal Swamp. It was a damp, utterly dreadful place, redolent with rotted vegetation and stagnant water. The croft itself was on the verge of collapse. Supposedly an old hermit had lived there for years upon years. It was said that he'd just walked into the swamp one night during a mighty storm, singing to heaven that he was on his way. There was one window, long since stolen and now boarded up, but even the boards were sagging and loose, one constantly swinging by its rusty nail. He pulled off his gloves and strode into the one room. There was a packed dirt floor, one narrow rope bed, one table, and two chairs. Sinjun was tied securely to one of them. He'd brought the table and chairs. He didn't fancy sitting on the dirt floor to eat his meals. There were rats to eat the remains. He imagined that they'd kept Sinjun excellent company whilst he'd been gone.

Sinjun eyed the huge man when he walked through the door. His head barely missed the frame. He looked very pleased with himself, damn him. She closed her eyes a moment, picturing Colin and her brothers. They would find her. She didn't doubt it for a moment. On the other hand, it would never have occurred to her not to try to escape. She was nearly ready.

"Not long now," MacDuff said as he sat down on one of the chairs and rubbed his large hands together. The chair creaked ominously under his weight. He cracked his knuckles, a ripping sound in the silence. He opened a brown bag and pulled out a loaf of bread. He tore off a huge chunk and began to eat. "No," he said, his mouth full, "not long. I saw Colin riding back from Edinburgh just a while ago. I left the letter on the front steps. No sense waiting until morning. Perhaps he wants you back alive, my dear. Who can say?"

"He is very honorable," Sinjun said, her voice carefully neutral. She wasn't stupid. She was afraid of MacDuff.

MacDuff grunted and swallowed the bread. He ate steadily until the entire loaf was gone. Sinjun felt her stomach knotting with hunger. The bastard didn't care if she starved.

In that moment she found herself wondering if he truly intended to let her go as he'd promised.

"I'm hungry," she said, eyeing the other brown bag.

"A pity. I'm a big man and there just isn't enough for you. Maybe a bit for the rats, but not for you. Yes, a pity."

She watched him eat until both bags were empty. He wadded them up and threw them into the far corner. The air was redolent with the smells of sausage and bread. "If the rats want the crumbs, they'll have to eat through the bags." He laughed at that.

Nearly free, she thought. Nearly there. He rose then and stretched. With his arms over his head, they touched the sagging roof of the croft.

"Perhaps you'd tell me now why you're doing this?"

He looked at the bruise on her jaw where he'd struck her the previous afternoon. "I was tempted to strike you again when you asked me that last night." He made a fist and rubbed it against his open hand. "You don't look like such a lady now, my dear Countess of Ashburnham. You have more the look of a frowsy slut from Soho."

"Are you afraid to tell me? Do you think I can somehow free myself and kill you? You're afraid of me, aren't you?"

He threw back his head and laughed.

Sinjun waited. She prayed he wouldn't hit her again. Her jaw hurt dreadfully. She prayed he wouldn't go ahead and kill her now.

"So, you want to taunt me into talking, huh? Well, why not? You're not stupid, Sinjun. You must know that, if I please, I can easily kill both you and Colin. You are so very different from Fiona. Colin must believe he's already died and gone to mighty rewards. You have an independent spirit and you have money, an irresistible combination. I will think about it. But, you know, telling you makes no difference to the outcome and we must pass the time. So why not tell you?"

He stretched again, then took a turn around the small room. "What a filthy place," he said more to himself than to her.

She waited, working her hands that were tied behind her.

"Colin is a bastard," he said abruptly, grinning hugely at her. "Ah, yes, a real bastard, as in his mother was a whore and slept with another man. Arleth knew but since she nurtured hopes of marrying the earl herself after Colin's mother died, she feared he'd turn on her if she told him the truth, so she just made up that story about Colin's mother and her kelpie lover. Ah, some kelpie! A flesh-and-blood man with a flesh-and-blood rod.

"The old earl never married Arleth. He bedded her, but nothing more. Then he died and Malcolm became the earl. Arleth loved Malcolm, none of us could figure out why. Malcolm was a rotter; he was petty and mean-spirited. He was occasionally quite cruel. Ah, but then he, too, passed on to his just rewards in Hades and Colin became the earl of Ashburnham.

"But you see, he was a bastard. It is I who should have become the next earl, I who should have inherited Vere Castle. Arleth was distraught when Malcolm died. She hated Colin, oh aye, she certainly did. She promised to give me proof of his illegitimacy, the old hag. She promised me the proof so Colin would be set aside and I would be the earl of Ashburnham."

Sinjun held perfectly still. She didn't even blink. He was furious, nearly out of control. She was more afraid than she'd ever been in her life.

He seemed to calm. He was sweating profusely. When he spoke again, his voice sounded a bit singsong, as if he were reciting words that had been in his mind for a very long time, playing themselves over and over. A justification, perhaps, for any guilt.

"Arleth tried to kill you through neglect. It was revenge against Colin because he was alive and Malcolm was dead. You survived, more's the pity. Then the old witch had an attack of conscience. After all these bloody years, an attack of conscience! I killed her because she refused to give me the proof. I wanted to snap her scrawny neck, but I thought perhaps you would all believe her guilty of killing Fiona if you believed she'd hung herself."

"You tied the knots much too tight at the base of the chandelier. She wouldn't have had the strength to do that."

He shrugged. "It doesn't really matter now. I will have fifty thousand pounds. I will go to America, I believe. I will be a wealthy man there. I've decided not to kill you or Colin, unless you force me to it. Then again, perhaps I shall. There's no reason to really, though. I've never hated you or him. But killing—it exhilarates me, makes me happy in those precious moments."

"Did you kill Fiona?"

He nodded, his expression suddenly dreamy. "Perhaps I should kill Colin. He always had what I wanted, even though he never realized it. Fiona was besotted with him, but he didn't give a good tinker's damn about her. She drove him mad with her ceaseless jealousy. She shrieked at him if he even looked in the direction of another woman. She didn't care about Vere Castle or any of its people. It was just Colin, only Colin. She wanted him to be her lapdog. He should have just beaten her, it would have helped, but he didn't. He just withdrew from her. But I wanted her, loved her, but she rejected me. Yes, Arleth gave me a potion to pour into

Colin's ale. Since the old earl and Malcolm were both dead, she didn't care if the whole bloody castle died; she was quite ready to assist all of them to the grave. Colin drank it and passed out. I broke Fiona's pretty neck and tossed her over the cliff. She pleaded and promised she would love only me, but I didn't believe her. Perhaps I wanted to for a moment or two, but then there was that odd exhilaration again. I couldn't stop once I'd begun. I was quite the artist, Sinjun. I arranged Colin's unconscious body right there, nearly over the edge but not quite. Had I been lucky, he would have fallen; had I been lucky, he would have been hung for her murder. But I wasn't lucky at all."

He stopped then, as if the spigot had turned off.

But Sinjun had to know. "Did you hire a man to kill him in London?"

"Yes, but the fool failed. I came to visit my dear cousin all happy as a clam in the home of the damned earl of Northcliffe. Safe from me, he was, but I was busy. I thought, were he to die in London, far away from Scotland, things would be easier for me, and they would have, damn him. Your brother behaved as I suspected he would when I sent the letter accusing Colin of killing Fiona. But you, Sinjun, you were completely unexpected. Whisked your lover away from London, away from your family's interference, away from me.

"Colin blamed Robert MacPherson for everything, though all Robbie did was steal a few sheep and butcher a couple of Kinross crofters. He did try to shoot Colin in Edinburgh and even botched that up. He hit you, the blundering sod. He believes himself so cruel and wicked, does Robbie. He does it because he's so pretty. The meaner he is, the less pretty people will see him to be. I told him that Colin had killed Fiona and he believed me because I also told him a very real truth—that I loved his sister and that I couldn't bear that Colin get away with her murder. I convinced him that it was his responsibility to avenge his sister's death."

He turned then and yawned. "I don't wish to speak any more. Indeed, I've told you more than another living soul. If you have more questions, my dear, perhaps you can ask God when you reach heaven—if I decide to send you there, of course. Ah, a decision to sleep on." He laughed.

"I think I'll take a short nap. Perhaps a long one. You just relax, my dear, listen to the rats and their gnawing. I'll try not to snore."

He unfolded several blankets, spread them on the floor, and careful not to touch his clothes to the dirt, he lay down. His back was to her.

She gave him twenty minutes. She'd needed but ten minutes to work her hands free, finally. Her wrists were raw and bleeding. It didn't matter. Soon now, very soon.

CHAPTER
══ 21 ══

HE DIDN'T SNORE, damn him. If only he would, she could be certain that he was really sleeping.

She couldn't afford to wait longer. If he was pretending in order to catch her, then so be it. She had to try. Slowly, Sinjun leaned down and began to untie the knots at her ankles. It took longer to untie the knots than it took the rats to eat through the paper to get to the crumbs.

At last she was free. She rose. Quietly, very quietly. She immediately collapsed back onto the chair. Her legs wouldn't hold her. She rubbed her ankles, rubbed her legs, one eye on her hands, the other on MacDuff. He shifted suddenly. Her breath stuck in her throat. He turned onto his back now.

Oh God, don't let him awaken.

She tried to rise again. This time she succeeded. Slowly, she walked toward the croft door.

A rat shrieked. Sinjun froze in her tracks.

MacDuff stirred, then groaned in his sleep.

She had her fingers clutching the handle. She pressed it down. Nothing happened. She pressed again and shook it.

There was a loud squeaking noise. MacDuff jerked and sat up. "You little bitch," he screamed at her, and jumped to his feet.

Sinjun had sheer terror in her favor. She jerked open the croft door and plunged into the darkness outside. Thank God for the fetid damp night, deep and fathomless. The ground beneath her feet was suddenly spongy, then wet, the wetness slapping against her slippers, sucking and loud. Her feet suddenly sank into quagmire, the dank muck pulling at her skirts, weighing her down. Smells were all around her, awful smells and strange sounds from creatures she would rather not see.

He was right behind her, yelling, "You damned bitch! You'll die in the swamp! I told you it was unlikely I would kill you! Come back here, all I want is the money and you'll be free! Surely even you don't think I could get away with murdering both you and Colin and perhaps your brothers, as well! Don't be stupid, get back here!"

Oh no, she thought, oh no. He sounded close, knocking against branches behind her. She turned, panicked, and ran into a tree. She nearly knocked herself out. She stood there, trying to get her bearings again, hugging that damned tree. It was bent forward toward the still, thick water and its trunk felt slimy. She felt herself being drawn deeper into the thick mud. She clutched the trunk, trying to pull herself free. It didn't work. She was sinking, the filthy slime nearly to her knees now. Her great plan, all for naught. Either she would sink here in this swamp or MacDuff would kill her. Why didn't he sink like a stone? He weighed three times what she did, why the devil didn't he sink?

"Jesus, you stupid bitch, I should leave you here to be sucked under."

MacDuff hauled her free of the muck and without hesitation threw her over his shoulder. "Any more trouble from you and I'll strike you again."

She was breathing hard, her face hitting his shoulder. She wanted to be sick but she had no intention of succumbing. She swallowed hard. She had to do something. She'd wanted only to run away from him. Damnation, all for naught.

Then, quite suddenly, she was flying off MacDuff's back, striking the ground and rolling onto her stomach. She heard Colin's voice and it was cold and furious. "All right, you damned bastard, it's all over."

Sinjun turned over quickly. She saw Colin holding a pistol on Mac-Duff. Thank God he hadn't tried to fight him. MacDuff would have broken him in half. Then there were her two brothers and Sophie and Alex, all of them there in a half circle, watching, silent as stones. All of them holding pistols.

Colin dropped to his knees and gathered her up. "Sinjun, are you all right?"

She stared up at her husband. "What did you call me?"

"I asked you if you were all right, damn you. You're filthier than a Loch Ard goat."

"Yes, certainly. Colin, you called me Sinjun."

"It was a slip of the tongue, done in my excitement. Now, MacDuff, we will all go to that dismal little croft and I want some answers from you."

"Go to the devil, you filthy devil's spawn! How did you manage this? Damn you, I saw you riding Gulliver to Edinburgh and coming back to Vere Castle. I saw you! It isn't possible that you knew I was there!"

Douglas spoke for the first time. "It was me you saw. As for discovering your hidey-hole, we had a dozen or so lads stationed all about the perimeter on the lookout. Jamie spotted you. It was quite easy after that."

MacDuff just stared at Douglas. Then he turned back to Colin. "I wouldn't have killed either you or Sinjun. I just wanted to leave. My father left me little money, Colin. You could afford fifty thousand pounds since you married her. I just wanted a little bit of her fortune. It was all Aunt Arleth's fault."

"You killed her," Colin said, his voice shaking with fury, with betrayal. "God, I trusted you. All my life I trusted you, believed you were my friend."

"Yes, was. Only, things change. We became men." He looked down at his feet, then, with a fierce cry, he rushed at Colin, grabbed his gun arm, jerking it upward, and crushed his cousin to him, his massive arms tightening around his back, cracking his ribs.

Sinjun was on her feet in an instant. She froze in midstride. The gun went off.

Sinjun screamed.

Slowly, so very slowly, Colin pushed free of MacDuff. He crumpled to the ground. He didn't move.

There was utter silence. The night sounds became louder. Sinjun fancied she heard one of the rats shriek.

"He knew he couldn't get away from all of us," Douglas said slowly, looking at the pistol he held in his own hand. "He saw that Ryder and I were armed."

"We were, as well," Alex said.

Colin stared down at his cousin, the man he'd loved as a boy and respected as a man. He was dead. He looked over at his wife. A look of intense pain crossed his face. "So many people lost to me, so many. Did he tell you why, Sinjun?"

She felt his pain, his wrenching betrayal. No more, she thought, no more. She looked at him straight in his beautiful eyes. "He told me that he murdered Fiona because she rejected him. He killed Aunt Arleth because she had proof that he'd killed Fiona. He was in financial difficulties, as he told you. He wanted to leave Scotland and he had to have money. We were the likely source. That's all there was to it, Colin. Nothing more."

Colin's head was bowed. "Nothing more?" he asked, not looking at her.

"No, nothing more. He didn't want to kill either of us, Colin. I think he was sorry for all the tragedy he'd caused. Thank you for saving me."

"Ah," said Douglas, "then you're not going to claim that it was the damned Virgin Bride or the absurd Pearlin' Jane who sent us here to save your white hide?"

"Not this time, brother dear." She smiled up at her husband. He looked at her closely. He lightly ran his fingertips over the bruise on her jaw. "You're a mess," he said. "A beautiful mess. Does your jaw pain you much?"

"Not much now. I'm all right. Just dirty and awfully tired of these foul swamp smells and sounds."

"Then let's go home."

"Yes," Sinjun said, "let's go home."

Two days later, Sinjun went to Aunt Arleth's bedchamber. No one had been in the room since they'd found her body. Thank God the rope had been taken away. There was no sign that a tragedy had occurred here, yet the maids wouldn't even come as far as three feet from the door.

Sinjun closed the door quietly behind her and stood there for a moment, just looking around. She saw signs quickly enough that MacDuff had searched in here to find his proof that Colin was illegitimate. But he hadn't found that proof. It was still here, unless Aunt Arleth had lied to MacDuff about it, and Sinjun didn't believe she'd lied about that.

She searched methodically, but at the end of twenty minutes she hadn't found a thing out of the ordinary. She had no idea what she was looking for, but she knew she would know when she found it.

Another twenty minutes of searching and she was nearly ready to concede that Aunt Arleth had spun the fantasy from her own tortured brain.

She sat in the chair that faced the small fireplace, leaned her head back, and closed her eyes.

What would the proof be?

Suddenly, she felt a warmth steal over her, a prodding sort of warmth that made her rise instantly from the chair. She stood perfectly still, wondering what the devil was going on, and then, just as suddenly as the warmth had come to her, she understood it. It was Pearlin' Jane and she was here to help her.

She walked directly to the long brocade draperies that hung from ceiling to floor on the far east side of the bedchamber. She knelt down and lifted the hem of the drapery. There was something very solid sewn into the wide hem.

The thread wasn't all that secure. She gently pulled it open. Out fell a small packet of letters tied with a faded green satin ribbon.

They were letters from a Lord Donnally and they were yellowed with age, the paper crinkly. They covered a three-year period, the first one dated nearly thirty years before.

Well before Colin's birth.

All the letters were from Lord Donnally's estate in Huntington, Sussex. She read a few lines, then hastily folded the paper and slipped it back into the ribbon. She withdrew the very last letter in the packet. It was dated after Colin's birth.

She read the faded black ink written in a spidery hand:

My dearest love,

If only I could see my son, hold him, just press him against my body once. But I know it can't be. Just as I've always known you could never be mine. But you have our son. I will abide by your wishes. I will not seek to see you again. If ever you need me, I am here for you. I will pray that your husband will cease his cruelty, that he won't hurt you . . .

The handwriting was blurred here and she couldn't make it out. But it didn't matter. She'd read quite enough.

Sinjun dropped the letter into her lap. She felt the wet of her tears slowly drop on the back of her hands.

The warmth seemed to swirl around her. She knew of course what she had to do.

Sinjun left Aunt Arleth's bedchamber ten minutes later. The room was warm from the fire that had burned briefly.

She went into the drawing room and walked directly to the fireplace. She stood there, looking up at Pearlin' Jane's portrait. It was between the earl's and his wife's, just as Pearlin' Jane demanded that it should be.

"Thank you," she said softly.

"Who are you talking to, Sinjun?"

Her name on his lips was wonderful. She turned around to smile at Colin, her husband, her lover, the man she would willingly give her life for. Now he was safe and so was she and they had life ahead of them.

"Oh, I was just talking to myself, really. I think that Pearlin' Jane's portrait needs a good cleaning. Is there someone qualified at minor restoration?"

"There must be. If not in Kinross, why then, in Edinburgh."

"I think Pearlin' Jane deserves the best. Let's take the portrait to Edinburgh. Also, it just occurred to me that I would have been sorely in the wrong had I sent Robert MacPherson to Australia."

"It would doubtless have improved his character, but it wouldn't have been justice. I'm rather relieved that you failed in that particular endeavor. Incidentally, I saw him this morning, told him all about MacDuff."

"Don't tell me he apologized to you."

"Oh no, but he did offer me a mug of ale. In his house. And none of his men or servants held guns or daggers toward me. Also, it appears he's trying to grow a beard."

"Did you see Serena?"

"No. He sent her posthaste to Edinburgh to take charge of their father's household. He fancies he's washed his hands of her, but somehow, knowing Serena, I doubt it."

Sinjun grinned at him. She walked into his arms and hugged him close. "Did I tell you yet today that I adore you? That I worship you? That I would peel grapes for you if any were available and pop them into your beautiful mouth?"

"That would be nice," he said, and kissed her mouth and the tip of her nose, and smoothed his fingertip over her eyebrows.

"I love you, husband."

"And I you, my lady wife."

"Ah, that sounds wonderful, Colin."

"Before I attempt to have my way with you here in the drawing room, where are the wives?"

"The last time I saw the wives, Sophie was arguing with Alex about where the rose plants would be best situated."

"Douglas and Ryder are out working with the crofters. Indeed, I had planned to come in and simply say hello to you and perhaps just give you one kiss. I told them that they were old married men and thus didn't deserve the same benefits that I was entitled to. Kiss me, Sinjun."

She did, with gratifying enthusiasm.

He kissed her until she was breathless, then he squeezed her tightly against him. "Jesus, if anything had happened to you I couldn't have borne it."

She felt his big body shake. She hugged him more tightly, kissing his neck. Then she felt the soft warmth again, swirling around her, about both her and Colin, but he didn't appear to feel it. Then it began to recede, but there wasn't any coldness in its place. No, in its wake was perfect stillness and a sort of softness in the air itself. Then, suddenly, Sinjun heard a faint lilting sound that could have been a laugh, perhaps.

Colin said as he nibbled on her earlobe, "I like your laugh, Sinjun. It's soft and warm and as sweet as a moonless night."